Jenny Maxwell is a Scot, was born in Egypt, educated in England and now lives in Germany. Her first novel, *The Blacksmith*, was chosen for the W H Smith Fresh Talent promotion.

Praise for *The Blacksmith*

'Ann Mayall is the first female blacksmith at Anford forge, and the owners of the neighbouring manor see her as a threat, although she doesn't know why. Hostility and intimidation fail to move her, and so they revert to violence. If she will not leave, she must die, but they have not reckoned on Ann's formidable strength. It's a saga of one woman's fight for friendship and independence'
Birmingham Evening Mail

'Initially the ordinary tale of a woman struggling to come to terms with her crippling shyness, *The Blacksmith* swiftly becomes a powerful thriller that gallops along at a pace'
Shropshire Star

'a good family saga with lots of detailed background and excellent character developments, this first novel develops into an exciting tale . . . first rate'
Portsmouth News

Also by Jenny Maxwell

THE BLACKSMITH

THE
BLACK
CAT

Jenny Maxwell

LITTLE, BROWN AND COMPANY (CANADA) LIMITED
Boston • New York • Toronto • London

First published in Great Britain in 1997
by Warner Books
This Canadian edition published by
Little Brown Canada
148 Yorkville Avenue
Toronto, Ontario M5R 1C2

Canadian Cataloguing in Publication Data

Maxwell, Jenny
The black cat

1st Canadian ed.
ISBN 0-7515-2009-8

I. Title.

PR6063.A98B52 1998   823'.914   C98-930384-5

Typeset in Palatino by M Rules
Printed and bound in Great Britain by
Clays Ltd, St Ives plc

For Maddy Gozman, with my love

AUTHOR'S NOTE

To write a book involving the production of Shakespeare's plays without mentioning Stratford-upon-Avon, the Royal Shakespeare Theatre and the Royal Shakespeare Company would be contrived and pointless, and I have not attempted to do so. However, none of the characters is intended to represent any member of the company or the theatre staff. Nor is the theatre in Cambridge intended to be a depiction of the Arts Theatre in that city.

Over the past few years many religious sects have sprung up, and some of them have been known as the Children of God. To the best of my knowledge, none of them bear the slightest resemblance to the sect described in this book. It was certainly not my intention to depict any existing organisation.

Nor does the charity Reconcile represent any genuine charity or charitable association.

The Black Cat is a work of fiction, and any resemblance between characters portrayed in it and any existing person is purely coincidental.

ACKNOWLEDGEMENTS

Of the many people who helped me while I wrote *The Black Cat* I would in particular like to thank the following:

My stepmother, the painter Rosalie Loveday, not only made her expertise available, but was also, as always, encouraging and kind.

Jo Hancock of Stratford-upon-Avon, with the support of those members of the Royal Shakespeare Company to whom she turned for additional information, was a tower of strength. It was not always possible for me to take her advice, but so far as I know errors that remain in the text do so because I decided to leave them in place, not because they were not noticed.

And to the many friends who answered my questions, or knew somebody else who could, once again, my thanks.

PREFACE

The roof of the forge shines dark green in the rain. I can see it from my window. I can stand behind the dark green curtain and look at the dark green roof, and nobody can see me.

The fire from the forge reflects yellow on the concrete in front of it, and I can see a little of that, too, although the corner of the building cuts off most of it. I can see the chestnut tree. The leaves are bright. The blossoms have gone now. They were white. In autumn, children come to collect conkers.

I can watch the horses as they walk up the concrete path. I can listen to their hooves. I can hear what Ann says, and what people answer. They can't see me. They can't hear me. I am very quiet. They don't know I'm here. I watch, and I listen, and they don't know.

Ann knows I am here, but she will never give me away. If there is anybody there, she doesn't look at my window. She promised. If she's alone, she looks up at my window. Her head is turned a little to the side. Are you all right, her head asks, and I move the curtain just a little. Yes, all right.

On a good day, if there is nobody there, I come down. I come down the narrow stairs, listening. If I hear somebody, I go up again, and close the door quietly, so nobody hears, and I slide the bolt on the door, quietly. But if I hear nobody, I help Ann. I get the duster from the kitchen drawer, and I dust the living room. I listen as I dust, I listen for the gravel on the drive. Nobody can come up that drive without me hearing. If I hear a car on the road I stop, and I listen, and wait. If it goes on along the road, I listen until I can't hear it any more, and then I go on. Dusting. Softly, quietly. So I can listen.

Polishing makes too much noise, I can't hear. But I can dust.

When there is nobody, and I am alone, and Ann is in the forge, I can go there. I go to the kitchen door, and I stop, and listen, and look, and then I run across the concrete path, round the corner, and into the forge. I can stand at the back of the forge, in the dark corner, in the shadows by the door to the workshop. The door is open. If somebody comes, I go into the workshop, and I shut the door, quietly, and I slide the bolt, and I wait until they have gone. I can listen, and I am very quiet. They don't know I'm there.

In the evenings Ann closes the big iron gates, and puts a chain around them. Closed. Go away. Sometimes she puts the padlocks on the forge door. When I hear the padlocks I know the work is finished. We go for a walk, where nobody else is. We go into the park.

I talk to Ann. It's easy to talk to Ann. My voice doesn't hurt then. I ask questions, and she answers them if she can, and I tell her what I've been doing, and what I want to do, and she listens. When I talk to other people, my voice hurts.

I talk to Uncle John, a little. My voice sounds funny, it creaks, and after a while my throat hurts. And Dr Mantsch, I talk to him. Every week, every Wednesday afternoon, we go to the hospital, in the van. I sit in the back. Ann welded a seat into the back of the van, I sit there. Nobody can see in. We drive into town, and Ann stops the van outside the door, by the grey stone steps, and she sounds the horn. Then the nurse comes out, and opens the back of the van,

2

and we go in. The nurse says there's nobody there. I have to trust her, but it's hard, because she tells lies. There was somebody there, one time, in the hall on the dark polished floor, a woman. We went into the room, quickly, but she had said there was nobody there, and somebody had been there.

Roly Mantsch says it doesn't matter if there is anybody there, and one day soon I will understand that again.

I talk to Ann, easily, and my throat doesn't hurt. I ask her questions. What will happen? What is the future? And she says nothing will happen, and the future can be like the present, or different if I want it to be different.

If Ann is here, the future can be like the present. I thought my life in the past would go on, but everything changed. If Ann is not here, everything will change.

I watch from the window. I watch the horses coming out of the horseboxes, and Ann with the horses, and I want to cry out with fear, not so near, please, not so near. I see her, standing by the horses, talking to the people, and she is touching the horses. Ann, be careful, not so near. Horses can kill people.

If Ann is killed, the future will not be like the present.

We walk through the paddock in the evenings to go to the park, and I watch for the horse. I don't like it to come too near. I'm afraid. Lyric, she's called. If she's in the stable, I'm not so frightened. I can even stroke her nose, if Ann's there, and Ann smiles, and tells me not to worry.

Ann rides her. She comes in from her work, and tells me she's going for a ride, and there's a happy look on her face, excited, she loves to go for a ride. And I smile, and nod, and I'm so terrified I can't speak. If Ann is killed. Horses can kill people.

Does nothing frighten Ann?

I stand at my easel and I paint. Flowers, and water, and blood. I listen for the gate, for Ann coming home. I want to do something for her. I dust. I try to keep the house clean.

3

A farrier was killed last week in Norfolk. I heard a man telling Ann. She nodded. Ned, Ned Sewell, kicked in the head by a horse he was shoeing. Ann was shoeing a horse, bending down, crouched over its foot. Only a few minutes later another man said something, I couldn't hear, and they all laughed.

How can they stand so close to death, and laugh?

Somebody thrown from a horse at a show, his neck broken. A jockey, trampled.

I look at those horses, I look through my window, behind my dark green curtain. They are so big, so strong. Under those smooth skins, muscle, powerful muscle, and nobody can ever know what a horse is thinking.

Don't stand so close.

A machine pumps, power and weight, but controlled, predictable. You can stand by a machine. You are safe. A machine won't think. A machine won't say, I am angry, I am frightened, I want to get away. A horse got away here once, a big white horse, standing by the door. I watched. Suddenly it was wild, running backwards, jerking the rope, rearing up on its back legs, and somebody had fallen over, there was a lot of noise. I watched. Ann, don't go, stay away. The horse was running in circles, somebody holding the bridle, shouting, and Ann did come. I wanted to scream, but I was quiet.

She caught the horse, the other person let go, a young woman, backing away and then going to the man who had fallen, leaving Ann with the horse, holding it. Those hooves, hard and dangerous, and the horse was kicking, close to her, she was holding it.

Let go, Ann, run away.

The horse stopped, it stood still, and Ann was standing at its head. It was still frightened. Then she led it back to the forge, I heard its hooves on the concrete, and I couldn't see it any more. The man got up, rubbing his arm, and limped round the corner. The young woman told him to stop making a fuss, I heard her.

4

They could have been killed. Stop making such a fuss, she said.

Ann holds their hooves between her knees. Even if they struggle, she doesn't let go. She talks to them, tells them to be still, she grips their hooves between her knees, and they are still again. They can't kick if you've got one of their feet off the ground, she says. And then she lets the foot go, and she stands beside them, and I watch from behind the dark green curtain.

1

My father left before I was two years old, and people say I was much too young to remember him. But I think I remember him, a tall man, with a thin brown face and flaxen hair. Most fair-haired men go red in the sun, but this man, my father, was brown. He was looking down at me, and his face was tense and angry.

You couldn't possibly remember him, they said. Much too young.

There were often men in our house, and I liked them. They played with me, and brought me presents. I can remember many of them, tall and smiling, some in uniform, calling me a little princess, saying I was pretty. But the thin, brown-faced man with the flaxen hair seems special. I think he was my father.

My mother, Lucille, wouldn't talk about my father. She said we don't need him, we three, we'll manage without him. Lucille, Gloriana and Antoinette, my baby sister. There are plenty of better men than Peter Mayall, my mother said, and we've got our share and more.

There was an American who used to take her dancing in the evenings. He came in a big car, and his driver stayed in the house, reading and smoking, until they came back in the early hours of the morning. He was supposed to look after us, but if I came down in the night he would growl that I should get up the stairs right now, hear?

Antoinette never came down the stairs when Lucille was out in the evenings. She stayed in her room. Sometimes I'd go into her room, and she was always awake, looking towards the door as I opened it. I'd snuggle into bed beside her and go to sleep. She was always awake before me in the mornings. I hardly ever saw Antoinette asleep. Even when she was a baby, when I looked into her cot her eyes were nearly always open. Big, dark-brown eyes. She and I would stare at each other. My baby sister.

I had dolls, and a Little Miss Clever sewing set, and some other toys. There was a red wooden fire engine in the toyshop window, and I said I wanted it. Lucille was annoyed. That's a boy's toy. Don't try to play with boys' toys, they don't like it.

I remember Lucille talking about what boys, or men, didn't like almost as soon as I could understand her. I asked why I couldn't climb trees, like the boys from the house down the road. I was standing in the garden watching them, and I wanted to try. I think I was about three, Antoinette was still in her pram. One of my first memories, standing in that garden, watching the two boys in the apple tree, one of them reaching tentatively for a branch above his head, the other perched in a fork of the tree almost at the top. I said I wanted to be in a tree too, and Lucille forbade it. Girls don't climb trees. Men don't like it.

Antoinette had a doll, too. It was very pretty, in a red velvet dress, and it said 'Maa maa' and closed its eyes. She put it on the table and looked at it. She didn't cuddle it. I cuddled my dolls.

I had a party dress made of real silk. The American man bought it for me, he said it came from Louisiana because I was a little Southern Belle. I kissed him to say thank you, climbing on to his lap pressing hard up against him and swaying the way I had seen my mother do it when he bought her presents. He laughed, but she was annoyed, and said I mustn't do that.

By the time I was five Antoinette was taller than me. My baby sister, I used to call her, but Lucille said I shouldn't call her that any more, not now she was bigger than me. Antoinette was only three. She was very dark, not like me and Lucille. She was quiet, she hardly ever laughed, she didn't speak much. I went to school in the mornings, and she watched me putting on my school hat and waiting for the doorbell to ring, Miss Merton on her way to the office, taking me to school for five shillings a week. Kind Miss Merton, who'd been hurt in the Blitz, and had a big white scar on her face that we weren't allowed to look at or ask about.

I didn't like school very much. I didn't like wearing the grey gymslip and the white shirt, I didn't like the red tie, and the black lace-up shoes. I hated the hat. I had to sit next to a dark, scornful girl who wore glasses and who said she was going to be a famous doctor when she grew up, like her father. When I came home in the afternoons I'd throw my uniform into the corner, and put on a pretty dress. When I told my mother about the scornful girl she laughed, and said I'd never have to worry about being clever. My face would be my fortune. My face, and my figure.

There were two men in army uniform, smart and brisk, clipped voices, trim and crisp, brass and brown leather shining, khaki smooth and flat. My mother danced away between them, her arms linked in theirs, her chiffon dress drifting like smoke around her slim legs, her laughter sparkling in the air around their smooth, bent heads.

Antoinette was away, staying at the forge with Aunt Ruth and Uncle Henry, and I was lonely. I sat on the stairs and waited for them to come back. I grew cold as the grey dawn light crept in through the windows, cold, and stiff, and sleepy, and when the car pulled up outside the house I woke suddenly from a doze, and I slipped and fell on the stairs. I hit my face on one of the treads, and cut my lip.

Here's a pretty ring for a brave little girl, silver and amethyst from Scotland, a present from the handsome soldiers. Smile and say thank you. There won't be a scar this time, but be careful, Gloriana, take care of your face. Stay in your bed at night, sleep through the night, don't wait up, don't listen.

Antoinette lay awake at night. Sometimes I crept into her room and she would be watching the door as I opened it, awake, listening. But Antoinette was very quiet. I think she listened. She went to school by then, walking between me and Miss Merton, and one day she asked, what happened to your face? and Miss Merton didn't mind. She told us she'd worked for the fire service in London during the Blitz, driving a van to take hot meals and drinks to the men who were fighting the fires. One night part of a roof had collapsed, and some of the lead on the roof had melted in the fire, and splashed against her before she could get out of the way. She had scars on her stomach and her legs as well. She said it didn't matter. How could she think that? She would have been pretty. Of course it mattered.

A man from London in a shining black car, grey-haired and handsome, black evening clothes, and my mother in a dark dress that showed her shoulders, an orchid pinned with a gold brooch to her breast, her hair smoothly piled on her head, new jewels gleaming. I was frightened of him, and shy, and I stayed in my bed and pulled the blankets over my head and wanted him to go away.

Antoinette was good at school. She listened. Even when she was a baby she listened. Once, when I was still taller than her, she told me that if she listened very carefully she could hear the air breathing. She liked school, she liked knowing about things. She told Miss Merton she wanted to know how everything worked. Miss Merton said that would be grand, knowing about how things worked. I couldn't see why, except if you had to mend them.

9

A man brought me a pearl brooch, and said it came from the South China Seas. I asked him to pin it on my dress for me, and he said I was a little flirt, just like my mother. Lucille laughed. He'd brought her a pearl necklace with a diamond clasp. Worth hundreds, she said after he'd gone.

Antoinette grew very tall, and Lucille was upset. She took her to doctors, and she wouldn't give her very much to eat. Men don't like women to be too tall, Antoinette mustn't grow too tall. Lucille was angry with the doctors, she said they were all fools, there must be something wrong with Antoinette, it wasn't natural for a girl to be so tall. Antoinette wasn't very pretty, but she was clever. In the school holidays she went to the forge, to stay with Aunt Ruth and Uncle Henry. She said she liked it there. I was lonely when she was at the forge. I liked Antoinette. I asked her why she went away to the forge in her holidays instead of staying home, and she said it was because Aunt Ruth and Uncle Henry loved her. I love you too, I said.

I went to a party with Lucille. There was supposed to be a baby-sitter, but she didn't come. Lucille said I'd be all right on my own, but the man in the black evening clothes said something quite sharp to her, so she dressed me in my white party dress and took me with them. There was a piano at the party and I sat on it while an old man played music, and everybody danced. They all said I was a beautiful child. I was tired, and I started to cry, so somebody put me on a bed in another room. There were coats piled up on the bed. I fell asleep, but a man came into the room in the dark, and when I woke up he was kissing me and pulling at my legs. He smelt nasty. He frightened me, but the light went on and the man in the black evening clothes came in. He took me and Lucille home. He was angry. I thought he was angry with me, but when I was in bed he came in to say good night, and he said I could forget about the smelly man, he was just being silly. He told me that if somebody tried to kiss me and I didn't want him to, I

10

should punch him on the nose. He was nice. I never saw him again.

I didn't like school, it was boring. Lucille said it didn't matter. I quite liked reading, and I liked painting too, but we only did painting twice a week. I liked painting shapes, I liked the way the paint swirled off my brush on to the paper, making shapes and colours. Miss Lawrence said I had a talent. When I'd finished and the others were still working she'd give me another piece of paper and say I could paint my patterns while I was waiting. That was the time I liked best.

An Australian, a sandy man in brown clothes, off to the races with Lucille, loud and laughing, bring the kids next time, why not? Come on, beautiful, don't keep the gee-gees waiting. Will the sprogs be okay on their own? You sure?

When I was nine we went to boarding school. Lucille took us on the train the first time. She was angry about it all. Our school uniforms had cost over two hundred pounds each, she said, and God knows what the fees were, just to stuff our heads full of useless nonsense, there were better ways of spending money than that. I asked her why she was sending us to school if it was so expensive, and she said it wasn't her idea, it was the trust fund, nobody asked her, she was only our mother. When we got to the school there seemed to be dozens of people, parents and other girls, and teachers writing names on lists. I was told to go and stand with a group of girls, and Lucille kissed me and said, 'For God's sake, don't turn into a bloody thundering English rose.' Two of the teachers stared at her in astonishment, and one of the mothers raised already arched eyebrows and watched down her nose as Lucille walked back to the taxi.

Antoinette was in the baby class, and I didn't see much of her. I'd stopped thinking of her as my younger sister, she was so much bigger than me, and cleverer, too. She wanted to learn. I wanted to have fun, and there wasn't much happening at school that I thought of as fun. I envied her sometimes. She never had to do her homework again, sitting in the classroom with the other dunces with a prefect on the dais at the teacher's desk while everybody else had free time, reading or playing table tennis in the common room. She was never at the bottom of her class, nobody called her lazy and inattentive.

But I was popular, and pretty, and schoolwork never seemed worth the trouble.

Most of the other girls had parents in the armed forces, some of them came back to school from foreign countries, Africa and the Far East. I was no good at schoolwork, but when we had the dancing class I already knew the dances we were taught, and more besides. Lucille had taught us, and she had sent us to dancing classes. Men like girls who can dance well, even if they can't dance themselves. Mrs Hill took me as her partner to demonstrate the foxtrot, and then told me to help the others. One of the girls whispered:

'I suppose you think you're *really clever*.'

'Clever enough to teach you to jive, if you want to learn,' I answered, and some of the others heard. That evening in the common room I showed them, and the Charleston and the Black Bottom too, which they thought was hilarious, they'd never seen it, it was well out of fashion by then. After that I had friends, and I was quite happy at that school, even though I never learned very much. I could never see the point.

Antoinette could make things. She told me, she made things when she was at the forge, staying with Aunt Ruth and Uncle Henry, but it was a secret. She made things out of hot iron, and she mended things, too. I didn't like the forge, it was dirty, and there were animals. I don't like animals very much, they smell, and they can be dangerous. But Antoinette liked it at the forge, she spent most of her holidays there. I spent them with Lucille, going to parties, meeting people. Learning how to handle men. Learning about lipstick and mascara, about not sitting facing a strong light because it made my eyes look small. Thinking about my silhouette against the light behind me. Learning about listening with my lips slightly parted. That a hand, just touching a man's wrist, would make him notice how slim and white my hand was against his broad, strong one. Little tricks, Lucille called them. Useful little tricks. I learned them. I accepted them.

I used them.

Every day there were men at our house, and Lucille was never at home in the evenings. Sometimes she'd take me to parties with her, but usually I was left behind. Do your nails, darling, she'd say. Don't grow them too long, talons are vulgar. Or wash your hair. Don't stay up too late, be sure you're asleep by the time we come home.

Sometimes there were presents from the men, especially if I was asleep by the time they came home. A silver good-luck token for my charm bracelet, a dressing-table set, and once a gold chain with a little sparkling stone.

My first diamond.

I was ten years old.

I won a beauty contest, Miss Golden Days. It had been organised by a small publishing company, Lucille told me, and it was very professional, just like the Miss World competitions. We had to wear swimming costumes, and then party dresses, and walk on a stage. Lucille taught me how to walk like a model, throwing my hips forward, turning my head high, my hands and arms graceful. A man measured us, and as we walked on to the stage he read out our names, and our ages, and our vital statistics. There was a golden crown and a sceptre, and the man gave Lucille a cheque and said she must be very proud of her beautiful, sexy daughter.

After the contest I had my photograph taken in the publishing company's studios. First in my party dress with my crown and the sceptre, then in my swimming costume. Then in a pair of knickers. Turn your back to the camera, darling. Yes, good, now pout. No, darling, purse your lips, try to look cross. Don't frown, sweetie, just your lips, lovely, that's lovely. Now face me, one foot on that chair. That's right, sweetie. Now, hips forward, legs a little apart, good girl. Pout again. Now try a smile. Lovely, darling, good girl. Now, just slip those knickers off and sit on that chair.

But I wouldn't. I hadn't been happy about the knickers, but I'd been swimming like that on the beach the summer before, so I supposed it was all right. The man with the camera told me not to be silly, having my photograph taken was part of the contract, my mother had signed the entry form. It was against the law, to break contracts.

I began to cry, at first as Lucille had taught me, just two teardrops sparkling on my lashes, stop before your eyes get red, and the man was there with his camera immediately, clicking and whirring in my face, muttering to himself.

'Knickers off,' he ordered. 'That's the contract, that's the law. Or I'll call the police.'

Then I really began to cry in earnest, and to scream. I heard Lucille calling my name outside, and she threw the door open and came into the room. She was very angry with the man, she tried to take his camera away, but he pushed her off and told her to take her dreary little cream tartlet home, he'd finished anyway.

Lucille helped me dress, as quickly as I could, and then she hurried me out of the building and we went home in a taxi. She was hugging me all the way home, saying she was sorry, so sorry, darling. She'd thought it was just going to be photographs of me in my party dress with my crown and my sceptre, a nice photograph to put in a frame on the mantelpiece. So sorry, darling Gloriana.

She was even more upset than I was. She made us tea when we got home, and she telephoned the man who was taking her out that evening and told him not to come. We'd have a nice evening together, she told me. We'd have chicken salad, and jelly and ice cream, and we'd watch

14

television together. And we did, and she hugged me and kissed me when she said good night.

When I was back at school a week later I told my best friend about the beauty contest and the photographs, and I said it was a deadly secret. The next day everybody knew about it, and I told Rosalind I'd never speak to her again as long as I lived.

'My *God!*' said Carol Burnett, who lived in Berkeley Square and thought herself very sophisticated. 'Glory's been photographed for a *porno* mag.'

That afternoon I was called in to see the headmistress.

'Sit down, Gloriana,' she said as I went in. 'Do you know why I asked to see you?'

'No, Miss Oakroyd.'

'School rumours, my dear. Sometimes I have to look into them. A beauty contest? Photographs?'

In the end I told her all about it. She said I wasn't to worry, I'd done nothing wrong, but she would have to write to my guardian. My Uncle John.

I'd never met John Mayall. Lucille was dismissive of him, she said he was a typical London solicitor, a dried-up, sexless old stick, but he controlled the purse strings, which meant he ran her life and made it a misery.

He came to the school the next day, a tall, thin man with grey hair, and a grave, formal manner. My housemistress introduced us in her sitting room, and then told me to sit down and not to worry. She stayed with us, sitting beside me on the sofa while Uncle John sat at her table, writing.

He knew what had happened. He asked me questions about the contest, whether all the children had been about my age, whether I could remember who had been in the audience, what had happened to the other children afterwards, the runner-up and the girl who'd won third prize.

And where Lucille had been while I was in the studio.

'There was a party,' I said. 'They had champagne and things. They said they wanted to interview her. They

15

wanted to take some photos of her, too. The man said they'd take my photos in the studio while they were interviewing her, then we could all enjoy the party. She didn't know.'

'Of course she didn't,' he agreed. 'You were both the victims of a trick. She's very upset and angry about it. There won't be any more beauty contests, Gloriana. Not for a few years, anyway.'

Mrs Russell patted my shoulder and smiled at me before turning to Uncle John.

'Will that be all, Mr Mayall?' she asked. 'Gloriana should be in class.'

I stood up and walked to the door.

'Uncle John?'

'Yes?'

'Will I ever see my father?'

He was startled, and so was I. I hadn't realised I was going to ask the question. It was several moments before he answered.

'Your father's in China, Gloriana,' he said gently. 'He has responsibilities there, and he doesn't want to disturb the family. You and your mother and sister. But he's interested. I give him news of you all when I write.'

And then, when I still hesitated, he added, smiling:

'He would like you to work rather harder at your studies.'

For a little while I did try harder at school, but it was all too difficult, and boring. I was top of my class in art, and my work was quite often pinned to the studio wall. I liked to draw patterns, angles and lines and curves, and then fit my picture into the pattern so it became a part of it, and you didn't notice the pattern, just that the picture seemed right. Some of the people I drew and painted were very strange, but if they fitted into my patterns I liked them, even though the other girls said they were weird.

Uncle John sent me a paintbox for my eleventh birthday,

16

not just school paints but real artist's colours, and two sable brushes. The colour was smooth and deep and even, and it glowed on the paper. I spent all my free time that weekend in the studio, painting my swirling patterns and my weird people, and when I wrote to thank him my letter was genuinely enthusiastic. I loved my paintbox and my brushes.

I didn't tell Lucille. Somehow, I didn't think she'd like me having a present from Uncle John.

She didn't mention the beauty contest and the photographs, not even in her letters. We had to write home once a week, on Sunday afternoons, sitting at our desks with our writing cases, dutifully listing the week's happenings and asking for new gym shoes or fountain pens. It was a chore. I certainly never expected Lucille to write to me once a week, but she did send letters sometimes, addressed to both of us, me and Ann. They were written on thick creamy paper in light blue ink, and her writing was wildly scrawling. Sometimes I couldn't read it at all.

On visiting days she usually came with a man. Lucille could drive, quite well in fact, although we never had a car. Sometimes she hired one for a day to take us to Brighton. For some reason she loved Brighton. But on visiting days she would nearly always arrive at the school in a smart car with a smart man at the wheel. She felt herself at a disadvantage without a man beside her. With somebody good-looking and well dressed to open doors for her and to give her his arm, Lucille was confident, and comfortable.

I overheard two of the teachers talking about her and her men. They were standing at the window in the gallery over the entrance hall, looking out at the cars.

'Mrs Mayall,' said Miss Costick. 'A Jaguar this time. Another new man. Do you suppose she keeps them tied up in a stable and takes them out at need?'

'She *is* very beautiful,' commented Mrs Bayer.

'My dear, successful tarts usually are.'

I felt my face suddenly hot, and I went quietly out of the

gallery back to my dormitory. A tart. I'd always thought Lucille was lovely, and charming, and popular. A tart, she'd said.

Matron came into the dormitory a few minutes later and found me sitting on my bed.

'There you are. Come along, dear, your mother's here. She *does* look nice, always so well groomed, isn't she? Now, have you got a clean hankie? Come along, then.'

So I followed her down the stairs to greet my well-groomed mother. And her new man.

That time she took me aside, leaving Ann with the new man in the hotel dining room where we were having lunch and sitting me down in an armchair in the coffee room.

'Darling,' she said, 'I'm afraid you're going to have to swot a bit. For God's sake, don't strain your eyes or get frown lines, promise me, but these exams, you know. You've got to pass them or you can't go to Storrington. You'd have to go to some dreary little second-rater. Do you think you could, my pet? I mean, maths, and English, and all that stuff? Just for a few months?'

As we went back to the dining room she remarked that she hoped there'd be men at the school interview. I felt my face growing hot again, and I turned on her.

'I'm *not* a tart!' I said.

She stared at me, aghast.

'Darling, of course not! My God, my pet, what on earth do you think I'm suggesting? Men *like* you, my sweet, they always have. Please God they always will.'

I did work a bit harder for the remainder of that term, but it was an unhappy, restless feeling. I wanted to leave Harts Hill, where the teachers thought Lucille was a tart, and start again somewhere else. In a bigger school, maybe nobody would notice that she always came with a new man.

I passed the exams, and I got a place at Storrington, but nothing changed. It was a big school, and I missed Ann. Lucille still came on visiting days in smart cars, with new men, and I listened, alert to remarks, but nobody said anything.

I had extra art tuition, where I learned about perspective, and how to paint in oils. I thought perspective was boring, like geometry, but suddenly I saw my pictures standing out from the paper, real and deep, as if they'd come alive. I stared at what I'd done, the street scene, the shops and doorways, the car at the corner. I could walk round that corner, there was something behind it. I could step off that kerbstone into the gutter. Somebody might come out through that shop doorway.

Miss Elphick stopped and looked over my shoulder at my drawing. She laughed.

'Yes, my dear,' she said. 'I think you've got it. That's very good. Well done.'

There were oil paints from Uncle John for my thirteenth birthday, and two art boards. Miss Elphick showed me how to prepare them, and she put them in the store room to dry. At the weekends I was allowed to use the studio with the sixth form. Only prefects had keys, but I had permission to go in on Sunday afternoons when they could use it, unsupervised. I painted my street scene on one of the art boards. No people, just the car in the road, and the buildings.

The head girl, Phoebe Corbett, looked at it as it stood on the easel.

'That's creepy,' she remarked. 'Has everybody died?'

I said I didn't know. I looked at it again. She was right, it was a bit creepy.

'Gives me the shivers,' she said. 'But it's good. You should frame that.'

Miss Elphick made me a frame, and showed me how to mount an oil painting. I sent my street scene to Uncle John for Christmas. He wrote to me to thank me. He said he'd hung the picture in his office, and several people had asked who had painted it.

I didn't mention it to Lucille, and I left my oil paints in the studio when I went home for the Christmas holidays.

There was an actor, Lance Allodyne, suave and graceful, but friendly, a practised smile, an angle of arm and shoulder, a profile. Lucille was tense, manoeuvred out of the chair she had set in the most flattering light on to the sofa, while it was the actor who bore his silhouette in mind, the hard, lean jawline, the wide shoulder, the long leg. But the talk of famous names, the locations, the travel, the casual invitation to a party on a film set. The magnificent white Lagonda. Two signed photographs in silver frames, mine inscribed to the loveliest of fairy princesses, Lucille's consigned to the waste-paper basket with an angry comment about fairy princes, the silver frame discreetly taken to the jeweller's for repair, never seen again.

But I liked him. He was friendly, and he made me laugh. Once, when he was waiting for Lucille, he acted for me, different characters he'd played, and I was fascinated. A moment's pause, a little frown as he thought, and then suddenly he was somebody else, as if he had reached down deep inside and moulded himself into a different shape. Shylock, he said, and avarice gleamed from his cringing lips. Long John Silver, violence only just hidden behind the jolly laugh. Scaramouche, and Cyrano. I begged him to teach me.

I told Ann about him. She asked me to call her Ann, not Antoinette, at least when we were alone. Ann listened, and asked if I wanted to be an actress. Yes, I said. Yes, yes. And I practised, in front of the long cheval glass, turning and posing and looking at myself, dissatisfied, and Ann watched and listened as I read plays, and sometimes she read the other parts for me. I was Juliet, gazing rapt at an Eastern sky as she obediently read the part of Romeo. I remember her reading Othello, Troilus, even Macbeth, but I can't remember myself as Desdemona or Cressida, and my last memory of the final week of that Christmas holiday was Lucille coming into my bedroom and finding me wringing my hands and declaiming, 'Yet who would have thought the old man to have had so much blood in him?' She said it sounded disgusting, and that Shakespeare should have known better. She couldn't see that he had meant it to sound disgusting, it was a play designed to shock.

That Christmas we went to a pantomime, and then my life changed.

2

We'd been to the theatre before, of course, but this was the first time I'd really looked at it. It was *Aladdin*, not a very good production, a back-street theatre in a Midlands town with a pantomime designed to last through December and not much further, but this time I was, quite literally, on the edge of my seat. I was trying to see how the scenery was hung, and how the genie swooped across the stage. When the comedian took half a dozen children from the audience to do a few conjuring tricks and hand out balloons, I was clamouring to be one of them, and I suppose the blonde curls did their trick because I found myself on stage, by far the oldest; the other children were mostly about six or seven, I think.

Not that I was a great success. I was far too interested in the people standing in the wings, and in the dazzling lights overhead, to listen to the poor comedian's patter, and I've always hated balloons. I was back the next day, snooping around the courtyard behind the theatre and begging the bad-tempered man who was sweeping it to let me in. He saw no reason why he should, and was impervious to the blonde curls, the blue eyes, and even the pleading smile. I was on the point of giving up when three girls huddled in winter coats scurried around the corner from the street into the courtyard. Two of them ducked straight in through the door, hardly sparing us a glance, but the third stopped. She sneezed, swore, and then looked at me.

'What does she want?' she asked the man.

'Wants to come in,' he answered. 'Reeve doesn't like it, not in the mornings.'

She sneezed again, and wiped her nose on a dirty handkerchief.

'Tra bloody la,' she muttered.

'You're Aladdin!' I exclaimed, suddenly recognising her. 'Louise de Vere, aren't you? I saw you last night. You're beautiful.'

'Let her in,' said the girl.

'Reeve doesn't like it.'

'Oh, fuck Reeve,' she said. 'Bloody old tart. She said I'm beautiful, let her in, she can have the royal box.'

The man shrugged and turned away, saying he wasn't letting me in but he couldn't see what happened behind his back. Slightly shocked at her language, I followed her. Only the night before she'd been so glamorous, shining and long-legged with flashing eyes and white teeth, and she'd danced and sung and cracked jokes with the children, and now she was swearing, and she had a runny nose and red eyes.

But she was friendly to me. She took me down to a dressing room, which was full of other women, smoking and chatting and trying on different costumes, and she explained, grinning, against a background of jeers and cat-calls, that although she was the star she had to share a room with the herd, because her proper dressing room was full of bits of old scenery.

Somebody told me to park my fortune on the end of a grubby plush-covered sofa, and I was handed a cup of black coffee. Nobody took very much notice of me, apart from smiling if I caught their eye, and I was content to sit and listen and watch. People came and went, and I recognised some of them from the performance.

When the man came in saying second act, chorus, on stage in five minutes, I left. I didn't want to be told to go, and I knew I might be in the way.

But I was back the next day, let in by the girl who'd given me the coffee, and this time I wandered around, looking and listening. I could hear somebody playing the piano from the stage, and then a crashing angry chord and a man shouting.

'For God's *sake*, girl, can't you kick higher than that? Swing your bloody *arse*.'

And the piano started again, with somebody else chanting:

'And *one*, two, three and *kick*, and *one*, two, three and *turn*.'

I crept away, and found myself in another corridor, green paint peeling off the walls, doors closed, one with the legend 'Sod off' sprayed across it, and from behind another the sound of a man reading loudly in a monotone, laying an exaggerated stress on some of the words.

It was like a rabbit warren behind that stage, little corridors leading off each other, all the doors looked the same, and the acoustics were strange. In some places I couldn't hear anything from the stage, and in others I might have been standing right beside the piano, even though all I could see were painted brick walls. Along most of the corridors there were big cupboards with labels on them with the names of plays, and there were stacks of props, a skip full of top hats, a wooden wheelbarrow, a grandfather clock.

I heard the piano again, quite close, and the man who'd been playing it said that would do, back at two please, and then there were footsteps. I found the stage again, dark and deserted now, and I stood in the wings looking at it, imagining what it would be like to be standing there waiting for my cue, with the auditorium full and all those brilliant lights blazing down.

I listened carefully, but I could hear nobody near, and so I stepped out on to the stage.

Immediately, a big bank of lights over my head came on, white and dazzling, and a voice from above me called down.

'Who the hell are you?'

'Gloriana Mayall,' I answered, startled, and squinting up into the lights to try to see him.

'Well, Gloriana Mayall, bugger off.'

Even though he had sworn at me he didn't sound unfriendly, so I raised my head and called back to him.

'I'll remember you when I'm famous!'

He laughed.

There was a huge space off to that side of the stage and it was full of big pieces of scenery. There was a complete cottage, with doors and windows, mounted on a platform with rollers, and there were trees, real wood with dark green cloth leaves. There was a strong smell of paint and of new canvas, turpentine and linseed oil, a little like the art studio at school.

I heard footsteps, and I turned to see a man walking towards me, trailing a length of electric cable.

'Gloriana Mayall again,' he said. It was the man who'd been up in the flies when I'd gone on to the stage.

I nodded.

'What are you doing here?'

I shrugged.

'Just looking.'

'How old are you?' he demanded.

'Thirteen.'

'Thirteen,' he echoed, busying himself coiling the cable over his arm. 'Gloriana Mayall, thirteen years old, wants to be an actress, doesn't she? All normal thirteen-year-old girls want to be actresses. Film stars. Wealth and glamour and handsome men falling all over them and kissing them. Looking for autographs, were you?'

'No, I wasn't,' I shouted. I was furiously angry. 'I wasn't looking for autographs, why are you being so silly? I don't want autographs and I don't want to be a film star. Yes, I want to be an actress. I wanted to see what it's like back here. I want to learn how to act.'

He was surprised by my outburst. He stood looking down at me, and then he turned away and hung the cable over a big hook on the wall.

'Did you say "learn"?'

'Yes.'

'You don't think you could . . .' he gestured in the direction of the stage, '. . . just, sort of, walk out there and do it? Because you're pretty, and you fancy yourself in a love scene with the current heart-throb? You don't think it's just learning the lines and saying them and moving around?'

'No, of course not. Of course you have to learn, I'm not stupid. I've pranced around in front of a mirror enough to know I can't act yet. But I think I could learn.'

There was a look of mild admiration on his face, but not the sort of admiration I'd been used to. He'd noticed I was pretty, but it didn't matter, not to him.

'Well, Gloriana Mayall, you're a refreshing change, aren't you? What made you decide you wanted to be an actress?'

'Lance Allodyne. My mother knew him. He acted for me once, in our living room, it was wonderful. He changed himself, right from the inside, just by thinking about it.

'Do you know, when he was Long John Silver, you'd swear he was about seven feet tall, honestly! You would, he was huge.'

He was nodding at me, and smiling.

'I remember him in that part,' he agreed. 'He played it well.'

A telephone rang, the bell sounding faint and far away, and he cocked his head and listened until it stopped when somebody answered it. I noticed things about him, he had very arched eyebrows, like semi-circles over his round eyes, and when he raised them there were deep, wavy wrinkles on his forehead. There were deep lines on his cheeks too, his face seemed to be made of wavy lines. I found myself thinking of how I would paint him, one of my pattern pictures, he would fit into one of them quite well.

I suddenly realised he had asked me something, and I hadn't heard.

'Sorry?' I said.

'Like to go out on the stage and act something now, would you? There's nobody using it.'

'Are we allowed?'

'You're not. I am. I'm the stage manager. Jim Priest. Call me Jim. Like to try, would you?'

I didn't know what to say. I thought I'd be stupid to refuse, a chance to act on a real stage when I'd said I wanted to be an actress, but I found the idea baffling. Act what? How, act? It didn't make sense. I made a helpless gesture.

He smiled. He seemed to be considering me, his head was on one side. I noticed there were hollows under his cheekbones, they made crescent-shaped shadows. I was getting the idea for a pattern.

'What are you thinking?' he asked, and I jumped. I realised I'd been staring at him.

'I'm sorry,' I said, and he shook his head, dismissing my apology, still smiling, waiting for an answer.

'I was thinking about how to paint you.'

'Were you, now? And did you come to a decision?'

I was embarrassed. I didn't want to mention how the wrinkles on his face made a wavy pattern, it seemed rude. Lucille had told us since we were tiny children that it was rude to make personal remarks, particularly about people's appearance. I felt myself blushing.

He looked at his watch.

'Things to do,' he said. 'Got to go.'

'May I stay and look around?' I asked.

He hesitated, half turned away from me, and then looked back.

'Keep off the ladders,' he instructed. 'And don't touch anything electric, this place needs rewiring.'

After that I went back to the theatre as often as I could. I became a sort of stray cat around the place, tolerated, sometimes sworn at for getting in the way, but usually treated kindly. I ran messages, found lost props, passed hammers and screwdrivers to the stage hands, and was made responsible for cleaning and washing the paintbrushes, a job I could do well.

I made up some story for Lucille about having met the daughter of one of the producers at dancing class, and she was quite relieved that I had found something to do to keep me out of the house. One of her men had asked me to go to the fair with him, and she had not been pleased. I was allowed to borrow her make-up, her bath salts, even her stockings, but her men were hers alone, and Gloriana was perhaps becoming a problem.

So Lucille decided I might well learn things to my advantage in a theatre, and agreed to my spending my days there.

What I learned, in and out of the dressing rooms and up and down the stairs and corridors, was often explicit and scandalous. I learned that Terry had got herself in slightly darker print in the programme by going down to the printer's and giving a blow job to one of the typesetters. Two days later, I managed to persuade Louise to tell me what was meant by a blow job, and I was horrified and disgusted. I learned that a certain well-known actor, famous for his magnificent physique, had taken so many body building pills that his genitals had shrunk to almost half size, and I learned that it didn't matter, because in that relationship it was his butler who was the stud, even though the butler was a skinny little wisp and twice his age.

But I also learned to check the lists for the props table, and how to hang costumes so they didn't crease. I learned I must never whistle in the dressing rooms, nor quote from *Macbeth*. It's better to say 'break a leg' than 'good luck' to an actor.

I did my pattern painting of Jim Priest, and I gave it to him, the day before I went back to school. I wasn't sure if he'd like it, but he found a frame for it, and hung it on the wall of the Green Room, alongside a tinsel picture of Henry Irving.

Back at school in the special art classes I asked Miss Elphick to teach me about scenery painting and stage design. She told me to concentrate on perspective, she said it was extremely important on stage, and she ordered two books for me to study.

On the first day of the Easter holidays I was back at the theatre. Two of the stage hands welcomed me with broad smiles, and told me Jim would be pleased to see me, we were rushed off our feet. He was in the paint store. On the way there I met Louise, who hugged me, and said it was good to see me back, time I stopped skiving off at school and got on with my work.

It was warm in the theatre, enclosed and exclusive. And I was part of it.

Then I bumped into somebody, who told me sharply to look where I was going, fool brat, and some of the happy excitement died. Raymond Clancarron, one of the actors, a nervous man with pale eyes and a long, thin neck.

'Opening night tomorrow,' said Jim, 'better get your skates on, hadn't you? Things to do. Right, four bouquets of carnations from Springtime, give them to Mrs Pasmore, then get back here. Brushes to clean, aren't there?'

It was as if I'd never been away.

Opening night came and went, and reviews were read in secret with the usual anxious avidity. It had gone far better than anybody had expected. The notices were good, all except those for Raymond Clancarron, whose performance was described as 'wooden'.

'You brought us luck, darling,' said Mrs Pasmore. 'And we're very, very glad to have you back.'

Raymond Clancarron apologised to me.

'I was nervous,' he explained. 'You're not a fool brat, sweetie, I'm sorry I said that. Lovely to have you back.'

And so I got my reputation for being lucky for the theatre. I felt sorry for Ray, the only one who'd been left out, and I painted a picture of a black cat for him for a mascot. He stuck it to the mirror of his dressing table, and said I was an absolute darling. I hope it brought him luck.

We were frantically busy. There were rehearsals for two more productions going on, and every minute of the day seemed to mean heavy scenery to shift. I was learning. The massive coils of rope and cable that at first had seemed untidy muddles took on a pattern. I knew which ones raised and lowered which of the long metal racks that carried the heavy canvas backcloths. I knew how to dim the house lights, and how to lower the iron, the safety curtain.

Most importantly, I knew where to find things.

Once or twice, I even acted. Only in rehearsals, and only when somebody was missing. None of the actors ever missed rehearsals if they'd been called, but sometimes there was an impromptu run-through of a bit that hadn't been scheduled, and then I might hear my name shouted into the scene room, or up into the flies, wherever somebody had seen me last.

The ban on climbing ladders and touching anything electric had long been lifted. Normally I hate heights, but when I was fifty feet over the stage on the metal grid catwalks I was always thinking of something else, and it never occurred to me to be scared. I was forbidden to carry anything when I was in the flies, the safety rules were very strict and everybody observed them, tools were attached by light nylon lines to the stage hands' belts.

But when I came home for the Christmas holidays that year, there was a late fourteenth birthday present on the table of the Green Room. My own tool belt, with some tools, from everybody in the theatre.

I never took it home. Sometimes I worried a little, not telling Lucille about what I was really doing in the theatre, or about the presents Uncle John sent me to help me with my painting. I'd come home in the evenings to find her preparing to go out, sitting at her dressing table carefully applying her make-up, or staring censoriously at her reflection in the mirror. Faint lines had begun to appear at the corners of her eyes and her mouth, and she would touch at them with the tips of her fingers, dismayed. There were jars of cream and bottles of lotion in the drawer under the glass-topped dressing table, all of them guaranteed to smooth away the signs of ageing, and Lucille was trying them, one after the other, looking for magic.

She'd call out as she heard me in the hall, an affectionate greeting, a question about what I'd been doing, and I'd go into her room, and kiss the proffered cheek.

'Helping the wardrobe mistress. Mrs Pasmore, I think I told you. There's a gorgeous blue velvet gown for Louise to wear in *Lady Windermere's Fan*, you'd love it.'

And we'd talk for a while about velvet, and how difficult it was to clean, how it showed every mark, but, oh, my darling, there is nothing, absolutely *nothing* more flattering, if you've got the figure for it. But blue? For Louise? Yes. Yes, perhaps, but tricky, with those green eyes. With the right make-up, yes, perhaps.

And all the while I'd be wondering what she'd say if she knew I'd spent the afternoon fifteen feet up a stepladder, dressed in a man's old shirt and a pair of running shorts as I painted the moulding on a plaster cornice.

'Now!' she'd say as she put her earrings on and carried out one last critical inspection of herself in the long mirror. 'Come down and have a tiny glass of sherry while I wait for Clifton, and tell me some stage gossip.'

And I would make something up.

31

Stage gossip that day had been that Terry had had to go to London for yet another abortion, and Queenie, her understudy, was actually much better in the part than Terry, so Terry had better be careful. Ray had had a dreadful row with Tony, and Tony was threatening to move out of their flat and find somewhere on his own. Ray had accused Tony of being heterosexual. Anton, one of the stage hands, had told a particularly filthy, but very funny, joke about a Spanish fighting bull and an American tourist without realising I was in the dressing room next door and could hear every word. Every time he'd seen me since then he'd turned bright red.

But I told Lucille what truth I could, that Sue, whose face was round, had shown me how rouge applied low on the cheeks made it look thinner, and Lucille was interested, although her own face was an almost perfect oval and needed nothing to improve its lovely shape.

'And have you been learning any acting tricks?'

'But why "tricks"?' I asked. 'Darling Lucille, they're techniques, they're not dishonest, it's not tricks.'

The beautiful eyebrows rose a fraction.

'Oh, my! I'm sorry if I'm not quite *au fait* with the words. Well, then, techniques.'

Reeve had suggested only that afternoon that I should try harder to project my voice so it would reach to the back of the auditorium, something he had told me about before, but the paint had been drying on my plaster cornice and I had been anxious to get back to it, so I had just smiled, and nodded, and run back into the wings and up the stepladder as soon as he could spare me.

At home I was fragile, and delicate, and a little helpless, at least if there was a man in the place. If I dropped something I would look down at it with an expression of faint dismay, until he picked it up for me and earned a grateful and admiring smile. At the theatre I could carry a thirty-pound counterweight, and if I was asked to do so I would, with difficulty admittedly as I wasn't very strong, but at least without complaint. At home I had to be helped from a car, I rarely opened a door for myself if there was a man in the house. At the theatre I swarmed up the ladders into the flies, I helped fix the rings that held the heavy canvas on the long bars, I pushed scenery around, and, if it was heavy, I braced my shoulder against it and dug my rubber-soled running shoes down on to the floor and pushed harder. Like the other stage hands, I would swear at awkward flats, 'Come on, you bloody cow, *move!*' and nothing I heard in the way of obscenities or blasphemy at the theatre shocked me any more. At home, if anyone of whom Lucille did not approve uttered a swear word she would turn on them an amazed stare, leaving them in no doubt that they had committed a grave social crime.

During school terms I grew more and more exasperated with any lessons that took me away from the art studio, with the exception of English literature, provided we were studying a play of some kind. Foreign languages bored me to distraction, and I spent the lessons staring out of the windows, mathematics was simply incomprehensible and not worth the time I wasted on it, the sciences tedious, and often unbearably smelly.

But there was the school play, *Macbeth*, and Miss Malcolm, the English teacher who was to direct the play, asked me if I'd like to play Lady Macbeth, since I'd said I wanted to be an actress. But Miss Elphick said she hoped I'd help her with the scenery, and I certainly couldn't do both. I wanted to play the fiend-like queen, I could see myself tearing at my hands, frantic at the sight and the smell of the blood, but I could see myself as Lady Macbeth against the background of the stark black rectangles I had in mind as the scenery for the castle, and I had to make the choice.

I tried to play the part, but it was difficult. I knew what I wanted, I knew how I thought her voice should crack, but my voice wouldn't do it, it sounded squeaky and rather silly. I knew how I wanted to urge Macbeth to murder, the way I would change from persuasion to scorn, from caressing to goading, but saying the lines to Naomi Beech, who was to play Macbeth, and who was so far chanting the dreadful words as though she were reading a shopping list, I began to feel self-conscious and rather silly.

So I thanked Miss Malcolm, and said if she didn't mind I would prefer to help Miss Elphick with the scenery, and Isabelle Renton played Lady Macbeth, looking and sounding like a Dutch doll, and making the task of murdering the king as horrible and awe-inspiring as building a set of kitchen shelves.

I showed Miss Elphick my drawings for the sets, and she liked them, but she pointed out that our school stage only had a row of footlights and four spots mounted on a rail. I would have to think of shadows, where the light would be blocked off.

'It's not like the Royal, dear,' she said. 'You're going to have to tame your imagination a little.'

I did persuade the bursar to invest in two more spotlights on stands, but Miss Elphick was right, it was no good building my great stark blocks to stand as silhouettes against a lit sky if there was no way of lighting the sky. Nor was there the big space at the side of the stage to store the sets, there was only a little room with the grand piano in it, which took up nearly half the floor space and had to be protected against possible damage, and could not have anything put on top of it.

But we worked together, she and I, and our blasted heath was a place of bleak and wind-blown ghastliness, with a rotting body hanging from a gallows, the rope creaking in the wind, against a dirty yellow sky, and Miss Malcolm shuddered when she saw it, and asked if perhaps we weren't going a little too far, for a school play.

I thought she was stupid. It was she who had chosen *Macbeth*, if she wanted something mild and placid she should keep her refined little hands off Shakespeare. *Macbeth* is still the best horror story ever written.

Miss Elphick was sharply reproving when I voiced my opinion, but I saw her smiling to herself as she worked on the weathered grey stone of the castle walls.

On the programme our names appeared side by side, Stage Settings by Patricia Elphick RA and Gloriana Mayall. And we were called on stage and the audience of parents and visitors rose to its feet and cheered us. We bowed, and backed modestly off the stage, leaving it to the cast and to Miss Malcolm, but at the party afterwards, sherry for parents and staff, orange juice for us, we found ourselves treated almost like celebrities.

Lucille had come with someone she introduced as Lord Chendar, who said he looked forward to seeing me in the West End, yes? Lucille said of course she was tremendously proud of me, but darling, did it *have* to be so dreadfully gruesome?

Ann had helped make the props, the weapons and the armour, and her name was on the programme too, but she didn't come to the party. She said she was ill, and Matron let her stay in the sanatorium. Ann was never ill. She was over six foot tall, and she hated school events, she said people stared at her.

Lucille said, oh dear, poor Antoinette, but if she's ill we'd better not disturb her. She was relieved Ann wasn't there. She didn't want to introduce her to Lord Chendar as her daughter.

'Don't forget to give Antoinette my love, will you, darling?' she said as they left. '*Lovely* play,' she added vaguely as Lord Chendar's chauffeur handed her into the car. 'Pity it's so . . .'

3

Aunt Ruth died, and Ann went to the funeral. Lucille
said she couldn't go to the forge any more, it wasn't
suitable. Ann and I didn't often talk together when we were
at school, she was two years behind me, but after Aunt
Ruth's funeral I spent a few hours with her. She'd wanted
to stay on and help Uncle Henry, but Lucille had forbidden
it, and had sent the police to fetch her away from the forge.
We sat together in the Quiet Room, and Matron brought us
a pot of tea.

'I won't be allowed to go there any more, will I?' she
asked, and her voice was desperate. 'I won't be allowed to
stay with Uncle Henry. Why not? Why not, Glory? Other
people stay with their uncles. He's family, why can't I go
there?'

I didn't know what to say. I hadn't seen Uncle Henry
very often, but I knew I looked a little like him, Aunt Ruth
had said we had the same high cheekbones and the same
smile. But Ann didn't look like Uncle Henry. Ann's face is
broad, and her skin's dark and creamy. Her eyes are brown.
I didn't think Ann and I had the same father.

'I can't live with Lucille,' she said. 'Not all the time. I
can't wear dresses all the time. And try to be feminine, and
smile, and all that. I'm not pretty, Glory. I can't be like that.'

36

I hadn't realised before, hadn't seen how it must have been for Ann. Lucille bought us dresses, and pretty shoes, and took us to hairdressers. She sent us to dancing classes, and we had to learn deportment, and elocution. I hadn't minded, had quite enjoyed the dancing and the attention from the dressmaker, and Pierre the hairdresser who had told me he came from Newcastle, not Versailles. But Ann had endured it, silently and stoically.

Lucille usually left us at home when she went out. I was used to this, and anyway, since I'd been at the theatre there was always something to do, either there or in the evenings at home, costumes to finish for Mrs Pasmore, or something to paint for Norman Jack, the property man. But if there was a party we were often invited too, and I enjoyed them. Parties were fun, there was music, and we danced and laughed.

At parties boys had crowded around me since I was about twelve. And men, too. Sitting in that room at school, looking at Ann, I thought about it. Dancing, and talking, and laughing with the boys and the men, and Lucille doing the same, and sitting somewhere else, in a corner if there was one, Ann, in dark blue taffeta, smiling and quiet. No boys, no men. Sometimes I had wondered, briefly, why she didn't join in, but then somebody would ask me to dance, or raise a glass to me, and the thought would fly away, unexamined, unanswered.

What, I wondered, would I do if I went to a party and nobody talked to me? If the boys and the men did not crowd around me, if there was no admiration in the eyes, no invitations to dance, no happy laughter wherever I happened to be? How would I manage if I was ugly, and taller than anybody I ever met?

Ann isn't ugly, not really. But she is very big, and very tall, and she doesn't like meeting strangers. She does as Lucille tells her, she smiles, and she shakes hands, and she listens, very politely. We all three listen politely when men

37

are speaking. They like that, they like women to listen when they talk. I've known that since before I can remember, and that what men like is important.

I had a boyfriend. His name was Nigel Carter-Riley, and his father was an architect. I can't remember much about him, except that Lucille approved of him, and that I got him to write his name and a sloppy message across an agency photograph of a young and relatively unknown actor. That photograph was pasted inside the lid of my desk at school, and since the actor was very good-looking the other girls in my class were respectful to me. Nigel had no interest in the theatre, and I had none in aeroplanes, which were his passion, but he and I used to go to the cinema together, and sometimes to parties, which pleased Lucille.

Ann hadn't been to many parties with us. She'd spent most of the holidays at the forge. I could only remember one or two, and I'd been having fun, I hadn't wondered whether everybody else was, I just assumed they were, because parties were fun.

At Christmas there were lots of parties over the holiday season. I'd gone with Lucille for the last two years. That meant Ann would have to come too. I didn't know what to say to her. I remembered Lucille doing up the zip at the back of Ann's dark blue party dress, and then standing back to look at her as Ann obediently turned to face her, and the look on Lucille's face as she begged her to try to be a little more feminine, and Ann helplessly trying to smile, her big hands clenching and unclenching at her sides.

'I'm only happy when I'm at the forge,' she said. 'Only really happy. Glory,' and there was a look of horror on her face as she looked into her future, 'Glory, I'm never going to be happy again.'

Matron came back about an hour later, and told us she'd saved some supper for us, we could have it in the staff pantry by ourselves. I wrote to Uncle John.

'Can you do something?' I asked. 'You're our guardian, aren't you? Ann's very unhappy.'

He wrote back and said there wasn't anything he could do if Lucille refused to allow Ann to stay at the forge, but they knew the situation at Storrington, and would help Ann.

I spent a bit more time with her that term, and Miss Elphick tried to help. There was a handicraft class for Ann's year, and she bought a welding torch and a mask, and Ann made figures from sheets of steel and mounted them on wooden blocks. Lucille heard about it, and forbade it. When I wrote to her I said Ann liked working with metal, and Miss Elphick said her figures were good, but she wrote back a very sharp letter. Metal-working was not suitable for girls. It was time I learned to mind my own business; she, as Ann's mother, would decide what Ann could and could not do. Storrington was a good school, and we weren't there to learn to be metal workers.

We went home together on the train for the school holidays, Ann and I, and she sat in the corner, staring out of the window at the passing fields and houses, her face blank. For the last week at school there'd been excitement, with trunks being packed, and Christmas cards exchanged, and the common rooms had been bright with paper streamers and branches of evergreen. There'd been carol services, and the junior school Nativity play, and everybody had been happy, with the holidays coming and Christmas only a few days later. I hadn't seen much of Ann. Sitting opposite her in the train, looking at her expressionless face, I wondered what she thought about the Christmas holiday ahead.

Lucille gave her a dressing table set, silver gilt. Hairbrush, comb, hand mirror, clothes brush. Ann smiled, and kissed Lucille's lovely cheek, and said, thank you, they're beautiful. Thank you, Lucille. I gave her a new fountain pen, and she smiled, and said, thanks, Glory. It's a good one, I needed a new one.

There was a party on New Year's Eve, and Ann wore her dark blue taffeta, and Lucille lent her a silver necklace and did up the clasp for her. Ann stood as Lucille stepped back to look. She was huge and quiet, her hands clasped around an evening bag, waiting for Lucille to sigh, to tell her to be more feminine, to smile.

I thought the silver necklace looked silly.

I remembered Ann in the art studio annexe, working on the weapons for *Macbeth*. She'd been standing, concentrated on her work, a pair of metal shears in her hand, two leather straps over her shoulder, the sleeves of her smock rolled up to her elbows. She'd looked right. She'd been working, competent and relaxed. That was how Ann should be, with tools in her hand, not a tiny silver lamé evening bag. I wondered why Lucille couldn't see this, couldn't understand that Ann could only be ridiculous playing the part of a pretty young girl.

Lucille sighed.

'Antoinette, darling, please *try* to be a little more . . .'

Nigel came with us to the party, and kissed me under the mistletoe out in the hall during the party, clutched painfully at my breast and tried to put his hand up my skirt. I hit him on the nose, and made it bleed. He was furious with me, he was wearing a suede jerkin and blood would stain it. We sat on the stairs together, and he said he needed ice on the back of his neck, but when I got some he complained that it dripped down inside his collar. He said I was a frigid lesbian. He'd been expecting to have his face slapped, which would have got him a reputation for playing fast and loose, but when I asked him to explain what that meant he said I was stupid. After that I sat beside him in silence while he mopped at his nose with his handkerchief and muttered and sniffed, wondering why I had to be so polite to him just because he was a boy, and how far he would have gone if I hadn't hit him. I decided to go and find myself another boyfriend, so I stood up and walked across the hall towards the big drawing room.

'Where are you going?' he demanded. 'You can't leave me here like this.'

'I think I can,' I said. 'I like parties, I don't want to miss this one.'

I spent the rest of the evening dancing with an articled clerk from Maidstone, but all he could talk about was how much money he would earn when he joined his father's firm, so I gave him a false telephone number and made some excuse when he offered to take me for a drive in his sports car.

I wondered if I really was a frigid lesbian, as Nigel had said. At school, the other girls boasted about how far their boyfriends tried to go, and how they had to fight them off. I tried to imagine what it would be like to kiss another girl, or to have sex with one, but I didn't know how you could do it, and it seemed a bit ridiculous, as well as rather disgusting. There was a rumour at school that one of the games mistresses was a lesbian, and that a junior teacher had had a nervous breakdown and left because of her, but although we all enjoyed the idea of such a scandal I don't think any of us really believed it.

I decided I might be frigid, but I certainly wasn't a lesbian.

There was to be a party at the theatre a few days after New Year, and I wanted to go. It wouldn't start until eleven, and was likely to go on all night. I was usually supposed to be home by eleven, midnight on special occasions, and I couldn't see Lucille agreeing. And I wanted to go alone, not with Lucille, who might learn what I really did at the theatre, and might hear the sort of stage gossip I'd not repeated.

'Can you come to a stage party?' I asked her. 'It'll be great fun. Somebody said John Gielgud might look in.'

'*Lovely*, darling. When?'

'Don't know yet,' I lied. 'Depends on how long this pantomime runs.'

Ann spent her days in her room, reading. She'd brought some of her school books back. I asked her if she'd like to come to the theatre, but she smiled, and shook her head. She didn't like meeting new people.

The pantomime season at the theatre meant *Cinderella* that year, with two of the stars from a television series about the police playing the Ugly Sisters. Some of the actors hated pantomimes, even though it was the one time of the year when almost everybody could find work. It seemed to me that the production was designed less for children every year, most of the jokes were political, and that year they were changing almost every day. That meant rehearsals all the time, and backstage we were working as hard as we could preparing the scenery for the next production, a new play by a young writer who Reeve said was headed straight for the top, so we'd better use him as much as we could before somebody else spotted him. There was a scene with mirrors, and it was very difficult because of dazzle from the spots, the angles had to be exact and we had to set them up on stage. So we had the Ugly Sisters capering to and fro snapping *doubles entendres* about power cuts at each other while behind them half a dozen of us shouted instructions and swore and adjusted angles. It's just as well they were professionals, it must have been almost impossible.

We were wedging the mirrors at the right angles, and measuring distances, and making notes about the lights, and trying not to get in the way of the rehearsals, and Reeve sat as usual, in the darkness of the auditorium, calling out his instructions, and I heard my name.

'Glory, come and be Buttons for a moment, would you, dear?'

I ran down to the footlights, and I peered into the darkness, and I called back to him.

'Reeve, *please* get somebody else, we'll *never* get this damned thing right if you keep calling me off it!'

And I looked round at the two men, at faces I'd seen so often on the television screen, now they were smiling at me, and for a moment I remembered how I would have felt three years ago standing next to them on a stage with the lights blazing down on us, and I almost laughed.

I didn't want to be an actress any more.

Every night, when I got the opportunity, I'd open Lucille's handbag and take out her diary and look. And at last, against the date of the party, I saw something pencilled in, with an exclamation mark after it. Lord and Lady somebody, in Mayfair, with Andrew Tyrrell.

It couldn't have been better. A local cocktail party she might have dropped, but Mayfair, and titles, and Andrew Tyrrell, would certainly take precedence over anything I might have wanted.

I brought it up the next day when I came in, feigning excitement and running up the stairs to her room.

'It's the sixth! It's been fixed, and John Gielgud *is* coming, at least for a little while, and it's going to be on stage with the mirror scene, so wear that silver thing, you'll be a . . .'

And I let my voice die away at the dismayed expression on her face.

I was brave, and I was cheerful, and I said of course she had to go to Mayfair, there'd be other parties, it didn't matter a bit.

Within half an hour Lucille had decided I should go on my own. I was, after all, sixteen, and quite responsible, and it was a special occasion. If it meant coming home with the milkman, then so be it. We'd just have to hope that prissy old fusspot John Mayall never heard about it.

The next day I saw Peter Clements for the first time.

It had been errands, errands all day, it seemed. Telephone calls to the paint shop for more burnt umber, deliver this afternoon without fail or else, run down to Fabrics and see if you can match this red cotton sheeting, back to Springtime for flowers, tell Dave he's wanted for another rehearsal of that sword fight scene this afternoon, get Sue and Terry to come for a fitting at three.

I seemed to spend the whole day running around with messages.

He was walking along the passage, his head bowed as he rubbed the back of his neck, hunching his shoulders as though it hurt. As I approached I heard him muttering to himself.

I stepped to one side to give him room to pass, but he didn't see me, and he brushed against me. He stopped immediately.

'Sorry!' he exclaimed. 'I wasn't looking where I was going.'

Tall, with floppy brown hair falling over his forehead, wide shoulders and very long legs. I felt suddenly shy.

'It's all right,' and I hurried on down the corridor. I glanced back as I reached the corner. He was standing at the other end, watching me. I went on, quickly.

'Sue and Terry, fitting this afternoon at three,' I chanted as I went into the dressing room. 'Who's the new man with the brown hair?'

'Wow!' said Louise, carefully smearing eye shadow into the little hollows at the corners of the sockets. 'Isn't he just? He's called Peter Clements, don't those legs go on for *ever*?'

The room was blue with cigarette smoke, and I coughed. I wished they'd open a window sometimes.

Terry was smoothing a pair of skin-tight trousers over her hips.

'Who'll bet me I'll have those jeans off him before opening night?'

I was remembering dark brown hair falling over a pair of dark brown eyes, and I answered without thinking.

'I think they'd be too big for you.'

They all screamed with laughter, and suddenly realising what she meant, and how naïve I'd been, I joined in. Sue smiled at me, her nice face kind and amused, and Louise reached back and punched me lightly on the arm.

'Well,' said Terry, shrugging herself into a fur jacket, 'if I come in here one day in a pair of Levis, rolled up, and a bit baggy, you'll know I did it. No takers? I'll offer five to one?'

Sue rolled a sardonic eye at Louise as Terry left.

'She's getting herself a nasty reputation, that girl.'

Louise blotted her lipstick with a tissue, and considered her reflection with her head on one side.

'That's her business,' she answered. 'But I hope she doesn't get Peter Clements. A reliable source has it that her last little fling gave her victim the clap.'

I threw myself down on the sofa and snuggled up against Sue. I really loved Sue. She was in her thirties by then, and saying she looked like a mother hen, but she still had the body of a girl, and she could dance as well as anybody, except Louise.

'It's not just her business,' Sue retorted, giving me a hug and smiling at me. 'Not when you find stinking drunk riff-raff around here asking for her. Is that true, Louise? Has she really got the clap?'

I can't remember what Louise replied, but I knew Sue was right. There'd been two men in the courtyard the week before asking for Terry, and the new security man had called the police. They'd started throwing bottles at the door when he refused to let them in.

'I'm coming to the party,' I whispered in Sue's ear. 'All night! She's going to be in London, and she said I could. I told her John Gielgud was coming.'

Sue grinned as she gave me another hug.

'You artful little cow! What are you going to wear?'

Before I could reply, Jim's voice came over the loud-speaker.

'Glory, will you *please* get back here to the paint room, wherever you are.'

'I'm coming to the party!' I told Jim as I squeezed detergent solution out of the brushes and swirled them around in a bucket of water.

'Good. Hurry up with those.'

'Who's Peter Clements?'

'Actor. Will you get on with those damned brushes?'

There was one stage hand I didn't like. Donald Flint. He was younger than most of them, a little overweight, and there was something furtive about him, like a snigger. If ever I had to speak to him his eyes used to slide down over my body, and then when he looked me in the face again there'd be a smirk, as if he could see through my clothes. Louise used to say she felt the palms of her hands itching every time he came near her.

He came into the paint room as I was leaving, and he stood against the door frame so I had to squeeze past him to get out. There was a sly look on his face. I turned my head away as I walked into the corridor, so I couldn't be sure I heard him correctly.

'Hello, *Cindy*,' he whispered.

I told Ann about the party, how I'd tricked Lucille into letting me go alone, and had said that John Gielgud was coming. Ann was looking tired. Lucille had put her on a diet again to try to stop her growing, even though all the doctors had said it wouldn't make any difference and might damage her health. Her hands and wrists were looking bony, and there were dark shadows around her eyes. I wondered if I should write to Uncle John, if there was anything he could do.

'Is John Gielgud really coming?' she asked.

'I don't suppose he's ever heard of us. Do you believe in love at first sight?'

We were in her bedroom. She was sitting at her desk, reading, making notes in pale pencil in the margin of a thick textbook, and I was lying on her bed, rolling to and fro on the eiderdown and wondering what on earth had induced Lucille to have it all decorated in pale blue and white when it was obvious to anybody with a quarter of an eye that Ann's colours were browns and creams and dark yellows.

Ann didn't know if she believed in love at first sight, but she listened attentively to my account of my meeting with Peter Clements, and said he sounded wonderful. No, she answered in reply to my question, she'd never been in love. She didn't suppose she ever would be. She tried not to think about things she knew she couldn't have.

But the book she was reading was about metal working, and Lucille had said Ann would have to go to secretarial college and learn shorthand and typing and book-keeping.

I took my party dress and my shoes and make-up to the theatre and left them in Sue's dressing room. She'd got three changes in that play and Reeve had said she had to have her own room, so Jim and Alan and I had cleared one of the small dressing rooms of old scenery and boxes of forgotten junk, and Alan had dumped it in the courtyard and arranged an accidental fire for the benefit of the insurance account. I painted Sue one of my lucky black cats, and she stuck it in the corner of the mirror, and said I was their very own black cat. She promised to help me with my make-up for the party.

'Knock their eyes out,' she promised, and, because she was perceptive and nice, she added, 'And we'll leave Terry nailed to a cushion, she can just weep. Peter's much too good for her, you get out there and drive him wild, sweetie.'

I'd seen him once or twice in the meantime, at rehearsals, waiting in the wings or hurrying away afterwards. He was in a television series and always worrying about being late.

'Stunt man,' Louise explained as I wrote down the measurements Mrs Pasmore called out to me. 'Giving it up, he's too tall.'

'Thirty-seven,' said Mrs Pasmore.

'It's *never* thirty-seven! You've got the tape twisted.'

'Thirty-seven,' repeated Mrs Pasmore firmly. 'Stand still.'

'Bugger it! Is it really thirty-seven? Bloody bleedin' hell.'

'Louise! *Language*, in front of the kid.'

'Thirty-six and a half,' I said. 'Stunt man?'

'You write down what I tell you, my girl, never mind stunt men. Thirty-seven, I said, and what's more, Louise, you're getting just a tiny, tiny spare tyre.'

'I *hate* you, Lindy Passion-Flower Pasmore! Oh, God. I'll be in corsets before I'm thirty.'

'Don't you call me Passion-Flower, I'll not have those rumours starting up again. Twenty-five. Glory, are you listening?'

Louise screamed.

'Twenty-five. Stunt man, Louise, *please* tell me.'

'Fights,' said Louise, eyeing the tape measure as though it was a poisonous snake. 'And falls and things. The taller you are the more there is to break. Or so I'm told. *Is* that thing accurate? Lindy, *please*.'

'It's the one I'll use to cut out. Thirty-eight, I'm sorry, dear, but that's what it is. Thirty-eight. "Curvaceous" I think the *Argus* said last time, didn't they?'

'You bitch! I'll have to starve. It's no good making the thing, I'll be thinner by then.'

'Yes, dear,' said Mrs Pasmore placidly, 'then we'll take it in. Don't worry.'

'Worry! Of *course* I worry, I'll have frown lines to go with the spare tyre. Oh, fucking hell.'

'Language, dear. At least it hasn't reached your ankles.'

'You're still the best dancer in the Midlands,' I offered. 'I think you're beautiful.'

'Love you, Glory,' said Louise absently, staring at the mirror and looking genuinely distressed. 'I'm already dieting. *Why* am I getting fat? I can't be, I should be getting thinner.'

'Are you on the pill, dear?'

'Of *course* I am.'

'That might be it. Takes some of them that way. Better come off it, dear.'

'I can't. Mark won't use anything else, he's a Catholic.'

'I thought they were against the pill,' I said.

Mrs Pasmore puffed herself up like an angry hen.

'Men! Catholics are the worst. Oh, yes, I know. Keep the women barefoot and pregnant, sweating over a hot, hot kitchen stove. If it was the men that has the babies it wouldn't be communion wafers they'd hand out, it'd be lots and lots of little pills. And there's some other religions I could mention, it wouldn't stop with circumcision, it'd be . . .'

She caught sight of me and stopped herself, red in the face with indignation, and patted Louise on the shoulder.

'Don't you worry, my lovie, I'll make you a beautiful, beautiful frock that'll have them saying you're thin as a rake. Men, all they're good for is sex, and there's not many that's much good at that, either. The times I've faked it just to stop myself falling fast asleep from sheer boredom.'

'Haven't we all?' Louise sighed, and turned away from the mirror with a rueful shrug.

'Barley water, dear. Flush yourself out, it's all fluid, that's the problem. Barley water, that'll help.'

I didn't want to talk about the pill, or barley water, or even why Mrs Pasmore was called Passion-Flower and what the rumour was. I wanted to talk about a stunt man who had grown too tall. I wanted to know why he was here, in fleeting glimpses, standing in the dark shadows in the wings, alert and still, and then, only moments later, or so it seemed, hurrying away as if he were late. None of the other actors did that, not even the ones who'd been taken on for one production only, in fact they spent more time around the theatre than any of the regular cast, hoping to be in the right place at the right time.

And sometimes they were. Ray had been taken on like that, and he'd been at the Royal for seven years now. But he still worried.

'Tell me about Peter,' I begged, and Louise looked at me blankly as though she couldn't remember who I was.

Mrs Pasmore ignored me.

'You chuck him, my dear,' she said to Louise. 'No man's worth your career, let alone your health.'

I gave up, and went back to the paint room, wondering what Lucille would have said about Mrs Pasmore's advice.

She'd been quite calm about Nigel, I'd thought she might be upset. All she'd said was I'd have to find myself another boyfriend, women on their own were a social nuisance.

I didn't go into the theatre on the day of the party. Lucille had said I should rest, as I was going to be up all night. Nigel telephoned, sulky and belligerent, and asked me to go to the cinema. He said he was having a rotten holiday. I told him I was going to a party and he asked if he could come, too. It seemed he hadn't found another girlfriend, as he had said he would do when I left him sitting on the stairs. He had said all cats are black in the dark, and you don't look at the mantelpiece when you're poking the fire, but I don't think he knew what the comments meant.

'No,' I said. 'You can't come, it's theatre people only.'

'Oh, you're a *theatre* person, are you?' he sneered. 'Don't *theatre* people have friends?'

I hung up on him, and I never heard from him again. I can't remember what he looked like, or why I got him to write that message across the agency photograph. I could have written it myself.

I got to the theatre halfway through the performance, and I went straight to Sue's dressing room. I was over an hour early, but I was excited, far more than I had ever been about any other party. I was in my own world here, with the people I liked, and we were going to celebrate. I listened as I sat, listened for the applause at the end of each scene. It was good, the play was going well.

Sue came in, planting a quick kiss on the top of my head as she stripped off her dress, with Mrs Pasmore bustling in behind her to help her with the lacing on the next one. She was intense and concentrated, and I kept quiet so as not to distract her. It was a difficult part she was playing, but she loved it, and Reeve said she'd got right down to the bones of it.

When she went out again I sat at her dressing table in front of her mirror and looked at the make-up, all laid out in rows on a folded white towel. Sue was always neat with her make-up. In the main dressing room the tables were a mess, with half-empty coffee cups and bottles of soft drinks lying around, ashtrays overflowing, stockings and tights hanging across the mirrors. The main dressing room was filthy. The men's dressing room was much tidier, but, as Louise said, they didn't have so many costumes to cram into it, let alone need to wash out their tights between performances and hang them up to dry. Even so, they could have kept it better.

I hadn't noticed at first that the door was open. It had closed behind Mrs Pasmore, she was funny about doors, pulling them shut until they clicked, and then pushing against them to test them. I sat at the dressing table and looked at the reflection of the door. There was a shadow on the frame, and it moved.

I felt uneasy. There was something furtive about that shadow, about the quiet way the door must have opened for me not to have heard it. Somebody was there, behind the door, watching me.

I turned on the stool, and looked. In the background I heard a burst of applause, and then voices backstage, footsteps thudding on the coconut matting, and the shadow on the door frame moved again, and disappeared. A voice, sharp in the corridor.

'What are you doing here?'

A mumbled reply, and then more footsteps, several people in the corridor, and Sue came back, smiling, so I got off the stool and stood aside for her.

'Who was that in the corridor?' I asked.

'Everybody,' she answered briefly, reaching for the powder box. 'Why?'

'Oh, it was a voice I didn't recognise,' I lied. I wasn't going to disturb her concentration just before her main scene. But the quietly opening door, and the furtive shadow, worried me. I didn't want to stay in the dressing room alone.

'Put on a hairband, darling,' she said as she touched at her mouth with a crimson lipstick. 'You'll find some in the drawer.'

She looked at her face with critical, narrowed eyes, and then glanced back at me.

'You could put your dress on if you like, you don't need make-up on your neck. Tuck a towel round the collar.'

She stood up, smoothed her hands down over the waistline of her costume, smiled at me, and was gone, her footsteps light and hurrying on the corridor matting.

I went to the door and watched as the cast came out of the dressing rooms, speaking softly to each other and smiling as they went back to the stage. They were all tense and excited, riding on the response from the audience, alert to the reactions. It was a good play, a good cast, an intelligent audience, there was triumph and a high-strung excitement in the air. I caught it from the way they moved as they went back to their places, in the lift of their heads and in the nervous hands, and I felt my pulse beating faster.

I closed the door, and pulled at it as Mrs Pasmore did. I wished there was a bolt, or a key, I felt nervous. I kept watching the door as I changed into my party dress. I'd thought she'd want to put the make-up on first, as she always did herself, I found I was fretting about that. Something seemed to be wrong.

I sat at her dressing table, and took several deep breaths to calm myself. I told myself I was being stupid.

There was a pile of stretch hairbands in the drawer, and I put one on, carefully settling it above my forehead, pulling it back over the temples. And a towel, she'd said I should put a towel around the neckline of the dress. There was one in my bag.

I was trembling.

I didn't hear him, but I saw the door opening, the dark line by the frame growing wider, and then light from the corridor, and the shadow on the white wood, and a pale blur of a face. As he saw me watching in the mirror he hesitated, but then the door swung wide, and he came in and closed it behind him, leaning against it and smiling, his eyes moving up and down over my body.

'Hello, Cindy.'

Why did he call me that? I wondered. Everybody knew my name. I stared at him in the mirror, thinking how disgusting he looked, fat and sly, and his tongue slid over his lips, and he smiled and moved towards me.

'You're not supposed to be here,' I said.

He was standing close up behind me, and I could hear him breathing, quickly, as he looked down over my shoulder and he smiled again.

'Nobody's going to come in,' he said. 'Not for a while.'

'Go away. You're not allowed in the dressing rooms.'

He licked his lips again, and his hands hovered over my shoulders, and then he was stroking them, and sliding his thumbs under the towel I'd put over my dress.

'My, Cindy, what a big girl you've grown into.'

I stood up quickly, and turned to face him, pushing him away.

'Get out of here! Don't touch me, you slug.'

He didn't seem to hear me. I backed away from him and he followed, until I was against the table at the back of the room and he pressed himself against me, soft and disgusting, and his thick lips were against my neck and his hands were on my shoulders pulling at the towel.

'I could teach you things those two never dreamed of, Cindy,' he whispered, and his voice was slurred, as if he was drunk. 'I could teach you, Cindy. You could learn how all over again, Cindy, little Cindy.'

He had an erection. He rubbed against me and nuzzled his lips into my neck, his hands were on my back, fumbling with the zip on my dress. I felt as if I couldn't move, I was disgusted and horrified, paralysed with fright, and he was mumbling, Cindy, little Cindy, come on, little Cindy, I'll teach you how, little Cindy, and I heard the zip opening, and suddenly I could move again.

I hit him, just as I had hit Nigel, with my clenched fist, on his nose, and there was a spatter of blood, and he staggered back, his eyes wide and shocked.

'Get out!' I spat. 'How dare you? How dare you *touch* me, you filth? I'll tell Jim about this. You'll never work here again, you'll never work *anywhere* in the theatre again, you foul slug. Get out.'

'You bitch!' He had his hand to his nose, and there was blood dripping through his fingers. 'You fucking bitch. You cunting little cock-sucker. You tell anybody, and I'll show them, don't think I won't. I've got copies. I'll show them, *Cindy*, little *Cindy*, I'll show everybody.'

'I don't know what you mean,' I said. 'Cindy, all this *Cindy*, you filthy slug. I'm not Cindy, I'm Glory. Miss Mayall to you and dirt like you. Get out.'

'I've got copies,' he said again. 'Oh, yes, I've got copies, *Cindy*, I'll leave them around. Yes, I will, I'll do that. I'd have kept quiet if you'd been nice to me. I might still. If you're nice to me. Little *Cindy*.'

'If you touch me again,' I said, sliding away from the table as he moved towards me, 'I'll scream. And they'll hear it on the stage. Maybe even in the auditorium. Reeve will *skin* you, if that happens.'

That stopped him. He stood staring at me, his eyes narrowed, and he sniffed, and looked at his bloody hand.

'Bitch. Dirty little bitch.'

'Get out.'

'I'll leave you a copy. In the Green Room. The first copy, for the star, that's right, isn't it? That's only right? And then I'll leave the others. Where they'll be found. You'll wish, Cindy. You'll wish you hadn't done that.'

He went out, and I sat on the stool in front of the dressing table, and tried to stop myself shaking. There was blood on the towel, splashed over my shoulder, and I took it off, and looked carefully to see if there was any on my dress. I looked at myself in the mirror. I was pale, and my eyes were staring and unnatural. I was very cold. After a moment I got up and went over to the gas fire, and lit it. I knelt on the rug in front of it, hugging myself, and taking deep breaths, telling myself I was calm, I was all right, everything was all right.

I wanted to change all my clothes, and have a bath, but I only had my party dress and my jeans and sweater in my grip bag. I went to the basin and washed my face, and my neck, and then I took off the dress and washed myself as much as I could, everywhere Donald Flint had touched me, but I hadn't got another towel to dry myself, and I didn't want to touch the one with his blood on it, so I stood in front of the gas fire, and then I started to shake again and my knees gave way, I found myself sitting on the rug in my brassiere and knickers and stockings, and I was fearful that he might come back.

I crawled across the carpet to the door, and sat against it, my back pressed against it, my feet braced to hold it shut. My teeth were chattering, and I clenched them. Shock, I told myself. It'll go. It'll go away in a minute. It would have to go away, the play was almost over, everybody would be back, I had to be normal.

I stood up, and walked back across the room, slowly, deliberately, one foot, then the other, one in front of the other, a straight line, no wobbling, no shaking. Good. Now the dress.

But I couldn't. He had touched it. He had fumbled at it,

55

had nuzzled his face against it, had scrabbled at the zip and almost pulled it down. I didn't want to touch that dress.

I took my jeans and my sweater out of my grip, and put them on. Then I bundled up the dress, trying not to touch the parts of it he had touched, and pushed it into the grip. I never wanted to wear it again. Lucille would be furious, it was wild silk.

I opened the door, and I listened. I could hear the voices faintly, Sue's, high and mocking, and Dave, a flat monotone in reply. Almost at the end now, and I'd never even seen it, just odd bits of rehearsal.

I went back to the dressing table, and I wrote a note. 'Sorry, Sue, not feeling well. Love, Glory.'

I left it on the towel by her make-up, where she'd see it.

There was nobody in the corridor. I walked along it, slowly and steadily, listening for footsteps, wondering where Donald Flint was, if he was watching me. If I saw him, I thought, I would scream. And then I told myself, I wouldn't, I would *not*, I would not risk being heard in the auditorium, I had never done that and I never would.

The door to the Green Room was open. I stopped, wondering if he was in there, waiting for me. Not many theatres have Green Rooms now, but the Royal was old, and there weren't enough dressing rooms, they were crowded, so Reeve had said the cast should have the Green Room, somewhere quiet to sit. Donald Flint had said he would leave it in the Green Room. I remembered that. The first copy for the star, he had said.

I stood on the other side of the corridor, and looked through the open door. The lights were on, but it seemed to be empty. Nobody sitting in the armchairs or on the sofa. The gas fire was unlit. But the lights were on, and there was something on the table. A book, a yellow book.

I pushed the door wide open, and then I went in, looking around to make sure the room was empty. I picked up the book. There was nothing written on the cover, it was cheap cardboard, a plain cover, nothing at all.

I opened it, at the first page, and my face stared back at me.

It was one of the photographs that had been taken after the beauty contest. I was getting off the chair, backing away as the photographer came at me with his camera, I remembered. I was crying. There were tears on my cheeks, and my eyes were wide and frightened. I was wearing my knickers, and one hand was on the back of the chair as I stood up, the other reached out towards him, as if fending him away.

There was a caption under the photograph, in blurred black print.

'Little Cindy Learns How! And How!'

I turned the pages. There were more photographs, I remembered him taking them. Sitting on the chair, standing, my hips thrust forward, one foot on the chair, and then the close-ups, a frightened face, tears. Captions. 'Little Girls Shouldn't Tease.' 'What are you Asking For, Little Cindy?' 'Time to Learn What It's All About.'

And then the photographs were of my face, frightened, and crying, and screaming, but it was only my face, the rest of the pictures were different, photographs I didn't know, never knew, had never known could exist. My face, on another child's body, and two men.

And they were raping her.

4

I went back to watercolours at school, and left the oil paints locked in the cupboard. I told Miss Elphick I wanted to do flower paintings and landscapes, and she looked at me in a funny way and said, whatever you like, Gloriana, but don't forget the perspective lessons.

It didn't seem important. It was my O level year, and I supposed I would pass art. I needed four others to get into art school, which was what I had wanted. I would have to do something. I wasn't clever enough to stay on at school for A levels. I would have to have some sort of career, or at least a job, as Lucille said, until something came up, by which she meant marriage.

I didn't want to think about it. There was plenty of time until the summer anyway, and I only needed to pass, I didn't need very high grades. Not unless I wanted to go to one of the best art schools, and it hardly seemed worth it.

I'd taken the book home. I wanted to throw it away, or burn it, but I kept looking at it. I kept it under my mattress, and I took it out, and looked at it, and put it away again, and then took it out, mostly at night, looking at it by torch-light, with a torch I kept in the drawer of my bedside table. Every time I looked I felt sick, and shocked, and unclean. I stared helplessly at the anguished child, half me, half not me. And I thought of everybody at the theatre looking at those same pictures, as Donald Flint had said they would when he left the other copies around for them to find.

'Are you all right, Glory?' asked Ann. I looked at her. Her eyes were sunken, her teeth seemed as if they were too big for her mouth. She looked dreadful, ill with starvation. Even Lucille was worried, almost frightened, she said Antoinette had better come off her diet for a while. But Ann said she wasn't hungry.

Scrambled eggs and bacon, and she pushed it around her plate, and smiled at Lucille, and said she wasn't really very hungry.

'Eat it!' shouted Lucille, and there was fear in her face. She'd gone too far, and Ann was ill.

I watched them both, Ann obediently chewing the soft eggs, trying to swallow, trying to control a retch, Lucille standing at the table, leaning forward, staring at her, telling her to eat.

Only three days to school, and Ann was ill. The doctors had warned Lucille that dieting wouldn't stop her growing and might damage her health, and now she was really ill. She was tired and listless, and she didn't want to eat.

I should have noticed. I'd been at the theatre almost every day, I'd been thinking about the angle of the mirrors, about the party, about Peter Clements and whether Terry might seduce him. I hadn't noticed Ann growing more and more ill, every day. My baby sister, I thought suddenly, remembering when she had been that, smaller than me, looking at me with her grave brown eyes. It was years since I'd thought of her like that, and I watched her trying to eat her scrambled eggs, quiet and obedient as ever, huge, and bony, and ill.

'Milk,' said Lucille, and there was panic in her voice. 'A glass of milk. Gloriana, get a glass.'

She was better by the time we went back to school, able to eat again, and the hollows around her mouth and eyes were no longer quite so noticeable. Lucille had convinced herself that Ann had caught an infection, the same one that had made me so quiet and pale for the last few days of the holidays. Obviously, we'd both caught something.

Sue had sent me a card, a picture postcard of a sailing ship in the mist.

'Get well soon,' it read. 'We miss you! The party was fun, everybody asked where you were.'

I wondered, as I read it, if she had seen the pictures yet.

Louise had telephoned. Lucille called me to the phone, but I wouldn't talk to Louise. I asked Lucille to say I was out. They'd have seen the pictures by now, I thought. Everybody would have seen the pictures by now. They'd think it was me.

I almost thought it was me. I looked at the pictures by torchlight at night, and wondered why I didn't remember. I looked at the man holding the girl, holding me, one hand in my hair, the other wrenching at a knee, he was laughing, why didn't I remember a man laughing? And the other man holding my arms behind my back, forcing me forward as he raped me from behind. Did I remember him?

I had been screaming for Lucille as the photographer came towards me, thrusting the camera at my face. There had been nobody else. The photographs were fakes. Those two men, it had been some other child. But sometimes, as I looked at those pictures, I almost seemed to remember, the laughter, screaming, violent hands wrenching my knees apart.

Mrs Pasmore telephoned the night before we went back to school. Did I know where the notebooks with the measurements for the *Goliath* costumes were? Ann took the message, and told her I'd ring back. I thought about it.

'In the second fitting room, on the metal rack behind the door, top shelf, on the left hand side,' I said, and I burst into tears. I was talking about my home, and I was exiled from it.

Another card from Sue, a black cat on a wall.

'Terry isn't wearing those jeans yet.'

'What does that mean?' asked Rosalind Back, reading it over my shoulder in the common room.

'Nothing,' I replied, and she pulled a face at me, and asked if she could borrow my geography notes. A different world, I thought. Like a dream now. They'd have seen those pictures.

I'd hidden the book under the carpet in my bedroom, under the bed. I didn't think Lucille would find it.

'What's the matter, Gloriana?' asked Miss Elphick, and I stared at her.

'Nothing,' I said. I was painting a tulip. It was quite pretty, I'd got the colour near enough. A bit solid, perhaps, you wouldn't think of putting it in water. But it was good enough.

'No shading?' she asked, lightly. And I thought, oh yes, I've forgotten the shading. Oh well.

Lucille wrote to me.

'Darling, they're making a fuss, they say you're not working. Honestly, it sounds like some kitchen gadget, as if you needed a spare part. I have to ask you, is something wrong? I told them about that infection you and Antoinette caught, but they insist it's not that. It seems you need a medical degree just to be a mother now, it'll be third degree next time I come, I suppose. What on *earth* did you do to that dress? Have you any idea what it cost? I am *very* angry with you, it's ruined.'

Mrs Russell invited me to tea in her study, something housemistresses sometimes did, and she asked me what I'd done in the holidays. I said I'd been to parties, the usual things one did at Christmas.

'Nothing at the theatre? No new productions?'

'Oh yes,' I answered. 'But, well, I got a bit bored with it, you know. I didn't go much.'

She looked at me in silence, waiting for me to continue,

but I just stared into the fire, and at last she offered me the biscuits, and changed the subject.

Matron took me to the doctor, and he took some blood for tests, and listened to my chest, and checked my blood pressure.

'What was this infection you had over the holidays?' he asked.

'I don't know.'

'What did your doctor say?'

'I didn't go to the doctor.'

He glanced up at Matron, who raised her eyebrows and looked over his head out of the window.

'Your sister lost a lot of weight, I'm told. Did she go to the doctor?'

I shrugged. Lucille wouldn't have taken Ann to a doctor, she'd just starved her, and I hadn't been ill. But I would go on pretending about this infection, since Lucille had thought it up.

I painted a landscape, part of the moor behind the school, in watercolours, and Miss Elphick told me it was damned lousy, a wishy-washy slop. She was really angry. She pushed me into the studio and took my oil paints out of the cupboard and stood me in front of the easel, breathing quite heavily.

'Paint me a rotting corpse,' she demanded at last. 'And, you listen to me, Gloriana Mayall, I want to be able to *smell* the thing.'

There was no point in pretending to be shocked, I'd worked with her on the *Macbeth* sets and we'd talked about worse than that. I squeezed some ochre on to my palette, and sketched in a flat figure. Then I thought for a moment, and scrubbed it off. Face down, one arm reaching out, so, fingers hooked into the earth. A scattering of rags, torn off the back. The shoulder hunched, one knee bent, and the foot, so.

Miss Elphick watched me for a while, still breathing

heavily, her eyes angry, and then she went away, into the handcrafts room. She came back about an hour later, and looked at what I'd done. She jerked her head, and grunted.

'I was beginning to think you'd got paralysis of the brain.'

For the rest of that term she made me paint weird subjects, a moonscape with the feeling that there were things waiting in the craters, an abandoned town, a woman sitting at a table waiting for the police.

'I want to know what she's feeling,' she said. 'Resignation, fear, something like that. And leave out that revolting powder blue colour, you're not illustrating nursery rhymes.'

It was easier to paint as she demanded than to resist, so I did as she wanted, and painted the alert and shadowy moonscape, and the wind blowing through the broken windows, and the tired woman, and I stood back and waited for Miss Elphick to look at them, and to comment, and to tell me what to paint next.

'What do you *want* to paint?' she asked.

'I don't know.'

'Design a stage set? What about that play by Pinter, the new one with the two old men. Would you like to do that?'

'No,' I said. 'No, I don't want to do that.'

She looked as if she wanted to hit something, there was baffled anger in her face.

I wondered if I could paint two men raping a child, a young girl with the wrong body. How would I paint the laughter and the screams? I could hear them. I could feel the hands in my hair, could feel my arms twisted up behind my back, I could remember screaming for my mother. Could I remember the laughter, and the pain? I thought I could remember, it was only that the body was wrong. Could I remember the men? I could hear them laughing.

I never wondered about the other child. There was no other child, there was only me, with the wrong body. And the memory that was almost there, of fear and laughter, of screaming, of pain and terror. I could almost remember now. Lips smearing across my shoulders, hot breath, the hands on the fastening of my dress, the slurred voice, Cindy, little Cindy.

If I painted it, I would remember.

'Gloriana? Are you listening?'

Could I paint that, here, in the school studio? Would I remember? Could I paint the laughter and the screams? Should I remember? Can I paint pain and terror?

'Gloriana! What's the matter?'

I looked at her, at the woman saying the name, Gloriana. She was staring at me. Her hand was on my arm, I felt her shaking it. Gloriana, she was saying. She was worried. Her eyes were wide and staring. My eyes had been wide. There had been tears. Gloriana, she was saying, Gloriana. I could paint the wide eyes and the tears.

She spoke to somebody else, and the door opened, somebody going out. Had somebody gone out? Had my mother gone out and left me to the men? No, it had been different. I could almost remember. Can I paint loneliness? Had I been lonely then? Was that part of the fear? Somebody had taken me away from my mother. The memory was nearly there.

Other footsteps, everybody going out, leaving me alone, standing at the easel, the woman beside me, talking to me, her voice steady, and slow, and quite clear.

'I think you should sit down, my dear. It's all right. Gloriana? Can you hear me? Come and sit down.'

It was a good voice, I knew that voice, a good, familiar voice. I looked at the woman. Short grey hair, lines around the eyes, I knew that face, I wasn't alone, I wasn't lonely.

'Miss Elphick.'

'Yes, that's right. Come and sit down. Matron will be here in a minute. Come on, dear. Sit down here.'

There weren't any comfortable chairs in the studio, only the stools in front of the drawing stands and a chair for a model, if we were doing life work. She'd put the sack of paint rags on it to make a cushion, and she led me over to it, talking to me, and I sat down and stared up at her. She brought one of the stools, and perched herself on it, smiling at me.

'What happened?'

I wondered if I could tell her, about the child that was me, and the memory that wouldn't quite come, and the wrong body. If I told her she wouldn't smile at me. She would be disgusted. If people knew, they wouldn't want to be near me. I couldn't tell a thing like that. I shouldn't be here, sitting on this chair, with a nice woman smiling at me. If I told, they would send me away.

And then I was in the sanatorium, and Matron was bringing me a cup of tea, pale and watery in the white china, and there was a thermometer, and her fingers on my wrist as she glared down at her watch, and nodded briskly, and looked at the thermometer, and nodded again, and told me I could drink my tea now.

The doctor again, the same one who had taken my blood pressure earlier in the term, who had asked me about the infection, and he was asking questions, but it was too difficult to answer his questions, too difficult to listen to him, so I closed my eyes, and I suppose he went away.

I tried to remember, I knew I had to remember. All my friends knew what had happened to me, I had been raped by two men, they all knew that, it was only me who couldn't remember. There was the wrong body, a thin body, I couldn't feel that body, with the concave curving of the insides of the thighs where the bruises were beginning to show livid against the pale skin, the jutting hip bones, but I knew the staring eyes and I could remember the tears. I had to remember, I had to know what all my friends knew, that I had been raped, it was true, it must have happened, the photographs were there, it was only the body that was wrong.

65

I was in the sanatorium for two weeks, sitting in an arm-chair by the window during the days staring out over the southern hills, wrapped in a warm blanket. There were books for me to read, and sometimes I turned the pages, but I can't remember them. There was a sketch pad, and some pencils, Matron said Miss Elphick had brought them. I drew Matron as she straightened the pillows on my bed, bending forward towards the black iron bedstead, her starched cap and apron standing out stiffly against the shadows on the wall.

'Am I really as fat as that?' she asked when she looked at it, and I turned the sketch and considered it, looking from it to her, and back again, and thinking. She was. She was fat, had she thought she was thin?

'It's the apron,' I said, and I laid the pad on the table, and the pencils rolled against it, and I turned back to the window and watched the early spring clouds blowing across the pale sky.

It takes time to recover from rape, I thought. Several years of sitting in a warm armchair looking at clouds, wondering if I would ever remember, if I could trust my memory, now that all my friends remembered better than I.

Ann came to see me once, looking at me doubtfully. She'd been told I'd had a bad case of influenza, it had left me very weak, and perhaps a little confused. She sat on the bright rug on the floor, and I watched her, and then I picked up my sketch pad. She didn't say much, but I liked having her there. She'd been to a lacrosse match, she was still in the kit, with the scarlet sash around her waist, and mud on her knee where she'd slid on the ground. A blue Aertex shirt, open at the neck, navy blue pleated divided skirt riding up over her thigh, the scarlet topped socks over the canvas and rubber shoes with their black studded soles, clogged with drying mud. I still have that drawing, of Ann sitting on the rug in my room in the sanatorium.

And Lucille, angry and flustered, complaining about

being cross-examined by schoolmarms, who did they think they were, and then asking what on earth I'd been doing with myself to get into such a state, with everybody fussing at her, it was enough to drive her mad.

'Darling, honestly! Have you looked in the mirror? Surely you could at least brush your hair, you look dreadful. *So* unkempt.'

And she had a quarrel with Matron, and refused to leave the room to discuss anything further, she'd said all she was going to say on the subject, would Matron please leave immediately, she wanted to talk to her daughter *in private*.

Matron was rigid with fury, standing by the door, holding it open. At last Lucille swept through it and I heard it close behind them. I heard Matron's voice as they walked away down the corridor.

'Antoinette lost nearly two stone in five weeks, madam. If you don't consider that sufficient reason to call a doctor, I have to . . .'

Lucille would be furious with Ann, I thought. Lucille could never tolerate criticism, she would feel Ann was to blame for laying her open to it. But Ann had tried to eat, and she'd drunk the milk Lucille had given her, even though it had made her vomit. I could remember the Christmas holidays now, quite clearly. Lettuce and oranges, that was what Ann had been given to eat, Lucille had said there were plenty of vitamins in lettuce and in oranges, but nothing fattening, nothing that might make her grow even taller.

Ann hadn't been fat. There'd been nothing for her to lose, from Lucille's diet. My drawing of Ann sitting on the bright patterned rug when she came to see me after the lacrosse match shows her wrists bony, and the sinews in her neck standing out thin and clear above the hollowed collar bone where the neck of the shirt had fallen open.

But Lucille would blame Ann for whatever had been said to her, for the searching questions she had been asked, for Matron's steady, accusing eyes under the level brows.

I stood up, and folded the blanket that had been wrapped around my shoulders, and I went to the basin in the corner, and I washed myself all over, carefully, and slowly, and deliberately, and I dried myself and cleaned my teeth, and I dressed in the clothes that were hanging in the locker, and I brushed my hair until it felt soft and shiny. Then I stripped the bed, and folded the blankets, laying them tidily stacked with the pillow on top, the sheets and the pillowcase rolled ready for the laundry, the damp towel on the edge of the basin, and I stacked up my books and my sketch pad, and packed my soap and my toothbrush in the sponge bag, and everything except the books into my canvas holdall, and then I looked around the room to make sure I had forgotten nothing.

'I'm all right now,' I said when Matron came in and stood in the doorway staring at me. 'I'm all right. I'd like to go back to school now. I've got a lot of work to catch up.'

'What do you think was the matter with you?' she asked as she helped me carry my books and my bag down to the hall for the porter.

'I think it was probably that infection,' I replied. 'Maybe it came back.'

She didn't answer, just gave a wry little smile with one eyebrow raised. She told me she got bored sometimes, sitting in her room in the evenings, any time I felt like a chat she could probably wring another cup out of last week's tea bag.

The next time I was in the studio I coloured my sketch of Ann sitting on the floor, the blues of the games kit, the scarlet sash and stocking tops, a jazzy pattern of greens and golds on the rug, and Ann's creamy skin and her reddish-brown hair. As I washed in the shadows around her arms I realised I loved her, my big sister.

If only Lucille would leave Ann alone.

But she wouldn't. When we went home for the Easter holidays we hadn't been in the house an hour before she told Ann she was disloyal, she told lies, and had caused dreadful trouble with her stupid stories. Ann stood in the kitchen, in a pale grey dress, pearls around her neck, listening as Lucille raged of her embarrassment, caused by Ann.

'Telephone calls, and letters! What had the doctors said, and why hadn't we been to a doctor, and God knows what else. What on earth did you tell them? They treated me as if I was a *criminal*, I have *never* been so insulted, I was nearly *ill* with the worry of it all.'

I went into the kitchen, gave Lucille a vague smile, and asked Ann if she'd packed my pencil case by mistake, I couldn't find it.

'What about that ghastly matron?' demanded Lucille. 'I have *never* seen such a frump, she looks like an advertisement for flannel underwear. I do think Storrington should be a little more selective, they are *supposed* to be training the aristocracy, after all.'

'Darling Lucille,' I said. 'If you think Matron's a frump you should see the new junior games teacher. You wouldn't *believe*.'

Ann slipped out of the kitchen, murmuring about unpacking, and Lucille made a dramatic gesture, hand to forehead and eyes closed.

'My *God*. She looks like a *troll*. Six foot three, and she's only fourteen, how much bigger can she get? Darling, just *what* went on at that *bloody* old nunnery? What did she *tell* them, for God's sake? And *what* was the matter with *you*, stuck in the damned sick bay for nearly three weeks and everybody accusing me of driving you into a nervous breakdown, how *dare* they behave like that?'

The book was still under the carpet, I could see it as I lay on the floor beside my bed, the line of shadow rippling through the dense rose weave, the faint light on the hard, silky wool that marked the top edge. I leaned my head on my arms and watched it, almost as if it would move. There it was, the proof of the thing I could not quite remember, that two men had raped me when I had been in the wrong body.

'Are you going to the theatre this week?' asked Lucille. I hadn't heard her coming up the stairs, she'd had new carpets laid and the thick wool had muffled her footsteps. 'What on earth are you doing?'

'I dropped my brooch,' I lied. 'It's awfully *dusty* under there.'

'Yes,' she said vaguely. Lucille would never discuss housework. 'I've booked you and Ann for a manicure tomorrow morning, her hands look dreadful. All that jolly hockey, I suppose. Somebody from the theatre telephoned, I said you'd call back.'

Don't think about it, I told myself when she'd gone. Thinking about it caused trouble. Try to forget, forget what you can't really remember. Don't think about the people you liked looking at the pictures and knowing. 'Leave it out', that had been the fashionable phrase at school last term, cockney slang, very good, the hard, ironic edge of the tough Londoner. Leave it out. *Don't* think about it.

Lucille and I had been invited to Lord Chendar's house in Somerset for the weekend. He'd forgotten she had another daughter, and Lucille had certainly not reminded him. Ann said she'd be all right on her own for the weekend, so Lucille sighed, and told her not to strain her eyes reading all the time, and try not to get another infection.

We were met at the station by a chauffeur with a shiny black Rover, which I thought was smart, but Lucille was offended. Lord Chendar had a Rolls-Royce; the Rover was almost an insult. She was only slightly mollified when he apologised, and explained that his son had crashed the Rolls, it was still off the road. She offered him her cheek, and said it didn't matter at all, with only a short hesitation to indicate her affront. He should have met her personally, not sent the chauffeur.

He did his best to placate her. She was, I had to admit to myself, very clever. She was charming, and friendly, and she admired the beautiful house, but there was the suggestion of a vague distance between them, a suspicion that perhaps she was beginning to drift away from him. And never had she been so lovely, so graceful, so perfectly groomed.

The son who had crashed the Rolls, the Honourable Francis, was to be my partner for the weekend. He was tall, and languid, and in his final year at school. He was destined for the army, and in his opinion any career outside the military was only for the plebs, or possibly for poofs. He was in the cadets at school, quite senior actually, and head prefect, which was really rather boring but it might look good on a CV, if I knew what that was. But then, as I was the arty-crafty type, I wouldn't need to know that sort of thing.

I arranged myself gracefully on the silk-covered sofa, and listened to him, my lips slightly parted, my eyes wide and admiring, my shoulders low to show off the line of my neck and the glossy blonde hair, and when he made amusing jokes about art and all that sort of rot, I pictured him in a white tutu, pirouetting under a spotlight. It made it possible for me to laugh quite convincingly at his witticisms.

'How did you come to crash the Rolls?' I asked, and Lucille frowned at me for the tactless question, but I pretended not to notice, and she turned away and spoke softly to Lord Chendar.

'Oh, wet leaves, you know. Suddenly no bloody traction, the back end got away, and right there, in just exactly the wrong place, this damned great tree trunk.'

Lord Chendar looked up from bending an attentive ear to Lucille and raised a sardonic eyebrow.

'Oh, it happened abroad?' I asked. 'Wet leaves, in April?'

Lucille threw me a disapproving and angry glance as

Francis coloured and said something unconvincing about a heap left over from last winter blowing across the lane, and his father let out a sharp crack of laughter.

'She got you there, by God! Not all blondes are dumb, my lad.'

Later that night Francis followed me out into the hall and tried to corner me by the stairs.

'I say, you're really rather attractive, aren't you?'

'Oh, no,' I replied. 'That's for magnets. What I am is very beautiful, and well out of your range. Please don't come any closer, or I shall have to kick this gong.'

Lucille was very angry with me. In the train on the way home she alternately sat in cold silence, staring out of the window, or raged at me.

'How dare you behave like that? The Chendars are one of the oldest and wealthiest families in the south of England. Have you taken leave of your senses? Do you imagine sarcasm and rudeness are attractive?'

'I don't. He did.'

'Don't answer me back! Don't say another word until we get home. I'm ashamed of you.'

But I had enjoyed myself. When I had seen Francis flush at my responses to his remarks I had also seen Donald Flint's face, his sly eyes, and every minor stabbing point I had scored over Francis had been a little retaliation against Donald.

It hadn't deterred Francis. He had followed me around like a dog, looking mournful and pleading, and had asked if he could write to me at school.

'Can I write to you?' he had asked.

'Can you? I don't know. Can you spell "Storrington"?'

Two days after we returned home he telephoned to ask if he could take me to a party in London.

'Why would you imagine I would want to go to a party with you?' I asked, and Lucille overheard, and stared at me in horror.

'It's all right,' I assured her. 'He's a masochist. He keeps coming back for more.'

It shocked her, and she became thoughtful. I caught her looking at me with a strange expression on her face, a little worried, perhaps frightened.

'You've changed,' she said. 'Darling, don't get *hard*, will you? Not all men are like Francis, they won't like it.'

5

I failed all my O levels except art. At least in that I got the highest grade, and Miss Elphick was pleased. But it meant I had to stay on at Storrington for another year to retake the other subjects, even the local art college, not a very well-known one, insisting on a minimum of four passes, including art.

I hadn't worked very hard during the summer. It had still all seemed rather pointless, and it was only Miss Elphick who had really encouraged me, telling me to build up a portfolio. She said my sketch of Ann was one of the best things I had ever done, but I found I couldn't take an interest in drawing anybody else. The pencil ran over the paper, the lines were fairly accurate, but there was no feeling of a living person.

I painted a crucifixion. Francis Chendar's spaniel eyes stared pleadingly from the bleeding face. Lucille, draped in black, pointed an accusing finger from the foot of the cross. You can't treat men like this.

Francis did write to me, boastful lists of cricket scores, and plans for his summer holiday, which seemed to involve shooting and fishing, in general killing a lot of animals, all of them smaller than him. I didn't answer any of his letters, but when Lord Chendar sent me a note inviting me to spend a week at the manor I thought I had better not ignore it, so I passed it on to Lucille, who accepted for me, and wrote me a long letter demanding and begging that I behave nicely. I thought about her letter, and I thought about the new thick carpets in the hall and the landing and on the stairs. No matter how I might feel about the languid Francis, I had better be charming to his father.

Rosalind Back's elder brother Tom took us both out to tea on one of our half-days, and tried to kiss me when Rosalind went to the Ladies'. I didn't resist, but he was panting with anxiety, and watching to make sure the waitress didn't come back, so the passionate salute landed on the side of my mouth, and the arm that tried to encircle my shoulders knocked my hat sideways. I smiled at him, distantly, straightened my hat, and dabbed at my mouth with a paper napkin. He looked embarrassed, and rather hurt. But Rosalind was my best friend, so I said nothing, and contented myself with making sure, and seeing that he noticed I was making sure, I wasn't alone with him again.

That evening Rosalind told me he had asked her to invite me to stay during the holidays.

'He's in love with you,' she announced. 'Do you want to come and stay? Mummy wouldn't mind, so long as you don't disturb Daddy.'

I toyed with the idea of disturbing Daddy, setting him off against his son and seeing just how much Mummy minded, but I let it go. Tom wasn't like Francis, and I was fond of Ros.

I wondered why, now, when I met a man, I thought of ways of belittling him. I'd never felt like that before, I'd liked men and been happy that they liked me. I genuinely despised the Honourable Francis, his stupidity, his ideas of witty conversation, making disparaging remarks about anybody he felt to be his inferior, which was most of the human race. It all seemed rather pointless now, but I never questioned Lucille's belief, as deep as knowledge, that men

75

ruled the world and had the entire right to do so. Sometimes the half memory came clouding back into my mind, two men had raped me, but I pushed it aside, I turned my face away, I refused to look at it. Leave it out. I would leave it out of my life.

Mrs Russell told me my best chance for the three other O levels were English Literature, Geography and History, and she gave them all their initial capital letters as she looked disapprovingly at me over the top of her glasses, and told me I'd fail them all if I didn't start working. English Language, she supposed I'd got a chance if I set my nose to the grindstone, but was I prepared to work? *Was* I, Gloriana?

I smiled at her, and said, yes, Mrs Russell, and she gave me an exasperated glare, and waved me away.

In the summer holidays the Royal closed down. I'd known that keeping it open had always been a gamble, each production, as Reeve put it, not only hand to mouth but heart in mouth, and a damned nasty taste it was. It had been a long time since they had dared gamble on anything new and daringly original, and reviews had begun to use words like stale, and tame. I took the local newspaper up to my room, and I lay on the floor, and I looked at a photograph of Reeve, and Louise, and Sue, and Ray, under the heading 'Royal Theatre to Close'. There was quite a long article, the history of the theatre, now destined for demolition, and interviews with some of the cast and the staff. Reeve was going to Australia to direct for a film company making documentaries. Louise had a part in a production in Birmingham and said she was excited about it. Sue spoke of needing a holiday, and Ray of his agent and a couple of scripts he was reading. I knew what that meant. What company would take Ray, with his irritating mannerisms, his watery eyes? And Sue, in her thirties, part actress part dancer, what was there for her that wasn't open to hundreds of ambitious teenagers with longer legs and whiter smiles?

There was a smaller photograph, Mrs Pasmore and Norman Jack in the main wardrobe room, Norman with two shields slung over his shoulder, half a dozen spears propped in the crook of his arm, Mrs Pasmore holding up a dress, spreading out the skirts and smiling at the camera. Our luck just ran out, she was quoted as saying.

I'd been lucky for that theatre, they'd said. My black cat cards were stuck in the frames of a dozen mirrors, I'd been welcomed when I'd come home from the holidays, lovely to see you, sweetie, nice to have you back, hi, Glory, good to see you, paint room, Glory, and hurry. Brushes to wash. Where's that sherry decanter they used in *Salad Days*, Glory? Glory, have you seen Dave? Ask Terry to come for a fitting, sweetie, three o'clock sharp, Glory, run down to Florian's for me, got a moment, please, Glory?

Busy, and happy, and popular. And lucky. But their luck had run out on them, party dress stuffed into a grip bag, filthy yellow-covered book under one arm, white-faced, frightened and ashamed, their luck had run out.

I lay on the floor and looked under my bed, at the square rise in the shadowed carpet, the first of many copies left lying around for my friends to see. It was six months now since I'd opened those pages and looked. I lay watching it, thinking again those drifting thoughts of the wrong body, the two men, the screams and the laughter. Can I paint terror? Can I paint defilement?

Luck running out through the sly, sliding eyes of a man who gloated over the rape of a child. Donald Flint, I hated him, Donald Flint.

I drew him. I drew a slug, sliding over a mirror, a trail of slime behind him, eyes slipping craftily sideways, thick wet lips. And the mirror image of the slug, blurred by slime or saliva, another wet lip, sliding over the smooth, clean mirror, sliding away towards the dark, to hide, to leave the trail of his defilement.

The drawing stood propped against the back of my chair,

and I stood back and looked at it. It wasn't very good. But I could see something of Donald Flint there, if I listened I could hear the slug moving across the glass, the faint whisper of its cold body, hello, *Cindy*, little *Ssssindy*.

I spat on it. The thin white foam trailed down the edge of the pencilled mirror, running slowly across the tail of the slug. I hawked mucus up from the back of my throat and spat again, slime on to slime, and again, and again, my throat becoming dry and sore, the paper smearing and buckling. Slug, filthy slug I had called him, man, man, dirty man, filthy slug, slug-man.

I sat on my bed and watched as the saliva dried on the buckled paper, the pencil lines of the slug blurred under slime. Slug, filthy slug, slug-man, I hate you. I hate you.

Francis met me at the station when I went down to Somerset for my stay at the manor. He was driving a white sports car, an E-Type Jaguar, a present from his father to mark his move from school to university. When I remarked that I had understood he was going to Sandhurst, he said the army had become tiresome about qualifications.

'Aren't you going into the army, then?'

'Oh, Lord, I suppose so. One has to do something. But I'm damned if I'll stamp around a parade ground with a bunch of grammar school oiks.'

I found I liked Lord Chendar. He was noisy, and opinionated, but he had a sense of the ridiculous, and a quick wit to go with it. I got up early on the first morning to look around the house and examine the paintings before Francis came downstairs, and I found him already at work at his desk in the study, glasses on the end of his nose, piles of papers in trays in front of him.

'Come in, my dear. Have a coffee. Up early, aren't you?'

'I wanted to look at the paintings.'

'Ha! Yes, Lucille said you painted. Ah. Now, just a minute, Madge's painting things, they must be around somewhere, just a minute.'

And he went out into the hall shouting for the butler.

'Bales? Bales, you up yet? Where's that damned bell? Ha!'

Before I'd finished my coffee the butler came into the study carrying an easel and a canvas and leather tool bag.

'Good man, that's it. Bloody marvellous, Bales. Where the hell was it?'

'Garage, my lord.'

'Yes, bloody marvellous. Garage, good God. Knows where to find everything, Bales does. Yes, thank you, Bales.'

Bales bowed to me as Lord Chendar lifted the bag on to his desk and let it fall open.

'He's even dusted it. Going to retire next year, old Bales, I tell you, my dear, I'm dreading it. Never mind, come and look at this, old Madge's painting kit. She bought this bag from the men who put the central heating in. I mean the proper workmen, not the architect. Said it was damned practical, what do you think? Come and look.'

It was very practical. A plumber's tool bag, strong, with big leather handles, and pockets packed with tubes of paint in flat tins, brushes, bottles of turpentine and linseed oil, and two small art boards.

'It's really good,' I said. 'Good idea. Was Madge your wife?'

'Aunt. Wife's still around. Gstaad. Yes, Gstaad, back next week some time. No, old Madge lived here. Died about five years ago. Liked painting. These any good to you? Use them while you're here?'

'Thank you. Yes, I'd like to.'

I used one of the boards to paint him at his desk. He seemed quite happy to have me working at the easel while he shuffled his papers and grunted at them, or leaned back in the big leather chair, holding a page at arm's length as he squinted at it, muttering to himself. He was a noisy worker, restless and fidgety, and I tried to capture this as I painted him. Sometimes he'd talk to me, short bursts of brusque comments, remarks about the writers of letters he was reading. He rarely seemed to expect an answer. I can't remember how he put it, but by the end of that first morning he had explained to me that, although the relationship between him and my mother was sexual, there was no suggestion that anything of that nature was expected of me.

Francis came down at about eleven, yawning and complaining that he was suffering from a mega hangover. He said we'd been invited to a tennis party that afternoon, had I brought my kit? And then, without waiting for an answer, added that, since I was painting, there was a horse in the stable he wouldn't mind having on canvas.

'Put it in a boxing ring, then,' said Lord Chendar. 'She's painting me, not your nag.

'Dozens of tennis rackets around the house,' he added to me. 'Francis'll buy you a dress and all that in Bridgwater on the way.'

Francis didn't buy me a dress, he bought me a gold bracelet. I had no intention of playing tennis and making a fool of myself; the only sport at which I ever showed any ability was running, I found ball games impossible. On the way to Bridgwater I told Francis I wasn't the good sport horsy type.

'I want to buy you a present,' he protested. 'You'd look marvellous in a tennis dress.'

He bought me the bracelet, and I rewarded him by sunbathing in a bikini the next day.

Lord Chendar told me to call him Patrick, not Pat if you don't mind, my dear, and he took me up to the minstrels' gallery to show me the family portraits. I've never been very interested in portraits, but I tried to be polite and intelligent about them. It didn't take him long to realise, and he laughed at me and then looked thoughtful, and a little hesitant. At last he said he had a few things that might catch my eye.

They were in the cellar, in a long, low room where air-conditioning vents hummed from the white painted walls.

Matisse, Miró, Degas. At the far end of the room hung a huge Tibetan thang-ka, with billowing clouds of purple smoke and a fanged demon god leaping forward over defeated armies. There were four tiles painted by Picasso, met him, my dear, liked the man. Monet's water lilies, cool blues and greens under shadowed willows, a cornfield, could that really be Van Gogh?

'Oh, Patrick!'

'Lend them to exhibitions. Rather you didn't tell anybody they're here, burglars, you know. Come down here myself sometimes. Feel it gets my head back into shape, know what I mean? Looking at them.'

'Yes, I know.'

There were racks with sliding rails down one side of the room, paintings hanging from them. The Chendar collection, started in the fifteenth century, added to in every generation.

'Got a couple of Turners, afraid they're in the States. See them next time you come. Like Munnings? No, you wouldn't. Ha! This, now. What about that? Yes?'

It was a horse by Blake, a thunderstorm of a painting, rolling into my mind and shaking at the barriers. Patrick stood at my shoulder, quiet for once, looking at it, and then at me, waiting until I sighed, and he reached out and touched the paint, gently, his fingers loving, and slowly slid the beautiful thing back into the rack.

He was a bit startled by the painting I had done of him.

'Good God, I'm an untidy bugger, aren't I?' he exclaimed. I wondered if he hadn't realised, scratching at his head and making the hair stand up in tufts, tugging at his shirt, one sleeve pulled up halfway to the elbow, the cuff of the other undone and hanging loose.

'Yes, Patrick,' I said. 'You are.'

He stared at it, taking his glasses off and standing back, then putting them on again and peering closely.

'Don't know,' he muttered. 'Don't know.'

The afternoons were spent with Francis, being paraded around various country houses like a prize-winning show pony, being polite, listening to the boys in the way Lucille had taught me, being acidly sweet to the girls. Swimming parties, and boating parties, and tennis parties. I was careful to be affectionate, and even deferential, to Francis in the presence of his friends.

But in private, when he tried to kiss me, when he told me he loved me, that I was beautiful, when he begged to be allowed to hold me, I was contemptuous. The more savagely sarcastic my remarks, the more devotedly he followed me, the more he claimed to worship me. It was only in public I allowed him to touch me, an arm around my shoulders, or holding me close when we danced, but never a kiss. If he seemed to be planning to kiss me I would look at him, a smile on my lips, my eyes cold and level, and he would hesitate, and then turn away. I might, I just might, say in public the sort of things I said in private.

'But I love you,' he said humbly, 'I really love you.'

'I will never love you, Francis. Not even if you grow out of adolescent pimples. And you smell.'

When I left to go home Patrick handed me a cheque for three hundred pounds for the portrait I had painted of him.

'I can't!' I protested. 'Patrick, I can't!'

'Decided I liked it,' he said. 'Eventually. You take that, my dear, it's a damned good painting.'

I had spent at least two hours every morning in that long white room in the basement, gazing at Patrick's lovely paintings. Like him, I felt it got my head back into shape. Blake's horse was, I suppose, my favourite, but I spent most of my time looking at the Monet water lilies, and at a Cézanne still life. They were cool, and clear, and infinitely peaceful. Love you, Paul Cézanne, I thought. I love you, Claude Monet. Love you.

The kiss I planted on Patrick's cheek was genuinely affectionate. My mother's lover. My friend, who had given me the means to get my head back into shape. And three hundred pounds.

When I got home my exam results were waiting for me. One pass, six failures. A disaster, but Lucille was quite calm and philosophical about it. Another year at Storrington would do no harm, the trust fund would pay, no doubt something would turn up for me even if I failed them again. I could take them again in the spring term. If necessary, once more in the summer.

'Don't you mind?' asked Ann, looking worried.

I found I did mind, but I didn't want to admit it.

'Oh, no,' I said. 'I'm not the brainy type. Maybe I'll scrape through next time.'

I lay on the floor in my bedroom looking at the square shape under the carpet, and I smiled. I've beaten you, slug, I thought. I've beaten you. Me, and Cézanne, and Monet. And Blake. What could you do against them, little slug, little slime?

I pulled back the carpet, and I picked up the book. It was dusty, the cheap paper smudged with the dust, the printing grey and ragged. I put it in a carrier bag, and that evening I went out. I took it with me down to the river, and I walked along the towpath until I came to the place where the anglers fished on Sundays. I sat on the bench, and very slowly and very carefully I tore every page into thin strips, and dropped each strip into the rippling water, and watched as it floated away, and curled, and flattened, and slid under the darkening river, and disappeared. It took a long, long time, and when it was finished I sat, my empty hands curled in my lap, and I thought, I will never try to remember again. It is gone, under the river, gone, washed away by the river, and by the clean strength of Cézanne, and Monet. And Blake.

6

I brought some school books home in the Christmas holidays, and tried to do some work. Lucille complained I'd develop frown lines if I read too much, she said Christmas was for fun, and parties, and meeting friends, not for swotting, but I wanted to pass my exams in the spring term if I could, so I could spend the rest of my time at Storrington painting in the art department, building up a good portfolio. I was beginning to feel a little more ambitious.

'But darling, *why*?' wailed Lucille. 'Honestly, I don't see the point. I mean, even if you don't pass them, any decent hotel would pay a fortune to have you on reception, with your looks.'

'And an indecent one would pay even more.'

'Don't be impertinent! It isn't attractive, Gloriana.'

I went to parties with her, and a young banker, Lucien Rathbone, asked me for my telephone number. I had begun to recognise the look, the humble eyes when nobody else was watching.

'Why do you think I would want to give you my telephone number?' Smile. Voice light and amused, eyes level.

'Please. I promise I won't be a nuisance.'

'I promise you won't be a nuisance, too. I don't tolerate

nuisances. No, Lucien, I won't give you my telephone number.'

He got it from Directory Enquiries, of course. And he took me to the opera, and to dinner in London, and to parties. He gave me a sapphire brooch for Christmas, he said the stones were the colour of my eyes, and so they were. I gave him a collar and lead, pale blue with diamanté decorations, designed for a poodle. I watched him open the box, wondering, behind my lifted eyebrow and the half-smile, whether he would rebel at the insult.

'*Don't* try to kiss me,' I said, turning my head away.

'Darling Glory. Gloriana, my darling, I'll walk to heel for you. To the ends of the earth at your heels. Please, Glory.'

'Can't you find a decent dentist?'

Francis sent me a dozen pairs of silk stockings from Paris. I sent them back, with a note telling him not to be presumptuous. But I kept the pearl earrings, and I wrote quite a long letter to Patrick to thank him for the lovely gold evening bag, although I didn't mention the hundred pounds he had tucked into the mirror pocket.

I didn't mention it to Lucille, either. She was preening herself in front of the cheval mirror in a long palomino mink coat, walking, and turning, and watching the heavy fur swing, and the light gleaming and shimmering.

'He really has got *marvellous* taste,' she said. 'What a colour!'

There'd been an envelope in the pocket of the coat, and she'd smiled as she put it in her handbag. We were both tarts now, I thought. At least Lucille gave value for money.

Ann offered to help me revise for the exams, and we read through *Julius Caesar* together. I learned the part of Brutus, a gamble; if there was a question on him I could quote big chunks of his speeches. It's a good play, but I'd never seen it. I knew I was missing the point in many ways, I almost wished I'd listened more carefully during the lessons, but I really needed to see it, a good production with a clever director. I read *Pride and Prejudice* through twice, and found it boring. And I read the poems, even Sir Patrick Spens, where every other word isn't even in the dictionary.

'"Skeely", skilful, I think,' said Ann, doubtfully. 'I think it must be. Or brave, maybe? What sort of skipper would you want? If you were the King of Scotland sending for a princess?'

'I wish I was brainy. I wish I could learn as easily as you.'

She was surprised. She looked back down at the book, and said something softly that I didn't quite hear. I think she said it wasn't easy. But she never seemed to have any trouble, or at least she liked reading her books, she found them interesting.

The trouble was, I found it so boring.

I had even failed needlework, a subject considered fit only for dunces, but when I thought about it dispassionately I realised it was hardly surprising. We had had to produce two examples of mending, a darned sock and a patch on a piece of patterned fabric, and a garment, which, Mrs York had decreed, was to be a sensible blouse, with set-in sleeves, neat buttonholes, and a patch pocket on the breast. I showed it to Lucille.

'Would you be seen dead in it?' I demanded, and she raised her lovely eyebrows.

'*Darling.*'

'And I am damned if I will darn socks or patch clothes.'

But it could be another subject, another of the essential four. The local art college simply specified four, including art. And even darning a sock had to be easier than trying to understand the Corn Laws.

I remembered the blue velvet dress Mrs Pasmore had made for Louise, and how I had helped her, drawing the design, then measuring it out on to the pattern paper, pinning and tacking, fitting it on the dummy, and later on Louise herself. It had been fun. We'd made cloaks, and dresses for a chess set, red and white, we'd tailored jackets, we'd worked with feathers and fur, velvet and cotton, leather and latex. We had not, however, made sensible blouses with set-in sleeves, neat buttonholes, and patch pockets on the breast.

'Could I make you a dress?' I asked Lucille, and she looked a little wary.

'Darling, would you be desperately hurt if I didn't wear it?'

'No, it's only for the exam.'

'Oh, well, in *that* case . . .'

It was black silk, and it didn't have set-in sleeves. In fact, it didn't have sleeves at all. It had a high mandarin collar, and an invisible zip fastening down the side; it fitted her like a glove, and we came close to quarrelling over it when I said I had to take it to school with me.

'If they spoil it, I'll sue,' she sulked. 'My sweetest love, I had no idea you were so clever. Fashion for you, my darling, is there a fashion course at that art school? There must be. The obvious choice, why didn't we think of it before?'

She asked me to make her an opera cloak to go with it, lined in sapphire blue, and for the summer a tailored suit in peach linen, and dresses, until I rebelled and said it would strain my eyes.

I did not darn the sock. I took one of the school's navy blue sports socks and cut a hole in it, and I sewed the edges of the hole together with thick scarlet wool, three huge blanket stitches secured at each end with a large knot, and a trailing tail of wool. Combined with the dress, the examiners would have to take the hint; I could only pray for a sense of humour.

I was restless and unsettled. I tried to spend some time with Ann, because I could see she was dreadfully unhappy, alone in her room when she could be, reading her books, but often called down to the drawing room by Lucille to be 'sociable', to try to learn at least a modicum of social graces, for God's sake, and *will* you sit more gracefully! She tried, but there was a weary, sullen look around her eyes that was new, although sometimes, when we were listening to men talking, I caught an ironic expression on her face, a suggestion that in her opinion they were perhaps not the lords of creation Lucille believed them to be. But if anybody looked at her directly she was smiling, and apparently listening with polite interest.

'What are you reading?' I asked, going into her room one morning. She laid the book down and smiled at me.

'Physics, was it?' I went on. 'Do you want me to test you on anything? Why do you work so hard?'

I stood at the window, looking out into the garden. It was raining, a heavy, black rain that slapped at the windows, the wind lifting it in sheeting waves across the road, lights from the other houses shining through it, dull and yellow.

'Shall I make you a dress? I could, you know. Something in your favourite colour. What *is* your favourite colour?'

She was a long time answering. Ann never answered questions quickly, she waited to see whether it was a genuine question, or just another bit of small talk.

'Copper, I think,' she said at last. 'Not when it's just been polished, but when it's going brown. Copper, or bronze.'

'It had to be metal, didn't it?' I said. I was joking, trying to be nice, trying to talk to her, but I saw the weary look come back into her eyes, and her smile was distant, and polite.

I still had the cheque Patrick had given me for the portrait, as well as his Christmas present, and I knew I would have to cash the cheque soon or it would be out of date. I didn't want to tell Lucille about it; she would have been jealous and angry, and anyway she would have argued that I should spend it on clothes. I didn't want to do that. I wanted to save the money, but I was too young to have a bank account of my own without Lucille's permission.

In the end I telephoned Uncle John. He was, after all, our guardian, and he'd helped me before.

'Come to London,' he said. 'I'll take you to lunch and you can meet my stockbroker. Thursday?'

'Stockbroker?' I was doubtful. 'For four hundred pounds?'

'People have started with less and made their fortunes. I think it's an excellent idea to invest it.'

'Thursday, then,' I agreed. 'Thank you!'

And I telephoned Lucien.

'Walkies,' I said. 'Take me to London on Thursday, and then get lost for a couple of hours.'

'I'll take you out to tea.'

'No. If there's a production of *Julius Caesar* anywhere between London and Birmingham, you can take me to that.'

'Of what?'

'*Julius Caesar*. The ancient Italian with the large nose and the toga. Shall I spell it for you? Can you remember how to make a J, or should I tell your secretary?'

Uncle John's stockbroker was a small, old man with wispy hair and pale eyes. Cameron was his name, Robert Cameron. I was disappointed; I had expected somebody brisk and efficient. But I smiled, and said I was very pleased to meet him, and it was kind of him to help me, and he replied, not at all, not at all.

Uncle John doesn't raise one eyebrow as Lucille does, a clear arch of gracious incredulity; but the outside end of his left eyebrow lifts slightly when he is amused and trying to hide it. I drew it once, in a cartoon of a judge, and Miss Elphick laughed and said it was wicked.

We talked about paintings over lunch, and Mr Cameron asked if I'd seen the summer exhibition at the Royal Academy the previous year, a question I thought of as entirely predictable and boring. But then he said he'd bought two of the works, a pen-and-ink sketch of factories in the Black Country, and a small painting by an artist I'd never heard of, a child with a kite. He had a photograph of it with him, and it was a lovely thing, clever and simple, with reflected light on primary colours, and a feeling of lively gaiety. So quite soon we were talking happily about the French Impressionists, and I said my favourite was Cézanne, and that I'd seen some of the Chendar collection when I'd been staying with them, and suddenly he changed the talk to finances, and my four hundred pounds, and asked if I'd like to put half of it into a new art gallery in Bath.

'It's a gamble,' he said. 'A horse race of a venture. You could lose the lot, but I don't think you will. I'm putting something in it myself.'

Uncle John's face showed nothing but polite interest, but I could feel his reserve. He had thought Robert Cameron would recommend something safe, something that would bring in a steady income, he wasn't happy with this talk of a gamble. But I was interested.

'It's a young man on his own,' Mr Cameron continued. 'That's the trouble, the banks don't greatly care for youth, so they won't back him. He's inherited a shop, a draper's I think it was, just the freehold and no capital. He needs money to buy stock.'

'He's not a draper, then?' asked Uncle John in a flat, polite voice, and Mr Cameron twinkled at him.

'He's a scruffy young art student,' he admitted. 'But he has health, and energy, and enthusiasm. Really enormous enthusiasm, it's engaging, John. One can't help but like him. Not to buy from him is like disappointing a happy child. It will carry him through while he gains experience.'

Uncle John nodded courteously, and stirred his coffee. He was neither convinced nor happy.

'Will he be selling his own work?' I asked, and Mr Cameron turned back to me.

'I don't think so,' he said. 'He's a bit dismissive of his own work. He calls it banal and obvious, which I think is rather brutal. But then, he is a rather brutal young man, when it comes to paintings.

'I think he'll make a great many mistakes, but he'll learn

from them. If he's got the guts to take the punishment the commercial world will undoubtedly inflict on him, he'll succeed. If not, he'll give up and we'll lose our money. What do you think, Gloriana? Two hundred pounds will buy you one per cent.'

But I wasn't sure. Uncle John wasn't happy, and I didn't want to lose my money, even in a venture that sounded fun. I hesitated, wondering what to say, and Uncle John coughed.

'It doesn't sound like a venture for a beginner,' he said, and Robert Cameron smiled and nodded.

'It isn't,' he agreed, which seemed to disarm Uncle John, who smiled back, and looked at me.

'It's your money,' he said. 'You ask the questions.'

'I'd like to know what he's going to sell,' I suggested. 'After all, it's going to depend on his taste, isn't it?'

'His taste, his luck, his selling ability, and the market. Is Bath the right place for an art gallery at the moment? Well, the answer to that is yes, it is. Just in case you were going to ask the question.'

Robert Cameron was enjoying himself, and I suddenly knew why. He believed the art gallery was destined to be successful, he knew what he was doing, he was like the trainer of a racehorse that has improved under his care just before a race, when he knows it is going to win. It was he who had called it a horse race, a gamble, but he was putting his own money on this horse race, and he did not expect to lose it.

I laughed, and he knew I had read his mind, and laughed back.

'Yes,' I said. 'Yes, I'd like to have one per cent of an art gallery, please.'

'Not the gallery,' he corrected me. 'Not the freehold, just the business being run in it.'

'Why doesn't he borrow on the freehold?' asked Uncle John.

'He's not allowed to until he's twenty-five.'

'Good God!' Uncle John was disgusted. 'He's a babe in arms.'

'It's going to work, though, isn't it?' I demanded, and Mr Cameron smiled happily.

'What about the other two hundred?' he asked. 'Something you know about, I suggest. Something that interests you. Any ideas?'

'Fabrics,' I said. 'Textiles.'

He nodded approvingly.

We walked back to Uncle John's office, and on the way Mr Cameron told me to learn from my investments, to read the accounts and consider what they meant, to think of the young man selling paintings when I looked at a profit-and-loss account. A balance sheet should be a picture book to a real investor, an informed investor, not just a list of numbers. I was to learn.

Wispy, pale-eyed, old. Robert Cameron. Appearances could be deceptive.

I did try to work in the spring term, I even made an effort to understand the Corn Laws, and to learn about the Gulf Stream and its effect on the British climate for geography. Four O levels, at least four, and Mrs York's fury at my impertinence over the sock had convinced me needlework would not be one of them. I was banned from the domestic science room for the rest of the term.

I read *Pride and Prejudice* again, trying to find the satire, and thinking instead of the triviality of women's lives at that time.

'But that's the whole point!' explained Rosalind.

Robert Cameron sent me some photographs of the art gallery, of a corner shop in a back street, a haberdashery, dim grey paint with faded black lettering on the board, knitting patterns and a hardboard display of bias binding and reels of cotton behind the plate glass. But there was another photograph taken from the same angle, and the paint was glossy black, with thin white lettering picked out in red on the board. 'Revelations', it read, and, underneath, in smaller letters, 'Ch. VI, vv. 1–8'.

I looked it up in the Bible, and it was about the Four Horsemen of the Apocalypse. I puzzled over the choice for a little while, and then I noticed the phrase, repeated four times, 'Come and See', and I smiled.

There was a photograph of a young man standing by a stepladder, stiff and posed, his expression one of embarrassment and exasperation. Red hair stood out in all directions around a long white face. He was wearing a chalk-striped suit that had obviously been made for somebody else.

'His idea for the window display is to set two small paintings quite far back, and light them only dimly with spots, so that people have to peer through the windows to see them,' wrote Mr Cameron. 'He thinks that will arouse interest and curiosity, and I believe he may be right.

'He hopes to be ready to open early in May. He would like to have an exhibition, but museums and most private collectors are being hard about security and insurance. I noticed the cheque you gave John was signed by Lord Chendar, and I wondered, since your interest in the French Impressionists sprang largely from your acquaintanceship with him, whether you might enlist his aid.

'Intelligent support of an investment in a small business is often extremely helpful. Are you in a position to effect an introduction?'

No, I thought immediately, no. That is asking too much, both of me and of Patrick Chendar. Robert Cameron had no right to ask such a thing. It would be an impertinence.

But I felt trapped. He had sent me balance sheets with notes attached, explaining. And a prospectus about a company in Northampton expanding to take in Scottish tweeds, with a share offer, and his letter had suggested I learn a little about tweeds before deciding. When I had asked Uncle John about stockbrokers' commission, Uncle John had said it would all be lost in the trust fund accounts, since technically he had to administer it, at least until I reached the age of majority.

'That sounds like "Don't bother your pretty little head",' I commented, and he winced.

'I'm sorry.' It was a genuine apology. 'Robert and I were on the same destroyer for a long time during the war. I sorted out an abominable tangle over his father's will, and he helped me with investments. Quid pro quo. Commissions and fees between us have always been on a rather informal basis. But of course you should know. I'll work it out and write to you.'

What he sent me instead was a list of the investments the trust fund owned, as well as a commentary on his own shareholdings, and copies of old letters. I read through the letters, and a picture emerged, two men who had lost their youth through the war, who had gained a strong friendship and the loyalty that went with the shared experiences, embarking on a new adventure, and treating it like a schoolboy dare. They were out to make their fortunes, and they took risks, and sometimes they lost, painfully, more than they could afford, and sometimes they won, at first only just a little more often than they lost. They had been gamblers. Ships, and lorries, and an early risk on air freight that had quadrupled their holding in less than a year. Then a paper mill that had burned down, uninsured. A new type of security lock, followed by a takeover bid, and a huge gain; Uncle John had sent Robert Cameron a share certificate in a champagne vineyard as a celebration present, and Cameron had responded with a share certificate in a Highland distillery. The letters that enclosed them had simply read, 'To your very good health', and the reply, 'To yours'.

They had never lost their sense of fun, the thrill of the adventure.

Robert Cameron had spoken of the art gallery as a horse race, a gamble. They had owned two racehorses once, kept them in training in Yorkshire for a year, but had agreed to sell them, neither of them having the time to spend at races, a decision taken with a little regret, they'd liked the horses. But the profit had been handsome.

They were rich men now, I realised. Between them, they held controlling interests in five companies, and a wide range of shares in organisations all over the world. Four hundred pounds must have been a tiny sum to Robert Cameron, and yet he had taken an interest, and had written to me about the art gallery.

And had asked me to use my friendship with Patrick Chendar.

I did write to Patrick, as he suggested. I spent a long time trying to find the right words, and I threw away several drafts of the letter. In the end I told him the whole story, how I had wanted to invest the money, not just spend it, and how we needed a good exhibition to support the opening of the gallery.

The examinations were in February and March, and I tried very hard. This time, I read the questions carefully, I made sure I understood them. When I finished the first of them, history, I sat waiting for the time to pass, and I remembered how I had felt the last time I had sat at a desk in the long room, with the big clock at the end over the adjudicator's desk, when it had all seemed so pointless. This time, I hadn't been able to remember many dates, I'd forgotten the difference between Pitt the Younger and Pitt the Elder, or was it Older? but I thought I had done well on the question about the Industrial Revolution and the cotton mills, so maybe I'd scraped through. Maybe. Last time I'd known I'd failed, I hadn't even bothered to read through my answers.

'Well, Gloriana, what did you think of the paper?' asked Miss Mortimer as we left the hall.

'I don't know, Miss Mortimer,' I answered. 'Maybe.'

'I think maybe, too,' she smiled. 'You've been working quite hard. I'm hopeful.'

There was a short letter from Patrick Chendar, saying he was getting in touch with Robert Cameron about the exhibition. He didn't make any promises, but at least he wasn't angry, he didn't seem to feel I was exploiting our friendship.

I passed history, English literature and needlework, and Lucille tried to persuade me to leave Storrington at once, and stay at home for the summer.

'They can't force you,' she said. 'You're seventeen, you don't have to go to school.'

'But I want to.'

'I thought you *hated* school. You always used to. That ghastly uniform. You could make yourself some nice clothes. It would be good practice, for the fashion course.'

She had had a face lift. There was a taut look to the skin over her cheekbones, and a thin line under her eyebrows, pink, fading to white. It only showed when she wore no make-up, early in the mornings, or at night when she had creamed her face, and it was blank and shiny with moisturisers. She spent longer at her mirror now, and she went for a massage once a week. She was beautiful, and elegant, and charming, but sometimes, when I watched her looking at herself in the mirror, I thought I saw panic in her eyes.

I tried to make her the peach linen suit, but she had definite ideas about how it was to look, and I couldn't find a pattern. I'd never tried to make anything without a pattern before, except with Mrs Pasmore, when it had been she who had done the measuring and drawn out the pieces on the paper, and although the skirt was good I couldn't make the jacket. It was too tight under the arms, and then it puckered across the back, and the lapels would not lie flat.

'I'm sorry,' I said.

'Never mind, darling. The skirt's lovely.'

But I noticed she stopped trying so hard to persuade me to leave school and stay at home during the summer.

Then I saw Mrs Pasmore.

The sheets hadn't been ready for the laundry van, so Lucille asked me to take the box in on my way into town. When I went into the reception the door into the back room was open, and I saw her working at a big steam press. She was wearing a white overall, it was too tight for her, the buttons tugged and there were gaps. Her hair, which had always been in a neat bun, was wisping over her forehead, damp tendrils.

I stared at her. She didn't look up, she pushed something forward on to the board, and reached up for the cover, and pulled it down. She looked so weary.

'Madam? Madam, can I *help* you?'

Oh God, no, I thought. Our Mrs Pasmore, working in a laundry. I ran out on her, and this is what happened. A bloody laundry, a bloody stinking laundry, our Mrs Pasmore, who could make anything, standing in a bloody laundry ironing sheets. Her luck ran out on her. Ran away.

'Madam! Are you all right?'

'Oh, yes, of course,' I whispered. 'I'm sorry. Mrs Mayall, we missed the van.'

'Right. And the book? Madam? Your laundry book?'

But I was already leaving, in case Mrs Pasmore should look up and see me. See her luck running away again.

Mrs Pasmore, who'd helped me, who'd called me sweetie, who'd shown me how to make clothes, who'd been teaching me, standing at a steam press in a laundry, bedraggled and tired, when she should have been briskly happy in the wardrobe room, making lovely, outrageous costumes and gossiping with the chorus girls.

When the taxi driver dropped me at the shopping centre he asked me to go for a drink with him, and I swore at him, violently, shocking him. I ran up the escalator, and across the pretentious great wasted space they called the Terrazzio into the Ladies', and I stood at the basins and glared at myself in the mirror.

'Hell and *bloody damnation*!' I yelled, and I burst into tears.

I'd wanted to stay there until I felt calmer, but the attendant came out of her cubby hole, officious and indignant about the noise and the language, and told me to leave. I swore, shouting my rage about Mrs Pasmore at her, and she threatened to call security, so I walked out, tears on my face, and people stared at me. The only place I could think of to go was the car park. I pushed through the crowds, keeping my face lowered, hating everybody, until I came to the passage to the car park, which was dark, and dirty, and smelled of urine. I was disgusted at the stink; the lavatories in the shopping precinct were free, why did people have to be so filthy?

It was almost dark in the car park, and the smell was even worse. But it was quiet, just a man and a woman getting into their car, the woman stacking bags on the back seat, and when they'd gone I stood in the shadows in the corner of one of the parking bays, and I shivered, hugging myself, and scrubbing angrily at my tear-stained cheeks with the heel of my hand.

I was trying to tell myself it was not my fault Mrs Pasmore was working in the laundry, the Royal hadn't closed down because I'd run away from Donald Flint, slug-man Donald Flint, I hate you, Donald Flint. Leave it out, I said. Mrs Pasmore's shining, tidy hair in its neat bun, draggled across her forehead, rats' tails sticking to her face, damp from the steam and the sweat. In a white overall too small for her, so she looked fat and sloppy, a slattern in a dreary job, worthless. Not my fault. Donald Flint, slug-man, filth.

'Leave it *out*.'

'What's that? Who's there? What are you doing?'

A sharp voice, a man at the corner of the bay, staring at me.

'What are you doing there?'

He was walking towards me, threatening, bullying. I'm in charge here, I'm taking care of this. I watched him. Grey suit, polished shoes gleaming in the dim lamplight. A glint of light on a cheap stone in a tie pin.

'Are you deaf? I'm talking to you. Come out of there, I want to see you.'

I stepped forward, away from the corner, past the car and into the roadway. He hesitated, and then came closer.

'What were you doing there? Is that your car? Were you waiting for someone?'

I didn't answer. I wiped my hand across my eyes again. There was a trail of mascara across the palm. I'd have to go back to the Ladies', face that angry harridan, deal with my smudged make-up.

'*I* see. Yes, well.' He glanced at his watch, and then back at me, looking me up and down, grinning. I turned away and began to walk towards the door.

'Hey, wait a minute! Wait a minute, you, Blondie, hang on a minute!'

I looked at him. His suit was quite new, but cheap, shiny fabric, it wouldn't do, it would catch the light, no good under the spotlights. And that tie, no good at all.

'Tenner?' he asked. 'A tenner? Have to be my car, haven't got long. Come on, Blondie. What's your name? What do they call you?'

Walking alongside me, an irritating voice, demanding, hectoring.

'Hey, look, Blondie, just *stop* walking, will you?' and his hand was on my arm, pulling me around to face him.

'Don't just *ignore* me, see? I'm talking to you. Don't you just walk off as if I didn't exist. You stop, and you listen to me, that's manners.'

I stared at him, at his big pale face, at the sweat shining on his forehead. He looked green in the glare of the lights. He was angry, and a little uncertain.

'You got to learn some *manners*, Blondie. Now, what's your name?'

'Please take your hand off my arm.'

He blinked in surprise, and for a moment his grip slackened. Then he laughed, and I felt his fingers tightening again.

'That's good. "Please take your hand off my arm",' he mimicked. '"Oh, I say, old boy, please take your hand off my arm." What's that, then, Blondie? Roedean, is it? Right, fifteen then, extra fiver for the five bob accent.'

'Please let me go.'

'You can't be that bloody exclusive, not cruising the car parks.' He was becoming angry again, there was a reddish flush on his cheeks and he was breathing fast. 'Fifteen quid for a five-minute bang, no bloody overheads, that's good money. That's the best offer you're getting, so take it or take it, and get back here in my car, Blondie, or you'll get the back of my hand.'

I tried to prise his fingers away from my arm, and he grunted, and seized my wrist, bending it back and pushing me against the wall.

'Don't you come that with me,' he said. 'Bloody tart. Bloody street walkers, flaunting it and backing off, trying to jack the price up, fifteen quid's what you're getting, Blondie, you going to walk or get dragged? Your choice.'

He was hurting my wrist, and I couldn't free my arm, his fingers were digging hard into it. He was big, powerful, and he was pressing against me, forcing me against the wall, pushing me back, threatening and angry. I began to panic.

'Let me go.' I struggled, and he forced my wrist even further back so I lost my balance and I was almost down on my knees.

He stepped back, pulling me towards him, and his jacket swung open as he turned, dragging me.

He had a camera. A small, black camera on a leather strap

around his shoulder, swinging towards me, the lens shining in the light, and he was swearing, telling me to come on, dragging my arm, bending my wrist, and he turned towards me, his hand raised, and the camera swung again, and I began to scream.

'Let me go!' I screamed. 'No! No! Let me go! Lucille, help me! Mummy, come and help me! Please, Mummy, Lucille, please come, please come, come and help me!'

Somebody shouted, and my arm was free, and I fell forward, crying, and there were running footsteps, somebody running past me, shouting, shouting stop, and a car engine starting, and there was a woman beside me, bending down, a grey wool coat.

'Lovie?' A voice, hesitant, concerned. 'You all right? You all right?'

So stupid, I thought angrily. So stupid, panicking like that, and screaming for Lucille.

'You all right?'

'Thank you,' I said. 'Yes, I'm all right, thank you.'

She was quite old, a little anxious, and she was looking along the roadway, worried.

'Jimmy?' she called. 'Jimmy, you all right? Jim?'

He was older than she was, panting hard as he came back, but triumphant.

'I got his number,' he said. 'Dirty beast. You all right, lovie?'

'Yes, I'm all right, thank you.'

'Got his number, I got it. Dirty beast.'

'You all right, Jim? You shouldn't run, you all right?'

'I'm all right.'

I stood up, brushing at the knees of my slacks, wondering if they would ever stop asking each other if they were all right, and then pushing the thought aside. They had helped, they had probably saved me, if this was how they needed to talk in order to calm themselves, then I was the last person who should criticise. And the man, Jim, he was

101

breathing far too fast, perhaps she was right to be anxious.

'Thank you so much,' I said. 'Thank you very much. For chasing him off.'

'I got his number. Dirty beast. You sure you're all right?'

'I dropped my shopping,' said the woman. 'There was eggs.'

The man wanted to call the police, and the woman wanted him to drive me home first, but she had to get some more eggs, and was I sure I was all right, and was Jim all right, he shouldn't run, and we stood under the lights in the roadway, the talk going round and round, until I stopped talking, and just waited in silence.

I could feel tears running down my cheeks, but I didn't try to wipe them away. I didn't really care. When I had seen that camera I had screamed for Lucille, as I had done years ago in the photographic studio. I wanted to think, I wanted to untangle this confusion, this stupidity, and all I was doing was standing in a car park while two kind and concerned old people, who understood nothing about it, talked, and argued, and would not go away.

The woman noticed my tears first, and hushed her husband, and touched my arm gently, then said they would take me home, I'd had a nasty shock. But the man was stubborn. The police should be called, the dirty beast might go looking for another poor girl, we should remember that.

'I don't think so,' I said. 'He thought I was a prostitute.'

The word shocked them. They both stared at me, silent for the first time, and then the woman looked away, her face growing pink, muttering she wouldn't know anything about that.

'Well,' said the man doubtfully. 'Well, if you're sure you're all right, then. We'd best be getting home.'

'Thank you,' I said. 'That was really brave of you, chasing him off like that. He was quite tough, too.'

They both lifted their chins at that, and the woman

managed a smile, although she was still pink with disapproval and embarrassment.

They walked away from me, slowly, the man holding the woman's arm, back towards the entry where two plastic carrier bags lay on the concrete, and I watched them go, and wondered if I would ever free my mind of this confusion, and if I deserved to be raped, because I was a tart, like my mother, and because it had happened before, when I had been in the wrong body.

7

Revelations opened early in June, a few weeks later than Robert Cameron had anticipated, because Patrick Chendar had agreed to lend five paintings once they were returned from an exhibition on Cubism in Berlin. I had been given special leave to go, Lucille believing it might help me get into the local art college where I was to study fashion. And then, I supposed, I was destined to spend my time dressing her.

By then I had other ideas, and Ann had given them to me, although she had probably forgotten.

Lucille had been out when I got back from the shopping centre that day, and I had walked through the kitchen door and collapsed in tears at the table before I even noticed Ann standing by the window.

'Somebody tried to rape me,' I choked, and she came over quickly, and put a hand on my shoulder.

'But didn't succeed?' she asked, and I shook my head, and scrubbed at my face with a kitchen towel she handed me, and told her about the kind old people who had helped. That made me cry again, I hadn't even offered to pay for the broken eggs, and he really had been brave, that old man, chasing after somebody so big, and even having the presence of mind to write down the number of the car.

Ann didn't make a fuss. She poured me a cup of tea, and

sat quietly beside me, passing me clean squares of kitchen paper and saying nothing, until I looked up and smiled at her.

'I must look dreadful,' I said.

'Dreadful,' she agreed, and I managed to laugh.

'I saw Mrs Pasmore.' I couldn't laugh or smile about that. I looked down into the cup of tea, and stirred it, watching the ripples swirling out to the rim of the cup, the smooth movement of the yellow light on the brown tea, watching the pattern, storing it in my mind. 'In a laundry, a machine. I think it's called a steam press. An ugly big thing, you pull down a cover and steam hisses out.'

Tears began to slide down my cheeks again, and drip on to the table. I didn't try to wipe them away. I could cry, for Mrs Pasmore.

'She looked old. She looked, sort of, nothing. As if she'd never been happy, as if all her life had been that machine, always had been, always would be. As if she'd never made lovely dresses, never put ostrich feathers in Louise's hair. She made Louise look like a million dollars that day, all in rhinestones. But it's as if it's all gone and forgotten.'

I looked up. Ann was watching me, listening, her dark brown eyes steady on my face.

'She shouldn't be doing that,' I said. 'She shouldn't, Ann. How did that happen? I thought she'd be working in a fashion house or something. Or another theatre. And there she was, in that laundry, that stinking laundry, just as if she was nobody. Nobody at all, our Mrs Pasmore. Our Passion-Flower.'

We sat in silence for a little while, and then I drank my tea, and looked at Ann again, and thought of Mrs Pasmore.

'I know it's not my fault, her being in that laundry,' I said. 'But I can't help thinking it is.'

She didn't say anything. She just watched me, and waited for me to go on, to explain if I wanted to.

'Everybody said I was lucky. For the theatre, I mean, not

for myself. The first time I went back there, after school broke up, it was a new production, they hadn't expected it to do much. But it did, it got good notices, it made quite a lot of money. All except one of the actors, his notices weren't so good, and he'd been rude to me. So everybody said I'd brought them luck. They called me their lucky black cat. It was a joke at first, but they really are superstitious, actors. They started to believe it.'

Ann nodded. Yes, I can see that. I can understand.

'Then I left. And six months later, the Royal closes down. Well, I know, it's been on the cards for years, it's always been struggling, there was never enough money, but when I left, it happened. It closed down. And in that article in the paper, they had interviews, and Mrs Pasmore said their luck had run out. It was stupid, but I thought she was talking about me. Running out, their luck had run out. Run out on them. Me. Dumped them, let them get closed down. Now they're pulling down the Royal, and Mrs Pasmore's working in a laundry.'

And there's been a man with a camera, in a studio, or in a car park, and Donald Flint the slug-man, and two men, laughing as I screamed in the wrong body. But I didn't tell Ann about that. It was all confusion and noise in my mind, screaming, and laughter, and a sort of buzzing, until sometimes I held my hands over my ears, and I pressed the heels of my hands so hard against my ears, against the side of my head, that it hurt. That could stop the noise, the pain could stop the laughter, and the screams, and the maddening buzzing.

'He thought I was a prostitute,' I said, and Ann looked blank for a moment, her eyes moved away as she thought, and then she nodded, and looked back at me.

'The man in the car park,' I said, but she had already caught my meaning.

'Do I look like a prostitute?' I asked, and she smiled, and then, seeing me waiting for an answer, shook her head. But

106

I wondered. I'd seen a prostitute near the station, a young woman, dark brown hair piled on her head, cascading on to her shoulders, it had to be a wig. She'd been wearing a short, tight dress in tomato-coloured wool, it had clung to her, exaggerating the high curve of her breasts, the rounded outline of her buttocks. She had been walking along the road, strutting, so that her breasts stood out and her curved haunches rose and fell, high-heeled shoes clicking, along by the taxi rank, crossing at the zebra crossing, over the lanes where the buses waited, back towards the station in front of the shopping arcade, and crossing the road again at the lights to start the same circuit again, never standing still, never stopping, except at the kerb, never speaking. I'd watched her as I waited for a taxi, and at last a car had circled the block twice, and then pulled up alongside her. She'd leaned into the window, talking across to the driver, then she'd drawn back and walked on, tossing her head, walked away from him, the round buttocks taut under the red dress, bouncing disdainfully under the supple waist and the waterfall of shining hair, and the car had moved on again, drawn up alongside her. And this time she had got in beside the driver, and it had sped away, the tyres squealing on the wet road.

But I'd been standing still, in the shadows. If I hadn't spoken he wouldn't have seen me. He hadn't heard what I'd said, just some words, perhaps he thought I'd been speaking to him. I was wearing slacks, grey slacks, and my blue sweater, not a tomato red wool dress that clung to me. I'd walked away from him. But so had she.

'I wish I could do something about Mrs Pasmore,' I said.

'Maybe you can, one day,' said Ann at last. 'If you go into the fashion business, you may hear of something. You could recommend her.'

That was what I was going to do. I would study fashion and design, and one day I would have my own business, but before that, as soon as I could, I would find a job for Mrs

Pasmore, where she could make her lovely clothes, and gossip, if not with chorus girls, at least with models.

Now I stood in the little art gallery and I stared at a Braque still life, corners and angles and light and shade, and I asked it to get my head back into shape, and I wished it was the Cézanne.

Not even Patrick Chendar, kind and generous and now listening with an air of absorbed interest to a local councillor talking about the town hall art collection, would lend the Cézanne to Revelations, despite the three large young men who spoke in the clipped accents of Sandhurst, whose champagne glasses never needed refilling, and whose eyes never stayed for more than a few moments on the faces of the people to whom they were talking. Military Police, Patrick had whispered to me, special invitation with strings attached. He had lent the big Braque, two Modiglianis, a tiny Signac and a Gleizes. But he had added his name to the invitation, and the town art gallery had as a result lent two paintings from their collection of Cubists, and there were seven works on loan from his friends. Not all the art critics were from the local press, either.

Robert Cameron introduced me to Martin Orek, the young man whose photograph he had taken standing beside the stepladder, and who was now in an agony of excitement and tension over the opening of his gallery.

'But is anybody ever going to *buy* anything?' he kept saying. 'I mean, it's all very well coming to look at Braque and all that, but will they *buy* anything?'

He wrung my hand and smiled, abstracted and anxious to get away into the second room of the gallery, where the paintings that were for sale were hanging.

'Miss Mayall is a shareholder,' Robert Cameron reminded him, holding him back almost physically by laying a hand on his arm.

'Oh, yes, it's the three of us, isn't it? Well, hello, yes. Look, please, do excuse me, have a champagne or something, but there are people in there, they might want to *buy* something.'

He was, as Robert had said, very engaging, like a puppy presenting a ball and begging for it to be thrown for him, but I did not want to be distracted.

'The three of us,' I said. 'Does that mean you put up all the remaining nineteen thousand eight hundred pounds?'

'I wanted you to be in on this,' Robert explained. 'I liked that painting you did for John, and we needed the contact with Patrick Chendar. That's all right, isn't it?'

Of course it was all right. But it was my first contact with his quick-thinking opportunism, and at first I felt patronised, and then exploited, and it was only later I recognised the truth, that it had been, quite literally, a fair deal.

I smiled at Robert, wondering what to say, and he smiled back, puzzled, and followed Martin into the second gallery. One of the military policemen, crisp and handsome, came over and introduced himself. Lord Chendar had promised to introduce us, but Lord Chendar was swamped in art critics and town hall dignitaries, excuse him for not being able to wait any longer. Derek Brindley.

'Gloriana Mayall,' I answered. 'I understand you're here to make sure nobody smuggles the Braque out in a handbag?'

He smiled politely, and his eyes moved quickly over the group of people coming in through the door, watching as they called greetings to each other, looked around, and dispersed among those already standing in front of the paintings.

'Lunatic fringe with Stanley knives,' he said.

'What did you say?'

'Not theft, vandalism. That's the danger in this sort of situation.'

I thought about it, wondering who would want to destroy a painting.

'How do you spot them? What are you looking for?'

'Anybody who doesn't know the people here. Saying "Hello, darling" to someone who doesn't answer, or who hesitates about it. Anybody trying too hard.'

I stood beside him for a while, looking for people trying too hard, wondering if I should be angry about Robert Cameron letting me have a share in Revelations just for an introduction to Patrick Chendar, thinking about a lunatic with a Stanley knife suddenly lunging at the Braque. Then Derek asked if he could take me out to dinner when the viewing was over, he knew a French restaurant, and I smiled, and said some other time perhaps, and wandered off into the second gallery to see whether Martin had managed to sell anything.

There were little red dots on two of the paintings, and Martin was looking dazed, as if somebody had hit him and he was just about to fall down. They were small paintings, crowded with colour, one of farm animals in blues and reds and greens, all outlined in yellow and fitting together like a jigsaw puzzle, the other a seascape with two trawlers under a brilliant blue sky, black and red funnels belching white and gold smoke.

'It's working, my dear,' said Robert as he passed me on his way out into the main gallery, and Martin, hearing him, threw me a smile of bewildered happiness, and then turned back to an old woman with huge tortoiseshell-framed glasses who wanted to know if he could recommend somebody to paint her daughter's portrait.

Patrick Chendar raised a champagne glass to me from across the room, and I raised mine in reply. He seemed to be enjoying himself, he was engaged in a noisy argument with a critic, and they were both grinning fiercely, inviting support for their views from the people around them, and there was laughter, and the occasional satirical jeer, and one or two people clapping at what they saw as telling points.

I went back into the main gallery and found the town

councillor who had been talking to Patrick. I thanked him for lending the two paintings, and he said he was delighted, delighted. Glad to support local enterprise. Very glad. Delighted.

Another of the military policemen introduced himself, and said he was interested in the painting of horses at Newmarket, did I know the one he meant? In the far corner of the second gallery, could I tell him something about it? I said he would have to ask Martin Orek, or look in the catalogue. I hadn't meant to be unfriendly, but he and Derek grimaced at each other when they thought I wasn't looking.

It had become very crowded, and the waiters were having to squeeze between people to take the little trays of canapés around. Champagne corks were popping quite frequently, and there was laughter, a party atmosphere.

Then Martin Orek was in front of me, talking so fast I could hardly understand him. He'd sold another painting, it was going well, did I think it was going well? Did I really? There were some more in the store room, downstairs, should he change them over, take down the ones he'd sold? What did I think?

'Leave them,' I said. 'Don't look so anxious. Enjoy yourself.'

But he was an anxious person, he couldn't relax, couldn't believe this would last. He seemed to be everywhere, talking, and explaining, and thanking people for coming, and as he darted from group to group, flashing his bewildered, happy smile at his guests, I watched their faces. They were amused, they exchanged smiling glances and small, suppressed laughs. But they liked him. They were pleased his opening party had been a success. They would be kind.

By the time the party ended, and Martin and Robert and I were alone, with just one normal security guard to stay overnight, Martin was exhausted. The waiters cleared away the glasses and the plates, packing them into boxes in the basement, but the floor was scattered with broken biscuits, and the galleries smelt of cigarettes and alcohol. Robert threw the doors open to let in some fresh air, and Martin went to fetch the vacuum cleaner. Ten minutes later I went to look for him, and found him in a chair in the basement, fast asleep.

There was half a bottle of champagne in the office. Robert poured it out into two coffee mugs and we drank it standing in the doorway, watching the sky growing pale with the coming dawn, listening to the sounds of the traffic in the town. I heard the security guard rattle the windows at the back of the building, and then his footsteps going down the stairs into the basement to check the store rooms.

'I love this part of it,' said Robert. 'Something new starting up, looking as if it might go well. Have you enjoyed yourself?'

I had. Being part of it had been exciting. Watching the interest and the activity, wondering if it would work, seeing it coming to life, I had liked it. I had done something for it. By bringing Patrick into it I had helped to make it a success. I had earned my part it in. I only had one reservation.

'What does Patrick get out of it?' I asked.

'For the moment, nothing, but one day Martin will find something for the Chendar collection. Where Patrick Chendar's concerned it's bread on the waters. That's how it works, my dear. You can ask favours of your friends in business, you just remember you owe them a favour. When you can, you repay it, with interest.'

I could hear a milk float at the other end of the road, and lights were coming on in some of the windows. I was very tired. I had never stayed up all through the night before. But I wasn't sleepy, I felt light-headed, perhaps from the champagne, and certainly from the success.

I wanted this to be part of my life, helping to start things, with money, with ideas, with contacts and the right people. I felt the sense of adventure that had inspired Robert Cameron and Uncle John, and I wanted to be rich, too. Not in the way that Lucille did, to buy expensive clothes and jewels, to try to remain young for ever, to be loved and admired, but so that I could be part of things, part of starting something good, and exciting, and useful.

I hadn't answered Robert. I wondered if, now he had achieved what he wanted, I would be of any use to him, and if not, whether he would help me in future. Revelations was destined to succeed; he had given me the opportunity to profit from that, because I could help it on its way. A favour had been given, a slightly larger one returned. The terms of the contract had been fulfilled.

'I don't want to invest in that textile expansion,' I said.

'Why not?' He didn't sound annoyed, or surprised; simply curious.

'They did something similar a few years ago, with printed silk from China. They didn't make much of a success of it. And I couldn't understand some of the figures, their operating costs last year were much higher than before, there didn't seem to be an explanation for it.'

'You looked, then?'

'That's why you sent me the prospectus, wasn't it? And three years' annual reports.'

He drank some champagne, and brushed a hand across his face. He looked tired, and wispy, and very insignificant.

'Mostly to see if you'd spot it,' he said. 'It was embezzlement. They tried to cover it up. It was incompetence, the managing director should have seen it earlier. No, we won't touch that one.'

He glanced at me out of the corners of his eyes, quick, considering, a little hesitant, and I smiled to myself. I have very good peripheral vision, I can see the expressions on people's faces when they think I'm looking in quite another direction. Robert was wondering if I was ready for another gamble.

'There's a woman in Chester producing printed silk. Very good quality, very little money. She needs a good marketing company, she can't afford it. Five thousand should do it.

113

Two per cent for two hundred. She wants to keep fifty-one per cent, the stock and equipment has been valued at five thousand.'

'That's a bit pat, isn't it? Surprisingly convenient.'

'From the arithmetical point of view? It's a rather generous valuation. Very generous, actually. The real value is about three thousand, but what about her expertise? She's been working at this for years.'

'Why hasn't she succeeded?'

'Because she's not a very nice person.' He raised the bottle, gesturing at my coffee mug, eyebrows raised in a question. I shook my head. 'She's a plain, middle-aged, bad-tempered woman. People don't like her. But she's almost pathologically honest when it comes to money, declares every penny to the Inland Revenue, that sort of thing, and I think the fabrics are lovely. Are you interested?'

'What do I have to do?' I asked, and he laughed.

'John has faith in you. You're going into the fashion world?'

'I hope so.'

'Then I hope that answers your question. What about mine? Are you interested?'

'Yes.' I looked at him, and raised the coffee mug in a toast to him. 'Yes, please, Robert. I'm interested.'

Back at school I went straight up to the dormitory and fell asleep. I didn't hear the bells, and I only woke several hours later when it became crowded, everybody changing into skirts and jerseys for the afternoon. Matron came in, and told me to stay where I was. Once everybody had gone I admitted I hadn't been to bed at all the night before, and she tried to look disapproving, but laughed instead, and called me a shocking little stop-out-late.

After she'd gone I pulled the bedclothes over my head, and started to drift off to sleep again. It was nice, being treated almost as an equal by Matron, I thought. When so many other people thought she was such a dragon.

114

About a week later a letter came for me, from Chester. Mrs Alexandra Martin, introducing herself, and thanking me, a little stiffly, for investing in her business. There were two photographs, which she had probably taken herself, of some fabrics draped over a table. The colours were beautifully balanced, clear and exciting, or serenely blended, but the display was amateurish. The edge of the table showed through the fabric. She also enclosed a price list, and she'd written on the bottom of it, a short scribble to tell me that I could have a discount if I wanted to buy some.

Mrs York had been slightly mollified by my pass at needlework, although she was still inclined to snap that it was more than I deserved. I showed her the photographs of Mrs Martin's fabrics, and the price list. She said they were far too expensive, but a few days later said she thought she would have three yards of the blue after all. I wrote to Uncle John to ask if the trust fund could buy me some too, and he agreed. I wanted to make myself some clothes, I wanted to try to design them myself, I needed something different. Even though Lucille claimed to be allowing me a free hand when it came to choosing clothes, everything I had somehow mirrored her view of me, fragile and gentle, and entirely helpless.

She had enrolled me in the local art college, I was to start in the following September. Fashion and Fabrics was the name of the course, and it lasted a year, with two secondary courses. Lucille had sent me the prospectus, and suggested I should take interior decoration, and portraits, or perhaps commercial art. I read the prospectus, and grimaced. Nobody could possibly learn enough in one year. The banality of the course descriptions made it quite clear that they were not intended for anybody who took the subject seriously. Fine art was the only course that seemed worth the time spent on it.

But there were other art colleges.

There was one in London offering a two-year course in theatre design, with fashion and fabrics as an auxiliary.

Miss Elphick had a prospectus for it, and she lent it to me. At first I passed over the section on theatre, that wasn't my world any more, and I looked at the pages on magazine drawings, models who must have been nine feet tall in clothes that defied gravity, colour washes of illustrations for romantic fiction short stories.

Was that to be my world instead?

I left the prospectus in my desk, and picked up my geography textbook, feeling vaguely depressed.

That evening I read through it again, and turned back to the theatre section. There were photographs, and the descriptions were enthusiastic. There was a set for *Antigone*, broken columns of stone washed with pale light, another made of scaffolding, and there were sketches, properly drawn designs of sets with measurements and angles in thin writing. At the end of the section was a list of results, names with a short paragraph under them. Ten students, six had passed with distinction, two were working in the United States, one in France.

Miss Elphick said I could keep the prospectus, I was the only one that year interested in art.

But they wanted six O levels.

'Geography,' said Mrs Russell, 'and English language. You could, you know, Gloriana. If you set your mind to it, you could.'

I wished there was somebody I could tell. When I thought of going back to the theatre I felt sick with dread and shame, and yet the longing was so strong it was like a pain, dragging at my mind.

I looked at the photograph of the *Antigone* set, and I wanted to do that. I wanted to know how they'd done that, and I still had my own ideas, my *Macbeth* castle, I knew it could work, and I wanted to see it, massive and ominous, not just in my mind, in my imagination, but completed, in wood and canvas, boards and struts, properly painted, with good lighting, and on a stage.

In the theatre, I might see Louise. Or Terry, or Ray. Jim Priest perhaps, any of the people who had seen the pictures. It's quite a small world, the theatre. I had been part of it, and I had loved it. They had liked me, I had been their lucky mascot, I had worked with them and been part of their world, enclosed and exciting, and warm.

I might see the slug-man, Flint, Donald Flint.

I put my hands over my ears and pressed, until it hurt, until the buzzing died away.

'Time to take control of your own life, Gloriana,' said Miss Elphick, and I stared at her. Taking control of my own life was something I had never really thought about. Other people were in control.

'Two more O levels won't do you any harm,' commented Mrs Russell. 'Even if you do end up in a job fit only for a silly little ninny, bored to tears and jumping into marriage just to get out of it, what possible harm could it do? Kick yourself in the bottom, my girl, and get on with it. You might even manage three.'

I wrote to Uncle John.

'If they accept me, could I go? It's two years instead of one, and more expensive.'

He wrote back telling me there'd be no difficulty.

Miss Mortimer offered me extra coaching in English language, she could manage an hour a week. I'd always thought she despised me, and suddenly she made an offer, not just of tuition, it seemed, but of friendship. I was so startled that for a moment I couldn't speak.

'Yes, please,' I said, and she smiled.

Take control of your own life, Miss Elphick had said. It was a strange idea, taking control, a little frightening, but exciting.

I wrote to Lucille, and said I thought the course at the local college would be useless.

'I want to make good clothes,' I lied, 'not cheap third-rate stuff for chain stores. Darling Lucille, you wouldn't be

seen dead in the things they used to illustrate their catalogue, would you? But the college in west London, some of
their clothes are really quite good.'

She agreed. If I didn't mind getting up while the milkman
was still asleep to catch the train every day, and provided
the trust fund would pay, it might be quite a good idea, she
thought. I'd meet nicer people, perhaps.

'I won't cancel the entry just yet, darling. After all, you
may not pass those dreary exams. Why on earth does West
London want six? How silly! After all, if you can paint, it is
an art college. For God's sake, don't strain your eyes. No
matter how they try to pass it off, women look hideous in
spectacles, and you might get frown lines.'

I looked at the prospectus again, at the pages on fashion
and commercial art, and felt the leaden, dreary boredom
and depression. Two years, learning to paint to sell. Facile
and banal, tomorrow's fish and chip wrappings.

I painted a watercolour of a man and a woman kissing
under a flowering tree, and I stood back and looked at it. So
what? I thought. So what? And I ripped it off the board
and crumpled it, and dropped it into the waste-paper
basket.

'Theatre Design', I wrote on the application form, and I
felt my heart thud in my chest, and my eyes were stinging
with tears, and I was very afraid.

But I signed the form, and I addressed the envelope, and
I took it down to the hall and posted it in the box for outside
collection.

I am going back, I told myself as I walked to the art
studio. I am going back, and I will make them accept me
again, even if they despise me. I will make them take me
back. I will go back.

8

I never did tell Lucille I was studying theatre design at the college. For all the time I was there she thought my courses were fashion, and fabric design. After a while I stopped feeling guilty about deceiving her; I had never actually lied.

If I had told her, there would have been trouble. It seemed simpler to leave things as they were, and face that trouble, and the angry scenes it would bring, when it happened. If it ever did happen.

During those two years I made her some clothes, the simple and elegant dresses she preferred, and I designed some hats; she had them made up, I think at Patrick Chendar's expense. Some of those dresses were made of Alexandra Martin's printed silks, and I used them myself. People asked me about them, and then I told them where they could be bought; now, they were to be found in some of the more exclusive shops. The marketing company was doing well by Alexandra.

I met her once, at a trade fair. Robert Cameron telephoned me and asked me to come, and bring some friends from college if possible. Alexandra was a big, rather fat woman, with a belligerent look and a hairy chin. Her voice was strident, and she looked unhappy and uncomfortable standing by her table, trying to smile at everyone. I'd managed to persuade two of the lecturers from the fashion department to come with me, and they bought some of her silks. They would have bought more if she'd been quieter, and perhaps prettier. But she seemed pleased, she thanked me for bringing them, and gave me a beautiful length of silk, dark green with thin waves of silver grey. I told her she shouldn't be so generous, and at first she smiled, but then a look of dismay crossed her face.

'I shouldn't, should I?' she exclaimed. 'Not now we're a partnership. I never thought of it. I've been giving some away. Oh, hell! I'll work out what it was, I'll pay it back.'

As Robert had said, she was almost pathologically honest, and as we both agreed, she was no saleswoman. We would have to get the marketing company to arrange professionals for the trade fairs.

Lucien Rathbone had been enthusiastic about my decision to study in west London. He said it would mean we could meet more often. We could meet for dinner in the evenings. We could go to parties.

He was doing well in the City. He gave me a sapphire necklace for my birthday. I held it up to the light. The stones were lovely.

'Sapphires,' I mused. 'Yes, I suppose I like sapphires.'

'Glory, you are so beautiful. I dream about you. I love you so much, it's making me ill. Truly, I'm going crazy.'

Spaniel eyes in a pleading face. I let him put the necklace around my throat, and I bowed my head as he fixed the clasp, trying not to shiver at the touch of his fingers. Fingers, on my shoulders, sliding. Cindy, little Cindy.

I stepped away, turning to face him.

'*Don't* touch me.'

'Glory. Please. Beautiful Glory, just let me . . .'

'No.'

I did do some work in the fashion department, part of the theatre course covered costume design, and when I went home in the evenings I would take swatches of fabric samples for Lucille, to stroke, to consider, to appraise; toys for my mother. And I was asked to model some of the students' designs at the Christmas show, and to be photographed wearing them, for portfolios, and for agencies.

I hadn't been in a photographic studio since the Miss Golden Days competition. It had seemed easy to agree when Jane Targe and Penny Ingles asked me, of course I'd wear their designs, why not? And photographs, yes. So they'd measured me, and fitted the clothes, and I'd stood on the table as they pinned and tacked the fabrics, and listened to them talking about camera angles, and lights, and when they could get the studio, and which photographer, and gradually the nightmare grew and took shape.

Backing out would have been stupid, and unfriendly, as well as unfair to Jane and Penny. Stupid, I kept telling myself. Not much to ask, to have a few photographs taken, and the clothes were good, Jane's thing like a poncho, which I had described to Lucille as an amazingly chic horse blanket, and Penny's dress which looked magnificent, but only on a perfect figure. There wasn't anybody else who could do it, not now, not when they'd made the clothes to fit me, just me. There wasn't time.

The night before the photography session I could not sleep, and at four in the morning I got up, and I went for a run in the park. There were lights alongside the path, but I did stumble occasionally on uneven patches, and I tired quickly. I stopped when I reached the lake, and I found I was crying.

I was terrified.

I sat on the bench with my head in my hands, counting, and breathing as deeply as I could, all the tricks I knew to try to bring myself under control. No matter what, I would not go to college that day with swollen, red eyes. I would be calm. I would do what I could. There was nothing to fear. No strangers in the studio, only students I had come to know, and I would not be alone, I need never be alone with a photographer again.

I ran on, around the lake and up the hill, through the gate and into the streets of the town. It was raining, a light, steady drizzle, and the cool damp on my face was soothing, gentle.

Outside, I could do it. I could stand outside, and let cameras come near, photographers clicking at me, I'd had snapshots taken dozens, hundreds of times, it didn't matter.

I was out of breath again, and I slowed to a jog, noticing for the first time the ache in my calves and thighs, thinking vaguely that I had let myself get out of condition. Stupid, I liked running, I could do this more often, it was good to run alone through the rain.

I stopped again, breathing slowly and deeply, my eyes wide to try to keep away tears. What, I asked myself, did I think would happen? A photographer would take pictures of me posing in Jane's poncho and Penny's dress, and Jane and Penny would be there, and perhaps other people too. I would not be alone. There would be no screaming, there would be no laughter.

This time my hands pressed against my ears could not keep out the noise, the buzzing, the screaming, and even with my eyes wide and staring down the wet, lamplit street, the pictures that were not quite memories were moving, my face pleading, laughing men, and a thin child's body.

Lucille was in the kitchen when I got home, in a dressing gown, her hair covered by a white towel, her face shining with scented cream. The thin scars from the facelift had almost gone now, just tiny white threads under the eyebrows, but there was a droop at the corners of her mouth, the beginnings of a look of heaviness in her cheeks. She was nearly forty.

'Darling, what on *earth*?' she exclaimed as I came in.

'Couldn't sleep.'

'But Gloriana! Out on the streets at this time of night, really. Dangerous.'

She turned away and went on looking for something in a wall cupboard. I sat down at the table.

'I'm modelling some clothes today.'

'Yes? Lovely. I always thought you'd make a good model. Why don't you? Instead of art, I mean. Wasn't Grace Kelly a model, before she was a film star? The one who married Prince Rainier?'

'I think so.'

'Well, then, there you are.' She looked at me, and smiled, puzzled. 'Why so glum? Gloriana? Have you been crying, darling?'

Could I tell her? Could I ask her?

I stood up, and smiled.

'I hate photographic studios,' I said lightly. 'All those lights, so hot and stuffy.'

Did I remember that? Yes, there'd been lights, a camera, a man pushing the camera at my face, muttering. And the laughter, and the screaming, and the camera in my face.

Lucille was still looking puzzled, but now a little amused.

'Yes,' she said. 'Well, yes, they are. Did you try that new anti-perspirant? It's quite good, isn't it?'

'Very.'

'Do you know . . .?' She was looking in the cupboard again. 'Where on earth? Have you seen that stuff that's supposed to unblock drains? The water takes a year to run out of the bath. Oh, yes. I heard they have to remake all the dresses after a Dior fashion show, because the models have sweated so much. Disgusting! I mean, can you imagine?'

'I don't suppose it's true.'

'Well, I hope not! I found the idea of wearing my cream silk quite off-putting after I read that. Or did I read it? Perhaps it was on the box.'

'The cream silk's Balenciaga.'

'You'd better have a shower if you've been galloping around. I do think track suits are unbecoming, so baggy and unfeminine. Couldn't you design something? Do think about it. I'll have to call a plumber, I suppose. What a nuisance!'

Shower, and comfortable loose clothes, and the new anti-perspirant, and two pairs of shoes in a grip bag, one to go with the poncho and the other for the dress, and my make-up in its square padded box, and my season ticket, and money, and the usual, careful routine of checking everything, plenty of time for the bus, and the train, and sitting listening to the rhythm of the rails, listening just to that, not to the buzzing it could not quite drown, not listening to the screams, not listening to the laughter.

'Have you got flu?' asked Penny anxiously. 'You're sweating, you're white as a sheet. Glory?'

So stupid. What on earth did I think could happen? In the college photographic studio, with my friends, and the other students, what could happen?

'Glory?' Jane's round eyes behind her thick glasses, her red face puckered with concern.

'I'm all right.' I tried to smile. 'Sorry, I think it's a bug, I'll be all right.'

'You look awful.'

Penny's lovely dress, on a padded hanger, carefully sheeted against the dust, and she hovered behind me as I sat at the mirror working on my face. Evening make-up, bright lights, dramatic eyes and dark lips, but not to draw attention away from the dress.

I'm a clothes hanger, I told myself. It is not me they are photographing, it is a dress. I will be holding up a dress.

'If you could sort of turn,' she said, 'so the skirt swings, it's weighted, so it should give a sort of swirl, you know?'

'Right.'

'And look back over your shoulder.'

And smile. And pout. And moments later I'd be screaming, and there'd be the laughter.

'Glory? Are you listening?'

'Yes. Turn, to make the skirt swing and swirl, and look back over my shoulder and pout.'

124

'And what?'

'Sorry. Swing the skirt, and look back over my shoulder.'

'Yes. Glory, you're sweating again.'

'Oh, damn!'

Cotton wool, thick pads of cotton wool, press them against my forehead. Cool, I am cool, and I am calm, think of icebergs floating on a cold sea, ice white, ice grey, ice blue. This cotton wool is cold, it is snowy, cold.

'And some photographs of you walking, if you could hold your hands away from the skirt a bit, sort of high, or something. You know? And then just standing, sort of, different poses.'

'Yes. Right.'

She was looking so anxious. I was being stupid, and selfish.

'It's a lovely dress, Penny.'

'We'd better hurry. We haven't got very long.'

It was a lovely dress. She lifted it over my head, carefully, not touching my face, not touching my hair, and my arms slipped easily into place, and the zip sliding smoothly, the cool fabric against my skin, fitting perfectly, a beautiful dress.

And students were turning and looking as we walked down the corridor, Penny looking at them, looking for reactions, and she was smiling, because they liked it, there were thumbs-up signals, and somebody whistled, but friendly, and we were at the door and she held it open for me.

'After you,' I said, and she laughed, thinking I was joking.

'Please, I'd rather come in after you.' My voice was pleading. I'd pleaded before, but it had done no good. Penny was looking at me, she couldn't understand, I could hear somebody laughing, and there was the buzzing in my ears, so I reached out and pushed her, I pushed her into the room.

There were lights, and stands, and screens, harsh white light and black shadows, and somebody laughing, but

Penny was there, just inside the door, looking back at me, waiting for me, so I smiled at her and I walked into the room, and stood beside her, looking down at the floor, waiting, and listening, and trying not to scream.

'Smashing dress!' I heard somebody say, there were a lot of people, they were moving around and talking, and Penny touched my shoulder. I flinched, and heard her speak my name, questioning, perhaps hurt. I tried to smile at her.

'Over here!'

An impatient voice, and I saw the cameras, two of them on tripods, but nobody with them, just light stands. Lights, just like on stage, I told myself. When I'd been with my friends. When people had liked me, and I'd worked under lights, on stage, now I was under lights again, it was no different.

'Over here! Come on, we haven't got all that long.'

Buzzing in my ears, quickly press the heels of my hands against my ears, hard. All right, here? Yes, this is where they're pointing, stand here. It's all right, Penny's there, stand, stand still, now smile, and I could hear the clicking, and I turned my head away.

Turn, she had said, turn, and I walked away from the cameras, I could hear footsteps, rubber shoes squeaking, and the cameras clicking, and whirring, and I turned, thinking of the skirt, she wanted it to swirl, so I swung my hips and felt the soft swinging cloth sliding across my thighs, and I turned again and looked back over my shoulder, straight at the camera.

'Glory?'

'What the hell's the matter?'

'Glory, are you all right?'

'She looks as if she's going to faint. Get her a chair.'

My voice, quite steady, and I was staring at the camera.

'I'm all right.'

And they were talking again, but subdued, I couldn't

make out the words, and the camera was clicking, and whirring, and it was coming closer, so I walked on, and turned again, and would not look at it but walked past it, Penny had said hold my hands away from the dress, and a long time ago I had known I had to walk with my hips thrown forward, and turn on the balls of my feet, and my head must be high and my shoulders low, and the dress had to swirl and swing, and I would not look at the camera, and I would not, I would not, scream, I had never done that, I might be heard on stage or even in the auditorium, I had never done that, I would not do that.

'Just stand still.' 'Right, that's lovely.' 'Look this way!' 'I say, are you *sure* you're all right?' 'Get her a glass of water.' 'Gorgeous dress, Penny!' 'Turn around, slowly.' 'Put your hands up on your head, yes, like that, fine.' 'Okay, I think that's okay. Great.'

Out. Out, away from there, out of the room and running along the corridor back to the changing room, with Penny running after me calling my name, and into the quiet little room, where Jane turned an astonished face towards me, and Penny came in after me, and I stood shaking, hands hard against my ears, blocking out the laughter, and the screams.

We hadn't got long, and I had to change the make-up, so Jane ran me a glass of water while Penny helped me out of the dress and hung it on its padded hanger and folded the sheet around it and told me I'd made it look wonderful, thanks, Glory, thank you.

'Can you do my poncho?' asked Jane, and her round red face was miserable with anxiety, so I nodded, and tried to smile, and didn't know whether to push the thought of going back into the studio out of my mind, or try to face it, so I wiped the make-up off my face, and smoothed away the cream, and put all my thoughts into foundation cream, and eye shadow, and rouge, shades and highlights, mascara and eyeliner, lipstick, and everything is cold, icebergs on a cold blue sea, cold grey sky over glittering icebergs.

Shoes, different shoes, and the grey dress which would be hidden by the poncho, and breathe very slowly, and count, I will not faint, I will not be sick, and breathe, and count, and Jane was fastening the clips against my shoulder, it was heavy, soft, heavy wool, and I shook my head to free my hair from the wide, deep collar, and tried to smile at her, and tried to smile at Penny as she opened the door for us.

I managed to look at the cameras as we went back into the room, and when people asked if I was all right I smiled, and I nodded, although I couldn't speak, but there was a backdrop for these photographs, autumn trees, and there were leaves on the floor, it was like a stage again, I was on a stage, these were my friends, a photo call on stage.

I walked, and I turned, and I stood as they told me, as they called out to me, facing them, head down, hands on hips so the poncho stood out away from me, showing the dramatic pattern and the sweeping lines, lean back and look up, turn in profile, look down, walk towards the camera, towards the camera, no, Glory, *this* way, for God's sake, right, good, now walk back, now come off the stage, okay, sit on the chair, elbows on knees, legs apart, stare at the camera, open your eyes!

'Is she all right?'

'Glory? You okay?'

Stand up, and turn, make the poncho swing, look back over my shoulder, Jane standing by a lamp with her hands pressed to her mouth, try to smile at her, the cameras whirring, and clicking, and the buzzing, and somebody laughing.

'Smashing thing, that. What is it? Cloak? Poncho? Cowboy stuff, yeah?'

'Wow, Jane, I'd buy that! I think it's great.'

Smile, head back, shoulders low, and walk.

'I'd buy what's in it. Glory? What's under the poncho, then, Glory?'

'Okay, that's fine. That'll do. Thanks, Glory.'

'What's under the poncho, then, Glory? Got time for a few more shots? Let's see what's under the poncho!'

Laughing, he was laughing, and his hand stretching out towards me, and a camera, laughing, and I screamed, and struck out, my hand hit his face, screaming, there was screaming, and lights, I struck again, he was backing away, but there were cameras again, I could hear them, clicking, and whirring, and buzzing, so I screamed, and I pointed straight at his face, and I screamed.

'Don't you ever try to touch me again! Don't you touch me!'

He was still. The camera had gone, it was on the ground, and he was still, staring up at me, he had stumbled back and dropped the camera, and there was real fear on his face, he was afraid of me. This time, he was afraid of me, his eyes were wide, there was blood on his cheek, a thin line of blood from a cut on his eyebrow, and I looked along the line of my arm, and slowly my outstretched hand sank, I was pointing at his face, and there was only my voice breaking the ringing silence.

'Don't ever try to touch me again.'

They were quiet. Nobody was laughing, the cameras were quiet, no clicking, no whirring, there was no sound, only the lights, and the man looking up at me, wide-eyed, slowly reaching up to touch the blood, and backing away from me, the sound of his breathing, uneven and deep, and this time it was his hand, his hand towards me, his palm towards me, he was fending me away, and his voice, unsteady and quiet.

'Okay. Sorry, okay? Sorry.'

I could hear people now, murmuring, moving around, somebody swearing, but I was looking at the man with the blood on his face, watching him as he backed away, as his eyes dropped and he turned away from me, trying to laugh, a shaky, whispering sound, and his hand up at his face again.

I had beaten him.

He had dropped the camera. He had backed off, had backed away from me, he had been frightened.

My hand dropped to my side, and I drew a deep breath and looked around. Jane was standing by the table, her hands clasped and pressed against her mouth, her eyes round. Two young men with cameras beside her, and a girl holding a lamp, all looking at me, and more people behind them, all looking at me, and then moving, and looking at the man I had hit, the man picking up his camera, the man I had beaten.

'Is that okay, Jane?' I asked. My voice was light, and steady, quite bright, friendly. 'Will that do? Or do you need some more?'

If she needed some more I could do them. They could take more, if they wanted to. But that man, that man I had hit, the one I had beaten, he would be on his knees. Only on his knees would he ever approach me again.

'No.' Jane spoke very quietly, and then she coughed, and cleared her throat, shaking her head. 'No. That's fine. Thank you.'

As we walked towards the door I smiled at them, at their wary faces, and Jane was thanking them, nobody was looking at the man behind us, the man who was checking his camera, his face flaming, his head lowered over the camera, hands busy on levers and knurled wheels. They were turning off the lights, and they were talking again, and one of the girls looked at me, and grinned, and then laughed, and I smiled back at her, and turned in the doorway and called out to them.

'Thanks! Thank you, everybody.'

Jane was very quiet as we walked back to the changing room, and I wondered if I had really upset her. But as I closed the door behind us she turned towards me, hesitated for a moment, and then placed both hands on my shoulders, leaned forward, and kissed me on the cheek.

'I have *dreamed* of doing that,' she said, and there was a broad, beaming smile on her face. 'I have dreamed of slapping his face, spitting in his eye, splitting his head open with an axe, and pushing him screaming into a furnace. Oh, Glory, that was wonderful.'

'I made your dreams come true?'

'Something like that. Every time he's happened to look in my direction, he's sneered at me. And every girl in this college who's halfway to being good-looking, he's pawed at her, and prodded her, and smeared his hands all over her body, and told everybody she loves it really, she's just playing hard to get. And you . . . Oh, Glory, did you see his face? Did you see?'

'I saw. Jane, this poncho thing is marvellous. It's so comfortable.'

'Will you model it for me at the Christmas show?'

'Love to.'

The photographs came out well, and Penny was pleased with the ones of her dress, the skirt had swirled around my legs as she had hoped, and the colours were good. The pictures of the poncho in the autumn wood scene made Jane smile happily, but it was the unplanned shot that made the posters, that set the theme for the entire show.

I was standing, one arm flung out, pointing, staring at something or someone in front of me, a look of fury on my face, the stance dramatic, and the fringe of the poncho swept back in a lovely line, by a happy chance exactly echoed by the line of my hair, the dark-blonde wool a few tones deeper than the light-blonde hair, compelling, and immediately eye-catching.

This Way!

It was the caption they gave to the photograph, and in the end it was the title they gave to the fashion show. The poster was just over life-sized, and it stood out in the street on a board backing, my hand pointing towards the main entrance, and then smaller versions in the foyer, on the stairs, in the corridors. *This Way! to the Showroom. This Way! to the Design Centre. This Way! to the Photographic Display.*

We rehearsed the fashion show. Most of the models were students, like me, but there were two professionals as well, and they showed us how to walk, and turn, and which poses showed the clothes best. They were nice women, friendly and helpful, and happy to share the tricks of their trade.

Everybody agreed Jane's poncho should be the last design to be modelled. I was to walk on to the stage, down the catwalk, turn, walk back towards the stage, and then turn again and point, exactly as I had done in the photograph, but this time straight at the group of designers, who would be waiting in the dark at the side of the stage. As my hand came up all the lights would be cut, apart from a spot on me, and then, immediately after I struck the pose, another would focus on the designers.

Lucille had said she would come to the show, but I telephoned Patrick Chendar and asked if he could do something to fend her off. I didn't want her finding out about my theatre design course. He was amused at my request, and said he'd see what he could do.

Lucien came, and brought friends with him. I hadn't given him a ticket, but he'd asked me to go out to dinner with him afterwards, and I'd agreed. I owed him something for the sapphire necklace. He would never get value for money, not from me, but he had told me that his friends envied him, having such a lovely girlfriend, and that seemed to give him at least a little satisfaction.

I noticed him as I walked down the catwalk for the second time. I was wearing a pair of white cotton shorts and a top like a cape that swung from my shoulders and left my midriff bare. Lucien was sitting at the back, very stiff and upright, as though he was nervous. He was quite tall compared to the two men on either side of him. I smiled at him, and raised my hand in a brief wave, and as I turned and walked away I put a little extra swing into my hips, a slightly longer stride. Giving him the envy of his friends cost me nothing.

There was a standing ovation at the end of the show. I stood in the pool of light, my arm held out stiffly, pointing at the designers, my head lowered as I stared along its line at the group, and they smiled, and bowed, and stepped back, and smiled again, and stepped forward to bow again while the sounds of clapping rose, and the shouts of 'Bravo!' began, and people were stamping on the floor, and the lights came up as I lowered my arm and turned to face the audience as the other models came in from the wings on either side, and we smiled, and bowed, and at last the noise died away and the lights dimmed on the stage and came up in the main part of the room.

We'd been asked to mingle with the guests for a while after the show. There were some buyers who might be interested in the designs, who might want to see them modelled again, and we'd agreed to help. But I went over to Lucien, and was introduced to his friends, and allowed him to kiss the air a fraction of an inch away from my cheek before I went back to stand beside Jane, ready to show the lovely poncho to anybody who asked to see it.

Lucien bought it for me.

We all went out to dinner together when the party finally broke up. It was a French restaurant quite near the college, and we stayed until after midnight, while Lucien grew expansive and noisy with his friends, treating the waiters as if he'd known them all his life, as if they'd served at the table in his nursery. I wondered what this demonstration was hiding, why he was so nervous. He'd bought champagne, he kept raising his glass to me, demanding toasts to the Loveliest Blue Eyes in the Northern Hemisphere, to the Pride of the Western World, and other extravagant declamations, and I smiled, and laughed when he or his friends made jokes, and listened admiringly to their boastful anecdotes, and watched Lucien, and waited to learn just what all this was leading up to.

He drove me home. He was slightly drunk, so we had the top of the car down, and I huddled into the poncho, wrapping the big, soft collar around my neck, watching the lights of the cars sweeping over the grass and trees beside the road, and listening to the radio playing smooch music against the background noise of the powerful engine.

He drove a slightly different way into the town, off the main road and through the older part where the Victorian terraces and corner shops were shaded by plane trees, slowly down the hill to the park, and then he turned into a short side road to the parking area and pulled up under the trees and switched off the engine.

He was breathing as though he had been crying, drawing in deep, soft, shuddering breaths, and letting them out in long sighs. He was watching me, his eyes huge and dark in his pale face, and I sat in silence, waiting. And wondering.

At last he reached behind him, into the back of the car, and brought out a long, thin box wrapped in silver paper, tied with a scarlet ribbon. He handed it to me, and his hands were shaking. I looked at him, and he gestured at me to open it. I untied the ribbon, and lifted the lid of the box, and looked into it.

It was a riding crop.

When I looked at Lucien again there were tears on his cheeks, and his eyes were imploring. He reached out, and touched the crop, running his fingers down its thin, supple length.

'I've been such a bad boy,' he whispered, and my hand closed around the plaited leather.

134

9

Christmas, and Ann came home, almost six foot five, and resigned immediately to Lucille's despairing recriminations. She stood listening quietly to accusations of unfemininity, of gaucheness, of a lack of social graces, and, as soon as she could, she went to her room and closed the door behind her. I stood in the hall listening to the sound of her footsteps on the carpeted stairs, the soft sliding of the door, and the click as the catch closed, and for a moment a feeling of desolation came over me; I had been shut out of her life, shut away from my big sister. Something had ended.

Lucille telephoned the beauty salon and made an appointment; cut, shampoo and set, manicure.

'Try to make her look human,' she demanded, not bothering to lower her voice.

She saw me watching her. She raised an eyebrow, a thinly pencilled arch over the cool blue of her lovely eye, faint amazement at my behaviour in listening to her private conversation, but I wouldn't look away.

'It's the Nestleys' party tomorrow night,' she said as she hung up. 'Will Lucien take you?'

'I suppose so.'

'Two men and three women,' she sighed, and then flashed an angry, spiteful glance up the stairs at the closed door. 'If you can . . .'

But she stopped short, and the look she gave me was uneasy, even a little frightened.

'I don't understand you these days,' she said.

When she had gone I went up the stairs and tapped on Ann's door. I heard movement, and then her voice, quiet.

'Come in?'

She was sitting at her desk, half turned towards the door. She smiled as I came in, a polite smile, nothing friendly or welcoming. She closed her book, but she left a slip of paper between the pages; as soon as this interruption was over, she would open it again.

'Hairdresser this afternoon,' I said, and I spread my hands, shrugging and smiling, trying to show her it was nothing to do with me, trying to tell her I understood. Or thought I did.

'Oh, yes.' She touched her hair briefly. 'Yes, of course.'

'She said a manicure, too.'

Ann's hands were broad, square-palmed, the fingers not very long or slender. Her nails were quite short. This afternoon they would be filed into ovals, and painted. They might even have false fingernails glued over them.

So stupid, I thought, and suddenly I felt passionately that it was wrong, it was not merely pointless, it was wrong.

'It's for the party,' I said helplessly. 'The Nestleys' party.'

But she was looking at me with that same polite smile, distant, faintly questioning, waiting for me to go. So that she could open her book at the page she had marked. When this intrusion, this interruption, was over.

'Why must Ann go to the party?' I asked Lucille. 'What's the point? She has a rotten time at parties.'

But Lucille refused to listen. Ann was to learn how to behave. It was nonsense to say she shouldn't go.

'She won't shrink,' I snapped, and saw from the sharp

136

tightening of her mouth that I had struck a blow at her fairy tale. Creams and lotions and massage would keep Lucille young. If Ann would only try, would be more feminine, would learn the social graces, she would no longer be too tall.

Lucille and Ann went to the party in a big American car, with some financier from New York. Lucille introduced us, and he smiled broadly, his eyes slipping quickly over the cleavage of my dress, and then back to Lucille.

'I can see the likeness.'

Lucille's gaze was cool and distant. He wouldn't last long.

I sat at the table sketching a set while I waited for Lucien. I was trying to remember how we had set up the mirrors at the Royal, there had been a particular effect with reflected light on white linen. It had come from two angled mirrors, and when somebody walked between them it cut off the light, there was a double flickering, the reflection in the mirror and the shadow on the pale fabric. It had been complicated, but it lent a feeling of uneasiness to the scene, restless and nervous.

White linen and light. If the linen was curved it would break up the reflection yet again, the change in the shape of the light could be effective. I could try this.

I never noticed time when I was working, and it was difficult to distract me when something was going well, an idea coming to life in my mind and under my hands. I don't know how often Lucien had rung the doorbell before I heard it, and when I first became aware of it I was irritated by the interruption, until I remembered him, and the party.

He'd brought me a diamond bracelet.

He was sweating, a greasy sheen over his face, and he looked ill.

I held the bracelet in my hand, and gazed down at the smoothly sparkling stones, but I was watching Lucien. How could he afford this? Thousands, for stones like this. And the poncho, the sapphires and the gold bracelet he'd bought me for my birthday. His pale, sweating face, and his eyes, they looked tired, bruised.

'Glory.'

I raised my eyes and looked at him.

'Glory,' he said again, and then quickly, 'have they gone?'

'We're alone, if that's what you're asking.'

'Glory.'

I waited, watching him, standing still with the beautiful bracelet in my hand.

He dropped to his knees, suddenly, thudding on to the carpet, and his eyes widened with surprise, as though he hadn't meant to kneel, as though he had been pushed. He looked up at me, his head tilted back, his arms hanging slackly at his sides. There were tears in his eyes, and he was breathing through his mouth, shallowly.

'I need more,' he whispered.

I said nothing. I stood looking down at him, waiting.

'More.' He reached out and touched my dress, his fingers trailing across the blue silk, and his eyes followed his hand. 'More than the whip.'

Diamonds.

I lifted the bracelet, and looked at it, holding it at arm's length.

'Diamonds,' I said. 'Yes, I see.'

'Glory.'

He was crying, silently, tears sliding down his cheeks, and there was a razor in his hand, an old-fashioned razor with a dark red wood handle, brass rivets gleaming. He opened the razor, and held it out to me, his hand shaking.

'I don't want your blood on the carpet.' My voice was contemptuous. Was that me, who had spoken?

'Glory. Please, Glory.'

'Go into the kitchen. You can wash the tiles, afterwards.'

Was that me, speaking? Me, following him out of the room? Me, watching him undress? My eyes on the thin bruises on his shoulders and back, remembering the riding crop?

Was that me, holding out my arm, giving him the bracelet to clasp around my wrist?

Did I take the razor from him, staring into his face, and make the first, sliding little cut low on his belly, and watch his eyes widen, and his lips tighten around his clenched teeth, as I drew in my breath, and listened to his whispering voice, and did as he asked? Was that me?

I wore the bracelet to the party, and I showed it to Lucille, and heard her gasp.

'Real?' she asked.

'Oh, yes.'

'*Darling!*'

How could he afford diamonds?

'Is Lucien all right?'

'What?'

'I asked if Lucien was all right. He looks ill. Why were you so late? I was quite worried.'

Blood. There had been blood, quite a lot of blood. Had that been me, doing that? How could he afford diamonds?

I was very small, and I was alone, and it was dark. Tiny threads of light linked me to other small people, far away, growing fainter. Lucille and Ann, drifting away, the thin threads flickering.

'Darling?'

It was dark, and I was alone, and drifting, and the little threads were flickering, soon they would be gone, I would be quite alone, there would be nothing. Had that been me, with the razor?

'Gloriana?'

I looked at her, and suddenly sound burst into my ears, music from the band playing in the big room at the other side of the hall, a woman's voice calling above the noise of laughter and people talking, and Lucille was looking closely into my face, puzzled.

139

'I'm sorry,' I said. 'I was miles away. There's this marvellous new fabric we've got, I've been thinking about it all week.'

And immediately she was interested, my peculiar behaviour forgotten, the questions about Lucien dropped, and her lovely smile and her pretty voice as she asked about the fabric.

'I'll bring you some.'

Lucien, leaning back against the banisters and looking down at a short girl with glasses who was talking to him. His face was white, his hair looked black against it, sleeked back and shining. There was a small, tight smile curving his lips. As if he felt me watching him he looked up, and the smile curved a little more, and he raised his glass to me. Sweat on his white face. The short girl looked at me too, and then back, reaching out to touch his arm, to regain his attention.

Ann, sitting on the end of a sofa, in a corner by the door to the drawing room, and Mrs Nestley stopping beside her, leaning forward to talk, Ann looking up at her. Lovely party, what a good band, I'm enjoying the music. Thank you. And Mrs Nestley, baffled, but with social conscience salved, moving away, her face breaking into a smile as she crossed the wide hall to speak to an old woman in a dark red dress.

Two men in front of me, smiling, the older playing the soulful clown, where have you been all my life? And I smiled back, a long, slow smile, languishing in outer darkness, I replied. But such brilliance can never be in darkness, it sets night itself afire, and laughter, and champagne corks, and did I know they were dancing in the next room? And would I like?

Lucien watched me as I walked past, only his eyes moving in his white face, and the short girl with the glasses glancing at me, irritated, but he looked down at her again, and shifted his shoulders against the rail of the banisters as somebody whom I remembered as Alec saw me and raised a drunken shout, Gorgeous Glory, Good God!

Dancing, the music good, I knew this band, and the trumpet player smiled at me as I danced past, appreciating the fast footwork of the quickstep, and my spirits began to lift, my partner was a good dancer, and he was making me laugh. But after a few bars the rhythm changed, and there were groans, and people began to leave the floor. A *pasa doble*.

I glanced at the trumpet player, and he waggled his eyebrows at me and stamped twice, one two, a challenge. My partner was asking me, did I know this dance? Did I want to try? And yes, I did, I would dance the matador's cape, the dance of the blood on the sand, so he smiled, and he echoed the trumpet player's stamp, his shoulders flexed and his back arched as his arm straightened and I swung away from him, two complete turns, full stretch as I threw my head back and leaned away from him, balanced only by his outflung arm, and back towards him as the drum rattled a fast tattoo, swing behind him, hands changing, the deep, plunging step and both our heads thrown back as my foot swept across the floor, laughter and applause from the people watching from the sides of the room.

He was very good, this man dancing with me, the strutting, arrogant steps, the lifted arms and the high shoulders, his hands quick and sure on the changes, as he circled, and swung me away from him, and caught me again, speed, and rhythm, and the scent of danger, and the sound of applause, and a drum solo, then the trumpet and the throbbing guitar, and people stamping in time to the music as it rose to a crescendo, and the cymbals crashed, and I was at his feet, the matador's cape lowered to the sand at the moment of truth, the time of triumph, and everybody was clapping, and the band was applauding, a few bars of a flamenco on the guitar and a drum roll.

Lucien had gone, Lucille said somebody had telephoned,

he'd asked her to apologise, of course I could go home with them, with her and Ann and that American financier in that huge and vulgar car. They were all smiling at me, somebody handed me a pair of castanets, wooden souvenirs, and laughed, and the man who had danced so superbly kissed my hand, but it had been a strange and exhausting evening, and my dreams that night were restless and uneasy, and there was no sense of shock when Lucille shook my shoulder and brought me out of the dreams to tell me, Darling Gloriana, wake up, darling, it's bad news. On the telephone just now, Lucien's uncle, darling. Lucien went home last night, and he hanged himself, his brother found him. Darling Gloriana, did you understand? Are you awake? Lucien's hanged himself.

10

He had been heavily in debt, and he had stolen money from the bank. He had transferred some of it from a client's account, hoping against all reason that in such a large account it would not be missed. But it had been missed, immediately, and he had been asked to explain, to sort it out and let Mr Barrett know what had happened, how the error had occurred, to which account it had been transferred, in error. There had been no suspicion of his dishonesty at that time. Not at once.

And then he had taken twenty-five thousand pounds, on that last day. He had made no attempt to disguise it, he had transferred the money directly into his own account, and then drawn it out, in cash, and walked out of the bank that afternoon with the money in his briefcase.

Sapphires and diamonds, he had given me. A gold bracelet, the lovely poncho. And it had never been anything less than champagne for Glory, champagne in the fashionable London restaurants, where people could see him, see the girl who drank his expensive champagne.

Lucille brought me tea, and sat beside me on the bed, saying, how sad, poor Lucien. She asked me if I knew why he had done it, but I didn't know, not then. Later, when the police came.

She refused to let them see me that day, she said I was far

too shocked. She watched me all that morning, trying to sympathise, asking me what she could do for me. Wondering, I suppose, why I didn't cry.

'Had you quarrelled?' she asked.

He'd watched me dance the *pasa doble*, she said. He'd stood in the doorway, and he'd smiled, and clapped, and when it was over and I lay at the feet of my partner, the cape on the sand at the moment of truth, he'd told Lucille he had to leave.

I'd never liked him. I thought he was a fool. I guessed what he'd done.

That afternoon I told Lucille I wanted to go out for a run, I thought it would clear my head, I felt a little confused. She seemed relieved, at last some sign of the shock and sadness I should be feeling, must, surely, be feeling.

I did run, I enjoyed the run, slowly, with short, bouncing steps for the half-mile to the top of the hill, and then down through the park, faster, the last quarter-mile as fast as I could until I came to the gates and stopped, gasping, bent over, catching my breath, and then on again, jogging into the town.

I went to a jeweller. I scraped my hair back under the hood of my track suit jacket, and I looked in windows, and I bought some jewellery. Two bracelets and a necklace. Quite good quality. Quite expensive, for costume jewellery.

It was crowded, Christmas shoppers, everybody busy.

Lucien's father had telephoned while I was out. Lucille had told him I was very distressed, and I had gone for a run. I was too upset to talk to anybody, she had said.

The police came back the next day, a policewoman in uniform and a tired young man in a dark blue suit, shiny, cheap fabric. He asked questions about Lucien, how long I had known him, how well we knew each other, did I know why he had committed suicide?

Teardrops, sparkling on my eyelashes. He said he was sorry, he knew these questions must be difficult for me.

Lucien, on his hands and knees in the kitchen, wiping the blood off the tiles while I watched him, and wondered if it was me, standing in the doorway, watching the crying man washing his own blood off the floor.

How had he seemed on that last evening?

I'd thought he was ill, I said. He didn't seem well. But he'd wanted to take me to the party. He'd given me my present, and we'd gone to the party, but he hadn't wanted to dance. He kept wincing, as if he'd been in pain.

The policewoman looked at me, and then at the young detective, who glanced back at her before writing in his notebook. He nodded as he wrote.

Had he been on time?

No, I answered, he'd been very late. Nearly an hour late. I'd almost given him up. He'd said his car had broken down. We'd stayed here about half an hour, because he'd said he felt a bit sick. Then he'd said he felt better, so we went to the party. But he'd left early, and I'd come back home with my mother.

There'd be an inquest, the policewoman said. I'd probably be called. I'd have to give evidence.

'Are you very upset, Glory?' asked Ann that afternoon.

'No,' I replied, 'Not really. I didn't know him very well. I was just for showing off to his friends, like his car.'

She nodded.

'I'm sorry he's dead,' she said. 'But I'm glad you're not unhappy.'

We smiled at each other, and this time there was some warmth. Perhaps she did care for me, a little.

Two men came from the bank where Lucien had worked. Lucille and Ann had gone to see Uncle Henry at the forge, the Christmas treat Ann had wanted, so I was alone in the house. They were very polite as they stood at the door, they insisted on showing me identity cards with their photographs and the name of the bank, so there could be no doubt who they were, but they said they had to talk to me.

'I'm sorry if it's inconvenient,' said the older one, 'but there are matters we have to discuss. Urgently.'

'By which we mean now,' said the younger.

I could have refused to let them in. I wondered what to do.

'May we come in?' asked the younger man. 'If not, it will have to be with the police.'

'With a search warrant,' added the other man, and neither of them was smiling.

They'd come for the bracelet.

'And any other jewellery Lucien Rathbone gave you.'

'Why?' I asked. I was looking bewildered, and a little frightened. 'Why should I give you Lucien's presents?'

'Because they were bought with stolen money.'

The older man sat forward in his chair and looked into my face.

'We're not accusing you of dishonesty, Miss Mayall,' he said. 'We have to repay the money to the clients. Anything valuable he bought with it, you understand. We must try to trace the money.'

'Lucien's Christmas present?'

'Somebody mentioned your mother admiring it. At the party, on the night he died. A diamond bracelet is certainly valuable. I'm sorry.'

I went up to my bedroom, and I took the costume jewellery out of the drawer of my dressing table, and looked at it, the pretty paste bracelet in the box that had held Lucien's present, the necklace on the black velvet pad with the discreet gold lettering from the famous London jeweller. I could feel my heart thudding in my chest, and I was cold. They were not stupid, these men. They were not at all stupid. I hadn't expected this. I'd thought there might be a polite letter, I'd even worked out my reply, what I'd say about dear Lucien's Christmas present, written in the upright, rather rounded hand Miss Mortimer had condemned as babyish at Storrington.

Would they believe me?

Another voice from Storrington. An amused voice, but with a bitter edge. Miss Mullins.

'There is no limit to the stupidity of which a man may believe a woman is capable.'

'Miss Mayall?' There was nothing amused about the voice from the foot of the stairs. It was sharp, suspicious. 'Miss Mayall? Is everything all right?'

'I'm just coming.'

Tears, wiped on the cheeks, faintly drying streaks. A brave smile. The breathing a little uneven.

'I'm sorry,' I said as I came down the stairs, 'I can't find the box for the gold bracelet. I've lost it, I'm sorry.'

They looked at the fake jewellery in the expensive boxes, and they looked at me, and they looked at each other, and they said I could, after all, keep Lucien's presents. Had he bought me anything else?

'A poncho, from the college fashion show. For the winter.'

A second-hand poncho made by an art college student was not, it seemed, likely to solve their problem.

Had it been that easy? I wondered, after they had left. Had it truly been that easy?

Yes. Lucien Rathbone had bought his dumb little blonde dolly bird costume jewellery and put it in expensive boxes, and told her it was diamonds and sapphires and gold. And she'd believed him. Dumb little blonde dolly bird. Clever old Rathbone.

After they'd gone I couldn't find the box for the diamond bracelet.

I didn't mention their visit to Lucille.

Two days before the inquest she said she had something to tell me, something rather unpleasant. I sat on the sofa and she stood by the fireplace, trying to find the words, the euphemisms.

Some men, she said, have habits most people can't understand. They like things that most people don't like.

147

'Spinach,' I said. 'And beetroot.'

'Darling, *please*. I don't mean that. It's that they don't make love like normal people. They like other things.'

I watched her, and then, from being mildly amused, I suddenly became bored.

'Lucien was a masochist,' I said.

'Yes,' and then, a little shocked, 'You knew?'

'I expect they'll have to mention it at the inquest. They found cuts on his body. On his genitals.'

Her eyes were wide and dark. She sat down, slowly, on the armchair, staring at me, and then suddenly looking away.

'Scandal!' she said, hissing and gulping, straining at the word, and again, 'Scandal!'

'It was the money that was the scandal,' I said. 'That's why he killed himself.'

She didn't seem to be listening.

'He told you? He told you?'

'About the money?'

'No.' A hand, flapping at me, frantic, her face behind it, pale and sick, not looking at me. 'The . . . the *other* thing.'

Lucien's voice, Lucien whispering, telling me what to do. Had it been me, with the razor, doing as he said? Had it been my hand, so careful, so slow, with the shining razor? Had I listened as he gasped, and whispered, and moaned, and finally screamed?

'*It was you!*'

She was going to be sick. Her hand was at her mouth, her eyes were wide, and staring at me.

'No!'

'*You* did it. You did that.'

I hadn't. I had not. It was the thin girl, it hadn't been me. But she had to believe it.

'No. Did what? I don't know what you mean.'

'You said.' She sounded savage with the accusation. 'You said it. The cuts, you said there were cuts.'

'He told me. And I said I thought it was horrible. I didn't want to hear. I said I didn't want to see him any more. He told me.'

She wanted to believe me. Her hand was pressed against her mouth, but her eyes were narrowed, staring at me.

I hadn't done it. It hadn't been me. It was disgusting, I wouldn't do that. The thin girl had done it, not me.

'I said we'd go to the party together. And then not see each other any more.'

'That bracelet.'

'Costume jewellery.'

'It was not!'

Lucille knew diamonds. She'd asked, was it real, disbelief in her voice, but she'd known.

I looked at her, coldly.

'Do you want to see it again?'

Her eyes dropped first, and she looked away, making a small, distressed gesture.

'Who, then? Who would have done it?'

I was ready for that.

'He said he'd been to his club.'

Relief on her face. She could believe this, yes. She could.

'I lied to the police,' I said. 'I told them Lucien had said his car had broken down. I didn't want to tell them what he'd said about the club. It was horrible, I was too embarrassed.'

Did she believe me? She wanted to believe me. She knew the bracelet was real, but Lucille was an expert at self-deception. She could forget the bracelet.

'For God's sake, don't tell Antoinette,' was all she said in the end. 'She's too young. I hope they can keep this out of the papers. His poor mother!'

Christmas, but I stayed away from the parties, at least at home. There were plenty in London, and those I went to, and Francis Chendar stayed in his father's Westminster flat and took me with him to addresses in Mayfair and

Belgravia, where hardly anybody had heard of Lucien Rathbone, and if they had, well, yes, I knew him, poor Lucien. So sad for his family. Financial problems, I'd heard. That's what I'd understood.

But the inquest was adjourned, and the police came to see me again, the same policewoman but an older man this time, more alert.

I'd led a sheltered life, I told myself as he questioned me. I'd been shocked. I was disgusted, and embarrassed. And I answered his questions, not looking at him, looking down at the carpet as I sat on the edge of the sofa, making nervous, clutching gestures with my restless hands. I didn't know where the club was, what it was called. It was just for people like him, like Lucien.

'Do you know if, apart from what you've told us, this was a gambling club, Miss Mayall?'

'Oh, no!' This time looking straight into his eyes, my own eyes wide. 'Oh, no, I'm sure Lucien didn't gamble.'

I watched his face, and knew I'd won. I'd played it right. I'm sure Lucien didn't gamble meant I wasn't at all sure, he may well have been a gambler, but I will not tell you so. I will not be so disloyal. I will not speak that ill of the dead man, having had to speak so much worse.

That was where the money had gone, that was why he had been in debt.

I gave my evidence at the inquest, quietly answering the questions, but there was whispering between the lawyers and the coroner, and nobody asked about a club, or spoke of razor cuts. When they asked me I said he'd seemed ill that evening, and had left the party early, leaving me to come home with my mother.

And the police inspector who had questioned me told the coroner they had reason to believe Mr Rathbone had been in the habit of visiting a private gambling club.

His parents were there, watching and listening, their faces expressionless. His father nodded to me when it was all over and we stood up to leave the court, but his mother didn't look at anybody. She walked out of the court, small steps, but very straight, her dark coat swinging from her narrow shoulders, her hands folded over her handbag. Her knuckles were white.

I sent a wreath to Lucien's funeral, small roses and maidenhair fern, with a silver and white card, 'With my love, Gloriana'. But I didn't put a card on the other flowers, the scarlet carnations and the white orchids which I tied with a chain of blue and white brilliants. If Lucien had a consciousness somewhere he would need no card to know from where they had come, or what they meant.

I didn't go to the funeral. I hate funerals, and there were two on that day, because Uncle Henry had died, and Ann had gone to his funeral, her face wooden with grief, her hands clenched into angry fists. I watched her walking down the path when the taxi came to take her to the station. She was wearing her school uniform, navy blue, she wouldn't wear anything Lucille had bought her, not to say goodbye to Henry.

I went back to London. I went to the college, and I stood in front of my easel and I painted a thin girl with bruised thighs, holding a razor. I was very tired by the time I had finished it, and somehow dissatisfied, although I think it was quite good. But the girl had no face, and I didn't seem to know what to do about that.

11

Uncle Henry had left Ann the forge, and Ann was going to be a blacksmith.

Lucille was frantic. The house seemed to whirl with her screams and with the sounds of running footsteps and slamming doors. She had telephoned a solicitor and demanded that he sue Uncle John, that he overturn the will, that he get a court order forbidding Ann to have anything to do with the forge or with metal working. She had called the doctor, and he had arrived with his black bag, an untidy, lumbering man, who had stood in the hall, scratching at his head as she sobbed and gasped, and had then gone upstairs to talk to Ann.

Ann seemed quite calm, but sometimes there was a sort of exultation in her face, and she had certainly changed. Lucille had insisted on taking her to a party on the day after the funeral, it was only an uncle after all, nobody would expect us to go into deep mourning, she said. And Ann had not sat quietly in a corner with a polite smile on her face. Ann had stood, and talked, and had drunk two glasses of champagne, and when a large and pompous man had tried to explain to me the importance of the financial institutions, she had said she thought all this money-shuffling was childish, just playing Monopoly and being given silly-money salaries for doing it.

Everybody had gasped, and Lucille had laughed, a shrill laugh, which she had stifled almost immediately.

'Darling! Rather a *schoolgirl* joke, don't you think?'

And the man who had brought me to the party, Edward, tried to look down his nose.

'Certainly rather aggressive.'

'You're some sort of soldier, aren't you?' challenged Ann. 'Spend your time learning how to kill people, don't you?'

'Hardly that, Miss . . .'

'Don't tell me I'm aggressive. Not unless you can back it up. Would you care to try? Indian arm wrestling, it's called, I think. This is me being aggressive, soldier boy. How's the defence fund? Running a bit low on courage, it seems.'

Edward was scarlet with embarrassment, trying to hide it with laughter, looking around for support.

'It's hardly that sort of party, Miss Mayall.'

Lucille took us home early, in a taxi, refusing her escort's offer to drive us. She was almost crying, apologising incoherently, saying that Antoinette had been to a funeral, an uncle, it must have unbalanced her, she was so sorry, and our host and hostess saying they quite understood, poor Antoinette. They hoped she'd feel better soon.

I said I'd come too, I was fascinated by this new Ann. Edward protested, he'd driven down from Manchester to bring me to this party and it had hardly started. Glory, my incomparable, for God's sake!

But I just smiled at him, and asked the maid to bring me my coat. Edward seemed to imagine he could treat me as a toy, not only in public, but also in private. And the diamond earrings he had given me for Christmas were certainly not fine enough for that, the stones were very small.

Lucille did cry in the taxi on the way home, she was mortified. Never had she been so humiliated, Antoinette must be mad. Mentally ill. She could almost hope so, the alternative was worse, people did recover from mental illness, what had Antoinette been thinking of, to speak to people like that? To insult an important man like Mr Baeling? And then to challenge Edward to a wrestling match.

Ann was quite quiet, very calm again, and she listened to Lucille, and looked out of the window at the lights on the motorway, and said she was sorry Lucille had been upset. She hadn't meant to upset Lucille.

But no, she would certainly not write letters of apology. Nor would she go to any more of these silly parties. No, she would not, not ever again.

'*Be quiet!*' screamed Lucille, and Ann was quiet, and she looked out of the window again.

It was the next day that Lucille learned of Ann's plans to be a blacksmith.

She telephoned Uncle John at his office, wanting to know what was being done about putting the forge on the market, and whether it was, once again, the trust that would have control of the money, or whether she, as Antoinette's mother, would be granted the tiny privilege of a say in the matter.

I listened from the kitchen. I heard her voice, at first angry and indignant about the stupid will, the ridiculous clause that made it impossible to sell the place. And then disbelieving. And then she began to scream abuse down the telephone, so I took my coat from the peg in the kitchen, and I went out, walking away from that house, leaving the screaming and the anger. I went down to the town library, where they had just started a collection of big photographs of famous paintings, and I took out a Pissarro landscape and stood it on the easel, and looked at it until my mind felt quiet and still again.

What would happen to Ann? Lucille would not tolerate this.

Ann had taken all her dresses into the town, and given them to a charity shop. She wouldn't need them any more, she said. She'd bought men's working clothes instead.

Lucille screamed until her voice cracked, calling her a monster, a perversion of nature, but Ann took her new clothes to her room, and quietly closed the door. Lucille sat in the kitchen, crying until she was exhausted, and then she went into the drawing room and fell asleep on the sofa, still gasping, her eyelids red and swollen.

There were lines on her neck, and the skin on the back of her hands was beginning to look a little crumpled, a little soft and loose. Could she still look at herself in the mirror and see the lovely girl who drew the men's eyes? Who could smile to herself and say, this one, yes. That one, perhaps.

Edward telephoned, saying he wanted to check that I'd got home all right, what a peculiar business that had been, how was my amazing sister?

Little chips of stones in those earrings he had given me, tiny little splinters.

'She's fine,' I said. 'Still quite intimidatingly strong.'

'Yes, my God, I bet she is!'

'Strong enough to tear your arm off, I should think.'

He didn't like that. His laugh was forced.

'I doubt that.'

'Pity you're too much of a coward to find out.'

'Glory! For God's sake, what did you expect me to do? Take her up on it? Start some sort of bar-room brawl in the Darlingtons' reception room? See which of us could lift the grand piano highest, me or Miss Hercules Mayall?'

'I love my sister, Edward,' I said. 'I don't enjoy remarks of that nature about Antoinette. She means ten times more to me than you could ever do.'

The telephone had woken Lucille. When I went in she was standing by the mantelpiece, smoothing her dress over her hips.

'Who was that?'

'Edward.'

'Oh.' She glanced at herself in the big mirror. 'Oh, dear

God, just look at me! Or, rather, please don't. How's Edward? What on earth he must have thought! Was he angry?'

'Frightened, I think. He's got shoulders like a hock bottle, had you noticed?'

'My goodness! You're becoming very critical these days. I think he's a nice young man.'

She'd called Ann a monster.

'I've just dumped him,' I said. 'You can have him if you like.' And then I added, more spitefully than I'd ever spoken to her before, 'Add him to your dwindling stock.'

'*Gloriana!*'

There were tears in her eyes. Did she still believe in fairy tales? Was she, at last, beginning to grow up?

What was Ann going to do?

I gave her Lucien's gold bracelet and told her to sell it. She was going to need money, and she didn't have any. I said she could buy herself an anvil, and her smile as she looked at me was wide and happy, her lovely brown eyes sparkling. Her best feature.

'I've already got one,' she said. 'Thanks, Glory, but I've got one.'

'Are you really going to be a blacksmith?'

She nodded.

'I wish he wasn't dead,' she said. 'I wish he wasn't, Glory. And I wish I could thank him. He's given me the forge. I love the forge, I love it so much. He's given it to me, he's given me a life.'

I had never seen her so happy, even though Lucille screamed at her, even though her beloved Uncle Henry was dead, even though she didn't know where she was going to study, didn't know what to do about apprenticeships, and she had no money, and Lucille was threatening to have her committed to a lunatic asylum. It was as if everything bounced off the shield of her bewildered happiness.

I hugged her, and she seemed surprised, and then she

hugged me back, carefully and a little clumsily; she wasn't used to gestures of affection.

'Thank you for the bracelet. Thanks, Glory.'

I shrugged, and grinned at her.

'Buy some hammers?' I joked, and she smiled.

'Got some.'

And we both laughed, and I was happy too, because I loved her.

She wanted Lucille to understand. She tried to explain, she stood in front of Lucille and said, look at me, Lucille, look, I'm six foot five, I'm not pretty, I can't be like that. She was wearing a dark red check shirt with the sleeves rolled up, and denim jeans, she'd had them made by Lucille's dressmaker, and she looked right, she looked right. Tall and strong, not feminine, not pretty, but right.

Lucille wouldn't listen. Always, in the past, Ann had done as Lucille told her, Ann had obeyed. Ann had starved herself, had made herself ridiculous, had been deferential to men she had despised, all because Lucille had demanded it, and now Ann was quietly but absolutely implacable. She would no longer try to be feminine, and charming, and pretty. She would not go to secretarial college, no, not even for one term. A blacksmith was what she would be, and nothing else.

Lucille could not believe Ann would not obey if she insisted, and she was frantic in her refusal to believe, in her fury at Ann's determination. There was something of terror in Lucille's disbelief and rage. She ordered Ann to go to her room, and to stay there until she came to her senses, and it was then that she called the doctor. She said Ann had had a nervous breakdown, and should be sent to a hospital. When the doctor came down Lucille was waiting for him, and he said Ann seemed quite calm. Lucille burst into tears, and he patted her shoulder, and said he would leave her something to help her sleep that night, she was looking tired.

157

She was looking dreadful. Her eyes were bloodshot and there were tight little lines at the corners of her mouth.

'I wish she would *die*!' she hissed when the doctor had gone, and I stared at her. She wasn't looking at me, she didn't see the expression on my face.

'I wish she'd have an accident and die. I wish this house would burn down, and she burn with it. I wish she was dead.'

'You'd better pull yourself together,' I said. 'You're beginning to lose your looks.'

She shuddered, and stamped her foot.

'She's destroying me,' she said. 'She's destroying me. Damn her. Damn her. I wish she'd never been born.'

'Who's her father?' I demanded.

'How *dare* you? How dare you ask me that?'

Perhaps I could draw a little of her anger away from Ann.

'She and I don't share a father. Who was he? Or don't you know?'

She threw something at me, seized it off the mantelpiece and hurled it at my head. It shattered against the wall behind me, her little Meissen shepherd boy, smashed.

'Oh, no!' she cried in distress. 'My lovely little boy! Oh, no. Damn. Damn.'

Ann stayed in her room for three days, eating her meals at her desk, reading, listening to Lucille when Lucille came to see her, to scream at her, but then she said she was going back to school. School started the next day, and she wanted to go back.

Lucille refused. Ann was not to go back to school, too much studying had caused this breakdown, this nervous breakdown. Ann was to stay at home, and rest. Until she was better. Until she had recovered.

Ann listened, and then stood up, and took her school trunk down from the top of her wardrobe. She began to pack her books into it.

Lucille screamed at her, a wordless shriek, and left the

room, locking the door behind her, and holding the key in her shaking hand as she screamed, shaking the key at the door in a gesture half rage, half triumph. Ann was her prisoner.

She telephoned the school to say Antoinette would not be returning to Storrington, and she was extremely dissatisfied with the education her daughters had received, the school could expect to hear from her solicitors.

I went out. I went back to the library in the town, and I took the big, cardboard-mounted photographs out of their hanging folders, and I set them on the easel, and I stared at them, but I could not block out the sounds of Lucille's voice, screaming at Ann.

I needed Patrick Chendar's Cézanne, and the Monet water lilies.

I tried to telephone him from the call box outside the library, but the new butler said his lordship was not at home.

'I'd like to leave a message,' I said, but the butler said his lordship was not expected home that week.

Could Lucille stop Ann going back to school? What was going to happen to her? I'd never heard of anything like this, I'd never heard of somebody going back to school if their parents had forbidden it. How would Ann live, in the holidays?

I stood in front of the easel, and I looked at the paintings. Degas, Turner, Manet. Colour, and form, and line, and my mind noted, mechanically and without love, without peace. Monet. Remember, the long quiet room, and the water lilies. Remember, and love.

One of the librarians was standing at my shoulder, looking at the painting with me. He was quiet.

'Could you get some more Cézanne?' I asked at last, and felt him shrug.

'Budget,' he said. And then, 'I'm sorry, we're closing now.'

159

I hadn't realised it was so late. I put the Monet back into its place and he folded the easel. A fat man, with thinning hair.

'Cézanne?' I asked again, and tried to smile.

'It's on my list.' He looked tired, a discouraged droop to his mouth, his shirt collar wasn't very clean.

Demoralised. He was demoralised.

'Not many people look at the ones we've already got,' he said as we walked towards the main door. 'It was an experiment, but now they're saying you can find all these pictures in the art books, we don't need the photographs, nobody looks at them. It takes space to store them, see? Some of them have already been vandalised. Lipstick on a Gainsborough, honestly, it'd make you weep. I dread it, checking them on Fridays, really, I dread it.'

Stanley knives, that had been the worry when Revelations had opened. Lipstick wouldn't have been a problem on an oil painting, but cleaning it off a photograph would take time, and care.

'Why?' I asked him. 'Why damage something beautiful?'

It was a stupid question, and we both knew it, but he was polite.

'If I knew that, I wouldn't be a librarian. I'd probably be ruling the world.'

Somebody unlocked the door to let me out, locked it again behind me. I turned to wave goodbye, but he was already walking away towards the dark rooms, the yellow light shining on his bald head, a tired fat man whose experiment had failed, too discouraged to respond to a friendly smile, even from a pretty girl who had been looking at his pictures, and who knew enough to ask for Cézanne.

If I stayed out until late, they might be asleep. It might be quiet in the house. Lucille couldn't scream all night. But it was cold, there was still snow on some of the roofs, thin tracks of black slush in the gutters, a dirty night in January.

They weren't asleep when I got home, and Lucille had

broken through Ann's happiness. Ann sat on her bed, her face still and white, and she watched Lucille, standing in the doorway of her room, standing with her hand clenched on the painted white frame, where broken splinters from the lock still hung, and Ann watched Lucille's face with its mask of loathing, and listened to the hate-filled words.

I looked at Lucille, and I looked at Ann, and I went into my room and closed the door. I sat and listened as Lucille told Ann that she hated her, that Ann was so hideous her own father had looked at her and left, that Lucille had done everything she could for Ann, but Ann had grown uglier, and uglier, so ugly that her own father could not bear the sight of her, that Lucille wished she, too, could have left, as Ann's father had done, one look at Ann lying in her cot, and he had left.

Ann's voice, very quiet, very steady, saying she was going, and Lucille would never have to see her again. And Lucille telling her to go, and saying she wished the devil might go with her.

So Lucille sent Ann away, her last words a curse and a vilification, and I sat in my room and listened, my fists clenched so tightly that the nails cut into my hands, and I hated Lucille. I hated her.

I sat until I could think properly again, and I thought of Ann, carrying that heavy trunk, going out into the cold night. Her face had been white when I had looked at her, white, with dark-shadowed eyes, sick with shock. She'd be suffering from shock, she'd be cold. She might be frightened. Had she sold the bracelet? Had she any money? I sat for a long time, thinking of Ann, waiting until I knew what I could do to help her.

I went downstairs, into the drawing room, where Lucille sat on the pretty blue sofa staring at the wall. I closed the door behind me, and she turned her head and looked at me.

'She's gone,' she said. 'She's gone.'

161

'Give me some money.' My voice was flat and hard, but she didn't hear me.

'She's gone. She carried that trunk down the stairs. Like some disgusting lumberjack, she carried it, on her shoulder. Troll. She's like a troll. Great lumbering troll. She's gone.'

'Give me money.'

'We're alone now, darling. Just us. I won't have her back, she's gone. We'll be better off without her. She's mad.'

'Listen to me, Lucille. Give me money.'

'What? Why? Why do you need money?' She was startled.

'For Ann. Antoinette.'

'Don't you understand? She's gone, I told you. Darling, listen, she's gone away to be a metal worker, a blacksmith. She's quite mad. It's disgusting. I won't have her back. I did my best, but she's a troll.'

'*Don't call her that!*' I screamed, and then, as she gasped at me, I spoke again, quietly. 'Don't call her that, Lucille. I love her.'

She wasn't listening to me. She had heard me scream at her, but the words had flown past her, she hadn't understood.

'Gloriana, please don't shout. It's vulgar, unattractive.'

Ann needed money. I hadn't any. I'd sent Patrick's Christmas present to Robert Cameron, to invest, but Lucille still had hers. I had to make her give me some.

'We could turn her room into a studio for you, darling. We could put your painting things in there, and there'd be room for a cutting-out table, and a sewing machine. There's quite a lot of space, once we've got that huge great bed out of it, it would make a lovely studio. Would you like that? Darling?'

I watched her, I listened to her, making happy plans, while Ann was walking away from us, leaving us, going through the cold night, going away. And Lucille sat on her pretty blue sofa, and talked of a little studio where I could

162

paint, and make nice clothes, we could look at colour schemes and choose something together, she'd been thinking about new curtains, perhaps something in old rose, what did I think? We might get a new carpet, something to tone in, something light, and the wallpaper, a self stripe on the long wall, and something plain and perhaps a shade darker on the other wall, it might improve the shape of the room, so it wouldn't seem so long. It could be such a nice room, so pretty.

'If the police come back,' I said, 'they might still find traces of Lucien's blood. In the kitchen.'

She was very still. She didn't look at me. She sat very still, her hands on the sofa beside her, resting on the pale blue brocade, and the smile that had been on her face as she made her happy plans was still there, her lips parted, lifted at the corners. She was looking towards the fireplace, what was she seeing?

'It was you,' she whispered at last. 'It was you, after all.'

'No. Not me.'

Had she heard me? She was moving, her head was turning towards me, but slowly, in little jerks, as if moving hurt her, as if there should be a sound of creaking.

'If not you, then who?'

Why was she so frightened? The thin child wasn't here, not now. There was only us.

'It was the thin girl,' I said. 'But I'll tell them it was you. I'll say I lied to protect you.'

How much money had Patrick given her? A thousand pounds? Two?

'I'll say he paid you to do it,' I said. 'And they'll find his blood, somewhere in the kitchen, they'll find some blood. I'll say he gave you a thousand pounds. I'll say you both made me watch.'

A thin, high, wailing sound was coming from Lucille. But her face wasn't moving, it was very still, just the faint wailing coming out from between her lips.

'What will happen to the trust fund, Lucille? Will it still pay you money? You've driven Antoinette away, what will happen if I go, too? You don't own this house, do you? It isn't yours. Where will you live, if I go?'

The sound had stopped, but Lucille still hadn't moved. I waited, but she made no answer.

'Give me money,' I said, very clearly. 'Give me some money for Ann. For Antoinette.'

She couldn't move. She could only sit and watch me, and the tendons in her neck were standing out, and there were lines around her mouth, and she had dribbled saliva on to her chin, and her hands on the sofa had little soft wrinkles on their backs and on the knuckles.

Her handbag was on the table. Only her eyes moved, at last, towards it, and then her lips moved, and there was a little, faint whispering sound.

'Take some. Take some.'

I took money from her purse, and I took the diamond earrings Edward had given me, and I followed Ann into the night, I ran down the hill where she had gone, down towards the town, and I wondered as I ran whether the thin child with the bruised thighs and the careful hands might one day come back and kill Lucille for what she had done to Ann.

12

I found her. She was in the waiting room at the station, sitting on the wooden bench, her hands folded in her lap, the heavy trunk on end beside her, her hat and her gloves set tidily on top of it. She was doing nothing, just sitting, still and quiet. She was very pale.

I went into the room, and she looked up at the sound of the door, and tried to smile at me, tried to say my name, but no sound came, and her face was frozen into its blank mask of shock. She tried again, so I sat beside her, and put my arms around her waist and hugged her. It was difficult, awkward, but I loved her, and I wanted her to know I loved her. I felt her take a deep breath, and then her arm was around my shoulders, and for a moment I did not know who was comforting whom.

'She didn't mean it,' I said. 'She didn't mean it.'

Another deep breath, and a slight movement, perhaps she had nodded her head.

'Oh, Ann. She's gone crazy just now. It's not just you. Do you understand? She says stupid things to me, too. Not just to you. She does love you really, she does. But she's just . . . Do you think it's the menopause? I suppose that might be it. I suppose.'

Her hand tightened on my shoulder, just a slight touch, but at least something. Some response.

'That's it, I think. Some women do go a bit potty, don't they? Change of life, well, I hope it changes back soon. Dear Ann. How did you get that trunk down here? It must weigh a ton. How did you?'

But she couldn't speak. Not yet.

'Look. Listen. I mean, look. I've got you some money, just a minute, it's in my pocket. Ann?'

She was trying to speak. She was trying. Soon, she'd manage soon.

'Oh, and these earrings. They don't look as if they're worth much, but they are diamonds, well, little ones. Anyway, real ones. Sell them. And, Ann? Are you listening?'

She did nod, that time. I saw her.

'Can you take them? Here, in your hand. And the money. You'll need some money, here.'

She took them, the earrings, and the money, and there was something almost like a smile on her face, and she looked at me.

'There's more. If you . . . I mean, when you need it, please tell me. I've got more. Men, you know? Stupid men, they give me silly toys. Sparkly things, men think women like sparkly things. Well, I do, I suppose. But I've got quite a lot of them, and I can sell them. Or you can. So, when you need more, tell me. Ann?'

She was looking at me, and trying to smile, and trying to speak. So I waited, and at last I heard her.

'Thanks, Glory.'

'Oh, Ann. She didn't mean it, what she said. She didn't mean it.'

'I know.'

She didn't want to say anything else, and it was enough. I sat beside her with my arm around her waist, leaning my head against her, wishing I could unsay Lucille's dreadful words. I was very tired by then, there had been days of unrest and screaming, with no peace except a little when I was looking at the pictures in the library, and even that had been destroyed in the end.

'What happened to your bedroom door?' I asked some time later, and I heard her reply.

'I kicked it open.'

After that I didn't remember anything, and when I woke she was gone, I was lying, cold and stiff, on the wooden bench, and Ann had gone.

I walked home. It was bitterly cold, but I had no money. I'd come out with nothing except what I'd taken from Lucille, so I walked as quickly as I could. It was still dark, with just a red line in the sky to the east, a single thread of light and colour, and I walked, and watched the sky as it turned to black, to steel grey, and to the sullen pearly colour of a winter morning, with the scarlet line breaking up, and fading.

Somebody was crying in the kitchen, and I could hear the sound of water, running water, and a soft noise.

It shocked me. I stood outside the door, listening, remembering the sounds, remembering Lucien, and I threw open the door and stepped inside, and stared down at Lucille, on her hands and knees, as he had been, washing the floor, washing the tiles, and looking up at me, her face bleared with tears, her mouth slack, open, pleading.

'Gloriana. Darling.'

Washing the floor.

'He's already done that,' I said.

'What? What do you mean?'

I didn't know what I meant, I didn't want to think about it. I took off my coat and hung it on the peg behind the door.

'This floor seemed so dirty, I thought I'd . . . I don't know what Mrs Hungerford can be thinking of, to let it get so . . .'

'Is there any coffee? It's bitterly cold out there.'

'Oh, yes, I'll make some. You should have worn something thicker than that, darling. Why don't you have a hot bath? That'll warm you up. The coffee should be ready by the time you come down. Try that new bath oil, it's absolutely gorgeous.'

I stood at the table, looking around the kitchen, feeling a little absent-minded, a little puzzled. I noticed, vaguely, how clean it was, all the work surfaces washed, and dried, and buffed until they shone, even the hinges on the door seemed to have been washed. And the legs of the table. I couldn't remember. I thought he'd only washed the floor.

I spent that day trying to contact Uncle John, but he was in court, and by the time I found out which court, he'd already left. I didn't know what to do about Ann. Every time I thought of her I saw her eyes, dark and wide with shock in her sick, white face, and I remembered the way her voice had sounded when at last she had been able to speak at all.

And Lucille. She telephoned the school, she kept telephoning, telling them she would sue them, they had deformed Ann's mind, that Ann was to come home, that she never wanted to see Ann again. She was screaming down the telephone, and she called the police and demanded that they rescue Ann, she told them Ann was being held at the school against her mother's wish.

But when she saw me she was quiet, and watchful. Then there was silence in the house when we watched each other, and her face would be still, and then her mouth would open and there would be a pleading look in her eyes, but I would turn away. And she would go, upstairs to her room, or back to the kitchen, and then there would be the sounds of running water again.

That evening I kept telephoning the number of Uncle John's flat, but it was very late when at last he answered, and I found it difficult to tell him what had happened. He sounded puzzled, because all I could say at first was that Ann had gone back to school, I kept repeating it. But then I managed to tell him she'd had a row with Lucille, and that Lucille had said she was ugly.

'There's more, isn't there?' he asked. 'Can you tell me? Glory?'

Everybody seemed so far away. I could hear his voice on the telephone, I could hear Lucille upstairs moving around in her bedroom, but Lucien had hanged himself, and Ann had gone, and they were all so far away, drifting away from me.

I put the telephone down and I sat on the stairs and tried to bring Ann back in my mind, to stop her drifting away.

There was a ringing in my ears, I tried to block it out, to ignore it, but then I realised it was the telephone, so I picked it up to stop the noise, and looked at it. I could hear a voice.

'Glory? Are you there?'

I would read it, I told myself. I would read it out of my memory as if it was a play.

'"Hideous",' I said. '"So ugly your own father couldn't bear the sight of you. Took one look at you lying in your cot, and he left."'

'Oh, no. Oh, God, no.'

'"You just got uglier, and uglier, and uglier."' Was that right? Were those the words in my memory?

'I'll telephone the school. Poor Ann.'

'"I wish I could have left, like he did."'

Then I couldn't remember any more. Only the sounds, Lucille's screaming voice, and Ann saying something, just once, quietly.

'Glory? Are you still there?'

'Yes.' And now there was something I had to ask him.

'He isn't her father, is he?'

'What?'

'Peter Mayall. He's got blue eyes. So's Lucille, so have I.'

'Peter's eyes?'

But he was lying. This bewildered question, it was a lie.

'Two blue-eyed people, I don't think they can have a brown-eyed child, can they? I'm not sure, but I don't think so. And Peter's got blue eyes, hasn't he?'

'What are you suggesting?'

169

'I want to know what happened, I don't want any more lies. Peter Mayall isn't Ann's father, I know that, I've known that for years. So what Lucille said to her, it was all a lie. And you, you too. "Peter's eyes". Stop lying.'

'All right. What do you want to know?'

But I couldn't form the questions, and he seemed to be drifting away again, far away from me, so that I was alone. I put the telephone down and sat hunched on the stairs, and I wanted Ann back, because I loved her, and because she didn't lie to me.

Love, it seemed a strange word now, I no longer knew what it meant. I'd thought I loved Lucille, because she was my mother; everybody loved their mothers. But she was remote, and somehow fearful of me, and during the next few days I would find myself watching her, analysing the way she moved, the expression on her face, or I would close my eyes and listen to her voice. I could learn a lot about Lucille that way, listening, and not watching. She lied. I'd always known she lied, but sometimes I'd believed her lies. When I closed my eyes and listened to her voice, and didn't look at her face, I knew. I could always tell.

I didn't think I could love a liar.

Francis Chendar offered me a flat, in a small town just to the north of London. He'd bought an old corn merchant's place, he wanted to convert it into an arcade of shops with flats above them, but that left a big granary under the roof, a wide, low room, with flour dust still hanging in the air over piles of soft folded sacks.

It smelt clean and airy. I wanted it.

'I'll tell my lawyer to do something about a lease,' he declaimed. 'Short term? Will that do? I suppose you'll only want it while you're doing this art course of yours.'

It amused Francis to be amused by my studies.

'Any chance of you marrying young Francis?' Patrick asked one day when he was in London, and before I could think of an answer that would not hurt his feelings, he sighed.

'Thought not.'

Patrick's taste ran to languid, elegant women, a foil for his bright energy. He'd married one, and their son had inherited her temperament. Sometimes I would see him looking at Francis with an expression of baffled wonderment. What would happen to the great Chendar fortune under Francis' stewardship? The lovely paintings that touched his father's emotions too deeply for words? Francis would never sit at that desk in the dark, panelled study, muttering as he read letters and contracts, sleeves rolled up, running fingers through untidy hair. Francis would leave all that to somebody else. He would accept the privileges of his status, not the responsibilities.

I looked at the plans the architect had drawn up for the conversion of the granary, and I told Francis the man was a halfwit. I did not want a Georgian-style balcony, nor any of the other silly, ostentatious trappings that seemed designed to impress the gullible.

'For God's sake, Glory!'

Francis was affronted. The architect was expensive, and very fashionable.

'I think I'd rather find somewhere else,' I said. 'I wouldn't be seen dead in a bijou residence.'

He sulked for the remainder of the evening, but then said I could do as I liked with the blasted place, just so long as I didn't expect him to come riding to the rescue if it all went wrong.

I sold Lucien's diamond bracelet and sapphire necklace for fifteen thousand pounds. When Lucille sold jewellery she usually said they were pieces her grandmother had left her, but I don't think she was believed; they were too new. The woman in Maida Vale assumed I was a call girl, and I let her believe it. She said she liked doing business with working girls, I should come again. She'd given me a fair price, so I did note her address.

I needed the money, but even more urgently, I needed to

get rid of the jewellery. I'd had a letter from Lucien's bank asking me to call on them, as they felt I might be able to help them in tracing the missing money. I wrote back to them, childish, rounded handwriting, saying I was sorry but I didn't want to come to the bank, I was trying to forget Lucien.

Jane Targe had been offered a junior partnership in a fashion studio in Birmingham if she could raise the money for it, and her parents hadn't got enough. Grey's of Birmingham. Gerry Grey, he'd been at the fashion show, he'd liked the poncho.

I lent her ten thousand. I was planning to use Lucille's story, selling my grandmother's jewellery, if she asked, but she didn't seem interested. Most of the students assumed I was quite rich, and perhaps I was, compared to them. I'd never thought about it. Jane was so delighted she was almost pretty, her eyes bright and shining, and I was pleased for her, but I saw the money as an investment, not a favour to a friend. The poncho was the best thing she'd done so far, but she was only just starting.

In my spare time, I worked at the granary.

Francis had given me a lease to sign, and I'd sent it to Uncle John. The trust would pay the rent for as long as I was studying, and give me an allowance.

The glass I put in the old windows was tinted gold, and when the floorboards were cleaned they too were pale gold, oak, bleached and polished by decades of flour dust.

I wanted light, and space, room to breathe, room to grow.

I told Lucille I was leaving, moving out at the end of the summer, and I closed my eyes and listened as she said she was sorry, she would miss me.

Lies.

Ann missed me. She spent the school holidays at the forge, staying in a bed-and-breakfast place in the village, but every day she went to the forge, and worked sitting at the bench, studying. Sometimes I went down for a weekend, once at Easter, and again in the summer. We hardly ever talked about Lucille.

The cottage had been let, an arty-crafty couple, she wore things like woollen sacks that she'd woven herself, he had a beard. They were trying to get back to the simple life, and finding it cost a fortune and took about twenty hours a day. I think they were book illustrators, children's books. But Ann seemed happy enough that they had the cottage, and the paddock, where they kept a few sheep.

Francis hardly glanced at Uncle John's amendments to the lease before he signed it.

It was green and gold, the granary, with hardly any furniture, just space, expanses of polished floor, and at night pools of golden light from big hanging lamps.

I could work there. Like Ann at the forge, I could work now. I used to lie on the floor, liking the feeling of the hard wood under my body, and read about lighting and filters, hydraulic jacks under staging, and I could remember what I had read. I could concentrate, and think, and remember. Studying wasn't boring at the granary. It was important, and private, a part of my life that mattered to me.

I wanted to do the set in white curves, the one I had been drawing on the night Lucien died. There would be no straight lines, everything would depend on shadow on white. I wondered if there was a play that could use a set like that.

And Camelot, the Chamber of the Round Table, one of the tutors, Tony Marks, had set us that as a project. The lighting for that, from behind, lights like swords stabbing outwards, reaching away into the distance, a great fan of swords made of light. The colours could change. It wouldn't work in a real play, it would be too distracting, but for the project it would be good, very good. The table, polished steel to reflect the lights, the knights in brilliant, gem-like colours, long robes, but the swords of light behind

173

them would be a constant reminder of the violence by which they lived.

I lay on the golden floor under the golden light, and sketched, and scribbled, and thought, and it came to life as I worked, I could see how they would move against the lights.

When I laid down my pencils it was brilliant morning, the golden lights were dim against the sun. I stared at the windows, puzzled. I had thought it was still evening.

Tony told me to apply for a grant so I could stay on at college for another year, he said I had a feel for the stage, I seemed to know what things would look like before I saw them.

But I'd already been offered a job by an advertising company by then, a job with quite a good salary, and prospects. I'd be starting as an assistant set designer, but the man who'd interviewed me said the company would be expanding, advertising was a boom industry, it wouldn't be long before I'd be running my own studio.

'You're young, of course,' he said. 'Nothing wrong with that. I like your work.'

'Thank you, Mr Treanor.'

'Call me Kevin.'

Sets for television advertisements, bath salts and corsets, tinned peas and garden furniture.

When I telephoned Uncle John he sounded pleased. It was a very good salary.

'Well done,' he said.

And Robert Cameron checked for me, and said the company was as sound as most of them, I should keep my eyes open but there was no sign of anything shaky.

'Alexandra Martin wants to expand,' he said. 'She's getting repeat orders from the USA. Are you interested? Have you got any money?'

'Five thousand,' I said, wondering if he'd ask where it had come from.

'Want to back Mrs Martin?'

I did. Now that she was free to concentrate on the designs, she was doing well, she had three people working for her and she'd spoken of taking on an office manager to handle the paperwork.

Jane Targe was almost incoherent with excitement over her junior partnership at Grey's, smiling radiantly whenever she saw me. She was planning the interior design of her studio and pestering her friends with her latest sketches and ideas.

Why was I so depressed?

Kevin Treanor sent me my employment contract, with a handwritten note asking if he could take me out to dinner one evening, and I left the contract on my bedroom table for two days before I read it.

Everything I did while I worked for the company was company property, every sketch I made, every portrait I painted, no matter when, no matter where, no matter what. When I telephoned Uncle John he told me it was quite usual, to prevent employees setting up their own businesses in company time.

But Tony Marks put his finger on the real sore spot, and made me wince. Tinned peas, corsets, shampoo. I would never see my swords of light, nor the *Macbeth* set that still lingered in the back of my mind.

'Tell him to stuff it,' said Tony. 'Oh, come on, Glory! For Christ's sake. Toothpaste commercials. "We need more light on her *teeth*." Tits-and-bums models and bathroom sets. I thought you had more guts.'

'Suppose I don't get the diploma?'

'Don't be stupid.'

'I mean it, Tony.'

'You stupid little cow. You *fucking stupid, stupider, stupidest little cow*. You'll get a first-class diploma, you've got more talent than the rest of them put together. And what will you do with it? Fucking advertising. You make me sick.'

I lay on the floor of the granary under one of the big lamps, and thought of working for Kevin Treanor, and where it could lead. What I might do. And staying on for another year under Tony Marks, with no guarantee of a job at the end of it, just the chance that I'd be better at what I wanted to do, and maybe even good enough. Maybe.

For the first time for months I thought of a yellow book with dusty covers, with filthy pictures of two men raping a thin child with bruised thighs and my face, and I thought of the people who had seen those photographs, people who had been my friends. I might meet them again, if I did as Tony Marks demanded.

I laid my forehead on my folded arms, and stared down at the dark flecks of grain in the golden wood, and wondered what to do. I thought of Kevin Treanor, boisterous and jovial, his eyes on my legs, his avuncular arm around my shoulders, the power I could hold over a man like that. And Tony Marks, who would throw snarling obscenities at me, and teach me all he knew, and make me take more risks than he could understand.

I lay all night on the hard floor, half dozing, jerking into wakeful alertness, trying to think, trying, and waiting for a decision to come.

13

He was watching me when I saw him, standing by the steps that led up to the main entrance, and although there was a half-smile on his lips there was nothing friendly about his face, no look of happy recognition. He was triumphant. He kept his eyes fixed on my face as I approached, even moving to the side, down a couple of steps, when a group of students walked between us, making quite sure he didn't lose sight of me in the crowd, ignoring everybody else, watching me, only me.

'Miss Mayall! How very nice!' he said as I tried to walk past him.

'I beg your pardon?'

'There are some questions I'd like you to answer, Miss Mayall. Haven't you recognised me?'

I had recognised him immediately, he was the younger of the two men from Lucien's bank, but I needed time to think. I turned to look at the other students, stepped back, was bumped into, tried to get out of the way, every move suggesting there was nothing important about this encounter, and I was in a hurry. I was just one of this bustling crowd of students.

'I know we've met.' I made my voice a little higher, clear and childish, carrying over the noise of the traffic and the

177

chatter of the people around us. 'I'm very sorry, I can't remember where.'

'Oh, quite good.' Was that genuine admiration, or irony? He seemed amused. Impossible to tell.

I tried a puzzled smile, and I glanced at my watch.

'Mrs Nestley remembers the diamond bracelet you wore to her party on the night Lucien Rathbone died. Not quite to her taste, she told me, but she noticed it in particular because it seemed, in her words, "just a bit much for a teenager".'

'But I showed you the bracelet! I remember you now, from the bank where Lucien worked. You said I could keep it.'

He had a thin face with hollowed cheeks, and very bright blue eyes, they were sparkling, I'd never seen eyes like that before. They almost seemed to flicker, he looked first directly into one of my eyes and then into the other, they were never still. And the smile, bright and triumphant, small, even teeth showing through parted lips.

You bastard, I thought, fighting down panic. You bastard.

'You said I could keep my bracelet,' I protested.

'Mrs Nestley's maiden name was Armstrong,' he said, and he laughed. 'Does that mean anything to you? Sebastian Armstrong's one of the five biggest diamond importers in Europe, and he's her father. Julia Nestley knows diamonds the way you know paint. Or pencils, whatever you work in.'

Think, I told myself. Don't drop the bewildered expression, but for God's sake, think.

'Lucien told me they were real diamonds,' I said.

He blinked, and for a moment seemed uncertain, but then he smiled again.

'Oh, you really are rather good. That was quite quick.'

Not very tall, pale brown hair, not light, pale, as though the colour had been diluted, falling back away from his forehead, and those bright, flickering eyes. What could he prove? Was there anything he could prove?

'I'm going to be late for my lesson,' I said. 'I'll have to go. It's been nice meeting you again.'

He winked at me.

'That was overdoing it. It's been nearly two years since you attended a *lesson*, Miss Mayall.'

I turned away, and hurried up the steps. What could he prove?

'I've got the riding crop,' he called after me, 'but I haven't found the club. That's quite funny, isn't it? Like a pun. Crop and club, do you get it? And what would you make of a box? A presentation box, could you work that into the joke?'

I looked back, down towards the pavement, where he was standing and laughing up at me, one foot still on the worn stone of the step.

'I've almost got enough. And I'm still looking. I'll see you later, Miss Mayall. We might have a coffee together.'

There was nothing he could prove, I kept telling myself throughout the morning, nothing. I'd never said the bracelet was fake. I'd always said it was diamond. I could keep up this act of bewilderment for as long as he could laugh at me. I wouldn't understand. This bracelet, this diamond bracelet, was my Christmas present from Lucien, he told me it was diamonds, Mrs Nestley said it's diamonds, I don't understand why you say it's fake. I can be the dim little dolly bird, for him and for anybody else. There was nothing he could prove. Nothing.

I don't understand, I always thought they were real diamonds, I never said they were fake. I don't understand. They said I could keep my bracelet. I don't understand, my lord.

Oh, God.

Julia Nestley, calm and utterly convincing. I saw the bracelet, I was quite surprised, it was obviously valuable.

Oh, I couldn't say for sure, but about twenty thousand pounds. Say, between fifteen and twenty-five thousand. No, this is not the bracelet she was wearing that night. This is costume jewellery.

And there would be others who saw the bracelet, wealthy women with experience of gemstones. Women with confident voices, who could stand in a witness box and speak clearly, and damningly, of a valuable diamond bracelet that was not this one. This is costume jewellery.

I looked for him in the lunch break, when I went out to a snack bar for a sandwich, but he wasn't there, there was nobody waiting on the steps of the college, no thin young man with flickering eyes and a triumphant smile.

That night I threw the bracelet into the river, and I went to the police and said I had lost a diamond bracelet. I had been out for a walk, along the towpath and back through the park, and the clasp must have broken.

Why had I been wearing a valuable bracelet to go for a walk by the river? Because something had happened that reminded me of the friend who had given it to me, I'd put it on because I'd been thinking of him. I'd just forgotten to take it off before I went for my walk.

Was it insured?

Unfortunately not.

The policeman seemed to relax. He looked up and smiled at me as he finished writing in the book, said he'd let me know if it turned up, he sometimes walked by the river himself, he'd keep an eye out for it. Would I like to come with him? We could search together.

Was it enough? Now nobody could compare the bracelets, would that be enough?

Two days later he was back, not on the steps of the college this time but waiting outside the underground station, and I didn't see him until he was walking beside me, beside and a little to the front so that he looked back at me, laughing at me.

'I've traced his movements for that night, Miss Mayall. What do you think? There's no club, not that night. Oh, no. No time to go to a club, certainly not that sort of club.'

I stopped, somebody bumped into me from behind and pushed past with a muttered apology, then a woman with a shopping basket grumbling about idiots blocking her way, a rush-hour crowd already nervous and irritated by the stress of movement and the lack of space, so I moved on, went to the kerb to try to cross the road, but there was no gap in the traffic, no chance to get away from him.

'It all points to you, Miss Mayall. I've got the crop, very safe. What could we find? Your fingerprints on the handle, his blood on the lash?'

I'd never drawn blood with the crop.

'Please leave me alone.' I allowed my voice to become forceful. 'If you don't leave me alone, I'll call the police.'

'Did you get rid of the bracelet?' he called after me as I hurried on down the street. 'Better safe than sorry, Miss Mayall.'

My fingerprints on the crop, oh yes. They could find them. Well, why not? The crop had been in his car. I had picked it up, handled it, why not?

Was there any blood on the lash?

Thin red weals on white skin. There'd never been any blood. I would have remembered. I would have remembered, if she'd ever drawn blood.

Who had seen the sapphire necklace and the gold bracelet? Who could say, the one I saw then was real, not this one? This is costume jewellery?

Lucien's friends, young men, girls. Nobody else. Nobody who could be convincing, nobody like Julia Nestley. He could prove nothing, this young man with the flickering eyes.

When I got back to the granary that night they were there, waiting for me, three men this time, in a big car, and they got out as I reached my front door. They wanted to speak to me.

181

He was one of them, hanging back a little, not excited and triumphant this time, calm, polite, as he produced identification, held out the card with his photograph for me to see. Wright, David Wright. With a signature over the bank's logo, spiky writing.

'I want you to stop harassing me,' I said, but the older man, the one who had come the first time, didn't even seem to notice that I had spoken.

'I must ask you to let us have the bracelet Lucien Rathbone gave you,' he said. 'Naturally, we'll give you a receipt.'

'I've lost it,' I said. 'Please go away. I don't want to talk to you.'

'When did you lose it?' The other man, fat, a face like a pig.

'Go away. Leave me alone.'

'We'll get a warrant. Bust your bloody door down.'

But the older man raised his hand to stop him, a look of distaste on his face.

'We'll do no such thing. I'm sorry, Miss Mayall. We don't mean to harass you, but we must have the bracelet.'

I took my key out of my handbag, and turned away from them, towards my door.

'I told you. I've lost it.'

The fat man snorted, said something I couldn't hear to the older one, and, when he was ignored, shrugged and walked a few paces away towards the car.

'Come on, let's get that warrant.'

'When did you lose the bracelet?'

'A few days ago. Tuesday, I think.' Voice high, not quite steady, a little frightened. Eyes moving between the fat man and the grey-haired one standing in front of me.

'Did you report it?'

'Yes, to the police.' And then my voice was getting angry, a little indignant. 'It's none of your business. It was my bracelet. It's nothing to do with you.'

'Warrant,' said the fat one, loudly.

'I'm going to telephone my lawyer,' I said, looking at him.

'Telephone the bloody Home Secretary if you like.'

'The local police station? The one in Berkeley Street?' The grey-haired man's voice was calm, he was standing very still, quite relaxed. The fat man might not have been there.

David Wright, he had warned me. I stared at him, but he wasn't looking at me, those bright blue eyes were fixed on the older man now, steady, they weren't flickering now, he was quiet, respectful, waiting to be told what to do.

'Was it the local police station? Miss Mayall?'

'She's lying.'

He wouldn't look at me. He'd warned me, and I'd taken his warning. Why had he done that?

I turned towards the fat man.

'I don't tell lies. I'm going to complain about you,' I said, and he snorted.

'Was it the local police station?' The voice was not quite so patient now.

'Yes, it was.' My key slid into the lock. My hand was beginning to shake. 'Berkeley Street police station. The policeman wrote it down.'

Why had he warned me?

I closed the door on them, and then I sat on the stairs, shaking, my arms around my knees, hugging them close to my chest, waiting until I heard the car start and the sounds of them driving away. I felt sick, I tried to think, but I was bewildered. He had warned me, and then they had come, demanding the bracelet. Their only proof, gone, because of his warning.

He came back late that night.

'I've got the receipt,' he said, and his eyes were flickering again, the smile triumphant. 'Take the chain off the door, Gloriana. We are going to be *very* good friends, you and I.'

'I don't understand. What receipt? Go away.'

'The *receipt*.' Exaggerated patience, the word drawn out, the smile widening. 'From the jeweller's, the same day as the party, for a diamond bracelet, he used his own name, did you know? Well, why not? He was going to choke himself to death that night.'

'Go away.'

'They only use their presentation boxes for genuine jewellery, none of your glass and paste muck from *that* shop, nothing under three figures and precious little under four. But there are five on this receipt, my dear Gloriana, and the first one's a two.'

'I never said it wasn't real. You were the ones. You lied, Lucien only ever bought me real jewellery.'

'Chain off the door, please, Gloriana. For a good friend. I've got the receipt, and I've got the box. I'm not going to hurt you, and I'm certainly not going to rape you. I don't fancy you myself.'

I closed the door, and immediately he began to shout.

'He didn't die fast, you know? He choked. I saw the report, I'm one of the few who did, they hushed it up. But he choked, Gloriana.

'Open this *door*, Gloriana! For a good friend, open this *door*! Or the whole damned street will hear. About the cuts, those razor cuts, and where they were, and who did it.'

I clapped my hands over my ears and screamed through the door.

'*Go away!*'

'He choked. He jumped, about eight feet it was, over the banisters, thought it would be enough. *Can you hear me, you murdering whore?* It wasn't enough. He thought it would break his neck, but it *didn't*, Gloriana. It didn't break his neck. He hung there, and he strangled. He choked. *His hands were raw, where he'd been clawing at the rope!* They were *bleeding*, Gloriana, the nails were ripped *right back*. Can you *hear me*?'

I opened the door, and he smiled at me, smiled at me, friendly, pleased, I'd done what he wanted.

'*There*'s a good girl.'

'I'll call the police,' I said, and he spread his hands, amazement on his face.

'But, my dear Gloriana, why *haven't* you?'

'What do you want?'

'I want to come *in*. Stand aside and let me in. Thank you. Your *virtue* is quite safe with me, I promise you. I won't lay a finger on you, not even in rubber gloves.'

Contemptuous disgust now, nothing friendly or pleased, there was revulsion in his voice.

'Up the stairs?' A guest, asking of an absent-minded hostess, polite again. 'Nice! Nice carpet. And I like these prints, *very* good.'

'Was that true? What you said about Lucien?'

'How he died? Oh, yes. I *say*! What a *lovely* room. Did you design this? Yes, I can see you did. *How* nice, I'm so glad you've got taste, Gloriana. Yes, it's true. About twenty minutes it would have taken, I understand. He'd have screamed, if he could. Of course, he *couldn't*, not with that rope. I wonder what he was *thinking*. Were you worth it? Do you think he *still* thought you were worth it, while he was fighting that rope? Fighting, and losing? I do *hope* so.'

'What do you want?'

He turned towards me, laughing.

'Didn't I *say*? How very stupid of me. I'm so sorry. I'm your new *pimp*.'

For a moment I could only stare at him. The word, I knew the word, but I couldn't understand. This had nothing to do with me, this word, this man laughing at me, his scornful blue eyes, that word. And then, when I did understand, rage, fury, I had never known such anger.

'I am *not* a tart.'

'No?' Astonishment in his voice, and there was something in my hand, I threw it, straight at his face, and he ducked, a cut glass vase fell to the floor behind him, landing on a rug, unbroken.

185

'If you can't throw better than *that*, Gloriana, you'd better not try. What a *feeble* effort.'

'Get out! Get out of my home!'

'He loved you.'

He'd turned his back on me, he was walking along the room, walking on my rugs, looking at my pictures, he reached out to straighten one, stepped back and looked at it, nodded, walked on.

'Degas,' he mused. 'Degas. Rather trite. You don't mind me saying so?' A bright, enquiring look turned in my direction, and then he'd moved away again, a hand stretching out and up to set one of my lamps swinging, the pool of light moving to and fro across the bright rug and the golden wood, he was walking towards my desk, towards the sketches of the Chamber of the Round Table.

'Thought the world of you. Talked about you. The most beautiful girl he'd ever seen, he said.'

He was looking at me again, his eyes calculating, head on one side, as though he was considering Lucien's remark, assessing my appearance, the beauty Lucien had claimed for me.

'He couldn't ride, you know. Tennis, that was his game. Quite good at it, I was told. But I suppose a tennis racket wouldn't have been the same, would it? Not for what you were up to.'

'Don't touch my work.'

'But these are good!' He slid the top drawing aside, lifted the second one, held it up to the light. 'Oh, yes, good. Better drop the dumb blonde act, Gloriana. If you can do this.'

'Put that down.'

'He wouldn't have bought you costume jewellery. Not Lucien Rathbone. Oh, no.'

He was walking back towards me, and he was not smiling any more. He reached out one hand to my face, and I flinched as his fingers flicked at my cheek.

'Listen to me, my *pretty*.' The word was an insult. 'I

186

know what you did to him. And I know what he paid you. We might drop this inquiry, or we might not. It's up to me.'

'You seem rather junior for that sort of decision,' I said.

'Oh, I *am*!' The smile was back, the eyes were flickering again. 'I am *very* junior, I am just the dogsbody, the *junior* dogsbody, who trots up to the top table bearing little titbits for the great and the good. But if the *junior dogsbody* doesn't find anything, then the great and the good get bored. And they tell him to go away and do something else. And so he does, he wags his tail, and puts the file away, and does a different little party trick. Unless, of course, he comes back again and says listen to what *I've* heard. Then the file gets taken out again.'

What did he know? What could he prove?

'It's a damned thin file,' I said.

'But *just* enough, don't you feel? Just enough to keep me digging. If Lucien Rathbone went to a club that evening, he did it in only half an hour. What do you think of that? A bit *hasty*, wouldn't you say? Why such a short visit?'

He raised a finger, wagging it in my face.

'I've only got to place him *once more*, Gloriana, just *one more* witness for that time, and that's your club *right out of the equation*. Listen to me, my sweet, my pretty, Lucien's beautiful love. I've got the *porter* from his flat.'

One finger held up.

'*He* knows when Lucien came home. From a shopping trip in the West End, where he bought we both know what. He stayed in his flat just long enough to have a shower, and change into evening clothes. How do I know that? Because the car park attendant remembers him collecting that big blue Lagonda. Just before he went off duty.'

Another finger held up.

'And . . . now listen carefully, my pretty . . . we have that same big blue Lagonda at a petrol station two miles away forty minutes later. On his way to you. He drove quite fast after that, it seems, must have been looking forward to seeing you. Yes?'

Now there were three fingers.

'If I find just one more witness, Gloriana, just one for Lucien Rathbone for those forty minutes, that's your club gone. And those wounds were *very* fresh. Some of them broke open again. Can you imagine? While he was strangling and choking on the end of that rope.

'I've hardly started yet. These three,' the fingers curled down again, a fist, and then one, two, three, they snapped upright, 'they were pure routine, two obvious people to ask, and a petrol receipt.'

He smiled, the same triumphant smile, and his eyes began to flicker again.

'I know a few things the great and the good at the top table don't know. I know Lucien Rathbone wouldn't have given you costume jewellery. I know you're not the dumb blonde you've made yourself out to be. And I know why you "lost" the bracelet.'

'It wasn't costume jewellery,' I said desperately. 'It was real.'

He shook his head, gently, reprovingly.

'I *saw* it,' he said. 'So did Brian Betherson. We both know what it was.'

'I don't understand,' I protested. 'I don't understand any of this. Why? Why are you doing this? Lucien stole some money, the police said that. I don't know. They said he lost it gambling, didn't they? Why is the bank still . . .'

'Lucien *worked* for the bank.' As though he was speaking to a child, explaining something carefully, something that should have been obvious. 'It's an *example*.'

He paused, watching my face, slightly questioning. Do you understand now? Have you got it?

'An example to the other staff. An example to our customers. If we have a thief, we get him.

'But they'll drop it!' Suddenly he was laughing again, his

hands spread wide as he stepped back from me. 'They'll drop it! It's only twenty-five thousand, after all. Peanuts, Gloriana, petty cash. He's dead, horribly dead, couldn't face the scandal, choked to death at the end of a rope, sliced up with a razor, and all *that*. Where's the razor, by the way?'

'I don't know. How should I know? You've said all these horrible things, as though it's all my fault. It's not my fault, I don't know. I don't understand. Why are you here? What do you want?'

'I've *told* you. Come on, Gloriana, I've already explained. I'm your *pimp*. I'm going to send you *customers*.'

I could feel my lips stretching back away from my teeth, I couldn't control it, the expression of revulsion, the hatred I had for this man, this creature, so confident and bright in front of me, so sure of his power over me.

'You think I will go to bed with your filthy friends? You think I would let you . . .'

'Oh, you don't have to go to *bed* with them! Of *course* not! Not unless you want to, I don't mind either way. You do as you like, my dear Gloriana. Just so long as you do as you're told first.'

'And what will I be *told*, you stinking little rat?'

That bright smile. He looked so happy. The child was beginning to understand at last.

'Riding crops,' he said. 'Razors. Needles. Soldering irons, perhaps. Whatever they ask. And if you don't, dear Gloriana, if you fail to give *satisfaction*, I will take the matter of the receipt and the presentation box to the top table, and I will *find* another witness, or *bribe* one, believe me, my dear. What I've got now is honest, it's all true. But I can set you up, and they can send you down. Slicing somebody up with a razor blade is quite seriously illegal. Prison, Gloriana. Prison.'

He would do it. He could do it, and he would. I stared at his blue, flickering eyes, half mad, half very sane indeed, and I knew he would do it.

189

And then, when he spoke again, his voice was very gentle, and his eyes were still, steady on my face.

'But for every customer, my dear, I will give you two hundred pounds. That is a lot of money, even for such a *specialised* service.

'You will have to be *good*. You will have to be *very good*. Do as you are told, and never, ever give any hint that I am there too. With my little camera.'

His finger was in my face again, moving slowly from side to side, and the eyes were beginning to flicker.

'And what I do with my photographs is absolutely nothing to do with you.'

14

I was to stay in London, I was to be a student, forget the idea of the advertising company, I might not have time to do as David Wright wanted if I had a full-time job.

Uncle John was surprised, and not very pleased, but eventually agreed I could stay on at the college for another year, if that was what I wanted. He said, and he sounded annoyed, that the theatre sounded rather risky compared to the offer I already had. Tony Marks wrote to him, said I had tremendous talent, used fulsome phrases, and at last Uncle John sighed, and said he hoped I knew what I was doing. He was a little happier when I got my diploma later that summer, a distinction, as Tony had predicted, and he invited Ann up to London and took us both out to dinner to celebrate.

I started work on my white set, everything curved, and I tried setting the lights right into the flooring of the stage, shaded and angled, hidden by the white curves, the only straight lines were to be the shadows.

David Wright gave me a key, and an address in a south London suburb. A few days after his visit he telephoned me, told me to go there that evening.

It was a long road, the houses would have been identical had it not been for the architect's determination to make them all different by adding bow windows or porches in various shapes to the basic design. Ugly little houses, anonymous behind their stucco façades, lace curtains, drab little squares of gardens behind laurel hedges and iron gates. I was shivering as I walked along the pavement, looking for the number, shivering from fear, from disgust, even from dislike of the place. I loathe stucco now. I hate little bay windows stuck on the fronts of anonymous houses, I hate glass porches with spider plants hanging in them, laurel bushes with variegated leaves, little square flower beds in the centres of little square lawns.

He was already there. He opened the door as he heard my key in the lock, and the triumphant smile was on his hateful face. Little white teeth, flickering eyes.

'How *nice* of you to come!'

I couldn't speak. I could only look into his face, walk past him as he stood aside, and go on into the lighted room behind him.

He followed me, catching up with me, and I turned quickly, my hands outstretched to push him away, so he stepped back, laughing. He was excited, he seemed happy.

'I shan't touch you, my dear! You're not here for *my* benefit.'

There was a table pushed up against the wall, a white cloth on it. A coil of rope. I looked at it. I was beginning to feel sick, I wondered if I would actually vomit.

'I'm going to *leave* you now,' he said. 'I shan't be far away. Don't forget to answer the door, will you? That *would* be a mistake.'

Heavy, dark red curtains hung from the ceiling to the floor, dense, no light from outside, the occasional sound of a passing car muffled, almost inaudible. Brown linoleum on the floor. A green tiled surround to a two-bar electric fire, dead and lifeless against dim, flowered wallpaper. A wooden ladderback chair. Two flower pictures on the wall. Nothing else.

I felt cold. I turned on the fire, and a few moments later there was a smell of burning dust, sparks from the reddening elements. I heard a cough from the back room. David Wright with his camera. The flower pictures, one of them must hide a camera lens. I would keep my face turned away from that wall.

Even though I was expecting it, the sound of the doorbell startled me. I jumped back from the fire, listening, wishing rather than hoping I had been mistaken, knowing I had not, and I didn't wait for the bell to ring again. I walked into the hall, opened the front door and came straight back into the room, not even looking at the man who followed me, only hearing as he closed the doors behind us. I could hear myself breathing, short and deep, I could feel the man behind me, coming closer, so I turned on him.

'What do you *want*?' I demanded, and my voice sounded savage.

He stopped, blinking at me, his mouth a little open. He was tall, a big man, grey-haired, in a dark grey suit. Quite good-looking, well dressed. I was surprised, but still my first feeling was one of fear. Fear and disgust.

'Oh!' he exclaimed, and his eyes were wide. 'But you are really lovely.'

'*What* do you *want*?' My teeth were gritted to stop them chattering, my fists clenched at my sides. I hated him, I dreaded hearing what I would have to do. The thought of touching him made me shudder.

'And good. Are you an actress?'

He was taking off his jacket, looking around for somewhere to put it, the chair, the table, he smiled when he saw the rope, and laid the jacket on the table beside it, carefully, and ran his fingers over the rope. Then he turned towards me, and reached out a hand.

I shuddered again, and stepped back.

'Don't touch me!'

A smile on his face, a nod, appreciative, and the hand

193

dropped, the smile disappeared, and he lowered his head.

He wanted me to tie him to the chair, and abuse him. That was the word he used, abuse.

I could think of nothing to say. I didn't even know what he meant. To me, abuse meant insult, verbally insult. Was that what he wanted? I could not even bring myself to ask.

He glanced up at me, humble and ashamed, but he was acting, as he thought I was. He thought I was an actress, a prostitute, beyond the reach of shock and disgust, thinking only of the money, but he was appreciative of my skills. My acting skills. This attitude I had struck, of revulsion and anger.

I stood in silence, shaking, as he undressed, trying not to think, remembering David Wright with his camera, on the other side of one of those insipid flower pictures, remembering to keep my back to them. But when he stood there, naked, his head lowered, I went to the table and picked up the rope, and I tied him to the chair, hands, and ankles, and the last of the rope around his chest and his stomach, and I dragged it tight, and if I felt some satisfaction as he hissed in pain as the rope bit into him when I tied it to the rung there was nothing sexual in my response. It was loathing, pure loathing, satisfaction at the sight of the suffering of a hated enemy.

And then I stepped away, wondering what I should say to him, and he raised his humbled eyes.

'Will you undress too?' he asked.

'*No!*'

He seemed surprised, even offended, as though he would protest at my refusal. Was this part of the deal, part of the agreement he had reached with Wright, my pimp?

When I spat in his face my anger was directed at both of them. When I called him the dirty names, I was thinking of Wright, when I told him how I loathed him, how I would punish him, I was thinking of Wright, that bright face was in my mind, that smile, those flickering blue eyes, not the humble, dark ones of the man in the chair. Filth, he was filth, I would scour him, I would scour the skin from his flesh, and it was Wright in my mind, and when at last those dark eyes closed, the head falling forward, and a spasm convulsed the pale-skinned body, I couldn't understand. I stared at him. I stared.

He raised his head, and he smiled at me.

'You can untie me now,' he said.

I bared my teeth, and he laughed.

'No, enough,' he said. 'You've done well. Enough. Untie these ropes, please. I'll pay you a bonus for this, you're far better than I'd expected. Even if it wasn't quite what I'd requested.'

He gave me money. When he'd dressed, he took out his wallet, and he handed me folded notes, smiling, friendly. Almost normal. But I couldn't touch him. I couldn't make myself touch him, and he laughed again, and laid the money on the table.

'Very good,' he said. 'What's your name?'

I couldn't even speak by then. I wanted him to go away. I wanted to vomit. I wanted to wash myself.

He smiled again, and walked out of the room, and I heard the front door closing behind him. Footsteps on the path. He had gone.

I went back to the fire, hugging myself, shivering. It was over. The rope lay on the linoleum where I had dropped it beside the chair. I looked at it, thinking to myself that I would not pick it up, I would not touch the thing again, Wright could clean up.

He came into the room, and he wasn't smiling.

'That wasn't much bloody good.'

I felt a small surge of satisfaction at his displeasure.

'He thought it was,' I said.

He went to the table and picked up the money, and my satisfaction instantly turned to fury. I threw myself across the room at him, screaming at him, striking at his face, fingernails reaching for his eyes, and he fell back, frightened and startled, his hands up to protect himself.

'Okay! It's yours, okay? My God, what the hell was that for?'

'Bastard!'

'Keep your damned *tip*, then. Next time you're told to take your clothes off, you do it. And abuse means something more than dirty language, don't pretend you don't know.'

'I do *not* take my clothes off, little rat.'

For the first time he seemed uncertain, as though he felt his power over me slipping away.

'Give me my money,' I demanded.

'You didn't earn it.'

I felt my teeth baring, I was shaking with fury, and he backed away again, holding up his hands as though I would attack.

'All right! I've got your money. Just calm down, okay? You don't have to be like this. Okay?'

He wasn't smiling now, and his eyes were wide, fixed on my face, almost fearful. He reached into his pocket, slowly, his right hand sliding across his chest into the inside pocket of his jacket.

'Okay?' he asked again.

It was in an envelope, a square blue envelope. He held it out to me. I shook my head.

'Put it on the table.'

'I won't hurt you,' he protested, and I laughed, a harsh and choking sound.

'Damned right you won't. You won't touch me, either. Put it on the table.'

He threw it, an attempt at bravado, trying to laugh.

I picked it up, it and the notes the man had left, put them into my pocket, and walked out of the room.

'I'll . . . I'll telephone you again, then,' he called after me. 'When there's . . .'

I slammed the door behind me, cutting off the sound of his voice, and walked down the path away from that revolting little house.

Tony Marks said my white set would make a better painting than stage scene, and he was right. I liked the patterns, the curves set off by the straight shadows, and so I bought a big canvas and painted it. I seemed to have lost the knack of reflected light, it had been too long since I had worked in oils, so I went to the fine art department, and spent a few days working there. It felt good, to be standing in front of an easel again, watching the shapes taking form under my brush, patterns and colours swirling. I lost myself in the lines on the canvas, it was like my first year at school when I had been allowed to make my pattern shapes after I had finished my work.

It felt as though I was working in a dream, slowly, without much thought, just standing back and watching while somebody who was me painted patterns.

'Costumes,' said Tony Marks when he next saw me.

'What?'

'Costumes, your weak point, do some work. What the hell are you up to? Farting around in Fine Art.'

'Oh, right.'

But I wanted to do my white set, I still hadn't got the reflected light. There was no hurry about costumes, I had plenty of time. Anyway, costumes didn't seem very important, just dress-making.

I painted a child. There were bruises on her thighs, and when I saw that I smashed the board into pieces and went home to the granary, and David Wright telephoned that evening and told me to go to south London the next night.

Once again, he opened the door as I put my key in the lock, and the bright smile was back.

'I want my train fares,' I said before he could speak.

'Take them out of your *tips*,' he replied, but when I stared at him he turned away, shrugging.

'Oh, all right.'

And I went on into the room, and looked at the table, where there were handcuffs and a whip, and there were two big ring bolts set into the wall behind the door.

'What about those costumes?' demanded Tony Marks the next day, and he was impatient and puzzled. 'What are you doing? What's the matter with you?'

I didn't know. I tried to think about costumes, they had to be important if Tony was worried, but he walked away, striding down the corridor, and I sighed, and my mind was on light on white curves, and angled shadows.

Patrick Chendar wrote to me and invited me down for a long weekend, 'If you can spare the time, my dear. I've got something to show you.'

What he had to show me was a painting of a hurricane.

It seemed to blast its way off the canvas, palm trees bent to the point of snapping, debris hurled through the turbulent air, a wrecked car cartwheeling. The colours might have been thrown by some angry wind god, brilliant, violent, wild.

'Wow!' I exclaimed, and Patrick beamed at me.

'First time I saw it, I wanted to duck,' he said. 'Looks as if it's coming straight at you, that car.'

'Who did it?'

'Young Trinidadian. Jonas van Deevan. Won't have heard of him, m'dear, not yet. Got it through Revelations. Young Orek.'

'That's all right, then, isn't it?' I said, and when he nodded, smiling his understanding, I asked, 'Patrick, can I stay for a while? I want to look at paintings.'

I stayed for a week. Patrick asked no questions, he gave me the key to the long room in the cellar, and left me alone. My good friend, my mother's lover.

The Cézanne was there, back from an exhibition in Madrid, still in its packing case, and the new butler helped me set it up on a big easel at the end of the room under the spotlights.

'All right for money, m'dear?' Patrick asked when the Rover came to the front door to take me to the station.

'I am, actually, Patrick,' I said.

And I was. Alexandra Martin was doing well, and the company had paid a good dividend. Revelations had not only found a painting for Patrick, it had found a set of sketches that was in the National Art Gallery being examined by excited experts. The publicity had brought in more business than Robert Cameron had thought possible, although Martin Orek had begged to be allowed to keep the money in the gallery to buy a set of seventeenth-century drawings. It was the sort of good fortune that comes once in a lifetime.

'You brought us luck, Glory,' said Robert when he telephoned me with the news, and I shivered.

There were two blue envelopes as well, and a small wad of folded banknotes, but they lay under a rug in the granary, making a shape under the dense coloured wool, a square shape where the light caught the edges, a shape that I watched sometimes in the evenings, watched, and remembered, and hated.

'I can't do reflected light any more,' I said to one of the fine art tutors, and she looked at my white set painting casually, not very interested.

'No?' she murmured. 'Doesn't look too bad to me.'

Twice in one week David Wright telephoned me, although he said nothing about the time I had been away. Bright, friendly voice on the telephone, happy to speak to me, pleased and excited.

'Are you ever going to do any work again?' demanded Tony when he saw me on my way up to the fine art department. 'You haven't been near us this month. What the fuck are you up to? Are you ill or something?'

'Of course not. It's reflected light, I can't get it right.'

'There's nothing wrong with your reflected light. You're just making feeble excuses. Feeble, feebler, feeblest. What are you doing? What the hell's the matter with you?'

The square shape under the rug in the granary was growing. I lay on the golden wooden floor and stared at it, at the faint light on the edge, where the blue envelopes lay under the green and gold wool, at the blurred edge on the other side, where the few thin wads of folded banknotes lay against them. So faint, those tiny lines of light on the green and gold wool, so faint, so clear, and growing.

Every time, those evenings, another blue envelope, fitted against the edges of those that already lay there, and sometimes the bank notes, laid on the table in response to my furious refusal to touch them, to touch the servile hand that proffered them.

Was that me? Scornful and angry, was that my voice? My hands?

It was such a long way away, that horrible little house in that mean street with its pretentions to gentility, its bow windows and glass porches. So far away. So very far away.

And yet the shape under the green and gold rug was growing, and the edges were harder, sharper, as the blue envelopes piled on to each other, there was no more room under that little rug, they lay two deep now, those square blue envelopes, and the folded notes beside them.

Christmas had come and gone, and I had hardly noticed. Two sable paintbrushes from Ann with a card she had drawn herself, as she had always drawn her own Christmas cards, and I set it on my desk and looked at it, a man with a sheep beside him, looking at a star.

I thought about Ann, studying some sort of metal working in a technical college in the West Country. What she'd always wanted, was she happy now? I loved Ann. She'd never lied to me.

One of the tutors asked me to come into his office, said it was time we talked. He said he was a counsellor, I wasn't sure at first what he meant, something to do with local government?

'Something worrying you?' he asked, and I shook my head, still waiting for him to tell me why he wanted to see me.

Tony Marks had asked him to talk to me, to find out why I wasn't working. I'd done nothing throughout the entire autumn and winter, nothing except my white set painting, which was now quite hopelessly overworked, fit for nothing but the dustbin.

'You were good in the summer,' he said. 'Spectacularly good in some respects. It's as though you're a different person. You hardly even look the same, you're far too thin. Can I help?'

Thin.

She came back sometimes, the thin girl.

That time there'd been the razors on the white cloth, and I'd turned on David Wright, one of the razors in my hand, slashed at his face, he'd only just got out of the way in time, I'd been screaming that I wouldn't do it, I wouldn't do it.

He'd been frightened, it had been in his eyes, fear, real fear, and I'd been elated by that, so when he'd offered me double the money, four hundred pounds if I'd do it, I'd said I would, and then he'd laughed.

'There's not much you won't do for money, is there?'

And I was still remembering the fear in his face, and the feeling close to joy it had brought me, so I'd agreed, bitterly, that no, there wasn't much I wouldn't do for money.

She'd known what to do, that girl, she'd held the razors and she'd been calm, and careful, and she'd listened as she had before, and the blades had slid straight, and the voice had been almost the same, the whispering, and the moaning had been almost the same.

Thin. Thin, and bruised, with careful hands, and she listened, and did what they told her.

Far too thin, said the man in the little office in the college. Perhaps I should have a check-up. He could recommend a doctor. No? Well, he was always available, if I wanted to talk.

Work, said Tony Marks. For Christ's sake, Glory.

He wasn't angry any more, he was sad. What the hell's the matter with you? Come on, Glory, what do you want to do? You want to do your white set? Okay, love, we'll do it. Somehow, we'll do it. Okay? Come on, Glory. Start tomorrow? Yes?

He came to find me, he looked for me and found me, and he took me back to the stage and said we'd start. We'd have to steam the frames to get the curves, he'd fix that up, this big sweep here, we'd have to do that in several sections, how would I join them so they'd still be smooth, there'd be no break in the curve? Glory? Or had I had another idea about the frames? Not wood, something else?

No, wood will do, I said at last. Yes, steamed. And the joins, well, I'd think about that. And then chicken wire and plaster, I suppose? Can it be smooth enough? If you cover it with canvas and size it? Or something else? Glory? Something else?

Glory?

Then he fell silent, he was watching me, and I was thinking, I was thinking of the curves, of the way the light could play on them, and Tony waited for me to speak. He waited until my eyes focused again, until I looked at him, and then he tilted his head, and smiled, questioningly.

Suppose we make it soft? Instead of canvas, Tony, what about soft padded cotton? That would cover the joins, too, and you could get some quite interesting effects if it's soft. The shadows would change if somebody touched them.

But the curves wouldn't be quite so true, would they, Glory?

Not up close, no, but from a distance they would. Especially if the lighting gave those straight shadows, look, on this diagram, do you see? If you have them together, the straight shadow and the curve of the white cotton in front of it, you'd never spot the curve wasn't quite true, would you?

This lighting in the floor, going to cost a packet, unless you've got a bright idea.

Grant? Could I get a grant, Tony?

Doubt it. But we could try. Is there some other way? No, you stupid cow, I don't mean the money, I mean some other way of getting those shadows. Use your brain, try to think of another way. Come on, clever clogs. Use those smart grey cells. Smart, smarter, smartest grey cells. Try. Think.

So I thought, and he was silent as my mind worked on the lights, on the shadows, as I groped through the problems and looked for the answers, as I finally began to work again.

Time passed, and Tony sat on the darkening stage, waiting for me, waiting until I grew aware of him again, until I spoke of the ideas that had come during those strange, long moments when nothing else mattered, nothing but what I was trying to create, nothing but the slow moments of clarity when I finally knew what to do.

She can do all that, the thin child, she can do those things with the razors and the ropes, all that stuff on the table, she can do that. I want to make my white set. I want to get this lighting right.

The thin girl, she can do those other things.

15

Somebody followed me.

I'd wondered, once or twice, when I walked along the road back to the busier streets and the underground station, and when I'd thought somebody might have been following I'd escaped them. I'd got off the train at a different stop, walked slowly alongside the brightly lit carriage, using the lights from the windows and doors to search my pockets or my handbag, as though I'd lost something, and then I'd jumped back into the train just as the doors were closing, and I'd watched, looking for someone also trying to get on at the last moment.

But since I'd let the thin child take over, I hadn't bothered.

'What's the matter with *you*?' demanded Wright that first evening when I'd agreed to use the razors, when he'd gone, that fat man, gone whimpering away, hobbling down the path.

I stared at Wright, and he shrugged, and tossed the blue envelope on to the table.

'More,' I said, and he sighed, and counted out the extra money.

'That was a bit different, wasn't it?' he insisted. 'Not like your usual routine?'

She did everything they asked. She took off her clothes, and they looked at her. Sometimes, she even let them touch her. They put money on the table afterwards.

Twice, three times, four times a week now. Double for the razors.

'You've changed,' he commented, and, later, in the early summer, 'You *really have* changed. What is this? A boyfriend? I hope he won't make trouble. Can't have that, boyfriend trouble. Glory?'

I had some friends. Tony Marks, he was a friend, and Jane Targe, who wrote to me every month telling me how she was getting on, paying back the loan, sending me photographs of her new designs, Jane was a friend.

Patrick Chendar.

But not the thin child. She had no friends. She was always alone. She didn't want David Wright. She didn't want anybody.

Now this man had followed me, and I hadn't noticed, I'd done nothing to prevent it, and he was standing in front of my door in the lamplight, looking at me, asking if he could please come in, just to talk to me. Please.

I wasn't alarmed, he didn't seem threatening, just standing there asking, very politely, if he could come in to talk to me. I didn't even know who he was. I didn't recognise him. The man that evening had been old, quite old, with bent shoulders, and this one was young, and tall.

'Who are you?' I asked, and he flinched, as though I'd said something hurtful.

'My name's Sam Cooper,' he said, and he looked away. 'Last week. You . . . Don't you remember me?'

One of her customers. In David Wright's house, one of those men. I remembered him now.

'You'd better make another appointment,' I said, and I started to close the door.

He didn't try to stop me.

'Please don't. Please don't close the door. If you don't

want me to come in, could we talk here? It's not cold, is it? Not too cold for you?'

I opened the door again and I looked at him, looked him up and down the way men so often look at women, and he glanced away, embarrassed, and then faced me again and waited, endured my eyes, patiently, until I had finished assessing him, waited for me to speak.

'What do you want to talk about?' I asked, and then I added, quickly, 'I don't do *anything* here.'

'No, nothing like that. That's not . . .' A deep breath, looking away again. 'When I want something like that, I'll make another appointment, as you said. I'm not trying to cheat you.'

I let him in. He followed me up the stairs and into the granary, stood looking around until I gestured at one of the chairs, and he sat in it, waited for me to go back to my desk, to turn on some lights.

'I'd like to see you sometimes,' he said. 'Not often, if you're busy, just sometimes. Take you out? Anywhere you want to go? I don't know what you like. But, whatever you like.'

He wasn't good-looking, this man. I hadn't taken any notice before, I never did notice that sort of thing, not on those evenings at that house, just in general, old, young, fat, thin, nothing more. But he looked nice, he had a pleasant face, wide-spaced eyes with laughter lines, a smile that might be friendly when he wasn't nervous.

'What did you say your name was?'

'Sam Cooper.'

He might be useful. If he met me a few times at the college, it might stop some of the students pawing at me, asking me to go out with them, being a damned nuisance. Sam Cooper was big, he looked fit and strong, he might be a deterrent. Glory's got a boyfriend, big as a house, take your head off with one swat.

Keep your bloody hands to yourself.

'Just take me out?' I asked.

'That's all.'

'Can you pay?'

He flushed, and there was a look of anger, quickly suppressed.

'No. I'm not asking for your *professional* time. I've got the telephone number for that.'

No powder-blue collars and leads for Sam Cooper. And yet he had gone to that house. An enigma, and I didn't like enigmas.

'What do you do?' I asked.

'I'm in the army.'

'Not enough discipline in the army for you?'

I'd meant it to sound scornful, I'd meant to put the contempt into my voice, to search him out, but it hadn't come out like that. I'd sounded amused, and he smiled, and raised his hand.

'"A hit, a palpable hit",' he quoted.

'"A *very* palpable hit",' I corrected. 'You could take me to see *Hamlet*, if you like.'

I'd been working on costumes, my weak point as Tony Marks had said, and there were fabric samples lying around. Blue velvet that I picked up sometimes and stroked, remembering the dress I'd helped Mrs Pasmore make for Louise, wishing somehow I could talk to her, study with her. I would lie on the floor with my head resting on the velvet, looking at that square shape under the rug, and thinking of Linda Pasmore and that other square shape under another carpet, the photographs she had seen. Blue velvet, and Louise laughing, Mrs Pasmore with her big tacking needle in her hand, and me holding the scissors, taking out the pins as the long white stitches flew into the fabric under her clever hands, me watching and listening, and laughing with my friends. When I had been their lucky mascot, their lucky black cat. Before I had run out on them.

I'd never be as good at costumes as Linda Pasmore. I did

207

wish I could talk to her, learn some more from her.

'That's your colour.'

I'd forgotten he was there. I looked at him, blankly, and he smiled at me.

'Oh,' I said. 'Oh. Yes, I suppose it is. Blue.'

'What were you thinking?'

He did have a nice smile, friendly. He hadn't been smiling last week, when he'd been crouched on the floor and she'd kicked him in the belly. He'd rolled away from her, groaning. I'd have remembered if he'd smiled, I'd have remembered that smile.

'Two people I knew a long time ago,' I answered. 'We made a dress from blue velvet. It was beautiful.'

'For you?'

'No. Not for me.' I stood up suddenly, went to a window, drew a curtain across it. 'My dress was wild silk. But it got spoiled. It all got spoiled.'

Shut out the light now. Curtains across the light. Draw the curtains across all that.

'I think you'd better go now,' I said. 'But I would like to see *Hamlet*, if you'll take me.'

He stood up. He was very big, he looked kind. Wild silk, I'd told this big, kind man about the wild silk.

'I don't know your name.'

'Gloriana. Glory, if you like. Gloriana Mayall.'

'I'll take you to see *Hamlet*. Good night, Glory.'

'Good night . . . um. Sam. Good night, Sam.'

Blue velvet, and wild silk, and a big young man with kind eyes, curtains shutting out the light. I lay on the floor with my face pressed against the blue velvet, and I looked at a shape under a green and gold rug, and there were tears on my cheeks.

I wouldn't use blue velvet any more. I would use black now, with frost on it, frozen black.

'Do you want to work on *The Merchant of Venice*?' Tony Marks asked me the next day.

'What?'

'Shakespeare, dear. You'll have heard of him. In August, there's a production in Chichester, I've been asked to do the set. Would you like to help? I need an assistant.'

That night I went home early, and I read the play. I read it through quickly, and then I started again, puzzled. Why was this called a comedy? Just because of all that silly business about the rings? It was dreadful, this story. I didn't think I wanted to do this. I set it aside, laid it on the top of my desk, and looked at the red leather cover on the dark wood. It gleamed in the lamplight, like blood. I picked it up again, and opened it.

Lucille came to see me.

She'd telephoned the day before, she sounded affectionate, called me darling Gloriana, asked how I was, had I made any nice clothes? I told her it was mostly theory this year.

She had something to discuss, she said. Rather important. Urgent, actually. Was I desperately busy, darling? Could she come tomorrow?

I'd been reading *The Merchant of Venice* again when she arrived, I'd been digging into the words, what had he been trying to say? The doorbell, the sound of a taxi pulling away, was an interruption.

She was smiling, and lovely, and gracious, exclaiming over the granary, saying it was charming, quite charming. What a lovely colour scheme, darling, how clever, to keep it so simple.

'Would you like a drink?' I asked.

'White wine.'

That was new. It used to be cream sherry. But I opened a bottle of Liebfraumilch, and we raised our glasses to each other.

'What's the book?' she asked as I closed it and put it back in the case on my desk.

'Shakespeare.'

She raised her eyebrows, a half smile on her lips, and started to speak.

'I'm sorry?'

'It doesn't matter.'

She was thinner than she'd been when I'd last seen her, in the spring, when I'd gone to the house to collect some books. The fashion demanded it, but I wasn't sure it suited her. When I'd commented, when I'd said she seemed to have lost some weight, she'd said she'd been to a health farm for a week. It had been gorgeous, a real holiday.

'It must have cost a packet.'

I'd been making small talk, just polite conversation, but her laugh, light and amused though she'd made it, had had overtones of terror.

'Patrick was surprised,' she'd said. 'By the bill.'

Now she was looking down at her glass, turning the stem in her fingers so the wine swirled, but her hand wasn't quite steady. She'd spill it if she wasn't careful.

'Do you want me to do something for you, Lucille?' I asked.

She nodded.

'What is it?'

She wouldn't look at me. She kept her eyes fixed on her glass, on the wine moving in the pale crystal.

'Patrick wants to buy me the house,' she said.

There was more to it than that. I said nothing, I waited.

'His plans for the future . . .' She broke off, and bowed her head.

'Yes?' I closed my eyes and listened. I wouldn't look at her now. I wanted the truth.

'He's an important man. He's going to be . . . He may have to go away. Anyway, very busy.'

She'd sent Ann away. Now she was lying again.

'He's dropping you,' I said.

There was no angry denial, no protest. She stopped

210

playing with the glass, laid it on the table, clasped her hands in her lap.

'Peter owns the house,' she said at last. 'It's in trust for you.'

'And you need his permission, do you? Or mine?'

But that was too much. She turned towards me, her small head raised high on her slender neck, and there was a look of disdain on her face.

'I'll tell Patrick I'd rather have the money. I'll buy somewhere smaller. What I wanted to tell you, Gloriana, was that there won't be room for you, when I move to a smaller place. I don't know what you'll do with the house, it's nothing to do with me. You'll have to remove your possessions before I go.'

'Do you want to leave?'

She didn't. She could hold the disdainful look, but I knew what she was thinking. Well proportioned, graceful, it was a lovely house. Lucille used to hint that it had been designed by Nash. It hadn't, but not everybody had disbelieved her.

Although I'd wondered about the house I'd never seriously asked. When she'd driven Ann away I'd challenged Lucille with it, with not owning the house, with having to leave if I moved out, but that threat had been based on a guess. In trust for me? That house?

And Patrick wanted to buy it for Lucille, he'd been her lover for years, he'd be generous in parting from her. Dear Patrick.

Lucille was still graceful, still very beautiful, but now there was something panic-stricken about her, and a new mannerism, a way of lifting her chin as her eyes slid from side to side, and as she drew in her breath it sounded uneven, shuddering. No longer quite to Patrick's taste, perhaps.

'You love him, don't you?' I asked.

Patrick Chendar could not love Lucille, not now. Patrick

had admired her beauty, wanted her body, and paid a fair price for it. Lucille would have no cause to complain of Patrick's treatment of her, but that would be no consolation, no recompense for her pain.

'If it's up to me you can stay in the house,' I said. 'I don't mind.'

If he had offered to buy the house for her, he would probably give her a lot of money in its place. Would she be able to keep it? Or would it slide through her fingers as she watched, wonderingly, not understanding where it had all gone, how it had disappeared so fast?

I didn't really care. There was nothing I could do anyway.

My thoughts turned back to *The Merchant of Venice*. I'd never seen it performed. It eluded me, this theme, this balance between justice and law, mercy and revenge. It was horrible, the old man sharpening his knife in the Courts of Justice, the trapped merchant, drugged with fear, watching, despairing, the love of his friends powerless against the dread that overwhelmed him.

I wanted to do this, with Tony. I began to see what I wanted from this.

Black robes they must wear, those lawyers. And there must be red, and white, but in the shadows, standing back, awaiting the judgment from the black-robed lawyers. Sombre and menacing, how could the old man fail? He would have his disgusting revenge, the merchant would die, and the loneliness of his misery must breathe from the shadows.

Lucille said something, and I looked up, irritated, distracted from my half-formed idea of a crimson slash lying diagonally across a table, the table must be the shape of a tomb, half hidden by books, legal tomes disguising the truth of the death, but what was the crimson diagonal?

'What?'

'I'd like to stay. If I may.'

What was she talking about? Stay? I hadn't invited her to stay with me. I looked at her.

'Will you want rent?'

Stay, in the house, yes. I didn't even like the house any more. Too many shadows, so much confusion, what was the crimson diagonal? A robe? Oxford, was it? Master of Arts, the crimson hood? Or light through a stained-glass window?

'I couldn't pay much.'

Rent the house, Lucille my tenant. Well, why not?

'Ask Uncle John,' I said.

Light, it would be light, that diagonal, reflected? Reflected off something crimson? No, through a stained-glass window, and when Portia cautioned Shylock against shedding Antonio's blood, somebody would open the window, the crimson would flash, and vanish, and daylight would take its place.

How would they play Shylock? The old man lost everything, where was Portia's mercy now? Even his religion denied him, how would they play that?

'Will you *please* discuss this with me?'

Lucille again. I jerked myself back to reality and looked at her. I didn't want to talk about this, I had work to do. I wanted to think about the crimson light, how to keep it clear and steady until that moment, how to stop the cast getting between the table and the window.

But Lucille demanded my attention.

'I *have* discussed it. I said. Ask Uncle John, I don't know. What do you want? What do you want me to say?'

'Please. You talk to him. John doesn't like me.'

Victim. Stupid victim, getting into debt to somebody who owed nothing in return, nothing but pain. Antonio, in debt to Shylock for the love of his friend Bassanio, Antonio at Shylock's mercy, thinking the old man had been joking. Not dreaming, as he signed the bond, that Shylock too might be a gambler, might be prepared to chance a small stake on a small hope of revenge. And chance had favoured Shylock.

213

'Gloriana?'

'Oh, for *God's* sake, Lucille! What do you want me to say? Yes, I'll ask Uncle John, but what should I ask? What do you want?'

'I want you to talk to John. Ask him if I may stay in the house at a rent I can afford.'

'How much can you afford?'

But she didn't know. She blinked at me, and looked away again. She had no idea.

'I had to sign an agreement,' she said. 'Once you and Ann move out, I have to leave as well. Or something.'

'What agreement?'

She'd lost it. She'd had a copy, Uncle John had given her a copy and she'd lost it.

Uncle John was not prepared to help Lucille.

'I can't do it,' he said when I telephoned him the following morning. 'I have a duty as your trustee to do the best I can in your interests. Selling that house now, with the market in its current position, is not in your best interests, and letting Lucille rent it, at anything remotely near what she could afford, would be criminal. I told her she'd have to leave when you moved out. I wrote to her, months ago, she didn't reply. I can't give her any more time.'

'All right,' I said. 'I'll tell her.'

He was surprised. Had he expected me to argue? To plead Lucille's case, the loving daughter trying to help her mother?

'I'm sorry.' His voice was uncertain. 'I really can't help. I've found another tenant.'

She cried when I telephoned her.

'I don't want to leave,' she said. 'This is my home, I've lived here for so long. Where can I go?'

'Ask Patrick to buy you a house.'

Silver on black, all the costumes for *The Merchant of Venice*, except for those comedy scenes which I didn't understand, I'd done them silver on black, and Tony was delighted.

'You clever little cow! What are you up to? What about the scenery?'

'That's your department.'

'Colour? That's what you're thinking, isn't it? That black against colour?'

I hadn't thought about the backgrounds. I'd left that to him, except for the courtroom scene, where I'd told him about the crimson light on the tomb-like table. He took my sketches, and he laughed, and then he gritted his teeth and scratched his head, and he swore, I'd never seen him so excited.

'I knew I was right about you. Dumb blonde, my arse.'

Lucille wrote to me.

'Please ask John again. I can't bear to leave. Please, darling, you've got so much money, and I've got nothing. It can't matter to you.'

So much money? I didn't understand. I telephoned Uncle John again.

'What does she mean?' I asked.

'She gets fifty per cent of the income,' he explained. 'The rest is yours, either to reinvest or to use for your education and maintenance. She's spent all hers. Most of yours is in gilt-edged stock.'

'Am I rich?' I was curious rather than excited.

'Comfortably off.'

I didn't even bother to ask him if Lucille could stay in the house. I knew he'd refuse again.

Chichester cancelled the production of *The Merchant of Venice*, and Tony was close to despair, saved from it only by fury.

'Bastards!' he yelled. 'Penny-pinching middle-class bastards!'

Middle-class was the worst insult Tony knew.

'*Hamlet*,' I said. 'Let's do a set for *Hamlet*, everybody does *Hamlet* sooner or later, we could have one ready.'

Sam Cooper had taken me to Guildford to see *Hamlet*,

the best production he could find, he'd looked at the cast. Good actors. He hadn't known, then, that I wasn't very interested in actors.

He'd brought me roses, and a box of chocolates, and we drove down to Guildford in a big, comfortable car, which he'd borrowed from a friend. He had no car of his own; he was abroad so often a car would have been a nuisance rather than a convenience.

I listened to him as he talked, and I found I liked him. I sat back in the deep leather seat of the car, half turned towards him, and I listened to him talking about army life in Germany, and sometimes I asked a question, but I wasn't really very interested in what he was saying. I liked the sound of his voice, it had been a long time since I had just listened to a man talking to me.

He didn't mention that house in south London, what he had wanted done, he didn't even mention following me home and the evening he had sat in the armchair in the granary and asked to see me sometimes. I wondered why I felt so comfortable with him, and in the end I thought it was because he reminded me of the men Lucille had brought home when I'd been a child, men who had expected nothing of me.

Little tricks, I tried on Sam, useful little tricks. My hand resting on his as he helped me out of the car, did he notice how slim and small my hand was against his big, broad one? Lips slightly parted so the light might catch white teeth as I turned my head, did he notice? My silhouette as I sat with the light behind me, my shoulders low, my head high, so my neck was long and graceful.

He met me from college, where I'd told him if some red-haired yob in a green leather jacket was hanging around he should push his face in, and Sam put his arm around my shoulders and looked at the boy, and said Miss Mayall had mentioned him. Sam spoke very gently, and very quietly, and the boy left me alone after that.

That was the only time Sam ever touched me.

He made no demands, he smiled, and he talked to me, and he brought me flowers and chocolates, he took me to the theatre and to restaurants in the West End, and apart from that time on the steps of the college he never tried to touch me, Sam never tried to touch me.

Sometimes he went to the house, and then she would look at him and she would be cold and angry, but she was strong, that child with the bruised thighs and the clever hands, she was strong, and savage, she didn't know Sam, she never saw the friendly smile or listened to that deep and gentle voice, she only did what he said, she didn't listen, she only heard the words, and she did what he said.

He took me on the river one Sunday afternoon, a picnic, he said. He had a rowing boat. There were big cushions in the boat for me to lie on as he rowed beside the willows, it was lovely, and peaceful, the sunlight on the water, and Sam was quiet, just watching me, and smiling, and rowing.

But we met a friend of his, and the friend said Sam shouldn't be rowing. He told me Sam had fallen off a horse, he was a mass of bruises, Sam should be taking it easy. Accident-prone, he called Sam, teasing him. Falling down a rock face, falling off horses, getting hit by motorcycles.

I smiled, and listened, and agreed Sam should be taking it easy. The afternoon was spoiled, and when the man had gone Sam sat in the boat, resting his arms on the oars and looking down, still, and silent, and somehow ashamed. When he looked up at me again my face was turned towards some cows in the field by the river, I knew he wouldn't realise I was watching him, waiting to see if he would talk of the thin girl, if he would ruin everything. And at last he just made a noise like a little sigh, and bent over the oars again, and rowed back down the river.

Nobody can go back to childhood, not even with Sam Cooper.

Patrick asked me to spend a few hours with him finding

a house for Lucille, give him advice about interior decorators and all that sort of thing, m'dear, if you would. He'd taken a lot of trouble finding somewhere that would suit her, and there were three he wanted me to see, to give him my opinion.

'Why not ask her?'

He coughed, and wouldn't look at me.

'Being a bit difficult, Lucille. Lovely woman, your mother, but a bit difficult. Just at the moment.'

We decided on a little Georgian house only a mile away from the one that was now mine, I supposed. It was pretty, and well proportioned, but small, compared to what she had been used to. We spent a few hours there together, I gave him some ideas about lighting and colours, and he tucked two hundred pounds into my pocket as he drove me back to London, consultation fee, m'dear. Don't argue.

'I shan't actually give it to her,' he confided when he dropped me at the granary. 'But she can live there for the rest of her life, it'll all be settled properly. Don't worry.'

'Won't you come in?' I asked. 'You've never seen the granary, have you?'

'Next time, if I may,' he said. 'Got to be going. Young Francis a good landlord, is he?'

Young Francis had only been to the granary once, dropping in uninvited one Sunday afternoon to see what I'd been up to, God, how much are carpets going to cost? Funny sort of glass in those windows, when are you going to divide it up into proper rooms?

'*Do* come in,' I'd said sarcastically as he strolled around with his hands in his pockets and his nose in the air, and he'd looked surprised.

'I do own the place, you know.'

'Read the lease.'

I'd been in no mood for Francis Chendar, I was due to go to that house two hours later, I'd been tense and nervous, and when Francis had told me we were having dinner together that evening, what do you mean, appointment? Cancel it, I'd turned vicious. I'd had some practice by that time.

I'd seen him once or twice since then, parties with his army friends when he'd been noisily possessive of me, bantering about art colleges, nothing against artistic poses, mind you. He'd never come to my home again. When he'd left that afternoon he'd been pale-faced and shaking.

As soon as he found an adequate substitute, Francis Chendar would be glad to forget Gloriana Mayall.

But David Wright would never forget, he was beginning to drive me frantic.

'I'm *sick* of this,' I said. 'Your filthy perverts, I'm sick of it. You go to hell, I won't do it any more. I don't care what you do.'

The smile had been bright, and hateful, and there'd been glee in the flickering blue eyes.

'Want to see some photographs?' he'd giggled.

The next time I went there were some photographs on the table, and he'd got her face. I'd thought she'd kept her back to those pictures, but he had got her face. And her hands. He took the photographs away before the doorbell rang, and he'd been laughing.

I hated him.

'I hate you,' I said. 'I'm going to kill you.'

'Special commission, my pretty.' I might not have spoken. 'Hotel room. Important customer.'

'No.'

There'd been different pieces of furniture in that room during the months I'd gone there, furniture and other things, but there'd never been a bed. And he'd always been there, in the back room, secret and silent with his cameras, but he'd always been there.

'Yes. Lots of money.'

'No.'

He'd grown angry then, he'd sworn at me, marched

around the room, shouting at me, threatened to beat some sense into me, but in the end he'd given up.

There was still some small balance in the power he held over me.

Lucille referred to the house Patrick had bought as a rabbit hutch. There wasn't enough room for her furniture, she said. She couldn't entertain there, how could she give a dinner party when there wasn't a dining room?

'Please let me stay,' she wept. 'Please don't make me go.'

'Uncle John says it's impossible, he's found new tenants.'

'How could you do this to me? Darling Gloriana, why are you being so cruel?'

I listened to her, waited until she had cried herself to silence, wondering if she would ever face reality, or if she would always believe that dreams could come true if she pleaded hard enough, if she stayed young and beautiful, if she did, and was, what men liked.

I wondered what I could say to her.

Sam Cooper took me to an exhibition of Impressionist paintings in Birmingham for my birthday, and spent the whole day by my side, watching me looking at paintings.

'Do you understand them?' he asked me as I turned away from a Matisse.

'Hmm?'

He gestured at the canvas.

'*Interior with Eggplants*,' he read from the label. 'What does it mean?'

He'd been kind, as always, driving so far to take me to something that was of no interest at all to him. I tried to explain.

'He's trying to use colour the way other painters might use line. To make the shapes with colours, not with out-lines. I mean, look. Those blues, do you see? They're not just colour.'

It was no good, I couldn't explain. Sam just looked politely baffled, waiting for me to tell him the untellable.

'They say something that I can't put into words,' I said, and then I remembered Patrick, looking at the lovely paintings the first time he took me to the long room in the cellar, I remembered what he had said. 'They help me get my head back into shape.'

He understood that. He smiled his slow, pleasant smile, and looked back at the Matisse, and the smile faded, and once again he seemed baffled.

'Bloody eggplants,' he muttered. 'Why the hell eggplants?'

16

Summer, and Wright told me to get a tan. His customers liked girls with suntanned bodies. Also, I was too thin, he said. He wanted some curves.

'Go to hell.'

Little sharp white teeth, and the flickering blue eyes. He looked like a rat. Rat Wright.

'I want to be your *friend*,' he said. 'Your *good friend*, my dear Gloriana. So listen to my advice, and do as I tell you. Put on some weight. And get a nice tan.'

He kept his distance from me, never closer than five or six feet away. Twice now I'd slashed at his face with the razor, the second time I'd almost got him. Sometimes I wondered why he never tried to retaliate, why he never hit me. He was frightened of me in some ways, frightened of me.

The thin girl listened to him, she did what he said, she didn't care. But when she'd gone and it was just me there with him, he was frightened, and wary, and he wouldn't come near me.

She was dangerous, too, but not to him. She was savage and vicious, they told her what to do, they told her what they wanted, and she did it, she even let them touch her, and she did what they said, but sometimes she wouldn't stop, when it was over, when they'd shuddered and there'd

222

been that spasm, she didn't stop, not even when they cried and screamed, and then at last she'd stop, and they'd go away, cursing and threatening, and Wright would be angry. She'd listen to him for a while, and then she'd go, too. When she went Wright would back away from me, out of my reach, he'd look watchful, and I'd take the money and walk away from him.

'You're mad,' he'd say. 'You're crazy. You'll cripple one of them one day, you've half killed him. And what about the noise? What about *disturbing* the *neighbours*?'

But they always came back, the ones who'd screamed and begged.

I hated him, but she didn't care.

Put on some weight, he said, but he didn't know, he didn't understand.

'Rat,' I called him.

'Lots of money,' he said. 'Nothing you won't do for money, is there, Gloriana?'

Tony Marks said I was too thin, he asked if I was ill, but I shook my head.

'I like being thin,' I said. 'I feel fitter like this.'

We were working together on a set for a company in Cambridge, he'd said it would do for part of my practical work, as stipulated in some complicated information sheet from the local education authority. He'd grinned at me when he'd said that; we just liked working together and he'd been quite enthusiastic about the play. He didn't think it would run for long, and it wouldn't make any money, but it had guts and bones and something to say for itself. Good enough. Bugger the money.

'Bugger the money,' I echoed.

Scaffolding at odd angles, an impression of enormous height and distance, stretching right up into the sky, perspective was to be the trick.

'Trick, trick, tricky,' chanted Tony under his breath as he scribbled in thick black pencil on to one of my sketches.

223

'You've ruined that,' I complained.

'Tricky, trickier, trickiest,' he muttered, ignoring me. 'Light, Glory. From where, clever clogs? Whence cometh the light? And this line here, too obvious. Come on, smarty-pants. Get subtle.'

I was so happy then, scrawling notes on sketches, thinking about light filters, reflections, angles. Don't tell me I'm thin, Tony. That's not me.

'Gargoyles,' I said.

'What?'

'Well. Look at it. It's all new, all this muck. But what about *old*, maestro? There's old in this play as well as new. Where's the old?'

And he glared at me, chin jutting, and his eyes moved away into the middle distance as he thought, and he grunted, and he muttered, and gargoyles were stupid and irrelevant, and what did I know about gargoyles anyway, and okay then, where?

Yes. Yes.

'Oh, *yes!*'

Sam took me to Cambridge, we went to see a play in the theatre which was to put on the production Tony was working on. Tony and I were working on. The play we saw was a farce, and I hated it, and I don't think Sam enjoyed it much either, but I did see the stage, and the lighting. I never could visualise stages, not from diagrams and measurements, I have to see them.

'You don't have to pay for tickets,' said Tony. 'Cretin. Just say who you are, go in and look.'

Who might there be, in that theatre in Cambridge? Who might have seen photographs in a cheap yellow book?

Leave it out.

'Glory? What the hell's the matter? You going deaf?'

'Sorry, Tony. What did you say?'

None of the names in the cast, nobody from the Royal. But what about the stage hands? Backstage, that had been

224

my world then, what about them? Who might there be, in that theatre in Cambridge? Whose names hadn't appeared in the programme?

Donald Flint? Slug, slug man, filth, Donald Flint, are you in Cambridge? Filth, are you there, slug?

I can't go back. I can't go back. They'll know, they'll have seen.

'*Glory!*'

Puzzled and irritated, Tony staring at me.

'I'm going home, Tony. Sorry. Got a period pain.'

Funny, Tony could be so prudish, so easily embarrassed. He was blushing, a brusque nod, not meeting my eyes. No further questions.

I can't go back.

But I was at that house that evening, the hooks had been screwed into the wall, leather manacles and a black leather riding crop I thought I recognised, and I looked at Wright, at the Rat, and he grinned at me, his nasty little sharp teeth all white and glinting.

'Bastard,' I said, and his eyes flickered, and he sniggered.

'"Waste not, want not."'

'Bastard. I'll kill this one. Hear me? I won't stop.'

'Glory.' He was uncertain now, the nasty grin a little worried.

'I'll fix him facing out from the wall. I'll flay him. I won't stop. I'll start on his great flabby belly and work downwards.'

He swore at me, threatened me, but he took Lucien Rathbone's black leather crop away, and he put the old bamboo stick on the table instead.

'Listen, Gloriana, my dear, I've got your photograph a hundred times now. You stop as soon as he's come. That's my advice to you, advice from a *good friend*, my dear. You stop when he tells you to stop.'

I knew the fat man's face, I'd seen it somewhere, but she didn't care. She didn't know. He left money on the table, but she didn't care about the money. When Wright came into the room he was grinning again, and he took the man- acles off the wall, watching me, keeping a safe distance away, and grinning.

'*That's* a good girl,' he said.

I was very tired. I looked at the bamboo stick, at the folded banknotes, at the blue envelope he'd laid beside them, I looked at Wright, standing by the wall with the leather manacles in his hand.

'How much longer?' I asked, and he blinked in surprise, and then grinned again.

'Until you're too old.'

But she was a child. She would never be old.

'Bastard,' I said again. I don't think he heard me. I was too tired even to hate him any more. I was thinking about a theatre in Cambridge, stage hands and technicians whose names never appeared in programmes, I was thinking about scaffolding and lighting, a perspective that reached into the sky and far over an unseen horizon, I was thinking about sly eyes sliding across my body as I stood in a little dressing room and heard voices from a stage, voices of people I had loved and never wanted to see again.

I was so far away from them now, and the little flickering threads that had held us together had gone, I was alone, and it was dark, and I was drifting in the dark, they had all gone and I was alone.

'Are you ill?'

There had been a red line of light in the sky as I walked away from the place where Ann had left me, when she had been sent away, and it had faded as I walked away through the cold, dark streets, it had faded quite quickly, broken up and gone. There was nothing to hold me to Ann now, but I loved her, and the line of light had gone, I was alone in the dark. But I loved her.

'Are you ill?'

It was very quiet in the dark. They had all gone. I could

remember voices, from a stage, from a distance, and I would not scream because I might be heard, so now it was very quiet, and the voices had gone, I could only remember, I couldn't hear the voices any more.

'Drink this. Come on, drink it.'

I had been alone because Lucille had gone. Had somebody sent her away? I had wanted my mother. I had been screaming then, but I mustn't scream because I might be heard, but I had screamed, I had screamed.

'*Don't touch me!*'

Blood, there was blood, and the Rat was shaking his hand, drops of blood flying, and he was cursing me and shaking the blood from his hand, broken glass on the floor.

'You bitch! You stupid bitch, I was trying to help you. God! What the hell's the matter with you?'

'Don't touch me.'

He had backed away, a safe distance away, looking at his cut hand, but never taking his eyes off me for long, flickering eyes, but he wasn't laughing now, there was no laughter now.

'Oh, I wouldn't touch *you*, my dear. Not with a ten-foot pole. You are not my type at all. Christ! You're mad. They'll lock you up one day. Fucking bitch. I was trying to help you.'

Blood on the floor, blood welling out from between his fingers, and he had backed away from me, he was frightened. I was between him and the door now, and he wanted water for his hand, water, and something to stop the bleeding. But he was frightened, and I was between him and the door.

'Bitch. Crazy bitch.'

I like blood. I like the colour of blood, I like the way it shines. I like the way it frightens people. I like the way it moves on his hand, running over the skin, I like that. I like blood.

'Get out and go home, stupid bitch. You need a doctor.'

'I'm all right.' My voice was quite light, quite happy. 'I don't need a doctor. You'll need stitches in that hand. That's quite a deep cut.'

'Get out of here.'

Between him and the door, and he was frightened. He'd clenched his fist, wrapped his other hand around it, but the blood was still running over his fingers, now there was blood on both his hands.

'I hope that hurts,' I said, and I felt happy, I was happy. 'I hope that hurts like hell. Stitches won't be any fun either, will they? Do you think you've cut an artery?'

He'd bared his teeth, but he wasn't grinning, not any more. He wasn't laughing now, there was no laughter, no screaming, it was quite quiet, and I was happy.

'A big vein, anyway. Does it hurt? Oh, I hope it hurts. You've learned so much about pain in these last few months, haven't you? Don't you like pain? I thought you liked pain. Shall I get the camera? Would you like some photographs?'

Pale hair, that faded pale hair, as though the colour had been diluted, and the pale blue eyes, and the pale teeth between the parted lips, but the bright blood dripping on to the brown linoleum, so bright, such a lovely colour, that bright blood.

Watchful, alert, wary, frightened, and very pale.

'Yes,' he said. 'Yes, get the camera.'

It wasn't running so fast any more, the lovely bright blood, it was still dripping, but not so fast. I heard his words, I listened to him, he wanted me to move away from the door so he could get out of the room, get away from me, but I watched the bright blood, and I was sad because it was stopping, it wasn't running so fast.

'Get the camera,' he said. 'I want some photographs.'

I wanted to watch the bright blood running, but I was tired again now, and the red line was fading, and breaking up, so I turned away, and I picked up the money, the folded banknotes and the blue envelope, and I went out of the room without looking back because I didn't want to see the brightness fading again, I didn't want to watch as it broke up and finally vanished.

I went back to the college the next day and I put blood red filters on the spotlights, and I trained them on to the scaffolding, and I sat back and looked. But it was all wrong, it made the scene small, compact, like a little room, so I took the filters off again, and sat hunched on the floor, thinking about the damned perspective, how to tell the audience about the vastness of the setting for this clever play.

'We'll have to do it in place,' said Tony. 'We'll have to see what they've got, anyway.'

I didn't want to go to Cambridge.

'Can't you do it without me?' I asked, and he stared at me in amazement, and didn't even bother to answer.

'Dinky little spotlights, here and there, all over the place, what would that do? How about that, then? Idea?'

'What?' I looked up at him and hugged my knees, still hunched on the floor, not looking at the scaffolding. 'What's the point of that?'

'I don't know.' I'd deflated him. His shoulders drooped. 'I don't know. We'll have to try it on the stage. See how it looks. It was only an idea.'

But dinky little spots, getting smaller and fading away, little lines of light, flickering and breaking up. Holes in the backcloth? With the strong lights at the base, and low wattage higher up?

Could I talk about this?

I drew in my breath, and I closed my eyes, and I tried.

'Tony. Listen,' I began, and he looked at me, and then looked away into the middle distance, and I spoke, and I tried to describe what I sometimes saw, and never had talked about before. I was stammering as I spoke of the little lines of flickering light breaking up, and of distance, and loss, but he didn't notice, and I went on, trying to tell him the feelings of the little red lines of flickering light, I was watching him, wondering if he could understand, and his eyes became unfocused, and something like a smile lifted the corners of his mouth.

'Yes,' he said at last. 'Yes. That's the starting point. Oh, yes, clever clogs. Now keep thinking, now you've finally started.'

We went to Cambridge the next day, the bits of scaffolding loaded into the back of his old van and tied with lengths of clothes line. We got lost twice before we left London, Tony wasn't a good driver and he'd been too impatient to get started to plan the journey. I tried to navigate, but the map was out of date, and there were roadworks which closed two of the streets we needed. Tony was furious with me by the time we got on to the A1, shouting that we should have come a different way and we'd be late.

'The Great North Road,' he yelled, hammering his hand onto the steering wheel as we waited at traffic lights. 'The fucking Great North Road, that's what they call this goddamned cart track. What is that stupid cunt doing? Bloody women drivers. Can't you find a fucking road they aren't ploughing up? Look at the fucking *map*, you dumb bitch!'

I jumped out of the van, slamming the door as hard as I could, and I walked away, stuffing my hands into my pockets and ignoring the sounds of the horn and Tony's furious shouts. He could go to Cambridge by himself, if the van didn't fall to pieces on the way, and if he didn't get lost again. I was shaking with rage.

He caught me up half a mile down the road, running down the pavement after me and grabbing my arm. I shook him off, I was still very angry with him, although calmer than I'd been when I'd left him at the traffic lights.

'Oh, clever clogs!' He was wailing at me, half laughing, half pleading. 'I'm sorry, I really am. Sorry, sorrier, sorriest. Sorriest wretch in London. In England. Come on. Come to Cambridge.'

'No. Bugger off.' But I was almost beginning to laugh, and he saw it, and he went down on one knee, spreading his arms wide in a ridiculous gesture of supplication and making all the passers-by stare at him.

'Darling smartypants, come to Cambridge with me! Come and enrol at the university, get yourself a degree. Nuclear physics. Get yourself a *doctorate*. Clever clogs? Please? Come to Cambridge?'

There was a parking ticket on the van's windscreen, and he swore again, told me it was my damned fault, and then he apologised. He'd made me laugh, he'd persuaded me to come back to the van, but I really had meant to leave him to go on his own, and he knew it.

We got lost on the outskirts of Cambridge as well. Tony hadn't got a map, and he flatly refused to stop and buy one, he'd been told it was easy to find the theatre. We ended up in the suburbs, and I insisted that he park the van, and go and ask for directions. He was gone for nearly half an hour, but he came back triumphant, he said he'd found an intelligent *native*, not some fucking mentally retarded undergraduate, and he'd got directions, it was easy, he'd written them on the back of his petrol receipt.

He went through all his pockets, he began to grind his teeth and swear, he took off his anorak and shook it so all his loose change fell out into the road, he even insisted on looking in the glove locker, but the petrol receipt had vanished. We were over an hour late, we were lost, no, he would *not* go and ask somebody else, he thought he could remember. It wasn't that fucking difficult. It wasn't that fucking far either, so shut up and let him concentrate.

After another ten minutes he admitted he was lost again. He sat at the wheel, melodramatically despairing, there was nobody at all in this entire damned city from whom he could ask directions, he might as well call it a day and shoot himself.

I got out of the van and walked over to a telephone box. I telephoned the theatre.

'Christ, we'd just about given you up.'

'Sorry. We're completely lost. We're opposite a pub, the White Horse, Downham Street. How do we find you?'

He laughed, asked what we were driving, told me to go back and sit in it. Five minutes later there was a rap on my window, a smiling young man who asked me to move over so he could sit beside me, and he told Tony to drive on, turn right, park here.

We hadn't been more than fifty yards away from the theatre.

They were very understanding about us being so late, I think they were simply relieved that we'd arrived at all. The stage manager sent two men back to the van with Tony to help unload the scaffolding. Tony began to say we could manage on our own, then he looked at me, and changed his mind.

It was the smell that was so achingly familiar, the smell of paint and glue. I hunched my shoulders and stared down at the floor, worn linoleum and coconut matting, peeling paint on the walls. Was this theatre destined to close, too? No money for anything the audience couldn't see? Frantic prayers before each fire inspection?

Voices from the stage, distant but clear, a notice on the wall about smoking in the corridors, it was so familiar, but now I was remote from it, I was a stranger here, I was lost in these beloved surroundings, I could only stare at the floor, and listen to the voices I loved but didn't know, and I hurt with longing and with love, but I wanted to get out, to run away, run out on them, I was so alone, I felt so sick, so ashamed, I wanted to run away.

But the smell of the paint, there would be brushes to clean, errands to run, messages to take to the dressing rooms and the paint shop and the props store, things to find, there was so much to do. So much to do, and I wanted

232

so much to be a part of this, to come back into this warm and exciting world, to know those voices that I already loved, to be familiar again, familiar, and not remote.

I wasn't even surprised when I heard her speaking, against that background of the smell of paint, of the voices from the stage, it seemed so right, even though I was a stranger in this beloved setting, her voice was so right, saying my name.

'Glory! Glory Mayall! Sweetie, is that you? It *is*, it *is*, it's our Glory!'

She shouldn't be here, I thought frantically, she shouldn't be here, her name wasn't on the programme, she was in a laundry, she was all bedraggled and tired and working a machine in a laundry, not like before, brisk and bustling with her lovely determined black hair newly dyed and fixed high on her head in its tidy smart bun, she couldn't be here, not Mrs Pasmore, she'd have seen the photographs, she'd know, she couldn't be here.

'Glory? Sweetie, it's *me*! Mrs Pasmore, you remember Lindy Pasmore? From the Royal? Glory?'

It was her, and I loved her, but she'd have seen the photographs, so I was trying to smile at her, but I wanted to run away, and I was crying, and she didn't notice, she was hugging me, holding me so close, and now I was taller than her, much taller than her, I hadn't realised she was so small. She was hugging me and laughing and exclaiming about how lovely it was to see me, and what was I doing there, and where had I been, and why had I vanished like that, they'd all missed me so much, sweetie, how lovely to see you, you look gorgeous, but why are you crying? Sweetie, what's wrong? Come on, lovie, come and sit down, tell Lindy all about it. Darling, darling Glory. What a lovely, lovely surprise. Don't cry, my pet. Come into the wardrobe room and tell Lindy all about it.

I was following her, I'd always done what Mrs Pasmore said, come into the wardrobe room, Glory, go and find my scissors, there's a pet, pass me that tape measure, lovie, hold this, fetch that, sit down there, my sweet, let me look at you. Well! Our Glory! Come back right out of the blue and looking like a top model, what a lovely, lovely girl you are, and what a wonderful, wonderful surprise. Now, don't say a word, there's a fresh pot of coffee on the ring, paper hankies behind you on the shelf, my pet, don't rub, don't make your eyes red, just a little wipe, that's my love, do you take milk?

She was so lovely, all brisk and bustling and doing everything just right, so expert and clever in her own world, and she was smiling at me, happy to see me, and chatting on so I didn't have to say anything.

But she'd ask soon. Those photographs, Glory. Yes, we all saw them, we hadn't thought you were like that. Had she forgotten? And when she remembered, that lovely smile would fade, it would vanish, and her eyebrows would level and she'd look at me from under them the way she had when Terry said she needed another abortion, another week away in London, when she remembered the photographs.

So I looked down into the mug of coffee, and I listened as she told me how Reeve had got himself nicely settled in Australia with the film company, got himself married to a pretty, pretty lass from Ireland, and Norman Jack had gone over and joined him only a year later, not on props now, logistics or something they called it, but that was all right. And Louise, she'd married, she had four kids now, one a year it seemed, silly, silly girl, no better than a rabbit and her figure all gone, but still, she was happy. Sue was teaching drama up north, drug addicts or something nasty, but sometimes she gets a little part in something, panto, or advertisements, see her on telly sometimes, and Terry, oh, my *dear*. One of her nastier men friends, beat her up, broke her jaw and her nose, well. That's her looks gone, and I do have to say, my sweetie, she didn't have much else. Bad,

bad business, but not much of a surprise to anybody. And Jim Priest! Would you *believe* it, my pet, *Hollywood*. Truly, that's where he is, and doing very nicely, thank you. Sent me a box of ostrich feathers for Christmas, extravagance!

'What about you?' I asked.

Oh, what a business! Done a bit of everything, selling shoes, alterations in a tailor's shop, laundry work, then Sue put me on to this agency, well. I was very, very doubtful, you know agencies. Don't ring us, we'll ring you isn't the half of it, but, my lovie, I haven't been out of a shop since! Now they've booked me for this one, and I just don't know. Well! Cambridge, and the writer's a don, ever so clever, I just don't know, I really don't. I mean, clever's all very well, but he's not a *professional*, he doesn't know what can be done and what can't.

She hadn't remembered. I was feeling sick. I couldn't drink my coffee, I was feeling so sick. I had to know.

'Donald Flint?'

Donald Flint, she didn't seem to know, had she forgotten him? Have you been forgotten, filth, slug, slug man, are you oblivion, Donald Flint?

But then her chest swelled, Mrs Pasmore's angry hen look, she had remembered, oh yes, Donald Flint, dirty, dirty beast. Out on his ear, no more of that sort of nonsense, thank you very much. The Goliath play, the two little girls, nice girls they were, from that Red Roofs school, not like some of the brats they tried to push on to the stage, very nice, polite little lasses, and Dave had found that dirty beast Donald Flint down by the wardrobe room, her wardrobe room, trying to put his hand up the little girl's skirt. Didn't even give him time to collect his things, Dave and Jim and Alan had him out through the stage door, about fifteen seconds it took, Reeve telephoned the agency and told them, that poor, poor little lass, so they didn't call the police, thought she'd been through enough, never mind questions from the police. Oh, yes, that's enough of Donald Flint,

235

thank you very much, but why was I asking? Glory, sweetie? Don't cry, sweetie, what's the matter? Tell Lindy, what's the matter?

'I ought to be going,' I said. 'I'm here to work.'

I was already working, she insisted, I was with her, she was the wardrobe mistress and something of a power in this place, oh yes. Paper hankies, Glory, just a little wipe, that's right, now. Behind you, in that little cupboard, no, dear, at the back in the dark corner, there's a tiny, tiny bottle, and it's a secret, please, sweetie, just for emergencies. A few drops in your coffee, now drink it, my pet, good girl.

She was thinking while she was talking, and her face grew very pink, and her chest swelled up again.

He didn't! Try it on with you, did he? That dirty, dirty beast, trying it on with our Glory? But, pet, why didn't you say? They'd have broken every bone in his body, trying it on with our Glory, well! You poor, sweet love.

Then her eyes were wide and anxious, and she sat down beside me, her hand on my knee, and looked up into my face.

Didn't succeed, did he? Sweetie, he didn't rape you, did he? My pet?

She hadn't mentioned the photographs. Had she forgotten? Nobody could have forgotten the photographs. He was going to leave them for people to find, everybody would have seen them. He'd got copies. The first copy for the star, he'd said, that was only right, the one he'd left in the Green Room, for me, but the others, left around for everybody to see.

She was distressed, she was taking my silence for assent, her fingers were digging into my knee and her mouth was working.

'No,' I said. 'He didn't succeed.'

Somebody was calling my name, I could hear a voice in the corridor outside, and then there was a crackling, buzzing sound from a loudspeaker high on the wall in the corner, and Tony's voice.

'Glory, will you please stop playing hide and seek and get up here to the stage? Where the . . . Where *are* you?'

'I'd better go,' I said, and she nodded, there was relief in her smile, and she patted my knee and nodded again. Shining black eyes, and her hair freshly dyed and smart and tidy, pinned up in its bun, our Mrs Pasmore, where she should be, in a wardrobe room, busy and brisk, and important.

'Our Glory! How *lovely*, our Glory back again.'

Tony was impatient and exasperated, the man who had written the play would want to ask questions, and so would the director, where had I been, for God's sake?

'With the wardrobe mistress,' I answered, and I was trying to listen to him, and I was aware of two stage hands putting up our pieces of scaffolding in front of another set, checking our diagrams, but I was thinking of Mrs Pasmore, who hadn't mentioned photographs, and Donald Flint, who had molested a little girl in the Royal and would never find another job in the theatre, and I could not understand. It was not until we were driving back to London in the evening that I asked myself whether he hadn't after all left other copies of the book lying around for everybody to find, and with that question came nothing but blankness. I could not think beyond it.

'Are you ill?'

Who had asked that? Rat, Rat Wright, was that him?

'*Bastard!*'

'What?'

Tony, startled, looking across at me.

'Sorry, Tony. So sorry, I was thinking of something else.'

It was all right, he said, I was welcome to call him a bastard if I wanted to, but what the hell was the matter? I hadn't said a word for hours.

Tony Marks was my good friend, might even have given me back my life by taking me to Cambridge, by making me do my best, making me work, and think, and dig into my mind through my own life to find answers.

237

'One day I may be able to tell you,' I said. 'But not just yet.'

He glanced across at me again, curious and puzzled.

'Anything I can do.' It wasn't a question, just a statement from a good friend, anything he could do, he would. I had only to ask.

I didn't know what to ask, even of myself. I sat in the van, watching the cars coming towards us, trying to find something to hold on to, something my mind could grasp, somewhere to start.

Lindy Pasmore, in the theatre again, not weary and bedraggled in a steaming laundry, but smart and tidy again, happy. I could think of this, not considering yet what it all meant, but I could think of our Mrs Pasmore, I could just picture her in her new wardrobe room with the ironing boards and the sewing machines and her patterns and drawings on the board by the window. I could remember her voice, happily gossiping and passing on the news and the opinions, while the steam rose from the coffee machine, and her smile, and her bright, sparkling eyes. I could remember that.

I could start there. Perhaps I could start again, there.

17

We had only three weeks in which to finish the set. The play that was running when we first went to Cambridge was a disaster, the house three-quarters empty, agencies returning tickets by the block, the manager declaiming he was bankrupt, ruined.

'Two months, you said,' argued Tony. 'What the hell do you think we are?'

'Busy,' answered the manager, narrowing his eyes. 'Busy. Which is a fucking sight better than out of work, sorry, Miss Mayall, didn't notice you there, I do beg your pardon. So sorry.'

'Busy, busy, busy,' muttered Tony, defeated. 'Busy, busier, busiest. Come on, Glory. Come and be Superwoman, or Boadicea, or someone.'

'I'd rather be Einstein.'

I was feeling discouraged. We hadn't solved the problem with the lights, we'd tried every trick we knew, but either the effect was lost from halfway back in the auditorium, or the feeling of unending distance vanished.

I knew what I wanted, I knew it would work, I could close my eyes and remember the desolation and see the faint lines of light, and I knew it would call up the effect of vast spaces, of isolation.

'Bloody gargoyles,' growled Tony, but he was just avoiding the real problem.

Some of the gargoyles were rats. I'd alternated them around the plinth of a building that stretched up into the sky, a rat and a bloated, puffy face with a slack mouth and upraised, pleading eyes, a rat and an old, lined face with a humble smile, a rat and something blurred, eroded by time, half turned away, was that a dog collar around its neck? Should there be a sparkle, something blue?

'Getting too interesting,' warned Tony. 'Going to distract them from the play. Why all the rats?'

Rats with flickering blue eyes? Little red flickering lights?

'Wherever man has been there are rats,' I answered, avoiding his question. 'I don't know which are the bigger pest. Lights, Tony. Or do we have to start again?'

We had no time to start again.

And David Wright was beginning to threaten me.

'Be *available*, my sweet,' he said. 'I don't want to lose my customers. There are other *tarts* around offering specialist services, and I am tired of getting no reply to your telephone.'

'I have other things to do, Rat.'

He smiled, gleeful and triumphant.

'Could you do them in Holloway? I've found *such* a helpful man, he sells newspapers. Lucien Rathbone knocked his stand over one winter night, slipped on the ice, he remembers *exactly* which night it was because of the headlines, and he'd just had his second delivery of the *Evening Standard*, regular as clockwork. That's your club, Gloriana, my dear. That's my third witness.'

'He's a damned liar.'

'Oh, yes, of course.' He had won this time, and he knew it. His hand reached out and flicked at my cheek, contemptuous. 'But blandly convincing, and no criminal record. Oh, yes, I do have access, I have *very* good contacts.'

'Bastard.'

240

He affected to stifle a yawn, and turned away from me.

'Tomorrow, *and* the next day, and the day after that, which is one of your double pay customers, you'll be glad to hear. But I think you can have Friday night off. Unless something comes up, of course.'

Tony was furious.

'This is *not* a part-time job, you stupid cow!' he yelled. 'What appointments? For *Christ's* sake, be realistic, this is your *career* we're talking about here.'

'I know. Sorry.'

'"Sorry",' he mimicked. 'She's "sorry", she's not the only one. You just *cancel* these fucking appointments, Gloriana, you have *important work* to do, and I mean in *Cambridge*, where all the clever people sit on their arses arguing with each other.'

I couldn't meet his eyes.

'I have got to be in London for the next three evenings, Tony. I can't get out of it. I really can't.'

He couldn't believe me. He shook his head, turned away from me, looked at me again, helplessly bewildered.

'I don't understand. I thought you took this seriously. Don't you see? Please, listen. This is your career. And it's mine. Tony Marks, not bad but turns up with part-timers, so don't rely on him.'

'Sorry.'

He wasn't listening.

'Glory Mayall, all right when she's there, but that's not when you need her. Forget it.

'They won't *beg* you, Glory. They'll just make do with somebody not as good, somebody with a bit of commitment, somebody they can depend on. Are you hearing me?'

That night I lay on the golden floor of the granary, my head resting on my folded arms as I looked at the shape under the green and gold rug, and I thought, Rat, this is a card you can only play once. And when you do, you've lost me. What am I worth to you, Rat?

What am I worth to myself? What do I dare risk?

Hundreds of photographs of my face, of the thin child's face, three witnesses to say that Lucien Rathbone could not have gone to a club on the night he killed himself, but if the Rat used any of this he had lost me.

How much money was there lying under the green and gold rug? Blue envelopes, folded banknotes, never touched, never counted. How much had he made from me, Rat, Rat Wright, how much money had I earned for him?

What am I worth to him? What am I worth to myself? What do I dare risk?

Mrs Pasmore was working with velvet again, grey this time, I had seen it, I had run my hands over it, and remembered when we had made a dress from velvet together. Mrs Pasmore had been telling people I was lucky for a theatre, the new play, it would go well.

It was called *A Long Time Away*, and she joked with me about it, how long I had been away, wasting my time at school when I should have been working properly. A long time away, a very long time.

Iron scaffolding, and I had set a long, precise curve into the main strut which had made Tony grind his teeth, and then grin and call me clever clogs and smart alec. He had walked the length of the auditorium backwards as I set it up, calling out directions.

'Right. That's about it, that *is* it, right, righter, rightest. Good, better, best, you are the *best*, smarty pants, that's *it*.'

Grey velvet, plaster gargoyles on painted plywood, it was coming together, this set, it was difficult, but it would work, the curve in the scaffolding had almost done it, but we still had to find the lights.

'Oh!' exclaimed Mrs Pasmore when she saw the scaffolding. 'Oh, my pet, that *is* a clever, clever bit of work. The *moment* I saw you I knew we were in luck.'

Was it worth the risk, to be lucky for a theatre again? If I challenged the Rat, defied him to take his little bits of evidence and his photographs to the police, would he do it? Would he lose me, find somebody else, and use the example of me in prison to strengthen his hand against the next girl he could blackmail?

I didn't know.

There was a row the next day, the director wanted part of a scene rewritten, preferably cut, the writer called him obtuse, obstinate and obfuscated, and damned him to 'the obscurity you so richly deserve'.

'Julian . . .'

'Doctor May to you.'

The cast was on stage, smiling brightly at each other, or frowning over scripts, or staring into the middle distance with pursed lips as they rethought their approaches to their roles, all perfectly and carefully oblivious to the verbal storm in the darkened auditorium.

'I am *not* asking you to drop it completely . . .'

'Half the characterisation rests on that speech.'

I was working on my plaster gargoyles, wondering if I dared put glass in their eyes, if they weren't becoming too important, too interesting, as Tony had protested. Plaster is difficult for me, it dries so fast, it doesn't give me time to think as I work. And the raised voices were a distraction, as was the nice middle-aged actress who was watching me. It gave her something to do rather than listen to the quarrel.

'Clever!' she remarked brightly. 'Why rats?'

'They'll take over the world when we're gone.'

She shuddered delicately.

'Plaster,' she remarked. 'When I broke my ankle I had it in plaster for six weeks, I got a part in a hospital drama, wasn't that lucky?'

'Fantastic,' I agreed.

A plaster cast. Hospital.

'Dreary part. Still, can't have everything. At least it was work.'

A plaster cast. A cast of actors. A cast of the dice.

'"Slave! I have set my life upon a cast,/And I will stand the hazard of the die!"' I exclaimed.

She laughed delightedly.

'Oh, how silly! *Richard III*, and do you know, I broke my ankle in Richmond? How does it go on? Just a moment.'

And from behind her, the leading actor, Stephen Ainsley, speaking rather diffidently.

'"I think there be six Richmonds in the field/Five have I slain today instead of him." Isn't that it?'

'Yes!' exclaimed Felicity. 'Of course it is.'

And she threw out her arms as they chanted in unison,

'"A horse! a horse! my kingdom for a horse!"'

And we all laughed together, delighted with our cleverness.

Later that afternoon they made the telephone call for me, Felicity as Sister Frank from the Accident and Emergency Department of Cambridge General Hospital, Miss Mayall had been most insistent that she telephone, was she speaking to Mr Wright? Yes, an accident, a fall on the stairs. Yes, quite a bad break, it seemed, the elbow, Dr Martello had said three days. No, Miss Mayall was not available to speak on the telephone.

And Stephen, brusque and impatient as Dr Martello, at least a month in plaster, Mr Wright. No, not a day earlier, are you questioning my professional judgement? Miss Mayall is under sedation, you most certainly may not speak to her.

In the background the cast called out to each other, rattled objects to sound like trolleys, spoke into an enamel jug which echoed just like a public address system, and played tapes of telephone bells. Not a smile passed between them while they were doing this, they were professionals, and even though they were acting as a favour for a friend, they were working, seriously working.

But when Stephen put down the telephone, they grinned at each other, and I hugged him, dear Dr Martello, and Sister Frank, I kissed her, and we all laughed.

Although I was laughing with them I knew it was a huge favour they had done for me. Actors are shy about their skills, particularly with each other.

It was a conspiracy, and my refusal to give them any explanation only heightened their speculation. Jealous boyfriend was the most popular suggestion, but the theories grew wilder as the day progressed.

He did, of course, telephone the hospital, and when I got home at the end of the week there was an envelope in my letter box, filthy photographs of naked, bleeding men tied to chairs, hanging by their manacled hands from wall hooks, lying on the floor, and in every one the thin child appeared, watching them, and in those steady, careful hands a whip, a rope, a knife. Sometimes a razor.

There was a message written on the envelope.

'Your last chance. Be there on Saturday night.'

Plaster casts were easy to make, although in the theatre we usually stuck the two halves together and covered the join with Blanco. This wouldn't do for Wright, and I spent Saturday afternoon making as good a job as I could of the real thing on my right elbow. I held it stiffly away from my body, trying to imagine how a broken elbow might feel, and when he opened the door I flinched away from him, as though afraid he might knock into it.

'The Cambridge General Hospital has never heard of you.'

'Did you try the private patients' wing?'

He hadn't. I saw the hesitation, and knew that, this time, I had probably got away with it.

'Do you want to see the X-rays?' I demanded, forcing anger into my voice. 'Do you know why I fell? Because I was in too much of a hurry, trying to get through the work in time to get back here. Because a rat is blackmailing me. Rat Wright. Bastard. What do you want me to do tonight?'

My voice was rising, I was beginning to shout, so he stood back and motioned me into the house. I stayed where I was, in the vile little coloured-glass porch.

'Club him with a plaster cast? I can't hold a whip.'

'Come in here!'

'I might manage a razor with my left hand. Or maybe a branding iron. What about that? Would that do?'

He seized my shoulder and dragged me into the hall, and I screamed, and kicked out at him, and remembered what Sue had once said about thinking of something sad to make yourself cry, and I thought of Ann sitting in the waiting room of a station on the night Lucille had driven her away, I told myself that was the last time I had lived with the sister I loved, and by the time Wright had slammed the door and turned towards me there were tears running down my cheeks.

'Bastard!' I said again, choking on a sob. 'You bastard. If you've damaged that break it could be six weeks before I'm out of this cast. Six weeks. I've got important things to do, and I don't mean your disgusting perverts.'

He believed me now. His lips were pulled back over his bared teeth, but his eyes were steady, staring into my face, at the tears, at my anger and pain. And then he looked away, he was thinking.

'Three weeks, you said?'

Would I argue with him? In pain, and angry, would I argue?

'*Do what you like!*' I screamed. '*I'd rather be in prison than here!*'

'Don't be silly.'

I kicked him, and as he backed away, slashed at his face with my left hand, the fingers curved into claws, and I spat at him.

'May you *rot*. I hope you die in a sewer, Rat. And I'll see you in court, I may be in prison clothes, but I'll see you there, for blackmail, standing in the dock. You bastard.'

'I'll call you a taxi,' he said, and he smiled. 'My treat, my dear Gloriana. You may have a little holiday, a little time to think, three weeks. I'm not quite stupid enough to have left

246

evidence around, so you can forget about the blackmail.'

'Then who took the photographs, Rat?'

And he spread his hands in helpless bewilderment.

'My dear Gloriana, how could I possibly know that?'

Three weeks would at least get this play set up, if we could sort out the lights, and if the writer didn't take a 'sue and be damned to you' attitude and tear up the contract, as he had already threatened. The gargoyles were finished, glittery eyes setting off the rapacity of the rats and the help-less supplication of the pleading faces, the curve in the scaffolding worked well; we had got the feeling of distance, but still the problem with the lights hung over us. Without it, nothing would be anything more than adequate. If we could find the little lines of flickering red light, this set would be something far better than merely good.

'Come on, clever clogs,' pleaded Tony. 'Think. Use the brain.'

I went to the writer instead.

'Doctor May? Could you help me?'

He was looking for somebody to talk to.

'Do you know this director?' he asked. 'This so-called director? This . . . this . . . Frederick Grafton?'

'Not very well. I've heard he can bring out the best in actors. Can you help me?'

He was middle-aged, and very polite. Somebody had told me the subject he taught was history.

'Of course, if I can.'

I sat down beside him.

'It's a problem with the lights. We've got a good idea, but we can't seem to make it work. We need them to flicker, you see. To give a feeling of distance.'

A woman had asked for his help, and he was the sort of man to regard an appeal from a woman as a claim on his chivalry; he could not refuse. But as I talked about theatre lighting I could feel his thoughts as clearly as if he had spoken them.

247

Oh, God. Secondary school physics.

I began to stammer.

'It's as though you're losing something,' I said. My throat was tight and dry. I had to make him understand. 'It's all breaking up. That's why we need the effect. Do you see?'

He nodded, but it was a polite nod. Do, please, go on.

'It's as though something is connected to you, but it's drifting away.' Ann, going away, driven away, alone. Lucien, gone. Think. How to explain this? This man might help. 'It breaks up. It's a line, little red lights. Like darkness, before sunrise? When the sky's really dark, except for the line of red light. Do you see? In a dark sky, a line of red light? And then it starts to break up.'

He wasn't looking at me now, he was looking down at his hand, at the back of his hand, as though he'd written something there. I'd seen him do that before, when he was thinking. I waited.

'I'm not sure,' he said at last. 'I think I see what you mean. There's somebody I know who's working on . . .'

And again, looking at the back of his hand, and thinking.

'Yes,' he said. 'I'll ask him.'

Piped light, they called it, and it had been on the market for a while, but this was a development nobody had seen yet. He brought it to us rather shyly, Dr May's friend Simon Azinski, as though he was afraid we might laugh at it, or perhaps at him. He wouldn't look at us, and he couldn't explain it, he could only shrug, and say, vaguely, that he thought it might be what we were looking for. Perhaps, if he could show us?

We took him to the light board, and he became another person. I'd seen this before, for a while I wondered who it was he reminded me of, and then I realised, it was Ann, with the metal shears in her hand, at Storrington, working on the set for *Macbeth*. As soon as this man was given the tools of his work, he became a craftsman, sure, and quick. He knew exactly what he was doing, and the theatre lighting technician, at first suspicious, then relaxed, and finally extremely respectful, turned himself into an apprentice, and took advantage of a situation in which he could learn from a master.

It was exactly what we needed. The lights moved, and shimmered, and the effect was what I had seen at those times when I was lost, when I had lost something of myself, or something I loved.

I couldn't stay in the theatre, I went out and walked the streets of Cambridge, and it was raining, so nobody noticed the tears on my face. It hurt, it hurt so much, it was like cutting into my mind and laying it open for everybody to see, I wondered if it could be worth this, just for a play, for an effect. Showing my mind, my pain, my loss. Just for an effect, for a play.

The next day Jacob Goldman came to Cambridge.

'I'm Fagin,' he said in a pantomime voice, thick and throaty, leering at everybody. 'I've got gangs of girls and boys working for me.'

Old, and bent, with a hooked nose that nobody would have dared to put on as stage make-up, in a long black coat, with a black hat on his head, Jacob Goldman loved the part he had cast for himself.

Everybody was delighted to see him, Felicity hugged him, Stephen grinned at him and pumped his hand, and Frederick Grafton called him dear, dear Jacob, how super.

He looked at our set, and he leered again, making Felicity giggle.

'Oh, *yes*,' he said. 'Oh, I think so. Who's got the brains, then? Who thought *that* up?'

Everybody looked at me, and he bowed, blinking his hooded eyes, wringing his hands.

'I've got no arms and no legs,' he said. 'That's how I don't chuck the money about. I pay your wages as though it's my last penny and I'm starving. Would you like to work for me, you clever little darling?'

'You'd be a fool not to,' said Tony as we drove back to London that night. 'Yes, smarty pants, it was me who telephoned him. You, Gloriana Mayall, are something special, and Jacob Goldman is the man to recognise it.'

'Why haven't I heard of him?'

'You haven't been in the theatre, have you? You can't work in the theatre for long nowadays and not hear of Jacob. One of the biggest of the angels, he backs winners, too.'

Mrs Pasmore was even more enthusiastic.

'My sweet, sweet girl, you'd be *made*,' she said. 'You have to be good, mind. No second raters for Jacob, oh no. But if you *are* good you'll be on oiled wheels. Don't be fooled by the act, he's got lots of money, he's a very, very clever man with money.'

'Would I be in London?' I asked him when he came back again the following week, and he wagged his head, and his eyes twinkled at me.

'Hmm, hmm, hmm. West End, you mean? You have to be a very clever girl to get into the West End, even for Uncle Jacob.'

'Where, then?'

'You'll have to travel, my dear. Theatre digs, it'll be. Not got cats, have you?' Suddenly he was anxious, his eyes a little wide as he peered at me.

'No. Why?'

'Oh, that's good. I've got cats. They don't like travelling and they don't like being left alone, so I have to be home nights, otherwise there's merry hell to pay. That's why I can handle leading ladies, my clever darling. I've got five Persian cats, and they all have to be humoured and treated like ladies. If I can handle Sonia and Flora and Canticle and Jemima and Abracadabra, actresses are a doddle, no trouble at all, not compared with those cats.'

'At least cats don't drink champagne,' I offered, and he grasped my arm, a caricature of terror on his face.

'Don't tell my cats about champagne, my clever darling!

250

Please don't tell my cats about champagne, lobster's nearly bankrupted me, champagne, oh, *please* don't tell them.'

'Has he *really* offered you a job?' asked Frederick Grafton, but I didn't know. There'd been leers, and grins, and he'd told me horror stories about starving in garrets. Members of the cast had looked at our set, and looked at me, and made thumbs-up signs.

'Jacob Goldman!' exclaimed Felicity. 'You lucky girl.'

'He really has got five Persian cats,' said Stephen. 'He adores them. He grooms them himself every day, it takes about two hours.'

I'd have to travel. I wouldn't be in London. I'd have to live in theatre digs.

The Rat. Rat Wright.

'Oh, I don't *think* so,' he said when I telephoned him. 'I don't think I can have you running all around the country, not for weeks on end. Oh, no, my dear Gloriana, I need you here, in London. Available. How's the elbow? Nearly healed, I hope?'

When I told Tony Marks that I didn't think I could move away from London, I thought at first he hadn't heard me. I was about to repeat myself when I looked at him and saw his eyes on me, an expression of cold dislike on his face.

'Your course ends in six weeks,' he said. 'I shan't want you back after that.'

'Tony, that wasn't . . .'

'I should start looking for a job in advertising. Bathroom cleaners and pizzas. That way, you can stay in London.'

He walked away from me before I could answer, and I felt tears starting to my eyes. I hadn't realised how much I valued his good opinion until I earned his contempt.

'Not *take* it?' exclaimed Mrs Pasmore. 'But, my dear, dear Glory, why not? There's nothing better, you know. Nothing, nothing at all, not in this work, nothing better than Jacob. Oh, my *dear*. I don't understand. Not take a job with Jacob Goldman?'

I told Sam Cooper that everybody was pleased with the set, and he smiled at me, and said it called for a celebration. Where would I like to go?

He took me to Stratford, and we went to the theatre to see what was playing. It was *Titus Andronicus*, and we looked at the posters, and looked at each other, and shrugged, and went for a walk by the river instead.

'Even Shakespeare . . .' I said.

My *Macbeth* set. Would I ever see it? Would I ever be able to make a set with white curves against a white backdrop, shadows and shapes? Would I see my swords of light reflected on shining metal?

Would I run out on another theatre?

'You're very quiet,' said Sam.

I wasn't thinking about Sam as we drove home that evening, but there was an army cap on the back seat of the car he had borrowed and a Sam Browne belt tucked into the padded leather pocket of the passenger door. Sam Cooper, an honest soldier, a decent, kind man, who had never touched me, except once, on the steps of the college. He went to that house sometimes, he made appointments, never spoke about it when we were together, never mentioned the thin child.

That evening I invited him into the granary, I offered to cook something for us, and he said that would be grand, he'd help, he could peel potatoes or chop onions.

When I asked him if he would do something for me I didn't know what it was I was going to demand of him. It was quite a casual question, but my hand was on his arm, just resting on his arm, slim fingers against the white cotton of his shirt, had he noticed how slim my fingers were? How the nails were polished, and almond-shaped, what a pretty hand it was, resting on his arm?

He had noticed. He was smiling as he looked down at me, and he answered my question.

'I'd die for you,' he said, and he said it simply, so I

252

believed it. He meant it. Then she was there, the thin girl, she shouldn't have been there, she was never there, not in my home. I didn't know what she was doing, but I heard her voice, the way she spoke in that other house, the contempt.

'Oh, die. Everybody's got to die. Die for me, that's a bit passive.'

Then I knew what she would say, I watched his face, a little surprised, he had never heard her here, not in the granary, but he smiled again, his nice smile on his honest face.

'What then?'

I watched the nice smile fade, I watched his eyes, I saw sorrow and something like shame, I watched him as she spoke, as she framed the dreadful question.

'Would you kill for me, Sam? Would you *kill* for me?'

18

Jacob Goldman wanted to send me to work in Bolton, with a little company that only did theatre work as a sideline.

'A little bit of everything, my clever darling,' was how Jacob described it. 'Advertising, bit of television, bit of film, making pretty dresses for pretty ladies. But you're one of Fagin's theatre gangs, don't you worry. You won't forget the smell of greasepaint.'

'In Bolton?'

The subservient leer that he used to express amusement crossed his face.

'Get the *experience*, my clever darling. It's a graveyard, so what? If you're going to die, do it out of sight, don't be messy in public. Get your flops out of the way in a place where nobody will *notice* them.'

I didn't intend to have flops, but Frederick Grafton said I should wait until I'd seen the scripts before I got cocky.

'The things some people want to put on,' he said, 'you wouldn't believe. You just wait, Glory Mayall. Wait until somebody too important to snub turns up with a "Rehally rahather *good* little piece" written by his favourite grand-daughter.'

He wiped imaginary sweat off his brow, and asked me to go and be nice to Dr May, 'who's having a tantrum in a

254

broom cupboard somewhere. You seem to exert a soothing influence.'

I'd telephoned Robert Cameron to ask about Jacob Goldman, and he'd known the name well.

'Jacob Goldman? *The* Jacob Goldman?'

'I think so.'

'Good heavens, girl. Well, not quite the richest man in the country, but nudging it, nudging it. Yes. I think I can safely say, yes, you should take that. Good heavens! You *do* seem to land on your feet.

'By the way, Revelations. Do you need money out of it this year?'

'Not especially.'

'Orek's begging us to let him use last year's profits to bid for a collection, nineteenth-century prints, he wants the collection intact if possible. I think he's right. And if you could ask Lord Chendar not to go after it?'

When I went home in the evenings during that last week before the opening night, I wasn't thinking about Revelations, or Patrick Chendar. I would sit on the floor of the granary, and shiver. I couldn't sleep properly, I had vague nightmares, vivid as I jerked awake, fading almost immediately, as though I tried to grasp water, it ran away through my fingers, leaving only a feeling of cold, a memory of shamed eyes and voices calling through the dark.

I waited for a telephone call, from the Rat, or from Sam. It was nearly two weeks now. Which would it be, that gleeful, triumphant voice? Or Sam, subdued and weary?

He had sat in the armchair, listening, sometimes asking questions, he had the photographs, he held them, looked at them, his hands were slack, sometimes he dropped them and then bent to pick them up again, and he looked, he said nothing, he just seemed tired, looking at pictures of those other men, naked, bruised and wounded men, and the thin girl, he listened, and he asked.

255

Careful questions. He was thinking, he was planning, had he learned this? How to kill, not on the battlefield, but in secret, shameful and dark? Had he learned this? Those careful questions, nodding slowly as he listened to the answers, thinking. Long, silent pauses as he thought, but always in his eyes the look of sorrow, he was already grieving for something precious to him that he would lose, grieving for himself, for the man he had been.

A decent, kind man, and she had turned him into a murderer.

There was no telephone call. There was an envelope, a ticket from a left luggage office at Paddington station. When I presented the ticket, there were three big cardboard boxes, and they were heavy. The taxi driver helped me, carried them up the stairs to the granary, waved away the tip I offered.

Two of the boxes were full of photographs, the other contained negatives, and notebooks. Names, addresses, dates.

Was it all here? Was this everything? Was I free?

I should have been relieved, but suddenly I was terrified. Had Sam found it all? Was Wright dead? What had happened?

Frantic, I looked through the boxes for a letter, for something from Sam, some explanation, but there was nothing. I looked through the notebooks, searching for something to tell me what he had done, but there were just names, and addresses, telephone numbers, dates. And cryptic notes in spiky handwriting. Nothing from Sam.

I sat on the floor, shaking and shuddering, and I looked at the photographs, the first, the second, and then threw them back in the box, feeling ill. So sick, all that pain, all that need, that pleading and begging, the tears, I could hear them, those men. I could hear them. Were those the voices, calling in the dark? Were those the voices in my dream?

All that night I sat by the three boxes, cutting photographs into tiny pieces, cutting negatives into tiny pieces, cutting notebooks into tiny pieces. My hand was bleeding. At first it had been sore, from the handles of the scissors, then blisters had appeared, and burst, and the raw flesh under the torn skin began to bleed. I didn't notice until the blood dripped on to the golden floor, and then I stopped and looked down at it, at the bright, bright blood, and I watched for a while until it stopped, my mind was drifting, slow and far away, and then the bright blood darkened, I climbed to my feet and fetched a cloth to clean it off the shining wood, and I bandaged my hand.

The blood soaked through the bandage and dripped on to the floor again, but this time I didn't stop, I went on, cutting, and cutting, tiny pieces of paper, of hard cellulose, the scissors growing blunt, so I threw them away and found another pair, and sat on the floor, and the blood spread as I watched it, drops of blood spreading, and running together, a little pool of blood, spreading to the drops beside it, the bright colour, the light shining on the red blood and the golden floor, and the little pieces of paper. But I went on, and on, and when I had finished, when there was nothing left but the blank, hard covers of the notebooks, and the drifts of paper, and the blood on the floor, it was daylight, bright daylight, sun through the windows, and I should have been on my way to Cambridge, I would be late.

I telephoned. I've hurt my hand, I ought to go to a doctor. Can Tony manage without me today? I'll be there tomorrow, is that all right?

I washed the covers of the notebooks, washed them and rubbed them dry, the cardboard peeling in little rolled flakes under the cloth, and I put them in a paper bag, I carried them with me and tipped them into a litter bin, and crumpled the paper bag and dropped it into another bin, and I caught the underground train and for the last time I walked down that road in south London, the road with the small, dreary stucco houses.

But that house was a burnt shell, blackened and filthy, the roof half collapsed, smoke stains around the door and the holes where the windows had been. The nasty little garden was trampled and soaked, a ruin of charred wood and broken tiles, and there was still a smell, the smell of fire, a smell of disaster.

I stood on the other side of the road, and stared.

Fire. Had the Rat burned? Had he died screaming, and squealing, and fighting flames and choking on smoke? Was this what Sam had done, to buy my freedom?

A man walking an old dog stopped beside me, looking across at the house.

'Shocking,' he said. 'Shocking.'

'Was anybody hurt?' I asked.

'Oh, dead. He was dead, poor chap.'

And then he looked at me, eager with curiosity, eyes beady behind his spectacles.

'Did you know him, then?'

'Oh, no,' I said. 'I was just calling on a client back there. What a dreadful thing. When did it happen?'

'Monday night. Tuesday morning, rather. Early hours.' He shook his head again. 'Shocking. You an estate agent, then? Lots of houses going up for sale around here.'

I smiled at him, thinking quickly. I'd been stupid to come.

'This one's buying, not selling,' I answered, and then I looked back across the road. 'But she wants something in better condition than that.'

He snuffled a laugh, and followed his dog a few paces down the road to the lamp post.

'I bet. Oh, well, keep smiling, eh?'

I went home and tried to telephone Sam. There was no reply.

My hand was stinging, the raw flesh weeping a clear fluid when I soaked off the bandage.

It felt like a burn.

I went to the surgery at the bottom of the street that

evening, I'd never been there before, I hadn't needed a doctor since I'd moved to the granary.

'How did you do this?' he demanded as he looked at my hand.

Too many lies, too many plausible explanations on the spur of the moment, I couldn't think of any more. I just looked at him.

'It hurts,' I said.

'I'm sure it does. How did you do it?'

His tone was sharp, I have a right to interrogate you, I am a doctor, I am your superior, answer my questions when I speak to you.

'That's none of your damned business.'

He looked as though I had slapped him, shocked and startled.

'I *beg* your pardon?'

'You certainly should. Don't take such a tone with me again. They're friction blisters. I expect that's what they're called.'

He was still staring into my face, his mouth slightly open, breathing as though he had been winded.

You are not *my* superior, Dr Levett. I am Gloriana Mayall, Jacob Goldman calls me his clever darling, and with good reason. I bet nobody as important as Jacob Goldman ever called *you* a clever darling, Dr Levett.

'It will need an antiseptic ointment and a clean, dry dressing.'

I spoke clearly, slowly and carefully, and he swallowed, and turned away.

'I know how to treat blisters, thank you.'

I walked home, and dialled Sam's number again. There was still no reply.

Three days to opening night, and Julian May and Frederick Grafton were barely on speaking terms, but Julian had rewritten the scene, and Fred had enthused, overdoing it, super, really just what he'd wanted, great. And could we, Tony and Glory, put some dinky little spots in the foreground? He wanted Felicity's jewellery to sparkle.

'What's it called, when you can see into the future?' I asked Tony.

'Precognition. Why?'

'Your idea. Your words. Dinky little spots.'

'Sounds more like acne than lighting.'

He hadn't forgiven me. He had persuaded Jacob Goldman I was worth seeing, worth considering, and it couldn't have been easy, not to bring Jacob to Cambridge to look at a set designed by somebody he had never heard of, an unknown, and a student at that. Even thinking about not taking a job with Jacob, after everything Tony had done to try to bring the two of us together, was some sort of blasphemy. He could not forget, and would not forgive. He didn't swear at me any more. He was polite, he talked to me as a colleague, but he was no longer my friend.

On the night before the dress rehearsal, Sam answered his telephone.

'It's Glory,' I said. 'Hello.'

'Glory. Yes. Hello, Glory.'

He sounded tired. He wasn't glad to hear my voice. He didn't want to talk to me. There'd been a pause before he answered, a long silence, as though something was dragging.

'I've been trying to contact you all week.'

Silence again, and then, when he spoke, there was distance, he had turned his head away, he was looking at something else, not speaking straight into the telephone.

'I've been away. In Scotland.'

'Did you have a nice time?'

What a stupid, stupid question. But my throat was tight, and dry, I couldn't think properly, I could only picture Sam holding the telephone, looking away at something else, not wanting to talk to me, for the first time, not wanting to talk to me.

'I did as you asked,' he said at last. 'It's all done.'

'Are you sure? Are you absolutely sure?'

'He told me everything I needed to know.'

Oh, Sam. What did you have to do to him before you killed him? Decent, kindly man, what did you have to do?

'I'm going away,' he said. 'I've been posted. To Hong Kong.'

'Oh. Hong Kong?'

'Yes. Very soon. I may not have time to . . .'

His voice faded away, vague, not really thinking of what he was saying. Then he spoke again.

'So I'd better say goodbye now. I may not . . . I may not have time . . .'

'Sam, the photographs. There would have been you, too.' I was crying. 'He would have had photographs of you. You know.'

But Sam had gone.

He had never lied to me.

I wanted time to think, but there was no time, with the dress rehearsal, opening night, Fred was still worrying and fretting about Felicity's jewellery, it was an important factor in the play, he wanted to draw it to the audience's attention. Little spotlights, we had to have little spotlights, he insisted.

Time to think, but all I could find to grasp was that Sam had never lied to me, and he had gone. I tried to remember his face, I knew it was kind, and that he had a nice smile, but the details were blurred, I couldn't even remember the colour of his eyes. He was kind, he had never lied to me, he had gone.

Tony was distant, and cool, and he, too, had never lied to me. He had contacted Jacob Goldman and told him there was somebody special working in Cambridge, and Jacob had come to Cambridge to see. My clever darling, Jacob had called me. What had Tony told him? Jacob wouldn't have taken me into one of his Fagin's gangs on the strength of one stage set.

261

And I had said . . . What had I said?

I had said I didn't want to leave London.

The dress rehearsal went well. Fred Grafton had said he did not, absolutely did not, believe the stage superstition that a bad dress rehearsal meant a successful run. A bad dress rehearsal all too often meant bad preparation.

He stared severely at the cast and the technicians.

'Any questions?' he demanded, defying them to disagree.

It wasn't easy. The new spotlights blew a fuse on the light board, the technician only just managed to rig up an extra cable from another power source half a minute before the curtain went up. A pulley jammed up in the grids, and my efforts to free it made my hand bleed again, blood dropped down on to the stage, only just missing Stephen, who was wearing a white shirt. One of the dressers scorched the front panel of a dress, and Mrs Pasmore was still tacking a new one over it as the actress put it on, wriggling to avoid the needle.

'It looks quite, quite dreadful!' exclaimed Mrs Pasmore. 'That silly, silly girl.'

But at last it was over, and we all crowded on to the stage to listen to Frederick's comments.

He was fidgety, not sure whether to be pleased, he had small criticisms, he came up on to the stage and chewed his fingernails saying, yes, well. But Felicity and Stephen looked at him, and looked at each other, and Felicity turned towards the auditorium, and called out in a screechy cockney accent, totally at variance with the character she was playing and the costume she was wearing.

'Julian? Julian, me old cock? You pleased? You bleedin' well oughta be!'

He came up to the stage, looking down at his feet, then shuffling and looking up at us, he seemed shy, and embarrassed, but he was smiling. Then he looked down at the back of his hand.

'I thought it went quite well,' he said.

And everybody started to laugh.

There were some changes to be made. Some of the dialogue was to be delivered more quickly, a couple of pauses to be put in, for emphasis, but on the whole he had to say it had gone well, he was pleased. They'd discuss this in detail the next morning. Thank you, cast.

Now, the set. Those spotlights, still not strong enough on the jewellery. The gargoyles, those rats, could they be highlighted a little more? They gave a suggestion of impending decay, he wanted them a little more important. Glory, can you do that?

And that curved piece of scaffolding, it needed to be raised about a foot at the front, when Stephen stood in front of it . . .

'No,' I said, and I spoke far more loudly than I had intended.

They stared at me, and I felt myself flushing.

'Sorry. But if you raise that end of it you'll lose the sense of distance.'

'Yes,' said Fred, after a slight pause, 'nevertheless, it does take away something from Stephen's entrance in the second act, so it will have to be . . .'

'Listen to Glory.'

Tony's voice, quiet, but insistent.

I walked to the front of the stage. I had to explain this properly, so he would understand. If he raised that curved piece of scaffolding, he would destroy the set.

'The sense of distance depends on that curve,' I said. 'If you raise that end of the scaffolding, it's going to look straight. From the auditorium, I mean. If you raise both ends, the perspective . . .'

He was looking irritated. I was just making silly difficulties.

Stephen and Felicity were still on stage, and Stephen stepped forward.

'I could come in from *there*.' He pointed. '*That* way I'd be

263

further away from the scaffolding, it wouldn't show.'

It would take him straight to centre stage as well, I thought, and I knew Fred would see it that way.

'Yes,' said Felicity brightly, 'and if I moved downstage we could simply have that bit of business a little closer . . .'

She waved her hands, explaining. She would, in that way, keep star position.

'No.' Fred was decisive. 'Leave the entrance as it is. Sorry, Glory, that bit of scaffolding has to be higher.'

We'd lost it. If he moved the scaffolding, he lost the whole set. All the sense of distance depended on that curve, on the curve and the little red lights, and we'd lost the curve. Just to save one unimportant entrance, we'd lost the whole set.

I looked at the curved scaffolding, telling myself I should be feeling anger and despair, but I felt nothing, only blank. Weeks of work, I told myself, the best piece of work I had ever done, and I'd lost it.

'Listen to Glory.' Tony's voice again, insistent. 'For God's sake, Fred, listen to Glory. She *knows*.'

But he wouldn't. I watched a stage hand uncoupling the bolts on the scaffolding, raising it nearly a foot, lowering it, up a bit, yes, that'll do, fixing the bolts again, and it was gone.

I turned my back on it, I looked at the gargoyles, at the rats, I told myself how I would make them more important, give them more definition, deepen the shadows here, add to a highlight there, but I was thinking mechanically, because it had been destroyed, I was just doing as I had been told now. Blankly, and obediently, I was doing as I had been told.

Tony drove me home, and we said almost nothing on the way. He was the only one who knew what had been lost, and what it meant. That curve in the scaffolding had been my idea, and from it had come all the perspective, everything that gave the dimensions to the play, and now it had gone.

The play was good. It might run. But our part in it had gone.

The set was adequate, I told myself, it was a background to a good play, and that was all a set should be.

But I didn't believe it. Our set had given that play its depth, it had stated the distance and the time, and it had been destroyed. A long time away, the title of the play, reflected in the set. Gone.

Tony tried again the next day, but Fred was impatient, busy with last-minute details, and not inclined to listen to what he thought were trivial objections. I found it difficult to speak to anybody, although I tried to be cheerful, the tension before opening night was hard enough to bear without somebody being miserable in the theatre. At least I was busy, checking bolts and toggles, working with the little spotlights, but when I had a few minutes I went to the wardrobe room and drank coffee, listening to Linda Pasmore as she sewed the new front panel into the scorched dress.

'You do land on your feet, my sweet,' she said. 'First time in a shop, well, as a proper professional anyway, and Jacob Goldman offers you a job. *Well!* Lucky, lucky girl. You must be feeling like the cat who's swallowed the canary.'

'Some canary.' I tried to smile at her, and she bit a piece of cotton thread and looked at me over her spectacles.

'So why is our lucky Glory looking so glum? Because Fred wanted the set changed?'

I smiled.

'Directors always want last-minute changes.' Her voice was brisk and matter-of-fact. 'It's a nuisance. I sometimes think the theatre would be a lovely, lovely place to work if it weren't for directors and actors.'

Would it really make such a difference?

I went into the auditorium, I stood in the shadows by the doors, and I looked at the stage, brilliant under its working lights. I listened to a young man talking about the measurements for the next production, the stage manager arguing about storage problems.

The next production.

It was still a good set. It said this is old, and this is new, and that is far away, and the rats glinted from the base of the plinth, lurking, waiting their turn, which would inevitably come. It was a good set.

Jacob Goldman, looking at that set, might have said, oh yes, not at all bad. But I didn't think he would have called me his clever darling. It did all depend on that curve, on that precise and careful curve.

'Hello, are you admiring your work?'

The manager, what was his name? For God's sake, I said to myself, working in a theatre and forgetting the manager's name.

'Hello. No, I'm not admiring my work, I'm feeling sorry for myself, if you must know.'

He stood beside me, looking at the stage, his head on one side. Nigel Byron? Not Byron, Birone, that's it.

'Something's different. What have you changed? I think I liked it better the way it was before.'

I didn't know him well, but that made it easier to talk to him. I told him about the curve, how difficult the perspective had been, how in the end it had worked, and how that small alteration to the height of the scaffolding had ruined it.

'Your first set?' he asked.

'Yes. Well, apart from student things. And school. First one on a professional stage.'

He was silent for quite a long time.

'You're right,' he said. 'It has lost that sense of distance. Have you tried shouting at Fred?'

Shout at the director?

'I don't want to get a reputation as a troublemaker,' I protested.

He shrugged.

'Sarah Bernhardt had a reputation as a troublemaker. So does Maria Callas.'

He pointed towards the stage.

'Is this the best you will ever do?'

'No!'

'Will you always let directors spoil your work? To save an unimportant entrance?'

I didn't know. I looked at him, puzzled.

He smiled, and shrugged.

'You're a good designer,' he said. 'If you're going to be a troublemaker, you'd do well to be a good troublemaker, too. Your choice, Glory Mayall. Lump it, or make it stick.'

I went on to the stage and put the scaffolding back as it had been, and then I found a stage hand.

'Weld it,' I said.

'What?'

'Weld it. That join, those bolts.' I pointed, and then held my finger against them to emphasise it. 'These bolts here. Do you see? *Weld* them.'

'But how you going . . .'

'Just do as I tell you.'

I watched him drag the big metal bottle on to the stage, set up the torch, adjust the flame, lower the visor on his helmet, and then turn the torch and the metal welding rod on to the scaffolding. My heart was beating so hard and so fast I thought I would be sick, I thought it would show, hammering in my chest like that, couldn't anybody else hear it?

The welding rod was white-hot, and he was curving it around the bolts, the flame too bright to watch, so I turned away, trying to stop myself shaking, trying to stop myself thinking I had gone mad, defying a director in a theatre, I had ruined my career, nobody would ever take me on again.

The roar of the torch died, and I turned back, saw the join red-hot, turning black. When it was cool I'd have to repaint it. Or somebody would.

I might have been thrown out by then. Out in disgrace, told never to come back.

The stage hand was looking at me.

'Okay?'

'Yes. Thank you.'

He shook his head, and bent to pick up his equipment.

'Bloody hell,' I heard him mutter.

I went up to his office, and told Frederick Grafton what I had done.

He turned white with rage.

'You've done fucking *what*?' he whispered.

'I've had it welded.' How could my voice be this steady? How could I stare him straight in the face? 'I'll highlight the silly gargoyles until they're far too interesting and important, because you say so, we'll fart around with your frigging spotlights instead of asking Julian to write in a couple of lines of dialogue about the diamonds, because you say so . . .'

He was standing up, leaning over his desk towards me, and he was shuddering with fury.

'You'll do *any* bloody thing I *tell* you, because *I say so*, Miss Mayall, because I'm the . . .'

'You're the fucking *director*, but you will *not*,' I slammed my hand on to his desk, 'you will *absolutely not* screw up the *entire fucking set* just to save *one bloody entrance*, and I *swear* I will . . .'

'*Get out of here!*'

This time when I slammed my hand on to his desk it upset the coffee over the papers he had been reading, and he looked down and grabbed at them.

'*Next* time we're talking about the fucking set, bloody well *listen*, and I mean to *me* or to *Tony*, not to your actors jockeying around for the best position. I will *not* be bloody *ignored*, not by *you*, not by any other bloody *director*, not by *God Almighty*, and *don't you damned well forget it.*'

I turned on my heel and strode out of his office before he could reply.

Troublemaker, that was the reputation I would have before I had even started. But he wouldn't be able to change that scaffolding now, there wasn't time.

'You did *what*?' Tony was aghast and horrified. 'Jesus, Glory, you just don't *do* that sort of thing. Have you gone mad?'

'Hopping mad,' I said defiantly. I was going to be sacked, I was sure of it, I told myself it would be worth it to save that set, but I still felt sick, and suddenly desperately weary.

'Christ!' Tony shook his head. 'I don't know.'

Was there something of reluctant admiration in the look he gave me?

I was still in the theatre. No apologetic stage door keeper had approached me to say Mr Grafton wanted me to leave.

I collected paint and brushes, and started to work on the blackened metal. I could hear people talking, and there was only one topic. What I had done was unthinkable. Who did I think I was? Just because Jacob Goldman had been nice to me.

But still, she'd tried to explain, and Fred hadn't listened. For God's sake, he is the director.

I went on working on the join, brushing in the paint so that it blended with the rest of the iron. I told myself I was deaf.

Frederick Grafton walked across the stage on his way to the prompt corner, threw a furious glare in my direction, and strode on, saying nothing.

Brushes to wash, I told myself, and went back to the paint store.

19

I didn't go to the pub with the others that night, and later Tony accused me of storming off home in a temper. In fact, I had run away.

I had stayed for the performance; I had had to do that, with the problems that had arisen during the dress rehearsal. Both Tony and I had hovered anxiously in the wings, he with half an eye on the light board, waiting for warning lamps, and me watching the problem pulley up in the grids.

We had been too busy with our own work to take much notice of the performance, but we would have had to have been blind and deaf not to have caught the tension, or to have been unaware of an audience as still and silent as they only can be for something special on a stage.

I had waited for the curtain calls, the applause for Felicity and Stephen, carrying a happy hint of affection for two pop-ular actors, the yells of 'Bravo!' for Frederick Grafton, and a genuine standing ovation for Julian May, but by the time Julian was making his speech, apparently reading it from the back of his hand, I had been on my way to the stage door.

I was back the next morning to supervise running repairs to the set, and also to make sure that Fred did not organise a cutting torch for the scaffolding. Having risked everything by defying him so blatantly, I braced myself to defend that action.

'My sweet, sweet love, you just don't do that sort of thing,' Mrs Pasmore said before she even greeted me. 'Surely. I mean, darling Glory, you must know? Don't you?'

'I know.'

She looked at me helplessly, shaking her head.

'Can I have a coffee?' I asked, and she sniffed.

'I suppose you think you can hide in my wardrobe room,' she said. 'And I suppose you're right. You wicked, wicked girl. And silly.'

She'd dropped a broad hint about a lucky black cat a few days earlier, and I'd painted one for her and pinned it to her board.

We were all anxious about the reviews.

The play was clever, very clever, but it was demanding, it called for an audience with a sharp appreciation for its intellectual qualities, and such work always carries a risk.

'It wouldn't have gone in the West End, you know,' I heard Fred Grafton remark as he and somebody I couldn't see walked across the stage behind the backcloth. 'For God's sake, Julian, don't let them move it there.'

Julian. Christian name terms again.

I went into one of the store rooms, and three stage hands fell silent. The same thing happened as I walked past a small group standing by the coffee counter.

'Glory?'

Nigel Birone. He drew me into a corner.

'Listen, when I said it's worth making a fuss . . .' He looked around to make sure we weren't overheard.

'Yes?'

'Well, my dear girl, I didn't mean you to go that far. I mean, defying the director like that! I do hope it wasn't anything I said that led you to . . .'

I waited, watching him grow more and more uncomfortable.

'Well, I certainly don't feel responsible for any of this,' he snapped at last, making himself angry. 'It was a ridiculous thing to do, and you'll just have to accept the consequences.'

'Don't worry,' I said, as evenly as I could. 'I wouldn't dream of letting anybody think that you have the slightest influence on me.'

But Jacob Goldman telephoned, and he didn't call me his clever darling.

'I want a word with you,' he said. 'You'd better come here now.'

I closed my eyes, feeling my lips beginning to tremble.

'What about this evening's performance?' I asked.

There was a long silence, and then he spoke quite gently.

'You'll probably be back in time for that.'

He lived in Leicester. I went up by taxi.

He opened the door almost as soon as I rang the bell, as though he had been lurking in the hall, waiting for me. He had some sort of brush in his hand, and he used it to gesture at me.

'Come in,' he said. 'Come in here, Gloriana Mayall.'

A small room, with two deep armchairs and a long sofa, the chintz covers a ruin of torn and frayed holes. There was a little television set in one corner, and a gas fire was burning, even though it was quite warm.

There were cats in the room, and I stared at them in amazement. I had never seen such enormous cats, and their fur seemed to wave around them, flowing, like silk fibres.

Jacob Goldman sat in one of the chairs and pointed with his brush at the other one.

'Sit down there. You'll be covered in cat hairs, you'll have to put up with that.'

I sat down, and a black cat with amazingly brilliant copper coloured eyes walked across the worn carpet towards me, and leapt lightly on to my lap. Copper on gleaming black, it was a beautiful combination of colours. I ran my hand over the silky fur, and the cat began to purr.

'That's Abracadabra,' said Jacob. 'Now, where's my Flora? Where's my beautiful Flora? Come along, my darling. Come on, come here.'

He was fussing around, looking for his cat, but after a few moments he gave up, and sat forward in his chair. He pointed the brush at me.

'This is my day off,' he said. 'One day a week, I like to sit around here and relax. And what happens? I have to deal with you.'

I said nothing. I watched him, and went on stroking the cat.

'I put money into the theatre,' he said. 'I don't mind that. It's my hobby, being a silly old pantomime Jew in fancy dress, I like it. But I don't like wasting time, because time is money, and I don't waste that, either. Do you know what the biggest waste of time in the theatre is?'

I shook my head.

'People who think they're important. Prima donnas, they call them. I don't bother with prima donnas, I don't care how good they are, they're not worth it. They're never worth it. Do you know why I recommend Felicity Sheldon and Stephen Ainsley? You just shut up and listen, because I'm going to tell you anyway. It's because they don't make trouble. When a director tells them to do something, they do it. They may not like it, they may have other ideas, but they do it, because they are *professionals*, Gloriana Mayall, and that means they do their best even if they don't like what they're doing. They hate the script, they want to strangle the wardrobe mistress, the director never knew his father, but they do it, they get on with their jobs.'

He fidgeted in his chair, looking around on the floor and muttering to himself.

'Flora? Where's my beautiful Flora, then?'

And then he sat upright again, and pointed the brush straight at my face.

'Now, you, Gloriana Mayall. Which are you? Are you a prima donna or are you a professional?'

I stared back at him.

'There's a white cat under the bookshelf behind your chair,' I said. 'Is that Flora?'

'Aha!' He got up and bent over, looking under the bookshelf. 'Come on, Flora, you've been spotted. Come on out, my beautiful.'

With the cat in his arms he sat down again, arranged her on his lap, and began to brush her, gentle, sweeping strokes.

'That play, *A Long Time Away*, that was one of those things I go in for sometimes, I say it's good for my soul. It was going to cost me money, that play. But it was good enough to be worth it.'

He was watching me again, and I nodded. I understood him, Tony and I had both felt the same way about it. Bugger the money, was how Tony had put it.

'I was enjoying that production,' he went on. 'Tony Marks told me to come down and look at the set. What the hell for? I can see a hundred sets a week if I want to. Come on down, he said. It's special. She's the best I've ever taught.'

The black cat seemed to have gone to sleep. I went on stroking her, not looking at Jacob Goldman, but listening.

'That play isn't going to make a lot of money, but it's going to break even, and a bit more. The notices are good.'

I glanced up quickly, and he nodded at me.

'Oh, yes, I get the papers in as soon as they're on the stands, you'd have been on your way here. They'll be pleased, that lot down in Cambridge. Most of the critics mention atmosphere, and that means the set. Those notices will bring in all the pseuds and the theatre snobs, they all have to pretend they know what it's about, ninety per cent of them won't understand one word in three, the other ten per cent won't care. Are you listening to me?'

274

'Yes.'

'Fred Grafton telephoned me, disturbed me on my day off. Fred knows better than that, so I listened. Now you listen to me. You have been a very, very lucky girl. You are lucky because it's Fred. I don't know another director who would have taken it this way. "I didn't sack her, because she's right." That's what he said. Fred's no Fellini, but he's fair.

'And talking about Fellini,' he was becoming excited again, waving the brush at me, 'I know the man, so don't interrupt, he wouldn't have sacked you either, he'd have *shot* you, and so would most other directors, so I want to know now. If I send you up to work for Simmie Lawley, am I just buying myself a pack of trouble? Are you going to go on defying directors and making a nuisance of yourself and wasting time, or are you going to be a professional? Answer me.'

'I've always been professional,' I answered.

'Hah!'

'I'm not docile and obedient, if that's what you're asking. No, I'm not like Felicity and Stephen, much as I like them. No.'

He was glaring at me, his face was turning red.

'I don't always do as I'm told. Usually, but not always. I *am* a professional, Mr Goldman, which means I'll be treated like one. Not simply overruled without a discussion.'

His eyes were narrowed, but he was brushing the cat again as he watched me.

'If there'd been a discussion with Fred? What then? What if he'd *still* said raise the scaffolding?'

'I don't know.'

'Ho! You don't know? You don't know?'

He brandished the brush at me again, and the white cat jumped off his lap and ran back under the bookshelf.

'You're a blasted nuisance, Gloriana Mayall, a blasted nuisance. Get yourself back to Cambridge.'

'Do you still want me to work for you?'

He spluttered at me, and threw the brush down on the floor. But then he picked it up and pointed it at me.

'Don't you make a habit of this. Defying directors and setting the whole theatre by its ears, don't you make a habit of it, Gloriana Mayall. Take care how you lift up that cat, I've taken a lot of trouble over her.'

'She's beautiful,' I said. 'Copper eyes against that black coat, it's lovely.'

'I want you safely up in Bolton by the end of next month, out of the way, being quiet, and behaving yourself, do you understand me?'

'Yes.'

He looked at me closely as we stood in the hall, his hand on the door.

'You don't look well,' he said. 'You're too thin, you look ill. What's the matter?'

'Nothing.'

'Working too hard?' He seemed to be asking himself. 'No. You love your work. Can't sleep?'

Voices calling out in the dark, a feeling of desolation. When I had woken up in the night, suddenly, still hearing the voices, I had looked at the chair and seen the silhouette of a man sitting there, a big man, his head bowed, his hands falling slackly at his sides.

Sam? A ghost? Is Sam dead, then?

The Sam I knew is dead, she killed him. She turned him into a murderer. Sam wasn't a murderer. Driving him to become one had killed him. What was left wasn't Sam, it was just a shell, just a someone. Not Sam. He hadn't wanted to talk to me, whoever it was, the not-Sam that was left after the killing.

'Gloriana?'

He'd loved me. He'd loved me enough to kill for me. He'd destroyed himself, and he'd destroyed the love he'd had for me. It was all gone now. There was just the silhouette of a

276

big man sitting in a chair, Sam, before he became what she had made him, because he loved her. Loved me.

'Come with me.'

I followed him, into a kitchen. It was bright and modern, very clean. I wasn't thinking, he told me to sit down, and I looked at him, blankly, wondering why he was small and bent with such a big nose. Sam didn't have a big nose, he had a short nose, slightly crooked where it had been broken. Then there were hands pressing on my shoulders, and I was sitting in a chair beside a table, and it was Jacob Goldman standing in front of me.

'Silly girl. When did you last eat? What do you want, then? Bacon and eggs? Don't look at me like that, I know Jews who'd kill for a pork chop, of course I've got bacon.'

'Why are you like this?'

My voice was vague, I was talking to Sam, why was Jacob answering?

'Because it amuses me, of course. Why do you think? You're one of my theatre people, so I'm Fagin. You think I'm like this in the boardroom? You'd be lucky.'

I knew it was Jacob, I had to stop myself talking to Sam. I sat in silence instead, smelling bacon frying, suddenly realising I hadn't eaten for days, I'd been living on coffee, I was hungry.

'Silly girl.'

'Am I still your clever darling?'

Oh, please. I had to be. I had to be something to somebody. I had to be his clever darling.

'You think just anybody sits in that room with my Abracadabra on their laps getting cat hairs all over their clothes? Oh, yes, you're my clever darling, no question. Why aren't you crying? What is all this? Boyfriend trouble?'

'Oh, *Christ*.'

He was putting a plate in front of me, three fried eggs, rashers of bacon, I'd never eaten as much as that. He waved a fish slice under my nose.

'So I'm being trite and banal? You're thin, you're not sleeping. What's the alternative? Eat your breakfast, don't tell me it's the middle of the afternoon, I already know. Breakfast is the first meal of the day. By the look of you, it's the first meal of several days, so eat your breakfast and don't argue.'

He didn't ask me again, but he talked as I ate, and he cleaned the frying pan, rubbing it with kitchen paper.

'You're going to work for my friend Simmie in Bolton,' he said. 'Little bit of everything. When you're not designing sets you'll be making clothes, doing backdrops for advertisements, helping him. Doing what he tells you.'

There was a stern look as he said that, and I nodded.

'You've got a lot to learn. Not every play that needs a set's like *A Long Time Away*, you've got to make sets for bad and boring and banal plays, too. Then we'll see. We'll see how professional you are when you're making sets for three-scene farces written for amateurs to perform in village halls. Whether you still do your best and use your brains.'

'Shakespeare,' I said.

'Oh, yes? What about him?'

My plate was empty, I was still holding my knife and fork, and looking down at the smeared white china in surprise.

'I'll do your three-scene farces. Well, I'll try. We should have done more of that sort of thing.'

I was beginning to ramble, so I stopped talking, and laid down the knife and fork. Shakespeare, I'd said. We should have seen *Titus Andronicus* that afternoon instead of going for a walk by the river, there was always something to learn. But I'd read the play, and been revolted by the violence, I hadn't wanted to see it. I'd missed an opportunity.

Jacob picked up my plate and carried it to the sink.

'Not been eating, not been sleeping properly. What am I going to do about you, then?'

'Nightmares,' I said, and then stopped myself.

He didn't seem to have heard me.

'Loves her work, so don't suggest holidays, Jacob. But a change of scene.'

'Shakespeare,' I said again. 'That's the man I want to work for.'

What was I talking about? He'd been dead for, what was it? Three hundred and fifty years?

'You're going to be moving about,' he said. 'Based in Bolton for a little while, but moving about, we don't know where you'll end up. Don't put down roots. And you need a change of scene.'

He was facing me again, pointing a finger at me.

'Nightmares, exhaustion, starvation, I don't know what you've been up to, I'm not asking. You need a fresh start, my clever darling. Any problems with moving? Nasty clauses in the lease?'

I thought of the lease Uncle John had amended and Francis Chendar had signed without reading, and I shook my head. Golden floor, golden light through the windows, the place I had worked, where I had been able to study for the first time, I had loved the granary. I knew I didn't mind leaving now. It was haunted, whether by a ghost or by my own regrets I didn't know.

'Shakespeare.' He shook his head. 'If you do *The Merchant of Venice* I want to play Shylock.'

Black and silver, with the blood-red stained-glass window casting light across the table. A table like a tomb. Why was I thinking of Lucille?

'Such a character,' I said, and my chest felt tight and constricted. Shylock. 'Lost everything. Would you know how to do that?'

He didn't answer, but his eyes were very steady on my face as he watched me.

'I've seen that,' I said. Lucille, the man she had loved, her beautiful home, gone. Her beauty fading. Why could I feel so much pity for Shylock, and none for Lucille?

'She took everything from Shylock.' My voice sounded vague and dreamy. '"Quality of mercy". What happened to it? I hate Portia. Bitch. Everything he cared for, she took it. Why didn't she just kill him?'

'Portia's very thin,' I explained. 'Did you know that?'

There was pain in Jacob's eyes, and I tried to stop myself talking. I was rambling again.

'I don't understand that play. Why did that happen? I thought he'd seen what it must have been like for Shylock. Why did he write it like that? I thought he'd understood. Shakespeare always seemed to understand.'

He didn't say anything for a long time. He was looking over my head, he was avoiding my eyes, hiding his pain.

'He had understood,' he said at last, very quietly. He pushed up his sleeve, and held out his arm. There was a number tattooed on it, the ink blurred and fading. I looked at it, and nodded. I didn't need to say anything, I felt very close to Jacob Goldman just then.

'Concentration camps,' I said. 'Yes. You could play Shylock.'

He shook the sleeve back down over his arm and smiled at me.

'I play at being a Jew now,' he said. 'I lost my wife, my children, my family, my country, I lost everything, because I'm a Jew. So now I'm a pantomime Jew, because I still hate them. Shylock and me, and the ones who walked out of Auschwitz beside me, these Jews didn't die, even though they killed us.'

The pain was still there in his eyes, but there were tears in mine, I couldn't see him through the tears. His hand was on my shoulder, it was he who was comforting me, his gentle old hand stroking my shoulder as it began to shake, and as I laid my head down on my folded arms, and cried for what we had both lost.

20

Simmie Lawley's business occupied an enormous space, but only employed about twenty people. There were cramped offices and design studios at one end of a huge warehouse, where echoes boomed from the domed roof, making it quite impossible to do any work with sound without setting up big mufflers of carpet felt, which were cumbersome and heavy, and needed several men to lift them on to their iron frames. The warehouse held the sets, each one roped off with plastic tape, and big pieces of scenery.

Even in summer it was cold and draughty.

One end of the warehouse was screened off and heated. This was the tailoring and dressmaking section of the business. It held big tables with thick felt covers, and several sewing machines where women worked at extraordinary speed, and in an almost eerie silence, to assemble the designs Simmie and his junior partner Mike Coster had created. Mike did nothing but design and make clothes, and resisted any efforts Simmie made to involve him in other aspects of the organisation.

The fabrics were stored in another part of the warehouse, on high racks and shelves, and had to be brought to the tables on trolleys, which was always inconvenient.

Simmie said he wanted to move, but town planning had him tied up in knots.

He was a young man, short and stocky, with enormous energy. He ran every aspect of his business himself, hating delegation, and, when forced to allow somebody else to take charge, worrying about it and interfering at every opportunity. But he apologised if anybody protested. Simmie's 'Oh, shit. Sorry' was to be heard several times a day. Everybody liked Simmie, his apologies were always accepted.

My studio was quite small, but it had good light, and I liked it. I told Simmie I wanted to bring my own furniture, and immediately he set about contacting a removal company to organise it, until I put my hand on the telephone, cutting him off.

'I'll do it,' I said.

'Oh, shit,' he responded. 'Sorry.'

He'd found me a flat on the outskirts of Bolton, and he'd booked decorators and chosen the wallpaper.

'Oh, shit,' he'd said on that occasion as well. 'Sorry. Yes, I'll tell them you'll choose your own wallpaper, shall I?'

'No. Tell them I do my own decorating.'

He'd stared at me, and then shrugged.

'Gosh,' he'd said. 'Well.'

It felt very strange, having a job that started at nine every morning and ended at five in the afternoon. Once I'd decorated the flat, and set up my furniture as I wanted it, I didn't know what to do in the evenings, I found myself tense and restless.

I took driving lessons, and learned quite quickly. I went running, five or six miles every evening, I started to eat properly, and found I took pleasure in my body's increasing strength and stamina. I began to look better too, the shadows around my eyes and in the hollows of my cheeks faded, and vanished. Men started to whistle at me again, and sometimes they followed me when I was running.

Usually they gave up after a mile or so, but if they persisted I would stop, and I would talk to them. I would use the voice I had heard the thin child use, and I would say the things I had heard her say, and the men would go away.

Advertising sets were Simmie's main source of income, and my main occupation for the first three months. They didn't have the sense of excitement that came from the theatre, but some of them were quite demanding, and Simmie himself was a perfectionist. Photographers often resented him, but the models loved him because he always did his best for them, and the advertising agencies came back to him every time. Satisfied clients were what counted, and with Simmie working on the sets they were nearly always satisfied.

My first theatre work for Simmie was indeed a three-scene farce for amateurs, and he asked me about it diffidently, inviting me to refuse if I wanted.

'It's to raise money for a hospital in Tel Aviv,' he explained. 'I'm sort of involved, well, it's my mother mostly, she drags me into that sort of thing. They asked if I'd help with the scenery and she said yes, so I'm sort of stuck with it. I wondered if you'd . . .'

'Yes,' I said. 'Of course I will.'

'Oh, great. Now, it's set in a country cottage, a sort of weekend place, so it might look a bit damp and neglected, but not too much . . .' He waved his arms around, and then caught my eye.

'Oh, shit. Sorry. You do it whichever way you think.'

I'd promised Jacob I'd do my best, and I did, but there wasn't much to be done with no money and only the scenery they could borrow to set up on a tiny stage in a church hall. Simmie lent some proper lights, which helped, and I modified the staircase, so that the leading lady, who was nearly fifty and weighed over twelve stone, didn't fall over as she tripped lightly down it in four-inch stiletto-heeled shoes.

Some of the problems were new to me. Never before had I had to contend with canvas scenery that billowed like a sail whenever anybody opened the back door of the hall. Nor had I set up lighting alongside a small troop of Boy Scouts, who alternated their semaphore practice with efforts to help me, nor had to dismantle the set by myself after the performance on the Friday afternoon because the stage was needed for a Women's Institute meeting that evening.

'I do appreciate it,' said Simmie apologetically, 'and so does my mum. You're to come to tea, she says. That's rather sort of Royal Command. Do you mind? I mean, this play. The tea's good, you won't mind that, you'll like my mum.'

I didn't mind. I'd had to think, there'd been difficulties to overcome, I'd needed to improvise and to coax help out of amateurs when previously I'd had the equipment I needed and professional staff to carry out my plans. But my amateur helpers were willing, if not always competent, and improvisation was surprisingly challenging. I found I could be quite resourceful, under pressure.

Ruth Lawley told me the play had made a profit, and I was a pet. So was dear Jacob for sending me to Simmie, have a piece of fudge cake, would I very sweetly paint a picture for her raffle for the hospital, was my cup empty?

'Oh, Mother!' Simmie protested.

She was an enormously entertaining and determined woman, and by the time I went home that evening I was committed to painting a picture, to designing a playroom for the hospital, and to drawing a logo for the charity that was raising the money, something to kick them in the heartstrings, dear.

'Oh, Mother!'

I didn't mind that, either. I'd never been involved in anything on a personal basis, as a friend. I felt needed, and appreciated, and I liked it. For the logo I drew a simplified child's face, the eyes questioning. I painted a moonlit snowscape, white on white, and I spent an afternoon in the children's ward of the local hospital, watching and listening, so I would know what would appeal to a tired child, and what would seem too difficult or demanding.

I've never liked children, which made it easier. I could observe them without being distracted by feelings of sympathy, or whatever it is that attracts people to children, something I've never understood.

The nurses liked my ideas.

Mrs Lawley said I was an absolute pet, it was obvious I loved children, and was Simmie treating me well?

'Oh, Mother!'

I invented a fiancé in London, and she twinkled at me, not in the least deceived, but quite happy to take the hint.

I passed my driving test.

Ann sent me a horseshoe as a lucky mascot when I wrote and told her I was taking my test. She was doing well at her course at Hereford, learning her trade, as she put it, and she spent weekends at the forge when she could. It seemed money was a problem for her, and I telephoned Uncle John.

'She's managing,' he said. 'Don't worry, I'm keeping an eye on her. I'm very fond of Ann.'

'Couldn't I send her some money?'

'She needs to succeed on her own. I'll let you know if she gets into real difficulties.'

I had quite a lot of money. I didn't need much to live on in Bolton, and Simmie paid me a good salary, subsidised by Jacob Goldman, because he wanted first call on my time. I saved more than half of it, and I found ways of investing it. Sometimes I asked Robert Cameron, but more often I left the money in the bank until I heard of something. My bank manager knew I liked good ideas.

Ian Sark, a retired motor mechanic with a stock car racing son, needed money to convert a row of garages into workshops. There were young men who repaired their own cars, or raced them, who would be regular customers if they could hire workshops with pits or hydraulic hoists by the afternoon. Ian supervised the workshops himself, and he liked his customers. He spent more time up to his elbows in oily bits of engines than sitting in his comfortable office reading the paper, which is what he had claimed to want to do with his retirement.

'Tools go missing,' he complained. 'I'd expected it. But you wouldn't believe. Battery charger. Trolley jack. How did I miss? Last week. Wouldn't believe.'

'Never mind,' I said.

'Do mind. Trolley jack! How? Wouldn't believe. Sorry, Glory.'

I owned ten per cent of Sark's Workshops, and Ian had what he called a 'divvy-up' every three months. The paper-work was careful, and honest, but very oily.

When I'd left the granary I'd given a party, and Ann had come up from the West Country and helped. She'd spent most of the time in the kitchen, I'd put up a parti-tion to screen it off from the rest of the room, but she said she'd enjoyed the party, most of it. I think she meant she'd enjoyed the preparations, setting up the lights for me.

Lucille had come to the party, which I'd told her was to celebrate my being offered a job. It was true, in a way. She was still beautiful, but her make-up was thicker, her hair a little more careful. The man who brought her was older than Patrick Chendar, and very deferential towards her.

She'd treated Ann with a sort of distant amazement, but she'd wanted to talk to me.

'Darling, when you're twenty-five the house will be yours. John Mayall won't be able to dictate to you any more, you'll be free of him. You'll be able to do as you like.'

Her hand had been resting on my arm, and I looked at it as she spoke. Little pads of wrinkles on the knuckles, and the veins beginning to stand out over the sinews.

'Yes?'

'I want to go home. Darling Gloriana, I can't live in the rabbit hutch for ever. You will let me, won't you?'

I'd smiled at her, and murmured something, and walked away.

The granary had been almost bare by then. I'd packed away as much as I could, there were boxes lined against the back wall. One of the last items to be put into them was the green and gold rug.

Thousands of pounds, folded notes, blue envelopes. I'd sat at my desk, slicing open the envelopes with a paper knife, laying the notes flat as I sorted them, and I'd begun to count. But after a while I'd stopped, it seemed pointless, and my mind was beginning to drift, so I'd forgotten how much there was in the pile I'd already counted, and I'd felt too tired to start again. It didn't seem real anyway. But during the party I'd sometimes glanced at the boxes, at the blue apple box that held the rug, and the money. I'd put the notes in an old school shoebag, I'd just looked around vaguely for something that would hold them, and the shoebag had been lying in front of my wardrobe, so I'd used it. It had only just been big enough, I'd had to stuff the money into it, and pull the drawstrings tight. Then I'd rolled the rug carefully, and put it in the box, and I'd put shoes in the box, and at some time while I was packing it I'd thrown the shoebag in with the other things. I'd have to do something with the money, I supposed, but in the meantime I'd had my books to pack, and I'd wanted to sort out the sketches I'd done of the costumes for *The Merchant of Venice*. I'd wanted to send them to Jacob.

Now the green and gold rug lay on top of a beige fitted carpet in a nondescript modern flat on the outskirts of Bolton, and somewhere in the wardrobe was a shoebag full of money, I couldn't remember exactly where I'd put it.

Thousands of pounds, I told myself sometimes. Don't be silly, leaving it around like that. Do something with it.

Jacob telephoned me at the beginning of December.

'Come and spend Christmas Day with me and my ladies, my clever darling,' he said. 'I want to see you again.'

'Your ladies?'

'My cats.' Exasperation in his voice, had I forgotten his beautiful darlings? 'I hate Christmas, you'll make it bearable. Can you come?'

He'd sounded hopeful, almost wistful, and I said I'd love to spend Christmas Day with him. I'd thought of going south to spend it with Lucille, but I hadn't really wanted to, and Ann had already said she ought to be with her landlady, who sounded completely crazy to me, obsessed with the idea that the Martians were about to land. But Ann was fond of her.

'I'll do a turkey,' said Jacob. 'I'm a good cook. We'll talk about the theatre, don't forget to bring the brain.'

We had a lovely Christmas, although Jacob wasn't quite as good a cook as he thought. He wanted to talk about my drawings for *The Merchant of Venice*.

'I like them. I think they're good, my darling, but I think you need a reputation before you show them to a director. They're too unusual to come from a beginner, and I don't want them rejected. I want to put them in my safe, and have a little gloat now and then.'

I was disappointed, but he was right.

'Oh, and another thing. I can't see me wearing a black frock with a silver lamé collar, so I'm withdrawing my offer to play Shylock. I'm very sorry, but there's no use arguing, you'll just have to be brave and make do with that upstart Olivier.'

'But Shakespeare?' I pleaded, and he shook a finger at me.

'Yes, I know, I know, I know. Shakespeare, the big man himself, I know. You will have to be patient. When you start working for Shakespeare I want you working with a *good* company, not some third-rate bunch of tourists with a cast of six and two suitcases full of plywood props.'

He looked at me, and smiled.

'It's going to take time. I promise you, Gloriana, I promise you, I haven't forgotten. I'm aiming for Shakespeare, and I want you at the top, but it's going to take time.'

In the end, it took seven years.

There were times when I almost gave up and told Simmie to forget it, he could have me full time, working on his advertising sets and his fashion shows. Jacob sent me all around the country, productions he'd turned down financially, some he was backing, anything that he thought might broaden my experience. He even sent me to Europe for a month one rainy autumn, a town in the middle of France I'd never heard of, and to Brussels.

I remembered what Fred Grafton had said about plays written by somebody's favourite granddaughter, and tried to swallow my disappointment when the reviews, and later the ticket sales, turned out to be as bad as everybody had anticipated. I designed sets for directors who simply didn't notice them, and for directors who flatly rejected them, demanded a completely new approach and then disliked that, tried to modify it, and finally said they'd take the first one anyway. I made costumes, and I painted canvas scenery, I quarrelled with lighting technicians and flattered stage managers, I drank coffee with wardrobe mistresses and champagne with actors, and I began to wonder if I was ever going to be given a play worth my work.

In the meantime, I worked on making money. I wanted to be rich. Sark's Workshops could have expanded, the workshops were booked up weeks in advance, but Ian didn't want to buy any more garages. It would have meant taking on staff, and it would have needed managerial skills that he didn't have.

'Don't want to,' he said at our next divvy-up. 'That okay, Glory?'

'That's okay, Ian.'

But there were three young women working out of a

basement flat in an old residential backwater who wanted to expand very much, and needed money to buy the lease of a shop in the town centre for their 'My Office' business, a secretarial agency, and my bank manager asked me if I was interested.

Once again, I thought of the shoebag in the bottom of my wardrobe, and I clenched my fists.

'All right? Are you all right?'

He was leaning over his desk, looking concerned, and I smiled, and turned my eyes back to the accounts.

'Fine, thank you. I'll need a loan if I'm to cover this.'

'I'm sure we can arrange that.'

When I was twenty-five the trust that had handled my money came to an end, and I went to London to see Uncle John and Robert Cameron. We went through the accounts and the shareholdings together, and by then I knew enough to be able to make the decisions for myself. I'd done well, with Robert's help and advice.

Revelations had never paid a dividend; every financial year Martin had telephoned us and begged to be allowed to keep the money. Once in a lifetime opportunities would be lost and squandered were he not to invest immediately in a new artist, a collection of prints, an exhibition. Martin had made mistakes, to which he'd admitted immediately and apologetically, but he'd done well. My two hundred pounds was now worth nearly four thousand.

Alexandra Martin had bought us out, paying generously and thanking extravagantly, and she'd moved to the United States. Her fabrics had suddenly become a sort of cult, turning her into a millionairess within three years, and when her company had gone public she'd written to us both privately, again thanking us for our early help. Mike Coster bought fabrics from her sometimes, and often the documents that came with the bales contained a personal letter to me, with photographs and catalogues, and sometimes a length of a fabric she'd printed and liked enough to want to share.

Lucky, Robert Cameron called me. You bring luck to your investments. Uncle John said he was superstitious. I smiled, and wished he wouldn't talk about luck.

'I want some capital,' I said. 'I want fifteen thousand.'

'Fast cars and fur coats?' asked Uncle John.

'Fashion,' I said.

Jane Targe had repaid her loan, and had asked if I'd like to invest in the studio. They were expanding, looking for investment capital, and Jane thought it would pay well.

'Grey's is growing quite fast,' she'd written. 'We've taken on four designers this year. It would have been six if we'd found anybody who was good enough. The order book is full for two years. I've got you to thank for this, and I do thank you, I really do. I've designed a coat for you to thank you properly. Can you come for a fitting? You could see the studio then, and maybe think about the money. You'll want to see the accounts, too. I hope you'll like the coat.'

I had liked the coat, and I'd liked being right about Jane. She was rounder and pinker than ever, and still living in a glow of happy excitement about her work. We'd spent a day together, a Sunday, the only day we'd both been free, but the studio hadn't been deserted. The people who worked there lived for their work, and loved their work, and I'd worn my beautiful golden coat home that evening because the senior seamstress had been there, and had been enthusiastic.

'Jane, I'll model it for you if you like,' I'd said. 'Fashion show? Or I'll lend it back to you. Whatever you like. It deserves its moment in the limelight.'

She'd turned bright red with pleasure, and three months later I'd been back on the catwalk, at a fashion show I'd helped design. Simmie had another client.

'Fifteen thousand,' said Uncle John, and he tried to look disapproving. 'That's a lot of money.'

Robert Cameron laughed.

'Can't you get it somewhere else?'

A shoebag in the bottom of a wardrobe. I turned my head away, I turned the thought away. Still sometimes I dreamed of voices calling in the dark, of pleading eyes. Almost every day, as I took something out of the wardrobe, I remembered the money, told myself I was crazy to leave it lying around. Would I really care if somebody stole it? So dirty, that money. So much pain, so much need.

'How much do you think I earn?' I asked lightly, and Uncle John looked puzzled. He'd noticed my reaction.

I was tired, too. Lucille had telephoned me months before, to remind me that I'd promised her she could move back into the house.

'I didn't,' I said. 'I didn't promise you any such thing, Lucille.'

'Darling, at the party. When you moved away, we talked about it. Gloriana, you *can't* have forgotten.'

'The Courtneys have a twenty-year lease on the house.'

She started to cry. I'd promised, she said. I'd promised she could go home.

Since then she'd telephoned almost every week. John Mayall had had no right to agree to a lease that long when I was due to come into my own property, I should talk to a lawyer about it. It was an illegal lease. It was her home, why was I being so cruel?

Had I talked to a lawyer yet?

She'd been to the house, she'd met those people, they were quite dreadful, they were common. They'd decorated the drawing room with some ghastly floral-print wallpaper.

'Lucille, leave the Courtneys alone. They can decorate the house in any way they like.'

'It's my home.'

The Courtneys could be bought off, they were those sort of people, vulgar. *Nouveau riche*. It only needed money. Darling Gloriana, you've got so much money. Please, darling, I want to go home.

What was John Mayall thinking of, to allow people like

that into a Nash house? They should be in a council house. Or some revolting executive housing estate, whatever they were.

'It isn't Nash.'

'Don't tell me! It's my home. Why are you being so hard? Darling, *please*.'

I bought a telephone answering machine. For two weeks I heard her voice in the evenings, as I sat in my flat and watched the little red light winking.

'Oh, God. What's the matter with this thing?'

'Gloriana? Oh, no. Oh, *damn*. Gloriana, are you there? Is that you? Hello? Hello?'

And then:

'Hello? Gloriana? This is some sort of tape recorder, isn't it? The telephone people told me. Will you please telephone me *at once*. I've been to see those dreadful people again, I told them they'd have to leave. They said they'd call the police if I came back. How *dare* they? Are those the sort of people you want in the house? In *my home*?'

'What can I do about Lucille?' I asked Uncle John, and he smiled, not unsympathetically.

'I'm afraid she's your problem now, Gloriana. Or are you asking for legal advice?'

I wrote to her.

'Leave the Courtneys alone. They are excellent tenants, I don't want them harassed, and if they call the police you'll have to deal with it yourself. Lucille, you couldn't possibly afford the rent for the house. The rabbit hutch, as you call it, is quite lovely, even if it is smaller.'

She telephoned again, and sobbed into the answering machine.

'How can you be so hard? You really are your father's daughter, Gloriana. Peter was hard, and cruel. Please, telephone me.'

'*Trojan Women* in Harrogate,' said Simmie at the end of my sixth year with him. 'Uncle Jacob says you're on loan.

293

They want your help. He says don't worry, you may be the junior collaborator but he's the senior financial muscle, he wants some imagination.'

'Ah!' This sounded interesting.

'"Tell my clever darling to find her sketchbooks and her brains, she's on the road again." Those were his exact words.'

I smiled.

'You'll have time to finish the staging for the Berkeley Fashion Show, won't you?' Simmie asked anxiously.

'I will if you keep your fingers off it.'

'Ah. Sorry.'

Trojan Women, wasn't this the play set at the end of the war, when they were to be dragged off into slavery? A city ruined by fire, roofs collapsed, charred beams like black spears, filthy smoke-stained holes in those walls that were still standing?

I shivered.

'Euripides,' Simmie was saying. 'I bet they're doing it modern. You'll need the flames behind the skyline, of course, I'll ring up and ask about . . .'

'Simmie!'

'Oh, shit. Sorry.'

Flames behind the skyline, I didn't think I wanted that. It was too dramatic. These were women in despair. Rain, there should be rain, the women's clothes would be wet, and clinging to their bodies, everything would be filthy, everything not destroyed would be defiled by smoke and dirt.

Could it be played on a stage, in the rain? Real water?

The cast would protest, it would be horribly uncomfortable. But it would work, if I could overcome the practical problems.

The cast did protest about the wet clothes, and the management at first refused point blank to entertain the idea of rain, they said it would ruin the stage, and was dangerous, it could get into electric points.

But their set designer said it was possible, and he liked the idea, what about canvas on the stage? And nobody had said the wet clothes had to be cold, they could wet them with warm water, which was stupid, they'd be cold moments later, but I didn't mention that.

The director was enthusiastic, and patient, and one by one he overcame the objections.

'Gloriana Mayall?' asked one of the actresses. 'Didn't you do that thing in Cambridge a few years ago? *A Long Time Away*? Was that you?'

'Yes,' I said. 'Me and Tony Marks.'

'Ah.' She raised her eyebrows, and nodded. 'Ah.'

The grumbling over the wet clothes subsided, and I painted her a lucky black cat.

The critics loved it, Jacob Goldman's pseuds and snobs flocked in, and he told me I'd doubled his investment.

'You've done yourself no harm at all, either, Gloriana,' he added. 'We're getting closer. I haven't forgotten.'

But after Harrogate it was back to Bolton, Simmie had three Christmas fashion shows to handle, and Jacob had said I was to help with a pantomime in Birmingham, his clever darling was to be conventional, keep the brains on a short lead.

'Never mind pantomime,' said Simmie, panic-stricken. 'I need help with Christmas displays in shop windows. Jackson's want us to do theirs this year, I can't turn it down, they're too big. *Glory*, I'm *talking* to you.'

'I'm listening.'

'You don't *look* as if you're listening, will you do the Jackson's windows?'

'Yes.'

'And help me with the fashion shows?'

'Yes.'

He gave an exaggerated sigh, and patted me on the shoulder.

'When you first came here, Jacob said you might be sort

of difficult,' he said. 'He's potty. You're an absolute pet.'

Christmas displays in shop windows, and fashion shows, and four nights a week in digs in Birmingham working on a set for *Babes in the Wood*, tinfoil leaves with toffees stuck behind them for the comedian to throw to children in the audience, I was so busy I never did really learn the story.

Ruth Lawley was giving a party for all the people who'd been involved in the hospital fund-raising venture, they'd finally reached their target, and two years earlier than everybody had said was quite impossible. Would I help her with the Christmas decorations and the tree?

'Oh, Mother!'

And come to the party, of course. Simmie would bring me himself, and take me home afterwards. Don't forget a mistletoe bough for the front hall, young people like mistletoe boughs.

Ruth was eternally optimistic. Simmie and Mike allowed her her blind eye, told her they shared a flat because the mortgage was easier with two incomes, and tactfully brought girls to her various social events.

After Christmas Jackson's wanted me to do their windows for the January sales, nobody else would do.

'What they're *paying*,' said Simmie, round-eyed. 'I mean, I sort of said to myself, Simmie, think of a number and double it, and I did, and they just said yes.'

'Well, good.'

'Yes, but I wanted them to say no, because Uncle Jacob wants you to go to Brighton and do a Molière season, well, two months anyway, and we've got four television commercials, I need you *here*.'

'We'll manage.'

I'd never read Molière, and it wasn't easy to find the time to do so. The days of nine-to-five work had long passed. Jackson's wanted me to do a presentation of my ideas and Simmie said for what they were paying it wasn't unreasonable.

'Sell yourself,' he said, and then turned bright pink. 'I mean, you know, sort of, sell your *ideas*.'

But there were still his advertising sets, two of them with sound for television, which meant scheduling them so we could transfer the big sheets of carpet felt between takes, and Mike had his own fashion show only a month later, when I was due to be in Brighton. He wanted my help before I went.

It was to be his last solo. He and Jane Targe loved each other's work, and had decided that Lawley's and Grey's should merge their shows the following year. If Glory would design them, please.

Simmie was becoming tense, he was under too much pressure, and he actually snapped at his mother when she asked me if I'd help her choose new curtains for her dining room. She was startled, and upset.

'I *can't spare* her, Mother,' he said. 'I'm *sorry*.'

I was worried and disturbed by that. He'd never spoken to her in such a way. My achievements, and my reputation, seemed to be bringing him problems rather than success.

He'd asked me to come into the business as a partner.

'You don't need a designer, Simmie,' I'd said. 'You need a manager. Somebody who can take some of the problems off your shoulders. That's not me.'

Simmie was putting on weight, and his hair was greying too quickly.

Brighton in winter, bravely trying to keep its holiday air, with the lights failing on the pier, the Pavilion being cleaned, and the flower beds along the front bare, the roses pruned, the only colour the identifying labels tied to their stumpy twigs. I had digs in Hove, with a landlady so hostile and sour that I left after two days, spent one night at the Grand because I couldn't find anywhere else, and then rented a furnished flat in a house in Kemptown, looking out over the sea. Once it had been a lovely home, part of a graceful crescent, but all the houses had been broken up into flats and single rooms, and mine was dark, with blackened varnish on oak panelling.

There was a cocktail club in the basement, and when I got back from the theatre late at night the members were usually leaving.

One of them accosted me the first time he saw me. He was drunk.

'I've seen you before,' he asserted. 'What's your name?'

I pushed his hand off my arm, and ran up the steps to the front door. I was shaking.

'Don't be unfriendly,' he called after me. 'I'm sure we're friends, I've just forgotten your name. Temporarily, I do assure you.'

Pleading eyes, voices calling in the dark. That night I slept badly, jerking awake every few minutes. I got up very early, and went for a run along the front, in the rain. It was still dark when I came back, and I dropped on to my bed in my wet track suit, and fell into an uneasy doze.

Two days later I was ill, I had a fever and a sore throat, and my head was throbbing. I took aspirins, and went on working, draping red plush and gold tassels across plywood backing, checking spotlights for dazzle on mirrors, trying to concentrate on the more complicated sets.

'You look awful,' said the stage manager. 'Take a day off.'

'Can't.' I was losing my voice, so I coughed, and tried again. 'Can't, we're short of time.'

'Always are.' He shrugged, smiled, and walked away. Nice man. What was his name? Wright?

No. No.

That night the man from the cocktail club was waiting for me, and he was sober.

'I've remembered,' he said. 'You were thinner.'

'Excuse me, please let me pass.'

'But I'd like to make an appointment. Is there a telephone number?'

I pushed past him, and ran up the steps.

'I want to make an appointment,' he called.

The flat seemed darker than ever. My reflection in the varnished panelling made me jump, I thought there was somebody there, waiting for me. And voices, I could hear voices, down in the hall. Had I shut the front door? Or was he there? Had he followed me into the house, were those his footsteps coming up the stairs?

My head was hurting, there were red spots in front of my eyes.

Move, I told myself, find somewhere else.

Coffee, and aspirin. I was tired, I didn't want to think. What was the stage manager's name? Not Wright. Who was the man downstairs? I'd never known his name, I'd never asked for names, didn't want to know. Who was that, standing in the room? Only my reflection. My reflection in the black varnish, was it only me? There were two. Who was that?

Lucien, is that you? Are you there, Lucien? Pale face, dark hair, I can't see. Is this place haunted? Why are you here?

Late, it's late, it's dark. Just the light from the hall, and a reflection, there's nobody here.

Coffee, and aspirin. Rixon, that was the stage manager's name, a nice man, not Wright. Rixon. Wait, don't turn on the light, not in here, the man might be watching. There's nobody here, just me. A fever, aspirin will deal with that. Stupid imagination. Get some sleep.

I'd drunk too much coffee, I couldn't sleep, and there were people outside in the crescent, footsteps, and voices. I was cold and sweating, and I could hear voices, somebody calling out in the dark.

Was he still there?

'I am haunted,' I said aloud. 'I am haunted.'

The sheets were soaked in sweat. I got out of bed, staggered as I stood up, went for a shower, and then dressed and spent the rest of the night in the armchair, wrapped in a blanket, and shivering.

Flu, I told myself. Aspirin, hot drinks. Only flu.

Pneumonia, they said. The taxi driver took me to the hospital when I fell trying to get into the back seat. He was very kind.

'Got to go to work,' I said, but they wouldn't listen.

'Shut up,' said a doctor, smiling at me.

'Who are you?'

I wanted to know who they all were, these people around me, and they told me their names, but I couldn't remember them.

'Who are you?'

My head was hurting, a long, deep pain overlaid by the throbbing, like drums. I could hear drums, I could hear music, there were people all around me. Fast drums, a fast rhythm, all the people, and the lights, I'd been dancing, hadn't I been dancing?

A pale face bending over me, dark hair falling forward over a sheen of sweat on a white forehead.

'Lucien? Is that you?'

'No. My name's Dominic. Don't try to talk.'

I am in hospital, I told myself. Don't talk. Be quiet.

'Oh, stop the drums.' My voice. 'I don't want to dance any more. Lucien's gone home.'

Be quiet. Be quiet.

'I'm going to give you an injection.'

'I am haunted. I am haunted.'

'Yes, dear, so am I. Nurse Mary Beech haunts my dreams. Now, just keep still.'

I must be quiet, don't talk. Don't tell them, don't tell them.

Hands on the pillow, lifting my head, something in a cup at my lips, but I couldn't swallow, my throat hurt. Somebody smiling down at me, I don't know this face, freckles, red hair, I don't know this face. I can be quiet now. Hold this hand, don't let her go. Make her stay. I don't know this face, I can be quiet.

'All right, stay with her, go up to the ward with her. You probably remind her of somebody.'

Oh, no. No, you don't. Please, stay.

'All right, dear, you can let go. I won't go away.'

'I can be quiet.'

'Yes, of course you can, dear.'

Cool white cotton, and flowered curtains, and the hands, lifting me, lifting me on to a bed, cool white sheets, and hands smoothing the sheets, it was quiet, and the drums were dying away, I was tired, and Lucien had gone home, Lucien wasn't there any more.

Be quiet. Be quiet.

I woke in a panic, trying to fight my way out of bed, it was evening, I should have been at work hours earlier. A staff nurse pushed me back on to the pillows, reassuring me. The taxi driver had told them where he'd been taking me, they'd telephoned. It was all right, now lie down again, it was all right.

Hundreds of people had sent their love, she said. Well, it seemed like hundreds.

People from the theatre came to see me, bringing armfuls of flowers, extravagant and generous. They apologised to the nurses for coming outside visiting hours. There were wry smiles and shrugs, explanations about eccentric working conditions, and the nurses laughed, and said, all right, just this once. Well, perhaps tomorrow too. Wednesday, we'd have to see, and did they know it was only two visitors to a bed, not seven?

Rixon came, and I knew his name at once. He came during the official visiting hours, bringing a copy of Molière's plays for me, and taking a notebook out of his pocket.

'Are you up to this?' he asked diffidently. 'It's just a few points so we can get on with the sets.'

I was more than up to it, I wanted to get back, and I desperately wanted to leave the hospital.

'Do I talk in my sleep?' I asked the nurse on the second morning, while she was making my bed, and she laughed.

'Never stop. This boy Lucien must be quite something.'

'What did I say?'

But she only laughed again, and went on to the next patient.

'Does everybody talk in their sleep?' I asked the doctor, and he said the fever had made me delirious. It wasn't uncommon.

'What did I say?'

He didn't know, he hadn't been there.

But the fever had gone, I was almost better. Just a couple of days more, they said, then I could go home. Perhaps a week, and I'd be back at work, better not to rush it. I'd been quite ill. Lucky I was young and fit, it could have been worse.

Two more days, said the doctor. And then a week at home, in bed.

'Who was Sam?' asked a student nurse the next morning as she brought me a cup of tea.

I looked down into the tea as I stirred it.

'He's a friend.'

'You said he was dead.'

I gripped the teaspoon, but it rattled against the cup.

'Oh, no. Sam's not dead. He's in Hong Kong.'

She pushed the trolley towards the door.

'Funny. You said he was dead.'

I put the cup on my locker, lay back on the pillow and closed my eyes. What had I said? What were these people hearing, while I was asleep?

'It was the other one you said was dead.'

The woman in the next bed, she was looking at me over the top of her spectacles while she sipped her tea. Her face was censorious, disapproving.

'Funny sort of dreams you have. You drink your tea while it's hot, my girl. They don't make it for fun.'

I discharged myself that afternoon.

The cocktail club was closed, just a pink neon light in the window, a champagne glass. I walked slowly up the steps and let myself into the hall. I didn't like this house any more, it was too dark and gloomy. The walls up the stairs were painted dark brown, in gloss paint that was chipped and damaged. When I'd seen the flat I'd taken it at once, a short lease was all I'd wanted, but now I hated it.

I turned on all the lights.

It was cold and stuffy, so I lit the gas fire and opened the windows. The tail end of a February gale was blowing out in the Channel, and I leaned on the window sill and watched ragged clouds as they ripped across the sky, and foam flying off the waves.

Jacob Goldman had said I needed a change of scene, and he had been right. That had been nearly seven years ago, and I had been all over the country since then, and to France and Belgium, too.

I couldn't remember the dreams, but I knew they'd been there. Lucien, and Sam. What had I said?

There were papers blowing across the floor behind me, so I pulled the windows closed, and latched them. The gas fire was roaring red, heat was beginning to spread, so I turned it down, and sat in front of it, a blanket wrapped around my shoulders.

What had I said? Who had heard me?

I went back to the theatre that afternoon, and there were expressions of consternation, and delight. I looked dreadfully ill, I looked marvellous, I was really damned silly, I was absolutely wonderful.

I was home.

I slept in the Green Room that night, on the sofa, under two sleeping bags borrowed from the property master. Rixon had shrugged when I'd asked him.

'Rules are made to be broken. I'll tell Security.'

They put flowers on the table for me, and a bottle of

champagne in case I was thirsty in the night. I was offered the loan of a huge fur coat to keep me warm, and most of the cast came in to kiss me good night before they left.

I loved them all. My family.

I felt safe in the theatre, I didn't want to leave.

I never wanted to leave.

21

I returned from Brighton six weeks after my stay in hospital to find three cartoonists in my studio. They were working on an advertisement for a new drink. The campaign was to be launched at Christmas.

'Where am I supposed to work, then?' I demanded. I was annoyed, I felt he should have asked.

'We're *expanding*, Glory.'

'That wasn't my question. I know you're expanding.'

'We've got to move. I can't stand this place any longer. I could kill those town planners.'

'Simmie!'

'Oh, shit. I know, I should have asked. Sorry. Can you work in with Su-Su for now?'

'Who's Su-Su? And no, I can't. I need my own studio.'

'I'll sort something out tomorrow.'

'Then I'll come in tomorrow. Damn you, Simmie Lawley, this is *ridiculous*.'

I was really angry with him this time.

'What about the Home Ware set?' said Simmie. 'They're starting tomorrow. Oh, shit, Glory, don't go home. Please.'

'Get those damned cartoonists out of my studio, and telephone me when you've done it. I'll see you half an hour after your call.'

It wasn't Simmie who telephoned me, it was Martin Orek, from the new branch of Revelations in Gloucester, and he was almost incoherent.

'I can't find Robert Cameron,' he said. 'I couldn't find you. Where've you been? I've needed you, it's a crisis.'

'What's happened?'

'I need thirty thousand pounds in cash, this afternoon, and Barclays said no. Sod Barclays. Have you got any money?'

'Thirty thousand?'

He was almost crying with exasperation.

'Yes, thirty sodding thousand, thirty thousand pounds in cash, how much have you got? Where's Robert Cameron?'

'I don't know. Look, Martin, just calm down. What's the money for?'

'It's for a *painting*, of course, what do you think it's for? Glory, just *listen*. Are you listening? Are you there? *Glory?*'

'Yes.'

'She's putting it in an auction tomorrow, well, tomorrow's the deadline for withdrawing it, they're coming to get it this evening, and I know what'll happen, there's a dealers' ring, they'll outbid me and then smother it, they'll *export* it, Glory. It'll go to America, we'll never see it again, it'll be on some Mississippi millionaire's wall. I've got to get the money now, and I can't find Robert Cameron and Patrick Chendar's in Australia.'

'Martin, I don't understand. What is this painting?'

'It's a *Cézanne*. Some lunatic gypsy offered her a hundred quid for it, and she got suspicious.'

'Cézanne? Are you sure?'

'Will you *listen*? She wanted it valued. This gypsy, he was buying antiques. That on the knocker business, she's not stupid. So she telephoned me. I said I didn't know what it was worth. But one like it, if you can say that about Cézanne, fetched forty thousand two months ago.'

'Are you sure it's Cézanne?'

'I told her it was anything between twenty and forty thousand, I couldn't be more exact. She said she'd split it, I could have it for thirty if I could raise it by today, otherwise it's in the auction. Glory, it's already in the catalogue. Where can I get the money? And where have you been? I've been telephoning for *two bloody weeks*. You didn't even switch on your *bloody machine*.'

Cézanne. Martin had been running Revelations for nearly ten years, he wouldn't be mistaken, not about this. Paul Cézanne.

I felt the hairs rising on the back of my neck.

Cézanne. Paul Cézanne. Martin had been lucky in the past, he might have found a Cézanne. He'd been clever, too, not just lucky. Robert Cameron had said Martin had the sense to ride his luck.

'Glory? *Glory?* Can you get the money?'

'Just be quiet and let me think, Martin. I'll call you back.'

'I need to know now.'

'Half an hour.'

I had money. I had quite a lot of money, by most people's standards I was rich, and Robert Cameron's advice had helped me to make the most of everything I could invest. Part of his advice had been to make my money work twice, to borrow from the bank against the security of my investments and invest that money, too. I'd done it. I could only draw two hundred pounds before I reached my credit limit.

A little paper empire, I told myself savagely. Now I needed money, I hadn't got any. Just a lot of paper.

But it was there in my mind, all the time. Half an hour, I had said, half an hour to look for an alternative, to fail to find it. And thirty seconds to push shoes and boxes out of the way, and find a dusty old school shoebag on the floor of my wardrobe. A big shoebag, packed and lumpy, I didn't know how much there was, and I couldn't calculate. My

307

mind slid away from the sums, like water on sloping glass, I didn't know whether there was enough.

Martin met me at the station, anxiously hopping from foot to foot as he looked for me, and then diving forward to meet me, only just remembering to shake my hand.

'How much did you get?'

'I don't know.'

'You *don't know*?'

I pushed the shoebag into his hands.

'Glory, I've got to go *straight there*.'

'I can't help it.'

I was beginning to cry, and he looked aghast, and scuffled into his pockets, hunting for a handkerchief.

'Never mind that,' I said. 'Take the money and try and get the painting. I'll meet you at Revelations.'

I'd never been to the new branch, but it was like the one in Bath, shining black paintwork with the same white lettering picked out in red. By the time I got there in a taxi I was calm again, although my eyes looked a little swollen when I examined them in the mirror of my powder compact.

There were two girls working at the gallery, one at a desk, the other in an office at the back, and they were polite and friendly. There was coffee, freshly ground and smelling delicious, and crisp little biscuits, the crockery was thin white bone china.

These were details that wouldn't have occurred to Martin.

There was something familiar about the girl in the office, the long, thin face, and when she smiled at me I realised what it was.

'His sister?' I asked, and she nodded.

'Samantha. Sammy, please.'

'Glory.'

She looked around the gallery, and gestured, a little awkwardly.

'Do you like it?'

Pale grey carpet, darker grey walls, details picked out in white. The lighting was warm and clear, the paintings glowed against the sombre background.

'Yes,' I said. 'I do. Very much.'

She seemed to relax, as though relieved.

'I was a bit scared when Martin said you were coming,' she said. 'Coming yourself. I mean, you know. Gloriana Mayall.'

'You've heard of me? Professionally?'

'I'm studying interior decoration. We did a course on theatre.'

I thought about that as I looked at the paintings. She said she'd been scared. I wasn't sure I liked that. Over the past few years I'd scared one or two directors, the episode with the welded scaffolding had turned into something of a legend, and had been exaggerated in the process. I hadn't meant to be overbearing or threatening, and it was very rare that I refused to do as a director asked. Never, if they discussed it with me.

'Have you done the gallery in Bath like this?' I asked.

'Yes. But I think Martin wants to talk about selling it, he could take a bigger place in Bath. It's a bit cramped now. And he needs somewhere with a proper secure vault, we can't keep anything really valuable there. He can't, I mean.'

That was typical of Martin. 'He', she'd said, not 'we'. He would think employing his own sister was dishonest, he wouldn't pay her a salary. But she was worth it. The atmosphere of the gallery spoke of prosperity, but it was welcoming and friendly, there was nothing intimidating about it.

'Has Robert Cameron seen this?'

'No. Not yet. Do you think he'll like it?'

'I'm sure he will. He ought to see it.'

Two people came into the gallery, and Sammy excused herself and went to meet them. I watched and listened for a few minutes. She was like a woman in her own home, pleased that somebody had called, happy to see them. She was relaxed, confident, friendly. She was worth a good salary.

I went into the office, and from there down the little staircase that led to the vault. I sat on the bottom step and leaned against the railing.

I hadn't asked Martin where the woman lived, I had no idea how long he'd be. I wondered if I should telephone Simmie, but I was still angry with him, and decided to let him worry.

I liked Revelations. It had been my first investment, and my first taste of starting something new. I thought about the party at the shop in Bath, with Patrick Chendar duelling with art critics, and young men from Sandhurst doing duty as security guards. It had been exciting, and happy.

Revelations had been successful.

Sark's Workshops had been successful, and so had My Office.

Robert said I was lucky with money. I didn't think it was luck. I tried to be careful, I tried to be alert, and I did understand balance sheets and accounts. I liked to invest in things I knew about, textiles, and design. Paintings. The workshops and the secretarial agency had been much more of a gamble for me because I didn't know about them, but I'd liked the people, and I'd trusted their enthusiasm.

I rested my head against the painted iron railing, and closed my eyes. I thought about a shoebag full of money, paper notes. Money is neutral, neither good nor bad, but I'd hated that money.

Cézanne. Paul Cézanne. The beautiful still life in Patrick Chendar's house, it had been so cool, so peaceful. When I had been confused and disturbed, a bit crazy, feeling dirty, Cézanne had healed me. He had been clear, and calm, and at last I had been clear and calm, and I had torn up a dirty yellow book and watched the little shreds of filth float and curl and sink below the surface of the river.

I had thought he had healed me.

I love you, Paul Cézanne.

Money, laid on a table by a rat with flickering blue eyes, by men with humble eyes, I still saw those eyes, I still heard voices calling in the dark.

Money is neutral, neither good nor bad.

I was so tired. But I was safe here, in Revelations, there were beautiful pictures behind that locked door, Martin had found some lovely pictures, and was keeping them safe. I was safe.

I jerked awake, startled, frightened. There was somebody on the stairs, and it was getting dark. Had I been talking? Had I said something?

'Glory?'

It was Martin.

'I was asleep,' I said. 'Did you get it?'

'Yes. Why are you sitting here in the dark? Come upstairs.'

I stood up. I was stiff, and my face was numb where it had pressed against the iron railing. I rubbed it.

'Did I say anything?' I asked.

'What? Come on up. Are you all right?'

He was silhouetted against the pale wall behind him, one arm reaching out as he fumbled for a light switch. I blinked and turned my head away as the light came on, it was too bright.

'There was enough money, then?'

'No. I gave her a cheque for the rest. I'll sort out sodding Barclays tomorrow. There was just over twenty-seven thousand. Why was it in a shoebag? Glory?'

'Hmm.'

'Sammy thought you'd gone. I was going to bring it down and put it in the vault.'

Now that my eyes had adjusted to the bright light I could

311

see him, he was looking worried, frowning down at me.

I thought for a moment.

'I've been ill,' I said. 'I was in hospital with pneumonia. I'm all right, I just got a bit tired.'

He was concerned, but the worried frown had gone.

He came down the stairs and took my arm.

'Come and see,' he said. 'It's filthy, and the frame's an abortion, but it's worth seeing. Come on, I'll help you up the stairs. Sammy's making coffee.'

He'd stood it on a easel in the small gallery, and Sammy had trained a spotlight on to it. The varnish was dark, and cracked, and somebody had painted the frame with cheap golden gilt.

I was still confused with sleep, but I looked at it, I stood quietly, and looked.

How had he made yellows and reds so calm? How was that hot Provençal sky so peaceful?

Martin and I stood side by side, silently looking at our lovely Cézanne, and I felt tears on my cheeks, and once again I felt he had healed me, and I was happy.

Sammy came in behind us, quietly, I heard her put the tray down on the table, and she was standing behind us, looking. I could feel her smiling.

'Oh, God,' I whispered at last. 'It is perfect.'

'Well . . .' Martin was trying to shrug, trying to think of something to say.

A soft laugh from Sammy behind us.

'It's certainly Cézanne.'

Then I was laughing too, and so was Martin.

'Oh, yes. Yes, it's certainly Cézanne. Oh, Martin, well done. Well done.'

'Coffee. It should be champagne, but there's coffee.'

'It'll taste like champagne. Thank you, Sammy.'

'Oh, hell!' Martin, clapping a hand to his forehead. 'I left your shoebag in the taxi.'

'Good. I'm glad.'

'They'll find it, I'll telephone . . .'

'Martin, I don't want the shoebag. I very seriously don't want the shoebag.'

'But . . .'

I took his lovely, ugly white face between my hands, and kissed him on the forehead. Then I hugged Sammy and kissed her on both cheeks, and then we all turned and looked at our Cézanne again.

'Quite late, I think, don't you?' said Martin. 'Late nineteenth, early twentieth?'

'Yes,' I said. 'Yes, probably. Maybe. Don't know. Don't care.'

Sammy grinned beside him.

'He doesn't care either,' she said. 'He's a pretentious fraud. Oh, sweet Jesus, isn't it lovely?'

Martin had an arm around each of our shoulders, he'd never touched me before, this triumph had turned us into something more than friends.

'I don't know what I'd have done if I'd lost it,' he said. 'I'd have gone mad. But I didn't believe it. When I couldn't get you, or Robert, and that moron at sodding Barclays wouldn't let me have the money, I didn't think I'd get it. And here it is.'

His arm tightened around my shoulder, and he turned a smile of pure delight on me.

'Thank you, Glory. For getting the money, thank you.'

I shook my head. I couldn't take my eyes off the picture.

'Martin, take it out of that foul frame,' said Sammy. 'There's many a good bonfire needs a frame like that.'

'Yes,' I agreed. 'Have we got something that'll fit?'

'Oh, God, yes, I'm sure we have. Look, Glory, that big cupboard in the office. There's some more in the vault, but I think there's a silver-grey frame in the cupboard, it'll do until we get the right one.'

So for a few minutes we were all busy, and then our Cézanne was back on the easel, the wonderful calm colours

313

glowing through the dirty varnish, and we drank our coffee, and stood together looking at it, and Sammy spoke of getting it cleaned, and properly framed, and I could hardly speak at all.

'When have I got to pay back the money?' asked Martin at last.

I shrugged.

'When you can,' I said, and then, because it did have to be said, 'When you sell it.'

Some of the warmth died away, but he nodded, and Sammy drew in a deep breath.

'It's ours tonight, anyway,' she said.

'Oh, yes.'

'And a bit longer,' added Martin. 'I don't want it to go anywhere . . .'

He waved an arm vaguely, looking for a word.

'No gloaters,' I agreed. 'No bank vaults.'

They both smiled at me, and we were happy again.

I was still happy, still remembering our lovely picture, when I went in to work the following morning, and Simmie met me, looking a little apprehensive.

'You look nice,' he said tentatively. 'I've always liked that jersey. It suits you.'

'Oh, yes?'

'The cartoonists are out.'

'Good.'

'It's just Su-Su. She only needs a small corner, just that table by the window. Now, Glory, please. Honestly, it's only for a little while, just while the cartoonists are in her room.'

We were walking up the stairs by then.

'No,' I said.

'Oh, shit, Glory. There honestly isn't anywhere else, there *really isn't*, I know she's a bit weird, but she doesn't talk. Well, I mean, that's weird, isn't it? Glory? Please?'

I walked faster, leaving him behind.

'No.'

'You haven't even *met* her!' A despairing wail. 'If we put up a screen you won't even *see* her.'

I stopped outside my studio door. Simmie caught me up and stood in front of me. He was red in the face, out of breath. It wasn't a very long staircase, and Simmie wasn't old. His shirt buttons were straining across his stomach.

'Just a couple of days,' he pleaded. 'I'll try to find somewhere else for her. Please, Glory. Oh, *God*. I *wish* I could find some decent *premises*!'

There was sweat on his face, too, and something desperate in the way he pushed his hair back from his forehead.

'I wish you'd find a decent manager,' I said. 'I wish you'd delegate. I wish you wouldn't try to do everything yourself. I wish you'd lose four stone, I wish you'd give up smoking, I wish you and Mike would spend a bit more time relaxing, I wish you'd listen to your mother. How's that for a letter to Father Christmas?'

He blinked at me, and tried a smile.

'Does that mean you'll let Su-Su have the table by the window?'

'Oh, *Simmie*. You bloody, *bloody* man. Two days, not a minute more.'

She was very quiet, but not particularly weird. She was working with clay, modelling reliefs of faces on wooden boards, and she looked up as I came into the room. Small, and slim, with very dark eyes in a brown face, and brown hair tied back at the nape of her neck with a piece of coloured rag. She was wearing a long cotton skirt and a T-shirt, even though it was still winter.

'Good morning,' I said. 'I'm Glory Mayall.'

'I'm Su-Su. Good morning.'

We hardly spoke to each other again for the rest of the day.

She'd been there for a week before I even learned she had a child, a boy, five years old. She didn't know who the

315

father was. It had been a party, she'd been drunk. Any one of half a dozen men. Or, more probably, boys.

'You're not interested in who the father is?'

'No. Danny's mine. I won't share him.'

Su-Su wasn't deliberately mysterious, she just didn't like small talk. Most conversation was small talk, it seemed.

'How's Danny?' I would ask her in the mornings, as seemed polite.

'He's well, thank you.'

Those might be the last words we would exchange for several hours, and yet she wasn't unfriendly, and I found I didn't mind her working in my studio. There was nothing distracting about her. I could almost forget she was there.

I came in one morning feeling sick and ill, with a pain running from my neck through both shoulders and down my spine. I hadn't slept well, the nightmares had been bad, and in the end I'd given up, got dressed and sat at my table, trying to think. But I'd fallen asleep, and when the eyes and the voices jerked me back into wakefulness my neck hurt, I'd been lying awkwardly, and there was a draught from the window. I was coughing, too, and coughing was painful.

'How's Danny?'

'He's well, thank you.'

Jackson's wanted something new for their autumn window displays, I was to give a presentation, it had to be completely different, but not too unconventional. Exciting and eye-catching, but it mustn't worry their older, more conventional customers, who didn't like change.

Business as usual, in fact.

Storm, I thought. Dark grey background, the dummies leaning forward as though struggling against a strong wind, brightly coloured leaves to set off brightly coloured winter and autumn clothes. Everybody knows storms, it wouldn't worry anybody. How would I give the impression of movement?

I felt so sick. My neck hurt.

There were hands on my shoulders, firm, fingers probing into the muscles.

'Sit up,' said Su-Su.

I hate people touching me, even people I know. I have to be very happy before I let anybody touch me, and even then I find it hard not to flinch away.

This wasn't friendship from Su-Su. She seemed to know exactly what she was doing, just where my neck hurt, where my shoulders were stiff.

'Take off your sweater,' she said, and I did, and she took a bottle out of the big cotton bag she always brought with her, and rubbed some oil into her hands.

'Try to sit up straight.'

She had very strong hands, most people who work with clay develop strength in their hands, but she was clever. Her fingers hurt as they dug into the muscles, but gradually I could feel my shoulders sinking, lower and lower as the tension was massaged out of them, and I could hold my head straighter, and then her thumbs were working down my spine, vertebra by vertebra, small pressing movements, and the knuckles were hard against the muscles. After a while I began to breathe more easily, I could turn my head without pain, I could move my shoulders. All that was left was a soreness in the muscles from the probing fingers.

She went back to her table, she didn't say anything, and when I looked at her she was wiping the oil off her hands on a piece of rag, and looking down at the clay face on the board.

'Thank you,' I said, and she glanced at me, and smiled her slow, grave smile before turning back to her work.

I hadn't liked to ask Su-Su what she was doing, I felt she probably shared my aversion to talking about important matters to people who might not understand, but when I found myself standing next to one of the cartoonists who'd been turned out of my studio I asked him. We were

317

both queuing at the coffee machine, and I wanted to say something friendly, because I thought they might feel resentful about me refusing to work alongside them. I asked him if he knew why Su-Su was making the reliefs of the faces.

'For a film, isn't it?' he said. 'Pinewood. They're masks. Well, moulds for masks, I dunno, something like that. They get sprayed with this sort of rubber, latex. Good, aren't they? Those faces. Creepy. Simmie thinks the world of Su-Su. She's weird, isn't she?'

I rubbed my hand over the sore muscles in my shoulder, and murmured something non-committal.

I didn't think she was weird. I thought she was restful. I'd begun to look forward to seeing her when I came into my studio in the mornings.

'How's Danny?'

'He's well, thank you.' And then, after a long pause, 'Would you like to meet him?'

I was so surprised I could only look at her, and nod.

I don't like children, I never know what to say to them, but I couldn't tell Su-Su that, and I was curious.

We walked to her home that evening, and it was five miles. She didn't ask if it was too far for me, she just slung her big cotton bag over her shoulder, waited for me, and then we set off together, side by side, out of the industrial estate, across the small park, and then on to the rural roads to the north of the town.

'Can I bring anything?' I asked. 'Shall we stop at a shop?'

But she shook her head.

'I've got everything,' she said.

'A present for Danny?'

Again, she shook her head.

We collected Danny from a child-minder in the village, and Su-Su waited in silence as he put on his coat and his boots. He was a fair-haired child, with broad shoulders and a square face, nothing like his mother. He also seemed quiet, although he had shaken my hand politely when Su-Su introduced us.

But as soon as the door closed Danny launched himself at his mother with a yell and a big smile on his face, and she caught him and lifted him on to her hip, laughing at him, and Danny began to talk about his day, about a painting of a train, and what he had had to eat. He was, after all, a very normal little boy.

Su-Su answered his questions as we walked along the road, and if she didn't know, she turned the question to me. I tried to remember about migrating swallows, about why bees only came out in summer, and to give intelligent answers, but I could only shrug helplessly when challenged with questions about aeroplanes, and Su-Su laughed when Danny complained that I didn't know much, did I?

Su-Su lived in one half of a semi-detached farm cottage, an ugly red brick house. The other half was almost derelict. There was a Jersey cow tethered in the front garden, lying placidly on the bare earth, and Danny ran over to her and climbed up on to her, bouncing up and down on her ribs until she heaved herself to her feet. He seemed prepared for this, scrambling on to her shoulders as she moved, so that by the time she was standing he was sitting astride her, swinging his legs and crowing with triumph.

'Poor Naomi,' commented Su-Su as she lifted him down. 'She was having such a nice rest.'

The house was filthy. There were two rooms downstairs, the living room had a kitchen range in it, covered in dusty grease, the fire door open and spilling litter on to the hearth. There was a broken sprung sofa with clothes scattered over it, a square table with four chairs set around it, and shelves with books and toys. Nothing seemed to have been cleaned, ever.

Su-Su put the cotton bag on the floor beside the range and walked on into the kitchen, peeling off her T-shirt as she went. She was naked under it. Danny went to a shelf and pulled a box of toys on to the carpet.

I followed Su-Su into the kitchen. There were blackened potato peelings all over the floor, and she was walking around on them in bare feet.

'Can I help?'

'Would you like some tea?'

I hesitated. There didn't seem to be any clean crockery.

'I'd love some. What can I do?'

'You could get some vegetables if you like.'

'Where?'

'In the garden.' Su-Su was filling a kettle from the single tap over the stone sink. I didn't like to question her further, so I found a knife, wiped it on a rag, and took a cardboard box from under the table.

I recognised spinach, and purple sprouting broccoli, so I cut what seemed to be enough for three, and then looked around. The garden was far better tended than the house. It had been dug over recently, and there were glass cloches over a few rows of seedlings. There was a chicken run at the end of the garden, a few brown hens scratched at the earth, and some rabbit hutches.

I didn't want to go back into the house, so I walked down the path to look at the rabbits. They were big white rabbits, some of them in a covered cage on the grass, and they stood up on their hind legs as I approached, their whiskers twitching.

Su-Su came out a few minutes later. She glanced into the box as she came down the path, and smiled at me. She was still naked from the waist up, even though it was April and not very warm, and I wondered what she would do if somebody came down the road. We could be seen.

She picked up one of the rabbits, ran her hands over its fur, and carried it back towards the house. Danny came out of the door to meet us, carrying a wooden toy.

I suppose I thought the rabbits were his pets.

There was a stick in her hand.

She held the rabbit by its hind legs, it hung for a moment,

and then arched its back, and she swung the stick and brought it down, fast and hard, on to the back of its neck.

It jerked sharply, and then quivered, a sort of fluttering, and blood dripped from its mouth and nose on to the path. Su-Su still held it at arm's length.

'Potatoes, Danny,' she said, and he nodded, and put down his toy.

'Bake 'tatoes?' he asked. 'Big bake 'tatoes?'

'Yes.'

She was hanging the rabbit on a hook, she rammed the hook through the skin of its hind legs over the hock, and she had a knife. She cut its belly open, and a slippery mass cascaded out.

'I hope you like rabbit,' she said politely.

I thought I was going to be sick.

Danny had gone into the other house, through the open kitchen door. I could hear him in there, he was singing.

'Ten green botters, hangin' on a war, ten green botters, hangin' on a war, an' if one green botter should sassidenty faw . . .'

There were birds chirping in the hedge and in the fruit trees, a child singing, and Su-Su was skinning the rabbit, blood smeared on her forearm. As she pulled the skin down over the legs she cracked the bones, and sliced through the joints and the tendons with her sharp little knife.

Baked potatoes, I said to myself, rabbit, spinach and purple sprouting broccoli. Why not? An excellent meal. Nutritious, and fresh. Oh, God. Fresh.

'Do you produce all your own food?' I made myself ask, and Su-Su shook her head.

'Not flour, sugar, dairy products.'

'But the cow?'

She smiled at me.

'She hasn't calved yet.'

I eat meat, I told myself. I eat meat. I will eat this rabbit, this evening.

'There's some rosemary growing by the gate,' said Su-Su.
'Ah. I'll pick some, shall I?'

She smiled again, and there was a gleam in her dark face. She knew her lifestyle had shocked me, and she found my reaction amusing.

Danny came with me to pick rosemary. He'd found three big potatoes, all much the same size, which he told me was important. He said he was good at finding potatoes in the other kitchen, it was his job. His other job was putting grass in sacks for Naomi.

I saw him doing that later. The potatoes and the rabbit were in the oven. A Calor gas cooker, even dirtier than the range in the living room, stood against the wall of the kitchen. Su-Su put on her T-shirt again, picked up the big cloth bag, and Danny came into the room, dragging two big sacks.

'Takin'. Naomi for a walk,' he said. 'Comin'?'

Danny rode Naomi, and Su-Su led her. I walked beside them, carrying the sacks and a sickle.

'Most people take dogs for walks,' I commented inanely, trying to bring myself back to normal, but Su-Su just nodded, as though agreeing with me.

'Naomi, Naomi, very hairy,' chanted Danny loudly. 'Hairy Naomi, Naomi hairy.'

He was swinging his legs, his arms were crossed over his chest. He was balanced perfectly.

'Poem,' he explained when he saw me looking at him.

'I was just thinking how well you ride,' I said, but the compliment meant nothing to him.

'Like my *poem*?' he insisted.

'Yes.'

We kept stopping. Every time we came to a stretch of grass verge Su-Su stopped, and the cow grazed.

'How do you come to have a Jersey cow?' I asked Su-Su, and she looked thoughtful, and Danny laughed.

'Have to *talk*,' he said, and then crowed with delight. 'Su-Su's got to *talk*.'

She grinned at him, and nodded.

'Okay,' she said ruefully. 'Su-Su's got to talk.'

She'd been to the farm market to buy gardening tools at the auction, and then she'd gone to look at the animals. There'd been a Jersey heifer in a stall by herself, and she'd been curious. Most of the cattle were beef bullocks, you didn't often see Jerseys at the meat auction. The bullocks were wild-eyed, backing away when anybody approached, but the heifer was quite calm. She seemed puzzled, but she wasn't afraid, until she was driven into the ring.

The men hit her with sticks to make her go into the ring, and she couldn't understand, she was bewildered and frightened, she obviously hadn't been hit before, she kept crashing into the sides of the ring, trying to get away from the sticks, or turning to face the men, and then they hit her in the face.

Su-Su had bid for her. A barren heifer, small and rather thin, she wouldn't make a high price. Jerseys don't make good meat, they're not worth buying in to fatten.

Twenty pounds. Su-Su only had three and some small change, and an hour before she had to pay. So she'd gone down to the station, and stood on the corner of the main street, and taken off her shirt. She'd stood there, half naked, flaunting her breasts, in the middle of the afternoon, in the town centre. A taxi driver had picked her up just before the police arrived.

'I need twenty pounds,' she'd said, and he'd laughed. But he'd paid her.

She'd made a halter out of some old rope, and led the heifer home. Naomi, she'd called her. Whither thou goest, I will go, because Naomi had followed her out of the market, the rope from the halter slack.

It had taken them four hours to walk home. Naomi had been exhausted, and thirsty, so they had kept stopping to rest, and at houses where Su-Su could ask for water. Naomi's face had been swollen where the men had hit her, so Su-Su had been looking for herbs in the verges, and that had delayed them, too. Danny had been quite worried.

We'd reached a wood by the time Su-Su finished speaking, and Danny slid off Naomi's back as Su-Su tied the halter rope around the heifer's neck and let her walk free under the trees. Su-Su was beginning to sound hoarse, and I realised she probably hadn't talked as much as that for a long time.

She took the sickle from me, and started to cut grass. I watched her, she was quick and supple, the sickle moved in an easy rhythm, and the grass fell behind it. Danny scampered through the trees, still chanting his Hairy Naomi poem, and Naomi cropped at plants, moved on, browsed on leaves on low tree branches, and turned to look at Danny as he played among the trees.

'You said she hadn't calved *yet*,' I said, remembering. 'Isn't she barren, then?' and Su-Su shook her head.

'Due in January.'

She coughed, but I remembered her amusement when I had seen her kill the rabbit, and I smiled.

'How did you find out she wasn't barren?' I asked, and Su-Su stopped cutting the grass and looked up at me. I returned her gaze, and we stared at each other under level brows. Then she smiled, and I knew she had recognised my small revenge.

She coughed again.

'Okay,' she said.

She'd known nothing about cows, she'd never imagined she'd own one, but she'd hated the bewilderment and the fear she'd seen, she'd had to take Naomi out of that. All she knew for sure about cows was that they were herbivores.

She and Danny had spent that evening cutting grass for Naomi.

She'd gone to a farm the next day, a small place where they had Jerseys, and by chance it was the farm where Naomi had been bred.

'She's barren,' said the farmer. 'What are you going to do with her?'

Su-Su had shrugged, and he'd raised his eyebrows.

'Bit big for a pet, isn't she?'

'They were hitting her in the face with sticks,' said Su-Su, and he'd winced. Su-Su remembered Naomi had been bewildered because she'd never been hit before.

He'd sold her some hay, and brought it round in the trailer that evening. He'd rubbed the heifer's forehead, and said he was glad to see her. He'd noticed the swollen bruises on her face.

Su-Su and Danny had talked about Naomi, and decided to let her feed herself in the wood. Danny had thought she might know what plants she needed to eat.

Danny heard his name, and came back to us, jumping over clumps of grass with his arms outstretched.

'Grass in sack?' he asked Su-Su, and she nodded. He picked up the two sacks, and tried to spread them out. They were tangled, and heavy, and he couldn't free them. Su-Su looked at him, but she didn't go to help. Danny dropped the sacks on the ground, and stamped his foot in exasperation.

'Bloody! Bloody!' he exclaimed.

When Naomi had come into season, bulling, they called it, Su-Su had led her to the farm.

'What about a stud fee?' the farmer had asked.

Su-Su had thought for a moment, and then pointed at the bull.

'What's his name?' she'd asked. 'Gigolo?'

He'd laughed.

'Go on, then. I told you, she's barren. No calf no fee's the usual arrangement.'

But Naomi hadn't been barren.

'Beginner's luck,' the farmer had said, but he'd been pleased for her. 'You'd better have her papers, I've still got them somewhere.'

Danny had untangled one of the sacks and was stuffing the cut grass into it.

'I made Naomi better,' he said, and Su-Su nodded.

'How did you do that?' I asked.

'I let her eat what she wants.'

I looked at Su-Su enquiringly as she straightened up and pressed her hands into the small of her back, but she shook her head. I'd had my revenge, and she would say nothing more.

'What will you do with the calf?' I asked.

'Eat it.'

The gleam was back on her face.

22

I was to go to Birmingham straight away, drop everything, Simmie said, this is important.

A play, of course, what did I think it was, a Punch and Judy show? A play, an important play, please, Glory. Your best.

He and Mike were both looking anxious, and Mike was drinking too much coffee. He wasn't usually in Simmie's office at all, but he seemed to have taken over the armchair usually reserved for visitors.

'Northern Theatres, Inc.,' he said. 'It's an Inky.'

'Yes?'

'They're big.'

I waited. I knew they were big, everybody remotely connected with the theatre knew Inkies were big. They had a chain of theatres across the north of England and up into Scotland, and they even managed to make a profit from them.

'They want us to design the set for a play in Birmingham. Well, you, they want you.'

'Simmie, will you please come to the point?'

I was beginning to feel exasperated. It was hardly the first time I'd been sent off to design a set, even for a big company.

It was Mike who explained.

Inkies wanted to drop their design section, they wanted somebody outside the company to handle it. There was a valuable contract, and Simmie and Mike wanted it. Needed it. Hoped, desperately, to get it.

'Listen, we could rent their studios in Birmingham and take over their staff, well, that's actually part of the contract, one of the terms. But that's okay, we can use them, and God knows we need the studios.'

I looked at Simmie. He was sweating again, he hated the heat, and the weather was oppressive. He'd put on even more weight during the spring. Whenever the pressure became too much Simmie ate sweet cakes or chocolate biscuits.

'Wouldn't it mean splitting up Lawley's?' I asked. 'What about Mike and the clothing section? What about the advertising sets?'

Simmie shook his head.

'We could get a grant. They're putting up new factories, they want new businesses. They're offering grants. We'd all move. If we get this contract, we could get a big enough loan to move.'

I began to shake. I didn't want this responsibility, this was too much.

'It all depends on this play?' I asked. 'I mean, on my design?'

'Oh, no. No, listen, Glory, don't worry.' Mike was trying to be reassuring. 'No, nothing like that. We'll try for the contract anyway, I mean, that's mostly financial, that's accountants and lawyers, leave it to them, thank God. But, listen, when we contacted them they said they'd like to see what we can do. And this is the play they want us to do.'

It sounded very much like a test production to me.

'They've got their own managers, too,' said Mike. 'They're very good. Simmie would be able to concentrate on the advertising side. He'd like that.'

He was looking at Simmie, and there was anxiety in his face. He loved Simmie very much.

'Do your best,' said Simmie. 'I'm not worried about that. You *are* the best. There's just one problem.'

'What's that?'

'The play. It's shit. Sorry.'

I took the script back to my studio, and read it.

It was even worse than I had expected. It was banal and predictable, and most of the dialogue consisted of clichés. They could not possibly expect this thing to run.

I looked at the specifications, particularly at the budget, which was miserly.

This was exactly what I had feared, a test. A test of my abilities.

I telephoned Jacob Goldman at his office, and left a message with his secretary asking him to call me back when he could. It only took an hour.

'Valerie said you sounded worried. What's the matter?'

I told him about Northern Theatres Incorporated, and the contract, and the horrible play with its tiny budget.

'I'll do it, Jacob, but I don't want Simmie landed with a white elephant, he's already under too much pressure.'

'Yes, I see. I know his mother's worried about him. I'll find out. Where are they putting it on?'

'It's called the Queen of Sheba, is it a pub, or something?'

'Oh, that dump. I thought they'd pulled that down. I'll call you back this afternoon.'

In the meantime I contacted Robert Cameron.

'Are you phoning about the Cézanne?' he asked when I finally reached him through a battalion of switchboard operators and personal assistants. 'Martin isn't hurrying to sell it, do you need your money back?'

'No, Robert, I need information. Northern Theatres, I need to know why they're contracting their design department out, I'm looking for elephant traps.'

He laughed.

'Where did you get that phrase? It's rather good.'

'I made it up. Can you help?'

'I can try. Glory?'

'Yes?'

'That's a *lovely* painting.'

'I want to talk to you about Revelations,' I said, 'but not today. Today it's Inkies, please.'

A cast of ten in the play, God, who never actually appeared but who boomed from the heavens, a monk, and eight angels, who gradually turned into demons as the play progressed. I wondered whether part of the script was missing, I couldn't believe anybody would want to produce this play.

But Jacob told me they were serious.

'Don't pass this on because you're not supposed to know. There are four other plays being put on in dumps like the Queen of Sheba, so yes, my clever darling, it's a test.'

'Oh, Jacob, that's mad. You don't put on five losers.'

'No, you don't. I'm afraid you've drawn the short straw. They wanted five new plays, so there'd be no pre-conceived notions. They got one good one, three possibles, and yours. They've got to pay the staff anyway, the actors are still under contract, and they're pulling down all five theatres this autumn.'

'God.'

'Also, my darling, as you know, about one in four rubbish plays catches on and makes a bit of money.'

'It won't be this one, and what about their reputation?'

'I was coming to that. They've formed a shell company, and it's a "nothing to do with us, thank you very much". Except for the designers. Simmie's company is one of the smallest. If you don't get the contract, don't blame yourself, it won't be your fault.

'Don't get in a state about it. I hope the other lot aren't counting any chickens. I wouldn't be if I was up against my clever darling. Just one more thing, Gloriana. Don't *trust* anybody.'

Jacob only ever called me Gloriana when he was saying something he wanted me to remember.

'I've got nothing concrete to tell you, I'm afraid, but you be careful. It's a small world, theatre management, but in a case like this you don't always know who's backing what. Sabotage is a dirty word, but you'd better learn it.'

'Thank you. I'll remember.'

'Use the brain,' he said, 'and break a leg.'

There would have to be quick changes between the scenes in this play, impossibly quick changes as the angels became demons, although whoever had written the thing gave no indication of how this was to be achieved.

I told myself to stop thinking about the quality of the play, and get on with my own job.

Robert Cameron called back. There was no problem with Inkies, it was a slimming exercise. A good idea. Streamline, concentrate on what they did best, farm out everything else, but they were behaving well. They weren't dumping their staff, and they were making sure the contract went to a firm that could handle it.

'Oh. Good,' I said bleakly. I'd been hoping I could go back to Simmie and Mike with a tale of impending disaster in Inkies, a clear warning not to get involved.

'There's a big deal with Inkies and Firmline Construction. They're demolishing five old theatres this autumn, and putting up smaller ones on the sites. Has this got anything to do with your information?'

'Only as a sideline. Five new plays in five condemned theatres. I'm told they're just using the people who're still under contract.'

'Let me know if you hear any whispers. It might be worth buying into Firmline.'

I pulled a sketch pad towards me, and picked up a thick black pencil. In this play God could take care of Himself, that wasn't my department, but His angels were trouble.

Simmie nearly locked me into my studio that night. I was

still sketching, and throwing away nearly everything I drew. Whenever I had an idea that seemed possible, the ridiculously low budget put it out of my reach, and anything I could do within the budget was hopelessly conventional.

'Hey!' I yelled as I heard the key turn, and he unlocked the door again and came in, looking surprised.

'Still here?'

'As you see.'

'All right, no need to be sarcastic. Is that the Inkies play?'

'Yes.'

He hovered by the table, wanting to look at what I was doing, knowing I didn't like it.

'Su-Su cleared all the clay away, then?'

'Yes, thank you.'

'Well.' He tugged at his tie. He'd been meeting clients that afternoon, he was wearing a suit. 'You'll lock up then, will you? When you go?'

'Yes.'

'When do you think you'll go to Birmingham?'

'When I've got a *bloody idea* of *something* to *show them*. Not *one bloody day earlie*r.'

He looked hurt, and I apologised.

'I'm doing my best, Simmie. I know it's important. I've got to take some ideas with me, otherwise I'll just look incompetent.'

I went three days later.

The Queen of Sheba was as Jacob had described it, a dump. It had been built just before the war, and the architect had tried to avoid straight lines, so the corners were rounded, the roof was a flattened dome, and the frontage was broken up with wrought iron balconies, which had rusted, leaving brown streaks down the grey concrete.

'They're going to pull it down this autumn,' said the caretaker. 'They're going to build a new one. It's going to be smaller. It's going to have a car park.'

'Just so long as it's going to have a stage,' I said, and he stared at me.

'I'll let you in then, shall I?' he asked. 'I'm going to have my tea break.'

I hadn't told anybody I was coming. I wanted to explore the theatre alone, to see which of my ideas could be made to work, and which I could discard immediately.

The auditorium smelt musty, and the seats were hard, and lumpy. The audience was likely to be depressed even before the curtain rose on to the scene of a monk's cell, not a sight that was likely to lift their spirits.

There were two stage hands working in the wings, slapping cheap whitewash on to the concrete walls, which had been covered in graffiti.

'Is the stage manager here?' I asked, and and one of them turned and looked me up and down.

'Who wants to know, gorgeous?'

'I'll find him myself.'

I walked away, and the other man called after me.

'He isn't here.'

The place seemed bare. Most of the doors were locked, and there were big pale patches on the walls of corridors where cupboards must have stood. A few torn posters were stuck to notice boards. The floors were either concrete, or covered with worn linoleum; even the carpeting had been stripped out.

'Shit,' I muttered as I looked around. 'Oh, shit, shit, shit.'

At least the stage was clean. It was big, too, which meant I could expand the sets, working outwards from the monk's cell of the opening scene to Hell at the end. There might even be backdrops that would work, I could save something of the budget.

The stage hand who'd called me gorgeous stood in front of me.

'You can't go up there, darling.'

He was grinning at me, leaning across the stairway with

one hand against the wall, barring my way. Once again, he looked me up and down, his eyes lingering on my breasts.

'I'm the designer,' I said quietly. 'I think you'll find I can go anywhere I like. Please stand aside.'

He laughed, but he pushed himself away from the wall and stood back. I walked up the steep iron steps, knowing he was watching me, trying not to be alarmed. If I looked down at him he would follow me. He would see it as an invitation.

He's a rapist, I thought to myself, and I shivered.

I didn't know why I was so sure. There was something about the attitude, it wasn't the boastfulness of a man who lacked confidence with women, it was the arrogance of one who took what he wanted, and sometimes wanted women.

There were only two backcloths hanging from the bars. Both were torn. One was a forest scene, the other plain black.

Footsteps behind me on the grids, he had followed me. I didn't turn round.

'Are these the only backcloths there are?' I asked.

'I didn't come up here to talk about backcloths, beautiful.'

Don't look at him, don't react. Fifty feet above the stage, this is a dangerous place for a struggle. Don't react.

He was standing close to me. I could feel his breath on my hair. There was a whisper of cloth, he was reaching out towards me.

I began to walk away, along the grid over the stage.

'Lower the black one, please,' I said.

Would he do as I told him? Or would he follow me again?

He was hesitating, thinking about it. Then I heard him move away, and there was the shrill squeaking of rusty pulleys.

'Oil those while you're up here,' I called back.

There was a man waiting for me at the foot of the steps, small and middle-aged, in shabby working clothes.

334

'I didn't know you were coming today,' he said, and he stuck out a hand. 'Robert Larwood. Bob. Stage manager.'

'Glory Mayall,' I answered, smiling back and shaking his hand. 'Designer. I didn't tell anybody I was coming.'

'Ah. Secretive type. Cup of tea?'

'Coffee, if I may.'

'No problem, but it's instant. Paint store do you? I'd say my office, but I haven't got one.'

He'd already turned away, so I called after him.

'Talking of problems, Bob, have you had any with that stage hand up there?'

He seemed surprised at my question.

'Which one's that?'

'The dark one with the moustache.'

'Ned Fleming? No, I don't think so. Why?'

Was it worth making an issue of this? What was there to complain about?

'He seems a bit pushy. I don't like stage hands who make passes at me, particularly before they even know my name.'

Bob smiled again, and gestured towards a corridor.

'Paint store? If I may say so without seeming to make a pass, I'm sure you're used to handling that sort of situation.'

Bob found an empty dressing room that would do as an office for me. It was clean, and bare, and he promised there'd be a desk in it that afternoon.

'They've stripped just about everything out,' he said. 'But the office stuff's still here. I know it's a dump, but I'll be sad when they pull it down.'

Everybody called the Queen of Sheba a dump, it was the only word I'd heard used to describe it.

'I want a new lock on my door,' I said. 'And I don't want keys to it left lying around.'

He was genuinely startled. I looked for an explanation.

'I'm paranoid,' I said. 'I hate people looking at my drawings. Bear with me, take it seriously.'

'All right, anything you say.' He was still surprised,

perhaps even a little hurt, but he would do as I asked. I didn't want to worry about Ned Fleming cornering me in my own room.

We spent the rest of the morning looking at what was left of the scenery and props. As Bob had said, everything had been stripped out, unless it was too worn or damaged to be worth moving.

'The lights are all right,' he said, trying to find something encouraging to tell me.

I already knew that, but I affected the relief I'd felt when I'd first checked them. I would have to rely heavily on those lights.

'No plans to strip them out before the play comes on?' I asked.

'Oh, no.' He laughed. 'No, they wouldn't do that to you.'

'I want the black backcloth.'

'It's torn.'

'I know. I'll tear it even more before I'm finished. I only want the top half.'

He did a good job on my office. There was a desk and a table, and the lights were clear and bright, and carefully placed. Somebody had put a pot plant on the windowsill and a vase of flowers on the table. I was touched by that; he was trying to make me feel welcome, and the gesture told me he would do his best for me.

The lock on the door had been changed, and two keys lay on the desk blotter. I thought of asking who had installed the new lock, and whether there had been time to have another key cut, but I rejected the idea. It really would have been paranoid, I told myself.

Ideas were, at last, beginning to come. I sketched, and sucked my pencil, and thought about lines and angles and lighting, and the simplicity with which it would have to be put together. The costumes would take most of the budget. The speed of the changes, not all of them even between scenes, would dictate the designs. Even the make-up, we would have to bring in professionals, the actors wouldn't have time. They probably wouldn't like it, most actors prefer to do their own make-up, but it would be impossible, at that speed.

Another chunk of the budget.

I read through a part of the script, reading aloud into a tape recorder, and timing it.

Fifteen seconds was the time the angel was off the stage, and there had to be a change of costume and make-up in that time.

It simply wasn't possible. He'd hardly have time to take off the first costume.

I sucked my pencil and stared at the ceiling.

He would have time to take off part of it. And with a good professional make-up artist in the wings, given a bit of practice and a cast willing to try, we might do this. If, instead of a change of costume, we stripped it down, there would be time. Just.

There was a knock on my door, and I shook my head in irritation.

'No!' I shouted. 'Not now.'

'Sorry.' An affronted grumble, and footsteps on the corridor floor.

Bloody carpeting, they'd have to bring it back. Nobody could put on a play with a noise like that backstage.

The same system with the scenery, it could work. The walls of the cell could be make of glass, or clear plastic, the stone painted on gauze behind them. Layers of gauze, several layers, they could be lifted throughout the play, and the flames of Hell would gradually begin to show through. It could do something for this totally feeble script, it could help. In the final scene the monk would be left with only the illusion of the stone walls between him and the Hell that he and his God had created, and surrounded by the demons of his selfish solitude. Everything stripped down to reality, or delusion, whichever of the two the audience preferred.

'Yes!' I exclaimed. 'Yes.'

Over the next few days, the theatre seemed to come to life. Various people connected with Inkies, or the play, came and went, the actor who'd been cast as God arrived, sat at various points in the wings, on the staircase into the flies, and up on the grid itself to try out his lines, and left every evening looking glum. He had a beautiful baritone voice.

Bob Larwood retrieved the carpeting from a warehouse in an industrial estate, and Ned Fleming unrolled it along the corridors. I tried to stay out of his way, but it wasn't always possible. Often he would be waiting for me, around a corner, behind a door, and always on those occasions he would step in front of me, barring my way.

'Hello, beautiful.'

'Please let me pass.'

An insolent smile, and his eyes lingering on my body. Sometimes a hand reaching out, as if to stroke me, but I always managed to back away, and walk off.

'No good running, darling. What I've got in mind for you, you're going to love.'

I mentioned him to Bob again, but Bob seemed dismissive, a little impatient; this was a problem, if problem it was, that I should be handling myself.

'Haven't you got a boyfriend who could warn him off?' he asked.

'He's in Hong Kong.'

I wondered why I had lied. Was Sam still in Hong Kong? He might as well be. Big, quiet-spoken man with a slightly broken nose, who had put his arm around my shoulders only once. Miss Mayall has mentioned you to me. But Ned Fleming was no immature art school student.

I ripped the lower half of the black backcloth away, and I tacked red and yellow flame-shaped pieces to what was left, with sheets of reflective foil between them. I played with filters and coloured spots, and low, glowing red lamps to light the flames from behind.

I painted grey brickwork on gauze.

The rest of the cast arrived, and from then on I was working around them, but the old Queen of Sheba was waking up again, it was as though there was a movement and a stretching in the damp-stained walls and the flaking woodwork.

'Hello, darling. Beautiful as ever.'

'Please let me pass.'

'I'm beginning to lose patience with you, my gorgeous. I don't mind playing games for a while, but it's time you started being nice to me.'

The wardrobe mistress was no Linda Pasmore, but she understood my drawings and said she could make the costumes. Dense white cotton, over white muslin, and more white muslin, and dark grey muslin fitting closer, and then skin-tight black, to look like skin, or leather.

'Ooh!' she exclaimed. 'Dead sexy. I hope they've got the bodies for it.'

The assistant director arrived, and seemed to like everybody except me. Graham Fitch. I'd never heard of him.

'Haven't Lawley's got anybody more experienced than that?' I heard him ask of the director. 'Do you think they're taking this seriously enough?'

'Come on, Graham. She's very good.'

Inkies were playing fair. Ronald Harmer was directing the play, and he was good. There were no star names in the cast, but they were all professionals, Jacob Goldman's definition of professionals. They worked hard, they didn't complain about the script, they made the best they could of their lines.

'Hello, gorgeous. No, don't run off, not this time.'

'Let me pass.'

'There's no hurry, my beautiful, and there's nobody here. Just you and me, like it's meant to be.'

I looked down at the floor, at the running shoes he was wearing, and I drew in my breath before raising my head and staring him in the eyes.

'Fleming, isn't it? Is that your name? Well, Fleming, if you approach me one more time, if you even speak to me again except on matters relating to your work, I shall report you to Mr Harmer. And I shall insist that you leave.'

His insolent smile was broader than ever, and this time when he reached out he was quick, I didn't manage to back away, and his hand brushed against my breast.

'All woman, no padding,' he said. 'All the bluff's in the mouth. That's all right, I don't mind mouth. So long as the body's all right, I don't mind mouth. I might even listen, if you say the things I like. I do listen to women sometimes. When they say the right things. Do you know what to say to a man, my gorgeous? To make him listen?'

He was standing very close, and I was pressed up against the wall, pushing myself against it, trying to keep as far away from him as I could. He was right, there was nobody there, nobody in this part of the theatre at all. If I screamed I might be heard, but I would have to scream.

He seemed to recognise the thought, because suddenly his hand was in front of my face, hovering close to my mouth. The idea that I might scream seemed to amuse him, or perhaps arouse him. The smile had tightened, his eyes were bright, and narrowed, and he began to breathe faster.

'Do you think I'd notice rape from a thing like you?' I asked. I kept my voice light. 'I doubt it. All it would need would be a bath, and you'd just be a rather grubby memory.'

He laughed.

'You'll notice, my darling. You'll never forget. You'll be begging.'

Begging. I'd heard men begging, I still heard their voices in the night, I still saw their eyes, but I closed mine, and I waited, and then she was there, and her voice was hard and quiet, and violent.

'You are filth, and you deserve what I am going to do to you.'

His eyes widened.

'I have knives and I have whips. You will bleed, filth. You will bleed, and you will cry. You will scream until your voice breaks, and then you will whimper.'

We both heard the footsteps at the same time, and he turned his head quickly. I ducked under his arm and walked away.

'Gloriana? Miss Mayall? *Madam?*' he called after me, and I looked back. He was smiling.

'That's what turns you on, is it, my beautiful? Well. That's good to know. That's very useful. I'll remember that, gorgeous.'

The pressure was growing. Coping with Ned Fleming was more than I could handle.

The angels' wings were the main problem. I'd designed them to pull apart with clips, light plastic to which I would affix feathers, but when we stripped them apart the clips broke.

I tried again, the property master suggested stronger clips.

Andy Gregson was his name, and he deserved a better job than this.

'Could we slide them together?' he asked.

'What about the feathers? They'd just strip off.'

'Clipped on to a backing?'

We couldn't find a way of hiding it.

Steel clips, they held, and then the plastic broke.

'It'll have to be metal,' I said. 'The whole frame, it'll have to be metal. Steel.'

He stared at me.

'They'll never do it,' he said. 'They'll never manage it. How much would it weigh?'

I didn't know. He calculated it, weighing a piece of sprung steel, and shook his head. Nearly forty pounds, absolutely impossible. I'd have to find another way.

But I couldn't. In fifteen seconds, there wasn't an actor in

341

the world who could change one set of wings for another, and strip off part of a costume, all the while having his make-up adjusted. It could not be done.

'Well, that means the damned play can't be done,' said Andy flatly. 'It's impossible, Glory. To hold that weight steady you'd have to have the straps across their chests so tight they'd hardly be able to breathe. I think you'll have to tell Inkies it's impossible.'

Sorry, Simmie. Sorry, Mike. I couldn't do the job. Sorry.

I went to the cast instead, and told them.

'How much would it weigh?' asked Darren Clark.

'It could be nearly forty pounds.'

They looked at each other.

'I did it once with fifteen,' said Nicholas Mack. 'Tree branches, that was. Speaking wasn't easy with those straps. Forty?'

They all shook their heads. Sorry, Glory. It can't be done. Sorry.

'Only for the first act,' I said. 'Then it gets lighter. After the first act the heaviest bit comes off, you could slacken the straps then.'

They were sympathetic, even apologetic, but it couldn't be done.

But neither could the change of wings, and anyway the budget only stretched to one set of wings for each actor.

'Tell them,' said Andy. 'You'll have to, Glory. It's an impossible play. I'll back you up. It's like saying have a demon king appear in a puff of smoke in the middle of the stage, but no trap door. It can't be done.'

I lay awake that night, worrying, and wondering.

I went shopping on my way into the theatre the next morning, a good rucksack from a camping shop, crêpe bandages from a chemist, and then a visit to a builders' merchant's, where a bewildered young assistant obligingly shovelled exact weights of sand into strong polythene bags, packed them into the rucksack, and held it for me as I pushed my arms through the shoulder straps and adjusted them.

'Now I need to tie it with these bandages,' I said.

'Pardon?'

'It's got to be absolutely steady. This is an experiment. It's got to be tight.'

I wasn't at all sure I could even walk to the end of the road with it, let alone the half-mile to the Queen of Sheba. By the time I arrived I was drenched with sweat and gasping, and the straps and bandages had rubbed raw patches on my ribs and shoulders. I leaned against the corridor wall, pushing the rucksack against it to take some of the weight, until I had caught my breath, and then I made my way to the Green Room.

'What the hell is that?' demanded Phillip Greaves. 'What are you playing at?'

'It's forty pounds of sand in a rucksack. I've carried it from Bridge Street.'

'Oh, good grief, Glory . . .'

'So? Good grief? Can we put on this play?'

'It's not that we don't want . . .'

The sweat was beginning to sting the raw patches on my shoulders, they were seriously hurting. I could feel tears coming into my eyes.

'I'm going to tell them,' I said, and there was a choke in my voice. 'We can put this angels play on, but not with a cast of fairies, I'll tell them that, shall I?'

John Hall vaulted over the sofa and peered at me over the back of it.

'Strewth!' he exclaimed. 'Who's auditioning for Godzilla today? They never warned us.'

Phillip was behind me, supporting the weight of the rucksack.

'Take it off,' he said. 'Come on, sweetie, take it off. Let me have it.'

'Surely,' I said as I slid my arms out of the straps, 'surely,

343

if I can carry that thing over half a mile in this heat, you could manage it for a little while on stage? You're all much stronger than I am.'

Phillip shook his head, but he was hefting the rucksack in one hand, and I'd hardly been able to lift it with both mine.

'God, but women are dirty fighters,' said Darren. 'Here, let me try that thing.'

I sank down on to the sofa, cautiously flexing my shoulders, longing for a cool shower and some soothing cream for the raw patches. Would the straps have to be tighter than those bandages? If so, it was true; they couldn't do it. I'd have to give up.

Darren grimaced as Phillip pulled the bandages tight, and shook his head at me.

'Did you really carry this from Bridge Street?'

'Glory, you didn't have to . . .'

'Give the girl a drink.'

Darren was walking around with the rucksack on his back, moving his arms, crouching and straightening as he had to do in the first act of the play.

'Orange juice, sweetie? Want a brandy in it?'

'What about it, Darren?' Phillip was beginning to laugh.

'Hell. Oh, bloody hell. Honestly, I don't know. It's going to be murder. I don't know if I can. I really don't know.'

But they would try. They didn't promise more than that. They wanted their own rucksacks and sandbags for the rehearsals, and they would try.

When they agreed, the tears did come into my eyes, and they mopped my face with paper handkerchiefs and called me an unscrupulous little blackmailer.

'You're all lovely,' I said. 'Gorgeous, every one of you. Thank you. Thank you *very* much.'

The wings would have to be made by a specialist. I couldn't do them myself. Andy Gregson was a good property master, but he couldn't handle these.

344

'Send them back to the studio,' said Bob. 'They'll do them.'

'I need a quotation. There's a budget.'

He noticed my wry smile, and grinned.

But it was Graham Fitch who took my drawings to the studio. He was going anyway, he said. I didn't like giving him the designs, but I could hardly refuse.

He came back the next day to say the work would have to be contracted out.

'Why?' I demanded.

He raised his eyebrows.

'Because they can't do it. I suppose you do realise how complicated those designs are? You drew them.'

And I heard him remark to Ronald Harmer when he met him on the stage:

'Another teenage tantrum from our little moppet. And what's this damned nonsense with rucksacks and sand-bags?'

'She persuaded them to try, Graham. I couldn't have done that, and neither could you.'

I'd wanted to tell Ronald Harmer about Ned Fleming. Now, it would seem childish. Please, Mr Harmer, a stage hand made a pass at me, I was frightened. Please, Mr Harmer, make the nasty man go away. It would have to be the stage manager, whether he was interested or not.

'Bob?'

He was splicing cables for the gauze backdrops to the monk's cell.

'Ned Fleming is becoming a poisonous pest, and I can't deal with him and all the other problems. Please sack him.'

He put down his marlin spike with a sigh, and spread out his hands helplessly.

'We've only got the bare minimum of staff as it is, where do you think I can find a replacement? Please don't be unreasonable.'

'Am I being unreasonable? He's threatened to rape me.'

345

'Oh, he's all talk. I'll tell him to lay off.'

He had picked up the spike, he was working again, his head bowed over his hands. I'd get nothing more from him.

I broached my next problem.

'Who's making the angels' wings?'

'I don't know. Didn't Graham Fitch organise that? Ask him.'

Damn. Oh, damn.

'Who usually does that sort of work?'

'It's usually done at the studio.'

'He said it was too complicated for them.'

Bob looked surprised, but he shrugged.

'Oh. Well, I don't know. Ask Mr Fitch.'

The actors were beginning to manage the rucksacks. Darren said it was almost impossible, but perhaps not quite. Not with a few more rehearsals. They still weren't promising, but they were doing their best.

'It's the sweat,' he explained. 'What about the make-up?'

'Don't tell her that, she'll have us in steel masks!'

'We have to prance around,' said Phillip. 'And those leather trousers, Glory, they're *indecent*. Any tighter and they'll show our religion.'

I went to see Graham Fitch.

'Have you got the quotation for the wings yet?' I asked.

'It's somewhere in my office. Please don't bother me now, I'm dreadfully busy.'

'Can you remember how much it was? I do need to know.'

'Between two and three hundred pounds, I think.'

He looked at me, and raised his eyebrows.

'Didn't you know how expensive that sort of work is?'

He made his voice sound amazed, even though I hadn't registered any surprise. Ronald Harmer must be within earshot, I thought.

'And when will they be ready?' I insisted.

'Miss Mayall, please. As I said, I am busy.'

346

'On something more important than the actors being able to rehearse with the props? Please, do tell me what that could be. I thought plays took priority in theatres.'

He gave me a dirty look. They'd be ready in time, he said. Some time next week.

The dress rehearsal was scheduled for the end of the following week.

The weather was sultry, it hadn't rained for a month and we were all feeling oppressed by it. There was no air-conditioning in the old Queen of Sheba, and the fans Bob Larwood brought in only seemed to stir the hot air, not cool it.

Anthea Bacon was beginning to worry about the wings.

'We ought to be fitting those costumes over them,' she said.

'I know. They're cutting it very fine. Sorry, Anthea.'

'It's the fastenings, Glory. They ought to be rehearsing with them, too. I don't know where to put the velcro tabs on the robes. It's got to be velcro, there's nothing else they can get off in time.'

'Yes, I do know. I'm sorry, it'll be a rush.'

'Well.' She sounded doubtful and unhappy. 'You're the designer.'

It was beginning to sound like an accusation.

'God, I wish it would rain. I wish it would rain.'

Everybody seemed to be praying for rain, or even a breath of wind.

'Hello, you sexy slut. Got some dirty talk for me?'

'*Get out of my way.*'

He called after me, he didn't seem to care if anybody heard.

'I'm going to tie you down and jack you up. You're going to love it. Leather manacles I've got for you, gorgeous.'

I went straight to Bob Larwood.

'If you talked to Ned Fleming it didn't work,' I said, and he clapped a hand to his forehead.

347

'Oh, God. I forgot.'

'Now, Bob. Right now, before you forget again, and please make it tough. I mean it, he's a menace.'

Pressure, too much pressure, I felt as if everything was coming to the boil, I wasn't in control. I was beginning to wonder how much longer we could bear the heat. The weather forecast was for a storm, but the sky was clear, the air completely still. There were warnings on the radio about heat stroke.

'We ought to be rehearsing with those wings.' A gentle nudge from Nick Mack. 'We can't even tell you if we can do this, not until we've got the wings.'

'I know. Sorry, Nick. I'm doing my best.'

A reassuring smile, and a wink.

'Good enough.'

'Bob, did you speak to Ned Fleming?'

'I couldn't find him, I think he's gone home. I'll see him tomorrow.'

I wanted to shout at him. If your damned stage hand rapes me you'll be responsible, it'll be your fault for not listening to me.

Gloriana Mayall, quite good, but can't take the pressure. Yells at the staff and thinks every man in the theatre wants to get inside her knickers.

Somewhere in the distance there was a low mutter of thunder. Anthea threw open the door into the alleyway and stood leaning against the frame, looking up into the sky. It was blue, but there seemed to be a shadow over it, a dark veil, and everything was very still, and very clear.

Far away, the sound again, like a muffled roll of drums.

I went up to Graham Fitch's office and walked in without knocking.

'I want to see the quotation for the wings,' I said, and he glared at me.

'I didn't hear you knock.'

I held out my hand.

348

'The quotation. And the deadline. Now, please, Mr Fitch.'

'Impertinent little chit,' he muttered, and he made a show of shuffling through papers on his desk. 'It doesn't seem to be here, it must be in my other briefcase.'

'I'll telephone them. What's the name of the company?'

'Don't you know?'

The same affectation of amazement.

'Ronald Harmer's on stage,' I said. 'I don't think he can hear you, and anyway I rather doubt if such an experienced director could ever have been taken in by your performance. The name of the company, please, Mr Fitch.'

'Can't it wait until tomorrow?'

'Why should it? Don't *you* know the name of the company? Or are you actually refusing to divulge it? Shall we go down and ask Mr Harmer to adjudicate on this?'

His face was flushing, a dark, angry colour.

'They're probably closed by now,' he said. 'Reddington's. Can you find the number in the book? Or should I deal with that, too?'

I used the telephone directory that lay on his desk. Reddington's Metal Works, I wrote down the number, nodded at Fitch, and walked out. I'd telephone from my own office.

There was no reply. As he'd said, they were probably closed.

I could hear people in the other dressing rooms, they were getting ready to leave. They were talking to each other, they sounded happy. It was cooler, the storm was coming, there was a little wind. I lifted my head to listen, and the thunder rolled again, died away to a muted mutter, and then rose, an angry rumble.

Outside my window, a pale flash, and again. Sheet lightning.

I sat on my desk, looking at copies of my drawings. It was true, the wings were complicated, there hadn't been a way to make them simpler. But they weren't impossible, not to a competent metal worker. I'd had far more difficult props made than these wings.

Doors were closing, there were footsteps, people were going home. They were calling to each other, hurry before it rains, have you got an umbrella? Quick, we can catch the six o'clock bus. Come on, quick, before it rains.

This was going wrong. I knew this was all going wrong. But it was fair, that my luck was running out. I'd run out on a theatre, it was fair now that my luck ran out on me. If only there weren't other people, depending on my luck, I could face that, if it weren't for the other people. Something was missing. Something was going to happen. There was a man. Where was the man?

I was very tired.

It always seemed strange, evenings at the Queen of Sheba, because there was no play. Evenings in a theatre should be busy, there should be movement and excitement. Here, it was quiet. Everybody went home, or back to their digs. I'd never been in a deserted theatre in the evening, it was so quiet.

Only in the dressing rooms, when there was a play, then it had to be quiet. You could hear, you could hear applause through the loudspeakers when you switched them on, you could hear the play, but it had to be quiet then. Sitting alone in a dressing room, I was waiting, I was waiting. I had to be quiet. I was listening for the applause. It was a good play, there would be applause.

Then I heard it, a quick patter, like a fluttering sound, it died down, and then again, louder, and I smiled at the sound, I was happy, they liked the play, the applause was growing louder, and louder.

The door handle turned.

I watched it, I felt dreamy, watching that door handle turning, there was something in my memory. What happened next? A line, a pale line, the door frame. I'd see the door frame next, and a shadow on the frame.

350

But nothing happened. The handle turned again, and then nothing.

The door was locked.

Why did I feel cold? It was hot, it was still very hot, but there should be a fire, a gas fire. I wanted a gas fire, I wanted to be warm. I looked around the room, I was looking for a gas fire, but I knew there wasn't one. There was a radiator, just an ordinary radiator, why was I looking for a gas fire?

They were still applauding, I could hear them, I could hear them clapping, there was a drumming sound, stamping feet, soon they would be cheering. It was wonderful, how they loved the play.

I was wearing jeans and a shirt. It was time to change. I had to be ready.

Where was my dress? A beautiful dress, wild silk, where was my dress?

I looked around the room, slowly, vaguely. It was as if it was under water, nothing was very clear. There should be a dress. There should be a mirror.

It was time to change, it was time to get ready.

Slowly, I undid the buttons of my shirt. I slid it off my shoulders, and I folded it carefully. I'd have to put it in my bag.

Where was my bag?

I was hearing a voice, Cindy, little Cindy, it was a whispering voice. That was right, that came soon, I would hear that voice.

My brassière, it was the wrong one for my dress, undo the clip, slide the straps down my arms. And my jeans, the buckle of my belt, the zip fastener, push them down over my hips, down my legs, step out of them, step away from the stiff denim. Fold them, carefully, fold them. That was right, that was what I did.

But where was my dress?

The door would open, and there would be a shadow on the frame.

351

He had a key. He was holding it out towards me, show-ing it to me, it hung between his finger and thumb, and he was grinning at me, and his eyes were looking me up and down, he was grinning.

'Hello, gorgeous.'

I frowned. That wasn't right. Something wasn't right, that wasn't what he said.

'Tonight's the unforgettable night.'

It was wrong, it was all wrong. He shouldn't have a key, the door hadn't been locked. And he was tall, he was tall and lean and strong, and he should have been short, and fat. Why was he so tall and so strong? The words were wrong, it was all wrong.

I was in the wrong body.

'Getting ready for me,' he said. 'I like that. Aren't you going to talk? Dirty talk, slut?'

She looked at him, the way she always looked at them, calculating, assessing, cold.

'Take off your clothes,' she said.

He was surprised, but he covered it quickly.

'Why don't you take them off for me?'

'I'm not your servant.'

Contemptuous, her voice. So contemptuous. He didn't like that. He lowered his head, he was looking at her from under his brows, the grin had gone.

'You'll be my bloody slave before I'm done with you, woman.'

Did he not realise what she was? How dangerous she was?

'On your knees,' she whispered.

The fool, the fool, what did he think she would let him do? Why did he smile like that, he reached out, his fingers in the waistband of her briefs, she was standing over him, she let him slide them down, her hands were in his hair, he thought she was stroking his hair, and he was smiling, he was raising his face towards her, smiling at her, her fingers were curled in his hair, he didn't even see.

She could kick so fast, he couldn't have seen, and her hands in his hair, dragging his head down, her knee in his face, there was blood, there was bright blood. It was on her legs, and she looked down at him, he was crouched at her feet, his hands clutched his crotch, he was rolling his head from side to side, there was bright blood, it was dripping on to her feet.

Her foot was on his shoulder, a hard shove, and he fell on his side. Blood all over his face, his nose smashed, his eyes were closed.

He was beginning to groan.

She looked down at him, waiting until he opened his eyes, and then she took off her briefs, and dropped them on the floor by his face.

'Tell me what you want me to do.'

23

He'd been found by the time I arrived at the theatre the next morning, and they'd taken him away. There were policemen, they were talking. The caretaker's face was white, he'd been sick. He was the one who'd found him.

One of the policemen stopped me at the stage door. He was wearing a cape, the rain ran off it, making it shine like silver.

'Not this way, madam.'

I looked over his shoulder. The caretaker had a handkerchief at his mouth.

'Oh, God,' he kept saying. 'Oh, God.'

'What's happened?' I asked.

'There's been an accident.'

Oh, no. She didn't do it by accident. She knew exactly what she was doing.

'I have to go in,' I said, shaking the rain from my umbrella. 'I'm the designer.'

'They've opened the doors at the front. Somebody'll meet you there. May I have your name, please?'

He wrote it down, looked at another list, and then nodded to me.

'Front door, please, Miss Mayall. They're expecting you.'

Bob Larwood told me what had happened, and I said it

354

was dreadful, quite dreadful, and I turned away from him and went back to the door, looking out through the glass into the street at the rain flooding down the gutters, the dirty rain.

The rain had come after the thunder. She hadn't cared when there'd been the applause, they'd liked the play, there'd been applause, and I'd been smiling, I was happy because they'd liked the play. She hadn't cared. She'd been looking down at him.

He hadn't screamed much. She'd told him his voice would break.

Somebody touched me on the shoulder, and I turned. Anthea, the wardrobe mistress, and she was crying.

'Oh, Glory. Isn't it horrible?'

It hadn't been horrible. The blood had been beautiful, the bright blood on her legs and her feet, it had been beautiful.

'He was so good-looking. I'd really fancied him. Oh, I shouldn't say that, not now.'

'I think he'd have been pleased, that you fancied him,' I said.

He'd got away from her. She'd been surprised, he was so strong, he'd managed to get away. She'd stood there, looking at the open door, and I'd been listening to the applause, and waiting. Something was going to happen. The blood was so beautiful, so bright. I was so happy, that the play was a success, that they liked the play.

She'd listened, too. She'd heard him. She'd heard him stumbling down the corridor, he'd been moaning. And she'd heard the door open, the door into the alleyway, where they kept the big bins.

The applause had been very loud when he'd opened the door, they must have been on their feet, stamping, and clapping, they must have loved the play. What was going to happen?

She'd followed him, and she'd taken the big scissors with her.

One of the policemen told Ronald Harmer that he hoped they wouldn't have to wait much longer. They should be able to use the stage soon.

'Are you all right?'

Bob Larwood, looking anxious, looking shabby, peering at me.

'Yes.'

'They're asking if anybody saw him,' he said. 'Last night.'

'You said he'd gone home.'

'I couldn't find him.' He shrugged, he lowered his eyes, didn't want to look at me. 'I didn't try very hard. I was busy.'

A bus drove past, its lights shining through the rain. The passengers were peering out, curious at the sight of the two police cars drawn up on the pavement. Pedestrians were hurrying on the flagstones, huddled under umbrellas, their feet raising small splashes in the puddles. Lights on wet tarmac, on windows, it was all very bright.

'He's got a record. Criminal record. You were right. Sorry.'

They said we could use the stage again, and the cast went down through the auditorium, Harmer wanted to go through the second scene. Their heads lifted as they took their places. Their voices were clear and steady.

They were professionals.

We could use the wings, we could go up into the flies if we wanted to. The offices, the lighting room.

The dressing rooms.

They hadn't searched very hard. He'd been found in the alley, between two bins, he'd died there, he'd bled to death. They'd searched the alley, but the rain had washed, and washed, and washed, and it was clean. It was all bright, and clean, and shining in the rain.

I walked out of my office, down the corridor, and I spoke to a detective as I passed him, I went on walking away.

'There's blood on the floor of my office.'

They closed that corridor again, they found blood on the carpeting, on the doorstep.

What had he been doing in my office? they asked, and I shook my head. I had no idea. I'd locked it when I'd left. It was a new lock. There were two keys. I had one, the other was at the security desk.

There were three keys, they said.

I shook my head again. I didn't know about that.

Did I know that it was Fleming who had installed the new lock?

No. Bob Larwood had arranged it. I'd asked for a new lock. I didn't like people looking at my work, I preferred an office I could lock.

Had I known Fleming? Had I liked him?

He'd been a damned nuisance. No, certainly I hadn't arranged to meet him, in my office or anywhere else. I'd asked the stage manager to reprimand him.

They already knew that, it seemed.

What time had I left? Had I been the last to leave? Had anybody seen me? Could anybody at the hotel confirm the time of my arrival?

Thank you, Miss Mayall.

They might need to speak to me again, and they needed the clothes I'd been wearing the previous evening, particularly the shoes.

Ronald Harmer asked if I'd like to change my office, and even Graham Fitch said that might be a good notion, my dear.

No, I said. I'd just like the floor cleaned, please.

I telephoned Reddington's to ask about the wings, but it was the lunch hour by then, there was nobody who could answer my questions.

When I telephoned again later, I already knew what they would say.

Yes, they'd sent the quotation, forty-five pounds for each pair, hadn't I received it? They'd sent it the following day.

It left me forty pounds in the budget, just forty pounds for contingencies. It was nearly double what I'd estimated they would cost.

And when would they be ready?

Well, they're quite complicated. It's not easy work. When did I need them?

I wasn't surprised. I was just resigned by then.

They're already overdue, I said.

Sorry, nobody had said it was urgent. End of the month at the earliest.

'Cancel it,' I said, and I put down the telephone.

Jacob had warned me about sabotage, he'd told me to trust nobody, and I'd let Fitch get away with it.

'I'm going out,' I said to Bob, and a detective wanted to know where I could be found.

'The design studios, Northern Theatres Incorporated. Mr Larwood has the address.'

I took my drawings with me, and I went to the chief designer, Jack Flowers.

'I've already seen these,' he said. 'They're good. Have they worked out all right?'

'No. Reddington's can't do them. I've got five days before the dress rehearsal.'

Other people in the room were listening. I heard indrawn breaths.

Flowers shook his head.

'I'm afraid you've blown it,' he said. 'Why didn't you check?'

He wasn't unsympathetic, but I could see he thought it was my own fault. Too bad.

'Why couldn't you have done them?' I asked.

Two or three people raised their heads.

'Fitch said it wasn't very urgent,' one of them commented. 'He offered to contract it out.'

I looked at him.

'But you didn't refuse to do them?'

He shook his head.

'We never refuse our own productions,' he said. 'Mind you, we weren't sorry when he offered, we were very busy.'

'You couldn't possibly manage them now?'

Silence. Their heads were down over their work again.

'You'd need about three good blacksmiths working night and day,' said Flowers. 'Sorry.'

Sympathetic murmurs from the other people in the room.

'It might be worth complaining about that,' he said as he showed me out.

Please, Mr Harmer, please, Northern Theatres Incorporated, it isn't fair.

I didn't go back to the theatre, I went to the hotel, and I sat on my bed, I wanted to cry.

I thought of Simmie, eating his way through stress and heading for a heart attack. I thought of Mike's anxious, loving eyes, watching him. I thought of Ruth, pretending she didn't know about them, worrying, confiding in her old friend Jacob Goldman, who had warned me, and I hadn't been careful enough.

Sketch pad, pencils, and use the brain, I told myself. Work very, very fast, get a new idea.

The telephone rang, and I snapped into it.

'What?'

'Ron Harmer. Why aren't you here?'

'I'm working on a new design. For the wings. Reddington's can't do them.'

He said nothing.

'So now I'm working here, I'm doing my best.'

He sighed.

'Pity. It seemed to be going well.'

Cardboard, plastic, cotton, artificial feathers, bent bamboo. Glue and string.

There were tears smudging the pencil lines.

Sorry, Simmie. Sorry, Mike.

The telephone again. Damn.

'My name's Celia Evans, you don't know me, I work at Inkies. We're all really sorry.'

'Thank you.'

'I thought you might like to know, I used to be Graham Fitch's assistant. His cousin's company is doing the design for the production in Sheffield. Graham owns part of that company.'

'Oh. I see.'

'Well, he won't get away with it with Inkies, but he's probably got a good job lined up with Fitch's in Sheffield. I should think so anyway, wouldn't you?'

'If they get the contract.'

There was a pause.

'Yes. Well, it's quite a good set they've done. Sorry.'

'Thank you.'

'We do wish we could help. But we've only got one black-smith, and he's already working overtime. For the Sheffield set, I'm afraid.'

Blacksmith.

Oh, my big sister, can you do the work of three men? In just five days?

She'd moved into the forge at the beginning of the year, she'd written me letters, happy letters, she'd been cold, she hadn't had any money, she'd been living off what the arty crafty couple had planted in the kitchen garden, and her happiness had shone through every word on the paper.

Ann. Please, Ann.

I telephoned her. I hadn't meant to cry, I hadn't wanted to put her under pressure, but when she answered the phone and I heard her voice, and I remembered her, so big and strong, so quiet, the tears ran down my face, I started to sob.

'I need help,' I said. 'It's a design, they say it can't be done.'

'Glory?'

I hadn't even said my name. I drew in my breath, and tried again.

'Yes, it's Glory. It's important, and they won't do it. They say it can't be done.'

'What is it?'

She was calm. I remembered her working on the *Macbeth* set at school, the way she'd stood there, relaxed, and concentrated, and everything had seemed so right.

'Wings.'

She was waiting for me at the station, standing very still against one of the posts in the shadows, Ann never liked standing out alone, people would stare at her. She was smiling at me, she was pleased to see me.

When I'd given up, when I'd known what Reddington's would say, I'd been resigned. Now, when there was just a hope that Ann might save this, I felt frantic with anxiety. I could hardly speak as we drove back to the forge in her van, and it was noisy, it rattled.

I told her a bit about it, I told her about Graham Fitch, and she listened quietly, and said we'd manage.

I unrolled the drawings on her workshop table, and she looked at them in silence, and I explained, and she nodded, and then she smiled at me.

'Yes,' she said. 'We'll manage.'

My big sister. I love you so much.

I couldn't help her, I could only watch. She didn't seem to be hurrying, but the speed was amazing, the metal seemed to grow under her hammer, it flowed into the shapes she wanted, and she'd stop, and look at the drawings, and turn back to the anvil.

I watched, I watched the big muscles in her back and shoulders rolling under her shirt, I watched the flames reflected in her quiet face, I listened to the steam hissing as she quenched the hot metal, and sometimes she'd look across at me, and smile.

I took three sets back with me that night, and I left money with Ann to send the others up by taxi. She was a little shocked at the extravagance, but she'd said the wings would cost twenty pounds a pair, so there was enough.

'It isn't my money,' I said.

I went straight to the theatre, and I was met at the stage door by a detective, who demanded to know where I'd been.

'Gloucestershire.'

'We're conducting a murder inquiry here, Miss Mayall.'

I'd forgotten all about it.

'I'm trying to do my job, too,' I replied. 'I've got a crisis on my hands.'

Even Bob Larwood looked shocked.

I worked all night in the property room, gluing the feathers into place, testing the clips, and when Anthea Bacon came in early the next morning two sets were ready. We kept one, we strapped it to a dummy and sewed the tabs on the costumes, I had to help her, she didn't have time to do it on her own, and the actors took the other, hefted it on to their shoulders, said they'd do their best, and they went to work, rehearsing, unclipping the sections, sliding them free, faster, and faster, until they could do it in the time.

One of the make-up girls said she could help Anthea, so I went back to the property room and spent most of the day working on the third set. I fell asleep at the table, and it was Phillip Greaves who woke me, shaking me gently by the shoulder.

'Glory?'

I jerked awake, and he apologised.

'Did I say anything?' I asked.

'No. I've just brought the wings back.'

'Are they all right?'

'They're fine. They're lighter than you'd said, we can manage them. Well, some of the feathers came off, sorry, we couldn't help it. When we take them off. We try to be careful, but we have to be so quick.'

I'd expected that. We'd be carrying out running repairs to the wings throughout the play.

'You can have three sets tomorrow,' I said, and he nodded, and smiled.

'Will they be ready on time?'

'Dress rehearsal?' I shrugged. 'Opening night, yes.'

'Are you all right?'

'Why shouldn't I be?'

He spread his hands, looking around, not meeting my eyes.

'This murder. It's a bit horrible. I keep thinking about it. Sorry, nasty subject, let's change it. I just thought you might be a bit shocked, it wouldn't be surprising.'

I thought about it, puzzling at it in my mind, wondering.

'I don't think I've ever had anything to do with murder,' I said.

He seemed to think that was a strange way of expressing myself.

'No, quite,' he said at last. 'Me neither. Hey, Glory, this is quite some set you've done here. We're, you know . . . impressed. So's Ronald Harmer.'

'Tight trousers and all?' I asked, smiling at him. I liked Phillip.

'God, I keep thinking I'll wake up a soprano,' he said, and then he screwed up his face, and turned away.

'Sorry.'

I felt vague and dreamy again. I must be tired, I thought. I hadn't really noticed what she'd done out there in the alley, I'd been listening to the applause, it had gone on and on and on, clapping and drumming, the sound of the applause, I'd been listening. I'd been thinking how beautiful the bright blood was, but it was washing away, I'd been sad to see it wash away, it was so lovely, so then I'd gone. Back to my office. I'd been wet. I'd been naked and wet, but I'd put on my clothes, except the briefs, my clothes were folded neatly, and I'd put them on, and still they'd been

363

applauding, and then I'd realised I was alone, there was nobody there. No audience, nobody. It was rain, it was the storm, the thunder still muttering in the far distance, and the rain on the streets outside, pattering rain, like hands clapping.

There'd been blood on the floor, but it hadn't been bright any more, it had been dark. It had looked dirty. I'd picked up my briefs, I'd wrapped them in a piece of paper. They'd been nasty, dirty, I hadn't really wanted to touch them, but I couldn't have left them like that for somebody else to find. It wasn't the cleaner's job to pick up my dirty, stained underwear. So I'd taken them with me, and I'd walked back to the hotel, and I'd dropped the nasty things into a litter bin on the way.

'I'd better go,' said Phillip, and I jumped at the sound of his voice.

'I'm sorry,' he said. 'I've upset you. Stupid thing to have said. I'm sorry, Glory.'

'No, no. We can't watch every word we say. That would be horrible.'

There was a knock on the door, the caretaker looked in, sniffed when he saw us together. A nice piece of gossip for when the horror of what he had found in the alley wore thin.

'Taxi from Gloucester,' he said. 'Big bundles in sacks. We're going to bring them in. In here?'

'Do be careful with them,' said Phillip. 'We don't want them broken.'

I smiled at him, and then I laughed.

'They won't break,' I said. 'My big sister made those. They won't break. They'll be very strong.'

24

It only ran for a week, that play, and the critics savaged it. They said it was banal, and predictable, and boring. But they praised the cast, said they'd deserved better, they praised the director, said he'd been wasted, and they praised the designer.

They said I was one of the country's most promising young designers. They said the costumes were excellent. They said I was imaginative, they said they wanted to see me given something better to work with.

The houses were full for the first two nights, but Ronald Harmer said it was just the ghouls because of the murder, and he was right. Once the police left, the public deserted us. Three-quarters full on the third night, a third on the fourth, almost empty on the fifth, and Inkies said that was enough. One week, they'd covered their outlay, take it off. Thank you, everybody.

The police had left the theatre, but they had not left us alone. I was the one they wanted to talk to. It was always me, I began to feel harassed, and exhausted.

Detective Chief Inspector Waller, he'd wanted me to come to the police station, but I'd said I had no time. It was the night of the dress rehearsal he'd first sent somebody to collect me, so I'd refused.

'I can't,' I'd said. 'It's the dress rehearsal.'

'This is a murder inquiry.'

I'd walked away. I'd still had two sets of wings to finish.

He'd come himself the next day, an angry-looking man with deep lines in his face, his shoulders hunched, he'd looked like a thin bull.

'It's opening night,' I'd said, and he'd leaned forward and slammed a fist on to my table.

'I'm not asking. I'm telling. Down at the nick, now.'

I'd telephoned Uncle John. By a miracle he'd been in his office, and I'd told him there'd been a murder, I was being harassed.

'Don't say another word.'

'I didn't kill the man.'

He'd said he was glad to hear it. He'd spoken to Waller, who'd answered in a series of grunts and monosyllables, and had then walked out of the property room without another glance at me.

They'd been back two days later, he and Detective Sergeant Coogham, could I spare them a few minutes of my inestimably valuable time, or was it closing night or some other precious moment?

I'd gestured at the armchairs in my office, and they'd started their attack.

I'd killed him, hadn't I? I hadn't liked him. He'd been attacked in my office, he'd had a key, he'd been killed with my scissors, my fingerprints were on the scissors.

'How do you know that?' I'd asked, and Waller had shot a venomous look at Coogham, who'd said, never you mind about what we know.

'Did he try to rape you?' Waller had asked, trying to sound gentle and understanding.

I'd shaken my head, and said I'd been told he had a criminal record, but no, he hadn't tried to rape me, he'd just threatened to.

'How do you know about his record?' Coogham had

demanded triumphantly, and I'd said Bob Larwood had told me. Wasn't it true?

'We want the clothes you were wearing the night he died,' Waller had said. 'Will there be a problem?'

'You've already got them.'

Several of us had been asked for our clothes. Anthea Bacon had cried, but she'd been crying most of that day.

'You don't seem to care much about this,' said Waller.

I hadn't cared, and I didn't care now. Why should I care about Ned Fleming? It was stupid, to expect me to care.

They'd left. Waller had looked even more like a thin, angry bull.

'I know you did it,' he'd said threateningly, just before he'd slammed the door behind him. 'I'm going to get you for it, too.'

Stupid man. They'd never find her, she wouldn't say anything.

Simmie telephoned, he wanted to congratulate me.

'You're the best,' he said. 'You're great, Glory. They sent me photographs. Under those circumstances, it's a miracle.'

'Close,' I said, and I told him about Graham Fitch. He was indignant.

'Shit! Conniving, back-stabbing bastard! Who knows about this?'

I couldn't give him an answer to that.

'Leave it with me,' he said.

Ronald Harmer and Bob Larwood said we'd have a few drinks after the final show, to say goodbye to each other and to the old Queen of Sheba.

'I'd planned a bit of a party,' said Ronald, 'but with the murder I don't think it would be appropriate. So, just drinks.'

'Please don't invite any policemen,' somebody pleaded, and there was laughter.

Uncle John telephoned that day, sounding worried.

'What about this murder? Do you need help?'

His voice had been cautious. I thought for a moment, and then realised he didn't want to hear the wrong answers to any questions.

'I've told them everything I know,' I said. 'The problem is there was blood on the floor of my office, and the murdered man had a key to the door. He shouldn't have had one, but he did.'

'I see.'

'He was a nasty type. He kept making passes at me, rather threatening ones. Waller may think I killed him in self-defence.'

'Yes. Yes, I can see he might, if there's no better theory. Glory, I don't suppose you've got anything to worry about, but if you are arrested, please don't say anything until I get there. I'll make sure I can be reached at any time.'

Waller and Coogham came back as I was packing.

'You're a cool one,' Waller commented, and there was something like admiration in his face. 'It's a long time since I've met one as cool as you.'

There didn't seem to be any point in answering him. I went on wrapping my brushes in foil.

'Lucky, too. Didn't you wonder where the caretaker was?'

'I don't understand.'

'He's a stupid little berk, that one,' said Coogham. 'When he thought everyone had gone, he sloped off over to the coffee bar in Grant Street. Fancied the waitress. God, you were lucky.'

'I wasn't here.' I made my voice sound a little weary.

'Cool, and lucky.' Waller shook his head, and rose to his feet. 'I hope you're not going to make a habit of this.'

He turned at the door.

'You can pick up your clothes from the front office at the Cheltenham Road nick. Forensics've finished with them.'

There seemed to be something valedictory in his words. I

knew the case would never be closed, not officially, but I suspected Waller would find something else to occupy his time. He thought I'd killed Fleming, and knew he couldn't prove it. He wasn't the man to chase rainbows.

I had the vision of rainbows in my head all that day, I was trying to think of some way of making one in the theatre, wondering whether there was a play that could use it, apart from *The Wizard of Oz*.

'You're very preoccupied,' commented Phillip as we stood together on the stage with Ronald Harmer's wine glasses in our hands. 'What are you thinking about? The next production?'

'I don't even know what it'll be. I was wondering how to make a rainbow on stage.'

He raised his glass to me, a slightly rueful smile on his face.

'You never stop working. I think you work in your sleep. For three weeks I've been wondering when I could ask you to come out to dinner with me, and every time I've seen you you've been working.'

'Oh, Phillip, I'm sorry. I'd love to have dinner with you some time. The next production we're in together?'

It had been two years since we'd last worked together. With a little luck Phillip would have forgotten before we met again. But I liked him.

Ronald Harmer made a short speech, thanking everybody for their work. He proposed a toast to me, which was kind of him. Graham Fitch raised his glass in my direction.

I hope it chokes you, I thought.

The party was beginning to break up.

'Am I right in thinking it's difficult for a man to get close to you, Glory?' asked Phillip.

'I suppose it is, a bit.'

He gave me the same rueful smile.

I went back to Bolton the next day, but it was more than a week before the meetings with Inkies began. Only two of the productions were still running, one of them the Sheffield group, where a young actress who had hardly been heard of until then was being hailed as the discovery of the decade. The reviews centred almost exclusively upon her.

'It takes an actress of quite exceptional quality to find the far from obvious depths in this difficult play,' one of the national dailies commented. 'Such perception in one so young is rare indeed.'

Simmie condemned her to seven kinds of hell. A production that ran and showed a profit held a distinct advantage over one that had not.

'Leave it to the lawyers and the accountants,' pleaded Mike.

But Simmie was desperate with tension, and with hope deferred. He'd been trying to diet, he'd promised Ruth he'd lose weight, so he was smoking more heavily. He was sweating, and the diet didn't seem to be having much effect.

'Glory's set was good,' said Mike.

'So's Fitch's. And they're bigger than us. And the damned thing's running. Oh, *shit*.'

I went shopping. I wanted a present for Ann. What I would really have liked for her was a new van, but Uncle John still insisted that Ann needed to succeed on her own. I'd asked her what she wanted, and she'd said toenail polish. She'd been so pleased for me, that the reviews about the set were good.

I bought the most expensive rug in the biggest saddlers in town. Ann had a horse. There was a peculiar business about the forge. Some time back in the Middle Ages a king had granted the blacksmith the right to ride over the land of the local lord of the manor. I think it was Henry VIII. There'd been a bet, the forge had been one of the stakes, but the forge was surrounded by manor lands, so the winner hadn't been able to use it. Henry VIII, if it was him, granted the smith and his family the right to ride on the lands so that they could shoe their new lord's horses. They had to collect them on the boundary of the manor lands, take them back to the forge, shoe them, and then ride or lead them back to the boundary.

Uncle John had insisted that Ann buy a horse, because the manor was for sale, and if the right to ride on the land fell into disuse it might be overturned in a court case. Uncle John, being a lawyer, always looks for the worst, but Ann seemed to love her horse, and her dog, a big mongrel somebody had given her when she was still at college.

'When did you and Simmie last have a holiday?' I asked Mike, and he shook his head.

'We've never had one. Not since we founded Lawley's.'

Simmie was asked to a meeting with Inkies in Manchester. Exploratory talks, they said, just a preliminary. No need for anybody else to come.

He bought himself a new suit. He said his old one had shrunk at the dry cleaners.

I told him I was taking two days off, and I went to see Robert Cameron about Revelations. Martin was still jealously hoarding our Cézanne, waiting for the right buyer, he said. Patrick Chendar had regretfully refused it; the collection didn't need another Cézanne.

'Are you desperate for the money?' asked Robert.

'No, I'm not. Samanatha Orek's the one who's probably desperate for money.'

Martin was hurt, and annoyed at what he saw as interference, but Robert agreed with me, and we that insisted that she be given a salary.

I was relieved. I'd been worried about Sammy, she'd done such a good job.

'I understand you're a roaring success,' commented Robert over lunch that day, and I said he was exaggerating.

He smiled.

'I didn't find any elephant traps, by the way,' he said. 'I think your friend Simmie's safe.'

Simmie had a heart attack on his way home from Manchester that evening. Mike telephoned me at my hotel. He was quiet, but I knew he'd been crying. He didn't want to talk for long. His voice was becoming choked, and he said he wanted to get back to Simmie.

I went back to Bolton immediately, I took a taxi straight to the hospital. Mike was holding Simmie's hand, and Ruth was not noticing. Simmie was trying to be light-hearted, but he was finding it difficult to speak.

'They're starving me to death,' he said, and then he stopped, his breathing a little shallow, and tried to smile at his mother. 'I keep telling them I should be keeping my strength up.' Another long pause, another smile. 'They're determined to kill me. Has anybody been intelligent enough to bring me a nice suet pudding?'

Ruth tried to twinkle at me, but it was a poor effort.

'Hello, Poppet,' she said. 'I hear you've been a great success.'

Simmie looked dreadful. His face was yellow, and there was a sheen of sweat on it, but his lips were blue, he looked as if he was in pain. There was an oxygen tank on a stand by his bed, heavy polythene draped behind it.

A nurse came in, and told us only two visitors were allowed.

'I'll go,' I said, but she looked at Simmie doubtfully, and said she thought he ought to be in his oxygen tent again, perhaps we should all leave for now.

Ruth cried as we waited for a taxi, and Mike hugged her. She turned her face into his shoulder.

'Darling Mike,' she sobbed. 'Darling, darling Mike. Oh, my poor Simmie.'

'He'll be all right,' said Mike helplessly. 'He'll be all right.'

I could think of nothing to say to reassure either of them. He'd looked terrible. Surely he should have been in intensive care?

'Do you want to stay on here?' I asked Mike. 'I'll take Ruth home.'

I slept in her spare bedroom that night, waking up every hour or so to check that she was asleep. I think part of the night she was pretending to be, she was so quiet, but sometimes I heard faint snores, so I know she slept a little.

'Come to the studio for the morning,' I suggested, but she wanted to go back to the hospital.

'Poppet,' she whispered over her coffee. 'Oh, Poppet, that was a dreadful heart attack.'

I couldn't answer her. I didn't know much about heart attacks, but I did think Simmie had looked very ill, and both she and Mike were frightened.

'Poppet, I'm so fond of you. Thank you for staying with me.'

'I'm fond of you, too, Simmie's Mum.'

She smiled at the silly nickname I'd given her years earlier.

'I'd hoped Simmie would fall in love with you,' she said a little while later. 'You're so beautiful, I didn't see how he couldn't. But when he said once something like, what was it? "I think she's the most beautiful woman I've ever seen", and it was so admiring, his voice. It was just the voice he uses to talk about a film set, or a piece of sculpture. I gave up.'

She gave me a watery smile, and I smiled back.

'Well, I've known about him and Mike for a long time. I was dreadfully upset. I tried to believe all that nonsense about sharing the mortgage, I really tried, wasn't that silly of me?'

She was crying again, fumbling in the pocket of her dressing gown for a handkerchief, so I got up and found the kitchen towels and gave her one.

'And Mike's such a darling. So silly of me, to be so upset. What is it they call it? "Gay". Such a stupid word, when so many of them are made so unhappy, by silly people like me, being upset, and having to be lied to. And other people, asking me if Simmie isn't married yet, I always think they're making nasty hints, and perhaps they're not. Why shouldn't I just be able to say, "No, Simmie won't marry, he's . . ."'

But she couldn't bring herself to say the word.

'What's the time?' she asked.

'Seven. Just past.'

'Oh. It's too early to go to the hospital.'

'Shall I telephone?'

She nodded.

'Oh, yes please, Poppet. I'll make some more coffee.'

The hospital was, as they usually are, non-committal.

'They say he had a comfortable night,' I said when I went back into the kitchen, and Ruth snorted, to disguise the muted sobs.

'They said that about me when I broke my hip. I heard the nurse when Simmie telephoned. "She's quite comfortable, thank you." I wasn't at all comfortable, I was thoroughly uncomfortable. I was *bloody* thoroughly uncomfortable.'

I laughed, and she managed to smile at me.

'Poor Simmie, being hospital-speak comfortable,' she said.

I drove her to the hospital in Simmie's car a couple of hours later. Mike met us at the door of the ward, he didn't look as if he'd slept, but he hugged Ruth and smiled at me. He was obviously tired, but the shocked expression I'd seen on his face when I'd first come to the hospital had gone.

'Can you hold the fort at Lawley's?' he asked. 'I don't want to leave Simmie.'

'Of course.'

I went back to my flat for a shower and a change of clothes.

There was a message on my telephone answering machine. It was Martin Orek. He sounded, as always, awkward, talking to a machine.

'Could you please telephone? Yes. I expect you've got the number. It's about the Cézanne, I've found a buyer.'

I had my shower first, washed my hair, sat on my bed and dried it, and felt like crying, more for our lovely Cézanne than for Simmie.

It was a private collector in Sussex, he said when I called him back, but he sometimes lent his paintings for exhibitions, and people could go and see them at his home if they had the right references.

This time Martin had no reason to refuse the offer.

'Fifty thousand,' he said miserably. 'Robert and I thought we should split the profits between you and Revelations. Does that sound fair?'

'More than fair. When does he want it?'

'Six weeks, when the York exhibition closes. They'll deliver it straight to him from the museum. So, I'll say yes, then, shall I?'

Was there just a little hope in his voice?

'Yes, Martin,' I said. And then, 'We always knew it would have to go some time.'

I heard something in the background, and then Martin spoke again.

'Sammy sends her best wishes.'

'Send her mine. We'll find another one. One day, you'll find another Cézanne.'

'Or a Turner.' He was trying to sound light-hearted. 'Or a Van Gogh, a da Vinci, or something.'

At Lawley's I told the receptionist to pass all telephone calls for Mike or Simmie through to me, to cancel whatever appointments they had, or postpone them if they were important, and then I went up to my studio.

The telephone was already ringing as I walked through the door.

It was impossible to work at all that morning. Most of the calls were business, deadlines for sets, appointments for models and photographers, lame excuses from suppliers and ridiculous demands from customers, but a lot of them were from friends with enquiries about Simmie, and messages to pass on to him.

He should have had a personal assistant. I became impatient with the words 'I'll tell him you called', I became impatient with Simmie, so much of what he seemed to do could have been handled by somebody else.

Jacob Goldman called, and came straight to the point.

'How is he, and how's Ruth?'

'He looks dreadful, and she's worried sick. So's Mike. The hospital says he's comfortable.'

'Gloriana, have you considered their partnership offer?'

'Not very seriously,' I said. 'It's been a while since they repeated it.'

'They're going to need somebody to negotiate with Inkies. Simmie's ill and Mike's no good. You'll have to do it. If you were a partner you'd have a stronger hand.'

'Oh, hell.'

'You'll have to decide quickly. This heart attack of Simmie's isn't helping the deal. They're obviously going to ask themselves what would happen if he died. Mike can't carry Lawley's. Gloriana? Are you still there?'

'I'm here. I just don't know. I don't know if I want to tie myself to Lawley's. Where would it leave me, if Simmie died?'

'Looking for a good manager.' There was a smile in his voice. 'Listen, my clever darling, I know about your ambitions, I'm not trying to stop you. Being a partner in Lawley's won't hurt, I promise you. You've got to decide now, today. If you deal with Inkies as a partner, I think you can get the contract. If you do it as an employee, I'm not so sure.'

There were two lights winking on my telephone, two incoming calls. If I were a partner, one of my first actions would be to sack that adenoidal receptionist and find somebody intelligent to take her place, somebody who washed her hair a little more frequently.

The first call was another well-wisher for Simmie, the second, who'd given up by the time I managed to get back to him, was from Inkies.

'He said he'd call back later,' said the receptionist. 'He'd been hanging on for ages.' She sounded reproachful.

'He should have been put through before Mrs Jameson,' I said.

Marilyn couldn't be expected to know that, could she? She just put through the calls as they came, she wasn't psychic, was she?

'There's another call now,' she added, and put it straight through without asking who it was.

'I really wanted to speak to Miss Beattie in the dress making,' whined some anonymous youth, 'but I suppose you'll do, if you can give her a message.'

Did Simmie have to handle this sort of thing every day? Why did he tolerate it? Surely Lawley's could afford someone better than Marilyn?

'The only calls I'm prepared to take for the next hour are from the hospital or from Northern Theatres,' I told Marilyn. 'I'll be working on the Luxor set, send someone to find me there if either of those calls comes through.'

I could think with a paintbrush in my hand. Sitting at a desk watching telephone lamps seemed to paralyse my mind.

A forest glade set, to advertise a household cleaning fluid. It was hardly an intellectual challenge, but the customer was important.

A partnership in Lawley's, heads or tails. If I pulled off the deal with Inkies we would all make a lot of money. If I didn't I could find myself trying to nurse the company along for the next ten years.

Watch the colours flowing off the end of the brush. Don't force it. Let it grow.

Let the dilemma resolve itself.

Green, or brown?

Yes, or no?

There was a telephone call from the hospital, it was Mike. Simmie was asleep, so he was taking a break.

'When did you last sleep, Mike?'

He didn't seem to understand the question. Simmie had been fretting about Inkies, he'd wanted to know if they'd been in touch, he'd wanted to know if I'd go to the next meeting for him, I could get the fast train, he'd said.

'I know how to get to Manchester.'

'Just Simmie being Simmie,' said Mike, sadly. 'Glory, can you handle this for us? I don't want to leave Simmie. Anyway, I'm hopeless at meetings, I can never find the right papers, I always look a fool.'

'What papers?' I asked. 'I haven't even seen any papers.'

'Oh. I expect they're here, in his briefcase. Anyway, I don't know. I don't know what happened at that first meeting. Oh, Glory, please take this damned deal over, any terms you like, I don't care.'

There were tears in his voice, he was exhausted, and frightened, and he loved Simmie very much.

Oh, damn. Damn.

'The first terms are that I take that partnership,' I said. 'Forty-five thousand for ten per cent of Lawley's.'

'Oh, yes. Yes, please, Glory. Oh, God. No. Just a minute. I've got to think.'

I could still hear him on the telephone, little thumping noises, was he hitting his head with the heel of his hand as he did sometimes when he was trying to remember something? And sighs, and his feet, scuffling on the floor, then he was muttering, and he spoke again.

'We were going to open a goodwill account, weren't we? Glory, I don't know, if we get this contract we'll need all the money for the move, I don't know.'

'I've got the money,' I said. There was no point in trying to explain goodwill accounts to Mike, not while he was worried and tired. 'I can raise forty-five thousand.'

He was so pleased, so relieved.

I found somebody else to finish the Luxor set, I told him how I wanted it done, echo those lines the leaves make, into the background, get a couple of the books, the water lilies, Monet, okay?

'Okay,' he said.

I went back to my studio. Marilyn said there'd been a lot of calls while I'd been in the warehouse.

'But not from Northern Theatres?'

'No. Not unless it was in my tea break. Janet was on the switchboard then, so I wouldn't know.'

Enough, I told myself, that was enough, I would not allow myself heart attacks or grey hair or weight problems, I would not be like Simmie.

I sacked her then and there, over the telephone, told her she could have a month's pay in lieu of notice but she'd be unwise to apply to Lawley's for a reference.

It took an hour to get the outraged Marilyn off the premises and to put the scared little mouse of an office junior on to the switchboard and assure her that it was only temporary and she wouldn't be sacked for making mistakes. I was shaking with sheer irritation by the time I returned to my own studio, to find a messenger had left the papers from the meeting on my desk. Nobody had thought to tell me.

I contacted Phyllis Sands at My Office and asked her to find me a replacement for the dim and adenoidal Marilyn.

Simmie seemed to have offered Inkies the earth, the moon and the stars in exchange for the contract. I read the draft minutes of the meeting he had had with them, and wondered how we could possibly meet the deadlines he had agreed, the employment conditions for the design studio staff, the financial commitments.

'Take my mind, take my heart, take my soul, take my body,' I muttered. 'Take my life.'

I was staring at the model I had made of the set for *Trojan*

Women. Ruination and desolation. Slavery.

Inkies had been kind. They had sent flowers and a sympathetic message to Simmie in hospital, and Jonathon Reynolds, the managing director, had arranged for the draft copy of the minutes to come to me. Guidelines, he had called them, agreed in principle.

'We'd like a meeting as soon as possible,' he said when he telephoned me. 'Will Mr Lawley be able to handle this? Or perhaps Mr Coster?'

'I'll be representing Lawley's,' I said.

'Ah.'

There was a long pause. He was trying to find the right words for his next question. I decided to save him the trouble.

'We're negotiating a partnership agreement,' I told him. 'But before that Mr Lawley and Mr Coster will authorise me to represent the company.'

We made an appointment for a meeting. Me for Lawley's, for Inkies him, Leonard Thompsett, his assistant, Charles Ingold, the company secretary, and Sean Hope, the financial director. His secretary would be happy to arrange hotel accommodation for me, perhaps my secretary could speak to her.

My Office had sent us Liz, and a telephoned apology.

'Hair the colour of brass, and a laugh to match,' Phyllis Sands had said.

'That's kind of you, Mr Reynolds, but I think we can manage from here.'

Manage. I wasn't managing, I was sinking. I tried to reassure Mike every time he telephoned, but I was not coping with running the company. I was making a mess of it.

A magazine had sent a letter complaining that one of our advertising cartoons was a direct copy of one that had appeared in their previous Christmas edition. Breach of copyright, what compensation were we prepared to offer? In addition to a published apology, of course.

I tackled the cartoonist about it, and he admitted it. He hadn't thought anybody would notice.

I called him a cretin, and sacked him.

Two sackings in five days.

I overheard somebody referring to me as 'that bitch'. Simmie never sacked anybody.

I contacted two employment agencies, the local college of art, and the labour exchange, looking for a replacement. None of them could help me. The woman at the labour exchange asked me to spell cartoonist.

Vandals smashed a window in the middle of the night, the rain ruined a half-finished set that was needed in four days' time. Janet had forgotten to turn on the window alarms. My fault, I should have checked.

I asked the two painters to repair what could be repaired, start again on what could not. Could they manage some overtime?

No, they replied in sullen triumph, they couldn't.

I worked on the set myself, all night, and fell asleep at my desk the next morning.

Nightmares. Voices calling in the dark, screaming, somebody screaming, and rain. Pleading eyes, and then a frantic face, and hands, fighting.

Mike came in, briefly. Just to say hello, and thanks.

'Go and talk to Sue Beattie?' I asked.

'I can't. I don't want to leave Simmie.'

'It's the yoke for the Duchess of Fife's evening dress. Sue can't get it right.'

But he wouldn't.

'You do it,' he said. 'Please, Glory. I don't want to leave Simmie.'

Janet came to me and whispered that Liz smoked in the office, something Marilyn never did.

'I know,' I said. I'd already asked her not to smoke when she was speaking to customers on the telephone, I'd tried to be nice about it.

'It sounds like passionate sighing,' I'd explained, and she'd looked at me as though I was mad.

Janet said the smoke was giving her a cough.

I telephoned Phyllis Sands at My Office again.

'It's Liz or a teeny-bopper with the IQ of a woodlouse,' she said. 'I'm doing my best.'

Colin claimed his back trouble was the result of lifting heavy objects in the warehouse, he was entitled to compensation. I looked at his employment contract, and found it specified 'moderately heavy' manual labour. I told him so.

'That fucking cow,' somebody called me, not bothering to lower his voice sufficiently.

I hired a car, and drove up to Manchester. I'd asked the staff at Lawley's just to hold on, I'd be back in a couple of days.

'Please don't hurry,' one of the cartoonists had said loudly, with a saccharin smile, and everybody had laughed.

Get well soon, Simmie.

'Comfortable,' said a staff nurse, but this time she added, 'Doctor's quite pleased with his progress.'

At least his colour had been nearer to normal, the last time I'd seen him.

Northern Theatres Incorporated occupied two floors of a good office block in southern Manchester. Their receptionist was smart, friendly, efficient. Jonathon Reynolds' secretary was just as I had pictured her.

Apart from Jonathon, who I liked almost immediately, the four men tried to patronise me. Sean Hope said that I had produced a really very good design, dear. Very good indeed, considering the difficult circumstances.

'You mean Graham Fitch?' I asked, and he looked a little shocked.

'I was referring to the murder.'

'That was beyond anybody's control,' I said. 'Nobody could have anticipated that. The matter of the assistant director's financial interest in a competitor for this contract, and his attempt to sabotage our design, is something that we do need to discuss. It was either unfair, or incompetent. Can anybody tell me which?'

Leonard Thompsett looked affronted. The words 'Mind your manners, young woman' seemed to be almost on his lips.

'I think you can leave that to us,' he said.

'No, Mr Thompsett, I'm sorry, we can't. Since it has come up let me make our position clear. We are asking for Mr Fitch's resignation. If you consider it carefully, I'm sure you'll see we cannot be expected to work with him. He has a financial interest in a rival company, and he has shown himself to be unscrupulous in furthering that interest.'

They were silent, the other three staring down at the papers in front of them, Thompsett watching me, a little warily.

'We do take your point,' said Ingold at last. 'We'll discuss it, and get back to you.'

We went through the draft minutes of the meeting Simmie had had with them. I used Reynolds' word, guide-lines.

'These deadlines are provisional upon us obtaining the grants your people informed us were available,' I said, and Hope and Thompsett exchanged startled glances, quickly suppressed. Was it Inkies who had told Simmie about the grants? I did hope so. At least I had sown a seed of doubt.

The commitments to their staff was not quite so easy.

'Believe me, gentlemen, we shall be only too glad to obtain the expertise of your management team at the design studios,' I said. 'As you know, Mr Lawley has been under great stress, and you also know the outcome. As for the work force, we should have to see. I am not in a position to offer guarantees.'

They argued, and insisted. I said nothing, I listened, and tried to give the impression that I was taking part in the discussion. The work force was excellent, very experienced, invaluable. Not one member, just a moment, Leonard, actually apart from two. Yes, apart from two members of staff, they had all worked for Inkies for . . .

'I do wish you wouldn't use that name.' Ingold, irritated, the American accent stressed for the first time.

'It's a nickname,' said Reynolds. 'Charles, it's affectionate.'

Ingold muttered something of which the only word I heard was 'disrespectful'.

'Donkeys' years, anyway,' said Hope. 'Bloody good team. Sorry, Miss Mayall, I apologise.'

I smiled at him, but it was a cool smile. Just stay on the wrong foot for a moment, please, Mr Hope, I prefer you that way.

I skirted around the financial aspect.

'I have to ask you to excuse me on this point, gentlemen. I'm not yet in a position to commit the company to any financial agreements. I hope to be able to clarify these matters at our next meeting.'

'Can you confirm that you agree, in principle, to what Mr Lawley said at our last meeting?'

Sean Hope, financial director, trying to stabilise Inkies' strong position.

'I'm sorry, Mr Hope, but I don't think I can. Mr Lawley is still very unwell, I haven't been able to discuss this with him in detail, but I do have to say he seemed puzzled by this part of the draft.'

Reynolds passed a hand over his mouth. I wondered if he'd studied at the Royal Academy of Dramatic Art, I'd seen that gesture so often. Hidden amusement.

'I think we've made as much progress as we can expect today,' he said, but Leonard Thompsett broke in.

'May I ask, Miss Mayall, where you got your information about Graham Fitch?'

Thank you, Thompsett, I thought.

I looked down at the table, and tried to give an impression of deep deliberation.

'When Mr Coster and Mr Lawley asked me to design the set and costumes for that . . .' I raised my eyes, and stared Thompsett straight in the face, '. . . perfectly appalling play, I made a few enquiries.'

Reynolds was hiding a smile behind his hand. Ingold was grinning, quite openly.

'Your company has an excellent reputation,' I said, 'and I could not understand why you were producing this rubbish about angels. I asked Robert Cameron and Jacob Goldman about it.'

Now I had their attention, they were all very alert.

'Jacob Goldman?'

'Yes, I'm one of his theatre gang, as he calls us.'

'Well, we knew that, of course.' Hope was leaning forwards across the table, his eyes fixed on my face. 'Naturally, we knew that, but what I'm getting at, Miss Mayall, what I think we'd all like to know is, if we award this contract to Lawley's, could we expect backing for our productions from Mr Goldman? Would you be in a position to exert any influence, I mean?'

I was looking at Hope, but I could see both Reynolds and Ingold, and Ingold was staring up at the ceiling with an expression of exasperated resignation on his face. Hope was making it all too clear that Jacob's name was one that meant a great deal to Northern Theatres.

I smiled at him.

'The influence between me and Mr Goldman is entirely one way, I'm afraid, Mr Hope. His on me. What I can tell you is that it was Jacob Goldman who placed me with Lawley's, and he refers to Mr Lawley as "my friend Simmie", although I believe it's Mr Lawley's mother, Ruth, who was the original connection. Further than that, I can't offer you anything. Apart from the fact that I always spend Christmas Day with him, and I call him "Uncle Jacob".'

Jonathon Reynolds picked up his cue.

'What does he call you?' he asked.

'"My clever darling",' I said.

I drove back to Bolton, telephoned the hospital, and left a message for Mike; the meeting had gone well, I thought.

Janet had left a note on my desk; she was taking the rest of the week off, she had a cough. I told Liz she would have to stop smoking in the front office, it was affecting other people. She became defiant; nothing had been said about not being allowed to smoke, and there wasn't anybody else who could work the switchboard while she went out for a fag, so she'd have to smoke at her desk.

The damaged set still wasn't finished, and the new paint-work was poor, unimaginative and stale. I looked at it, and felt depressed; Simmie always got people to do their best, but I couldn't. At the Queen of Sheba I'd persuaded eight young actors to attempt the impossible, and they'd succeeded. Here, I couldn't even get people to do their own jobs. I'd have to work all night again, and I was tired.

The realisation shocked me. I'd never looked at work in that way before, that I didn't want to do it, that I was tired. I'd thought tiredness was an excuse. Now, I wanted to go home, I wanted to rest.

Four wings and a backdrop, third-rate work.

The Duchess of Fife's damned evening dress, with a yoke that looked as if somebody had pulled it together with a drawstring.

Two cartoonists who should have been trying to do the work of three, and weren't bothering. Two painters who should have finished a damaged set, and hadn't made the effort.

I went to the dressmaking section, asked for a copy of the drawings for the dress, and then I wrote a short note to Jane Targe.

'Jane, why doesn't the yoke work, and what can we do? Simmie's had a heart attack and Mike's at the hospital with him, we're stuck. This is a plea for help! Glory.'

The franking machine had run out, and there were no stamps.

'That's Janet's job,' said Liz, and looked me straight in the eye as she lit a cigarette.

Then Lucille telephoned.

'My lawyer's been talking to the Courtneys. They'll accept twenty thousand pounds to give up the lease, I said that would be all right. Darling, peasants can always be bought off. When can you pay them?'

I listened to her voice, I didn't even try to think of what to say to her. I felt puzzled, it was as though I had opened my desk diary and been confronted by a children's book. This has nothing to do with who I am now. Lucille shouldn't be here, in this part of my life, on the other end of this telephone, here in my office.

'Are you there? Gloriana? Darling?'

I had to find somebody to replace Liz, and if Phyllis Sands couldn't do it I'd have to go to another agency. I had to talk about the financial aspects of the Inkies contract with the accountants, and I didn't like Mr Summerfield, I didn't want to talk to him. I'd never even met Simmie's lawyers, they'd have to be involved soon.

'Gloriana?'

Another cartoonist, where do I find a cartoonist? Chris had been a cheat and a liar, but he could draw. I'd try the art college again, anybody who knew which end of a pencil to sharpen. Please, just send somebody.

'Gloriana! I can *hear* you, I know you're there. Will you *please* speak to me! This is so rude.'

Lucille. Get out of my life.

'Pay them yourself, Lucille. The rent for the house is seven and a half thousand a year, and there's a deposit of two thousand. I'll want bank references and a good guarantor. The rent is payable three months in advance. Do you understand, you stupid bitch?'

She was too shocked even to cry.

I put down the telephone, and picked up a pencil. I hadn't drawn a line for nearly two weeks, I was beginning to feel frantic, if I don't make something soon I'll lose everything. I wanted paints, I wanted to paint something for myself, to see colour swirling out from my brush, to watch it, to control it, to let it live.

The telephone again, a deep and passionate sigh, Liz blowing smoke as she told me Mr Summerfield was on the line wanting Mr Coster.

'Put him through,' I said.

Simmie, get well soon.

It wasn't Mr Summerfield, it was his secretary, playing petty power games, passing messages to and fro between us rather than connecting her boss, her God, to a subordinate.

'I'll speak to Mr Summerfield, I will not continue to speak to you,' I said at last.

A consultation, muffled by a hand over the telephone, and then her voice again.

'Mr Summerfield would like to know when Mr Coster . . .'

I put the telephone down.

I've got to have some help. I can't do this. I don't know how to run this place, everybody's starting to hate me, nobody will work for me. I'm ruining Simmie's company.

Liz on the telephone again, one of the reps from a textile company wanted to know if we were to repeat the order, Mrs Beattie didn't know. Should she put him through?

Another passionate sigh.

'Do you know what that sounds like, when you blow smoke around?' I demanded. 'It sounds like an explicit sexual proposition. But then, perhaps you haven't had enough experience of them to recognise one. Put out that cigarette, and don't light another one in that office, do you understand?'

The line went dead. I picked up my pencil again, and

began to draw a rather cruel caricature of Liz, floating on a cloud of smoke, her lips pursed as though ready to receive a kiss.

Half an hour later Su-Su came into my studio, a gentle tap on the door, and she was there, a slight smile on her dark face, waiting for me to speak first.

'Hello. How's Danny?'

'He's well, thank you. Liz has left.'

Damn. Damn, damn, and damn again. Three in less than two weeks.

'Su-Su, can you operate a switchboard?'

She shook her head. It had been a stupid question, Su-Su would never take on a task that involved talking.

'I can paint,' she said.

'That set? That set they've nearly ruined?'

She nodded.

'Oh, Su-Su, please. Yes, please.'

I telephoned Phyllis Sands. She was coldly furious with me.

'I'm not surprised she left. What you said to her was unforgivable.'

'Phyllis, she was impossible.'

'She was a nineteen-year-old, not very bright and not very pretty, which makes your remarks even more cheap. So, Glory, you won. You reduced her to tears, you made her feel small, you confirmed her very low opinion of herself. Please collect a silver cup at the rostrum. I'm charging you for her time until the end of the week, and I haven't got a replacement for her. If you want a good receptionist perhaps you'd better look at the salary you're offering. Goodbye.'

Nobody had ever spoken to me like that before. I found I was breathing in a strange way, as though I'd been winded. It was the tone of her voice more than her words, her disgust with me, her anger. Until I'd tried to run Lawley's I'd been popular, people had liked me. I hadn't realised that was important, until I'd lost it.

I didn't know what to do.

I went down to the front office and sat at the switchboard myself. Heads turned as I took my seat, and then everybody went on with their work, their backs towards me. The silence was both hostile and amused.

I contacted the two other employment agencies in the town. I was looking for a receptionist who could operate a switchboard, I needed a temporary replacement urgently, and the position might be a permanent one for the right person. I named a salary over a thousand pounds per annum more than we had paid Marilyn.

'A non-smoker,' I added. 'That's essential.'

I spent the rest of the afternoon at that switchboard, trying to ignore the air of dislike. Luckily, nobody who really mattered telephoned. At half past five I turned on the answering machine, made no mention of the fact that everybody had started to pack up their work at least a quarter of an hour earlier, and went into the warehouse.

Su-Su had done quite a competent job. Her talents lay with clay rather than paint, but she knew enough, and she had tried.

What was more important to me then was that she was still working.

'Danny?' I asked, and she shook her head.

'Another hour, if I can take a taxi.'

Another hour from Su-Su, and I should be able to finish it by midnight.

'Another hour and you can have the Coronation coach.'

We worked together in silence for nearly the hour before Su-Su spoke again.

'Glory, be nice to people.'

I looked at her, put down my brush, and waited.

'Simmie tells people he likes their work.'

She went back to painting shadows on the grooves of a Greek column.

'What does Janet like doing?' I asked.

390

She shrugged.

When Su-Su had gone I telephoned Janet. She lived with her parents, but she answered the telephone herself, and there was no hint of a sore throat in her voice, although she did manage a rather artificial cough.

I told her Liz had left, I said we needed her desperately, we were stuck without her. A good office junior is like an extra right hand, I said. Also, once we'd got a proper replacement for Marilyn, I wanted the front office made to look nicer, would she like to do that?

'I like arranging flowers,' she said, and she wasn't whispering.

It was well after midnight when I got home, and there was a message on my answering machine.

'Telephone me if you're back before two, I mean in the morning.' Jacob never bothered to introduce himself, he knew I'd recognise his pantomime Jew voice. 'I hope the reason you're home so late is because you're out on the town with a brave, handsome, charming, and extremely rich young man.'

'I was out in the warehouse with a sticky paintbrush,' I said when he answered his telephone. 'How are the lovely ladies?'

'They've decided they like salmon,' he said. 'The fresh sort, preferably Scottish. Their taste is impeccable. Now tell me about Inkies.'

I described the meeting, and he listened, muttering to himself as I spoke.

'Right,' he said. 'That sounds as if it's under control, I thought it would be. There's a fair hint of poison seeping around Fitch's at the moment, I think you're responsible for that, aren't you? Yes, quite a nice little low blow, that one.

'So, now we can put in the killer, and you can start to smile again, my clever darling.'

'Jacob, I do hope this is good, I'm ruining Lawley's.'

'It's as good as it comes. It's Shakespeare, you're on the road properly this time, so you'd better find a manager for Lawley's, and find one fast.'

I closed my eyes, I could feel tears under the lids. Shakespeare. At last, Shakespeare.

'Stratford-upon-Avon,' he said, 'you know where I mean? That place in Warwickshire. And the Royal Shakespeare Company? You've heard of them?'

I couldn't speak.

'*The Merchant of Venice*, they rather like your drawings, it would be tactful not to tell them you did them eight years ago when you were a student, they like to think their designers have some experience. I hope you're still there, Gloriana?'

'I'm here.'

'If that goes well, and it will, you've got Solomon Crawley directing and he's good enough to listen and clever enough to know what to listen to, they'll want you to do *A Midsummer Night's Dream* in the spring. And after that, are you still there, my clever darling?'

'Yes.'

'*Macbeth*.'

25

Simmie and Mike and I signed our partnership agreement two days before we wrote our names under the long and complicated contract our lawyers had negotiated with Inkies. The consultant said Simmie could have half a glass of champagne in celebration.

Even Ruth agreed Simmie was looking better. His colour was back to normal, he was breathing easily, and he had lost weight.

'It was a bad one,' the consultant told Ruth.

Simmie was to lose at least another three stone, preferably more, he was to cut out smoking, cut down drinking, lead a less stressful life.

'I may not live longer, but it'll seem like it,' he joked.

He was out of danger, and I insisted Mike come back to work. I'd lost two permanent members of staff and made most of the others miserable and angry, and I hadn't been able to do any of my own work since Simmie's heart attack.

Simmie decided to worry about the relocation. How would Su-Su find a house where she could keep a cow? What about Don's little boy, who was mentally handicapped, was there a good school for him? Would Janet be all right, living away from home for the first time?

'*Shut up!*' yelled Mike, suddenly furiously angry with him. 'Just shut up, Simmie. You are so *hellish* arrogant. Do you really think nobody can manage to live their lives without *your* help?'

He seemed to run out of words. He glared down at Simmie, his breathing so strained it sounded like sobbing, then he made a helpless gesture, turned and walked out of the room.

'Oh, *shit*,' said Simmie. 'Glory, tell him I'm sorry. I don't know what for, but tell him.'

'What will Mike do if you die?' I demanded. 'You are *so* selfish, you and your damned interference in other people's business. Just stop it.'

I telephoned Ruth from my office, told her what had happened, and asked her to go and cheer him up, we'd both torn lumps out of him. She said she was glad to hear it, she'd have a couple of lumps for herself while she was about it, but yes, she'd go and be nice to him.

There was a letter from Ann. She seemed to have kept the schoolgirl habit of regular letter-writing, a dutiful list of things she'd been doing, ending with best wishes.

The manor had been sold to a religious order, the Children of God. She said they were unfriendly, they didn't like her riding on their land. She'd had to ask Uncle John to write to them, because they'd chained her gate to keep her out.

I telephoned her. She sounded a little subdued and worried. I asked if they'd threatened her, and she said no, but there was a doubtful tone in her voice. For the first time since she'd been at the forge she was unhappy.

'Is there anything I can do?'

'No. I'm just being stupid. It was great, riding in the park when there was nobody there.'

'And now it's been spoilt?'

She laughed, but it was a sad laugh.

I worked in my studio on my *Merchant of Venice*

drawings, leaving Mike to deal with anybody who wanted to tell him what a bitch I'd been. I'd put in an average of fourteen hours a day in that warehouse since Simmie had been ill, and it seemed to me that nobody else had done one single piece of decent work. Simmie was still trying to run everything himself, and I'd had to argue with Mike to get him to come in. The Cézanne was on the wall of a manor house in Sussex, Revelations had been paid, so had I, and the money had gone into my partnership in Lawley's.

I'd owed it to Jacob Goldman. I suppose to some extent I'd owed it to Simmie, perhaps even to Mike. Obligations, debts, I hate them. They weaken people, they take away their power and their freedom.

The pencil in my hand was a dark, soft black, and blunt. The lines were thick on the creamy paper, thick and angry. Bassanio, and his stupid craving for that thin and evil bitch Portia.

Mike came up for a cup of coffee half way through the afternoon. He was looking shaken.

'Did you have to sack Marilyn?' he asked.

'Yes.'

Portia, lean and vicious, a skeletal finger stabbing towards the broken Shylock. Would they do this? Or would she be the wise, the merciful, the beautiful, the utterly boring and totally conventional?

You can do anything with Shakespeare, please look hard at this nasty little creature. Please, this time, look at Portia again.

'And Chris?'

Mike's voice, pulling me away from Shakespeare and back to Lawley's. Cartoonist Chris, damned plagiarising Chris, and his sarcastic colleagues who wouldn't even try to do his work.

I swivelled my chair towards Mike, and pointed my pencil at his face.

'Four hundred pounds compensation,' I said, 'and a damned humiliating apology, in print, a furious client who we very nearly lost, and would have done if they'd been able to find somebody else in time. Don't tell me Simmie wouldn't have sacked Chris, because I already know. That's probably why he did it.'

'All right, all right.'

He was fiddling with the pen tray on my desk. I tried to ignore him.

Antonio, a victim. I don't like victims, they're always portrayed as gentle, helpless, life's losers, but I don't like victims. They're stupid, and very often they're vindictive. It was Antonio who started this conflict with Shylock. I do not like Antonio.

Why does my drawing of Antonio have Mike's gentle eyes?

Friendship. Antonio's friendship for Bassanio was certainly more than that, and Portia knew it. It was homosexual love, and it was physical desire; probably, but not certainly, hopeless.

A scrape of glass on wood.

'Mike, what's the matter?'

He muttered, and said it was nothing really, and it wasn't until I told him to go away that he asked me to telephone Jane Targe. She'd completely redrawn the bodice for the Duchess of Fife's evening dress, and Sue Beattie had sewn it to Jane's design. Mike didn't feel he could put his name to it.

I gritted my teeth.

'Mike, I'm not your nanny. Phone her yourself.'

'She's your friend.'

'Make her yours. You like Jane, what's the matter with you?'

He scratched my pen tray across my desk, scoring the varnish, and swearing to himself.

'Listen,' he said, and then stopped.

I wanted to work on my drawing of Jessica. I wished Mike would go away. The divided loyalties of a daughter. Was Jessica exhausted by the demands Shylock made on her?

When could I talk to the director? Solomon Crawley, how did he want to do this? He was clever and original, flexible.

'Go on, Mike.'

'What about a merger between us and Grey's?'

My first reaction was one of exasperation. I didn't want to talk about this, I wanted to do my own work. I'd handled the entire deal with Inkies, and now Mike was throwing another major negotiation at me. Even if I could persuade him to try to handle it, he'd almost certainly give up half way through the first meeting.

'Have you talked about this with Simmie?'

'Not yet, he isn't well enough.'

If Mike had the right reasons for this, it was not a stupid idea.

'Is this just because you work well with Jane?' I asked.

'Well, partly. But, listen. You and Simmie do their fashion shows, you do them beautifully, you really do. Jane and I can work together quite well. No, listen, better than that. We're both good.' He turned a little pink at that, Mike hated vanity. 'Together, we're more than good. Well, aren't we? Listen, if we merge, before we move to Birmingham, we can get a bigger grant for bigger premises.'

It made sense. Lawley's and Grey's both in Birmingham as rivals could suffer; merged, working in the same premises, particularly if Grey's could adapt to theatre work as well as fashion, we could do well.

I pushed my drawing of Jessica towards Mike.

'How do you think you and Jane would like working on this? And Gerry Grey, of course.'

'Ooh!' His eyes were round. 'I say! Can I see some more?'

He looked through all the drawings, glancing at me a little quizzically after he'd studied Antonio very closely, and then laid them down on my table.

'Well,' he said. 'I don't know. Gerry, maybe, but I think Jane's a bit too subtle for theatre. Don't you?'

Please, go and talk to Simmie. Please leave me alone. Somebody else find a manager for Lawley's, let me do my work. Let me go to Stratford and talk to Solomon Crawley, I never want to speak to another personnel manager again, let alone a labour exchange clerk.

He didn't want to bother Simmie. Simmie was still unwell, the consultant had insisted he cut down on the stress. He wanted me to think about it. Make a decision. Approach Gerry Grey, talk to Jane Targe, see whether there was still a bigger building on that new industrial estate and what the grants could be.

'Yes,' I said. 'Okay, Mike, I'll think about it. But please go away now. I have to do my own work too.'

He went, reluctantly, reminding me twice on his way to the door that it was urgent.

Nerissa, smugly witty, sycophantic.

I closed my eyes over the drawing of a plump young lady with a smirk, aware that I was becoming ever more negative about this play. I had to talk to Solomon Crawley, soon.

But Patrick Chendar spoke to me first, a rare telephone call. He didn't enjoy talking on the telephone.

'Go and see your mother,' he said. 'I need a sit. rep., m'dear.'

'I can't,' I answered. 'I haven't time, and I don't want to. What's a sit. rep.?'

'Situation report. I wouldn't ask if it wasn't important.'

She'd told the Courtneys I'd pay the twenty thousand pounds, and they'd found a house to buy and exchanged contracts. Now they were threatening to sue her, and she wanted to sell her house to pay them off.

'Oh, Patrick. What on earth can I do about this?'

'If you can make her see sense, I'll pay the Courtneys. It won't be a huge amount, m'dear. They just want her to leave them alone. Nice people. Bit middle-class for your mother's taste, that's all. Go and see her. Be nice to her. Don't call her a stupid bitch, Gloriana, she can't help being what she is.'

I left Nerissa smiling up from my table, and telephoned the car hire company.

Lucille had had another facelift, and I suspected something had been done to her neck. She kept touching a place under the line of her jaw, stroking at it with the tips of her fingers. But she was still slim and graceful, and if her pale golden hair had been dyed it had been done by an expert.

She had certainly not forgiven me for the way I had spoken to her, and probably never would, but she knew she was in trouble, and that she needed my help.

'I don't understand why you wouldn't pay them,' she said, and there was a tremble in her voice. 'I never brought you up to be so mean. I thought you'd be glad to have me back in the house. I could have made it beautiful again.'

'Oh, I know,' I agreed easily. 'It's only paint and wall-paper they've changed. They're not allowed to do anything structural to the place.'

There was a sudden look of hope in her face, so I shook my head and spoke before she could.

'No, Lucille. No.'

She could still cry quite beautifully.

I stayed with her for an hour. I read the letter she'd received from the Courtneys' lawyers, and the one her own solicitor had written to her.

'All people ever seem to think about these days is money,' she said frantically. 'I don't understand. Money, money, money, why are they all so vulgar? It's dreadful. I can't deal with those sort of people, I've never had to associate with them before. How dare they demand money from me?'

'They believed your promise,' I said, and she shot me a glance at once accusing and pleading.

'I never *dreamed* you wouldn't let me go home.'

Tears again, carefully dabbed away with a lace handkerchief.

'You are home. This is a lovely little house. Patrick went to so much trouble to find a house for you, why are you so ungrateful to him? It's a beautiful house.'

'So small,' she sobbed. 'I can't even give a proper party here.'

These were genuine tears, her eyes were growing red. I hadn't seen her like this since the time just before she drove Ann away.

'Patrick won't let me sell it.' Her voice was choking.

'He wants to keep it safe for you.'

'I can't pay this money. Gloriana, I haven't got enough money to pay these dreadful people. They'll take me to court, and everybody will know. They'll know I haven't got any money. I can't bear this, I can't bear it. I don't know what to do.'

I waited until she was calm again, until the storm of tears had gone, and she was sitting quietly, just the occasional sob shaking her slim body.

'Leave the Courtneys alone,' I said.

'I wish I'd never . . .'

'Leave them alone. Do you understand? Don't ever get in touch with them again. Not by yourself, not with lawyers, not with anybody.'

Another sob, but she nodded her head.

'This is your home now. It's a lovely house.'

She turned away from me, and her shoulders were shaking again.

'Lucille, you will have to accept that you will never live in the big house again.'

She tried to break in, quickly turning towards me, her drowned blue eyes wide, so I spoke sharply.

'No, Lucille! Never. I mean it, never. Accept it before you do any more harm. To yourself, you're only harming yourself.'

400

'But why? Oh, why? You've got so much money. Why can't I go home?'

It was nearly ten years since she'd lived in that house. It was the house where men had visited her, been delighted by her grace, her beauty, her charm. There had been lovers who had adored her, they had bought her gifts, they had paid her bills, she had been happy, and loved; she had been young in that house.

Lucille still believed in fairy stories. If Ann would learn social graces she would no longer be too tall. If Lucille made a promise, somebody would keep it for her, because everything ended with happy ever after, romance had always promised that.

If she could go back to the palace, she would be a princess again. Young, and beautiful, and desired.

Make her see sense, Patrick had asked.

I didn't think it could be done.

I telephoned Patrick and told him what had happened. He sounded depressed, but said he was sure I'd done my best.

'What did you expect?' I asked.

'I'd just hoped, m'dear. I'll deal with the Courtneys anyway. Poor Lucille.'

Mike wanted to know if I'd thought about the merger with Grey's.

'Telephone them yourself,' I said, and he protested wildly. He wouldn't know what to say, he'd make a mess of it, he'd never done . . .

'Ask for Gerry personally, and say, "Hello, Gerry. How do you like the idea of a merger?" Mike, I'm going to Stratford, I'll see you when I get back, and I don't know for sure when that'll be.'

I walked out on him, ignoring his outcry.

If I didn't go now, there'd always be something to delay me. I had to go. I had to go now, not make appointments, which could be postponed because Mike had found an emergency and couldn't manage it; because Simmie was

401

ill; because Ruth needed me; because everybody else's lives seemed to be collapsing, and I was the only one who could handle it.

Because Patrick Chendar wanted me to go and see Lucille, and not call her a stupid bitch, because she couldn't help being what she was.

By the time I reached Stratford I was thinking a little more reasonably, my mind was a little quieter. I looked at the famous theatre, and I drove on, parked the car, and walked down to the river, where Sam and I had gone because I couldn't face the violence in *Titus Andronicus*.

It had been summer then. Now it was autumn. There had been swans, and people in boats, but I couldn't remember what Sam and I had talked about that time, the last time I had been here. Why had I been away for so long? Why had I never come back to Stratford?

I sat on a bench and watched the river, tried to think and to remember, but I could only see the ripples on the water, and something that looked like small pieces of yellowed paper, curling, and flattening, and sliding down through the brown river, lost.

Dreaming, I must be dreaming.

I want to paint this river, this old, brown river, with the sun making little yellow curls on the ripples. There is something I have to remember.

I walked back to the theatre, in through the stage door, and a doorkeeper asked who I was.

'Gloriana Mayall,' I said. 'I'm expected.'

My name was on a list, but he was cautious, and there were questions, and a telephone call to somebody to come and meet me, a nice woman from the office. She offered to take me to Solomon Crawley, but I said I'd like to be on my own for a little while, if that was all right.

How did I know my way around this theatre? Doors, and passages, staircases, turnings and corridors, how did I know? Why wasn't I lost?

People were working, I didn't want to disturb anybody, so I went through the pass door and sat in the stalls in the darkened auditorium, gazing at the famous stage, not thinking very hard, letting ideas and feelings drift quietly into my mind, musing on them, allowing them to slide away again.

I was here. I'd finally got here, the most famous theatre town in the world, sitting in this theatre, as part of it, about to play my role in Shakespeare's 350-year-old story.

I felt tears on my cheeks.

Two men and a woman walked across from the wings, and I watched them, carefully. There were only working lights playing down on to the stage, but they were clear.

My silver patterns on black would work well here, with the real lighting. And the reflection from the stained-glass window, it could show up brilliantly. Or perhaps be muted, just a hint, the blood on the tomb. I could experiment here, I could try them out, see which one was best.

Somebody had come into the row behind me, I smelt aftershave lotion, heard a faint rustle as he sat down, but he was quiet, he didn't want to disturb me. I let the awareness of his presence drift away, I watched the stage, and I listened.

A voice calling from the wings, and the woman had come back.

'Can you move that . . .? Yes, forward just a bit? Right. Thank you.'

What were they playing? It was a flat set, stylized, modern. It could be anything.

'*Troilus and Cressida*,' said the man behind me, so aptly I wondered if I'd spoken aloud.

Then he leaned forward, and a long, pale hand was offered over the back of the seat.

'Solomon Crawley. Hello, Glory, they told me you were here. Welcome to Stratford.'

I looked into his thin, intelligent face, lit only by the lights from the stage, a glimmer of teeth from a friendly smile, a firm grasp on my hand, and I knew he'd seen the tears shining on my face, and I also knew it didn't matter, because he would understand.

I had never been so happy before.

26

I had never before worked as I did through that autumn and into the winter, in a company where there was time and space and the will to create something lasting, at least in theatre terms. This production of *The Merchant of Venice* was intended to be part of the repertoire, not something that was to run for as long as an audience could stand it, and then vanish for ever.

Five years, I was told. Well, roughly. Give or take a month or twelve.

It was an ordered whirlpool of ideas, from actors young and old who had played roles in *The Merchant of Venice* many times, or were doing so for the first time, from a director who had done it three times, from lighting technicians and stage managers who had seen just about everything and had never lost the desire to see something new, and from a designer who was quite hopelessly out of her depth, suddenly once again a complete beginner and a newcomer, and who was spending her days in some kind of panic-stricken fairyland.

I was urged to give my ideas, nobody believed I had none.

Antonio was to be played by Donald MacFarlane,

405

middle-aged, burly, and about as effeminate as Stonehenge. Portia, Julie Stepping. I looked at her wise young face sadly.

But I did tell Solomon Crawley of the ideas I had had, and he smiled, and nodded, and mentioned that Portia the vindictive bitch, and Antonio as Bassanio's homosexual lover had been done before, once or twice, and then he laughed at my crestfallen expression, and told me there was still plenty of time for me to be the *enfant terrible* of the RSC, if that was where my ambitions lay.

It wasn't, I muttered. It was just, he'd wanted to know how I saw the play. So I'd told him. In a coffee break, when nobody else was listening.

Even these ideas were used, nothing seemed to be rejected here. I watched Donald frowning as Solomon talked of the relationship between Antonio and Bassanio, something a bit subtle, and then Donald did what I had, as a child, watched Lance Allodyne do, which had first kindled my fascination. He looked for something inside himself, he became withdrawn and remote for a few moments as he reached for it, for experience or intuition, and then he came back, different. There was a smoothness and a suggestion of fluidity in the way he moved, the turn of his head and its angle as he looked at Bassanio. It was more than friendship, even if only for a moment. It suggested a sudden realisation of what might have been between them, had he or Bassanio been only slightly different.

He kept it, I saw it throughout the rehearsals, and I thought, that's mine.

Julie Stepping looked at my drawing of Portia and Shylock, and asked if she could have it. Please, Glory. May I, when you've finished with it?

'It isn't you,' I said, but that didn't matter.

When Portia spoke the line 'Then must the Jew be merciful', there was a threat in her voice that hadn't been there when they'd first read the play, and when they all looked up at Donald as he asked a question, Julie glanced at me, and winked. That's yours, she said in the smile that flashed briefly towards me. She took it on through the scene, building up the menace in her voice, line by line, Shylock too avid to notice, only some of Antonio's friends alerted by it, waiting for something that might even be hope. Terence Bourne, as Shylock, playing to it, building the tension, it seemed as if everything was moving faster and faster, could the Jew be this blind to his danger, with the young doctor setting trap after trap?

There's more than one knife here, old man.

Mine, that was mine.

The courtroom scene was mine, too. Black and white, and the crimson diagonal of light lying across the table that was a tomb. They blocked it all out, chalk marks on the stage, cardboard cartons, pacing around and arguing, from the back of the auditorium, would they see? Black on black, if I stand here. How? Yes, all right, two paces backwards just here. Here? Yes, that's at least half black on white. Right, keep that.

Lighting technicians. Can we . . .? Could you . . .?

So many experts, thinking, and talking, and testing, all for my idea. These people had lived their lives in this work, now they had taken my idea and they were trying to make it good. They were making it come to life.

I stood in a fold of curtain, watching, making myself as small and inconspicuous as I could, and I had never felt so proud, and yet somehow so scared. My idea. Fifteen actors, some of them world famous, one of the best directors in the country, so many technicians, bringing my idea to life.

Solomon Crawley, shouting at me and grinning.

'Come on out of there, you! This is all your fault. Right, now, where do you see this red window, if we don't want half the cast getting between it and your damned table?'

I was on the stage, tongue-tied with shyness, trying to explain without seeming to disagree, but actually they'd got the lights wrong for this idea. Well, sorry, but actually the whole scene had to be set at a different angle.

'Right, start again,' called Solomon, and aimed a cuff at my head. 'You might have *said*. "But actually".'

It was beginning to take shape, the ideas, the voices and the figures, all held together by Shakespeare, strong enough to be broken down and built again, changed, and moulded, and polished, until it was ready. Solomon had stripped this play down to the bones, and left it spare and clear, and demanded of us that we all do the same.

It was almost good enough to take its place in this long history.

When I threw my frost pattern drawings into the bin, along with an old property list and a fabrics catalogue, I didn't regret them. They had played their own part, and it had been a good one. Many ideas had been tried and discarded as we had worked together, none of them had been wasted.

They were no longer my ideas, Antonio and Bassanio, Portia as a vengeful menace to Shylock, the red light on the table. They were part of the whole structure, indistinguishable from the rest. I no longer thought, that's mine, I no longer noticed. It was running and flowing now, it was beginning to live, each rehearsal was new and different, it was almost ready.

I'd persuaded the wardrobe department to discuss some of the costumes with me, although the wardrobe mistress had looked at me incredulously when I'd first broached the idea.

'You can *sew*?'

'Yes. Yes, I can.'

She muttered something about a designer who knew which end of a needle to thread had to be breaking some sort of record, and probably a regulation as well, but she agreed to look at my drawings, and then said something might perhaps be done with one or two of them.

'Where did you learn this?'

'From Linda Pasmore.'

So there was coffee in the wardrobe mistress's room again, because Heide Carter and Linda Pasmore had known each other since Noah landed on Ararat.

'I got this job just a nose ahead of Linda, and she retaliated by pinching my best boyfriend. Do you take sugar?'

Head cocked on one side as she looked at me, she was very like Linda in these mannerisms.

'No, thank you. Just a little milk.'

'Now, this golden dress for Portia. Why gold? It's a horrid fabric, it slips around, I hate it.'

But she was discussing it with me as an equal now, not as an experienced wardrobe mistress trying to explain technical difficulties to a newcomer.

'Happy?' asked Julie Stepping as I worked on the set for Portia's house, and she posed in front of the draperies in the golden dress Heide had finally agreed to make.

'Hmm,' I tried to reply through a mouthful of pins.

'When I first came here I kept thinking it was a ghastly mistake,' she mused, putting her head on one side and looking keenly into the mirror. 'They'd meant somebody else. I was an impostor. They were going to find out.'

I nodded.

'Well, they haven't yet. Isn't it amazing? Here in Stratford, they're so thick they still haven't realised I can't act. Oh, God. I think they may find out, this time.'

I spat the pins into the palm of my hand.

'I can't design,' I said.

'Can't you? You'd think somebody would notice, wouldn't you? I mean, the stage manager, or at least one of his assistants.'

'Is that dress comfortable?'

'Yes. God bless velcro. Hell, Glory. Portia! Me. Whatever next? Do I look as scared as I feel?'

'You look very, very wise and very, very merciful, fuck it.'

'*Glory!* Language.'

I stood up, and we both looked at her image in the long cheval glass.

'I could diet, I suppose,' she said. 'Get all scrawny and crabby, and play your nasty bitch Portia.'

I laughed.

'You still remember that? Anyway, it's been done.'

'But has it been done *well*?'

We smirked at each other.

'We could always ask Sonia Loveday to try,' I said, and Julie drew her face into a ferocious snarl.

'So fuck you, too,' she said, and then she turned towards me.

'Glory, there's a rumour about you, may I ask if it's true?'

'What is it?'

'Did you persuade a cast to play with angels' wings weighing twenty-five pounds?'

'No.'

'No, I didn't think you could have done. I wonder where that story came from? I shouldn't think it could be done.'

I smiled at her.

'I persuaded them to play with wings weighing forty pounds. That's how they rehearsed it, with rucksacks full of sandbags. Twenty-five pounds was what they actually did weigh. They turned out lighter than we'd thought.'

Her response was a soundless whistle, and rounded eyes.

They were all nervous. Hadn't I expected it? Why had I thought it would be different, here?

'They'll say it's conventional,' said Solomon Crawley over his third cup of coffee, which always made him edgy. 'They'll say it lacks innovation. Does it lack innovation?'

'"They say. What say they? Let them say",' quoted Donald, and chewed irritably at a fingernail. 'Anyway, it's too late to change it now.'

410

'Oh, God. They're never happy. It's incomprehensible or it's too conventional. Damn their eyes, and their pens.'

'We've still got three days to draw up a suicide pact,' I suggested, and earned a wan smile from them both.

It was conventional, I thought. All my sets, they were boring and normal, there was hardly anything new. Well, in a lot of the scenes there was hardly anything at all. Spare and simple, Solomon had said, not bare. Everybody would hate it. They'd drop it and go back to the last one, with its iron columns against a blue sky, until they found a proper designer who could do a decent set.

It wasn't going to succeed, and it would be my fault. They'd all worked so hard, and they were so good. All that work, and their good reputations, all spoiled by boring sets and boring costumes. How had I ever been arrogant enough to believe I could work here?

'Is it always as bad as this?' I asked, and Solomon nodded and Donald shook his head.

'It's usually worse,' said Donald.

Solomon looked at the coffee machine, and shuddered.

'I started in Punch and Judy shows at Eastbourne when I was eight,' he said. 'I wish to God I'd stayed there.'

'I wanted to be an actress,' I offered, and Donald gave a short, despairing laugh.

'At least you changed your mind.'

The dress rehearsal went smoothly.

'Bad omen?' I asked the stage manager.

'No, it's not. Shut up. I *hate* designers. This would be a lovely place to be a stage manager in, if it wasn't for designers. Bugger off.'

I telephoned Jacob.

'Hello, my clever darling. They're pleased with you,' he said.

'How do you know?'

'I asked, they said so. Got ideas, but uses her eyes and her ears more than her mouth.'

411

'Uncle Jacob, I'm scared.'

'Can I believe my ears? Is the girl human after all? So? You've never been scared before? You think nobody else is scared? This is one of the most terrifying professions in the world, the theatre. Anybody who never gets scared in that game is plain stupid. You don't get to Stratford if you're stupid.'

We were to have two previews, just two performances in front of invited audiences, and then it was press night, with critics from all the national papers.

'The night of the long knives,' said Terence. 'I wish I was dead, I hate this job.'

Timon of Athens was playing that night, and then there were three days before our first preview. There were photographers, and anonymous people in suits, or jeans and anoraks, asking questions and talking to each other. Somebody asked me how it felt to be working here, and I mumbled something banal about the great honour, and a sense of history, and the fool wrote it all down. A camera flashed, and somebody thanked me.

I didn't sleep at all for two days before the press night. I lay staring up at the ceiling, wondering if there was anything I could do to improve the sets or the costumes, feeling cold and sick with apprehension. Everybody else was so good. It was only me, who had let them all down. I should never have come to Stratford.

We were all brittle with tension, hiding it behind smiles, the lovely cast suddenly artificial, playing the part of actors just before a first night because there was no other defence. Julie said she was drunk, she'd decided it was the only way to play Portia, would the rest of the cast please note. Somebody snapped at her, not *now*, please, darling, and then apologised, and the fragile edifice of everybody loving each other had to be rebuilt. Julie's hands were trembling, she was hurt and upset. She never drank more than half a glass of white wine.

I spent the afternoon painting black cats, cats stretching, jumping, sleeping, sitting, and I tried not to think. Black cats are important, I told myself. Think about the black cats.

Steam irons hissing, lights around dressing table mirrors, carefully folded head cloths, the theatre was coming to life, stretching, flexing its muscles.

Was that somebody praying? Oh, dear God. What have I done, coming here? Please, oh please, let this be all right. All the things I've done wrong, please let nobody notice.

Oh, God, let me out of here. Let me get out.

Julie's calm eyes, wide and frightened.

'Love that golden dress,' she said to me. 'It wouldn't fit me if I dieted.'

'It wouldn't suit you, either.'

A brave smile, only trembling a little.

'I'll stay as I am, then.'

A deep, indrawn breath, eyes closed, a long silence, and a sigh.

I left her with her dresser, closing the door quietly behind me, and went to the property room. The stage manager and two hands, checking a list, looked up and smiled.

'Well. Tonight's the night.'

Could I manage to smile back? What's the matter with my jaw?

'Yes. As you say. Tonight's the . . .'

Oh, God. What have I done? How could I have . . .?

Lights, testing. On, off, on, off, white, and colours, and then the crimson, the bar of light across the table. So obvious, childish little bit of stage trickery, why had I ever mentioned such a silly idea? Why hadn't I learned to keep my stupid notions to myself?

I feel sick. I'm going to be sick.

Solomon Crawley, friendly, relaxed and confident, talking to everybody, how could he be so calm? He saw me, and smiled.

'Well,' he said, 'whatever else happens tonight, you did all right. It's a cracker, that set. Thanks, Glory.'

But he was white, and there were dark grey shadows in his eyes. As good an actor as any of them, I thought.

'Would you like a black cat?' I asked.

'A what?'

'Cardboard. One of my black cats.'

I was distributing the damned silly things like confetti, I had nothing else to do. Dressing table mirrors, with black cats stuck in the side clips. Was there anybody who hadn't got one?

Shylock's house, it was all wrong, it shouldn't be like that. And that street scene, it looked like a skeleton of a supermarket.

God, let me out of here. I want to die.

Word coming back from the front of house. Almost a sell-out. A good house.

Tight smiles. Make-up, hair, costumes smoothed down, breathing exercises, clasped hands, lucky incantations.

Good luck, everyone. Not that we need it, we superstars.

Five minutes. Five minutes.

No. No. Please God, no. I am going to be sick. I should never have come here. I'm sorry. I'm sorry.

The house lights dimmed and died, there was a brief patter of applause, then Donald's voice absolutely right, this is Antonio. Donald, I'm sorry.

'"In sooth, I know not why I am so sad: It wearies me; you say . . ."'

I sat at my desk with the papers spread open in front of me.

'*Shakespeare with form, and life, and depth, no pretentious distractions.*'

Well, he'd told me to keep it bare. At least they'd noticed that.

'*The menace in the courtroom scene was almost palpable. Julie Stepping plays Portia like a swordswoman.*'

Was that partly my idea? Did I have a little of the credit for that? Julie had been wonderful. It really had been wisdom with menace, there'd been a warning in her voice, right through that famous, difficult speech, and Shylock had missed it. She'd been watchful, and clever, and dangerous, and, in the end, utterly merciless. Shakespeare's cynicism had been deadly in this production.

'Shylock almost reduced me to tears of shame and pity.'

Yes, he had been good, Terence. He was a very clever actor.

'One of Crawley's better efforts.' 'This splendid cast were most definitely not wasted.'

They'd hardly mentioned the set, or the costumes.

Solomon came in to see me, and grimaced at the sight of the newspapers.

'Are you reading them? God, you're brave.'

'They're very good, but I'm afraid they missed all your pretentious distractions.'

'What? What are you talking about?'

I pushed the *Express* across the desk towards him, pointing at the paragraph, and he affected to flinch away, clenching his teeth and drawing in his breath, before reading it, and laughing.

'They're super notices,' I said. 'They really are. I'll put a little whisper around, shall I?'

'They expect the best here,' said Solomon. 'Believe me, Glory, if they don't get it, they damned soon say so.'

I smiled at him. Stupid, to be disappointed, when just over two days earlier I'd been praying not to be noticed. Stupid, to feel left out.

Stupid people don't get to Stratford. Or don't stay for long.

I was pleased for the cast. They'd done so well, they deserved these good reviews. I was very pleased, and relieved.

And disappointed.

'They don't mention the set if it's good.'

Solomon had noticed. He wouldn't have been such a fine director if he hadn't been very observant.

'It's a good set, you ask the stage hands. They know. They know more about theatre design than any critic. They have to shift it around. Clockwork, was what they said about yours, and that's why I'm taking you over to the Dirty Duck for a drink.'

The Dirty Duck. The Black Swan, one of the landmarks of Stratford, one of the landmarks of the theatre world. Some of the cast might be there, celebrating relief more than success. Press night was over, the long knives were back in their scabbards, almost unbloodied.

'Right,' I said. 'Right. Let's go and drink the place dry.'

I smiled at him, and stood up, reaching for my jacket.

'It's a damned good set, Glory. It is, you know. Damned good.'

But they hadn't said so.

27

Anti-climax and depression, they seemed inevitable, but nobody noticed. I did try very hard not to let my disappointment show, and the friendly atmosphere in the theatre hadn't abated at all. On the contrary, now that we could relax, the dressing rooms came closer to a resemblance of the 'big happy family' legend than I had ever known.

The design was complete, there were only running repairs to be carried out, a few minor adjustments, and then I felt at a loose end. I was no longer needed, and Solomon Crawley wasn't saying anything about *A Midsummer Night's Dream*. I didn't like to ask.

Designers usually leave after press night, but Solomon always liked to keep his team intact for a few days. It worried him if we weren't immediately available to handle alterations, or at least to discuss them with him.

I made Julie a copy of the golden dress, modified enough for the management to allow it with nothing more than a mildly disapproving sniff. Heide Carter helped me, she was right about the fabric, it was almost impossibly slippery. I'd never have been able to sew it myself. The original design wouldn't have done, it was too dramatic. This new one could be used for parties. It would turn heads, but not raise eyebrows.

'I'm still not going to be skinny and vindictive,' she said, preening herself in front of the mirror. 'Oh, Glory! When did you do this? Wow!'

I'd had to do something with my time. I couldn't just stand around, waiting to see if Solomon would mention the next production.

Julie struck various poses in her new dress, ending with a burlesque of a fifties film star, hips and breasts thrust out at opposing angles.

'Anyway, if I was going to be the bitch you'd have to persuade Donald to play a pooftah,' she said, 'and he doesn't like doing it.'

'That's rude, Julie.'

'Don't you tell me I'm prejudiced. Some of my best friends are filthy little perverts.'

I could hardly make Donald an adaptation of his costume to wear to parties. I did thumbnail sketches of the stage hands, and I drew an object that might have been a tree, or might possibly have been a gallows, and left it on Solomon's desk.

A forest glade, with all the trees resembling gallows? Just an idea, Solomon?

He didn't mention it.

It was a relief when Mike telephoned.

'Listen, can you come up this week and sign this agreement with Grey's?'

'Yes. On Thursday?'

'Fine. I'll tell them. Glory, it was easy!'

Suddenly I felt both impatient and affectionate. Dear Mike. As Ruth had said, such a darling.

'Of course it was easy, Mike. Gerry doesn't want us in Birmingham as competitors any more than we want to compete with him. Even so, you did well with that contract. And the new premises.'

In fact it had been Inkies who had negotiated the grants for the new premises on the industrial estate for us. I had

418

insisted Simmie had been told about grants by their people, and although they could find nobody who would admit to having done anything so rash, they weren't prepared to deny it outright. They certainly didn't want to antagonise us, and me in particular, at that time. Not with the Royal Shakespeare Company in the background.

At least that contract was sealed. The managers at the studios were handling the advertising sets so smoothly it seemed as though they had been doing it all their lives, and the two work forces were merging without any apparent difficulty, or antagonism.

Simmie had decided we no longer needed a third cartoonist.

'Just as well,' I'd said. 'They seem to be nearly extinct. We have the last breeding pair in captivity.'

Simmie was out of hospital, but not back at work. He'd been to the warehouse twice, and Mike had threatened to have the locks changed if he came again.

'But who's running the place?' Simmie had wailed.

'I am,' Mike had retorted, and told me later he'd prayed for forgiveness for the blackest lie he'd ever told. Nobody was running the place, unless you counted Janet, who was turning the front office into a greenhouse and spilling potting compost all over the carpet tiles.

We hadn't found a manager, despite Inkies' efforts. Simmie refused to consider anyone whose company had failed, no matter what the circumstances. If they'd been good enough, the company wouldn't have failed. The manager had to have experience, no snotty little university graduates, all theory and no practice. Nobody who'd been made redundant, good managers weren't made redundant.

Simmie didn't want a manager. He wanted to do everything himself, it would all be all right in the end.

Our decision to change our choice of premises to something larger had been greeted with eager relief by the industrial development department of the city council; the big units on the site were proving difficult to lease, the little ones were in demand. Our first choice was snapped up by a bakery within a week.

'Will it be all right if I go up to Birmingham on Thursday?' I asked Solomon Crawley, and he nodded. He was reading a script, he'd hardly noticed me standing in front of him.

Gerry Grey, Jane Targe, and two other partners whose faces I hardly noticed represented Grey's, Simmie, Mike and me for Lawley's. We signed several copies of a contract in a solicitor's office, and then went back to Grey's for what they called a celebration.

Half a glass of champagne for Simmie, Ruth had instructed. He had three, and smoked salmon sandwiches, two slices of blackcurrant cheesecake, chocolate mints, cream in his coffee.

I tried to be happy, I smiled, I talked to Jane, I asked her to design me some clothes, and she named a startling price and said it was a special offer, because it was me.

Success, and she was loving it.

I watched Simmie putting only three lumps of sugar in his coffee, I saw Mike watching him too, and I noticed a sad and strained look on Mike's face.

I had bought this partnership to try to save Simmie, and make Mike happy. I owed everything to Jacob Goldman, who had urged me to take the offer, to make the big merger possible. Jacob wanted me to help his friend Simmie, and this was a debt I had to pay.

Simmie would kill himself anyway, and Mike would grieve, and I would be left with Lawley's, trying to run it, and destroying it instead. Had I not been tied down to Lawley's I might have made a better job of *The Merchant of Venice*. The critics would have noticed a better set, better costumes.

Solomon Crawley would have been talking about *A Midsummer Night's Dream*, not simply reading a script, and nodding when I asked if I could go to Birmingham.

Simmie and Mike and I drove back to Bolton in the car I'd bought to celebrate being offered the design of *The Merchant of Venice*, Mike crammed sideways into the tiny back seat, Simmie complaining about lack of room.

'It's a sports car,' said Mike. 'What the hell do you expect? You're gross, Simmie. Stop whining.'

Simmie, a hurt and sullen silence.

Back to Bolton, and a crisis. Su-Su was in hospital, and dangerously ill.

Some sort of poison, said a nurse when I telephoned in response to the urgent message on my machine. Please could I come at once, there was the child.

'The child' was at the hospital, sitting on one of a row of chairs in a corridor outside the ward. He was pale, and stolid, and stoical, staring down at the floor, with the edge of the chair gripped tightly between whitened fists. Somebody from the Department of Social Services had tried to take Danny away, and he had fought her, bitten hard enough to draw blood.

'Hello,' I said, and he looked up.

' 'Lo.'

The staff nurse said it was the first word he'd spoken since he'd arrived, in the ambulance with Su-Su.

I sat beside him while she went to find a doctor.

'All right?' I asked, and he nodded, staring down at the floor again, gripping the chair.

The doctor was a furious little man, almost dancing with rage. This was the third time Suzanne Meyerling had been in hospital, the third time, if it happened again he'd have the fool woman committed, was I a relative?

'No.'

Using herself as some sort of guinea pig for herbal medicines, irresponsible lunacy, did I understand? Did I understand what he was saying? Poisoning herself, quite deliberately poisoning herself. Who was I? What was I doing here?

421

'A friend.'

What about that child? Had she no idea of what it meant to be a mother?

'Have you?'

I'd spoken very quietly, but he gasped, and stared at me with his mouth open.

'Keep your temper under control, you grotesque little clown,' I said. '"That child" can hear you.'

He snorted and blustered, but he had flushed with embarrassment, and his voice became quieter.

'How serious is this?' I asked, and he ground his teeth, and drummed his fingers on the table, and at last he spoke, sensibly.

'She could die. It is very serious.'

It was simply a question of wait and see. I could visit her if I liked, but she was unconscious, there was little point.

I sat with Danny instead, and after a while one of his hands stopped gripping the side of his chair, and sought mine. It was a firm little hand, but it was very small.

'We've got to look after the animals,' I said.

'Yes.'

He wasn't interested in the car. I asked him if he'd like to drive fast, and he nodded, quite politely, but he sat in the seat, looking down at the rubber mat on the floor, taking no notice of the passing scenery, the wind in his hair, or my trick of making the engine roar as I changed gear, something to entertain a small boy.

I stopped at the village shop and bought food, things that could be cooked quickly and easily.

'Danny, have you got a family? Granny or grandad? Uncles? Aunts?'

He shook his head.

'Has Su-Su got any friends?'

'You.'

The house key was tied to Naomi's halter. Danny showed me, and watched as I struggled with the knot. Naomi was

422

huge and ponderous, heavily pregnant. She was wearing a blanket under a canvas cover, a strap around her ribs holding it in place, and there was a rack for hay tied to the window frame of the other house. It was wet, that winter, I thought she should be under cover. At least it wasn't too cold.

'Goin' to have her calf soon,' said Danny.

'How soon?'

He shrugged.

A five-year-old child, a pregnant cow, chickens and rabbits, all to be moved to Birmingham. Had Su-Su found anywhere to live?

'Danny, you'll have to teach me about the animals. I don't know about looking after animals.'

He showed me where the food was kept, in the kitchen of the other house, in big bins. I didn't know how much to give them, and Danny just shrugged when I asked. I put what seemed to be enough in the troughs and bowls, filled up the water tins, collected two eggs, and asked if we should clean the hutches.

He shrugged again.

There was hay stacked in bales under a tarpaulin beside the door of the other house. I carried half a bale to the front garden, and tossed it into the rack, pulling it apart so she could drag it through the bars.

'Is that enough?'

'Yes.'

A big plastic bucket, and a water bowl. I used the bucket to fill the bowl, and Danny said Naomi had special food, too. It was a mixture of grains in another bin, I didn't know how much to give her. This wasn't the sort of thing I'd ever thought I'd be doing.

Danny was watching me.

'Su-Su going to die?'

I didn't believe she would lie to Danny.

'I don't know.'

What do I say to him? He is only five years old, so stoical, standing there holding the torch for me, waiting for me to tell him.

'She's young, and she's strong, and she loves you very much. She won't die if she can help it.'

I saw him nod.

We carried the big bucket back to Naomi, and she left the hay and started to eat, eagerly. I thought I ought to take her blanket off for a while, so I undid the buckle, handed the strap to Danny, and shook it out. In the torchlight Naomi looked huge, her belly was enormous. What would I do, if she went into labour? There wasn't a telephone here, I couldn't even call a vet.

'Hungry?' I asked, and Danny hunched his shoulders.

'Bit.'

We ate our supper in near silence, but he was very hungry, almost everything on his plate vanished. There was no electricity, but there were oil lamps and candles, and it was quite warm in the room, with the kitchen range burning. There seemed to be enough coal. The last time I had been there Danny had told Su-Su about his morning at school, and she had listened carefully. Danny had explained to me that Su-Su earned the money and he learned, so he taught Su-Su what he had learned, so she could learn too, because that was fair.

They had looked at books after supper, and he had explained about letters, and reading, and drawn some to show her what he meant.

'Do you want to tell me about school?' I asked, but he shook his head.

'Didn't go.'

We shut up the chickens and the rabbits, to protect them from foxes and weasels, and then I boiled a kettle on the Calor gas cooker and gave Danny a bath in a plastic tub. He folded his clothes quite tidily, and stood still as I soaped him, and rinsed him, and then lifted him out and dried him, and dressed him in his pyjamas.

He led the way upstairs, I followed him with an oil lamp. He shared a room with Su-Su, there were boxes of clothes, two beds, no other furniture.

'Why did Su-Su eat whatever it was?' I asked, but it was too difficult for him. He knew, but he couldn't explain.

He thought about it, sitting on the side of his bed, his chin in his hands, then he told me to wait. He went downstairs, I heard books thumping on to the floor, and when he came back he was carrying one.

'In here, it says.'

The Ballad of the Sad Café, Carson McCullers. I'd read it once, a long time ago.

'In here?' I asked, puzzled, and he nodded, and climbed into bed, pulling up the blankets.

'Story,' he said.

'You'd like me to tell you a story?'

'I start.'

I sat on the edge of his bed, looking down at him and waiting, and he closed his eyes and frowned as he thought.

'Once upon a time,' he said, and then opened his eyes and looked at me. 'There was a zebra.'

I smiled, and waited, but there was nothing more.

'My turn?' I asked, and he nodded, and watched me, expectantly.

What could I do for this child? This tight stoicism, everything held in and controlled, this wasn't right. What could I do?

'He lived at the bottom of the sea,' I said. 'And he rode round and round and round on a bicycle.'

He looked at me, and then he looked towards the window as he thought, back at me as a smile broke out on his face, and there was a great shout of laughter.

Then, at last, tears.

I spent the night lying on the bed beside him, hugging him close until he stopped shaking, I washed his face for him, and cuddled him until he fell asleep, and then I read

The Ballad of the Sad Café by the light of the oil lamp.

It was almost at the end of that marvellous little book, Miss Amelia trying out her herbal medicines on herself, feeling her own reactions to them, judging which organs had been affected.

Su-Su had done the same, but without the skill and knowledge of Miss Amelia.

Danny didn't want to go to school the next day, so I took him to work with me. I had Su-Su's table and some clay brought up into my studio, and asked him to make something while I worked, but he only tried for a few minutes, and then came over to me.

He didn't like being alone.

We went down into the warehouse together, and I tried to work on one of the last sets. There were only three, the others had all been dismantled, some of them were already in Birmingham. It was impossible to paint, with a small boy holding my hand.

The hospital said Su-Su had gained consciousness briefly during the night.

I told Danny that was a good sign, and he nodded, but he didn't smile. I picked him up, held him against my hip as I had seen Su-Su do, and looked into his eyes.

'If Su-Su dies I will make sure you are all right,' I said. 'I promise.'

'Stay with you?'

'I don't know if I'd be allowed to have you, Danny. There are rules. But I promise I will make sure you're all right.'

He was sucking his thumb. I'd never seen him do that before.

Mike didn't think Su-Su had found anywhere to live near Birmingham. He said he thought she was squatting in the house they had, nobody had tried to evict them because the place was almost derelict anyway.

I telephoned estate agents in Birmingham, and told them what I wanted. Their reaction was disbelief. A *cow*? How much land would that mean? Well, yes, of course. What price range was I thinking of, madam? To *rent*? Oh, no, madam. Most unlikely. Of course, if something does come up . . .

'You'll just have to sell the cow,' said Mike. 'Listen, Glory, it's impossible. Listen.'

Danny was rigid on my lap.

'No,' I said. 'I won't. Naomi comes too.'

'But how? You'll never find a place.'

'I won't sell Naomi,' I said, and felt Danny sigh.

I telephoned the hospital. Su-Su had come round briefly, spoken Danny's name, but was unconscious again. There was a slight improvement, but she was still on the danger list.

'Bit better,' I said to Danny. 'She's trying very hard.'

I telephoned the National Farmers' Union and told them of my problem. They were doubtful. Most farm cottages were used by agricultural workers, or else rented out very profitably as holiday homes. But they gave me the telephone numbers of two farmers who might be able to help.

One of the estate agents telephoned. A sixteenth-century farmhouse, listed building, with twenty-five acres of land, was I interested?

Not remotely, I said, and hung up.

John Flanders was the second of the two farmers on my list, and he said he did have a cottage, it needed a lot of work, but it was for sale, not to rent.

I'd already concluded I'd never find a place for Su-Su, where she could keep Naomi. I'd have to buy a cottage, and rent it to her.

'May I come and see it?'

'Now?'

'A couple of hours.'

The cottage looked as if it was about to collapse. There was a hole in the roof, the front door hung off its hinges, and not one pane of glass in the windows was unbroken.

Flanders stood at the front gate looking at it cynically.

'Last people in it were tenants,' he said, and spat into the hedge. 'Never again.'

'They did all that damage?'

'Most of it. It's not as bad as it looks. The timbers are still sound.'

It was L-shaped, one storey, and there was a garage which could be adapted to house the chickens and rabbits.

'How much land?' I asked, and Flanders shook his head. 'Garden.'

'We've got a cow, we need a bit of land.'

He shook his head again, and looked away.

'They had goats. Christ. A cow.'

Scarlet paint scrawled across the front door. 'Fuck off, fachist shit farmer!'

'They couldn't even spell,' he said, and I laughed.

'If the timbers really are sound, and the walls haven't got nasty cracks, I will buy it, but only if you can let me have some land as well. For the cow.'

He looked mildly interested.

'What sort of cow?'

'Jersey.'

He spat into the hedge again.

'Useless things. Yellow meat.'

Danny was suddenly furious.

'Naomi *not* useless,' he screamed, and aimed a wild kick at Flanders' shins.

'Sorry.' Flanders was laughing, backing away from the angry child. 'Sorry, young man. Naomi's a quite exceptional Jersey cow. Not useless.'

'Land,' I reminded him. I let Danny go on kicking at his shins, he'd started the quarrel and I wasn't responsible for Danny's behaviour.

He dealt with Danny by picking him up and throwing him over one shoulder. Danny hung there, looking surprised.

428

'I don't sell my land. Two quid a week, let her run with my Herefords. That's just grazing, no extras.'

He put Danny down, squatted in front of him, and pointed a finger at his face.

'Kick me again, you get kicked right back. You shouldn't keep a cow on her own, she gets lonely. How would you like it if you never had anyone to talk to?'

'Naomi not useless,' said Danny sullenly.

'Danny, go and look at the house,' I ordered. 'Tell me if you think Su-Su would like it.'

He looked at me suspiciously, and his thumb was back in his mouth again as he walked slowly down the path.

'It's not for you, then?' asked Flanders, sounding a little disappointed.

Danny looked back at us from the front door. I waved at him, and called out.

'Go on, Danny. I'll be here, I promise.'

He hesitated. He looked very small, standing in the door-way, but I had to talk to Flanders alone.

'Danny's mother's dangerously ill in hospital,' I said. 'I should sell the cow, but it's too much. Danny's fond of Naomi.'

'Sorry to hear about the boy's mother.'

'That cow looks as if she's going to calve any day now, and I don't know anything about cows.'

'Oh, Christ.' He spat into the hedge again, but he was grinning.

I smiled at him.

'I think I was lucky to find you,' I said, and held out my hand.

He let me telephone the hospital from his house, where his wife gave Danny a slice of fruit cake and a mug of milk. She was a pleasant woman, but she didn't look very happy when Flanders said I'd buy the cottage if the survey was all right. I wondered whether she had reason to be jealous.

429

I had to wait for a long time to be connected to the ward, and I was becoming very anxious. Danny put down his cake, and looked at me. His eyes were round, and solemn.

'Miss Mayall?' A nurse's voice, the one I'd spoken to the day before.

'Yes?'

'She's conscious. Can you come? She's anxious about the child.'

'Is she out of danger?'

But she wouldn't commit herself. I would have to ask the doctor about that.

'She wants to see you,' I told Danny. 'We'd better go.'

Flanders walked back to the car with us.

'I'd better warn the Herefords about this most particular Jersey cow who's worth such a big fight,' he said, and Danny hung his head.

Su-Su was white, and sweating, but she was still conscious. She held out her hand, and Danny ran to the bed and buried his face against the blankets.

'Been in a fight,' he said, and burst into tears.

It was unforgivable. Violence was for the stupid and the inadequate, and Danny was neither. Even if you won a fight it only showed you were more violent than the other person, therefore more stupid, less adequate. It was a matter of shame, and a disgrace, to fight.

'Always?' I asked, and Su-Su nodded.

'Always.'

Danny howled in misery.

A nurse came bustling in, officious and busy, now then, what's all this about, we can't have this, young man.

'Go away,' I said. 'It's a private matter.'

She was indignant.

'I can't have my patients upset like this.'

'It isn't your patient who's upset. Go away.'

'Well, really!'

She'd have slammed the door if it had been the right sort.

430

'I wondered why he was so embarrassed with John Flanders,' I remarked.

Su-Su took Danny's hair and pulled his head back so he had to face her.

'You must apologise,' she said, and he sobbed.

'Yes. Yes.'

I'd had enough.

'What about your apologies?' I demanded. 'He's been through a day and a half of hell because of you and your stupid experiments. What about your apologies to Danny?'

'She did!' bawled Danny. 'She did! Shut up.'

Su-Su's hand was gentle on his hair now, stroking him, and she was smiling.

'Danny. Danny.'

I stood up.

'I'll leave you alone,' I said. 'I'll wait outside. Sorry, Danny.'

He came out half an hour later, still hiccuping from the tears, but calm again, and he managed to smile at me.

'Home?' I asked, and he nodded.

I looked at Naomi anxiously when I took off her blanket that evening to shake it out. She was shifting from leg to leg as though she was uncomfortable. Is this the first sign of labour?

I gave her half a bale of hay, and Danny held the torch as I scooped grain into the big bucket. I told him she would go to the farm the next day, so that Mr Flanders could look after her when she had her calf.

'Not you?' His voice was very small.

'I can't,' I said. 'I don't know about cows. Mr Flanders knows about cows, he'll help her if she needs help. He'll be kind to Naomi.'

He nodded, but he wouldn't look at me.

He had his apology to make.

We wrote it that night. He sat at the table, crying, telling me the words he had to say, to apologise for fighting. It

431

seemed a dreadfully long task for such a small boy, but I wrote it all down, and then wrote it again, in the big letters he could copy.

It took him two hours.

We told each other a story about polar bears that night, as far away from cows and farms as we could get, and Danny fell asleep as I spoke of the iceberg carrying our family of bears away from the hunters to a safe island where nobody was allowed to hurt anybody else unless they had to eat them, which seemed reasonable, to Danny.

Naomi went to the farm the next day, in a horse trailer from a thoroughbred stud farm, with a groom in attendance. It was all I could find at short notice. Cattle trucks were almost as expensive, and none was available for nearly a week.

To my eyes, Naomi looked as if she might have her calf at any minute.

I took Danny to Birmingham with me, to the new building, where the offices were still being decorated but the main floor had already been divided up into the spaces needed for the sets, and racking for equipment and fabrics had been installed. There were telephone engineers putting in cables, there were electricians, and plumbers.

There were also two secretaries, one from Grey's, who was to work for Mike and one of the other partners.

I told her I was borrowing her, I needed her to arrange repairs to a house, and she blinked in surprise, but nodded.

'Our house?' asked Danny.

'Yes.'

Then there was the bank, I'd have to sell shares to raise the money for the house. There was no time to arrange a mortgage.

There was no time for a survey, either. I would just have to trust John Flanders, and my own luck.

Danny and I drove to the farm to see Naomi.

She was in a loose box, up to her knees in straw, and off her food. Flanders said she'd arrived just in time.

I left him and Danny in the loose box, and walked down to the cottage. Danny's letter had gone with Naomi, the outcome was between the two of them.

Apart from the room under the broken tiles the cottage seemed dry. There was no smell of rot. Filthy graffiti, mostly aimed at Flanders or farmers in general, was written on the walls. Everything in the bathroom and kitchen had been smashed. More work for Mike's secretary.

Four rooms, a small kitchen with the bathroom behind it forming the shorter leg of the L-shape. Quite a big garden, there were some fruit trees. Danny could have a swing.

'Going to buy it, then?'

They were standing in the doorway behind me. They'd come in very quietly. They both seemed rather subdued.

'Oh, yes. Danny thinks it'll do.'

Flanders was looking around. He jerked his head in disgust.

'I'll get this muck off the walls. I don't want Danny reading this.'

Danny had his hands stuffed into his pockets, but he was looking up at Flanders. They'd sorted it out, it seemed. The misery had gone from the boy's eyes.

Back to the hospital to see Su-Su, who was lying propped up on pillows, a drip in her arm, a little colour in her face.

Out of danger, the ward sister said. Doctor would like a word with me.

I didn't want a word with Doctor, so Danny and I left quite soon. Danny was beginning to smile again.

Chickens and rabbits to feed, but no Naomi, so I drove him back to Bolton, and we had supper in a restaurant. Danny had never been in a restaurant before, and was a little over-awed.

'We'll telephone about Naomi tomorrow,' I said. 'She might have her calf tonight.'

He nodded. He was eating a fricassee, suspiciously. He didn't know what it was, under that sauce.

433

'Chicken,' I said, but he wasn't reassured. He didn't see how I could know, either.

I was beginning to like Danny.

Back to the house, shut up the chickens and the rabbits and give Danny his bath. I didn't notice that the chickens were flapping about in the henhouse, perhaps that was normal behaviour for chickens.

A story about an elephant who wanted to be a dentist, that left me completely confused but seemed to satisfy Danny.

I slept in Su-Su's bed, which was cold, and lumpy. Could we move back into my flat?

There'd been a weasel in the henhouse, seven of the chickens were dead.

'Hell!' I exclaimed, revolted by the blood and the feathers, the corpses lying on the slatted floor, but Danny just shrugged.

'Sell them,' he suggested. 'Rabbits and chickens, sell them.'

'Wouldn't Su-Su mind?'

He shook his head.

'Buy more when we moved? Keep money, buy more when we moved?'

He thought I should kill them, and clean them, and take them to a butcher.

'I can't!' I said, shuddering, and he was disgusted.

'Can't do much, can you?'

Stupid, to be resentful of a five-year-old, just because I'd bought a house because I liked him, and because his mother had entrusted him to me.

I used a garden fork to put the dead hens on to the compost heap, and then I followed Danny into the house.

'We are going to work,' I said. 'Go and get in the car.'

The second butcher I telephoned agreed to kill the rabbits himself, but wasn't interested in the five remaining chickens.

I wanted to get out of this, back to a modern flat with a proper bathroom, where chickens came deep-frozen, eggs in cartons, food out of supermarkets.

'Will you just kill the things and put them on the compost heap for me?'

The voice was slightly affronted.

'All right. I suppose so. Seems a bit of a waste.'

I gave him the address of the house, hung up the telephone, and turned back to Danny, who was sitting at my desk.

'That's sorted,' I said, and he hunched his shoulders.

'Don't be so intolerant.' I sat down opposite him in the chair reserved for visitors. 'Nobody can do everything. Could you design a theatre set?'

'Yes. Anybody could.'

His face was red and furious.

Five years old, I reminded myself. Brought up by Su-Su. Landed on me without my permission, and had already taken up three days.

I pushed a pencil at him.

'Do it, then. Do me a theatre set. On the blotter.'

Tears in his eyes, and I was ashamed.

'Let's go and see if the drinks machine still works,' I said. 'I think there may be Coca-Cola.'

'Want Su-Su.'

Five years old, I'd defeated a five-year old. I could be really proud of myself.

'We'll visit her this afternoon. She has to see the doctor this morning.'

There was no response. He was looking downwards, very still.

'Shall I telephone and ask about Naomi?'

After a moment he nodded.

A heifer calf, John Flanders said. Healthy, Naomi was fine.

'Could you tell Danny?'

435

Danny listened to the telephone, nodding solemnly as John told him about the birth. When the sounds of John's voice stopped I took the receiver back.

'Thank you,' I said. 'He seemed to understand all that.'

'Nice boy. Somebody's fixed the front door to the cottage, I've got the keys here.'

'Were you up all night with Naomi?'

'No, I wasn't. I left her to get on with it. She's all right. They usually are.'

'And if they're not?' I was annoyed, I'd entrusted Naomi to him.

'Then I find out about it in the morning. I deal with it, or I call the vet. Cows aren't as fussy as women, they manage on their own, and they don't ask for clean sheets.'

He hung up on me.

I laughed, and Danny scowled at me.

'Not to put chickens on compost heap,' he said, and he began to cry again.

Wearily, I telephoned the butcher.

'Don't kill the chickens,' I said. 'Just the rabbits.'

'Tomorrow,' he said. 'It's Sunday. I'm entitled to my day of rest, aren't I?'

I'd lost track of the days. Sunday, and I hadn't bought any food. It would have to be a restaurant again.

I couldn't even throw the damned chickens away. We'd have to live in that filthy house until we moved, just because of five chickens.

'I've got to do some work, Danny.'

He nodded, and rubbed his eyes with his fists. I passed him a paper handkerchief.

'I can't do it with you holding my hand or sitting on my lap. Can you watch? Or do some of Su-Su's work for her, with the clay?'

'Su-Su's work,' he mumbled.

He liked working with clay. He liked splashing the water on to it, watching it smooth out under his fingers when it was wet. He used a lot of water, working with that clay.

Sunday was usually the day when I managed my best work, when there was nobody else in the place, no distractions. Danny was very quiet compared to most children, being Su-Su's son, but he did demand admiration of his models, and some sort of conversation.

'I think you'd better go to school tomorrow,' I said, and he nodded.

It poured with rain that night, and the roof leaked. Danny woke me, water was dripping on to his bed. There were buckets downstairs, he said. I put him into my bed, lit the oil lamp, and looked at the ceiling. Brown stains were spreading across the plaster from three patches of damp, and as I watched a water droplet formed in the centre of the largest of them, trembled, hung, and fell.

The ceiling was uneven, it seemed even more distorted in the lamplight, but I wasn't sure it was only the light. There was another water droplet, they were forming faster, and a crack from one corner, had it been there before?

As I watched, it spread, and water began to drip from it. The ceiling was collapsing.

I shook Danny awake, wrapped him in blankets, and carried him downstairs. 'We're moving,' I said.

'New house?' He was sleepy, a little puzzled.

'Old flat. Wait there.'

I went upstairs again to collect the blankets from his bed, but there was a huge three-cornered tear in the ceiling plaster, and water and filth from the rafters had poured in. The blankets were soaked, and ruined.

'Just as well you woke up when you did,' I said, but he was asleep again, curled up on the sofa.

I draped the thickest of the blankets over us both, and carried him out to the car. He put his arms around my neck, mumbled something, opened his eyes, and then fell asleep again as I fastened the seat belt around him. I ran back into the house, wondering if there was anything I could do to protect Su-Su's belongings, but I had to get Danny into a safe, dry bed, so I just locked the doors. I could only hope the water would stay upstairs, not bring down the living room ceiling and ruin the books and toys.

The flat was cold, I hadn't lived in it for weeks, but at least it was dry. I turned on the fire, draped sheets, blankets and a quilt over the furniture to air, and left Danny lying on the bed in his coat. He sighed, turned on to his stomach, put his thumb in his mouth, and closed his eyes again.

He was incredibly beautiful. I stood by the bed, looking down at him, at the lovely curve of his cheek with the eyelashes lying softly, the rounded forehead under his fair hair, I wanted to stroke him, I wanted to protect him. The idea that anything might hurt this child was intolerable. He was so beautiful, so very beautiful.

I'd never liked children, before.

I waited until the quilt was warm, I made sure it was dry, and then I wrapped him in it, and I lay down beside him on the bed, holding him close in the warm covering, and I listened to his soft breathing.

I was beginning to love this boy.

It was still raining when we woke up, a heavy and steady rain with the sky dark above it, no sign of the clouds breaking.

I dressed Danny, I noticed his trousers were too short, I'd have to buy him some new clothes soon. There was nothing in the flat to eat, so I drove to a coffee bar and he had two sticky cakes and a milk shake. He was smiling, this was an adventure. I bought him another cake to take to school with him.

'Disgusting,' I said, and he giggled. I was sure Su-Su would never have fed him on sticky cakes.

I dropped him at school, checked that he would be taken to the child-minder as usual, and then went back to the house to feed the animals. They were damp, but unharmed.

438

I felt ridiculously guilty as I fed the rabbits.

In the house, I stacked the books on to the broken sofa. I'd have to arrange for them to be collected, and Danny's toys, which were in wooden apple crates. I didn't think the furniture was worth moving to Birmingham, but it belonged to Su-Su, I couldn't throw it away. There was hardly enough to make it worth hiring a truck, so I decided I'd send one of the lorries that was to take the last of the sets and the office equipment to the new building to collect it all. It could be stored there until the house was ready.

This is not my responsibility, I told myself, but I was still dreamy from the beauty of the sleeping child and the feelings of love that had overcome me, so I put his toys carefully on to the piles of books, and I locked the door behind me when I left.

Only two more days, and we'd be out of Bolton, tomorrow there were three photography sessions, and then those sets could be dismantled, the last of the furniture from the office taken away, and we'd close the place. Already, it was almost deserted.

But the telephone was ringing, and Janet was late, so I went to the switchboard and answered it.

It was Solomon Crawley, irritated.

'Where are you? You're supposed to be here.'

'Why? It's Wednesday before you're putting on *The Merchant* again, why have I got to be there?'

'I'm not talking about *The Merchant*, for God's sake. Haven't you got a diary? We're starting work on *A Midsummer Night's Dream*, you're supposed to be *here*. How long before you can get here?'

I couldn't get there. I couldn't leave Danny, and what about the blasted chickens? What could I do?

'Listen,' I said to Solomon, 'I'll have to bring a child with me, and I have to leave by late afternoon. I'm sorry, I'll explain when I get there. It's a crisis.'

'A child? I didn't know you had children. Is it an actor?'

439

'No. He's not mine, either. What do you mean, is it an actor?'

He'd been working on *The Caucasian Chalk Circle* with some brat from a detergent advertisement, who'd been shaking its curly little head and acting its damned knickerbockers off. I could bring the child, but he warned me, if it tried to act he'd strangle it.

I liked Solomon Crawley so much.

'Danny won't act,' I said. 'Danny's a realist.'

I collected Danny from school, promising him that I'd help him catch up, and meaning it. I'd hire a private tutor if I had to, but lose *A Midsummer Night's Dream* I would not.

The roads were clear for once, it didn't take as long as I'd feared, and I parked the car, grabbed Danny's hand, and ran for the stage door. Only an hour late. Better than I'd hoped.

An ideas session, bouncing ideas off the walls, as Solomon put it. At least he smiled when Danny and I came in, which was more than I'd expected, and he waved a hand around the room.

'You probably know everybody,' he said. 'Except, perhaps, Oberon.'

'I think we've met.' A nice voice, but had I heard it before? I began to turn towards him.

'A long time ago,' he said. 'At the Royal? Peter Clements. Hello.'

Long, long legs, and wide shoulders, and brown hair falling forward into brown eyes.

'Well, hello again,' I said, and I smiled.

28

'I told you I liked the set,' said Solomon. 'What more do you want? Gold medals and laurel wreaths?'

'You didn't say you wanted me back. It all depended on the set for *The Merchant*, and you didn't say.'

I was almost too happy to speak. He really had meant it, it hadn't mattered that my design had hardly been mentioned in the reviews, he'd liked the set. He wanted me back.

'You like working here?' he asked.

'Oh, God. Solomon.'

'Don't take on any commitments without checking with me first.'

I was here, I was back again, I was with the Royal Shakespeare Company at Stratford, fairyland again, and not the slightest idea of what to offer for *A Midsummer Night's Dream*.

But this time I knew most of the cast, I knew what they'd like. Terence Bourne was to play Puck, and Donald was to play Theseus as the battle-scarred warrior, somewhat brusque as Hippolyta's lover.

I could forget about fairies being miniature and fragile, with Oberon over six foot tall, and Titania the lean and powerful Sonia Loveday. Solomon had said he wanted to accentuate the danger of the fairies; they are like wild animals, they simply don't care.

Peter Clements. I wondered, fleetingly, whether Terry had ever won her bet, and pushed the idea away. Like the fairies, I simply didn't care whether she'd worn those jeans or not.

They wouldn't fit you, I thought, and giggled to myself.

'What?' demanded Julie.

'Nothing. Silly thought.'

'Don't you ever share your silly thoughts?'

She was sitting on my desk, fiddling with my pencils. She'd come to tell me that a fashion buyer she'd met at a party had asked if he could buy the design of her golden dress, but she'd decided she'd rather keep it exclusive.

'I've never seen you like this before,' she remarked. 'Why are you so bubblingly happy?'

'I'm back, that's why.'

'Oh, darling Glory.' She reached out her hand, and patted my shoulder. 'We're all so sorry.'

'That I'm back?'

'No, stupid! That we didn't realise you didn't know. We didn't say. We just thought, anybody as good as you *has* to know. You can't not know.'

It was only yesterday that I hadn't known.

I'd driven back to Bolton as fast as I could, but Danny and I had missed visiting hours at the hospital, and we'd only been allowed five minutes with Su-Su. She'd understood, but she'd been anxious, and unhappy.

'No stress,' the ward sister had said, staring at me in disapproval.

'Right. Sorry.'

'Doctor wants a word. And there's a social worker, about the child.'

Danny's hand had crept into mine. He'd bitten the social worker.

442

'Listen,' I'd said to him, not much caring whether my philosophy corresponded to Su-Su's, 'she started that fight. Fighting is stupid, but that doesn't mean you don't fight back if somebody attacks you. Do you understand?'

He hadn't answered. He'd just looked at me, rather solemn.

'Anyway, you certainly don't apologise.'

Doctor wouldn't be long, the nurse had said. I'd replied that I wouldn't be long either, and Danny and I had left. She'd been scandalised.

The rabbits had still been in their run.

I'd telephoned the butcher, furious.

'You fed them,' he'd said.

'Of course I fed them.'

'You don't feed animals for twenty-four hours before you kill them.'

It was a disgusting idea. It was bad enough killing animals, leaving them hungry first was intolerable. I was sure Su-Su didn't starve her animals before she killed them. I told the butcher to forget it. I'd call in and pay him for his time when I was next in town.

'I love you, Danny,' I said the next morning when I left him at the school. 'What are we going to do about these animals?'

He shook his head. He didn't know.

'Animal sanctuary,' said Sonia Loveday, and solved the problem.

Seven pounds a week for five chickens and fifteen rabbits, probably a hundred and fifteen by the time I got all this sorted out.

'The sex life of the rabbit is one of the most amazing things in the whole of creation,' said the young man at the Croft Lees Sanctuary.

'Please do feel free to feed them to the stray dogs,' I said, and he smothered a laugh, tried to look disapproving. Dogs and cats are carnivores, but it is not considered

443

tactful to draw attention to this fact in an animal sanctuary.

A Midsummer Night's Dream, what was I going to offer?

'Are you going to make me tremendously glamorous?' demanded Sonia, grinning at me, but there was something behind this. Sonia was in her late forties now. I'm cracking a joke with you, Glory. Glamour, for an old bag like me, that's a joke.

Please, Glory. Give me glamour again, begged Sonia.

Please, begged Glory, please something, somebody, give me some ideas to offer.

It happened the very next day, in the Green Room, in a crowd of actors and stage technicians, with the smell of coffee in the air, and Terence Bourne truculently defending himself from ridicule.

Terence carried his kit in a huge old leather grip bag, and he'd been rummaging in it, looking for something, becoming increasingly exasperated at his failure to find it.

'Turn it all out on the table,' suggested Sonia. 'When did the inside of that bag last see daylight, anyway? You might find something valuable.'

'You'd be more likely to get bitten,' said Terence. 'Right, stand back, everybody. Here goes.'

The contents of the bag cascaded out on to the table, and Sonia pounced on the dusty heap with a whoop of delight.

'Terence! Does the Victoria and Albert know you've got this collection?'

Terence tried to push her away.

'Hands off, you unscrupulous woman! You're just jealous.'

'But what's this? Ooh, yuck. It's all stuck together. Gum Arabic, the tube's burst.'

We all gathered around the table, prodding at Terence's heap of old make-up.

'Don't *touch* it!' he said. 'Honestly, have you *no* respect for other people's property?'

'Is this comb real tortoiseshell?' 'What on *earth* is this?' 'Did you ever wear this? What in?'

Terence threw out his arms.

'Oh, do come and join in, everybody. There's a mass loot going on here, it's open house on Terence Bourne's private property.'

'What the . . . good *grief*. Greasepaint. Your real, honest-to-God original Leichner.'

'Sonia, *leave* my greasepaint alone.'

'Is it meant to be that colour, or is it mildew?'

'Oh, hell.'

Terence sat down and glowered at her.

'My nanny said that everything came in useful once every seven years,' he said.

'It's a lot more than seven years since I've seen that stuff.' 'Sonia, is it really greasepaint? Hand it over.' 'Terence, did you have to wear this?'

'Yes. Yes, I did. All right? So I'm old.'

Sonia was drawing with it on the back of her hand.

'I've used it, too,' she said. 'God, this brings back memories. It smells of overcooked cabbage.'

'How much of it have you got?' 'Is there any more in there?' 'Do let me try.' 'How do you get it off again?'

'Cold cream,' said Sonia. 'I remember. It tasted like lard.'

'Well, don't taste that lot, you'll probably poison yourself.'

'What a charming remark,' muttered Terence. 'Anybody else got anything to say?'

Peter Clements was leaning over the table with the rest of us, laughing, and the bright lights cast strange shadows on his face.

I hadn't slept the night before. Danny had been restless, he'd wanted Su-Su, and he'd cried. She was still in hospital, he thought she was going to die, so I'd sat up all night, rocking him in my arms. Every day she lives she's stronger, I'd said. And the body heals itself, it really can, Danny. It really can.

Shadows under his cheekbones, was this how Oberon looked in the moonlight? Pattern pictures, it had been years since I'd painted pattern pictures, but those curved shadows, this could be Oberon in the moonlight. They were brown, these shadows.

Like this stick of greasepaint in my hand.

I stood up, I went over to him, I looked into his face, and he smiled at me. It made the shadow deeper, and I reached up with the greasepaint. I traced it under the line of the bone.

Yes. That curve, that could be Oberon, in the moonlight. Everybody fell silent, watching.

With a highlight, on the bone, and over the brow. Now, gold should be dusting in the eyebrow here, enough to glint in the light. Yes, like that. And the shadows, greys and greens. Where are the greys and the greens?

Somebody pushed the greasepaints closer to me. Green, a line traced down the jaw, with the brown shadow over it, like a tree, like a young tree. Shadows in the eyes, the same shadows in the throat, but the golden brown on those long muscles down the side of the neck, and the dark shadows in the hollows of the throat.

Yes. Yes, this could be Oberon.

A white shirt, in the way, get it out of the way, I was trying to pull it away, and then it was free, he'd taken it out of the way, and I was tracing the golden brown down the breastbone, on to the ribs, with the dark shadows between the ribs, the green and the brown on the muscles of his belly, with the gold on the hairs of his chest. Green and brown on his arms, on his shoulders, dark shadows under the collar bones, highlights on the bones again. A young tree, this had grown in the forest, half animal, half tree. The colours over the shoulders, on to his back. He'd turned, brown and green on his back, shadows, grey shadows on the spine, and brown between the ribs.

This is Oberon, King of the Fairies. Yes, this is Oberon, this is how it must be.

Smooth, under my fingers, the warm skin, and the smell of greasepaint in my nostrils, firm muscle, gold here. Gold on the firm muscles in his back, because this is a king, and then brown again, down the sides of the spine, gold, and brown, and green.

Turn, yes, gold and brown on his belly, a strong young animal, this king, and look up, gold in his hair. Brush the gold into the brown hair, brush it back from his face, yes. That's right. A young animal, a young tree.

Stand back, and look.

Gold, and brown, and green.

Warm young muscle under my fingers, colour tracing the movement of the muscles, a shiver in the skin, brush the gold into the hairs, this is a king.

Deeper, down the belly, gold and brown here, with the green shadows, not too much green, this is the trunk of the tree, brown, and grey, but there's something in the way, get this out of the way.

A hand stopping me, his hand on mine, he was laughing, everybody was laughing, my hand on the buckle of his belt, and he was holding my hand, his hand over mine, he was laughing.

'Bloody fantastic!' somebody exclaimed.

But they were all laughing, and I looked down at my hand, I'd been trying to undo the buckle of his belt.

'I'm sorry,' I said. 'I'm sorry.'

I could feel my cheeks flaming, I pulled my hand away, pressed my hands against my cheeks.

'Sorry,' I said again. 'I don't know . . .'

'Fan*tas*tic! God, that's fantastic.'

There was a mirror, he was looking at himself, at the paint I'd put on his body, I'd painted him.

I hardly knew him. I'd painted his body, his face, I hardly knew him and I'd put greasepaint all over his body. I'd taken his shirt off and painted his body with greasepaint.

447

I must have been mad, to do such a thing. Completely mad.

How could I have done this?

I backed away, backed into a corner of the room, looked around for the door. I had to get out, now.

'Glory, that's incredible. That's it!'

'Where's Solomon? He's got to see this.'

I wanted to cry. I'm sorry, I'm so sorry. I don't know what came over me. I'm so sorry.

'That's what he wanted, isn't it? An animal, that's it. Glory, that's fantastic.'

'Peter, go and show Solomon. Go on, now, go and show him.'

He went out, he and some of the other men, he still had the paint all over his body.

'*Wow!*' Julie Stepping, looking at me, laughing.

'Oh, God. I don't know what came over me. God. I just, sort of . . . I saw Oberon, I wanted to paint him. God, how awful. How could I have done that?'

She was still laughing.

'I've been wanting to get my hands on his body ever since I saw him,' she said. 'Now I know how to do it. Just throw myself at him and rip his clothes off.'

'Oh, Julie. Please, don't. Please don't.'

But she wouldn't stop laughing.

'There are shirt buttons all over the room,' she crowed. 'Wow, Glory! And *what* a body! What about those muscles, then, Glory? How do they feel?'

'Oh, shut up, Julie! Shut up.'

They were all laughing, Sonia, and Julie, and the stage hands, the rest of the cast, they were all laughing. My face was burning, I knew I was scarlet with shame and embarrassment, and they were all laughing at me.

'If we'd *known*,' said Sonia. 'If we'd only *known* what you were planning, we'd have helped you with that belt. I reckon the *three* of us could have held him down.'

I was beginning to laugh, too. I couldn't help it. But how was I ever going to face him again, after this?

The two stage hands, the ones we called Nervo and Knox, clowning at us.

'Ooh, *duckie*, you could have counted on more than three.'

Sonia spread her hands.

'See, darling? Let's set up an ambush, you get behind the door, I'll jump him from the table.'

'You wait, Sonia Loveday. I'll make you look like eighty years old. In black bombazine.'

'I don't care. I get Oberon. All muscle and bone. I get Oberon, he'll have to lump the black bombazine, I get him anyway.'

They all came back, Solomon Crawley with them, and he was grinning.

'Right, I want that photographed,. I want Make-up matching it with Aquatint. Sonia and the rest like this. Glory? Where's the dratted girl *now*?'

I was standing against the wall, looking down at the floor, wishing my face would stop burning, wishing I could be somewhere else.

Wishing I hadn't painted him, but remembering the way the skin on his belly had shivered under my fingers.

Solomon was demanding my attention, so I looked up, brushed the hair out of my eyes, stared at him. I did not look at Peter Clements.

'Right, Glory, what's the idea behind the body paint?'

There was an idea, at last. It had come. I'd remembered a cross-country run when I'd been at school, running across the heath. I'd wanted to be alone, so I'd run fast and left the others behind. It was very quiet on the heath, and I'd seen a stag.

I hadn't seen him until he'd moved. He'd blended so perfectly with his background, it wasn't until he'd raised his head that I'd noticed him, and then I'd wondered how I could have missed him.

I'd stopped running, and looked, and closed my eyes and counted, twenty-five. When I'd opened them again I couldn't see the stag, and then I'd heard the voices of the other girls, and he'd sprung away, and run across the heath and into the woods, he'd gone.

Now, to try to explain this.

'You don't see them against the background until they move,' I said. 'When they're standing still, they blend in.'

He wanted to see this, back on stage, get a backdrop down, a forest scene. Yes, that old thing.

Get over here, Glory. Peter, you too. Now, show me.

Alone on the stage with him, under the lights, Solomon standing in the aisle and watching, everybody else behind him.

But this wouldn't work, the paints on his body were different colours, this grass green and yellow, he couldn't blend into this.

I was tongue-tied, and I knew my face was scarlet again. I'd have to try to explain, so I walked to the front of the stage.

'The same colours for the . . . the make-up. Um. Well, you see, he's like a tree. Not like this . . .' I gestured at the backdrop, a bit contemptuously, it wasn't very good.

'When he's invisible, he's not really. Like a forest animal when it doesn't move. Or, if he's half tree, he just becomes another tree.'

'Peter, be a tree,' said Solomon, and I felt him move behind me.

'I know it's been done before,' I said. Had it? Surely, it must have been.

Solomon was shaking his head impatiently. He didn't mind doing things again, if he thought he could do them better.

I glanced at Peter. One arm raised, bent, head thrown back.

'The jeans aren't quite what we're looking for,' some-

450

body called, and then a falsetto squeal from the back.

'Get 'em *off*!'

An irritated gesture from Solomon, and they were quiet. He was thinking, his head hunched down.

'Have them on stage the whole time?' he asked doubtfully.

I heard a mutter from Sonia.

'Hell's bleeding teeth!'

I hadn't thought about it.

'Peter, how long could you hold that?'

I glanced back at Peter. There was a tremor in the bent leg.

'Not long enough,' and he straightened up, lowering the raised arm.

Solomon came on to the stage, gestured up into the flies, and the backcloth swung upwards.

'I like the idea, though. Cut that invisibility bit, let it speak for itself. Just turn into a tree.'

'Or a stag,' I said. 'I think, sort of, half and half.'

The way he'd stood, with his head thrown back, this was coming back, I was beginning to see what I could do here. I walked over to him, frowning at the green and gold make-up on his face, I reached out and smeared part of it upwards into his hair.

'A head dress, like antlers made of brambles,' I said. 'He's got to look dangerous, though, hasn't he? Anyway, you can hardly see a wild animal, when it's keeping still. The other fairies, they're more . . .' Another vague wave of the hand, I must look like a halfwit here, flapping my hands about.

I backed away from Peter. I'd touched him again, without even realising I was going to, I'd touched his face, changed the lines of the make-up. But he hadn't moved, he'd just watched my hand, and then looked at Solomon again.

'Sort of, conventional, the other fairies,' I said. 'I don't mean silly wings, but they could be trees. Or plants and things.'

'Hmm.' Solomon, chin cupped in his hand, shoulders hunched as he thought.

'Not like some tableau, though. I don't mean that.'

'Can I say something?' A voice from the back, Robert Yeo, who'd been cast as Demetrius.

'Yes, Robert. What is it?'

Robert walked down the aisle as he spoke. I watched him as he grew clearer in the reflection of the lights. He was nearly middle-aged now, and he'd look better if he lost weight. They'd have to be careful with his costume.

'If they're going to be holding these rigid poses, the audience is going to be watching *them*. Watching to see if they can do it. They'll miss the action in every scene.'

A long silence. When Solomon was thinking in top gear like this, nobody interrupted.

'Yes,' he said eventually. 'We'll have to compromise on the poses. But I do want Oberon holding still like a stag, I like that idea. You'll just have to practise it, Peter. Get fitter, if necessary.'

'Thanks a *bunch*, sweetheart,' Peter muttered, and I glanced at him nervously. The grimace he gave me was, at least, half humorous.

'Glory, I want to see some sketches,' said Solomon. 'Particularly the head dress, and the background he'll be standing against. By tomorrow, please. Peter, get that body paint photographed. Sonia, and the rest of the fairies, I want you thinking around this. Bear in mind what Robert said, too. I don't want anybody upstaged by a pantomime tree.'

He glanced at his watch.

'Right, that was your lunch break. Back to work.'

By tomorrow, he'd said. I'd have to work all night.

Danny, please sleep well tonight.

But he didn't. He was tearful and bewildered. If Su-Su was better, she should be home. Why was she still in hospital? He wanted her. Not me. He wanted Su-Su. He didn't want to go to a restaurant, he wanted proper food, out of the garden. He wanted his books, and his toys. He didn't want to be in the flat, it was silly.

'Shall we go to the coffee bar for supper?' I asked.

'No!' he shouted, and he started to cry again.

I said we'd buy some fresh vegetables, things that had been grown in a garden, but he wouldn't get into the car. Cars were silly, he didn't want to go in a car.

After we'd walked a hundred yards he was tired. I had to carry him. He grew heavier and heavier.

He said the vegetables at the late-night supermarket weren't properly fresh. The potatoes weren't big enough to bake, and he wanted baked potatoes. He didn't want chicken. He didn't want sausages. He didn't like fish.

'You choose, then,' I said, and I gave him the basket.

He came back with a bar of soap and a bottle of olive oil.

'Omelettes,' I said. 'I'll get eggs.'

'No!'

'Oh, shut up, Danny.'

He started to cry again, I wanted to slap him. I left him standing by the till, I bought eggs, and fresh salad from the counter, and the biggest potatoes I could find, to bake.

'If you don't stop crying I'll make you walk all the way home.'

'Want to go home,' he sobbed. 'Want Su-Su.'

I squatted in front of him and wiped his face. His nose was running.

'Blow,' I said, but he twisted his head away.

'The roof fell in,' I said. 'Remember?'

I carried him home. I wished I hadn't bought the potatoes. By the time we got back, the handle of the basket had left deep white grooves in my fingers.

Danny fell asleep on the floor while I was cooking the supper, so I set his to one side, ate mine, and got out my sketch book to start drawing the head dress.

Then he woke up.

453

'Hungry?' I asked.

'No.' He was sullen, and angry, and he began to cry again.

'Oh, Danny. You'd better have your bath now.'

'Hate you,' he sobbed. 'Hate you.'

'Just shut up, you.'

I'd had enough of this. I wanted to work, not cope with a snivelling brat. How could anybody work, with this going on? Tomorrow, I had to have these sketches ready tomorrow, I hadn't even started.

It was midnight before he was asleep, and I was furious and exasperated. He'd hardly eaten anything, he'd said he hated me. He wanted to go home, he wanted Su-Su.

'So do I,' I'd retorted. 'She's welcome to you.'

And he'd cried again, and I'd felt ashamed of myself.

'Poor old Danny,' I'd said, and tried to hug him, but he'd pushed me away, and stood alone, wailing miserably, so I'd walked away, and at last he'd got into bed and fallen asleep, still sobbing.

Su-Su was going to be in hospital for another week, they'd said. Doctor still wanted to see me, and so did the social services. Would I please make an appointment?

'No.'

'Miss Mayall, are you always this irresponsible? Doctor . . .'

I'd hung up.

Antlers, sweeping back from the line of the brow. His forehead had been rather flat, broad, but we could take the hair back under the band of the head dress. Perhaps a crest between these brambles, coming down low? It would balance better like that.

It was going to be heavy, this thing. And if he had to hold it, motionless, like a stag in a forest, he would need to be very strong.

I stopped sketching.

Golden brown, I'd made the muscles down the side of his

454

neck. Warm and firm under my fingers as he'd turned his head. Strong, yes, they'd felt strong.

I smiled.

He'd manage.

Danny woke up, he wanted a drink, he was thirsty. He felt hot, and he was crying again. His face looked flushed.

'Danny, don't you feel well?'

'Want Su-Su,' he wailed.

'Have you got a pain? Does it hurt anywhere?'

He snivelled, rubbed his eyes, wiped at his nose with his sleeve, a string of slimy mucus on the flannel. I sponged it away, trying not to mind.

'Have you got a pain?'

'No.'

His forehead was very hot. He fell asleep again, but he was murmuring, and singing. Delirious, he was feverish.

Two o'clock in the morning, what can you do for a sick child at two in the morning?

I looked in the telephone directory for a doctor, one not too far from the flat. A woman's voice answered, the doctor was out on a call already, was it really an emergency?

'I don't know. I'm looking after a child for a friend while she's in hospital. He seems very feverish.'

'How feverish? What's his temperature?'

'I don't know. I haven't got a thermometer.'

'Are you one of Dr Small's patients?'

I hadn't needed a doctor. I told her, I had no doctor, and she said she'd tell Dr Small when he called in. He'd come, if he thought it was necessary. Otherwise I should bring the child to surgery in the morning. Surgery started at nine.

I was supposed to be in Stratford at nine. I had to be in Stratford at nine. Solomon wanted these sketches.

Send them by taxi?

No good, he wanted the sketches, and he wanted me there, to talk about them, scribble on them, argue, and

455

listen, and bounce the ideas off the wall, see what stuck. The sketches without me were no good. I had to be there.

Thick black pencil, one thing at a time. Make the eyes long, and follow the line of the long eyes with the antlers. What shape were his eyes? He'd have to hold his head thrown back, or could I balance the antlers better, so he could look ahead? How does a stag stand, with a full head of antlers?

Think. I'd have to look at pictures, there must be a picture book somewhere.

Picture book, children. Check Danny.

Danny was moaning. He'd kicked off the quilt. His face was red, and he was sweating.

I pulled the quilt over him again, fetched a sponge and wiped his face. He pushed my hand away. A sort of choking cry, and then the singsong noise again, his head rolling from side to side.

What was the matter with him? How serious was this? Should I call an ambulance?

'Oh, Danny!'

He opened his eyes, but he didn't seem to see me.

I left the door open, went back to the table. A background for this head dress, something against which Peter should stand, as a stag, camouflaged but not quite invisible.

I know a bank whereon the wild thyme grows. Blows?

Danny was moaning again. I put down my pencil, went to the door. The quilt was on the floor.

Should I leave him uncovered, if he was so hot?

Plenty to drink, I seemed to remember that was one of the rules. I'd bought some orange juice, I went to the kitchen and poured some into a glass.

He knocked it out of my hand, it spilled on to my jeans and on to the carpet.

'Oh, Danny! Damn. Damn, damn, damn.'

He was crying again.

'Want Su-Su. *Please*. Want Su-Su.'

'Darling Danny.'

I tried to cuddle him, but he pushed me away, fell back on to the pillow, and his head was rolling from side to side again.

'Ten green botters, hangin' on a wall,' he sang.

'Oh, God. Danny.'

It was an hour since I'd called the doctor, where was he?

I dialled the number again. The same woman answered, annoyed at being disturbed again. She would tell Dr Small when he came in. He would decide whether a visit was necessary.

'If he doesn't think it's necessary, we'll be finding out whether the courts are of the same opinion,' I threatened. 'I mean that.'

Oxlips, and the nodding violet. And brambles?

Leave the damned bank, he wasn't sitting on the thing, I didn't need it. Just brambles.

Standing against them, his head thrown back like a stag. They'd have to be high, then, those brambles. There'd be a bank, there'd have to be. It could be useful. One of the banks for the lovers, they kept falling asleep, the enchanted sleep. Right, so they fall asleep against this bank, and high on the bank there are brambles, but Oberon is standing in front of them. They don't see him. Are they between him and the brambles? Or does he stand above them, looking down?

I threw my head back, held it back, tried to imagine holding it like that, with the head dress.

No. Not possible, no matter how strong he was. Less than a minute, and it really hurt, even without a head dress. So, looking down at them. Head forward, and those antlers, like brambles, high over the bank. There'd have to be a tree, he'd be standing against the tree. Yes, and turn the prongs inwards. Colour them golden, like a crown. He's a king.

'An' if one green botter should . . .'

Silence. Suddenly, silence.

457

Oh, Christ. Danny.

I ran into the bedroom, threw myself on my knees beside the bed, reaching out for his face.

'. . . sassidently fall, there'd . . .'

His skin was so hot, so dry. I'd better put some cream on it. What had I got? It would crack if I didn't do something. Danny, what can I do for you?

The doorbell rang. The doctor.

He was middle-aged, terse.

'I don't know anything about children,' I said as I led him into the bedroom. 'I don't know whether this could have waited until morning.'

'Where small children are concerned, you don't wait.'

A stethoscope, a thermometer, and Danny moaning and crying.

'How ill is he?' I demanded. 'Should he be in hospital?'

'Not yet. Hold him up, I want to look at his throat.'

Tonsillitis, he said.

'Is that serious?'

He shrugged.

'He's not in danger. He should stay in bed for a week or so. I'll call in again in the morning.' He glanced at his watch. 'Later in the morning.'

He was writing something on a prescription pad.

'Penicillin. Is he allergic?'

I doubted if Su-Su had ever given him penicillin.

'I don't know.'

A brief glance, not very friendly.

'No children of your own?'

I shook my head.

'How do I get hold of a private nurse?' I asked.

'You don't. He won't want strangers.'

'I have to go to work tomorrow.'

He was standing up, pulling on his gloves.

'You'll have to take some time off work. You can't leave a sick child with strangers.'

I followed him out of the room.

'Mine isn't the sort of work from which I can take time off.'

'Nobody's indispensable, Miss Mayall. Good night to you. I'll call after surgery, see how he's getting on.'

'I won't be here,' I muttered to myself as I closed the door behind him.

Four o'clock in the morning.

Danny was awake again, and crying. I went in to him, picked him up, cuddled him.

'Darling Danny. Poor old boy. Tonsillitis, rotten thing to have. Poor old Danny.'

I'd take him with me to Stratford, hire a big car, so he could lie across the back seat and sleep. A sports car, particularly my little TVR, wasn't meant for sleeping. I'd get that really efficient secretary at the theatre, what was her name? Glenda? Glynnis? A nursing agency, she could find a nurse who could travel with us. Two nurses, if necessary. They could work in shifts.

'Danny?'

'Hmm?'

He was suddenly alert, wide awake and looking at me.

'You are going to cost me a lot of money, young man. Do you want a drink?'

'Pounds and pounds?'

'Yes. Do you want a drink?'

But then he was crying again, and pushing me away.

'Want *Su-Su. Please*. Want Su-Su.'

I had some aspirin in the kitchen, I crushed a quarter of a tablet in water, and took it in to him, but he was asleep again. I sat on the edge of the bed, watching him.

'Pounds and pounds, Danny,' I said. 'I've bought a house, because of you. God, are children always this expensive?'

'Ten green botters . . .'

I sighed.

'Oh, what the hell, sweetheart. It's only money.'

Two days since I'd slept. I wasn't fit to drive. Think about that, carefully, and slowly. Danny in the car, trustfully asleep, on the back seat, with me at the wheel. I really wasn't fit to drive.

A chauffeur-driven car, to Stratford. And back again.

Pounds and pounds, Danny.

29

Danny and I both slept in the car on the way to Stratford. I got the chauffeur to stop at an all-night chemist so I could buy the medicines, and Danny swallowed them obediently, put his arms around my neck, and went back to sleep again. He seemed a little better.

'Always worse in the early hours,' said the chauffeur, who was a grandfather, and comfortably reassuring about Danny.

'He'll be all right. This car's probably warmer than your flat, and it's air-conditioned.'

I'd finished a few sketches. I hoped Solomon wouldn't think they were too bad.

Glenda, the efficient secretary, merely nodded when I asked her to find a temporary nanny for Danny, two if necessary. I felt she would have reacted in the same way if I'd asked her to find me an astronaut. Perhaps they were used to unusual requests, here.

Anna Watson arrived an hour later, with a suitcase, and a bundle of bedding. One nanny would be quite adequate, she assured me. Yes, she had experience of nursing sick children.

She hardly looked old enough to be out of school.

Half an hour later Danny was in a children's bed borrowed from the props room, in clean pyjamas, between clean linen sheets, under a fluffy blue blanket with a rabbit embroidered on the corner. He'd had his second dose of medicine, and a mug of warm milk, and he was sleepily listening to a story about kittens. He looked beautiful.

Whatever she, and the chauffeur-driven car, were going to cost, it had to be worth it.

'How do working mothers manage?' I asked.

'Most of them don't.' Sonia sounded terse, and a moment later she left. Julie watched her.

'Oh, dear.'

'Did I say something wrong?'

'Her nephew died last year. He had meningitis. The doctor said it was flu, so his mother left him with a neighbour. The coroner was foul. He said she'd been irresponsible.'

She looked down at her script, looked up again, closed her eyes, and mouthed a few words.

'Mothers are supposed to be madonnas. They're irresponsible if they work, and lazy scroungers if they don't. Are you busy?'

'Not for the next three seconds, anyway.'

'Could you hear me on this scene?'

Portia, and Helena. Dear Julie.

Danny was asleep when I looked in my office. Anna smiled at me, raised a finger to her lips.

I told Solomon I wanted to draw Peter, I needed to make sketches of him. Photographs would not do.

I wasn't sure whether they would have done, or not. I wanted to look at him, I wanted to listen to him, I wanted to draw him.

I wanted him to like me.

He seemed to like me, he smiled at me, he sat as I asked him, and he talked. He told me about the play I'd never seen at the Royal. He'd had to fall down a flight of stairs, that was why he'd usually been limping, or nursing bruises, when I'd seen him. His last appearance as a real stunt man, it had come a bit too close to real injury, that one. Bruises were one thing, broken necks quite another.

'Could you look at me, sort of menacingly?' I asked.

Lowered head, level brows, narrowed eyes, but then a smile that turned into a laugh.

'No, Glory, I don't think I could look at you menacingly.'

Two hours, I could have spent all day drawing him, but then Solomon needed us both back on stage.

An hour, pacing around, drawing chalk marks, measuring. Sonia, standing against a tree, stretched up against the trunk, her arms high.

'No, not for that scene, it's too long. I really can't.'

'Put your arms down, then. Just lean against it. Bend one knee. Turn your head this way.'

'So?'

'Yes. What about that, Glory?'

All the possible angles, Sonia blending into a tree, yes, it would do. We could do that.

'Yes,' I said.

The lunch break, he was sitting beside me, a faint smell of sweat, he'd been standing under the hot lights. He asked if he could have one of the sketches when I'd finished with them. Would I sign it, please?

'Yes, of course.'

He'd smile at Titania like that, in their last scene.

'Shall we go for a walk when we've finished here? Perhaps we could have something to eat. I know a café down by the river.'

'I must take Danny home.'

Damn. Not even my child.

'His mother's in hospital, they'll want to see each other.'

He nodded. Please ask again. Ask for tomorrow, or the next day?

463

Not the sort of man to ask straight away. It might have been an excuse.

I sketched Sonia that afternoon, I wanted her to talk to me. Yes, dear Sonia, I will try for the glamour, if Solomon will let me. Your own sort of glamour, like a leopard. Touch if you dare, but it might be worth it.

'Danny's a lovely child,' she said. 'He looks a little like you, no relation? Not even distant?'

'Not so far as I know.'

She has beautiful eyes, almost black, and a long, smiling mouth. Well cast as Titania, but this could be the last time she can play a part like that. Unless I can do something.

'I think you've gone all broody over him,' she said. 'It's a disgusting sight.'

'Huh.'

'Maternal instincts jumping around? Hormones acting up?'

I pointed a pencil at her.

'I'm trying to draw your mouth.'

Was that the answer? Was that why I, who don't like children, felt as I did about Danny, that I must protect him from anything that might hurt him? That he was perfect, and beautiful, and precious?

And was that why the memory of Peter's skin shivering under my fingers made me feel weak? Made me feel as though something inside me was melting?

The chauffeur said he'd had a lovely day in Stratford, thank you, madam, nicest day out for a long time. How was the little lad?

Danny smiled at him. Anna was carrying him, and a stage hand followed her with her suitcase and the bundle of bedding. Danny's face was still a little flushed, but Anna had smoothed baby oil into his skin, and the dry look had gone.

'Are you feeling better, Danny?' I asked, and he ducked his head, buried his face against Anna's coat.

Stupid, to feel jealous. Why shouldn't he like her more than he likes me? He's not my child.

Stupid, to resent it, when she'd done so well for him.

I sent them both to the hospital in the car to visit Su-Su. While they were gone I telephoned John Flanders to ask about the house. He was worried.

'The plumbers have left a lot of gear there. New bath, all that, and it's worth money. The thing is, the windows haven't been mended. Anybody could get in. With that new door, it looks as if it might be worth a try, obvious there's work going on in there. There might be tools, thieves look for that sort of thing.'

'There's nothing I can do about it. We'll just have to hope.'

'Yes. A couple of the frames are rotten. Sorry about that, I didn't notice. I told you the woodwork was sound. Tell you what, I'll get one of the lads to put plywood in the windows tomorrow. Have to charge you for the wood.'

'That's kind of you, John.'

'Roof's been done. How's Danny's mother?'

'Getting better, but he's been ill, he's had tonsillitis. He'll want to know about Naomi.'

'Oh, her. She's all right. Sorry about the little lad, give him my best.'

There was a letter from Ann, and she was in trouble. The religious order who had bought the manor had been harassing her all through the winter, they'd been unfriendly almost to the point of menacing her. They'd tried to buy the forge, but she'd refused, they'd offered her a lot of money to give up the right to ride over their land.

'I don't want their money,' she'd written to me. 'What can I do with money? I've got what I want, I've got the forge, I've got my animals, and I've got somewhere to ride.'

Now, they'd killed a horse. They'd thought it was hers, but it was a racehorse, it had been left with her because she'd found it was lame when she was changing its shoes.

'Christ!' I exclaimed aloud. I'd thought she'd been exaggerating about the Children of God. Why on earth would they be so hostile to Ann, just because she had the right to ride on their land? She wouldn't do any harm.

But they'd killed a horse, thinking it was hers.

'Now they've welded a security lock to my gate,' she wrote, 'and they've planted blackthorn against it. It might be Lyric they kill next time. I feel miserable about that horse. He was so friendly.'

I telephoned her, but I only got her answering machine. I'd told her to buy it, and she'd said she'd never regretted it.

'I may have some work for you,' I said. 'A head dress, quite special. To appear on the stage at Stratford. Fame at last, big sister, so put up a brass plaque.'

I scribbled a quick note to Uncle John, asking for information. I was worried about this.

Danny and Anna came back. Danny looked happier, but Anna was concerned. She needed to talk to me, when Danny had had his supper and his bath, and was safely asleep.

She'd seen the doctor, and he'd told her there was talk of taking Danny into care. Su-Su was not considered a fit mother, their housing wasn't adequate, her experiments with herbs might endanger a child. There was to be a case conference.

'Oh, God,' I said. 'What should I do?'

'Have you got a solicitor?'

'In London.'

I tore open my note, and wrote another one, more carefully. I addressed it to Uncle John's flat, and I wrote 'Urgent' on the envelope.

Anna said she and Danny should stay in the flat the next day. Danny should be seen by a doctor.

'Don't let anybody else in.'

She smiled, and shook her head.

'Hiring me was quite a good idea,' she said. 'So far as this social services business is concerned.'

466

God. I hadn't anticipated this. Danny. Over my dead body, you bastards.

I scribbled on the back of the envelope to Uncle John. 'I need the Knight in Shining Armour act.' He'd once said I was only ever flippant when I was really worried. I hoped he'd take the hint.

I slept on the sofa. Anna assured me the bed was quite wide enough for both her and Danny, she'd be perfectly all right. She got up a few times during the night, when Danny was thirsty, and hot and fretful. I woke up, too.

'It's always worst, at this time,' she said as she warmed him some milk. 'Don't worry. He's getting better.'

I forgot to cancel the car, and it arrived early the next morning.

'Damn,' I said to the grandfather chauffeur, who inclined his head politely. 'Come and see Danny, anyway.'

He'd brought him a jigsaw puzzle.

It was a fine day, I drove to Stratford with the car open, hoping the wind in my face would blow some of the worries out of my head. I was frantic with anxiety over Danny and the threat from the social services, and these Children of God sounded nasty, too. My big sister. Be careful, Ann.

'I won't let anybody except the doctor in,' Anna had promised before I left, but suppose they turned up with a warrant? What could she do?

Costumes for Moth, and Mustardseed, Cobweb and Peaseblossom, and the anonymous 'fairies'. All male, all to vanish against the background when necessary, so I'd have to discuss that background with Heide Carter. It was about time I bought her a packet of coffee, I'd drunk enough of it.

And Puck, Terence Bourne, saying he wished he could wear his Shylock costume for this one, it hid the paunch.

'Do you have to vanish, or can you be the exception?'

'Act three, scene one. Act three, scene two, and that one's a sod, it goes on for hours. You and your bright ideas.'

'All right. Sorry.'

'I want the body paint treatment, like Peter. Your own fair hands, please, Glory. After all, it was my greasepaint, I think I've earned that.'

It still made me blush, remembering that.

Terence laughed.

'It was creepy,' he said. 'Were you in a trance? It looked like it. I must remember that, I'll use it, one day. So focused, and yet so impersonal.'

Impersonal?

I met him in the corridor outside the props room.

'What about that walk?' I asked.

'This evening?'

'No, now. Isn't it your lunch break? There's rain forecast later.'

He looked a little surprised, but he glanced at his watch.

'Lunch breaks and Solomon Crawley don't always match,' he said. 'Right, why not? Let the sod suffer. Meet you at the stage door in five minutes?'

A pale blue sky, just the suggestion that spring might be coming, and the river brown and shimmering in the sunlight. His arm around my shoulders, mine around his waist, I'd never walked with a man like this before. I was very conscious of the way his hip bone moved against my hand, his ribcage as he breathed. He was warm, I was close against him, and he was warm.

What was he feeling, being close to me?

His lips brushed against my hair.

Good. That's good.

'Are you going to do the make-up?' he asked.

'Hmm?'

'The body make-up. I can't reach my own back.'

'Ah.'

'I hope you'll do it. It was one of the most exciting . . .'

'Peter?'

'Yes?'

468

I stopped, and faced him, my hands on his waist, looking up at him.

'Who took your shirt off?'

The lovely smile that was almost a laugh.

'That was a joint effort.'

Sunshine on the Avon, silver and brown. And the swans on the famous old river. This is something like eternity, his arm around my shoulders as we walked back. I won't have to ask him again, what about that walk? The minutes we can have together we will take. We don't have to ask.

'I'll paint your body,' I said, and we were walking slowly, but he was breathing as if he'd been running.

30

Not yet spring, but it seemed to me that the sun was shining almost every day, and my life was running more smoothly than ever before.

Oiled wheels, Robert Cameron said, tip me off next time.

I'd sold two blocks of shares to buy the cottage, and both companies had crashed within a month. It was no joke, but if I'd been superstitious I'd have crossed my fingers.

Uncle John had left a telephone message with Anna.

'I've locked horns with the social services,' he'd said. 'Phone me about Ann.'

I'd done so that night.

'These Children of God, whatever they are, I think Ann's in trouble here. I've told her to hire a private detective.'

'What could he do?' I asked.

'She, actually. She'll do rather more than the police, anyway. Well, they're stretched, I suppose. The thing is, Gloriana, I don't believe Ann can afford more than one, and if this is as bad as I fear it may be it needs at least three. I'll pay for one, what about you paying for the other?'

'Yes. Yes, of course. Will she agree?'

'We won't tell her. So far as Ann's concerned, Mrs Hunter's doing the lot.'

'Sorry,' I said. 'Stupid of me. Of course, that's the way to do it. Uncle John, do you think she's in danger?'

He did. Uncle John's one of the most undramatic people I know, but he was very worried this time. They'd killed a horse. This was an incredibly violent reaction, an extraordinary act of aggression.

'Leadbetter and Chase,' he said. 'They're very good, not very cheap, I'm afraid. Nicholas Leadbetter and Cynthia Hargrave, and their Mrs Hunter, who's the cheapest of the three. Once we know what they're up to, I'll know what to do about it.'

He sounded determined, and rather angry.

'Right, Glory, I'll tell them to go ahead, then. I'll send you the address. They'll need a five-hundred-pound retainer.'

'I'll post them a cheque,' I said. And then, because he was watching me from the doorway, 'What about Danny?'

'What they got from me has shaken them a bit. It should hold things for a few weeks. Mother and child are moving, aren't they? Don't give the social services a forwarding address, my dear. They won't get one out of me, I promise you.'

Three weeks later I was living with Su-Su and Danny. I hadn't had time to find anywhere else, and somebody had to help Su-Su until she was well again. Danny had wrecked most of my furniture, but I didn't mind. The only piece I cared about was my desk, and that was in my office in Birmingham.

'Are you going to pay me rent?' asked Su-Su.

'Are you going to pay me?' I retaliated, and she smiled.

'I don't think so,' she said. 'We like squatting.'

I wasn't sure if she was joking.

But I had to find a place of my own.

'Come and live with me,' said Peter, and I'd been

embarrassed, and flustered, shaken my head, and wouldn't look him in the face. I hadn't even thought about how I'd respond when he'd ask me, as he would.

I'd just dreamed of what it might be like, with Peter.

We'd been at a rugger match that time. Peter loved sports, cricket in summer, rugger in winter, he played for village teams. He'd been abroad, there were only the rehearsals for *A Midsummer Night's Dream*, and a few small parts in television plays.

It wouldn't always be like this, he said. Well, he hoped it wouldn't always be like this.

I'd stood at the side of the field and shivered. Wellington boots, I'd had to buy them specially, and Peter's duffel coat, I would not wear an anorak or anything like one. Nor would I buy my own duffel coat, no, not even for you.

By the end of the match he'd been plastered in mud, limping, and there was a cut on his knee that would not stop bleeding. But he'd been laughing. They'd won, and he'd been largely responsible.

'You look revolting,' I'd said, my teeth chattering. 'And I'm perished.'

Remorse, a quick shower, and he'd take me somewhere warm. Where there was tea, and hot buttered crumpets, and a huge fire in an inglenook fireplace.

He'd asked about my plans for spare time in the next week, and I'd said flat-hunting.

'Come and live with me?' His face was serious, he was looking me straight in the eyes, and I'd shaken my head, flushing.

The first evening we'd been out together, in a boat on our lovely river, he'd asked me to go to bed with him and I'd said no. He hadn't minded. He'd smiled, and kissed me.

He'd thought I'd rather wait.

And then later, two weeks later, when he'd asked again. 'Is it a religious thing?' he'd asked. He'd been puzzled.

'No.'

472

But I'd been trembling that time, and he'd understood. He hadn't said anything, but when I'd glanced up he'd been mouthing the word.

Wow.

We went for a run, and I was feeling wicked. He'd thought he was going to show off, but I'd seen him run, I knew I was faster than him.

His reaction was a mixture of delight and chagrin.

I stopped and waited for him, and when he reached me he bent over, gasping for breath, his hands on his knees, and some of the gasping had been laughter.

We walked back together, and Peter said that in his opinion virginity was something everybody should get shot of as soon as possible.

Am I a virgin? There's something I have to remember. There is something.

Two men, laughing. I'd been screaming.

'Glory?'

Shivering, close to tears.

'Hold me.'

'What is it?'

There was no point in saying, nothing, it's all right. There was something, and he knew it.

I couldn't speak, I thought I'd choke. He held me, I leaned my face against him, tried to breathe.

'Can't remember,' I said, but he shook his head, I could feel that. He didn't believe me.

'Can't remember, not clearly.' Try, try to tell him. Tell him something.

He is warm, his arms around me, but this is nothing. I am cold. He could be stone, this is nothing.

Rain in the afternoon, it's not spring yet, and two nights later there was a frost.

Don't touch me, Peter. It was nothing, just Danny, just broody over a beautiful child. Hormones playing games, like Sonia said. Don't touch me.

'Whatever I did, I'm sorry,' he said.

'There wasn't anything.'

Nothing now. Just a blankness where there had been something solid, and warm, and exciting. Just pain in his eyes, where there had been a smile.

Nothing now, when I watched the rehearsals and saw him, nothing where there had been weakness, and a feeling like melting, the soft drowsiness that might have been love.

Oberon. He must be brown, and gold, and green. I'd drawn the sketches, I'd coloured them, he could disappear against those brambles and the tree, he could stand so still now. He had to stand still against the tree, to hold that position so you could forget he was there.

'I want to see that,' said Solomon. 'I want to try that now. With the costume, and the paints.'

I'll paint your body, I'd said, and Peter was there, with the box of Aquatints.

'Do it,' he said, he was looking at me, he was sad, but it was a challenge. I'd said I'd paint his body.

He waited, watching me, standing still for a long time, and then he sighed, turned away and sat on the stool in front of the mirror. He took the green paint, drew it along the line of his cheekbone, down his jaw, smoothed it, and faded it out. Then the brown, into the shadows, in the hollows.

'No,' I said. 'Not like that.'

He turned away from the mirror, turned his face up towards me, and I wiped the brown lines away. The curved shadows under the bones of his cheeks, this was Oberon, and the gold in the eyebrows, the long eyes.

The brown and the gold on the muscles of his neck. The hollows under the bones.

'I think I was raped,' I said.

He kept very still as I drew the green shadows over his shoulders, I was standing behind him, grey in the spine, grey shadows on the brown, and then green again. I was behind him, he was looking in the mirror, looking at my face in the mirror.

'It was when I was a child. I can't remember clearly.'

Brown, on these long muscles beside the spine, this is the trunk of a tree. Brown, and grey, and gold.

'There were two men.'

I was standing in front of him again, drawing the gold and the brown on his ribs, the green shadows, this is Oberon, this is a king. Look up, Oberon. Brush the gold into his hair. You are a king.

His jaw was clenched, there was pain and anger, narrowed eyes.

Gold, in the hairs on his chest, gold down his belly, the muscles hard and taut, no shiver this time, no tremble under my fingers. Hard, cold muscle.

He is disgusted, I thought. He is disgusted.

Hot tears on the back of my hand as I drew it away from the hard muscles, I turned my back on him.

He is disgusted.

He was behind me, I heard him stand as I walked away, two long strides and he'd caught me, his arms around me, holding me back against him, trying to turn me to face him, but I couldn't, and I fought him, to free myself.

He let go, immediately, he let go, but he was still there as I turned, I hung my head and I backed away.

'Darling. Darling Glory.'

Somebody knocked on the door, I couldn't get out, there was somebody there. I went away from the door, I went to the window, and I heard the door opening, and Peter's voice.

'Yes? Oh, right.'

And then the door closing.

'Solomon wants us on stage,' he said.

I nodded.

He hesitated.

475

'Glory, there's make-up all over the back of your jersey, it wasn't dry. I'm sorry.'

'Oh. Oh, damn.'

My eyes were red and swollen, and now I had to go on stage, with Peter, to look at this camouflage effect, and there was make-up all over my jersey. I couldn't even get to my own office.

'I can lend you a T-shirt. Very fashionable, baggy T-shirts.'

'Oh. Yes. Thank you. Thank you, if you would, I'd . . .'

A drawer opening, he was behind me again.

'You'd better wash your face. Your mascara's run a bit.'

I went to the basin, washed my face, stripped off my jersey. Peter wasn't watching, he'd very carefully turned his back. A white T-shirt hung over the chair. It was new. It smelled of fresh cotton, it didn't smell of Peter.

'I love you,' he said.

This does not mean me. He is disgusted with me. His eyes were angry, and there was pain in his face, his body was hard, and cold. This does not mean me.

'I love you.'

'Solomon's waiting.'

'Will you come back? Glory, will you come back to me?'

I didn't understand what he meant.

He came to my office later that afternoon, he brought my jersey. There was a knock on the door, when I opened it he was standing there, looking down at me, he looked very tense, very anxious.

'May I come in?'

Julie was there. Heide had wanted to change her costume, and I was trying different fabrics against the mock-up of the forest scene, pinning them roughly into shape and hearing her lines for a part in a television play as I did so. I hadn't been concentrating, and she'd been growing impatient with me.

I couldn't look at Peter, I just stood aside, and he walked

476

into the room, and then Julie was leaving.

'Don't you just *love* them when they go all masterful?' she said, but he didn't laugh.

'Sorry,' she said, and the door closed.

'I want to talk to you,' he said. 'I must talk to you. Anywhere you like. Glory, please. Please, let's talk.'

'Oh. I don't know. I . . . I don't think I . . .'

'A coffee bar? A pub? Anywhere anonymous, safe. Public. Quiet.'

I didn't want to look at him, I didn't want to see the disgust and anger on his face.

'I want to be with you. Talk to you, listen to you.'

I was staring out of the window at the rainy sky.

'Anywhere. Anywhere you like. Please. Here? People keep coming in, but here, if you like. Where, Glory? Just somewhere. Say, please. Somewhere. Here?'

Turn my head just a little, and I can see him, but he won't know.

His face, misery on his face. He's looking at me.

'Glory. I can't *bear* the thought of anything hurting you.'

His voice, unsteady. Are those tears? Why am I so cold? I'm shivering.

He'd stopped talking, he was standing by the table, watching me, waiting. Then slowly he looked down, his hands and his arms were slack, hanging at his sides. He was defeated, it seemed as if he was defeated, he'd given up. There was nothing, now.

I'd seen this. Where had I seen this?

What was he looking at? Are there photographs here?

'I can't remember,' I said, and then, 'I'm cold.'

Had I been cold, then? I could remember screaming, I could remember laughter. Had I been cold?

He brought me my coat, held it out to me, he wasn't sure if he should help me put it on. The last time he'd touched me I'd fought free, I'd wanted to get away from him.

He was talking again, very quietly. He was quite close to

me, but he didn't try to touch me. I could smell him, the clean smell of his clothes, and the soap he used to wash off the make-up. Peter.

I listened to his voice.

'I never forgot you, the girl I saw sometimes in the corridors at the Royal. Louise said you were ill, then you'd gone back to school. I hadn't realised you were still at school. You looked older.'

He stopped, his face was sad. He wasn't speaking any more, I'd have to talk now. Could I remember? What can I say to him? I can't remember. Something happened, I have to say something to him.

'There was a bet about you,' I said. I was trying to remember, but I had to say something, he'd been talking to me. 'Terry. Five pounds that she'd . . . Oh, God!'

I pressed my hands into my cheeks, they were red again. What had I nearly said? Rambling on, just to make conversation, just to be polite to him. To Peter.

He waited, looking at me curiously.

'That she'd be wearing my jeans before the end of the run,' he said. 'Yes, I know. Those walls were like paper.'

He was frowning. What was the point of this? He was trying to understand, why was I talking about this?

'Hmm.'

What else had he heard, then, through those paper-thin walls?

'She lost,' he added. 'If that was what you were going to ask.'

'No. I was trying to remember something else.'

Donald Flint. Oh, I remember you. Slug man, filth, I remember you, Donald Flint. Dirty blood, splattered on to my shoulders, on to my dress. The book you left for me. First copy for the star.

The lie, that you'd leave other copies for everybody else. The lie that I'd been young enough to believe, and later I'd never thought to question. The lie that had driven me away

478

from the theatre, I'd run out on them, their luck had run out.

I'd been sick, and so ashamed, I'd taken the book, and run away.

If I hadn't run away, I would have known Peter then, when he was younger. More than ten years ago. Fifteen years, was it?

Too late, though. Donald Flint hadn't taken the photographs, it hadn't happened then. There'd been a camera, and lights, a camera in my face. Laughter, and screams?

'I'm trying to remember.'

It didn't matter if I talked, now. I had to be quiet, I wanted to remember. I had to remember, now.

'At the Royal?' he asked a few minutes later.

'No. The photographs were at the Royal.'

He waited again, watching me, and then, very gently,

'Tell me about the photographs, Glory.'

Remember, Glory. Remember.

'I was in the wrong body. It was the thin girl, it was . . .'

Then I was screaming, and he was holding my hands, because I was fighting him, he had to get away, she was nearly here, she was nearly here.

'*No! No! Not* here. Go *away*, *don't* be here. *Not* here, *not* with him, *not* with *Peter*!'

I was trying to fight him away, she was so dangerous, he was here, and she was so dangerous, Peter, go away, go away.

This time he didn't let go, he was holding me, it didn't matter that I'd hit him, he was holding me, holding my wrists behind my back, pinning my arms, I was close against him and he was holding me, this time he didn't let go.

'All right. All right. Tell me about the photographs.'

'Peter, she is so *dangerous*.'

'Who's dangerous, Glory?'

479

'The thin child. The thin girl. Peter, be careful, please be careful.'

'Yes, I'll be careful. Tell me about the photographs.'

Oh, I was so tired. I leaned against him, my head was heavy, resting against him. I could hear his heart beating, I could hear him breathing.

'I tore them up and threw them in the river,' I said. 'Not the Avon. Not our river.'

'No, not our river.'

'The Thames. I threw them in the Thames. Because Cézanne had made me better.'

'Cézanne?'

'And Monet. He helped. And Blake.'

'Ah. What were these photographs, Glory?'

So tired. Peter, be careful, she could come back.

'The two men. When I was in the wrong body.'

He was breathing very slowly, very deeply, I pressed my head against his chest, I could feel his ribs moving against my cheek.

'The two men who raped you?'

'Yes.'

Like a shudder, like a sigh, and his breath on my hair.

'Photographs.'

And then something I didn't hear, whispered into the air over my head. He was whispering something, I couldn't hear.

'What?' I asked.

'No, nothing, darling. Nothing. It's all right.'

He was very pale, but his eyes were dark, and wide. Not like Oberon, Oberon has long eyes.

He wasn't holding my wrists any more, his hands were on my back, he was stroking me. I reached up and touched his face.

'Oberon has long eyes,' I said.

'Yes, Glory. Oberon has long eyes.'

'I'm tired, Peter.' And then, 'Are you angry?'

'Not with you. But yes, I'm angry. I've never felt so murderously angry in my life. Truly, I could kill them. I think I would kill them, if I could find them.'

'I'm tired,' I said again, and then suddenly, 'She can kill. The thin girl, she can kill. Peter, be careful.'

'I'll drive you home,' he said. 'You can sleep on the way, I'll drive you home.'

'My home?'

'Yes. To Su-Su and Danny. Your home, not mine.'

I was thinking very slowly. It would be good to be home, with Su-Su and Danny. I wanted to be home. I was very tired now.

'I'm going to see my sister,' I said. 'Ann. I'm going to ask Ann to make your head dress.'

'Can't they make it here?'

'Oh, yes. They could make it here. But not as well as she can make it. Ann's a blacksmith, a very good blacksmith. She'll make it special. I want it to be special, Peter.'

I did sleep on the way home, I felt safe with Peter driving my car. It isn't far, between Stratford and Birmingham, not when the roads are clear, but I fell asleep, and when I woke I'd fallen against him, my head was against his arm.

'Hello,' he said.

Had I dreamed everything I'd told him? I'd warned him about the thin girl. I'd told him she could kill.

'Did I say anything?'

'No. We're nearly home now.'

But I'd told him about her. He knew, Peter knew about the thin girl.

I didn't know whether it mattered, I didn't have time to think about that, because Danny saw Peter and came running out to meet him. He wanted Peter to go to the farm with him and Su-Su, to milk Naomi and see the calf.

'I think you'll have to meet Naomi,' I said.

So the three of them went to the farm, and I fell asleep on the sofa. I was woken when they came back by squeals and

481

yells from the garden. When I went to the window to look, Peter and Danny were wrestling on the lawn, and Su-Su was ignoring them both, carrying the bucket of milk up the path.

I went to the door.

'Fighting's silly,' I said, and they answered simultaneously.

'We're not fighting, we're playing.'

'I wouldn't fight Danny anyway,' said Peter. 'He'd tear me apart.'

I drove Peter to the station. Once away from Danny, he grew very quiet again, and I didn't know what to say to him. I'd told him as much as I could remember.

'Could we go back to how we were before?' he asked when we were nearly at the station. 'Before you told me all this?'

It had been warm, and exciting, and we'd had fun together. I thought of the walk by the river, when I'd told him I'd paint his body, and the way he'd breathed, and I remembered the rugger match when I'd been so cold, watching him play. I remembered how he'd held me, I remembered the first evening we'd spent together when he'd asked me to go to bed with him, the way he'd kissed me when I'd said no.

The memories made me smile, and he saw the smile.

'I love you.'

Do I love you, Peter? Is this love?

'I'll never hurt you, Glory. I don't know what I can do about what happened to you. Is there anything I can do?'

'I don't think so.'

I was still smiling, and he answered it, a long, slow smile that seemed more in his eyes than his mouth.

'I won't give up trying to get you into my bed, that's not what I'm offering. But I want you to want me, too. Only then, Glory, I do promise you that. Only then.'

I went into the station with him, and we stood on the

482

platform waiting for the train, hugging each other. His chin was on my head; I was listening to his heart again. It was such a comforting sound, it was steady and it went on and on, repeating itself, the same rhythm, softly, against my face. I think I love you.

But I didn't say it.

31

I didn't go back to Stratford for three days. Jacob wanted to see me, and he still took priority, but now mostly because I liked him. Loved him, really; he was like a grandfather to me.

'You're glowing,' he said accusingly. 'You're in love, don't tell me, some hopeless young actor with no talent and less money.'

'Peter Clements.'

'Ah. I don't know about the money, I grant you the talent.'

Cat hairs all over my slacks. Flora on my lap this time, white hair, and a rumbling purr.

'Are you happy, my clever darling? With your fairy king?'

'I'm happy with everything, Uncle Jacob.'

He was grooming Abracadabra. She was old, now. I'd used that colour, copper on black, what was it? Electra, I think. In Cardiff. Yes, Jacob Goldman's beautiful black Persian cat, I'd said I'd use those colours, and I had.

'Stratford meeting your exacting standards? Or do we pull it all down and start again somewhere else?'

'It'll do.'

'This I am glad to hear. It cost quite a lot of money, that theatre. Word in high places is that you are dug in, and dynamite wouldn't get you out again. Are you glad about this?'

Flora, purring on my lap. Abracadabra, on his. It doesn't matter what clothes I wear in this flat, these cats go for contrast. Black, I am wearing today, and Abracadabra shuns me. Flora adores me.

'Yes, I'm glad. Uncle Jacob, what's behind these questions?'

'Smart enough to cut yourself,' he muttered. 'Never give an old man a chance of a surprise. Films, my clever darling, films is what's behind these questions, strips of cellulose with holes down the sides, you'll have heard of them, might even have seen one. This is quite an ambitious project, and the fuddy-duddies in the business are having fits. Locations, not stages, but it's still Shakespeare, and it's still the Royal Shakespeare Company. Most of the money's American, I think that's the rub. The fuddy-duddies don't like the idea of Hollywood getting its fingers on our precious RSC, they think they'll contaminate it.'

I laughed, and he leered at me.

'Your name has been mentioned. So has Solomon Crawley's, he's done a film or two before, he knows what a camera looks like. There's a whisper about a permanent contract.'

'Permanent?'

'Five years. This is as permanent as you get in this business, unless you are eighty years old with a knighthood. Then they might take a chance on something longer.'

I didn't know. A permanent contract, I'd never had one, I'd hardly been aware that they existed.

'That would mean I wouldn't be able to work for anybody else?'

'Not without permission, and I doubt if you'd have time.'

A contract, to work on films, with the Royal Shakespeare Company. Why was I hesitating? Why this confusion?

'Only Shakespeare?' I asked.

'The project is a series of what Hollywood regards as his best efforts, yes.'

But I'd done three designs since I'd started working at Stratford, two of them for Uncle Jacob's productions. I didn't know if I could only work on Shakespeare. I had to do something else as well.

'Are they offering a contract?' I asked, and he shook his brush at me.

'They are trying to get into my ribs for a lot of money for this project. It's a seven-figure sum, so if I say "contract" they'll write it in gold ink. What about it? Tell me before the end of June. In the meantime, there's a script I want you to look at. It's genius or rubbish, I can't decide.'

I nearly crashed the car on my way home, I wasn't concentrating on driving. I pulled up by the side of the road, shaking, the sound of the lorry's squealing brakes and the angry bellow of the horn still in my ears. Stupid, driving fast and not handling the little car properly. Stupid.

What was the matter with me?

Words in my head, don't put down roots. Uncle Jacob had said that to me, don't put down roots. But that had been different. He'd had roots, Jacob Goldman had had roots. They had been ripped out, torn off, left him maimed. He didn't die, even though they killed him. Shylock, and him, and those others who'd walked out of Auschwitz with him.

Don't put down roots.

I laid my head against the little wooden steering wheel and I looked for the link, those words, and my troubled mind. It was there. Let it come.

Let it drift. Wait. Wait.

I was so tired. Why was I so tired? What was the matter with me?

Ann had put down roots. She was there, at the forge, the only place she had ever felt loved, and she would not leave. Rooted there, in the memory of her beloved Uncle Henry, and they were trying to dig her out.

Ann was going to get hurt. They might not get her out, she might win, but they were trying, they were digging at her roots.

They had already hurt her. They had harassed her, spoiled her pleasure in her rides, and they had killed a horse. They'd thought it was hers.

She would have been heartbroken, if they'd killed Lyric.

All I'd done was send a cheque to a firm of private detectives. That was all I'd done for my big sister. A cheque.

I drove home, slowly, I sat on the broken sofa in the living room and tried to think.

The place was growing dirtier by the day. Su-Su wasn't interested in cleaning it, and I didn't think it was any of my business. I didn't care, anyway. My room was all right, although Danny had bounced on the bed in muddy shoes, broken the mirror, spilt something on the carpet. It didn't matter.

I'd said I'd feed the chickens, Su-Su was going to be late.

Danny hadn't minded about the chickens being killed, it was putting them on the compost heap that had upset him. Don't tell the butcher to put them on the compost heap. It's all right to kill animals, but don't waste them, don't be wasteful of their lives.

The Children of God had killed a horse, cut its throat and left it choking to death on its own blood.

Why were they harassing Ann? She was doing them no harm.

Uncle John had written to me again. He thought Ann should sell the forge and move somewhere else. They could make her life a misery, he wrote, there was no point in that. Better to accept their offer, find another forge and start again. She hadn't got enough money to fight them. If they could buy Gorsedown Manor they were very wealthy.

Ann would never sell the forge. Uncle John might not understand, but I could. Ann had loved Uncle Henry, he was the closest she would ever come to having a father,

487

and she wouldn't be happy anywhere else. She'd been loved at that forge, it was her home.

Think. Think carefully, and think slowly, but think now. Make a plan.

My big sister. I'm wealthy, too, Ann. If you want to fight them, I'm here.

Fighting isn't always stupid, Su-Su.

I went to see Nicholas Leadbetter at Leadbetter and Chase. Who actually owned Gorsedown Manor was one of the questions I wanted answered, and he smiled, and said they were already working on that. It was a company, there'd been some effort made to hide their tracks, but they were nearly there. They'd have an answer by the end of the week, he thought. Certainly by the end of next week.

And then I asked the quiet man on the other side of the desk for the name of another firm of private detectives, the least respectable he knew.

He looked at me over steepled fingers, and there was a slightly wary expression on his face.

'I've been told, by entirely unreliable sources, that the police would be happy if somebody would provide them with evidence against Alan Raven,' he said. 'My only recommmendation in this respect is the utmost caution.'

I asked him to send copies of any letters he wrote to both addresses, the theatre, and my office in Birmingham. I wanted to know what he uncovered as soon as possible, no delays while I travelled from one place to the other.

I didn't see Alan Raven, but the woman with the chestnut hair and the scarlet fingernails claimed to represent him.

'Do sit down,' she said, but I walked round her desk, pulled open the second drawer, and switched off the tape recorder. I'd designed the sets for enough third-rate modern melodramas to know the script.

She smiled.

'Let's go and have a coffee somewhere,' I said. 'You can leave the handbag here, I'm buying.'

She suggested a club, she wanted something stronger than coffee after the day she'd had. I took her to a hotel instead, and booked myself a room so that I could order her the gin she demanded.

'Something nasty against these creeps,' I said, 'so that I can persuade them to sell up and move.'

'Nuns and monks, are they? Shouldn't be difficult. Deviant sexual practices, Sunday newspapers.'

'I don't give a toss what it is, but it's got to be strong enough to shift them.'

I left her five hundred pounds in cash, and told her there'd be ten times that amount when the Children of God left Gorsedown Manor.

'I'll believe that when it's in my sticky little fingers, duckie.'

I stopped at the door and smiled at her.

'Find me something, and I'll top it up. Duckie. Every time you find me a little bit of dirt, I'll top it up. When I stop, you can. When we've got a big enough heap of shit, we'll see.'

I felt like something out of a Mickey Spillane novel as I walked back to the car, but I thought she might look, and I thought she might have the contacts to find out. There'd been a lot more than five hundred pounds in my purse, and I'd seen the quick lift of her eyebrows as she noticed. She thought I'd been looking in the other direction.

I took the drawings of Oberon's head dress down to the forge the next day. I wanted Ann to make this for me, for Peter. I wanted it to be special.

She was looking tired, and strained, but she was pleased to see me. She accused me of showing off, making an appointment through a secretary.

She looked at the drawings, and said she couldn't make it lighter than fifteen pounds. I tried to imagine what it would be like, holding that steady and still for ten minutes, fifteen pounds, on his head, braced against that weight. Could he do it?

No. Not possibly, nobody could. It would break his neck.

But I wanted to stay here and talk to Ann. I'd get the property department to make another one.

'He'll manage,' I said.

She smiled.

'Well, I hope he's a big strong lad.'

She had nothing else to tell me about the Children of God, except that they collected money for a charity. Reconcile, that was the name of the charity.

Reconcile. I'll pass that on. It might help. We'd better find out about Reconcile.

My big sister, I love you.

I think she loved me, too. I wanted to talk about the Children of God, somehow I wanted to offer my help. I didn't like deceiving her, I wanted everything to be honest between us. She turned the subject aside, not abruptly, but she said she'd rather talk about me. What about Stratford? Tell me about Stratford. Please, tell me.

So I did. I told her about *The Merchant of Venice*, and Solomon Crawley liking my set and not telling me because he thought I knew. Julie's golden dress that a fashion buyer had wanted, and the feeling of friendship in the theatre, the way they all worked so hard, for themselves and for each other, how nice they'd been to me.

And Ann smiled as she listened, and said that being the Royal Shakespeare Company's lucky black cat was a big step up from the old place where I'd started, wasn't it?

I smiled back at her, but I didn't like that. I don't like luck, I don't trust it.

I had the drawings for a fashion show to finish that evening, so I drove straight to Birmingham, and found Mike in my office, in tears.

Simmie was in hospital again, another heart attack.

'It's not as bad as the first one,' said Mike. 'Why won't he stop?'

I didn't know, I couldn't answer. Simmie had put on all

the weight he'd lost after the first attack, and another stone on top of it, he was smoking forty cigarettes a day, and drinking too much as well. He'd refused to accept a manager for Lawley's, and it had taken threats from me and Mike to stop him interfering with the management team for the Inkies design studio.

'Ruth's coming over,' said Mike. 'She wants to stay with me. Listen, there's only the double bed and the sofa, she'll find out.'

'Oh, Mike. Darling Mike. She's known for years. She doesn't mind any more.'

I sat beside him on the big leather sofa. Such a glamorous office, this, and I was hardly ever in it.

'It's all going so well,' said Mike. 'Why does he have to be like this? Listen, I'm sorry I came in here. I didn't want to be disturbed. I just wanted somewhere to go and think. I don't understand. I don't understand.'

There was a bar in the office, hidden behind the birch panelling, I had to think before I could remember which panel. I poured Mike a brandy, dropped a kiss on his head. He was beginning to go bald.

'Why won't he get a manager?' Mike sounded so desolate. 'Why can't we have a holiday? Listen, I really do want to see North Africa, he thinks I'm making it up, to get him to have a holiday, but I really do. I want to see North Africa. But with him. With Simmie.'

'We'll handcuff him and drag him on to the plane,' I said.

A wan smile in response to a feeble joke.

'Listen, can you handle things for a few days here?' he asked.

'No.'

'Glory, I can't. I've got to be with Simmie.'

'I've got to be in Stratford, and in London, and in Manchester. Remember what happened last time?'

Another wan smile.

'Sacked half the staff and antagonised the other half?'

491

At least he could manage a little joke.

'Mike, now is the time to get a manager, preferably that one from Durham University that Simmie called the smart alec brat. Kevin? Kelvin. Tom Kelvin.'

'Simmie won't agree.'

'You, me and Ruth together can outvote Simmie. Mike, this is another heart attack.'

At last he nodded.

'Right,' he said. 'Right. Another heart attack. Listen, thanks, Glory. Thank you.'

I telephoned Leadbetter and Chase and asked to speak to Nicholas Leadbetter. He called me back ten minutes later.

'They collect for a charity called Reconcile,' I said.

'Yes,' he replied. 'A five pound donation to it is on my list of expenses.'

He'd been quick, with that. He was good.

'Could you put somebody on to looking into them? While you're concentrating on the main group?'

'Yes, I'll arrange it. I must go now.'

Home, and Peter was waiting for me, smiling at me.

He and Danny had been telling each other stories about an enchanted island where a magician lived with his daughter, and some people were shipwrecked in a storm.

'Cheat,' I said, and he nodded.

He'd been in a television studio all day, playing a policeman, and he was stiff and stuffy. He wanted to go for a run.

'It'll be dark soon,' I said.

'Just a short one. Down to the village and back. Through the woods.'

It was an excuse. He wanted to talk to me.

'Please tell me about the thin girl,' he said, and when I tried to run on he caught my arm, and pulled me round to face him.

'Please, darling. Tell me about the thin girl.'

I stood in front of him, looking down at the ground at my

feet. There was leaf mould on the path. He was wearing running shoes, they were black and white, there were studs in them. His hands were on my arms, mine hanging at my sides.

'I want to run,' I said.

'Tell me about her, Glory.'

'Peter, I'm so tired.'

'No.' He put his hand under my chin, raised my face until he could look at it. 'No, you're not tired. Tell me.'

I tried to lean against him, to lean my face against his chest so I could listen to his heart beating, but he pushed me away.

'Tell me.'

'No,' I said. 'No. I won't.'

'Why must I be careful? Why is she so dangerous?'

'Oh, Peter, yes. Be careful.'

'Why, darling? Why?'

I shivered.

'I'm tired,' I said. 'I'm cold.'

'Have my jacket. Here, come on. Glory. Tell me about her.'

'No. I can't. I don't know.'

'Tell me something.'

His jacket, around my shoulders. It smelt of Peter. It was warm, from him. I liked it.

'Tell me something.'

'She hasn't got a *face*.'

I tried to turn away from him, I wanted to run again, but he wouldn't let me go.

'Why hasn't she got a face, darling?'

'I'm tired.'

'No, you're not tired, Glory. You're not tired. Why hasn't the thin girl got a face?'

'Because she uses *my face*! Let me *go*, Peter, let me *go*. I'm *tired*.'

I struck at him, I wanted to hit him, but he threw up his arm.

493

'Be *careful*!' I screamed, and then I wrenched my arm away from him, I jumped back, and I ran down the path, I ran away from him.

Be careful, Peter. Be careful.

He was at the cottage when I got back, waiting by his car. He'd run back through the woods, knowing he couldn't catch me, knowing I'd have to come by the road.

I slowed up when I saw him, dropped down to a jog, and then a walk. He must be cold, standing there.

He was watching me, and he didn't smile, even when I did.

'Hello,' I said. 'I thought you'd have gone. Oh, I suppose you need your jacket. Thank you for lending it to me. Would you like a coffee?'

He shook his head.

'I want to talk.'

'Come in, then.'

'No. We can't talk in there.'

'It's too cold to stay . . .'

'In my car, then.'

I tried to push past him, but he stopped me, his hands on my shoulders.

'I want to have a shower,' I said. 'I've been running, I don't want to get chilled.'

'You haven't been running that far.'

'I'm all sweaty. Peter, let me go.'

Then he was hugging me, I leaned against him so I could hear his heart, such a good sound. So steady, I could listen to that steady sound, not think, just listen.

'Darling. Please, talk to me.'

'Oh, Peter. I don't want to talk any more. I'm tired, I've had a very hard day.'

'Me too. I just thought I'd see you at the end of it, then it became bearable. Why does the thin girl use your face, Glory?'

I struggled out of his arms, pushing him away.

494

'God, you're becoming a *bore*,' I said. 'I'm tired, I'm cold, and I'm sweaty. I'm going to have a shower. Just *drop* it, Peter. *Drop* this *bloody boring* subject. I *don't* want to *talk* about her.'

I left him standing at the gate, I ran into the cottage and slammed the door. My throat and chest felt tight, I didn't seem to be able to breathe properly.

The bathroom was filthy, water from Danny's bath slopped over the tiles, a ring of soap scum on the porcelain. The shower curtain had been torn, it was hanging free from two of the rings.

I had to find a place of my own. Soon. As soon as I could.

I had a shower, and then telephoned the hospital.

Simmie was comfortable, they said. I left a message for him, I'd come and see him as soon as I could. There wasn't anything else I wanted to say. I was furious with him.

Danny had been in my room again. There was a smear of paint on the pillow and the quilt was crumpled. He loved using my bed as a trampoline. He'd been reading my books, too. Three of them were lying on the floor, one of them was still open. It was a book of drawings by Aubrey Beardsley, posters and Victorian erotica, some of it almost pornographic. Perhaps I shouldn't keep these books here, I thought. Perhaps I should make sure there's nothing here a child shouldn't see.

Perhaps Su-Su ought to keep Danny out of my room.

Find a place of your own.

There was a letter from Leadbetter and Chase on my desk at the theatre the next morning.

Gorsedown Manor is owned by a private limited company by the name of Stephenson Holdings, which has four registered shareholders, Jonathon Stephenson, Angela Stephenson, Samantha Grafton and Anthony Clinton-Smith. The house is a private residence. There has been no application for a change of use. Samantha Grafton has a criminal record for shoplifting and dishonest handling,

Angela Stephenson is an American citizen who holds joint nationalities, British and American, since her marriage to Jonathon Stephenson in 1968.

Mr Nicholas Leadbetter is continuing his inquiries on my behalf, and will forward any further findings in the near future.

In accordance with my instructions, inquiries are being made about a charity known as Reconcile. Any information on the subject will be forwarded.

In the meantime, they remain, most sincerely, Leadbetter and Chase, Ltd.

Nothing from Alan Raven or his red-haired assistant, but her commission might be more difficult to fulfil.

The morning was spent on the Palace of Theseus scenes, mostly on lighting, with Donald in make-up and costume as Theseus. The shadows were difficult. Solomon had said he didn't want any bloody columns, and I'd said I reserved my Doric columns for soap advertisements on television, I wasn't wasting them on the Royal Shakespeare Company.

I'd said it over Spanish red wine, late one evening in his office. With the rest of the company we were usually serious, and highly professional.

Peter was sitting on the bonnet of my car when I left late that evening.

'I didn't think you were here today,' I said.

'I wasn't. I want to buy you dinner. I want to dance with you. We've never danced. Can you dance?'

It was growing dark, I could hardly see his face.

'Dance? Oh, yes,' I said. 'I can dance even better than I can run.'

'I still want to talk to you.'

'Plato's theory of idealism?' I suggested. 'Is delegated legislation anti-democratic? Answer in three words or less?'

'Don't be flippant, Glory. You're too important. I don't want to swap clever cracks with you.'

'What *do* you want with me?'

He was standing in front of me, silhouetted against the car park lights.

'Everything I can get,' he said. 'Everything you'll give me. What do you want with *me*?'

I looked back towards the theatre, I shrugged.

'Cross-country runs? Rugger boots and a duffel coat?'

'Body and soul,' he said, and his voice wasn't quite steady. 'Body and soul. Yours, Glory.'

'Uncle Jacob said you'd got talent. He was right.'

'*Christ*. Stop this. Please, stop this. Do anything else you like, but don't do this.'

I was close to him. I could hear him breathing, I was very close. He was warm.

'I'm tired,' I said.

I leaned against him, leaned my face against his chest, I wanted to hear his heart beating. He put his arms around me. I listened.

'Will you tell me about the photographs at the Royal?' he asked.

'Hush,' I answered. 'I'm listening. I'm listening to your heart.'

He sighed. His lips were on my hair, I could feel his breath, warm against my head.

'What's it saying?' he asked.

'Thud-thud. Thud-thud. Thud-thud.'

'Glory. Darling. My lovely, lovely Glory. Please, stop listening to my heart, and tell me about the photographs at the Royal.'

'I'm so tired, Peter.'

'Did you take them there?'

'No. Silly. Of course not.'

'Who, then?'

'Slug man. Filth. Filth, Flint. I hate you, slug man. Filthy slug man, I hate you. Cindy, little Cindy. Peter, I am very tired.'

497

'Who's the slug man?'

'Donald Flint. Stop, Peter. Please, stop.'

'In a minute, darling. Donald Flint?'

Peter was wearing a leather belt. I hooked my thumbs into it, leaned against him, listened to him breathing, listened to his heart. He kissed my hair again, and then his head moved.

'A stage hand? Flint, wasn't he a stage hand? Glory?'

'Hmm. Let me listen to your heart.'

He stood quietly, just his breath in my hair, letting me listen. Then he kissed me again.

'Who was Cindy?'

'Stupid. Stupid slug man. Filth, I hate you, slug man. Sssindy, little Sssindy. Little Cindy learns how. And how!'

Quietly, standing, holding me, letting me listen to his heart. And then he sighed, and his arms were hard around me, his heart was beating faster, he wasn't breathing smoothly now, hard and shallow breathing.

'Oh, Christ. Captions. Captions to the photographs?'

'Hmm. Peter, please. I am so tired. I am so very tired.'

'Yes. All right, darling. Rest a moment.'

Rest here. Rest, leaning against him, he's warm, he's warm. Rest, with my thumbs hooked into his belt, his arms holding me against him. Peter, let me rest here. I'm very tired. Truly, Peter, I'm very tired now.

'You threw them away, my sweet,' he said. 'You tore them up and threw them away, into the Thames. You destroyed them, my darling.'

'Hmm.'

'Flint had the photographs?'

'I can teach you things those two never dreamed of. Sssindy, little Ssssindy. Filth. Slug. I hate you, slug man. Filthy slug man, I hate you. Don't, Peter. Please, don't.'

'Don't what, darling?'

'Don't be like that, don't . . .'

'Like Flint? No, never. No.'

'No. I know that. No. Just, I want to be here, like this. I want to listen to your heart. Not, when you go cold. You don't breathe properly. Please, just breathe properly. I want to listen.'

'Sorry, darling. Sorry. I'll try to breathe properly. I'll try.'

Deep, slow breaths, his ribs under my cheek, moving slowly, deep and slow breaths. But his heart, too fast. Too fast.

But then he stopped breathing, and he moved, suddenly, quickly.

'Glory?'

'Oh, Peter. I'm tired.'

'Glory, was the thin girl in the photographs?'

Slug man, I hate you, I hate you. Let me *go*. Let go of me, let me go.

'Glory.'

'Let me *go*. Let me *go*.'

'It's me, darling. It's me. No, don't fight me, it's me, Glory. It's Peter. Don't fight me. Was the thin girl in the photographs?'

'Let go. Let me *go*.'

'Was she there?'

'Yes! *Yes!* Let me go.'

'Yes, yes, my love. Yes, darling. In a minute, just a little minute, I'll let you go. Darling Glory, just a minute. Don't fight me, my love. Keep still, Glory. Keep still, stand still. Stand there. Listen, listen. Like before. Just listen. Listen to my heart. Listen to me breathing, like before. Just listen. Darling, listen.'

'Peter.'

'Yes, it's me. It's Peter. Just listen.'

'Peter. Peter, I truly am very, very tired now. Please, Peter, I am. Tired.'

'Yes. I know. We'll just stay here. Just stand here. You tore up the photographs, darling. They're gone.'

'Book. They were in a book. First copy for the star.'

499

I could talk about the book. If I talked about the book he might not ask any more.

'First copy for the star, he said. That was fair. Then he'd leave the other copies lying around for everybody else. If I wasn't nice to him.'

I leaned back, and looked into Peter's face.

'I punched him on the nose. That was as nice to him as I ever got, Peter.'

A gleam of teeth in the lamplight. Oh, Peter.

'I hope you smashed his nose. I hope it was just a bloody smear across his face.'

No. No. Just a nosebleed. No, I didn't smash his nose.

She did that. She did it, that other time. She smashed his face into her knee, both fists wound into his hair, smashed his face down into her knee, just after she kicked him, that crunching kick into his testicles. She did that. Not me. A bloody smear across his face, yes, and there was a little splinter of bone in the blood. Oh, yes.

But no, not me. Not me.

'Be careful, Peter,' I whispered.

'Do you want to go dancing?' he asked.

'Dancing where we hold each other? I don't want to jive. Not tonight.'

'Dancing where we hold each other, then. Waltz, quick-step, foxtrot. Tango?'

'Can you dance?'

'Most actors can dance, my sweet, it's one of the tools of the trade. Like riding horses, and sword fighting. You never know when you might need it.'

'Falling down stairs?'

A gleam of teeth again.

'Let's go dancing, Glory.'

32

Simmie was lying in bed, smiling up at me. There were vases of flowers on the tables in his private room, cards on the windowsill, magazines and books, a huge cut glass bowl of fruit.

There were gaps in his pyjama jacket between the buttons, and the buttons were straining.

'It's only a little attack,' he said. 'I'll be out quite soon. There's no need to worry.'

I hadn't sent him any flowers. I hadn't sent a card, either. The only reason my telephone message hadn't told him to go to hell was because I didn't think the nurse would have passed it on.

Mike, crying in my office, and Ruth, when I'd met her at their flat late the night before, pale and tense, trying to be brave.

'Just a small heart attack,' she'd said. 'He'll be all right, sweetie, won't he?'

'Of course he will,' I'd answered.

'Don't sign any contracts with that smart alec brat,' he ordered. 'Tell him we'll see how he shapes up. I'll be back soon.'

'I've got to go,' I said. 'Don't hurry back, Simmie. The smart alec brat is actually rather good at your job.'

'Glory?'

501

'What, Simmie?'

'Oh, shit. Sorry, Glory. Sorry.'

His apologies were a little too glib now. Simmie thought he could put everything right with his 'Oh, shit. Sorry.'

'Don't apologise to me,' I said. 'I don't give a damn. It's Mike who's frantic, and your mum who tries to hide the tears behind the brave smile. Not me. So far as I'm concerned you're just another fat slob. Oh, and in case you're interested, you're getting a dirty reputation as a drunk, too.'

'Glory!'

He was shocked this time. I'd never spoken to him like that before.

'Dry martini may be the sophisticated drink, I wouldn't know, I don't like the taste myself. Eight of them is just self-indulgence.'

'I don't drink eight dry . . .'

'Do you want to count the empties? A waste of time, I should think. It might take too long. I'll get over you, Simmie, in no time at all. Ruth will be sad for a while, a long while, I expect. Mike might cry himself into an early grave. I'm very fond of Mike. I wish I could say I admire his taste in men, but I don't. Goodbye, Simmie.'

I had to go back to see him again the next day. Ruth said he'd been seriously shocked by my words.

'Please, sweetie, just a quick visit. I know he deserved everything you said, I know you're busy, but please.'

'Ruth, I . . .'

'Don't apologise, don't take back a single word. Just smile at him. He's really hurt, poppet.'

I went back.

'Get well soon,' I said. 'We do need you, Simmie. It isn't Lawley's without Simeon Lawley.'

'What about the smart alec brat?'

Simmie was trying to be carefree about Tom Kelvin.

'We're signing his contract, Simmie. You're outvoted. Mike told you that. We need him for the times you're ill.'

502

'But I'll be out of here in a couple of weeks. Oh, shit, Glory. Only a couple of weeks.'

Half the bunch of bananas in the cut-glass bowl had gone. None of the oranges had been touched.

'And back again in two months. Listen to me, Simmie, if we'd taken Tom when we first interviewed him he would have cost us three thousand a year less. We had to outbid Texaco for him this time.'

'Oh, shit. Sorry. I mean, I really am sorry. Very sorry.'

'Mike needs a holiday, he's on his knees, have you noticed? He hates the place without you. Thank your lucky stars for Tom Kelvin, Simmie. He's the reason Mike can come and see you at all.'

Simmie was beginning to look distressed. I had to keep my temper. Ruth had asked me to smile at him.

I tried. I did manage something like a smile.

'Mike wants to see North Africa with you. He's worked so hard for you. Surely he deserves that?'

'He can go any time . . .'

'Listen to me. With you. Did you hear those two words? With you. With you.'

'As soon as the new place is running smoothly. I promise, Glory, you can tell him. As soon as the new place is running smoothly.'

I stood up. I smiled, as I'd promised I would.

'Give me those bananas,' I said. 'Our chickens like bananas. And you get well soon.'

I hadn't managed to persuade Lucille, either. I was hopeless, with people. Outside the theatre, I was hopeless.

I went to Manchester, and looked at light filters for *Who's Afraid of Virginia Woolf?*, and nothing seemed right, least of all the casting.

'I see myself as rather youthful, actually,' said the woman whose name I could never remember, who was to play Martha. 'Not just childish, but actually, rather a child. Don't you?'

Why was I hesitating about a contract to do films with the Royal Shakespeare Company?

Simmie had signed this agreement, with this third-rate company, there was a name he'd thought he recognised. He'd been wrong. Tom would have torn it in half and dropped it into the waste-paper basket.

I could be free of this. If Jacob Goldman said he could get me a five-year contract, he could do it. Why was I hesitating?

Back to Stratford for the rehearsals, and a big sacking-wrapped parcel in my office. Ann, my big sister, what have you done with those drawings?

It was magnificent.

I put it on my desk, and I stood back and looked at it. Antlers, they were antlers, they swept back, and the prongs stood proud and high, but it was bracken, and bramble, and the crown of a wild and barbaric king.

Thank you, Ann.

I put it on my head, just as it was, and it was sprung steel, it wasn't heavy, it felt alive, it moved. Even with no padding, it was so beautifully balanced I could hold it, I could move my head. The steel slid on my hair, but I could hold it.

Peter would manage this. Padded, with the leather strapped against the headband, it would be steady, and he could move his head like a stag, to blend against the background, to become invisible.

Yes, it was magnificent.

I took it down to the property department.

'Huh!'

Fred Greenhalge, property master.

'What do you mean, "huh"?' I demanded.

'Oberon? Yus. Yus indeed. Right, Miss Mayall, and what do we do with this?'

I showed him. Gold here. Like a crown, where the prongs turn inwards. But this is bracken, yes? In autumn? Right. And bramble. So, that's green.

'And red. Huh?'

'No. What do you mean, red? Why red?'

'Bramble in autumn, Miss Mayall.'

'Oh, God. This is midsummer.'

Damn. Think. Think again. Gold, in summer? There has to be gold.

'What colour are antlers?' I asked.

'Ivory. Sort of ivory.'

No idea. What about Fred, though? No fool, Fred Greenhalge.

'Fred, gold, like a crown.'

'Yus.'

'And the ivory. But it's bracken, and bramble, in mid-summer.'

'Yus.'

'Oh, and don't forget the padding, and the leather. Okay?'

'Yus.'

Why can't Simmie delegate? It's easy, here.

All you need is a gang of experts.

Back to my office, to find a letter from Alan Raven's assistant, Tracey Smith, yes, I bet that's your name. Mine's Susan Jones.

I only had to think of her to start talking like a melodrama.

Samantha Grafton, one of the co-owners of Gorsedown Manor. Shoplifting and fencing.

I wrote her a brief note.

Dear Ms Smith, thank you for your letter. I was already aware of Ms Grafton's slightly criminal record, which would not shift me off a molehill, let alone out of a stately home. Please find enclosed a cheque for twenty-five pounds for your not very impressive efforts. In order to save you further wasting your time, may I inform you that Gorsedown Manor is owned by Stephenson Holdings, Ltd, a private limited company.

Another half-page of sarcasm and information. But she wasn't a nineteen-year-old with low self-esteem, nor a five-year-old child. I felt slightly smug, as well as angry, as I franked the letter and threw it into my tray.

'Is Peter Clements in today?'

'No, Miss Mayall. Not until Monday.'

Oh, Peter. Just you wait and see what Ann's done for you. Ann, and Fred. And me.

He hadn't been lying, when he'd said he could dance. We'd laughed at each other, tried out the tricky steps, matched each other every time. Exhibition standard, my lovely Peter, so the hotel professional had said when she'd asked him to dance, and he'd refused.

'Love to, my gorgeous,' he'd said, and that time the actor's charm had been just a little obvious, at least to someone who'd seen it a few times before. 'But not tonight, I'm afraid. She's got the car keys.'

Liar.

He'd had the keys, and he'd driven me home that night. I'd drunk too much sherry and white wine, otherwise I wouldn't have danced like that, not the tango, not in public, with everybody whistling and cheering, Peter tall and slim and doing the snake-hips act as he grinned at me when the audience whistled and stamped and yelled for more.

No, Miss Mayall. Not until Monday.

Damn.

But on Monday he was there, and the head dress was ready, he tried it on, and it was right.

Yes, Ann, my big sister, it was right, and that's a better word than perfection.

On the stage, and Solomon walked around him, the rest of the cast looked, and whispered, and talked, and then they started to clap.

Ann, I wish you were here. I've never heard a compliment like this, not from an audience like this. I wish you could know what this means, to me, to you.

'Can you hold it still?' asked Solomon, and Peter tilted his head back, dropped his shoulders, and tried it.

'Yes,' he said. 'Yes, I can hold it still.'

Solomon, smiling, not the broad grin he uses when he wants to encourage someone, but the small, tight smile that means he's got exactly what he wants.

'Right,' he said. 'Right, Glory.'

Peter came to my office that afternoon, still smiling, carrying the head dress.

'Can I have it, when they drop this production?' he asked.

'It's not mine.'

'I'm going to ask my agent. I've got to have it, Glory. It's fantastic. I've got to have it.'

Oh, Peter. If they won't let you have it, I'll get Ann to do another one. Ann, and Fred.

'I want to draw you,' he said. 'May I borrow your pencils and sketch pad?'

I was surprised. He'd never said he could draw. He'd never really shown any interest, except when he'd asked if he could have one of my drawings, if I'd sign it for him.

'Draw me?'

'Yes. Why not? You drew me, why shouldn't I draw you?'

So I passed him the sketch pad and the pencils, and I sat by the window, and looked at him.

'How shall I sit?'

'Any way you like, my love. Just sit still. And listen. All right?'

Look out of the window, at the old brown river. Boats on the river. Spring will be here soon. It's March, it's windy, but spring will be here soon.

Peter, a pencil in his hand, sitting on the high stool, his legs crossed, one knee high with the sketch pad resting against it.

'Are you listening, Glory?'

'Mmm?'

He seemed very uneasy. Embarrassed. Yes, his face was red, and even though he was drawing me, he didn't seem to want to look at me.

'I think I have to tell you a story.'

I waited, sitting still, looking out of the window, but watching Peter and listening to him. It had been a long time since I'd posed for somebody to draw me. Not since I'd left college.

'It's about me, I'm afraid,' he said. 'It was years ago, and . . . Well. I wouldn't do it again. I really do think I'd rather starve.'

A short laugh, just a little forced.

'I was in California. I'd broken my leg falling off a horse, so I hadn't been able to work, and I wasn't insured either, so I was broke and . . . well. There wasn't much work around. Not for me, anyway.'

Tapping the pencil on the sketch pad, looking down at the floor. What was he going to say? I kept my eyes on the window, but I could see him. He didn't know that, but I could see him.

'I did a couple of blue movies. And, some magazines.'

'Oh.'

'Well, I never did get paid for the movies, if that makes it any better. Serve me damned well right, I had been warned. Quite a lot of struggling young actors, as we were known, do get those offers, and some of them take them.'

'Including you.'

'Including me, yes. I'm sorry.'

I shook my head. I couldn't imagine Peter agreeing to do that.

'You don't have to apologise,' I said. 'It's none of my business.'

He laid his pencil down on the table.

'Please don't say that, darling. Everything about me is your business.'

I had my own memories, I didn't need his. I would not talk about my memories to Peter.

508

'I don't want to hear any more about that, though, Peter.'

He picked up the pencil again, looked at me, and started to draw. I watched the boats on the river. There was a sudden flurry of rain, the brown water shimmered under it, the trees moved in the wind.

'I have to tell you something else, Glory.'

I didn't answer. He could tell me whatever he liked, so long as he did not ask me. Don't ask, Peter. Don't ask if I have ever done anything like this. Please, Peter, don't ask. I will lie to you rather than tell you, and then it is over.

'All right.'

I'd spoken very softly. I thought perhaps he hadn't heard.

'For one of the magazines, the woman was quite old.'

It was very quiet. I could hear the pencil scratching against the paper as he drew.

'She was a nice woman. I know that sounds strange, but she was. Not some blowsy old tart. She needed money, like me. She had a good figure, but her face wasn't very attractive.

'So they didn't use her face, Glory. They used photographs of another woman's face, they pasted them up and rephotographed them. Her body, another woman's face. Do you understand?'

'I didn't think they concentrated on faces,' I said.

He didn't answer. Just the pencil, scratching against the paper.

'Sorry,' I said. 'I'm sorry.'

'No. It's all right. Say whatever you like, it's all right.'

Somebody knocked on the door, the post had arrived. The girl dropped the letters on my desk, and went out.

'Do you want to say anything?' asked Peter.

'No.'

'Did you understand what I told you? About the way they did the photographs? Another woman's face pasted over the real one?'

'Yes, I understand.'

'I want to talk about the thin girl, Glory. No, don't move. You don't have to answer. Can you just listen? Don't move. I'm trying to draw your mouth. Just keep still.'

Peter. I don't want this. Be careful, Peter. She's so dangerous.

'You said she used your face. She hasn't got a face. She uses yours. Glory, you have such a lovely face. I've never seen a more beautiful face.

'Don't move, darling. Just keep still.

'The thin girl was in the photographs. You said that. You said you were in the wrong body. "When I was in the wrong body." I think those were your words.'

'Peter, I don't want to talk about this. I'm tired.'

'Don't talk then, my sweet. Just listen. Are you listening?'

'Yes.'

'You were in the wrong body. She uses your face. She was in the photographs. Glory, my darling, I don't know who the thin girl was, poor kid, but I don't think it was you. I think they faked the photographs. I don't think it was you the two men raped.'

Watch him. Watch his hand moving the pencil. Peter.

'Did you hear me, darling? Did you understand?'

No. No. I don't understand. I heard screaming. Didn't I hear screaming? Wasn't there any laughter? They'd been laughing. Hadn't they been laughing?

I'd seen it, in the photographs.

Cindy, little Cindy. Cindy learns how. And how!

Hadn't I heard it? Hadn't I heard the laughter? I'd been screaming, I'd heard the screaming. I'd heard the screaming, I'd screamed for my mother. I'd screamed.

'Glory, do you understand?'

'No. I don't know. I don't know.'

'How old were you, Glory?'

He wasn't drawing me any more. He was watching me. He still held the pencil, he still had the sketch pad, held it against his knee, but he wasn't drawing me.

Who is the thin child, then? Who is she? Who did those things to Lucien? Who was it who did those things for the Rat, for the Rat, Rat Wright?

No. No.

Who was it with the knives and the whips?

No.

Who followed Ned Fleming?

No. No.

'It was her,' I said. 'It was her.'

'Yes.'

'She did . . . She . . .'

I couldn't speak any more. I didn't dare speak. Peter, you are wrong. You are wrong, she is here. If I speak, you will hear her. She is here, she is dangerous. Go away, Peter. Please, go away.

He was watching me. He still held the pencil, but it wasn't moving, he was watching me. What can you see?

'Glory?'

Teeth bared, Peter, go away now. She is hissing between her teeth, Peter, she is dangerous. Don't speak, don't make her speak.

He mustn't know.

'Glory?'

He'd put the sketch pad and the pencil on the table, he was standing up, he was walking towards her.

No. No.

'What do you *want*?'

No.

'Darling?'

Go away. Go away.

'Darling?'

She struck at him, clawed fingers raking at his face, straight for his eyes, slashing out at his face.

He jerked his head back, he is fast, he can move fast. She missed. She doesn't often miss, and never twice.

Go away. Go away, Peter, run away. Run, please, run.

511

'I have knives and I have whips.'

No. No, please. No.

'Tell me what you want me to do.'

He was backing away, his hands were coming up in front of his body, he was half crouched as he backed away, watching her, watching.

'You will cry. You will beg. You will scream.'

'My love? Glory?'

Hissing through her teeth, Peter, get away, get away now. Don't try to fight her, Peter. You are stronger than Glory, but not the thin child. She won't miss twice, she never misses twice.

'Tell me what you want me to do.'

'I want you to love me.'

She doesn't understand this, she won't understand.

Peter, get away. Don't stand there, don't lower your hands, don't let her get close to you. Run away.

'What do you want?'

'I want you to love me.'

No. No. Nobody ever asks her that. Nobody.

'I love you. I want you to love me. Please, love me.'

She doesn't do that. She can't do that. Peter, she can't . . .

'Glory. I want you to love me. Glory.'

Peter. Peter.

I am so cold. Peter, I am so tired. I'm so tired.

'Peter. I'm so tired, Peter.'

'Glory?'

'I'm so tired.'

I could feel the tears on my cheeks, I was shivering, I was so cold, I would never be warm again, I was so cold.

'Darling?'

'I'm cold. I'm tired.'

He walked towards me, slowly, watching me, his head was turned a little to one side, he was very tense, his hands were curled up high in front of his chest. He was moving so slowly, so warily.

512

'Oh, Peter. Peter. Oh, no. Peter.'

'Yes?'

'She's gone, Peter. She's gone now.'

Ice, I felt like ice, only the tears on my face were warm. I was shivering, I could never be warm again. Never. Only cold from now on, only cold. For ever, cold.

'Who's gone, Glory?'

'The thin child. The thin girl. She's gone.'

I crouched down, I wrapped my arms around myself, and crouched low on the floor. So very cold. So cold. So tired.

I lay down, I curled my legs up close against my body, my face into my knees. Too tired, now. Too tired.

Peter's hand on my shoulder, he was beside me, half kneeling. Where have I seen this before? One fist braced against the floor, a foot curled under him. The start of a race, when they are lined up, waiting for the gun, this is how they are.

So they can get away, very fast.

Too late now. You should have gone before she came.

I closed my eyes. Can I sleep? Can I sleep, when I am so cold?

I heard him move, his hand had gone from my shoulder, a foot, sliding on the floor, and then he was back, he was putting something over me. My coat?

'Glory? Sit up, darling. Sit up. That's right. Come on.'

His hand under my head, lifting it.

'Sit up. Come on, Glory, get up. That's right.'

Hands under my arms, lifting me. But I want to sleep.

He picked me up, he carried me across the room, laid me down on the sofa and pulled my coat over me.

'You'll be warm again soon,' he said.

No, I don't think so, Peter. I don't think I'll ever be warm again.

'I'm so sorry, my love,' he said. 'So very sorry.'

His voice was shaking.

I closed my eyes again.

'Stupid amateur psychology,' he said. 'So stupid. I should have realised. I am so sorry. Darling Glory, I am so sorry. Can you ever forgive me? For being such a fool? Putting you through that?'

'I'm so tired.'

'I know, my love. Can you sleep? Do you think you can sleep now? I'll stay with you, darling. I'll be here. Are you warmer now? My poor love.'

His hand on my face, stroking my cheek.

'Yes,' I said. 'I'm warmer now.'

I slept.

He was still there when I woke up, sitting on the floor beside me, his arms around his knees, his head resting on them, watching me.

'Hello,' he said.

'Did I say anything?'

'Yes.'

It didn't matter. He already knew. He knew about her.

'You don't have to tell me anything,' he said. 'God knows I've done you enough damage, my sweet.'

He touched my cheek again, and smiled.

'I want to help you. I do, I truly want to help you. But I think it takes about seven years to learn what I'd need to know, and I don't think you should wait that long.'

'Seven's a lucky number.'

'I know.'

'What takes seven years, Peter?'

He hesitated, and drew in a deep breath. When he spoke again he wasn't looking at me.

'I think it takes about seven years to qualify as a psychiatrist.'

I was puzzled. I wondered why he cared about her.

'You think she should see a psychiatrist?' I asked. 'She isn't there all the time. She isn't there very often, really.'

'Hmm.'

514

He had so many different smiles. I hadn't seen this one before.

'Perhaps you could tell a psychiatrist about her,' he suggested.

I sat up, pushing my coat away.

'Oh, I don't think so. I haven't got time.'

He picked up my coat and carried it over to the cupboard. He was putting it away when he spoke next.

'It might be necessary, darling. When she's here she's quite dangerous, isn't she? I think you once said she could kill.'

'Yes,' I said. 'She's killed.'

He had his back to me. He stood still for a moment, and then he closed the cupboard door. He stood with his hand against it, he seemed to be looking down at his hand as it rested against the door, or perhaps he was looking at the wood, at the patterns of the grain in the pale oak. I like to do that too, look at patterns in wood.

'One man killed himself because of her,' I said. 'She turned another into a murderer, and he was destroyed by that. Not everybody dies, even if you kill them, did you know that, Peter? Then there was the man he killed for her, and the one who thought he could rape her.'

I thought about it.

'That's four, isn't it?' I said.

'Yes. Yes, that's four.'

He'd taken a long time to answer. It must be a lovely pattern in that wood, he was still looking at it. It was nice, that Peter and I liked the same things.

I felt quite light. The sleep had done me good.

'She used the knives and the whips?' he asked.

'Oh, no. No, she never killed anybody with those. Just, whatever they said, but sometimes she wouldn't stop. The Rat said she should stop when they'd come, but sometimes she wouldn't.'

I could remember. Sometimes in my dreams I heard

515

them, those men, but that didn't matter now. The bright blood, I could remember, the bright blood on her hands.

'The blood was very beautiful.'

He'd stopped looking at the wood, he'd turned away from the door, but he wasn't facing me, he was staring down at the floor. I wondered what he could see on the floor, there were no patterns there.

'Yes,' he said. 'Blood's a beautiful colour.'

The sketch pad was still lying on the table.

'May I see your drawing?' I asked.

'Yes, of course. Do.'

I picked it up, turned it over, and looked at it. I don't know what I'd expected, Peter seemed to be able to do anything, so I was puzzled. Perhaps this was a new sort of pattern drawing that I hadn't seen before. Perhaps there was something I was missing. I could usually understand what a drawing meant, if I looked hard. I was an outline, and my shoulders didn't match. I didn't think I'd been sitting like that, either.

It just wasn't any good.

Peter couldn't draw. He couldn't draw.

'I haven't seen such a talentless piece of scribble since I left school,' I said, and I smiled at him.

'I was never much good at drawing.'

He managed to smile back as he said it, but his face was white and sick, and his eyes were wide, and very dark.

33

Simmie was out of hospital and back in his and Mike's new flat in Birmingham. Tom Kelvin went there every afternoon to discuss the business with them, and Simmie left a message on my telephone answering machine.

'Thanks, Glory. Tom's okay, you were right. Um. I hope the chickens enjoyed my bananas.'

Very subdued, for Simmie.

The production of *Who's Afraid of Virginia Woolf?* had been cancelled. There was a rumour, which I believed, that the director had thrown a chair at that actress whose name I could never remember. At least Simmie had not forgotten the 'kill' clause in the contract; Lawley's got paid for my work whether the play went ahead or not.

I'd found a flat in Birmingham that I liked, but I was no longer sure. I could buy it. I could sell some more shares, and this time I'd warn Robert Cameron, just in case. I do not believe in luck.

'So how did you know?' he'd demanded. 'That time you sold those two blocks to buy the cottage, how did you know?'

'I didn't know,' I'd replied. 'I looked through the portfolio for the ones I liked the least.'

We'd been on the telephone, but I'd been able to picture him, sitting at his desk looking out over the North Sea. I'd been able to picture the grimace.

'Next time, tell me which ones you like the least, will you?'

'Would you like a rabbit's foot for your birthday?' I'd asked. 'I can get you one. Quite easily, actually.'

It had hardly been six weeks, and the cottage was filthy.

Su-Su was not paying me any rent, Su-Su and Danny were squatting. I supposed I should be angry. I should be taking legal action.

I should at least be doing something.

I was telling stories with, rather than to, Danny. I was washing paint stains off my pillowcases. I was replacing a torn quilt. I was feeding the chickens and the rabbits when Su-Su was late home.

The flat in Birmingham was exactly what I wanted. It had space, it had light. It had a wooden floor, which gleamed when the sun shone through the high windows.

I wondered whether I'd rather live in Stratford, with Peter.

'Come and live with me?' he'd asked that evening after the rugger match.

Ask me again, Peter.

Only a week to the dress rehearsal for *A Midsummer Night's Dream*.

I was confident, this time. It was going to be so good, this production. It was going to be part of Shakespeare's history, one that would be written in the long book. There would have to be a book, the best productions of Shakespeare. Some of the finest actors in the world, and Solomon Crawley breathed this play now, it was in his soul.

I was back on oiled wheels, I knew this was going to be good.

Macbeth, after this. *Macbeth*. With a team of experts, and a real stage, and all the technical equipment I'd need. Stark black blocks against a lit sky, if that was what I still wanted, if that was what Solomon wanted, and if it survived the ideas sessions.

There was another letter from Leadbetter and Chase, this time from Mrs Hargrave, a copy of one she had sent to Uncle John. Reconcile was a registered charity, and worked with refugees. The only connection that had been traced between the charity and the Children of God was that refugees occasionally visited Gorsedown Park for short holidays, and these holidays were financed by Reconcile. So far as she had been able to discover, the Children of God were the only people who collected for the charity, although some donations and bequests had been received.

Did Mr Mayall wish her to continue her inquiries into the charity, or was this information sufficient for his requirements?

I telephoned their office, and was told Mr Mayall had instructed Mrs Hargrave to continue.

There was also a letter from Tracey Smith. Her information with regards to the Children of God was that they smuggled art objects. These art objects were stored at Gorsedown Manor until they could be disposed of. Some of these art objects were stolen.

Miss Smith would be obliged by a further retainer, together with the supplement as had been agreed for information discovered.

Now why, I asked myself, did Tracey Smith imagine I was fool enough to fall for that?

I wrote another note. Vague accusations are hardly sufficient. Where is the evidence to support these allegations? Who smuggled the 'art' objects, refugees? Or were the Children of God bringing out Greek statuary in collecting tins?

Why was my irritation overlaid by such a feeling of unease?

Peter took me out to dinner, to meet a friend, somebody against whom he played rugger, he said. I'd like Roly.

I did. He had a dry sense of humour, he made Peter laugh. Peter had been a bit quiet, he'd been thinking about Oberon, he said. But with Roly, Peter was laughing again.

'What do you do?' I asked him.

'I'm a doctor, when I'm not on a muddy field getting my head kicked in by oafs like this. I had to stitch up my own leg last month, it was horrible. I thought I'd faint. I'm really squeamish about injuries, when they're mine.'

Peter had to make a telephone call to his agent, and when he'd gone Roly said he'd never seen Peter like this about a woman before.

'Over the top, frankly. It's disgusting, everybody's jealous.'

Then he became serious.

'Peter's a very old friend. What do you feel for him? I hope you don't mind me asking, I don't want to pry. But I'd hate to see Peter hurt.'

'I think he's gorgeous,' I said.

'You mean physically?'

'Yes.'

He smiled, and raised his glass.

'I'll drink to that. And suppose he wasn't?'

It seemed a pointless conversation, but he was Peter's friend. I shrugged.

'He wouldn't be Peter.'

Roly smiled again.

'When he's not there, how do you think of him?' he asked.

I wondered why Peter was taking so long over the telephone call. It wasn't like him, not when we were out together.

I didn't want to answer Roly's question. It was none of his business, how I thought of Peter.

Wide shoulders, long legs. The muscles in his back, when

I painted them, brown and gold, with the grey shadows in his spine. The shape of the hair on his chest, like a cross, gold in it, the way his skin shivered under my fingers.

'Why are you smiling?' asked Roly.

'Sorry. I was miles away.'

He asked me some more questions, but I turned them aside, and he realised I didn't want to talk about myself, or Peter, so he stopped. He had nice manners.

When Peter drove me home that night I told him about the flat I'd found in Birmingham, how big it was, quite old, with high ceilings.

'Do you think you'll buy it?' he asked.

'I don't know.'

Then, when he didn't say anything else, 'I can't go on living with Su-Su and Danny. I like Su-Su, I love Danny, but it's impossible.'

'You love Danny?'

'He is so beautiful, Peter. Don't you think he's beautiful?'

He didn't answer for a while.

'I think you're beautiful,' he said. 'Glory, I think you're incredibly beautiful.'

'You don't have to sound so sad about it.'

'Beauty doesn't last. Not for ever. I'm getting grey hairs, have you noticed?'

I hadn't. I hadn't been close enough to look, not for a little while. No, I hadn't noticed.

'You're tired,' I said. 'Are you overworking? You don't usually talk like this.'

He pulled the car off the road into a lay-by and turned off the engine.

'I must be mad, to love you like this,' he said. 'I can't understand myself any more. Sometimes I think it was a nightmare.'

'What was a nightmare, Peter? Do you have bad dreams?'

'I see you every day, you look just the same. You're so lovely, when you smile at me I feel as if I'm dying. I can't

521

stop thinking about you. I can't stop wondering about you. I want you so much it hurts, it's like a real pain. I don't know what to think about you, or what to believe about you. My love. My beautiful Glory.'

He wasn't smiling. Why wasn't he smiling? When he'd called me loving names before, he'd always smiled at me. He was hardly even looking at me, and his voice was strange. It was as though his throat hurt, he couldn't speak well.

'I love you. I can't help it. I love you.'

'I'll paint your body for the dress rehearsal,' I said.

That should make him smile. That should make him reach across and take me in his arms, and I could lean against his chest and listen to his heart, it would be fast, and his breathing, as if he'd been running. I liked listening to Peter's heart.

But he looked away from me, and his breathing didn't sound as if he'd been running. It sounded as if he was crying.

'Peter?'

'Did you like Roly?' he asked.

I didn't want to talk about Roly, I wanted Peter to hold me.

'He's all right. Shall we go dancing again?'

'Yes. Not now, though. It's late now. Did you talk to Roly?'

'Yes, of course I did. You were there. When shall we go dancing?'

'Tomorrow. When I get back from London. I'll pick you up from the cottage. Glory, listen to me.'

Why wasn't he holding me? Why was he sitting over there, looking across at me? I didn't understand.

'When I went to make that phone call, what were you and Roly talking about?'

'He asked about you. I don't know. Why? Are you jealous?'

He smiled. I could only see a little gleam from his teeth in the lights of the dashboard, but he did smile.

'Yes,' he said. 'I'll beat him up next time I see him. Glory, darling, would you tell Roly about the thin girl?'

'Why?'

'He'd be interested. He's a psychiatrist, he's very interested in that sort of person, like the thin girl. Would you tell him?'

'Oh, Peter. I really haven't got time, I've got two summer fashion shows, and there's a play I still haven't read for Uncle Jacob.'

At last he touched me. He reached across the car, and laid his hand against my cheek.

'Roly's such a good friend of mine,' he said. 'It would help him. Please, Glory. Try to make some time for him. Please, darling.'

'Oh, God. What does he want to know?'

'Darling, I've no idea. He'll ask questions, I expect. His practice is in Gloucester, it's not that far. Not the way you drive that little sports car.'

'All right,' I said. 'I suppose so. Not for a couple of weeks, though, I can't.'

Both his hands on my shoulders, now he was really smiling at me.

'But you will? Tell him about her? As soon as you can.'

'Yes, darling, I'll tell him. If he's interested.'

He pulled me towards him, and I leaned my face against his chest, and I listened to his heart, and to him breathing.

'Dancing tomorrow,' I said.

'Yes.'

'Close-up dancing.'

'Yes, my love. Close-up dancing. Very, very close.'

Danny had been in my room again, my books were on the floor. At least he never drew in them, he was careful with books. He'd done a painting of Naomi for me and left it on my pillow. It hadn't been quite dry when he'd put it there.

523

He'd also been playing with my telephone answering machine.

He wanted to show me the next morning before he went to school. If you press this button there's a red light, and if you press this button I can hear your voice, and if you press this button it makes a funny noise, and if you press this button it makes another noise and the red light goes out.

'I know, Danny,' I said. 'Sweetie, could you wait until I get home before you play with it? Sometimes other people leave messages on it for me.'

He knew that. He'd heard them.

Oh. Thank you, Danny.

We were late, so I took Su-Su and Danny in the car. We dropped Danny at his new school, it was a lot bigger than the one he'd been to in Bolton.

'Is he managing all right there?' I asked Su-Su, and she nodded.

'Chatterbox,' I muttered.

A slow, grave smile, but her eyes were amused.

'He likes it,' she said.

He never spoke of school friends, he never asked if he could bring anybody home. I was worried about Danny. Surely somebody would have had a birthday party by now, there should have been an invitation for him? Shouldn't children have friends?

The nanny I'd hired for him had said he was a nice, normal little boy. What was her name? Anna. Anna Watson.

But Danny didn't seem to have any friends.

There were letters from the detectives, copies of the ones I'd already received, and a new one from Leadbetter and Chase.

Stephenson Holdings had commissioned several estate agents to find them a large house with at least three square miles of land, and no public access. The stipulation about public access had been the most important condition. There

524

were no listed rights of way across Gorsedown Park, but the right of the blacksmiths and their families to ride on the land had not been on the local authority lists.

Stephenson Holdings had sought advice from solicitors in Cheltenham on the matter of that right, but had been advised not to take action in the courts.

Mr Leadbetter was continuing his inquiries, and, unless he received instructions to the contrary from me, would now concentrate on the reasons for Stephenson Holdings' requirement for privacy. In the meantime, they remained, and so on.

I wondered how Mr Leadbetter had gained the information about the solicitors. He really was very good.

I spent the day working on plans for a summer fashion show for Gerry Grey. I wanted it to be something extraordinarily good, more for Mike than for Gerry. Mike needed something to make him happy. Mike looked as if he was already in mourning.

Dear Mike. As Ruth said, such a darling.

I went home early, I wanted to have a bath and change because Peter and I were going dancing, and I knew the bathroom would be filthy again. I spent half an hour cleaning it, and then I had a long, hot bath, I lay back in the bubbles, thinking of Peter.

Dancing, very, very close, he'd said.

Peter, by the river, his lips on my hair, the way his hip bone moved under my hand as we walked together. Peter, laughing at the end of the rugger game, filthy with mud and sweat. Standing on the stage, motionless, his head braced against the weight of the antlers.

Peter.

He came early, and he was smiling at me, he didn't seem so tired any more. He said he'd had a bloody day, some television commercial for chocolate, he'd hated every minute of it, only the thought of dancing with me that evening had kept him going.

I laughed at him, and he laughed back.

Dancing, with Peter, a big hotel in the centre of Birmingham, and we danced a quickstep, and a cha-cha, and then Peter said we should stop showing off, and just dance together.

So we did, for the next three hours, danced close, and slow, and when the band played pop or Latin American we sat at our table, and Peter told me he loved me.

Dancing close, my arms around his neck, his head bent low against mine, I listened to him whispering that he loved me, that I was his beautiful darling, I listened to him breathing, I stroked his head, my fingers gentle in his hair, I felt his hands low on my back, pressing me close against him, holding me close, and I was drowsy, I felt as if I was melting, I was drowsy, and weak, but he was holding me, and he was strong, his arms were very strong around me.

'Let's go home now,' he whispered. 'My home, Glory. Let's go to bed together this time, darling. Tonight.'

'Yes,' I answered. 'Yes.'

I love you, I thought. Is this what love is? I love you.

I didn't want to let him go. We walked to the car, I was close against him, leaning against him, feeling every move he made, his arm around me, his fingers stroking my shoulder, the way he was breathing, his thigh against mine.

I thought, I have never been this close to a man before.

I held him closer, I turned my face against him, I stroked the side of his chest where my hand rested against him under his jacket, I felt the ribs moving, suddenly more quickly.

This is good, I thought. This is good.

In his car, I wanted to be close against him, I wanted him to hold me, and he did, he held me pressed against his side, and he kissed me again.

'You'll have to do the gear changes, then,' he said.

Close against him, watching his hand on the steering wheel, listening to him breathing, listening to the love words, feeling him warm beside me, knowing he smiled as I listened to the note of the engine and reached for the gear lever, watching the way his leg moved as he let out the clutch, touching, feeling the muscles in his thigh flexing as he moved.

Thinking, this is love.

I'd never been to his home before, I'd wondered what it was like, but I didn't even look, I was listening to Peter, listening to him breathing, I was feeling his lips on my hair, his arms around me, I was listening to him telling me he loved me.

I held him, and I listened.

'I've never been this close to a man before,' I whispered, and he answered me.

'I know. I know, my love. I know.'

Hands, and lips, and Peter smiling at me, and I remembered I had touched this body before, I remembered smooth skin and the curve of muscle, and I touched again, smooth skin and curving muscle, and I felt his hands on my skin, stroking, gentle, and slow.

Close against him, lying very close, his face close to mine, leaning over me, looking down, something like a question in his eyes, and a smile as I ran my fingers down his spine, remembering.

'Gold,' I said softly. 'And brown, and grey shadows.'

'Yes, but I'm not Oberon now, my love.'

Hands, I looked down and I watched his hand, stroking, caressing, I watched as it moved against my breast, I watched as he took the nipple between his finger and thumb, and he was gentle, and slow, but for me there was a surge of feeling, something wild and urgent, and I writhed under him, my arms around him, no longer stroking, I wanted more than this.

He was holding me down, one hand pressed against my shoulder, his lips on my breast, he was stroking me again, his hand moving on my body, over my belly, my back was

arching, I was pressing myself against him, I wanted more,
I wanted more.

'Peter, Peter.'

'Yes, my love, yes. Darling, yes.'

He is too gentle, he is too gentle, I need more than this, I
need more, Peter. Peter, more.

Hands slow, and gentle, stroking, and sliding, searching,
and questioning, caressing, and probing, and gentle.

Peter, more, I need more.

'Peter, please, Peter.'

'Yes.'

'Peter, please. Oh, please, Peter.'

'Yes.'

Then he was there, deep inside me, deep, this was what I
had wanted, this was what I had demanded of him, this
was his answer, deep, and strong, and surging, and I could
not speak, and I could not think, I could only feel, and feel,
and this was more than feeling, this was need, and answer,
and demand, and again answer, and more need, wild, and
urgent, Peter, please.

Yes, and yes.

This is why I am alive.

Peter, please, Peter.

Yes.

Every desire, answered, every need, every sense, yes, yes,
and more, yes, my love, yes.

More. More.

Voice, and hands, and lips, his body surging over mine,
close and hard and warm, and deep, deep, everything I
demand of him, answered.

Now, Peter. Now, please, now.

My love, my darling, no, wait, my love.

Peter, now. Oh, please, Peter, now.

Wait. Wait, my love.

No, Peter, now, now. Now.

Shuddering, rigid and shuddering, deep, deep, and

strong, yes, Peter, oh yes. This, yes, yes. This is what I wanted, this is what I needed, this, from you.

Yes. Yes, Peter. Yes.

Lying over me, breathing fast, his head beside mine, his face turned away, sweat in his hair, my arms around him, I can taste him, my lips against his shoulder, I can taste him, I can taste the sweat on his skin, he is smooth, and warm, and hard.

'Oh, Peter. Peter.'

'Glory. Oh, good God.'

'That was wonderful, Peter.'

'Was it?' He rolled his head on the pillow, looking at me out of the sides of his eyes. 'Then you're very easily pleased, my love.'

Half a smile on his face, he was still short of breath, I stroked him, I touched his face.

'Peter.'

He raised himself up on to his elbows, looking down at me, looking close into my eyes, he was smiling, he kissed me.

'Yes, well,' he said, 'you've no scale of comparisons yet, have you? Just as well.'

I wanted him to hold me. I wrapped my arms around him, pulling him down close against me, I kissed his cheek, tasting sweat again, his hair was in my eyes.

Then suddenly his eyes were wide open, he was looking at me.

'Oh, damn. Glory. Come on, shower. Come on.'

'I don't want a shower, I want to . . .'

'My darling, one day we'll talk about peopling the earth with little Glorys and Peters, but not right now.'

He pushed himself away, he rolled off me, and I tried to catch him, to hold him, but he was only half laughing.

'Come on. Come and have a shower.'

'Cuddle me.'

'Right, here's a cuddle.'

He picked me up, arms under my shoulders and my

thighs, and I nuzzled my face into his neck and clung to him, close, as he carried me out of the room.

There was water all over us, and we were soaping each other, his body was smooth and slippery under my hands, I wanted to touch and stroke him, I wanted hold him, I wanted to be close against him.

'Glory. My beautiful Glory.'

Soap, and water, and gentle hands, and Peter smiling at me, he was kneeling, and I was stroking his hair, his lovely head between my hands, I was looking down at him, and there was water all over us.

A big towel, and it was scratchy, and rather threadbare.

'This is not a luxury item,' I complained, and he looked a little doubtful.

'No,' he agreed. 'Sorry.'

'Carry me back to bed,' I demanded, and he wrapped the towel around me, and carried me.

He wanted to know which side of the bed I preferred, and I didn't know.

'Have both, then,' he said. 'Sleep on top of me.'

Dark brown cotton sheets, and they smelt of Peter. Two pillows, one each? No, share both.

Tired? No, not very. Chocolate commercials. What? Chocolate commercials, very tiring. Oh, exhausting, yes. I'd forgotten.

A clock that ticked. Noisy old thing, how can you sleep with that racket by your bed? Had it since I was at school. Never thought about it. Am I the first to complain, then? You mind your own business. Unless you really want to know, my love.

I want that side of the bed. Which side? Your side. You stay where you are, you're keeping me warm.

Do you snore? I don't know. I don't think so. If you don't stop talking you'll never find out.

Hold me close. If I hold you any closer you'll be right through me and out the other side.

530

Are you going to make love to me again?

Movement, hands, lips against my ear, suddenly breathing faster.

I know now. I love this body, I love the smooth skin under my hands, I love the way the muscles in his shoulders curve outwards into the palms of my hand. I love this hard, flat belly with the hair in the shape of a cross, the way it shivers under my fingers as I trail them across it, low. The ribs, the way they move under his skin, under my hands, I love, I love.

I love these long, hard thighs, I love the smile in the half-darkness, the way his head turns towards me. You missed. I'm a rotten shot. Try again, witch. Yes, Glory. Yes, like that. Aah. Yes, yes. More? Yes. And like this? Do you like this?

I love the movements, I love the way he lies beside me, I love his hands on my breasts, I love the way they ask questions of my body, like this? Like this? I love my own body, the way it answers, oh yes, like this, and more.

I love his voice whispering in my ear, darling, my darling Glory, yes. Like this, like this. More? Yes. And deeper. And slowly, my darling. Yes, now slowly. Oh, yes. Yes.

No, not yet. Slowly, yes, slowly. Not yet, my darling. No, not yet. Say after me, I will do as I am told. I will do as I am told.

And you? Will you do as you are told? Yes, darling, yes, my love. As soon as you know enough to tell me what to do, I will do as I am told.

Slowly? Still, slowly?

You don't like?

I like, but . . .

All right, my love. Yes, then do that, yes. Oh, God. Yes.

Like this? Will you tell me what you like? I won't need to tell you. You'll know, I promise. Tell me anyway? All right. Yes, I like that. Oh, yes.

Teach me. Teach me. Yes. My darling love. Put your hand

here. Like that, yes. Now . . . Yes. Oh, God, yes, yes. Stop, no, no more. Not yet. Not yet.

Later, yes. Yes, I'll tell you.

Slowly again?

Just for a moment. Yes, slowly. Yes.

Now again? No, wait, darling. Not yet.

I love, I love. I love his voice, I love his body over mine, his arms around me, I love the gentle strength of his body, I love his quiet voice whispering in my ear, I love the way he speaks to me, I love the way he listens. I love the way he answers me, I love the way his body answers mine.

I love. I love.

Like this now? Do you like this? Yes. Yes, I like that, and you? Do you like it when I touch you here? Or here? Now, like this? Is this right? Yes. Yes. Now? Yes, now. Yes, now. Now, oh yes.

Now. Now.

Yes.

34

The dress rehearsal for *A Midsummer Night's Dream* was not the smooth performance we'd had with *The Merchant of Venice*. It wasn't a disaster, but, as Solomon said, it was only a whisker away from it.

'I don't know if I can believe this,' he said as a pile of flats stacked in the dock fell down, the noise clearly audible over Julie's lines.

'Sorry,' he called. 'Take it back. Start the scene again. Sorry, everybody. Sorry, Julie. And will somebody please do something about whoever stacked those flats, something like murder.'

Fluffed lines, a light that blew at the wrong moment, some complete stranger who got in through the dock doors and walked on to the stage.

'I say, I'm sorry if I'm interrupting anything, but is there a Mr Robertson-Jones here?'

'Let's hope the superstition holds good,' I said, and Solomon did a double-take.

'Oh, break a leg,' he said. 'Please. Now. Go and jump off something, and break a damned leg.'

Sonia looked lethal and beautiful as Titania, and she'd been cast as Lady Macbeth. She was savage, she was fey, she was heartbroken.

Her sister had committed suicide. She could not bear never seeing her child again. She could not bear the idea that she might have been able to save him.

'Is there nothing that can be done about coroners?' Sonia had demanded. 'Is there really nothing I can do about that man?'

'Give evidence at the inquest,' said Julie, who'd been crying. 'Tell them he was responsible.'

'Yes, tell them.'

'Tell them. Tell them. We'll get the press there. Sonia Loveday's sister, they'll want to know.'

'Tell them, Sonia.'

Lucky black cats, I was painting my little black cats. Should I give one to Sonia?

'Make me glamorous, please,' she said. 'For Fiona.'

'Yes,' I'd answered.

'I don't mean now. You've done that. I will go to that inquest, Glory. I want headlines. Coroner accused of murder by famous actress. Glory, dress me for the inquest. Tell me how I must look.'

'Yes, I will.'

A tight, very brave smile.

'I don't think I'm going to get Oberon,' she said. 'Titania may, but Sonia doesn't. Does she? You lucky bitch?'

I'd done Titania in silver and pale green, not the browns and golds of Oberon, but the younger colours, spring not yet gone.

'Bless you, darling,' she'd said, when she'd still been happy.

Make Sonia catch headlines at her sister's inquest.

Make Mike happy with a fashion show design, to set off clothes that were not as good as the ones he had done last year.

Tell Jacob Goldman that the play might be genius, but only with a genius of a director, a genius of a designer, a cast of total brilliance. Forget it, Uncle Jacob.

Tell the estate agent I don't want the flat. I'm going to live in Stratford, in something half the size. I'm going to redecorate it. Change the décor from gas bill and pair of rugger socks on the television to something light, and bright. Move the cricket bats out of the larder.

'Why have you only got one roller skate?'

'I keep hoping I might find the other one.'

'When did you lose it?'

'About ten years ago.'

He likes his roller skate, don't be bossy. Leave it there. With the broken crash helmet.

'Do you mind if I redecorate the flat?'

'No, I don't mind.'

'I'll leave the bedroom dark.'

'Why? I like looking at you.'

Standing naked in front of the mirror, with Peter behind me.

'You are pink and white and gold,' he said. 'Why isn't that insipid?'

'Because you love me.'

That bloody, bloody clock.

So he threw it away, and bought something that didn't tick. Something with a bright-turquoise face and scarlet hands.

I love you, I love you, I love your silly damned clock.

'What? What did you say?'

Nothing. Nothing.

'Come riding with me one day.'

'I *hate* horses, Peter. I am *terrified* of horses.'

Arms around me, face in my hair, breathing gently.

'All right.'

'Horses broke your leg.'

'No, darling. Falling off a horse broke my leg. Not the horse.'

'Why did you fall off?'

'Because the script said I had to. I'd been shot.'

Peter in Birmingham, at Lawley's, looking around my office.

'Is this yours? All yours?'

'Yes.'

A long, silent whistle. And he was rather quiet for the rest of the day. When I asked him, he said he was having a brood.

'Maternal instincts,' I said, putting my arms around his waist and leaning against him. Waiting for his arms around my shoulders, smiling as I felt them. Broad chest under my cheek. Ribs moving, breathing. Heart beating.

'What?'

'Maternal instincts. That's what Sonia said.'

A long pause.

'Hmm?'

'Sonia said Danny had roused my maternal instincts. He'd made me go broody, and that had made my hormones start playing up. So, when you said you were having a brood I thought maybe you'd gone maternal.'

A sudden shake of laughter.

'No. I don't think so. I've gone chauvinistic, I think. Are you very rich, Glory?'

This was danger. I knew that, even only from reading scripts and novels, I knew this was dangerous.

'Compared to who?' I asked. 'Are you a gigolo?'

Yes, there was a difference in the way he was breathing. In the stillness, the long silence.

'I don't think so.'

'Then it doesn't matter if I'm rich.'

The silence and the stillness went on.

'Unless you're the sort of . . . *boy* . . . who can't stand the idea of a . . . *girl* . . . competing in any way.'

And then I stood back, and looked him straight in the face.

'I can run faster than you, too,' I said.

It took a little while, but he did laugh. And then he smiled, which was even better.

'I'm not rich,' he said.

'And I'm not six foot one.'

He would have to solve this one himself. I'd done all I could.

There was another letter from Leadbetter and Chase in my office at the theatre the next day.

Mr Nicholas Leadbetter was continuing his inquiries on my behalf, and now suspected that Mr Anthony Clinton-Smith and Mr Jonathon Stephenson might have been engaged in activities of a criminal nature. As Mr Leadbetter had informed me in our initial interview, confidentiality could not be guaranteed under these circumstances. Would I please inform them at my earliest convenience if Mr Leadbetter should discontinue his inquiries. In the meantime, and so on.

I telephoned.

'Never mind confidentiality,' I said, 'Mr Leadbetter must continue, as quickly as possible. This is excellent news.'

'Yes, madam. I'll inform Mr Leadbetter. If you could please confirm in writing?'

'Yes, certainly. Does Mr Leadbetter need an assistant? I'm quite prepared to pay.'

'Mr Leadbetter usually works alone, madam, but I will inform him.'

'Thank you. Please give Mr Leadbetter my *very* best wishes. I am delighted with his results so far.'

'I will inform Mr Leadbetter, madam. Thank you.'

I tried to telephone Uncle John, but he was in court. He called me back later that night.

'Ann's been hurt in a riding accident,' he said. 'No, she's all right, don't worry. Well, she's concussed, and she dislocated her shoulder. It happened in Gorsedown Park.'

I felt myself growing cold.

'An accident?' I asked.

'Ah. Quite. Well, that's the official explanation, but no. I doubt it. I'm not quite sure what she was doing, riding

537

there in the dark, but it seems these people set a trap for her. Impossible to prove, unfortunately.'

'How is Ann?' I asked.

'Well, she's out of hospital. She discharged herself, which is rather a pity. I wish she wasn't back at the forge right now.'

He sounded annoyed, which meant he was worried.

'Mr Leadbetter said something about criminal activities,' I said. 'They wouldn't tell me any more than that, but you're a solicitor, did they tell you?'

'Pornographic films,' he said, and I winced.

'Glory?'

'I'm here. What do you mean, they're distributing blue movies?'

'Making them, or so Leadbetter and Chase suspect. It's rather more than blue movies, as you call them.'

'Will it be enough to get them out of Gorsedown?'

He didn't answer immediately, and when he did he sounded even more annoyed.

'I *do* wish I could think of some way of getting Ann out of there for a few days. Oh, yes, I think it'll get the Children of God out of Gorsedown. Leadbetter doesn't know how widespread this is. I'll be in touch when we know more, Glory.'

I sat on my bed, staring down at the floor.

Ann. They'd hurt her. They'd set a trap, and they'd hurt her. A dislocated shoulder, and concussion, she'd been in hospital.

But she wouldn't leave the forge.

I wanted to telephone her, to ask how she was, to beg her to leave, but then she'd know about the private detectives, how else could I have found out about her injuries? She's not suspicious, but she's not stupid, my big sister. How do you know I've been hurt? she'd ask. Who told you?

How would she feel, if she knew that John Mayall and I were paying for the other detectives, the expensive ones, who might make it possible to find out enough? That her Mrs Hunter wasn't working alone?

Tricked, betrayed, belittled. The two people she trusted and loved had treated her as though she was a child.

She would understand our motives, but she would never forgive us, and the confidence she had built up in herself, in her ability to live her own life in her own way, it would be dreadfully damaged.

Oh, Ann, my big sister. Be careful, please be careful.

I wish I knew what to do. I wish I knew.

The first preview for *A Midsummer Night's Dream* was only two days away. Why wasn't I nervous?

Peter was almost frantic.

'Hell. Oh, hell. Hear me on these lines again, darling.'

'Peter, you've been word-perfect on those lines for six weeks.'

'Just once more. Please, Glory.'

'All right, Peter. I'll be Puck again.'

'Please. Oh, damn. Puck rhymes with fuck, and that was no accident, did you know that?'

'Yes, I did, Peter. Should I have dressed Terence as a penis?'

'No. Well, maybe. Sorry, come on. Give me the cue.'

'"I remember."'

'"That very time I saw, but thou couldst not, /Flying between the cold moon and the earth . . ."'

Solomon, stamping around his office and cursing.

'They'll say it's conventional. They'll say there aren't any new ideas. Are there any new ideas?'

Sonia crying, and then not crying, because she couldn't allow her eyes to become swollen.

I'd never ceased to be amazed at the discipline of actors. It was almost inhuman.

Julie, standing in front of her mirror with her hands on her hips.

'I'm going to get drunk, I'm going to get drunk, I swear

I'm going to get drunk. I'm not going on that fucking stage sober, I will not. Glory, where's the vodka?'

'Heide, I'm sorry, but this thing doesn't *fit*. I can't move my arms.'

'Has anybody fixed the lock on the dock doors? No? Because I will *not* open tomorrow if there is the *faintest* chance of some cretin marching on to the stage and asking for the Duke of Edinburgh.'

'Terence, would you like a black cat?'

'Fifty, please, Glory. And rabbits' feet.'

'And a broken leg?'

'Oh, *please*, if you could arrange it with an anaesthetic.'

'Darling, will you hear me on those lines again?'

'No. Go to sleep, Peter. Go to sleep.'

'I can't sleep. I feel sick.'

'Sleep, my love. Oberon, go to sleep.'

'"Macbeth hath mur . . ." Oh, God. Oh, *God*.'

'You're not in the dressing rooms, you're not in the theatre. You're in bed with me.'

'This is the first big part I've had since I got back to England.'

'I know.'

'If I blow this, I'm finished.'

'No, you're not. And anyway, you won't.'

'Hold me. Please hold me. Glory, I'm scared sick.'

'Everybody good always is. It's only the no-hopers who aren't.'

Julie, standing in the wings with her eyes closed, muttering her mantra.

'I'm going to get drunk, I'm going to get drunk. I will not go on that stage sober. I can't.'

Sonia, dry-eyed and savage, looking like spring, looking like a leopard.

Peter. Oh, Peter. Antler, and muscle, and leaves and bark, eye and bone, bared teeth, grinding in tension. Oberon, I love you.

I will not wish you luck. I will say, I love you. I will say, you are a king, Oberon, Peter. You are a king. I love you.

Solomon, pacing in the corridors. They'll say it's conventional, damn their eyes, that's what they'll say. Those *fucking* doors, they *still* haven't fixed the lock. Oh, shit. They'll say it's conventional, I know they will. God. I wish I was dead.

Five minutes, everybody.

A good house. It's packed, darlings. Yes, fine. Well.

Love you, Peter. You are a king, Oberon. I love you.

Donald as Theseus, a deep breath as the house lights dimmed, and then out on to the stage, and his lovely voice, sounding so confident, so clear.

'"Now, fair Hippolyta, our nuptial hour/Draws on apace; four happy days bring in . . ."'

Good, yes, good. They're listening, they are listening. They're looking and listening, he's got them. For now, he's got them. Oh, Peter.

Yes, all right. Good luck, and break a leg, and my fingers are crossed so hard they are hurting. Peter, I love you. I love you.

'I believe in fairies.' 'Solomon Crawley has triumphed. I was enchanted.' 'Sonia Loveday is not only beautiful as Titania, she makes it look easy, which most actresses find impossible. "Superb" is hardly a good enough word.' 'Where has Peter Clements been, and why has he been there so long? Welcome home, Oberon!' 'Trompe l'oeil *without the trickery. Solomon Crawley and Gloriana Mayall have established themselves as champions of the Shakespearian art.'*

Solomon had wandered into my office, looking shy and diffident. He hated reading reviews, but he knew I'd have all the papers, and he couldn't resist coming to ask.

'"*Crawley takes a four-hundred-year-old play and turns it into a slashing indictment of the modern monarchist establishment*",' I read as he hovered over my desk. 'Clever old Creepy. Did you know you'd done that?'

'Um. Subconsciously, yes, of course I knew. Knew it all the time. Naturally. What paper's that?'

'*The Star*, of course, what do you think?'

Solomon scratched his head.

'*Is The Dream* four hundred years old?'

This time. This time, they'd mentioned me by name, and they'd mentioned the set, and they'd liked it. This time I'd done it.

'Solomon?'

I was looking up at him, my face as serious as I could make it.

'Oh, God. They're dreadful, aren't they? Those notices, they're dreadful, I knew they would be. They've said it's conventional, I knew they would. Oh, hell. What about the cast?'

I relented. This was a cruel joke.

'Solomon, they're super. They are *fabulous* notices. Look. Look, read them. They won't bite, I promise.'

'I can't. It was conventional, I know it was.'

'Listen, then. Listen to this.

'"*I'm going to Athens for my holiday, and I hope it's half as good as this production.*"'

I pushed it across the desk towards him, and reached for another.

'"*I loved my evening in Stratford.* And, where's that one that talks about you? I think it was the *Telegraph*, it's . . .'

But he was already reading it.

'Solomon?'

'Uh. They could have been nicer to Terence.'

'Oh, please. Creepy? Please, I've got to tell somebody.'

'What? What is it?'

But I couldn't tell him. I could only show him, the letter I'd read so often that I knew it by heart, and that I still couldn't believe.

I'd been nominated for the new Equity Design Award.

It had been on my desk that morning, an expensive-looking envelope, heavy cream paper.

Thick, heavy cream paper, an embossed letterhead, I'd been puzzled when I'd started to read it. Then I'd had to read it three times before I understood.

I'd never thought about awards.

'Ah,' said Solomon as his eyes travelled down the page. 'Yes, I thought you must be one of the contenders. How nice to be proved right.'

He looked up and smiled at me, the smile spread into a grin, and then he was round my side of the desk and hugging me, and laughing.

'That is *really* great,' he said. 'This is one of the big ones. Oh, Glory! Well done. This goes up on the wall, this is a Roll of Honour thing.'

So he pinned my letter up on the wall by the stage door, and for the rest of the day people knocked, and looked in, and gave me thumbs-up signs, and told me it was no more than I deserved.

'Oh, darling!' said Sonia, who just bounded into my office without even bothering to knock. 'I mean, joking aside, that really is something. It's international, isn't it? Broadway, and all that?'

'What's Broadway?'

'Love it. *Love* it. I believe I heard it's somewhere in the colonies, but I forget.'

She rolled a wary eye at the newspapers on my desk.

'Are those, er . . .?'

'There's nobody you can sue, I'm afraid.'

'Oh, damn. I was counting on a nice libel action to top up the coffers.'

Julie, with an orchid for me.

'I'm one step ahead of the police,' she said. 'Drunk and disorderly.'

'You've read your notices, then?'

'*Hush!* They must have been blotto. Or maybe they weren't there, perhaps they all went to the wrong theatre.'

'That's the answer, of course. Why didn't I think of that?'

Julie threw me a delighted smile as she left.

I tried to bring myself back to reality by starting sketches of *Macbeth* sets, but it was impossible to concentrate. I laid down my pencil, and looked out of the window at ragged clouds blowing across the pale sky.

'This I am pleased to hear,' said Jacob when I spoke to him. 'This is a sign of intelligence and taste creeping into the theatre when nobody was looking. I'd have been surprised if you weren't on the list. I'd have been offended, too. None of my other pickpockets have been nominated.'

'Uncle Jacob, I think I do want that contract. I love these people. I love them.'

'Then I will see what I can do in the way of blackmail and bribery. Blackmail used to be cheaper, but now they just want the hype. Publish and be blessed, haven't you got a better photograph than that? It's heartbreaking.'

And Ann. I would go down and see her, I would see bandages, I would demand an explanation, and then I might get her to leave. I could still act a bit, I could become hysterical with anxiety. They tried to kill you, they tried to kill you, I'd scream. Come away now. Please, come back with me.

There'd be tears, I'd beseech her to leave, I'd threaten to go and see these Children of God maniacs, I'd make her leave with me.

My celebration of this nomination would be the only excuse I'd need. I'd telephone, I wouldn't listen to her protests, just tell her I'm coming down and bringing champagne, I've got something wonderful to celebrate and I want to celebrate it with you.

And hang up quickly, before she could shout me down.

I'd have to ask Solomon if I could go to Anford. I should be here, he might say he needed me here. Nothing had gone wrong on the press night, but that didn't mean it couldn't tonight.

I went back to the Green Room, and asked.

'Yes, you go. Come in early tomorrow in case we need repairs.'

It had been quieter by then. Most of the cast had gone, just a few sitting around the tables, talking quietly, drinking coffee, reading.

I went back to my office, I sat in the armchair and looked out of the window, and I was smiling. My nomination, and *A Midsummer Night's Dream*. It had been a success, the critics had liked it. This time they'd mentioned me by name, and the set, and Peter was their darling.

And Sonia.

'Sonia Loveday is beautiful as Titania.'

Dear Sonia. You looked magnificent. Perhaps her last chance in this sort of role, it's Lady Macbeth for the next one, and then you might be looking at the nurse in *Romeo and Juliet*.

It's a cruel world, this one, for a Shakespearian actress growing old.

I telephoned Ann, but she wasn't there. There was only her answering machine. I left a message telling her I was coming for a celebration and bringing champagne, and that I'd tell her all about it when I got there.

I was glad she hadn't been there. I hadn't had to lie to her.

I started to read the list of notes the stage manager had made on the first night performance. Time to stop dreaming and celebrating. Time to get back to work.

It was early in the evening when Nicholas Leadbetter telephoned.

'Miss Mayall, I can't continue with this inquiry. The police are now involved.'

'What's happened?'

'I'm afraid I'm not at liberty to discuss it with you, I did warn you that might happen. But I do very strongly recommend that your sister should leave the forge, immediately. Can you get her out of there?'

'Can't you tell me anything?'

545

'They make films, Miss Mayall, they're known as "snuff" movies. I can tell you that Mrs Hargrave has not managed to interview any of the refugees who've stayed at Gorsedown. She hasn't managed to trace them. This is very unusual. The implications are most unpleasant.'

'I don't understand.'

'Try to get your sister to leave. I'm sure the police will do their best to protect her, but if you can persuade her to leave, please do so. I don't think it will be for long.'

'All right. I'll try.'

'Please do.'

I didn't try to telephone Ann. I was going down anyway, Solomon had given me permission and I stood a far better chance of persuading her to leave if I could see her.

Tom Kelvin's secretary telephoned from Birmingham. A message from my sister, would I please call her, urgently.

'Alice, if she calls again, could you please tell her you didn't manage to contact me?'

'If you say so.'

She sounded doubtful, a little resentful. She didn't like lying.

'I really wouldn't ask if it wasn't absolutely necessary.'

No, Ann, I will not call you. You will tell me not to come. You will make an excuse to put me off, and I will not be put off. I think you are in danger.

I was about to leave when Peter came to find me. He wanted to congratulate me himself, and he said he wanted a little peace and sanity.

'Solomon tells me your notices were good,' he said. 'They don't often mention the set. Well done, my love.'

I tried to set my anxiety about Ann aside. Peter deserved my attention, too. Just for a few minutes, and then I must go. I must go and find Ann.

'And yours?' I asked. 'Did he tell you about yours? I always knew yours would be good. Oh, Peter, you did earn

546

them. I went weak at the knees just looking at you from the wings.'

'So now you fancy Oberon, do you?'

'God, yes. I always did. Right from the time I first put grease paint on him.'

I'm not very tall. I'm only a bit taller than the height of Peter's shoulder, which he said made me the ideal size for him to rest his chin on my head when he held me.

I always knew when he was smiling, when we stood like that, and I wanted to stay, holding him, close to him.

Ann.

'Peter, I must go. Listen, I have to go and find Ann. That detective, Leadbetter, he said I should get her out of there.'

'Why? Glory, what's happened? What's the matter?'

'I don't know,' I said. 'Honestly, I don't know. He telephoned and said he was having to drop the case. He said the police are involved, and I should try to get Ann away if I could. He really sounded worried. So, I must go, Peter. I must get her to come away.'

'These Children of God?' he asked.

'Yes. Peter, what are "snuff" movies?'

He was very still, he'd stopped breathing.

'Peter?'

I looked up at him. He was staring over my head, staring at nothing, and still not breathing.

'Peter, what is it?'

He shivered, his head turned, he tried to smile at me, but he looked so strange.

'Why do you ask about snuff movies, Glory?'

I reached up and touched his face. It was rigid under my fingers, and he was white.

'Somebody mentioned them. He said . . . Peter?'

'Oh, Jesus. Who? How did they find out?'

His jaw, clenched under my fingers, his face white, he was staring down at me. Peter. Peter, what is this? What have you done?

547

'Who was it . . .?' And then a great shuddering sigh, and he turned away from me.

'Oh, God. You didn't know.'

'Peter, what is this, please? Tell me.'

'Yes,' he said, almost as if he could not believe it. 'I'll have to tell you. I'll have to.'

But he turned away from me, he wouldn't look at me as he spoke.

'They kill people,' he said. 'To make films, pornographic films. Sadism. They kill people, they really do kill them. They torture them to death, and they film it. That's what a snuff movie is, Glory.'

She'd have done that. If the Rat had asked, she'd have done that, the thin girl. For Rat Wright, and for the money.

'And you?' I asked him.

'Yes. No. I don't know. Truly, I don't know. I don't think so, but I don't know.'

It was after he'd done the photographs for the magazine, there still hadn't been enough money for the hospital bills for his broken leg. He'd been telephoned, and offered money, quite a lot of money, to make the films. He'd made one, a group orgy, about ten people, they'd all been high on drugs. He didn't know which drugs, he'd been ill for about a week afterwards. He couldn't remember much about the film, about what he'd done, and he didn't try very hard. What he could remember was bad enough.

They'd come back and said he had to do the second one. He'd be paid for both when he'd done the second one. Not an orgy this time, just him and a girl. He'd be drugged again.

And he was. He was confused, and sick, and they told him the girl had agreed, and that anyway she'd had an anaesthetic. That they were paying her a lot of money, and that she'd agreed, and that she'd had an anaesthetic.

And that she was a very good actress.

And he was drugged.

'I can't tell you any more, Glory,' he said. 'I can't. I can't say . . . I can't tell you what I did.'

'Did she die?' I asked.

'No.' He shook his head. 'No, she didn't die. I stopped. I didn't believe she was just acting.

'They said I had to go on. They said she needed the money, and she wouldn't get paid if I didn't. But I didn't believe she was acting. She didn't speak English, you see. She was Chinese, I think. I was sick and confused from those drugs, I didn't know what to do, but I knew I was hurting her.

'So I wouldn't. I said I wouldn't. I was throwing up by then, I'd had a bad reaction to the drugs. I had cramp, I could hardly move. Anyway, I wouldn't do it any more.

'They put me in a car and drove me down to the beach. They threw me out. I never saw them again, any of them.'

'Oh, Peter. Oh, God. Peter.'

'A few weeks later the police found some bodies. They'd been tortured. Not the Chinese girl, thank God. Not her. But the people who'd made the films, they'd gone. They'd got away. I think it was Venezuela. South America, anyway.'

'Oh, Peter.'

I went over to him, I held him, but he hardly seemed to know I was there.

'When I think what I did. When I remember what I did. I can hardly bear this. Oh, God. God. I don't think I can ever forgive myself.'

'Peter, darling. My love. Darling.'

'Glory.' He was whispering, his voice was dry and tight, he was whispering my name.

'Glory, it was filthy. It was dreadful, what I did. It was filthy. And I don't know what happened to her. They didn't find a Chinese girl's body, but I still don't know. How can I know? Maybe they didn't find them all. I don't know.

'I've always dreaded somebody finding out. Oh, God. When you asked, I thought somebody had found out. I thought somebody had found out what I'd done, and told you.'

I held him, and I told him I loved him, I tried to comfort him.

Ann. My big sister. They kill people. They kill people.

And repeated, over and over again in the back of my mind, like some dreadful refrain chanted by a Greek chorus.

I am haunted. I am haunted.

35

Peter didn't want me to go. He begged me not go. He said the idea of me being in the same country as people who did this sort of thing was bad enough, next door to them was intolerable.

'Didn't you understand?' he begged. 'What they do, Glory?'

'I've got to get Ann out.'

He was shaking.

'I *hate* this,' he said. 'I hate the idea of you being any-where near them.'

'But I've got to get her out.'

'Don't go alone,' he said. 'Please don't go alone. Hire a bodyguard, or something. Please.'

'There's no time. I must go now. And what can happen? Darling, honestly, what can happen?'

But his eyes were frantic.

'There *must* be some other way. And don't ask me what can happen. I know what can happen, Glory. I've seen it. Christ. I *did* it.'

It's not a long way from Stratford, if the roads are clear, but to me it seemed as if I would never reach the village. There were road works and diversions, and a traffic jam. A lorry had shed a load of copper pipes, and I was blocked in, I couldn't get past and I couldn't turn round.

Half an hour, and then we were allowed past, slowly, about five at a time, with the police alternating the traffic flow from each direction.

Then I was behind the slow lorries that had also been delayed.

In the end I gave up trying to overtake them, and I left the main road and tried to find my way down the small country lanes, I wasn't sure of the way.

I stopped twice to check my map, but the roads were difficult, I couldn't be sure which of the small junctions were marked, where I was on the map. It wasn't even up to date.

It was beginning to get dark.

Little roads. The car was fast, but I couldn't see. Blind corners, little twisty roads, I couldn't see.

Don't let me be too late.

Glory, they kill people.

Ann, they kill people. Come away. Now. Right now.

There was a signpost, I slowed down and read it.

Anford, two miles.

I was nearly there.

There were people in the road, waving me down. Shouting. 'Stop! Stop!'

A group of young women, they were right across the road, I couldn't get past. What is this, an accident?

An ambush?

I threw the car into reverse, but they were there, all around me, behind the car. Beside me, tapping on the window, smiling at me.

'Are you the blacksmith's sister?' 'She sent us to look out for you, she said you'd be coming this way.' 'It is you, isn't it? You're the blacksmith's sister?' 'Hello, Glory! Hello, I'm Susie, hello, Glory!' 'It is you, isn't it?'

The passenger door was open, there were two of them there.

552

'It is you, isn't it?' 'It is, it is!' 'Doesn't look much like her, does she?'

They were giggling.

'We're going to have a party. You're coming to a party.'

'Get out of my car!'

They'd got the keys.

'We're going to have a party, a party, a party.' 'Come on, Glory.' 'Come to the party, Glory. Glory-Glory, come to the party.'

'Get out of my car, and give me back my keys. Now, please.'

'Your sister's waiting for you.' 'We've got her, Glory-Glory.' 'Hello, Glory. I'm Susie. Hello. Hello.'

Oh, God. They've got her. Ann. Ann, they kill people.

Peter, they've got Ann. They kill people.

Peter, they've got me.

'Get out of the car, Glory-Glory.' 'Hello, Glory, I'm Susie. Hello.' 'Come to the party. Come to the party.'

I tried to push one of them away, and she grinned at me, seized my hand, and bit, hard. I felt the skin break under her teeth.

'Get out of the car, Glory-Glory. Out of the car. Out. Out. Out.'

Hands wound in my hair, pulling.

'Let go, let go of me.'

'*Out* of the car. Right.' 'Hello, Glory, I'm Susie.'

Giggling, they were all giggling, and I was kneeling by the side of the road with my arms twisted up behind my back, and two of them holding my hair.

'We're going to have a party, Glory-Glory.'

They drove my car away. Two of them, in my car, giggling.

I watched my little car, weaving down the road.

Crash it, bitches. I hope it burns.

'It can go faster than that!' I yelled after them, and somebody kicked me.

'Hello, Glory-Glory. I'm Susie.'

'I could give you some tips about your acne, Susie. Like a face amputation.'

Another kick, this one harder, in my ribs. I thought I felt something break.

They kill people.

They dragged me off the verge, through a gate into a field, pulling my hair, twisting my arms. I gritted my teeth. I will not cry out. I will not let them know this hurts.

'Party! Party! Going to have a party, Glory-Glory.'

'What is this? What is this Glory-Glory nonsense? I'm not called Glory.'

Think. For God's sake, think of a name.

Another kick, this time against my knee, and a slap across my face.

'Who are you, then? *Who*, then? What's your *name*, then?'

There's a monogram on my powder compact. My initials.

'What's your *name*, Glory?' 'Hello, Glory, come to the party.' 'Glory-Glory, it *is* you, it *is*.'

Another slap, and one of them wrenched at my hair, hard.

'Grace, my name's Grace.'

A kick in my stomach, and for a moment I couldn't breathe. I couldn't catch my breath, but it gave me a moment to think.

'Grace Martin.'

It hardly sounded like my voice. But I'd given them a name.

'Why are you driving Glory-Glory's car, Gracie? Why are you driving her car?' 'It was her car, wasn't it?' 'Naughty Glory, telling fibs.' 'Hello, Glory, I'm Susie. Hello.'

How did they know about my car?

They were still giggling. One of them bent down over me, giggling into my face. I closed my eyes.

'*Look* at me, Glory-Glory. *Look* at me.'

Another slap, this time it made my eyes water. I blinked,

and tried to shake my head. The giggling face came closer.

'Tracey Smith told us about your nice little red car,' she said. 'Grace! *Liar!*'

She wasn't giggling, her teeth were bared, and she punched me hard, low in my stomach. I began to retch.

Tracey Smith. If Gloriana Mayall is prepared to pay for information, the Children of God, who own four square miles of land and a manor house, might pay more, to learn that someone is snooping.

What a fool I'd been. She'd do anything for money, Tracey Smith.

'Let me go.'

Was that my voice? That croaking gasp?

Tracey Smith. I'd even told her what I knew, what Nicholas Leadbetter had found out. I'd as good as told her she wasn't the only one checking up on the Children of God. How could I have been such a fool? He'd warned me, and still I'd told her.

And she'd told them.

'Let's go and meet your *sister*. Ins*tead*.'

Somebody spat in my face.

'Glory-Glory. We're going to have such a party, Glory-Glory.'

They hadn't got Ann. They wanted me to telephone her. I was to tell her, we were all invited to a party.

They pulled me to my feet, but there were three of them holding me, my hair, my arms, twisted high behind my back.

'Walk,' said the girl who had spat in my face. '*Walk*, Glory-Glory. Walk to the telephone box. And invite your sister to our party.'

Right, I thought, I will do that. I will telephone, and as soon as I can I will scream a warning to Ann.

They kill people.

They can only kill me once. I think I would rather they did that, quickly, than take me to a party.

I don't want to die at one of those parties. Not that way.
They had knives.

Good.

When I fight, and I will fight, they'll have to use them.

But I might get away.

Giggling at me, they were all giggling. They stood by the telephone box, holding the door open.

'Come on, Glory-Glory. Ask your sister to the party.' 'Glory-Glory.' 'Not much like her, is she?' 'Ask her to the party.'

Right. Get them off their guard, let them think I'm frightened.

God, I'm so frightened.

'Ann?' My voice was shaking. 'It's Glory. I'm at the . . .'

I put my hand over the telephone.

'Where the hell am I?' I demanded.

'Hello, Glory-Glory. I'm Susie.' 'Ask her to the party, Glory-Glory.' 'Go on, Glory, ask her to the party.'

'Sorry, I'm not sure where I am. They're giving a party for you. They want you to come.'

Ann, speak to me, I haven't heard your voice. Is this a trap? Ann, are you there?

'Who are? What are you talking about?'

Yes, it's Ann. They haven't got her. I may yet be able to warn her, even get away. If they think I'm frightened enough. If they think I'll go along with this.

Ask questions. Don't finish the sentence before you scream a warning.

'Your neighbours, they say.' Smile, a little laugh. Pleading. See how good I'm being. I'm doing what you say. See how good I'm being. Please don't hurt me.

'They're awfully insistent that you should come.'

She was silent. Ann, they kill people.

Don't finish the sentence before you scream a warning. Take them by surprise.

'Just a minute, one of them . . .'

556

They didn't use a knife, they used a torch, I think. A heavy torch, behind my ear, a hard, short blow, and they had the telephone, one of them was speaking into it, I was trying to think. I was shaking my head, trying to think. Everything was blurred, I couldn't think. They were talking, I couldn't think.

I had to scream a warning. Now, scream a warning.

'Ann, get away, they kill people!'

But I was too late. They'd hung up. She hadn't heard.

'Now, how did you know that, Glory-Glory?'

And giggling, they were still giggling.

'I've seen your picture, Glory. I've seen your picture.' 'Hello, Glory. Hello, Glory.' 'Seen your picture, naughty Glory. That poor man, all bloody.'

Giggling, and whispering behind their hands.

'Naughty Glory! Seen your picture. Seen your picture.'

They'd tied my hands behind my back. Wire. I could feel it, cutting into my wrists.

My head hurt, I couldn't see properly. There was blood in my hair, I could feel it, warm and sticky.

Get away from them, get away. Even if they kill you it'll be better. They're going to kill you anyway. At a party.

Wire, around my wrists.

Hands in my hair, dragging me, and a van, a white van, the doors open.

They hit me again, on the back of the head, and I fell.

I can't think, I can't think. How can I get away if I can't think? Stop hitting me, I can't think.

I was in the van, lying on the floor. They'd thrown me in the van, and it was jolting. Where are they taking me?

One of my ribs, broken, I could feel it grinding. Breathing hurt. I couldn't think. My head, everything was blurred. Sticky blood in my hair. My wrists were bleeding.

Two of them in the back of the van, no, more. More of them. How many? They were holding my hair, twisting it. That hurts.

I can't think. I can't think. How can I get away if I can't think?

Must get away. They kill people.

The doors opened, they dragged me out.

There was a fire.

Oh, no. No, not that. Don't burn me. I've never done that. I've never done that. I don't deserve that.

Again, a blow to my head, near my neck, everything was going dark, there were noises, there were loud noises, a roaring noise in my head.

Then club me to death, yes. But not the fire, I've never done that. I don't deserve that.

The knives, I've used knives, yes.

Wire on my knees. Cutting into my knees. A tree, they were tying me to a tree, with wire, and the wire was cutting, they were hanging me from the tree by my knees and my wrists. Knives in my clothes, knives, I could feel them sliding against my skin, I'm cold, I'm cold.

They were singing. The little knives were flashing in the firelight, and they were singing. I was cold, hanging from the tree by my knees and my wrists, I was naked, and the wire was cutting, and I was cold. I watched them dancing, and they were singing, I watched the little knives.

I've used knives, yes. I've used knives. You can do that, I've used knives.

That noise, am I making that noise? I remember this. I heard laughter, and I heard screams, I remember this. I was screaming, I remember this.

I've used knives, I've cut with knives. I deserve this, you can do this, yes, I've used the knives.

My body, moving, fighting the wire, my voice screaming. There is blood, there is blood, I can see the blood, I can see my body, writhing against the wire.

A pale face, sweating, with dark hair. Lucien, is that you? Lucien? Pale, a pale face, white. Lucien? Is that you?

Laughing, I've heard the laughter. I did hear them

laughing, then, I did hear, and I hear them now, I hear them, I hear the laughter.

You were wrong, Peter. I was there. It was me.

And screaming. So loud, so loud, these screams. Is this me, screaming? Again, is this me? This cannot be, this.

Lucien. Yes, Lucien, you're here. Is that you, screaming? You did scream, Lucien.

There is pain, there is so much pain it cannot be true, this cannot be pain, this, that is happening now. This is not. This is not true. This cannot go on, this pain, this can not be.

Faces, and voices calling in the dark, I can hear the voices. Those others, I don't know their names, I heard them. I can hear now. They screamed then. Yes, so now I must scream.

I had the knives, I had knives.

It is dark, it is dark, the faces in the dark. I hear their voices now. I hear them calling. I am haunted. There are faces in the dark. There are voices calling, I hear the voices. I am haunted.

You were wrong, Peter. I was there. It was me. I am the thin child, it is me. This body, thin. A child's body. In the dark, in the firelight, a child's body. Thin, and bruised, and screaming.

It is me, Peter. It was always me.

Don't be sad. Don't be sad, my love. I had knives, and I had whips. Tell me what you want me to do. Tell me what you want. You will cry. You will beg. You will scream.

Blood is beautiful. Yes, Peter, blood is a beautiful colour.

Screaming, and screaming, but this is not me. There is no pain now, I can be quiet. I can be quiet, and still, in the darkness, there is no pain now.

There were lights, there was noise, I could hear shouting. Blue lights, and shouting, people there, so many people, shouting, and running, and there were lights, bright lights.

So many people, but I want to be quiet now. Let me be quiet, now.

You were wrong, my love, Peter, my love. You were

wrong. This is me, this thin child. Bruised, and I was screaming. Thin. Where there were breasts, I can see bone. Thin, I am her. I was always her. I will always be her, now. So let me go. Let me go. I want to go, now.

I am haunted. I am haunted.

Let me go, now.

36

I wanted to die, and they wouldn't let me.

Let me go, I thought.

It was quiet, there was no more shouting, and the lights were clear and bright. Everything was white. There were brilliant lights, and the people were dressed in white, talking, and moving around. They didn't speak to me, only to each other. I could hear them, and I could see them, if I opened my eyes.

Let me go now. I want to go. I will die. I *will* die.

'Her heart's stopped again.'

'Right, stand back, everybody. Everybody clear?'

A jolt, the body gave a sudden lurch on the white table, and I was back again. They wouldn't let me go.

Please let me go, I thought. Please let me die now. I want to die now.

The lights were bright and clear and I could see. People were bending over my face, looking into my eyes. They were holding my eyes open and shining lights into them.

'Can you hear me? Can you hear me?'

'Do we know her name yet?'

Please let me go.

Then there was darkness, and quiet, a feeling as though the darkness was rolling through me.

Light again, daylight. Voices I could hear, people I could see, if I opened my eyes. But I wanted to be quiet, I didn't want them to know I am here, in this body, the wrong body.

Please let me go now.

Sometimes I opened my eyes, but if they were looking at me I closed them again. I didn't want anybody to see me there, not in that body. When they were looking at me, if I opened my eyes they came over.

'Can you hear me? Glory, can you hear me? Gloriana?'

There was pain, but I kept very still, so they would not know I was there. I couldn't stop the sweat. When they saw that, they wiped my face, and then there'd be the darkness again. I felt as if I was rolling in the darkness, and the darkness was rolling through me. Perhaps, then, perhaps there, I could go away.

Back in the light, I could hear again, I could see again. If I opened my eyes.

'Nurse? Nurse, she's sweating again.'

Uncle John. I knew that voice. Uncle John.

So I will not open my eyes, I will not be here in this body. I will go back into the darkness, where I cannot be found. I will try to stay in the darkness. I will try.

Let me go. Please, let me go. I do not want to be here, in the light, in this body. Please, let me go back into the darkness, let me stay in the darkness.

'Can she hear me?'

'We think so. Try talking to her.'

There was movement by my head and a shadow across my face.

'Glory, it's Uncle John. Can you hear me, my dear?'

No, I cannot hear, I cannot see, I will not listen to you. I will not be here.

He wouldn't go away, and I could not find the darkness again.

I opened my eyes.

'Hello, Glory.'

562

Ann was there, she was bandaged, on her head and on her neck. Her arm was in a sling.

Ann doesn't talk much, she's always quiet. She sat by the side of my bed, I liked having her there. Sometimes she'd speak to me, sometimes she'd just be quiet.

It had been a week, she said. I'd nearly died.

Nearly. I'd nearly managed it. I'd nearly got away.

There was a doctor who talked, even though I would not open my eyes.

'We can reconstruct quite a lot these days. You have been badly hurt, but you can look forward to a normal life, in most respects.'

Not in this body. No, not a normal life, not in this body.

'Do you think you could talk to the police now?'

I kept my eyes closed. If my eyes are closed, I am not here. They cannot see me.

'Can you talk? Have you hurt your throat?'

'Does anybody know, was there a throat injury?'

They moved me into another room. They said I was out of danger.

Ann came every day, and Uncle John. He was staying with her at the forge.

Uncle John asked if I could talk to the police, but I kept my eyes closed. I only opened my eyes if Ann was there, alone. Or sometimes by accident, because if I opened my eyes they knew I was there.

The police had caught them all, the Children of God, Stephenson Holdings. I'd driven into Anford as the police had raided Gorsedown, but they hadn't known the women were back in Anford, they'd thought they were still in the town, begging, for the charity. Reconcile.

'They knew you were coming. They listened to my answering machine. They heard you say you were coming for a celebration.'

They'd been in Anford, those women, looking for me. I was the blacksmith's sister, and it was the blacksmith who

563

had destroyed them. I was Gloriana Mayall, who'd set a private detective on them, who'd found out too much, who'd mentioned refugees. They'd have been glad I was coming. They'd have been glad to have given a party for me.

They'd been on amphetamines.

I listened, I listened to Ann, and I listened to Uncle John. There was a policeman, but I kept my eyes closed. He mustn't know I am here, in this body.

Yes, they had tried to kill Ann. They had set a trap for her in the park, and she'd only just got away. They'd killed her dog, and her horse had been hurt.

I opened my eyes and looked at her when she said that. There were tears on her cheeks. We were alone in the room when she told me about the dog, so I reached out my hand and I touched hers.

I love you, my big sister, said my hand. I'm sorry about your dog. I know you loved your dog.

After they'd tried to kill Ann the police had started to investigate. There was no proof it was anything other than a riding accident, and she'd been concussed, but the police had believed her then.

I nearly smiled when she told me about Mrs Hunter, who'd found out about the films they made. Yes, they'd been killing people, they'd been making their films, refugees sent to Gorsedown by the charity Reconcile, for a holiday, for a little break. Refugees can disappear. Nobody asks for long, when there isn't a family.

But Mrs Hargrave had been looking for refugees who'd been at Gorsedown, and she hadn't found any. Where had they gone, the ones who'd been there for their little holidays? Where had they gone, when the little holidays were over?

Nicholas Leadbetter, and Cynthia Hargrave, they'd found out enough.

And Mrs Hunter.

When they discovered what had happened, the police moved very fast.

Ann sat by my bed, quietly, holding my hand. When I opened my eyes and looked at her, she told me what had happened.

A little bit at a time, she told me.

Holding my hand. Crying, sometimes. Telling me what had happened, a little bit at a time.

The Children of God had been in Scotland and in Yorkshire before they went to Gorsedown. Drug addicts and alcoholics, they can disappear, they often disappear. Nobody looks for long. Just another junkie, just another drunk.

The Children of God, and Anthony Clinton-Smith had set himself up as a god, his followers were to worship him. There were sacrifices, and they were filmed.

The police had found films, and cameras. And they'd found bodies, buried in the grounds.

'It was the most appalling bad luck, you coming down that day,' said Uncle John.

No. I'd had knives, too. It was right, what had happened. It was justice.

They operated on me. I thought I might be able to die when I went back into the darkness, I thought this time I might manage to stay there, but there was daylight again, and more pain. More sweat, but no more darkness. Tubes in my arms, needles. It didn't matter.

Lucille, screaming and hysterical, saying it was all Uncle John's fault for allowing Ann to be a blacksmith. If Ann hadn't been a blacksmith this wouldn't have happened.

I kept my eyes closed, and they took her away. She was sobbing. There was an old man with her, but they didn't know I was there. I kept my eyes closed.

I had another operation, but I didn't want this. If I couldn't escape into the darkness I didn't want to go there any more. This body is nothing now.

Some people die even when you don't kill them.

I learned that. I learned it when the nurse came in and told me Peter was there, he wanted to see me.

No. No.

I was frantic, I had to get away. Not Peter. No. Please, not Peter, no.

Ann touched my face, and said she'd tell him.

Glory died in the wood that night. There's nothing for you here, Peter.

I will answer to the name, Glory. I can use that name. I have the memories, but Glory has died.

More operations, they said, they could do a lot for me.

Leave this body alone. It doesn't matter. I don't want it. Leave it alone.

I couldn't live with my eyes closed, I wanted to get out of there.

'Take me home,' I asked Ann.

But they said there had to be at least one more operation, because of the pain.

Yes, there's pain, but that's right. I know about pain. That's justice, too.

'Take me home,' I begged. 'Take me home now.'

I couldn't speak. My throat was tight.

Lucien hanged himself, perhaps this is why I cannot speak. My voice creaks, like a rope against wood. My throat feels tight.

Just one more operation, and I agreed, because of the tears in Ann's eyes.

Roly came to see me.

'You're going to need a psychiatrist,' he said. 'I'd like it to be me. It's your choice.'

Dr Roland Mantsch. He put his card on the table by my bed, but I just looked up at him.

Peter said you wanted to hear about the thin girl, Roly. Well, here she is.

'My practice isn't far from Anford,' said Roly. 'I'll come

and see you there until you can come to me. I don't usually make house calls, but Peter's a good friend.'

And will you tell Peter about the thin child who answers to the name of Glory? I wondered, still looking up at him.

'I don't discuss my patients, even with my very good friends,' he said, though I hadn't spoken.

'Ann, take me home with you.'

They took me to the forge in an ambulance, and Ann carried me up the stairs because climbing the stairs hurt too much, then. She laid me down on a narrow bed in a little room at the front of the house.

'You'll be all right here, Glory,' she said. 'You can live here with me. I'll take care of you.'

When she had gone I curled up on the bed, I pressed my face into my knees and wrapped my arms around them. I was cold. It was bright summer, but I was so cold.

Later that week Roly came to see me. He sat in a chair by the window, as I had liked to do, and I was on the bed, pressed tight into the corner of the walls, my knees drawn up close.

I watched him.

'Peter said you'd agreed to tell me about the thin girl.'

Roly didn't speak again. He sat by the window, waiting, not looking at me, not avoiding looking at me, just being there, waiting.

I watched him. I was close into the corner, sitting with my back against the wall, my knees drawn up to my chest. I was as far away from him as I could be.

Minutes passed. The shadows of Roly and the chair grew longer on the floor, and I watched.

Be careful, Roly.

He waited, not looking, not speaking.

'Here she is,' I said.

'Ah.'

A policeman came, and he had photographs to show me. I had razors, I had whips, I had knives. There were men

567

hanging from a wall behind me, men lying on the floor, standing, kneeling.

'We found these at Gorsedown,' he said. 'Do you recognise them?'

I shook my head.

'She's very like you.'

I couldn't speak to strangers. I could only talk to Ann, and a little to Uncle John. Roly. But I couldn't speak to strangers. The rope would tighten around my throat, and I would fight it as it creaked against the wood.

I could not breathe, I could only gasp.

'Well,' he said, 'there were hundreds of photographs. It was quite an industry. But we couldn't help but notice the likeness, in these ones. Sorry, we did have to ask.'

Ann carried me upstairs again, and sent the policeman away.

Ann had nightmares about the Children of God. I heard her at nights, and I crept into her room, and stroked her forehead.

Sometimes she cried for her dog, the one they'd killed.

In the evenings when she finished work she closed the gate and put the chain on it, and then I came down and we sat together on the little lawn behind the cottage, because nobody could see that lawn from the road. Ann had to do exercises for her shoulder, she'd dislocated it when they'd set the trap for her in the park. They'd told her two of her friends were being taken away. She'd ridden into the park after them, knowing it was a trap, but not daring to ignore it in case it wasn't, in case she could save her friends. They'd set a tripwire, and they'd made her horse bolt into it. She'd seen the wire and thrown herself clear, and the dog had held them off until she'd climbed on to the horse again.

They'd had hammers, they were going to kill her, if she survived the fall. She'd managed to get back on the horse, but it had bolted with her.

That was when they'd killed the dog. She grieved for her dog.

It's a strange story, the forge at Anford. It's so old, it's not surprising it's haunted. Ann doesn't know it's haunted.

I told Roly it's haunted. People have died because of this place, of course it's haunted.

Two of the women died in the wood that night.

Ann had tried to save me. She'd ridden into the woods on a gypsy pony she'd been shoeing, but she hadn't got there in time. Two of the women had been killed, the pony had reared and hit one of them in the face with its hoof, and Ann had killed another. Ann had been trying to reach me, and the woman had stabbed her. Ann had broken the woman's neck.

I'd been unconscious by then. I didn't know.

But I did remember the time in the hospital, when Uncle John had been there and I'd kept my eyes closed, so they wouldn't know. Ann would cry sometimes.

'If I'd had Lyric I'd have got there in time,' she'd say. 'I might have been in time, if I'd had Lyric.'

'Who haunts the forge?' asked Roly.

I was tired by then, I didn't want to answer.

'Lucien?' he asked.

That was stupid. Lucien haunts me, not the forge, he knows that.

I liked listening to Ann. She knew that. I could ask her questions, and she'd answer.

When Ann was better, somebody lent her a horse.

I smiled when she told me, but I was frightened. People can be killed by horses. She said the horse was like an arm-chair on legs, but she loved riding. Her shoulder wasn't strong enough for her to manage her own horse.

Another few months, she said, and she'd have Lyric back.

There was an inquest on the women who'd died in the wood. Roly wrote to the coroner saying I couldn't give evidence.

'You won't have to give evidence at the trials either,' he said.

'There's nothing I could tell them.'

'It's time I stopped coming here. You can come to Gloucester. Ann says she can bring you.'

'No.'

'Yes.'

'People will see me.'

'One day that won't matter. You'll understand that soon.'

People can look at me, and know. The thin child never pretended to be anything else. They can look, and know what she is and what she did.

Ann got my easel and my paints from Birmingham, and she made a drawing table for me. I looked at them, and wondered what to do with them.

I won the Equity Design Award, and for a few days the cottage was full of flowers. They sent roses, and champagne, and cards and letters saying they missed me, they wanted me back.

It made me cry, and I couldn't understand that.

'Would Glory have cried?' asked Roly when I told him.

'I suppose so.'

Ann welded a seat into the back of her van so she could take me to see Roly in Gloucester without anybody seeing me. I had to go. I had to see Roly.

'Why?' he asked.

I didn't know. It was something to do with a promise, I thought.

Ann wanted me to paint, so I tried. I painted flowers for her, I thought she'd like that. I started to help her with the housework.

'Why don't you buy some new furniture?' I asked, but she looked up, glanced around the room, and she seemed puzzled. She didn't answer.

Ann has everything she needs. The furniture is old and shabby. She doesn't think about that.

Autumn came, and I was stronger. In the evenings, when nobody was around, Ann and I started to go for walks in Gorsedown Park. I wondered whether she'd still want to go there, but she said yes. She liked riding there, too.

The house is locked up now, and there are shutters over the windows. We don't go very close to it, we walk on the tracks and the paths.

Roly asked if the thin girl was still dangerous, but I didn't know.

Ann was working again, her shoulder had healed, and she'd been careful about doing her exercises. People started to bring horses. I stayed in the house during the day, in case they saw me.

'Nobody could know,' she said, but Ann doesn't know about the thin child.

'What's going to happen to me?' I asked, but I was speaking to myself.

I didn't seem to know anything that winter. I looked at the paints and the easel, and colour came off the brushes, and made shapes on canvas. I listened to people who came to the forge, I hid behind the thick green curtains, I heard what they said, about their horses, and their work, but I didn't seem to understand.

'Why is that?' I asked Roly.

'Maybe you're changing again.'

When I was leaving he mentioned Peter for the first time since he'd seen me after I came out of hospital.

'Peter broke his arm on Saturday in a rugger match. I'm afraid it was me who did it.'

'*Don't* hurt him,' I said. '*Don't.*'

'Why not? You did. I never saw a man in such agony.'

And the next time I saw him.

'Anyway, why does it matter to you? The thin child never cared about Peter.'

'She never hurt him.'

'She sent him away. I think he'd sooner have faced the knives and the whips and the razors.'

Jacob Goldman sent me a script, and a note with it.

'Hello, my clever darling. Time to come out of there now.'

It was a good script, it was new and clever. Tricky.

Tricky, trickier, trickiest, Tony. This one would take some thought.

'I am haunted. I am haunted.'

I told Roly I was haunted, and he agreed with me.

'The ghost of Glory. She's coming back.'

I didn't know. Is this Glory, coming back? What is there for Glory, now?

'Are you still in pain?' asked Roly, and I looked at him, and nodded.

'Do you want to be?'

I thought, perhaps I've done enough now. Perhaps I've paid.

Ann got her own horse back, and I was very frightened. This horse is not like the one she was lent, this is a racehorse.

'What will I do if Ann is killed?' I asked Roly.

'You'd survive. You're a survivor.'

Then it was March, it was a year since that night in the woods when Glory had died, but it was warm, it was spring. I wanted to run again. I hadn't run for over a year.

When Ann and I went into the park I tried to run, but the pain was too much, and I stopped.

Then I cried.

'I've done enough,' I said. 'It's enough now. Please, that's enough.'

37

I would need three operations, they said, and then there should be no more pain, or only a little. Space them six weeks apart, or perhaps, since I was quite strong, a month would do.

'There's quite a long wait, I'm afraid,' said Dr Lawrence.

'I can pay.'

'You have private insurance?'

'I have money.'

Whenever I left the forge I wore a thick coat and a head-scarf, and I kept my face lowered.

'People don't notice me then,' I told Roly.

'That's good, Glory.'

I sat in the black leather chair, my legs stretched out and crossed in front of me, my hands pushed into the pockets of my jeans.

'What is Glory going to be, without her beautiful body?' I wondered aloud. 'That's what everybody noticed about Glory, Roly. Her looks. How's she going to manage without them?'

'The operations?'

'Skin grafts, and plastic mostly. There'll always be scars. It can never be a real body again.'

He didn't answer that. Roly can be very quiet, too. I like that.

'What about the pain?' he asked at last.

'They say they can stop that, or mostly, anyway. They can do something about it. I think that's good. I think I've paid now. I want to run again. I used to love running.'

There was sunshine coming through the window, I looked at the dust motes in the yellow light. They moved. There might be something there I could use. I watched them, the tiny specks of dust moving in the yellow light.

'Did the thin girl like running?' asked Roly.

'I don't know,' I said.

He smiled at me.

The dust motes danced in the sunlight. Maybe I could dance again, too.

'And the first operation's on Friday?' asked Roly. 'Well, break a leg, Glory.'

I smiled back.

London, a private clinic, I hadn't been in London for a long time, and I didn't like it. Ann couldn't take me, her business was building up again, and she said she hadn't time.

I was shocked, but I tried not to be. She'd always had time for me before, for anything I needed. Now, suddenly, she was too busy.

I had to hire a car and a chauffeur.

'Why don't you drive yourself?' she asked.

'I can't drive,' I answered, and she looked at me. When she looked away again it was with a shrug, and raised eyebrows.

'Your car's in a police pound in Cheltenham,' she said. 'You can have it back whenever you like. In fact, they'd be pleased if you'd take it away.'

I sat in the back of the Rover with my head lowered and the collar of my coat pulled up high. It was a comfortable car, but the woman wasn't a good driver. I didn't think she was very experienced.

I wouldn't use this firm again, they weren't good enough.
I was in the clinic for a week.

I read another script Jacob Goldman had sent. There'd been a letter with it.

'My clever darling, this is one I want you to do. Find the brain and dust it. At least do me some drawings. I want your ideas on it. Do you think you could drop the "Uncle" from my name? You and I have things in common.'

Yes, Jacob, I can give you some ideas on this. You're going to need good lighting. I wouldn't mind hearing what Fred Greenhalge has to say about these street scenes.

I'd have to go to Stratford to ask him.

But I'm too tired. And I'm cold.

I took a taxi back to the forge. The driver wouldn't stop talking. He wanted to go to a motorway restaurant, and buy me a meal.

'My treat, darling,' he kept saying. 'My treat.'

Ann took me to Cheltenham to collect my car. One of the police mechanics had serviced it for me, he said he'd wanted to make sure it started, and that it wouldn't break down. A year's a long time for a car to stand idle.

'Thank you,' I said, and I was touched. 'That's really kind of you. Thank you.'

I sat in it, and I ran my hands around the little steering wheel, I touched the gear lever, and I tried not to shake. They had got into this car, they had taken the keys, they had dragged me out of it, and driven it away.

But I liked my car. You don't see TVRs very often, and people look at them. I hadn't minded that, before. I would have to try not to mind it now.

I told myself, I will not let them destroy my pleasure in my car. I will drive my car, and I will enjoy it.

Ann was waiting in the van. I was to follow her, I wasn't sure of the way, and I was nervous of driving.

I turned on the engine, and I flashed the lights at her. She waved, and the van moved off.

Ann, I thought, I am going to buy you another van, I am sick of that rusty old bucket, it's an eyesore. You could buy a new one for yourself now, you just don't think about it. Well, now you can do it for yourself, so I can do it for you, without damaging your pride.

I followed her through Cheltenham, and out on to the main roads, I listened to the engine, and I played with the gears, smiling to myself.

Yes, I like my little car.

When I knew where we were I overtook the van. I waved out of the window at Ann, and she waved back, and I drove fast. On the sharp bends in the little lanes I remembered what I had learned, and I drifted my bright little car on the curves, my hands light on the wheel, feeling the faint shudder of the tyres on the road, and catching the steering again quickly as we came out of the bends.

I was smiling. I can do this again now. I'd forgotten this, but I can do it, and it's fun. I like this.

Bright summer, and it's warm.

Simmie died, in Algeria, on holiday with Mike. The heat had been too much for him, and he'd had another heart attack.

I wrote to Mike and I wrote to Ruth. I'm sorry, I said. I'm so sorry he died. And yes, Mike, thank you for your letter. Of course you can offer Tom a partnership, it's a good idea.

I lay on the lawn, with my sketch pad and my pencils, and I did my drawings for Jacob.

'Dear Jacob, The lighting has got to be good if this is going to work. It'll stand or fall on the shadows in the street scenes, where they're supposed to hide. That means the colours of the costumes will have be to be right, too, and no flashy wristwatches, did you notice? Who did you have in mind to play Sean? He'll have to be clever.'

He wrote back, Peter Clements.

I drove myself to London for the second operation.

When the surgeon came in to see me the next day he said

he thought something might be done about my chest. Breasts again.

'I've always hated anything false,' I said. 'I really don't like fake.'

'We couldn't give you back the originals.'

'No, I know,' I answered. 'I think they threw those on the fire.'

He nodded.

'Think about it,' he said. 'And when you feel up to it, you could see about running this time. Not too far, mind you. Just try.'

I went to see Roly. I told him what the surgeon had said.

'What about the thin girl?' he asked.

'Do you need to know any more? I think I've told you everything now.'

'What do you feel about her, Glory? That's what I want to know.'

I considered that, looking down at my sandalled feet on the wooden floorboards, trying to remember, and wondering how much longer our appointment had to last. I couldn't see the clock from there.

'I don't really want to talk about her any more,' I said, and then I added, with a flash of memory from somewhere, 'Poor kid.'

July was hot and sultry, too hot for Ann, working in the forge. She doesn't like hot weather.

'Couldn't you install air-conditioning?' I asked.

'I've never heard of a forge with air-conditioning.'

'Be a trailblazer.'

We went for walks in the evenings, and sometimes she rode the horse. I wouldn't walk too close to her, but Lyric never did try to kick. I suppose she was quite friendly, for a racehorse.

I could run, a little. About a mile, if I didn't try to run too fast. Or a short sprint, I could manage that, and the pain wasn't too bad. On those wide tracks in Gorsedown Park I

577

would run, and Ann would ride Lyric, for as long as she could hold her. Ann said Lyric had three paces; stop, dead slow, and flat out. So I'd run, and Ann would ride, and after a little while Lyric would take over, and they'd go, galloping away from me. I'd run on until I was tired, or until the pain became too much, and then I'd stop, and start to walk home. Eventually, Ann and Lyric would catch up, and Ann would either ride on ahead, or dismount, and walk beside me, leading Lyric.

The day before I was due to go back to the clinic for the final operation, I heard the gate as I walked back towards the forge.

Ann had made that gate when the Children of God were at Gorsedown.

It hasn't got any catches or locks, just three springs, and you have to be very strong to open that gate against the force of those springs. She'd made it of iron, a crazy gate, all covered with flowers and leaves, and when it swings shut it rings, like a peal of bells. She made it after they killed the horse, so she'd always know if somebody came through it from Gorsedown.

I'd never heard anybody come through that gate. Nobody was supposed to be in the park, except for the blacksmith, and her family. Nobody was supposed to come through that gate.

I stopped, and I stepped off the track into the trees. I waited, and I watched.

It was Peter.

I couldn't hide from him. I was wearing a white shirt, he saw me straight away.

I tried to run. I tried to run away from him. I'd always been able to run faster than him. I ran through the trees, but I was tired by then, I'd already run nearly a mile, and the pain was coming back.

He was fast too, and he was very angry.

I stopped, the pain was too much, I was beginning to

bleed. I crouched down by a tree, I wrapped my arms around the trunk of the tree and I pressed my face against it.

I heard him. He walked up to the tree, he was standing beside it, his shadow fell across me.

'Go away,' I said. 'Please, go away.'

I could hear him breathing. He'd still had to run quite fast, then. It hadn't been that easy, to catch me.

'No. I am damned if I will go away. I will see you in hell first.'

I was crying.

'Been there,' I said. 'You weren't there.'

'Did you look? Did you look, Glory? I was there. I've been there for over a year. It's enough.'

Hoofbeats, fast, on the track. Ann had heard the gate too, she was riding back. It was still an alarm signal.

She saw us through the trees, she pulled Lyric round and came through them towards us.

Peter looked at her, and then down at me.

I'd let go of the tree, but the pain was bad, I was crouched down, hunched over my knees.

Ann recognised Peter, and she stopped. She didn't say anything to him, but she stared at me.

'All right?' she asked.

'No.'

I thought she'd tell him to go away, but she just looked at him again, and nodded, and she rode off. Not far, only back to the trail, and then she stopped. She couldn't hear us from there, but she could see. She rode Lyric round in circles, the way she does when the horse is hot and sweating, to cool her down.

'Look at me,' he said.

'No.'

I could hear him. I could hear him breathing, and I could remember. There were hot tears on my face as I remembered, walking by the river when I'd said I'd paint his body, how he'd breathed like that, as if he'd been running. When he'd come off the rugger field that winter afternoon, I'd been so cold, and he'd been covered in mud and sweat, with his leg bleeding, laughing, and he'd breathed like that. When he'd said we should go for a run, and I'd been faster than him, when I'd stopped and he'd caught up, he'd breathed like that.

When we'd made love, when it had stopped being slow, and gentle, and it had been wild and frantic and we'd fought each other and we'd both won, gasping and holding each other as the shuddering and the spasms died away, and we'd both breathed like that.

'Who the hell do you think you are, to send me away?' he demanded. I'd never heard him speak like that, such rage in his voice. 'Just who the hell? What did you think you were to me? One more quick fuck? Took a bit longer than most to get you into bed, is that it? Thank you, sweetheart, that was great, see you around some time?'

'No.'

'Look at me, Glory.'

I looked up at him. He was white, his face looked rigid, lips tight against his teeth and his eyes hard and steady.

'I'm nobody's fuck,' I said. 'Quick or slow, or anything. Do you know what they did to me?'

'I know.'

'I tried to die. They wouldn't even let me do that.'

'Stand up.'

'I can't.'

'Stand up, Glory.'

'I can't, I'm hurt. Damn you.'

He saw the blood, and he knelt down beside me. I looked away, but I could feel him there, warm, beside me. Tears scalding on my cheeks, I turned my head away.

'How badly are you hurt?'

'I shouldn't have run so fast.'

'Damned right, you shouldn't. Shall I carry you home?'

580

'No. It'll pass in a little while.'

'I want to carry you. Glory. I want to carry you home. All the way to Stratford, I want to carry you. Are you in pain? Darling?'

'I've known worse.'

'Oh, my God.'

He didn't try to hide his tears, he knelt in front of me, he looked into my face, and he cried. He couldn't speak any more, but his hands were on my shoulders, then stroking my cheeks, stroking my hair, and his face wasn't angry, I had never seen such sorrow.

'Peter. Peter. I tried to die, they wouldn't let me. I tried to get away from them.'

I didn't know what I was saying, but he seemed to understand.

'I couldn't get away. How can you get away, when you can't think? They hit my head, I couldn't think. I wanted to go into the darkness, I wanted to stay there, but the daylight kept coming back. I couldn't get away. Peter, I'm sorry, I couldn't stay in the darkness.'

I leaned forward, I laid my head on his shoulder, and he put his arms around me, I could feel him breathing, I could feel him crying, but this was where I had to be.

'I tried to get away.'

'I love you,' he said. 'I love you.'

'Peter.'

'Don't say any more, darling. No more now. I can't bear it.'

My head on his shoulder, his on mine, just still, in the warm summer evening, waiting for something to end, or to begin.

'I love you, Peter,' I said.

And then, a little later, 'Did Jacob send you that script? Do you want to play Sean?'

'I don't know. Do you want to do the design?'

'I think so,' I said. 'Maybe, anyway. If you'll be there too.'

I felt him nod, I felt something like a smile.

'I'm not beautiful any more,' I said later, 'and I can never have children. Did you know?'

Again he nodded, and even though there was no smile, it was all right.

I looked through the trees towards the track where Ann was still riding Lyric in slow circles, waiting for us, and I held Peter, and I thought of going back to London the next day for the last of the three operations.

'I can't be how I was before,' I said. 'But I think perhaps I am going to recover. I think I'll be all right. I think I will.'

EPILOGUE

Autumn is here, and I am stronger now. I can leave the forge when I need to, and if I still believe that people can look at me, and know what happened, I can face them despite that belief.

I can even face the people who really do know.

I did the design for Jacob Goldman's play, and Peter accepted the part.

Sean.

'You'll need to be clever,' I said.

'So will you.'

I stayed at the forge with Ann, walking in the park, then running, short sprints, or longer runs. A mile, if I was careful. Two, and then three.

When he could, when he had time, Peter ran with us. He's as fast as I am now, but maybe one day he won't be able to keep up with me. Ann rides alongside us, for as long as she can hold Lyric, and Peter runs between me and the horse. I'm still nervous of horses, I'm still afraid of what they can do, and he understands that, even though I can hide it now. From other people, anyway.

When Ann finally responded to his hopeful admiration of Lyric by swinging down out of the saddle and handing him the reins, I managed to smile at him. He knew how I felt, but he couldn't resist the chance to ride that beautiful horse.

Ann walked beside me that evening, back towards the forge.

'Will you live with him?' she asked.

I didn't know.

The dress rehearsal of Jacob Goldman's play, Peter speaking from dark shadows on the stage, having to use his voice so carefully, so cleverly, hardly ever in full light. You need more than your good looks now, my darling. You need to be damned good, my love.

And the night before the play opened. Hold me. Please, darling, hold me. I feel so sick.

The good ones always do, my love.

Peter's hand rests on white scar tissue where once it rested on rounded flesh.

No, I will not pretend, my darling. Peter, I cannot pretend with you. This is what I am now, this is all I can be. But I love, I think I love.

No, Glory, we won't pretend. We won't ever pretend.

Peter, my love. This is not for ever.

We go to the cottage sometimes to see Su-Su and Danny. Danny is nearly eight now, strong and sturdy, an attractive child. He's shy of me, he doesn't want to come too close, but he likes Peter. They play football, and they wrestle in the garden. We're not fighting, we're playing.

Su-Su is silent. She watches, me, and Peter, and Danny, but there is a smile on her quiet, grave face.

Hold me, my love.

Peter likes children. One day he will say, let's get married. Let's adopt a child, Glory. One day Peter will want children.

Then I will know it is time to look away, but I am stronger now, and by then I will be stronger still.

This is as much as I can give, for love, and it is not for ever.

Hold me, my love. Hold me.